"... this epic drama exerts an excep[tional] engrossing and moving piece of histori[cal conver]sation." – Holly Kyte, *The Sunday Telegr[aph]*

"Moving and with an almost palpable compassion for its subject, yet clear-eyed and even humorous at times, this is a book I will be re-reading." – *Historical Novels Review*

"... one of those rare books that turns the reader into an admiring fan of both the author and her subject. You feel a compulsion to urge others to read it... Newman gives Mary a riveting voice... after reading *Mary*, you'll view stout little Mrs. Lincoln – and her 19th-century sisters – in a new, more respectful light." – *USA Today*

"... thoughtful and thoroughly enjoyable... Mary is not only a fascinating read, but also a touching love story." – *Chicago Sun-Times*

"... readers looking for a vivid, mostly flattering account of [Lincoln's] once-notorious spouse... will not be disappointed – and those who simply come upon it will be happily surprised." – *Publishers Weekly*

"... thoroughly engaging... it is what history doesn't tell us that makes this book sing – the inner, intimate world of a brave and fascinating woman." – *Constant Reader*

"This is no run-of-the-mill historical novel. Newman has done her research, and the result is a juicy, literary read... engrossing and enjoyable." – *Portland Tribune*

"... mesmerizing... a gripping read that vividly portrays history in a way we all wish our high school history teachers had. Grade: A." – *Rocky Mountain News*

"A gripping blend of fact and fiction, Mary's dramatic life story, the tragic tale of the woman behind one of the most popular American presidents, appeals to history buffs and casual readers alike." – *Pages Magazine*

"... presents a riveting portrait of Mary Todd Lincoln... [her] hopes, dreams, feelings, and thoughts are conveyed with depth and subtlety." – *Library Journal*

"Newman has no doubt done her homework... and she has created a page-turner. The reader is left feeling like they know and understand one of history's most misunderstood and enigmatic women." – *ForeWord Magazine*

Janis Cooke Newman lives in San Francisco, where she teaches classes in creative writing. Author of *The Russian Word for Snow*, a memoir about adopting her son from a Moscow orphanage, she has also written for numerous anthologies, including *Secret Lives of Lawfully Wedded Wives* and four *Travelers' Tales* editions. Newman's travel writing has appeared in a variety of newspapers and magazines, including the *LA Times*, *San Francisco Chronicle*, and *Backpacker*. *Mrs Lincoln* is her first novel.

MRS LINCOLN

A NOVEL

by Janis Cooke Newman

MYRMIDON

Myrmidon
Rotterdam House
116 Quayside
Newcastle upon Tyne
NE1 3DY

www.myrmidonbooks.com

Published by Myrmidon 2009

First published as *Mary* in the United States of America by
MacAdam Cage, San Francisco CA, 2006.

A catalogue record for this book is available from the British Library.

ISBN 978-1-905802-21-0

Set in 11/13.75pt Minion by
Falcon Oast Graphic Art Limited,
East Hoathly, East Sussex

Printed and bound by
CPI Mackays, Chatham ME5 8TD

1 3 5 7 9 10 8 6 4 2

To Mary

(May 20) Mrs. Mary Lincoln admitted today –
from Chicago – Age 56 – Widow of Ex-President
Lincoln – declared insane by the Cook County
Court May 19 – 1875.

—Patient Progress Reports for Bellevue Place
Sanitarium

(May 24) Mrs. Lincoln has seemed cheerful and is apparently contented – She took a long walk this morning – Sleeps well at night.

—Patient Progress Reports for Bellevue Place Sanitarium

I read today the account of my attempt at suicide. It was printed in the *Chicago Inter Ocean* – on the front page, where appear all the worst stories about me. This is not to say that Doctor Patterson allows the eighteen female lunatics under his care newspapers. Indeed, he believes all news of the outside world to be excessively agitating.

It is Doctor Patterson's opinion that the tumult of late-nine-teenth-century life is responsible for diseases of the brain. He explained to me during our first interview that female nerves – which are smaller than those of men – are more likely to be drained of their vitality by the chaos of modern life.

"Newspapers would only serve to overstimulate your already deranged mind," he told me.

Our interview was conducted in Doctor Patterson's office, which is fitted up like a lady's boudoir, with velvet chaises and a great many needleworked pillows. A décor designed to make comfortable the doctor's patients, all of whom are possessed of those female nerves.

"I do not believe that my mind is deranged," I said to the doctor. "Addled from too much chloral hydrate and laudanum, perhaps. Unsettled by the ten-year anniversary of my husband's killing. But not deranged."

The doctor pulled at his coarsely curled hair, which he wears quite full in the back, as if to give the impression of a very large brain. "Your bladder is hysterical," he informed me.

"My bladder, I believe, was damaged by the birth of my last son."

"You are also possessed of an irritated spine."

"It is an arthritic condition which has come upon me since I passed fifty."

"And you have engaged in the religious excitement of séance."

"As has Queen Victoria and fully one-third of the gentlemen of my husband's cabinet."

I had perhaps sounded too definite in defense of my sanity, for Doctor Patterson raked at his unruly beard with impatience.

"How long shall I have to stay at Bellevue Place?" I asked, in a tone more meek.

Doctor Patterson relaxed back in his leather chair, the only masculine furniture in the room. "You should not dwell too much upon leaving," he told me.

"But seeing an end to my time here will make the days more tolerable."

I watched the doctor handle the paperweight he kept upon his desk, a dragonfly caught in amber – an object which feels cruel to me, put before ladies who have been committed here.

"You will remain at Bellevue Place," said Doctor Patterson, "until I – and your son – determine that your reason has been restored."

"And how shall you determine such a thing?"

The doctor rose and went to stand before a lace-curtained window which looked out upon the lawns surrounding the asylum. "Treatment at Bellevue Place," he explained, "is based upon the wholesome benefits of fresh air, moderate exercise, and the therapeutic effects of cooling baths, in addition to the essential practice – particularly for those of the female sex – of moral restraint." He turned to regard me with a stern expression. "I shall decide your sanity by your willingness to participate in these activities."

"I shall do whatever you require to prove my underangement," I told him.

In the three days since that interview, I have every morning gone for a drive in the asylum carriage – which unlocks only from the outside – through the unpretty town of Batavia. Batavia is a quarry town, and everything in it – its clapboard houses, horse carts, and citizens – appears dulled by a fine powdering of limestone. I have also allowed Mrs. Ruggles, the matron with the forearms of a man, to soak me three times a day in cold, salted water, and have engaged in countless games of croquet with my fellow madwomen, games which are frequently halted so that Mrs. Munger, the wife of a Chicago banker, can shout at her ball. I pursue no moral unrestraint, and at the close of each afternoon, I walk the long path that traverses the asylum grounds all the way to the unfinished greenhouse at the edge of the property, returning by way of Mrs. Patterson's kitchen garden in the event that lady should wish me to dig up some radishes for the good mental hygiene of it.

It is because of these walks that I have come to know Doctor

Patterson's retarded daughter, Blanche, a twelve-year-old child with the facial features of an Asiatic. And it is because of Blanche that I learned of the story of my attempt at suicide.

Blanche is not an attractive child. Her face is too round and her eyes too lidded. Also, Mrs. Patterson keeps her weak-minded daughter's hair braided so tightly, the child's head appears too small for her chubby body. But Blanche possesses an affection which does not demand to be deserved, and seems incapable of judging anyone's actions; and over the days that I have been here, I have developed a fondness for her.

I visit with Blanche every afternoon, for she is a child of firm habits, and that is when she comes to sit upon the stone steps of the back porch with a pair of shears and her family's discarded newspapers. Newspapers which she snips into elaborately outfitted – though oddly shaped – silhouettes of ladies.

On this day – the day I read about myself in the *Chicago Inter Ocean* – I returned from my walk to find the girl sitting in her usual place upon the porch steps, a stack of newspapers at her side and her white lawn dress littered with snippets of black words.

"Abraham's Widow!" the child exclaimed upon seeing me. Someone – the girl's mother, I expect – must have explained to Blanche who and what I was, and this piece of information is all of the explanation which has fixed in her mind, for she uses it in place of my name.

"Good afternoon, Miss Blanche," I said in reply. I like to call her "Miss" in the Southern style for the way that it causes her to touch her tight plaits, as if they have miraculously turned into curls. I gathered my skirts and sat beside the child. "Let me see what you have done."

She handed me the newspaper she was cutting into a lady, and then rested her head upon my shoulder. At twelve, Blanche retains the warm, milky scent of a much younger child – a symptom, perhaps, of the undeveloped state of her mind. Whatever it is, I have found none of Doctor Patterson's treatments as soothing as his daughter's head upon my shoulder.

"You have made this lady very elegant," I told her. I held the paper to the sun to better see the silhouette, and also to read something of what that scoundrel Grant, who has astoundingly become president, might be up to. I have passed the whole of my life following politics and only find it agitating to my female nerves to be cut off from them.

The late-afternoon sun was low and shining into my eyes; and I nearly returned the paper to the frail-minded girl without reading any of it. But as I angled the page to set it down, I was stopped by what I saw there. For just above the place where Blanche had cut her lady's head was the headline, "Another Sad Chapter in the Life of the Demented Widow."

I gasped, a short intake of breath which made Blanche stare up at me with worry, as if she feared she had stabbed me with the scissors. But it was not Blanche's scissors which had so unsettled me; it was the knowledge that I am the country's only demented widow, and that the sad chapter reported in the newspaper could only be my own.

"Are you well, Abraham's Widow?" Blanche shouted into my ear. Almost all of the retarded girl's utterances are rendered in over-emphatic tones.

"I think an insect must have flown too near to me," I told her. And though the child waited, I did not return the newspaper, for I knew that once I let her take possession of it, she would cut the story about me into a paper lady's bonnet.

"Would this lady not be prettier with a hat?" I asked her.

"Yes, Abraham's Widow!" she exclaimed.

"Let me design one for you."

Carefully, I removed the shears from Blanche's awkward fingers, and while she watched closely, as if I were working magic, I cut a small flat-topped hat which took up very little of the page.

"Is that not more in fashion?" I said, putting the paper lady into Blanche's hand and tucking the rest of the page into my pocket.

At that moment, I saw Mrs. Patterson coming from the kitchen garden with a bunch of stunted-looking onions in her arms, and quickly worked the shears back into Blanche's fingers, for only the staff – and this retarded child – were allowed scissors. Then, I rose from the steps.

"You are going, Abraham's Widow?" asked Blanche.

"Yes," I said. I feared that if Mrs. Patterson encountered me, she was likely to ask me to return with her to the garden in order to enjoy the wholesomeness of weeding. "Cut a lady with a great long train," I told Blanche, "and show it to me tomorrow."

"I will!" she shouted.

I rested a hand upon her narrow head and then disappeared into the dank coolness of the limestone building.

I found myself in the corridor outside the asylum kitchen, where I could see the Negro cook pouring something pale and watery into a cauldron. Doctor Patterson believes in the benefits of a bland diet upon unquiet minds, and all the food we are served at Bellevue Place is tasteless and white and smells of steam. Although I was anxious to read the story about my suicide, I did not linger here to do it, for I believed Mrs. Patterson to be headed toward the kitchen with her onions – though not, I assumed, in order to add them to our lunatics' supper. I hurried toward the staircase at the end of the hallway and rushed up to my second-floor room.

I have been told by the doctor's wife that my room is one of the best of the asylum, in recognition of the position I once held. That may be so – I have not seen where the other inmates are kept. Still, the room makes me think too much of a second-class boardinghouse. The bureau is oak and was once decorated with acanthus leaves, which have long since fallen away, leaving behind their ghostly outlines. I have also a rocker which has been made to an odd geometry, and when I sit upon it, it makes me feel as if it wishes nothing more than to pitch me to the floor. The room possesses a table, covered with a cloth which has lost half its tassels, and a strange little desk decorated with the carved face of an angel at the joining of each of its legs. Only the mattress is new, for I had it brought here on my first day – less to keep myself from sleeping upon bedbugs, as to avoid placing my head where others have dreamt their mad dreams.

I have a view of the river from my one window, but there are bars over the glass.

Shutting the door behind me – although a desire for privacy is thought at Bellevue Place to demonstrate an unwillingness to participate in the institution's therapeutic activities – I dropped into the inhospitable rocker and took the newspaper clipping from my pocket.

"On the evening following her trial for insanity," I read between the cuts on the page, "Mrs. Lincoln, overcome by melancholy, eluded the Pinkerton guards stationed outside the door of her hotel room and escaped to the pharmacy of Squair & Company. Acting in appearance both anxious and uncoherent, Mrs. Lincoln demanded of the druggist a lethal mixture of laudanum and camphor. When Mr. Squair expressed concern over providing such a poisonous concoction, the despairing lady informed him that she intended to use the potion to bathe a neuralgic shoulder. Unable to dissuade Mrs. Lincoln from her request, the druggist retired to a back room, and after some short moments, during which the demented lady grew increasingly agitated, Mr. Squair returned with a bottle marked 'Laudanum – poison.' Grabbing the potion from the druggist's hand, Mrs. Lincoln rushed into the street; whereupon, she immediately poured the entire contents into her throat. Then, she returned to her hotel to await her death.

"The nation was only spared further sorrow by the fact that Mr. Squair had recognized the Widow of the Martyred President beneath her veil, and divining her purpose, substituted burnt sugar water for the laudanum."

No one would believe this of me, I told myself. *No one would believe that a fifty-six-year-old lady who is slightly arthritic and plumper than she should be could escape two Pinkertons. No one who knows me could believe that after all which has happened in my life, I would choose to end my life over commitment to the madhouse.*

But of course they will believe it. For now that I have been proven insane, anything might be believed of me.

It is a singular experience to be adjudged insane, to sit in a court-room in muddied skirts while seventeen witnesses swear to your derangement. My skirts were muddied because the man who had come to bring me to the courthouse, Leonard Swett, would not allow me to change my dress.

"I am not to let you from my sight," he explained. He was standing in the doorway to my room at the Grand Pacific Hotel with two policeman behind him. "We want no possibility of escape."

"We are on the third floor of the hotel," I said. "Even as a young woman, I could not have managed it." Mr. Swett was a former colleague of Mr. Lincoln, and his resemblance to my husband had always made me feel warm toward him. I recalled then that Mr. Swett had lately acquired the title of "The Insanity Lawyer," and I made myself smile into his stern face to remind him that we knew each other, and that I was Mrs. Lincoln and not his latest lunatic.

But Mr. Swett only fixed me with a hard look from behind his small, pince-nez spectacles. "I shall give you the choice of traveling to the courthouse in my carriage," he said to me, "or in that of the officers."

"Where is Robert?" I asked him. "Where is my son?"

"Mr. Lincoln is waiting at the courthouse."

Robert is waiting there to defend me, I told myself. *He will not let Mr. Swett commit me.*

The courthouse was filled; overflowing with people who had known I was to be tried for insanity before I had. They crowded the benches and stood in the aisles, staring at me with eager expressions, in hopes, I supposed, that I would succumb to a fit of madness before their eyes.

But I barely saw these men and women who had come to witness a mad First Lady. I searched only for my eldest son, finding him at last at the front of the courtroom behind a mahogany desk, well dressed and handsome in dark brown. Robert has inherited none of the homeliness of his father. His nose is straight and aristocratic, and his mouth is well formed. The only features he shares with his father are a small indentation pressed into his chin, which I always wish to put my finger to, and eyes of an uncommonly pale shade of gray. Robert's left eye, however, does not sit entirely straight in its socket. As a child, he was made by doctors to look through keyholes to straighten that eye, and now that Robert is a man of thirty-one, it is a little less inclined – save when he is overcome by some emotion, when it cants violently toward his nose.

"Please," I begged Mr. Swett, "take me to my son."

"You must sit with your own lawyer," he instructed me.

"Is Robert not my lawyer?"

"Your lawyer is Mr. Arnold." And as if Mr. Swett had conjured him out of the air, Isaac Arnold, a man who had been a friend of Mr. Lincoln's and of mine during our time in Springfield, stood beside me.

"Perhaps you do not consider Robert experienced enough," I said to Mr. Swett. "But I believe in my son and would prefer to have him defend me."

Mr. Swett made an irritated exhalation. "It is Robert who has drawn up the application to try your sanity."

"Robert wishes to commit me to a madhouse?" The noise of the courtroom grew deafening, and I found I could draw no air into my lungs.

"Robert only wishes what would be to your benefit," said Mr. Swett. "And Mr. Arnold is here to ensure that afterward, no one can say that what is decided was not to your benefit." He gazed pointedly at Mr. Arnold, and though I wished to understand the meaning of that gaze, I could not, for the gaslight which reflected from the lenses of Mr. Swett's pince-nez spectacles turned his eyes to opaque disks.

Mr. Arnold, however, seemed in no doubt of what he was to do. He led me across the room, where he settled me behind my own mahogany table, in opposition to that of my son, and sat quietly as Mr. Swett proceeded to call sixteen witnesses to testify to my madness.

I was light-headed from my inability to breathe and brain-numbed from shock; and as the witnesses spoke about my insanity, I sometimes believed that this was no more than a dream induced by laudanum, hoped that it was. Nothing the witnesses said of me was untrue, and while all that I had done and thought had felt sound at the time, now that it was spoken aloud, it seemed the behavior of a madwoman.

"Mrs. Lincoln spent more than six hundred dollars on Belgian lace curtains," declared a clerk employed at Mattock's Department Store. "Though she told me that she does not own a home."

"I have had to send men to search the rooms next door to Mrs. Lincoln's," said Mr. Turner, the manager of the Grand Pacific Hotel, "because she insisted there were assassins in them plotting her death. When my men found no assassins, Mrs. Lincoln swore they were living in the walls."

"One night," whispered the hotel housekeeper, her voice full of the excitement of relating scandal, "Mrs. Lincoln was found running through the hallway in her nightclothes, shrieking that her son was trying to murder her."

Once the hotel employees and shopkeepers had finished describing my lunacy, five doctors were called. I had been examined by none of these doctors, had only seen them over the past weeks coming from Robert's room at the hotel. Yet it was the opinion of each of these gentlemen that I had lost my reason due to excessive grief on the brain force.

The testimony of the doctors cut through my opiate-like haze like scalpels. *I am going to be shut away with madwomen!* I clutched at Mr. Arnold's hand to keep myself from acting as insane as I was being described – and to urge him to make some defense of my sanity. But Mr. Arnold only patted my fingers with a palm made slick from the pomade he uses to fix the hair combed to hide his baldness and did not question any of Mr. Swett's witnesses.

When the sixteen witnesses were done, Mr. Swett called Robert Lincoln to the stand.

He will not go, I told myself. And when Robert did go, taking the seat at the front of the courtroom and keeping a hand pressed over his flawed eye, I told myself that still, he would not tell this courtroom he believed me insane.

Apologizing first for obliging my son to speak about unhappy occurrences, Mr. Swett asked him to describe my spending since I had returned to Chicago.

"My mother has spent two hundred dollars upon soap and perfume," he told the court. "More than she will be able to use in a lifetime. She has purchased seven hundred dollars' worth of jewelry, which she will never wear, for she lives in mourning. The closets in her hotel room are so overfilled with purchases, she is in danger of being crushed by them."

"Does your mother suffer from delusions?" asked Mr. Swett.

"She hears voices. Men who argue about the most efficient method of murdering her."

My son told the crowded courtroom every irrational thing I had done these past months, every utterance I had made that sounded unreasoned. "My mother's behavior has become so erratic," he declared, "I have had to engage Pinkertons to follow her whenever she leaves the hotel."

"Can you tell us," said Mr. Swett smoothly, "why you drew up the petition to try your mother's sanity?"

Robert's left eye tugged furiously toward his nose. I hoped the emotion pulling upon it was love. Or at minimum, regret. But I had never possessed any skill for reading my eldest son's emotions, and could not say which one now worked upon him.

"My mother has long been a source of great anxiety to me," Robert told Mr. Swett.

"Do you believe she is insane?" asked the lawyer.

Please, say no. For I am your mother, still.

Robert rubbed again at his defective eye. "I have no doubt of it," he declared.

A lady seated behind me gave a small cry, as if she had come upon something shocking, a dead bird or other small animal; and for a moment I could not be certain that it was not I who had made the cry.

Mr. Arnold called no witnesses. It required only ten minutes for the gentlemen on the jury to decide me mad.

I thought then that I *would* go mad, for I was terrified of being locked up with lunatics. But for the moment, it was not fear I felt. Even the deepest dread could not be more powerful than the emotion which now claimed me, which overrode all other feelings. And when my son at last crossed the room to me, I found voice only to speak the one thought which pushed out all others.

"To think," I said to him, "that my son would ever have done this."

It is now well past midnight, and I am seated at the little desk carved with angels reading again the story I rescued from Blanche's scissors. As I read, I can hear above me Mrs. Wheeler's pounding. Mrs. Wheeler beats her fists upon the walls of her room every night until she is dosed with chloral hydrate. But Mrs. Ruggles, the mannish matron, is a heavy sleeper, and so the sound continues without ceasing for most of the night. During the day, Bellevue Place is subject to a different type of pounding noise, that of the machinery at the nearby quarry breaking up the limestone. I sometimes imagine that the asylum possesses a malevolent heart, and that those of us who are confined here will never escape the sound of its beating.

I do not sleep at Bellevue Place. But it is not only Mrs. Wheeler's ravings which keep me from resting. Since my arrival here, I have given up my nightly doses of chloral hydrate and laudanum, refusing them when Mrs. Ruggles comes with the bottles. I have long suspected that the drugs addled my thinking, even when awake, and since I have left off taking them, I have grown more clearheaded. However, I also cannot sleep.

And so I find myself awake, reading lies about myself printed in a newspaper.

None of this is new to me. From the time that I became a president's wife, I have come upon too many stories of myself which contain no truth. I have read that I spied for the Confederacy during the war and sold my husband's speeches to pay for my dresses. I have read that I kept slaves in the basement when I lived in the President's

House and stole the silver when I left it. I have read so much that is false and so little that is true, that I now believe paper cannot be made to hold one authentic fact of my history.

Perhaps it is this last thought which made me look inside the odd little desk for pen and ink, made me write the sentence, "I read today the account of my attempt at suicide," then made me write everything which fills these pages, more true words about myself than have ever been inked before.

I cannot say if it is this tally of words which decides me. Or if it is only the unfilled hours of my sleeplessness. Whichever it is, I somehow am decided. I shall spend my nights at Bellevue Place writing my true story. Every night, while Mrs. Wheeler pounds upon the walls and the other mad ladies cry out in their sleep, I shall write. And the exercise will help the night to pass. And make me forget that I am locked in a madhouse. And keep me sane.

My first strong recollection is of the summer my mother died. I was six years old and the month was July – cholera season in Lexington, Kentucky. The windows of our brick house on Short Street had been shut tight against the poisonous gases that drifted up from the lowland swamp, and my mother was forced to breath her last in a shuttered house filled with the scent of her own bloodletting – the smell of the big copper penny known as the "large cent," used to keep shut the eyelids of the dead.

For two days, the stifling house swelled with the screaming of my mother giving birth to her seventh child in twelve years. Usually when my mother's time came, my sisters and brother and I would be taken out of the house, sent up the road to Grandmother Parker's farm. But because the air was filled with cholera, we were forced to remain at home, shut in with the sound of our sibling being delivered. I passed most of those two days in the sweltering bedroom I shared with my three sisters, removing the dresses from my china-faced dolls – relieving them of their clothes made me feel cooler – and singing hymns to cover my mother's screaming.

During the night of the second day, the house went quiet, and I woke feeling panicked, for I had gotten used to the cries, which had come at intervals like the ringing of a clock. I slipped from the bed I shared with my eldest sister Elizabeth and crept into the hallway. There, I spied the thirteen-year-old wet nurse sent down by

Grandmother Parker coming from my mother's room, my just-born sibling in her skinny black arms.

"It be a boy," she told me. The squirming baby was wrapped in white sheeting and resembled a newly hatched cotton weevil.

"Where are you taking him?" I said.

"I got to feed him." The slave girl arched her back, pushing surprisingly large breasts against the worn cotton front of her dress.

"It is too soon," I told her. I remembered that my younger sister, Ann, had not been turned over to the wet nurse for at least a month.

"Miz Leuba give him to me herself," said the girl, invoking the name of the midwife who assisted at all my mother's lying-ins.

I did not want to believe the wet nurse. "You are lying," I said to the girl. And I pushed past her to my mother's door, which was shut but not locked, opening it upon a dark room hung with the scent of blood.

Mrs. Leuba hovered over the bed. My father, his linen shirt crisp despite the overpowering heat, stood in a corner. It was not common for my father to enter the birthing room so soon after one of his children had been born, not common for him to be here at all. And the fact of it made me search the darkened room.

On a small table I saw the pitcher of mulled wine which Mrs. Leuba made my mother swallow when the pain was too great. And in the corner opposite my father, I could make out a pile of cotton rags nearly as tall as I was – rags which in the darkness appeared black with blood. My mother was in the bed, shivering beneath the linked circles of her wedding quilt, though the birthing room was so filled with heat Mrs. Leuba dripped sweat upon the bedclothes.

"Go back to bed," said my father in his soft voice.

"Is Momma all right?"

He looked to Mrs. Leuba, who was wringing out a cotton rag over a bowl of water, turning the liquid dark.

"Your momma needs you to go back to bed," she said.

"But she is not dying?"

"You cannot make her better by standing here."

Still, I did not move until Mrs. Leuba put her hands upon my shoulders and piloted me out of the room. The wet rag, which she had kept hold of, left a pink spot upon the shoulder of my nightdress.

I slept little that night, and not long after sunrise ran across the yard to the kitchen building, where I knew I would find Mammy Sally.

Mammy Sally had been a present from Grandmother Parker, who kept a good number of slaves. She was tall for a woman and as angular as a teenage boy, although I suspect that her age was nearer to thirty than twenty. (It was always difficult to gauge the age of a slave. Some appeared older from misuse. Others hid the wrinkling of their skin within their blackness. And most did not know with any specificity the actual number of their years.)

Mammy Sally gave me beef tea. Beef tea was all we consumed during cholera season, for fresh fruit and vegetables were thought to carry the disease, and not even slaves would leave the safety of the house to buy cornmeal or flour. I moved my chair as near to Mammy Sally as I could. The slave woman was sitting at the table, polishing her shoes – a heavy pair of men's brogans – with cooking grease. I wanted to ask Mammy Sally about Momma—the colored woman seemed to know everything which went on in the house—but before I might, I was startled by the crack of a shutter opening and the sight of the lifeless body of our neighbor Captain Postlewaite flying past the window. The old captain was entirely naked, and his skin was tinged bright blue. He sailed through the heated air as if he were impatient to become an angel and was attempting to hurtle his way into heaven in his earthly form. With a shriek, I dropped my mug of beef tea, shattering it upon the stone floor, and ran to bury my face in Mammy Sally's skirts.

She placed a rough hand upon my braids. "Hush, chile," she told me. "That jest be poor Captain Postlewaite dead of the cholera."

"Why did they throw him out of the window?"

"They don't want no cholera gas leaking out his body and making nobody else sick. Anyways, he won't be there long. Gravedigger come by and bury him soon as he get a chance."

I raised my head from Mammy Sally's skirts – all of the slave woman's dresses were homespun, as she was too tall and bony to wear the cast-off frocks of my soft-figured mother. "Is Momma going to turn blue and have to be thrown out the window?" I asked.

Mammy Sally put hands which smelled of bacon grease upon my face. "Your momma don't have the cholera," she said. "Your momma got childbed fever."

"Is she going to die?"

The colored woman looked past me into the yard. "You got to pray for her," she told me.

I would not wait for Mammy Sally to force another mug of beef tea upon me, but went immediately to pray for my mother's recovery. I stationed myself in the hallway outside my mother's room, for I had determined that my prayers would be more effective if said close to where she lay. And I did my praying upon my knees – although we were Presbyterians and prayed sitting sedately in pews – for that, I believed, would make my praying more difficult for the Almighty to refuse.

At midmorning, Doctor Warfield arrived, carrying a porcelain jar filled with live leeches. He passed a long time in my mother's room; and while he was inside, I prayed that the creatures would grow fat with the sickness in my mother's blood. After Doctor Warfield came Doctor Dudley. Doctor Dudley brought with him a small amber bottle of calomel and a silver basin. While he was with my mother, I prayed that the mercury in the medicine would cause her to retch up the humors which were causing her fever. I prayed also that her teeth would not turn into blackened stumps, like those of Mrs. Cuthbert, who dosed herself daily with the stuff.

After Doctor Dudley came out, my mother was left alone. I had been saying my prayers for some hours, and I was anxious to know if they – and the leeches and mercury – had worked to make my mother better. Unsteadily – for my knees had grown stiff – I rose to my feet and approached the door, keeping an ear out for the heavy tread of Mammy Sally's brogans. If she discovered me in my mother's sickroom, she would threaten me with tales of the Jay Bird, who flew to "the Debil" every Friday night to report the sins of disobedient children. I was afraid of the Devil. But I was more afraid that my mother was dying.

My mother's room was hotter than the rest of the house. The heavy curtains had been drawn against the brightness of the day, and in the dim light my mother's shivering body looked indistinct, as if she were already more spirit than flesh. I crept closer to the bed and took hold of her wrist, lying limply upon the coverlet, to assure myself that she was still solid.

It was a rare thing to find my mother alone. I could seldom recall a time when I had her to myself, a time when I could crawl into the comfort of her lap without being dislodged by the tugging of another sibling, or the growing curve of a new sister or brother waiting to be born. I was the middle child, and as such had no claim upon my mother's attention. Elizabeth and Frances were older, and knew all the ways to push me aside, to make me wait while they spoke to our mother of French bonnets and velvet corselets. Levi and Ann were younger and could claim her with tears or by threatening to put a handful of weevil poison into their mouths. I had only my need to draw her to me, and it was never enough.

"I shall come to you later, Mary," my mother would promise. And when I made to protest, she placed fingertips upon my mouth and lightly traced the upcurving of my lip. But later, Elizabeth would require help unrolling her barley-sugar curls, or Levi would be caught tormenting Grandmother Parker's hogs with a poker, and that light touch upon my mouth would be the sum of all the affection I would receive.

I lifted a corner of my mother's wedding quilt and was struck by the rush of blood smell that had been trapped by the linens. The collar of her nightdress was marked by small red spotting – blood which must have been spilled when the doctor removed the leeches from her throat; and as I lifted the quilt higher, I saw that more blood seeped from the cotton bandages pressed between her legs. I had never seen my mother bleed before, never known her even to cut a finger of her white hands. And this blood, staining my mother's linen and her body, made her seem a stranger, made me want to run from the room and search the house for my real mother. But this woman who bled without ceasing and whose flushed cheeks bore traces of the yellow bile of which she'd been purged was my real mother. And for once she was alone. And mine.

Breathing through my mouth to keep the smell away, I crawled into my mother's bed. Blood-stiffened linen scratched my cheek, and I pulled at the sheets searching for a section which was unsoiled. My mother's shuddering body was as hot as the cast iron sides of Mammy Sally's stove after a morning of baking, and her chemise was transparent from the dampness caused by her fever. I pushed myself against her and inhaled the too-sweet mixture of violet toilet water and mother's milk, flowing hopelessly for the child which had already been given to the wet nurse.

I wished for my mother to put an arm about me, to pull me to her leaking breasts. I wished for her to touch my mouth. But my mother's only movement was the shaking of her body; and her eyes remained fixed upon the carved pineapples that topped her bedposts.

"Momma!" I called loudly, slapping my hands upon her overheated cheeks. "Momma, look at me!"

My mother gasped, as if drawing in her very spirit. Very slowly she turned her head upon the blood-flecked pillow until we were eye-to-eye and her breath, made bitter from the calomel, fell upon my face.

"Mary Ann," she said in a parched voice, calling me by the double name I'd possessed until my younger sister had been born and robbed me of it.

"Get close to me," I told my mother. I pressed my narrow child's chest against her shivering one. "I will make you warm." The sweat from my mother's body soaked the bodice of my cotton shift and the heat from her skin suffocated me, but I would not remove myself from her.

"I am dying," my mother whispered, her dry lips almost touching mine.

"You cannot," I told her. And I pressed myself so close, I could feel the struggle for her next inhalation against my own lungs. "I have never had enough of you," I whispered, too quietly for her to hear. "And if you die, I never shall."

My mother shut her eyes.

"I have prayed to God to make you well," I said in a loud voice.

"God has more pressing duties," she replied without opening her eyes.

"Look at me!" I cried. I put a thumb upon each blue-veined lid and tried to pry open my mother's eyes.

"What is going on here?" My father stood in the doorway.

"I am keeping Momma from dying."

"It is not proper for you to be here. Doctor Richardson has come to purge your mother."

Taking my eyes from my mother's face, I saw in the doorway a man dressed in the long black coat of a doctor.

"Please let me stay," I begged my father.

"You must give your mother her privacy," he replied. "And let the doctor try to make her well."

I could not stay then, though I wanted to. For I could not do anything which might stop my mother's getting well. I slid out from beneath the quilt, straightening my shift, which had gotten twisted about my legs. "Can I come back?" I asked my father.

"Later, perhaps," he told me.

For a while I lingered outside the door to my mother's room. But then began the hard sound of her retching, and I moved away so I would not hear it.

I intended to stay awake all of that night praying for my mother. But Mammy Sally brought me some warm milk which, I suspect, she had dosed with opium, for I slept deep and dreamless until the latemorning sun had heated the room to airlessness. As soon as I woke, I left my bed and stumbled down the hallway to my mother's room. But it was empty, and had been cleaned up of every sign of her sickness.

I found her in the parlor, laid out upon a bier. Her cheeks were no longer flushed with fever, and she was wearing a blue silk evening dress that foamed over the sides of the pine box in which she lay. She looked so well, and so much more like herself than she had in her blood-stiffened sheets, I took this as confirmation that she was not dead. Certainly she was uncommonly still. But my mother had always possessed the talent of uncommon stillness, listening intently when I came to her with some injustice inflicted by Elizabeth or roughness received at Levi's hands.

"Momma is in Heaven," Elizabeth announced. My sister was seated in a parlor chair beside our mother's body as if guarding it.

"No, she is not," I told her. "She is right here."

"This is just her *body*," said Elizabeth. "Her spirit is gone."

"No," I insisted. "It is not. Momma is only resting." And to prove my point, I lifted one of my mother's hands, ignoring its coolness, and pinched the white flesh.

"Show some respect for the dead," said Grandmother Parker, coming into the parlor. My grandmother was a large and imperious woman. She had run the Parker farm on her own for as long as anyone knew, and no Negro or hired man had ever questioned her authority.

"Momma is not dead!" I told my grandmother.

"She is." Grandmother Parker came to stand beside the bier. "Your mother has gone to God." Gently, she took the cool hand out of mine and placed it upon her daughter's heart.

"But she has not turned blue!"

"She is gone, nevertheless," said my grandmother.

Grandmother Parker stood at the side of the bier a moment

more, then called for Mammy Sally, instructing her to keep me occupied in the kitchen.

I stayed near to Mammy Sally all that day, and though she repeated the fact of my mother's death to me more than once, what she could not convince me of was that my mother's leaving was permanent. At six years of age, I had had too little experience of death, save for the victims of cholera, and over the course of that morning, I convinced myself that my mother's passing was something akin to her lying-in, during which she was always removed from me, only to be restored when all was over.

Because of the heat – and despite the cholera which hung upon the air – my mother was to be buried that afternoon. I was told to dress in a black linen mourning shift and sent to the parlor. And at four o'clock, my mother's brothers lifted her bier and carried it out onto Short Street. Grandmother Parker led my sisters, Elizabeth, Frances, and Ann, my brother Levi, and myself in an unhappy line behind the pine box, now with the blue dress tucked up inside. Trailing us was my aunt Ann, my father's sister, who had come to stay with us. In her arms she carried the last child Eliza Todd would bear, a boy named George Rogers Clark.

The church cemetery was four not-very-long blocks away, but before we reached it, my uncles were dripping sweat upon the dust which coated their shoes. The Reverend John Breckinridge, the pastor of McChord's Presbyterian Church, waited for us at the grave site, a handkerchief pressed to his mouth, a protection from the miasma of cholera in the air. My uncles lowered the pine box into the fresh-dug hole and stepped back, wiping at their foreheads with their sleeves. Only then did the reverend remove the handkerchief from his mouth.

Reverend Breckinridge spoke in a sonorous monotone, and as I did every Sunday, I let his words flow together until they became a soothing sound, like running water. When the reverend had finished with the eulogy, my father, handsome in a dove gray waistcoat, stepped to the hole and with a graceful motion dropped a handful of dirt upon my mother's coffin. Elizabeth followed him, sprinkling her handful of dirt over the pine box with the solemnity of a novitiate; afterward wiping her palm with great ceremony upon a black lace handkerchief which Grandmother Parker had presented to her that morning. Frances, as usual, attempted to imitate Elizabeth, but having no handkerchief, was forced to wipe her hand upon the hem of her skirt. When Frances again took her place among us, my grandmother poked me sharply between the shoulders.

"Mary!" she whispered. "You must throw your dirt upon the coffin."

But I could not move. For I saw now what it was they meant to do. They meant to cover my mother with dirt. Trap her beneath a terrible weight of blood-red Kentucky clay. So much that she would be unable to push her way out of the pine box and return to me.

"Levi!" hissed Grandmother Parker. "You go next."

My brother ran to the edge of the great hole and hurled his clod upon the coffin, producing a sound like scattered shot. My grandmother then gave a small shove to three-year-old Ann, whose handful of clay fell upon the ground just short of our mother's grave. A gentleman I did not recognize pushed Ann's dirt into the hole with the toe of his boot.

Again, there came a sharp poke in my back. "It is your turn," said my grandmother.

I squeezed my handful of dirt until the sweat from my palm turned it to mud.

From across the open grave, my father regarded me sternly. My father disliked any behavior which was not mannerly, which went against the rules of politeness. I tried to back away from his glare, but was blocked by the unyielding hoops of Grandmother Parker's skirts.

Reverend Breckinridge turned his gaze upon me. "You must accept God's will," he intoned. "You must accept that He has called your mother to Him."

"I do not want God to have my Momma!" I shouted at the reverend. "I want him to leave her with me!"

Reverend Breckinridge pressed the handkerchief to his mouth, as if protecting himself from the contagion of my blasphemy. From behind its linen he declared, "And must this body die, this mortal frame decay. And must this active frame of mine, lie moldering in the clay."

I could not bear to think of my mother being left to molder in the clay, could not bear to think of her beneath the earth at all. With a savage motion, I flung away my handful of dirt, meaning only to keep it from falling upon my mother's coffin. But the muddied dirt flew farther and with more force than I expected, and it spattered itself against the reverend's trousers.

No one spoke. Even Grandmother Parker was unable to utter a word to chastise me. It was Levi who made the first sound, a surprised and admiring "Huh," and before anyone else might find their tongue, I ran from the graveyard.

I sped back to the house, racing up the staircase to what had been my mother's room. Throwing open the door, I hurled myself inside as if I thought I might still find her there. But the room did not even feel like my mother's. Earlier that day, Grandmother Parker had sent down two colored women to remove the bedclothes and scrub the walls with lye, and while the room no longer smelled of bloodletting and vomit, it also no longer smelled of my mother's violet toilet water and the scent of her skin.

I spun around, searching for some sign of my mother, something to prove she had lived, had sometimes stopped long enough to put her fingers upon my mouth. I grasped hold of the glass handles of her dresser, surprised by their coolness in the hot room. Yanking open one of the drawers, I pushed my face into the weightless pile of her lace-trimmed bed jackets and crocheted shawls, burying my nose and mouth in the bits and pieces of my mother's clothing which the slave women had not yet had the time to remove. I pressed a satin bed jacket upon my eyelids until sparks of light flashed behind them, stuffed the fringed edge of a shawl into my mouth until it nearly choked me. I clutched at the silks and satins my mother had worn against her flesh, putting each to my nose, searching for her scent. At last, my hands fell upon an organdie bavolet, which my mother would attach to the back of her bonnet to protect her neck from the sun. It was in the stiffened fabric of the bavolet that I smelled most the toilet water my mother daubed upon the coiled hair at the base of her neck. Crushing the bavolet to my face, I inhaled the scent until my head began to swim.

It was then I swore that I heard the dull thudding of dirt falling upon the box that held my mother – although I knew that the cemetery was too far away for that to be true. I tried to stop the sound by covering my head with a cambric nightdress my mother had favored when it was summer, wrapping the fabric tight across my ears and pressing the bavolet with more force against my nose.

It was Levi who found me lying on the floor with the bavolet over my face. I did not recall how I had wound up there, or what Aunt Ann said to try and make me rise. I only remember my fit of temper when

Mammy Sally attempted to remove the bavolet from my nose and mouth. Her hands came at me – hands which my whole life had soothed me with their roughness, the way wood is made smooth by the roughness of a file – and as if by reflex, I sank my sharp child's teeth into their raised tendons. It was then my mouth filled with the taste of rancid fat which must have come from some pork the slave woman had been curing. And I let her go and retched onto the floor.

They put me to bed after that, and I remained beneath my blankets for more than a week. For some days, I did not eat. Later, I would let only a little broth or some uncooked egg to pass my lips, because if I did, Mammy Sally would leave me alone to cry into my mother's organdie bavolet.

It was Grandmother Parker who forced me out of my mourning bed. One afternoon she arrived with a young slave girl and, insisting it was high time I rejoined the world of the living, tossed me onto the floor with the soiled linens. Before I rose, I gathered my mother's organdie bavolet into a ball and hid it behind my back.

"Grief is an emotion you must acquire the ability to control," my grandmother told me. "Now give Pattie your nightdress."

I removed my chemise, which was stiff with spilled egg and tears, and delivered it to the slave girl.

Not ungently, my grandmother covered me with a clean length of muslin sheeting. For a moment, she allowed her hands to rest upon my shoulders, although it was clear she had no more to say. After a time, she sighed and said, "Mammy Sally has prepared a tub for you."

"Do you miss Momma?" I asked her.

My grandmother's hands felt more weighted. "It is better not to think of those who are lost to us," she told me. "Now go and wash this all away."

In the year that followed my mother's death, I was very much alone. My father, who seemed to find the house on Short Street too sorrowful, spent most of his time at the state capitol in Frankfort, where he held a position in the Kentucky legislature. And before many months had gone by, he began to take Elizabeth and Frances with him.

"Can I not come as well?" I asked him, as he and my sisters made ready for one of these journeys. I had dressed myself in a wool traveling costume and for nearly an hour I had waited for him beside the carriage.

"Your sisters are ladies already," said my father, "and as such require the more sophisticated commodities which can be found only in the shops of Frankfort." He smiled down at me. "It is only for a week. I do not think you will miss them too much."

"I will not miss them at all," I told him. "I shall miss you." I lifted my face to him, hoping that *he* would put fingers to my mouth. But my father had never done such a thing, and he did not do it now.

Of the white people in the household, only Grandmother Parker took an interest in me. But her interest was too much concentrated upon instructing me on ways to govern my grief and attempting to separate me from my mother's bavolet, which I had worn to tatters with the constant rubbing of my fingers.

"It is only a piece of organdie," she would tell me. "And does you more harm than good."

But I would not give up the bavolet. And once, when she tried to snatch it out of my hands, I fled to a hiding place beneath the sun-porch, where I remained for the rest of the afternoon, while Pattie called my name until she was hoarse.

I found refuge only in Mammy Sally's kitchen. The colored woman made me baby cakes, told me stories from the Old Testament, and replaited the hair which Aunt Ann was always too hurried to make even. During those months, it was common for my braids to be dusted with a fine layer of flour.

But even Mammy Sally wished me to give up my mother's bavolet.

"Lemme least wash that thing for you, chile," she would offer. "It ain't fitting for a girl of good family to be toting around a filthy rag."

But rather than allowing Mammy Sally to wash the bavolet, I coaxed her into sewing little pockets for it into the waistbands of all my dresses, so I could put my fingers upon it whenever I wished.

Though the bavolet helped keep my grief at bay during the daytime hours, it offered no protection at night. Within weeks of my mother's funeral, I began to be plagued by nightmares. Once, I dreamt myself in the parlor, playing with a majolica tea set. Raising my eyes from the little china cup, I beheld my mother's body, unclothed and colored blue like that of Captain Postlewaite, sail in through the window and take a seat beside me, reaching for one of the cups. Another time, I dreamt her standing at the side of my bed, her hair so plastered with red clay, it resembled a termite's nest. I woke screaming from these dreams, disturbing my sisters and bringing my aunt Ann, who rushed into the room clutching at the lace and muslin cap she wore at night to protect her earlocks.

One night, almost a year after my mother had been put into the ground, I dreamt that I woke in her old room to find her standing before her bureau, her foaming skirt now rotted and damp with mud. She was pulling open the drawers and crying as she tore through the shawls and bed jackets that had belonged to her. I knew at once she was searching for the bavolet, which lay ripped and crusted with dirt beneath my pillow, and I sprang up from my bed to return the bit of organdie to her. But no matter how loudly I shouted my mother's name or tugged upon her arm, she did not seem to know that I was there.

I woke from this dream with my heart beating wildly and my chest tight with terror. It was a moonless autumn night of such darkness it was impossible to tell whether the time was nearer to dusk or to morning. I leapt from my bed and ran down the steps to the kitchen, hoping that whatever the time, I might find Mammy Sally there.

Hurrying across the darkened yard, I saw a faint light flickering behind the drawn kitchen curtains. It was too faint to be sign that Mammy Sally was working – Mammy Sally liked her kitchen bright. It was only faint enough to show that she was tending to fugitives.

Mammy Sally often let runaway slaves into her kitchen. She kept an old purple rag tied to the horse fence at the edge of our property as notice that in the little brick building behind the house, whipped backs would be sponged clean, empty knapsacks would be filled with fried grits, and nobody would say anything to the "Pattierollers" if they turned up with their dogs. I believe that my father knew the meaning of that purple rag. And I think that certainly my grand-mother did, for little went on at our house of which she did not know. But neither of them could abide cruelty practiced upon Negroes, and so the rag was never untied, and no one of the family mentioned the cornmeal which should have been in the pantry but wasn't.

I had learned the meaning of the purple rag on account of the nightmares which so often sent me down to the kitchen looking for Mammy Sally. The first night I had come upon that oddly faint light, perhaps six or more months before, I had sensed that something secret was happening in our kitchen, and so had slipped into the pantry by way of the back door and hid myself behind an earthenware jar of limed eggs. From this spot, I could see most of the kitchen without being seen myself. And what I had seen was Jonas, who belonged to our neighbor Mr. Wilkinson, stuffing his mouth with Mammy Sally's leftover biscuits. Jonas ate without hunger, swallowing the biscuits just to know he had eaten. Then he shoved the rinds of salt pork Mammy Sally gave him into his pocket and disappeared into the night. The following day, Mr. Wilkinson turned up with a pack of dogs, but though the dogs barked frantically and circled the kitchen building until they were called off, he never did find his missing slave.

It was to this hiding spot that I now crept, entering the pantry from the back porch and stepping quietly past sacks of cornmeal and canisters of buttermilk until I reached the tall jar of eggs. Seating myself upon the stone floor, I hugged my knees to my chest and peered into the kitchen.

There, resting herself in Mammy Sally's Boston rocker, was a colored woman who possessed a face so ugly, it made me start upon viewing it. The woman's eyes were viscous, and they protruded from their sockets in such a violent manner, she appeared as if she were being strangled. Her nose did not look to contain any bone, for it spread wide and flat across her cheeks, with no discernable shape; while her mouth dipped lower on one side than the other. Her teeth, widely spaced and black at the edges, made me think of rotted stakes set into the ground at haphazard angles. As I watched, the woman glanced at the mug she held in her hand and a colored man who was tall and regular-featured leapt to his feet to fetch the water pitcher.

"Cady." The voice which issued from the woman's crooked mouth was low and throbbing. "Go outside and collect Miss Sally some kindling."

"Yes 'um," said the man. And pausing only to refill the woman's glass, he went out the front door.

Mammy Sally, who had been standing at the table, filling a knapsack with salt pork and grits, turned toward the woman. "How you make him do that?" she asked.

"You mean, how I make him do it when I so ugly?" replied the woman.

"You was the one say it," shrugged Mammy Sally.

"I got me a hoodoo hand." From between her shallow breasts, the woman pulled out a small, damp-looking calico sack which was tied about her scrawny neck with a shoestring.

Mammy Sally studied the calico sack with a wary eye. "You knows how to make up a hoodoo hand?"

"My mammy teach me all kind of conjure," the woman replied. "Say somebody done you some mischief. You jest write his name on a scrap of paper and stuff it in a dead bird's mouth. Then, you let that bird dry up, and nothin' good ever happen to that person again."

Mammy Sally wiped her hands upon her apron. "You done a trick to give somebody misfortune?"

"I done worse'n that," said the woman. "This young gal – she work up in the big kitchen – I see her be coming around my man, askin' him to carry the slop bucket for her, 'cause her arms be too weak." The woman laughed and spat a brown arc of chewing tobacco onto the floor.

I knew that Mammy Sally did not approve of women who chewed tobacco, nor did she allow anyone who wasn't white to spit upon her kitchen floor, and I waited for her to reprimand the ugly woman. But she said nothing.

"When laundry day come around," the woman continued, "I sneak up to the line and snatch that gal's underdrawers – stupid things with some scraps of lace she got off the Mistress and sewed on herself. She were no good at sewing, either – mebbe her arms be too weak for holdin' a needle too." Again the woman laughed. "Anyways, I hid them underdrawers in my apron till night come. After dark, I go out to the little plot of ground Marse done set aside for us to grow cabbages and such, and I turn them underdrawers inside out, and bury 'em in the ground – settin' a big ole brick on top so they don't get dug up by accident. Two weeks later, that young gal be drawing water from the well, trip on a broken step and tumble in. Drowned before anybody could pull her out."

I shivered behind the jar of limed eggs, imagining the girl falling headfirst down the shaft of a deep well.

"You know how to lay a trick to kill a person?" Mammy Sally whispered.

"Colored, or white," declared the woman with no little pride. She leaned forward in the rocker, letting her bushy hair throw the shadow of a big-headed monster upon the wall. "Also know how to make up a hoodoo hand to protect me from they's hant."

Again, Mammy Sally wiped her hands on her apron, as if the ugly woman's conversation had left something sticky upon them. "Preacher say they ain't no such things as hants." Mammy Sally went every Sunday to McChord's Presbyterian Church, where she sat at the front of the slave's gallery and listened more closely to Reverend Breckinridge than I.

"Preacher?" The ugly woman spat another puddle of tobacco juice onto the floor. "Preachers don't know the first thing about hants."

"The Reverend Breckinridge say the only hant be the Holy Spirit of Jesus who die for our sin and arose again," Mammy Sally declared.

"Well, your Reverend Breckinridge be wrong," scoffed the woman. "A powerful conjurer can raise the hant of any person that die."

I was so startled by this information, that I bumped the earthen jar, rattling the eggs inside. Mammy Sally looked into the pantry uncertainly, as if it were possible that a hant had gotten into the limed eggs. I held my breath and waited for the ugly woman to go on. I had to know if she spoke the truth. I had to know if there existed a charm which could raise the ghost of one who had died.

Mammy Sally settled her hands on her hips and glanced at the tobacco juice puddle upon the floor. "How come I ain't never seen one of these hants?" she asked the woman.

"Mebbe you ain't lookin'," the woman shrugged. "Or mebbe you don't have a powerful enough conjurer round here."

"We don't need a conjurer round here," said Mammy Sally. "We got the word of the Lord." Mammy Sally owned a small Bible that my mother had given her, and though she could not read, every night she opened the book to a different section and rested her eyes upon the words "so the prophecy of the Lord can speak directly to my soul."

"The word of the Lord?" cackled the ugly woman. "That be for white folks."

"Jesus' mercy be for black folks too," insisted Mammy Sally. "They the ones need it most." She turned away from the woman and resumed filling the knapsack. "I bet that gal just fall into the well on her own," she muttered.

"You don't believe I know hoodoo?" said the woman.

"I'm not saying one way or t'other," replied Mammy Sally. "But I know only Jesus can raise the dead."

With a sudden motion, the ugly woman threw the last of her water into the fire, where it hissed and spit. Then leaning so far forward in Mammy Sally's rocker I thought she might fall from it, she began to chant in a voice which stopped Mammy Sally's hands and raised the hairs at the back of my neck.

"Pinch of pepper, pinch of wool,
Two runner beans, rusted iron from a tool.
Wrap 'em in a rag 'pon which you have bled
Tie it up with hairs that come from your dead
Just afore midnight, bring the hand out
Wet it with whiskey, spit from your mouth
Tote it to the graveyard, where your dead one lay
Then call 'em by the name they carried on their dyin' day."

When she had finished, the ugly woman leaned back in Mammy Sally's rocker and shut her eyes. The kitchen stayed silent, save for the dry clatter of kindling being stacked outside.

"That be blasphemy," whispered Mammy Sally at last.

"It be conjure," replied the woman.

With a hard tug, Mammy Sally tied up the knapsack. "Either way, I don't want it in my kitchen."

From then until the time that the ugly woman and her man headed into the night, neither Mammy Sally nor the woman spoke a word. Only I moved my lips, silently repeating the recipe for the hoodoo hand the ugly woman had recited, committing to memory the conjure to raise the dead.

Even after I returned to my room, I did not sleep, afraid that sleep might erase a part of the ugly woman's conjure. And once it was light enough to rise, I began to gather the ingredients necessary to make the hoodoo hand.

For the pinch of pepper, I stole a small bit of cayenne from Mammy Sally's supply. Cayenne was the most powerful pepper I knew, and I imagined it would generate the most potent magic. I wrapped the pepper into the folds of my mother's bavolet, for I had decided that it would best serve to hold all the conjuring ingredients. Tucking the piece of organdie back into my pocket, I thought of my mother, of having her back, and without meaning to, ran my own fingers over the curve of my mouth. But the cayenne had left oil upon my hands, and almost immediately my lips began to burn. Crying, I ran to Mammy Sally.

"What you been suckin' on to make your lip swole up like that?" she asked, dragging me into the pantry for some butter to spread upon my mouth.

But I could not answer her. For Mammy Sally considered what I was trying to be a blasphemy, and I feared that a lie might further inflame my mouth.

My pinch of wool I took from the seam of my mother's woolen underthings – some of the few items which had survived Grandmother Parker's charitable impulses on grounds of indelicacy. My grandmother had presented most of my mother's wardrobe to her house slaves, and I was often unsettled by the sight of one of my mother's dresses disappearing around a corner. My mother's woolens were stored in a trunk in the attic, beneath a layer of camphor to prevent moths, and when Mammy Sally was preoccupied in the kitchen, I went there and scratched off a small pile of woolen fibers from the hem of a winter chemise.

The runner beans were the easiest ingredient to acquire. At all times of year, Mammy Sally kept in the pantry a row of wooden boxes filled with soldier beans and small reds, black-eyed beans and the white-tipped variety known as Jacob's cattle. At the times when Levi had cracked the china face of one of my dolls, or Elizabeth had scolded me for ruining her best bonnet merely by placing it upon my head, I retreated to the cool floor of the pantry and buried my hands in these boxes, taking comfort in the beans' polished surfaces and the light clacking they made as I sifted them through my fingers.

For my mother's hoodoo hand, I chose scarlet runner beans, because my mother had been fond of red. But when I returned to my room to add the beans to the folded bavolet, I found among them a single black bean, dark as night. Separating the black bean from the others, I hurried to the window and threw it as far from the house as I could. I could not bear even the sight of its blackness, for the black bean reminded me that what I was doing was dark magic. Still, if I did not make the hoodoo hand, I would have nothing of my mother at all. And it seemed to me that a haunt would be better than nothing.

The rusted iron from a tool was also easy to acquire. Like all refined Southern ladies, my mother had cut roses, and since she had died, her shears had gone rusty with disuse. When Mammy Sally was occupied elsewhere, I took the shears from the shelf and struck off some few shavings with a rock.

It was the "hair from your dead" which presented the most difficulty. All of my mother's hair which had been saved had been made into mourning brooches, which had been presented to my mother's sister and sisters-in-law, as well as to Elizabeth, as eldest daughter.

My sister kept the brooch, a gilt-edged oval with a curl of my mother's chestnut hair flattened beneath glass, in a polished wooden box – although I would have worn it always. It was my opinion that Elizabeth did not deserve the brooch, for I did not think she grieved our mother enough. Lately – since she had caught me clutching the brooch in my hands – my sister had taken to locking the box. But I knew that she kept the key in the top drawer of her bureau.

On the morning after the conjure woman's visit, Elizabeth and Frances left the house to attend a strawberry party, and before they had been gone many minutes, I was sitting in the garden shed with Elizabeth's mourning brooch in my hand.

I had hoped that I might be able to pry open the edges of the glass and remove a strand or two of my mother's hair without Elizabeth noticing that the brooch had been tampered with. But the gold band that held the glass together proved impossible to open, no matter how I worked at it with a file I had found in the shed.

I ran to the shelves for a hammer. But once I was seated upon the floor of the shed with the brooch laid before me, I could not bring myself to hit the thing. I cherished this keepsake of my mother as much as the piece of organdie in my pocket; and the sight of my mother's honey-tinged hair trapped inside the glass made me believe that smashing the brooch into pieces would be too like bringing the hammer down upon her own fragile form. I sat for some time amidst the dust and the spiders, my fingers gripped about the hammer's handle. When I still could not smash the brooch, I made myself imagine my mother's ephemeral caress, the soft brushing of her ghostly lips, affections which would be for me alone. For it seemed to me that if I were the one to raise my mother from the dead, then I would be the one entitled to her undivided love. Fixing that thought firmly in my mind, I raised the hammer above my head, then with a quick motion, I brought it down upon the brooch, shattering the glass and releasing my mother's hair.

I used that hair to tie up the bavolet, now filled with all the ingredients of the conjure woman's charm. Picking up a small shard of the glass, I stabbed it into the soft part of my thumb, dripping my own blood upon the hoodoo hand. The remaining pieces of glass and broken bands of gold I swept beneath the floorboards.

Elizabeth discovered that the brooch was missing upon her return from the strawberry party. She had opened the wooden box to replace a cameo she preferred wearing. Her shrieking brought Aunt Ann in to question me. Even Grandmother Parker was summoned from her house on the hill, the disappearance of the mourning brooch being of such seriousness. But no matter how severely I was questioned, I did not admit to having taken the brooch.

"I shall turn out your pockets to see if you are lying," threatened Grandmother Parker.

"Then you will see that I am not," I told her defiantly. I knew that Grandmother would not come near my pockets, for she had a horror of touching my mother's bavolet.

At length, Elizabeth was consoled with a small jet mourning pin in the shape of a beetle that had belonged to a Todd cousin. I was sent to my room, after enduring a forceful lecture upon the wickedness of lying from Grandmother Parker.

Alone in my room, I tied my completed hoodoo hand about my neck with a piece of kitchen twine which I had taken that morning.

By late afternoon, the air had grown thick and still, and I found that I could not sit for any length of time. Levi was so agitated, he threw rocks at the dogs, and then ran around a willow until he was staggering like a drunkard. Even Elizabeth flitted from her embroidery to the piano and back again, filling the house with irritable little crescendos.

"A lightnin' storm be coming," declared Mammy Sally, frowning at a tray of collapsed biscuits she had forgotten to leaven.

Her words sent me running outside to search the sky, for Mammy Sally was never wrong when she predicted lightning. The last time she forecast it, one of the neighbor's slaves had been struck and was found rigid on the seat of his plow. I told myself it would be too dangerous to go to the graveyard that night, decided I should wait a day or two for clear weather. But I had lived without my mother for a year; and I knew that I would not wait.

That night, I prevented myself from falling into sleep by repeating the conjure woman's rhyme into my pillow, fingering each ingredient through the organdie of the bavolet until Elizabeth told me to "stop rustling that nasty thing and go to sleep." When, after an eternity, I heard the clock in the parlor strike eleven, I slipped out of bed and stole downstairs.

I was happy to see that the kitchen was dark, and I felt around for the kerosene lamp Mammy Sally kept upon the table and lighted it. Keeping the light low, I brought it and a little three-legged stool which was always set before the stove into the pantry. My father's bourbon was stored upon a high shelf, and even with the stool, I had difficulty reaching it. The conjure woman had said to wet the hoodoo hand with whiskey "spit from your mouth." So, still balancing on the stool, I pulled the stopper from the bottle and poured a stream of whiskey into my mouth.

The harsh taste of the alcohol surprised me, and I choked upon the amount I did not dribble onto the front of my nightdress. My throat burned – and my stomach. But the hoodoo hand was dry. Again, I lifted the bottle to my mouth. This time, I was careful to take only a small sip. So small, that when I spit it onto the little bag tied about my neck, it was barely damp. I took a larger mouthful, and then another, swallowing some of the bourbon without meaning to, because I could no longer feel it in my mouth.

I also could no longer feel my tongue; and the objects in the room – the woodstove, Mammy Sally's Boston rocker – appeared to shiver and twitch of their own accord. Unsteady on the three-legged stool, I raised the bottle above my head to set it back upon the shelf. But when I let the bourbon go, it tumbled down – more slowly than seemed possible – to the stone floor.

The crash of the bottle was as loud as gunfire. I crouched upon the three-legged stool, my heart pounding, expecting at any moment to hear the scuffing of Mammy Sally's brogans hurrying from the slave cabins. But all was silent, save for the gurgling of the whiskey spreading across the floor.

I leapt off the stool, soaking my slippers in the puddle of whiskey. I could feel a dull ache in my foot, and lifting it, I saw that the bottom of my slipper had been pierced through by a piece of glass. I watched my blood bubble up around the glass, surprised at the dullness of the pain. Then the parlor clock chimed the half hour. Pulling the piece of glass from my foot, I picked up the lamp and ran out of the house.

By the time I reached the cemetery, the wind had risen. It blew across the tube which stood up from the grave of Colonel Vandermeer, the tube of his Bateson Revival Device, which was meant to keep him in contact with the outside world in the event he had been buried alive. It sounded like the moaning of the dead, and made me run faster through bristling grass in the direction of my mother's grave. But when I arrived at the spot I believed it to be, it had disappeared! And in its place, I saw only the crumbling tombstone of Charles Hosgood, who had "received his final reward in 1792."

In a panic I spun around, attempting to gain my bearings. Scroll-topped headstones and marbled cherubs whirled about my head, and I fell to the ground and vomited the little I had eaten of my supper upon Charles Hosgood's grave. Wiping my mouth upon the edge of my nightdress, I felt around for the lamp, which I'd dropped. But it had gone out, and I could not find it. I tried to stand, but I was too light-headed, and my foot pained me. I was forced to drop to my knees and crawl through the cemetery, searching for my mother's grave in the weak light of a slivered moon.

The whiskey fumes from the hoodoo hand burned my eyes and the hem of my nightdress caught upon the jagged edges of the head-stones, pulling at me like unseen hands. Once, my knees sank into the soft earth of a freshly dug grave, and I screamed and scrabbled at the ground, my nose filled with the smell of dank earth and worms. Then, amazingly, I was at the feet of the marble angel my father had commissioned for my mother's grave.

Putting a hand to the marble of the angel's foot, I pulled myself upright. I clawed at my own throat, took hold of the hoodoo hand, and raised it to the heavens. The twine which held it cut into the skin at my neck. And the wind grew stronger, strong enough to tear the words from my mouth as I cried out my mother's name, the name she had carried at her death.

"Eliza Parker Todd!" I shouted into the darkness of the graveyard.

I felt, more than heard, a deep rumbling, as if a massive carriage were approaching. The air turned sweet with the smell that precedes lightning, and in that sweetness I imagined I detected the scent of violet water.

"Momma?" I whispered.

But there was nothing.

Again I raised up the hoodoo hand, squeezing it between

my palms until the whiskey which soaked it burned the cuts I had made crawling across the graveyard. Again I cried out, "Eliza Parker Todd!"

The air crackled. The small hairs on my arms felt ready to spark.

"Come back to me, Momma!" I shouted into the wind. "Come back to me!"

With a sound like the disappearance of all breath, the cemetery was lit by a blinding light. I fell to the earth, my frantic heart feeling that it would fly from my chest, the last of my dinner choking up my throat. I heard then a thunderous crack, as if the atmosphere itself had been rent, and a scalding rain began to beat upon my legs and my back.

The rain smelled of blood, like the pennies meant for the eyes of the dead. I lifted my face and searched the graveyard for her ghost. But I had been blinded by that flash of light. Blinded until the next one came and showed me the marble face of the angel weeping above my mother's grave, a face which looked in the rain to be crying real tears.

I threw myself upon my mother's grave, pushed my face into the dirt which pressed upon her body. "Come to me, come to me, come to me," I murmured into the ground.

Lightning struck so near, the hair at my neck hissed with it.

"Come to me," I pleaded again.

The rain came harder now. Hot and hard, and turning the dirt to mud which threatened to drown me. But I would not raise my head.

It was then that I felt a pair of hands seize my shoulders. Hands which were much too strong to be my mother's hands. Much too rough.

These are the Devil's hands! Mammy Sally was right. I have done black magic. And now the Devil has come out of this storm to take possession of me!

Then came thunder which could only be the ground splitting open to send me into Hell. With one last gasping, I fainted dead away.

But the hands which had grabbed me in the graveyard belonged to Mammy Sally, who would not say what it was that made her come looking for me in the cemetery in the midst of the storm. Mammy Sally had no explanation either for what had happened to my mother's bavolet, which when I woke in my own bed was no longer tied about my neck.

"I didn't find nothin' round your neck, 'cept some old kitchen twine," she told me. "Though I am glad you're shut of that thing."

When I was recovered, and when Mammy Sally would allow me out of her sight, I returned to the cemetery and hunted among the tombstones for the bavolet. When I did not find it, I determined that it had been taken by my mother. Perhaps she does not wish me to see her as a ghost, I told myself. Perhaps she believes I will be afraid. And I decided that my mother would return to me in another form.

It was three months before she found a way to come back to me.

In the late autumn of 1826, my father sent his bride of five days to Lexington to meet her new family. She traveled under the protection of Nelson, our coachman. My father remained in Frankfort to attend to business.

Grandmother Parker did not welcome the news of the new Mrs. Todd. "Remarrying after barely a year?" she muttered to Aunt Ann, despite the fact that Elizabeth, Frances, and I were in earshot. "One would not be faulted for considering that an indecently brief interval of heartbroken widowerhood." Still, on the day our stepmother was to arrive, my grandmother insisted that all six of us be present to greet her, arranging us in row – from littlest to largest – upon the path before the door, as if to impress upon the new Mrs. Todd the precise nature of the bargain she had struck.

Betsey Humphreys Todd arrived at the house on Short Street in a well-appointed landau, a wedding present from her mother. She shared her carriage with six flowered bandboxes, five trunks, and two female slaves – another wedding gift from the well-born and socially connected Mrs. Humphreys. The day she arrived was chill – a harsh November wind was blowing – and I stood with my siblings before the house, shivering with both cold and anticipation. For I cannot deny that from the moment I heard about the new Mrs. Todd, I had hoped hers might be the fleshly form my mother would take to return to me. Indeed, I had hoped it so powerfully, I feared I might trick myself into believing it was true. But the ornate landau had scarcely come to halt before the house, covering the six children waiting to welcome it with dust, when I saw that I need have feared no tricks of desire. I could say without doubt that the straight-backed lady in the elegant carriage was my mother returned – for fluttering about the back of her freckled neck was an organdie bavolet exactly like the one I had lost in the graveyard.

"Say hello to your new ma," Grandmother Parker instructed us.

"Good afternoon, Ma," recited Frances and Elizabeth in voices made flat by the sullen politeness they'd acquired upon reaching young womanhood. Ann mumbled something in the direction of her shoes; and Levi said nothing, being preoccupied with stepping upon a colony of carpenter ants which had chosen a path too near his feet. Baby George Rogers Clark, who suffered from colic, howled his greeting. Only I spoke in the clear voice Grandmother Parker insisted upon.

"We are so very glad to see you, Ma!" I said too loudly. "So very glad you are here!"

My stepmother started, and looked to Grandmother Parker as if seeking explanation for being shouted at. But my grandmother only regarded the young woman with an unhelpful gaze.

Betsey Todd studied the six of us. "Good afternoon, children," she replied.

Levi took this as dismissal and ran off toward the icehouse. Grandmother Parker, who at any other time would have scolded him for ill manners, stayed silent.

Our stepmother remained in the carriage, making me worry that she had changed her mind, that she would not come inside, but return to Frankfort, taking her slaves and her landau and my mother's spirit with her. I almost spoke, almost shouted at her again, but before I could form words, she gripped the handle of one of the bandboxes and turned to speak to the colored women sitting behind her. "Jane," she nodded at the one who was as tall and broad-shouldered as a man. "Judy," she inclined her head toward the other, fine-boned and tiny as a child. At once, the women began collecting the remaining bandboxes; and Betsey rose from her seat, gathering her skirts and stepping from the carriage. She passed near enough to me to put a hand upon my braids, and I thought that she might. I thought she might make me some sign that she held my mother's spirit, brought back from the dead by my conjure. But my stepmother only gazed up at the house with an uneager expression, then swept inside, the bavolet waving in the wind behind her.

Betsey Humphreys Todd possessed a great many ideas about etiquette, and it was clear that she believed we Todd children possessed too little of it. From her first day as mistress of the Short Street house, Ma undertook the great work of improving our manners. We were chastised for humming at the supper table, speaking when someone was playing the piano, and laughing in the house of God. "It takes seven generations to make a gentleman or lady," my stepmother informed us. Although it oft seemed she was attempting to accomplish the work in one.

Within the space of very few weeks, my sisters and Levi had formed a strong dislike for our stepmother. Even baby George Rogers Clark seemed more stricken with colic whenever she was in the room. Ann hid from her behind furniture and in closets, and sometimes could not be found for hours. Levi disappeared every morning with a slingshot, coming back only when it was dark, his hands full of dead songbirds. Elizabeth and Frances spent the greater part of each day behind the door of the bedroom they had been given upon Aunt Ann's departure, where they sat before the looking glass, arranging and rearranging their hair.

Only I wished to be in Betsey's company. Indeed, I rarely wished to be out of it. I followed my stepmother from parlor to sitting room to bedroom, until she pleaded headache and pushed me into the hallway – the only time she put hands on me. Once she had locked her door, I sat myself upon the carpet near her room and waited – sometimes for an hour or more – for her to be recovered.

It required much faith to believe that Betsey Todd held the spirit of my mother. She was angular where my mother had been soft, and possessed eyes of a strangely faded color, which reminded me of a picture of a glacier I had come across in one of my father's geography books. Betsey did not resemble my mother in temperament either. She did not appear able to remain still enough to listen to anything I might tell her, but was always rushing away with a command for Judy or Jane, or interrupting my story with a correction regarding my posture or the cleanliness of my hands. Still, she possessed the bavolet. And I was in no doubt that it was an exact copy of my mother's, for whenever Betsey was out, I took it from her dresser and handled it.

Five months after becoming the second Mrs. Todd, my stepmother's tightly corseted body began to swell with her first child. I took this as further sign that Betsey was indeed my mother returned, for had not my own mother been pregnant during the greater part of my childhood? My stepmother was not easy in this first pregnancy. She sent often for Mrs. Leuba. The midwife recommended large dosages of wine suffused with fennel root – a concoction which was not only to be drunk, but also every night sponged upon the back and legs.

I begged my stepmother to allow me to perform this task – a petition which was readily granted, as I had no competition for the job. Elizabeth confided that she would rather sponge Grandmother Parker's sow, and Frances declared that it was a job for colored women. However, Betsey's wedding-present slaves showed no inclination toward sponging their mistress's back. Indeed, whenever she went looking for them with wine and sponge, they were always just setting off on an errand of immediate urgency. Thus, I was given the sponge and the bottle of licorice-scented wine, and granted permission to remain in my stepmother's bedroom.

I imagined that once my stepmother and I were alone in her bedroom, once she had removed all but her short chemise, she would become more my own mother. I imagined she might then grow still enough to listen to me, perhaps ask me to bring my face near enough to place her hands upon. On that first night, I passed the wine-soaked sponge over her bare flesh with great carefulness, describing for her all that I had done that day. But she only shifted herself about the bed, telling me, "Your touch is too light. It is making my skin itch." But when I pressed harder with the sponge, she complained that I pushed painfully upon a nerve in her leg.

When the time came for Betsey to deliver her child, I would not stay at Grandmother Parker's house, but slipped away across the yards to my own, hiding myself in the attic above my stepmother's bedroom. There I knelt before a dressmaker's dummy as if it were the Almighty, and said prayers for the howling woman laboring below. "Do not let her die," I begged the headless form. "I have already lost her once to childbirth."

Childbirth did not kill Betsey. But the child she bore – a boy named Robert Todd, after my father – lived only three days.

The house was made sad by the death of the baby boy. My father went to Frankfort and did not return for weeks. My stepmother remained in bed, waited on by Jane and Judy. Even Mammy Sally became more accommodating than usual about Betsey's frequent requests for lemon verbena tea and slices of white cake. "It is always sorrowful when a boy chile die," she declared, sending up another tray.

For my part, I was relieved that my stepmother had survived. And more certain than ever that she harbored the spirit of my own mother, who had also borne and lost a child named Robert Todd. This certainty made me wish even more to be in her company, and it was I who begged to carry up the trays of tea and white cake, I who sat upon the edge of the mattress until my stepmother claimed that the weight of me unseated her organs and slowed her recuperation.

Betsey's first act upon leaving her bed was to arrange for me to attend the Shelby Female Academy. I was nearly nine years old by then, and my stepmother declared that if I could not attract a husband with grace and manners, at least I might do it with learning. Attending the Female Academy would also, she continued, get me out of the house.

As my stepmother appeared so eager for me to depart each morning for the brick schoolhouse at Second and Market Streets, I concluded that it would please her if I excelled at my lessons. Thus, I set about studying all that Reverend Ward assigned us at the Female Academy, remaining up long past the rest of the house had fallen into slumber to memorize passages of *Miss Pilkington's Historical Beauties for Young Ladies* and *The Ladies Geography*.

After my first full week of study at the Female Academy, I pursued Betsey into the sitting room, with the purpose of recounting for her every major battle of the Revolution. But no sooner had I begun to describe Major Pitcairn's retreat at the Battle of Lexington and Concord, than she stopped me with a stern look.

"Stop slouching, Mary," she commanded. "And do not wave your hands about so. It makes you look like a foreigner."

I stood straighter, clasping my hands behind my back, and began again. But Betsey found such fault with the way that I dug my toe into the carpet and the faintness of my voice, that I mixed up the dates of several battles and left out the Siege of Boston entirely.

"You shall have to apply yourself with greater vigor," my stepmother informed me. She rose from the settee upon which I had obliged her to sit. "Perhaps Reverend Ward might agree to tutor you an additional hour a day."

My stepmother's words sent me back to my studies. And I memorized even longer passages of *Miss Pilkington's Historical Beauties* and *The Ladies Geography*, pouring over them until my candle burned itself into a puddle in the hope of learning one historical fact which might soften my stepmother. But though I won ribbons for recitation and could conjugate the most irregular of French verbs, I did not earn the affectionate touch of my stepmother's hand.

A year passed. The second since my mother had returned in the form of Betsey Todd. I was now ten years old. Too grown to wish to spend time in the company of my younger sister, Ann, and the baby, George Rogers Clark. Not grown enough – in the opinion of Frances and Elizabeth – to be allowed entrance into their world of dressmaking and décolletage. This was a world which had begun to tempt me mightily, and the pull of it made me invent business which took me back and forth before my sisters' door.

It was on one such afternoon that I spied a pair of dresses hanging before the open window in my sisters' bedroom. The dresses had been made of such weightless silk that the lilac-scented breeze caused their skirts to rise and fall like breathing. Indeed, the gowns were so lovely, it seemed to me that it was the fluttering skirts which breathed out the scent – skirts which had been fashioned from so many yards of material, they could be draped over the most extravagant hoops.

My sisters were sitting at their dressing table, their hair half-arranged in styles too elaborate for daytime. I was forbidden to enter this room, forbidden even to glance inside as I passed by. But the desire to stand nearer the dresses was too overpowering. Like one caught in the spell of a mesmerist, I moved without stopping to the window. The fluttering skirts pulled at me, and I put out a hand to touch the silk, certain that it would be as smooth as water.

"What do you imagine you are doing?" asked Elizabeth. My eldest sister had turned from the mirror to stare at me, and the serpentlike coil about her ear and her scowl made her look dangerous and half-mad.

I hid my hand in the folds of my muslin shift. "I came in only to see the dresses," I told her.

Elizabeth stood and approached me. "These gowns come all the way from St. Louis," she declared.

Still, I could not take my eyes from the dresses rising and falling in the perfumed breeze. "I wish that one of them was mine," I murmured.

My sister began to speak – some remark which would be mocking and dismissive – then stopped herself. She came a step closer and smiled wickedly. "Perhaps you should ask Ma for such a dress."

"She will say I am too young for hoops."

"Then you must show her you are not."

"How might I do that?"

Elizabeth lifted a length of the fluttering silk, held it very near my face. "Let her see how grown you are. Appear before her in a hoop-skirted gown."

I watched the silk slide over my sister's fingers. "Could I borrow one of yours?"

"Of course not," said my sister. "You must devise your own."

"Do you think it would please Ma?" I said. "Do you think she will be happy to see me?"

"Is she not forever insisting that we must become ladies?"

"Yes."

"And have you ever seen a lady dressed in anything but hoops at church?"

"I have not."

"Then use the intelligence which God has granted you," said my sister, employing one of our stepmother's oft-quoted instructions.

"I will," I assured her, and ran from the room.

I could not ask Mammy Sally to help me make a hoop-skirted dress to wear to church. She, I knew, would be of the opinion that it was unsuitable – perhaps even blasphemous – for a ten-year-old child to appear in the House of the Lord wearing such a garment. No, I would have to fashion the thing myself. I waited until my stepmother had gone for her nap, and borrowed a pair of her needlepointing shears. Later, when everyone had gone in to supper, I ran down to the slave cabins where I remembered there was a willow tree and broke off a long, thin branch. These I hid in my room, not taking them out until it was dark and my sister Ann lay so deep in sleep I might cut up the sheets with her still in them and she would not know it.

I chose my best dress – a damask shift with French broderie across the yoke – to alter, knowing that to impress my stepmother, I would have to appear as elegant as possible. Snipping open a section of the hem with the shears, I pushed the willow branch into the opening, working it around the edge of the skirt and tying together the ends with a piece of hair ribbon. My child's shift did not possess the yards of material of Elizabeth's gown; nevertheless, when I put it on and stood before the glass, I believed that the skirt belled prettily about my ankles.

I did not sleep that night. I was too occupied with imagining how pleased my stepmother would be to see me a lady, too excited by the notion that the hoop-skirted shift would accomplish what the recounting of Revolutionary battles had not. I saw myself twirling before Betsey in my homemade hoops, pictured her placing a hand upon the dress's waist, so very near to my skin.

I woke at dawn, yet did not go down to the carriage until the last moment, for I knew that until then my stepmother's attention would be taken up by the littler children. I waited until she had called me twice, sounding more irritated the second time, before I descended the stairs, holding up the hem of my hooped skirt as if it had not already been raised by the willow branch well above my boot tops. I found my stepmother in the foyer, twisting one of Ann's collapsed ringlets about her finger.

"I am ready for church, Ma," I announced.

Betsey did not glance up from the limp curl. "Then you may join your father and brother in the carriage," she told me.

"I should like to wait for you," I said.

My stepmother breathed out exasperation and tugged harder upon Ann's ringlet.

I stood in the foyer and waited for my stepmother to notice me. Before very long, Elizabeth and Frances, who were always the last to be ready for church, glided down the steps, wearing the gowns I so envied. I turned toward my eldest sister to show that I had followed her advice. But upon seeing me in my homemade hoops, Elizabeth let out a loud snigger.

"Elizabeth!" scolded our stepmother. She raised her eyes from Ann's falling curls, intending, I am certain, to chastise Elizabeth for making coarse noises. But before she could utter a word of reproach, she caught sight of my altered dress.

"What have you done to your best frock?" she exclaimed.

"I have given it a hoop," I said softly. "Like the ladies at church."

My stepmother glared at me, her pale eyes chill as the glacier they so resembled. "You shall make us the laughingstock of the entire congregation."

"You do not think I look a lady?" I asked her.

"I think," declared my stepmother, "that you look an ungrateful child who has ruined her best dress."

I hung my head. "I only wished to show you I was a lady," I told her.

My stepmother twisted her mouth into a scornful shape. "You, Mary," she replied, "are as far from a lady as a barefoot pickaninny."

Though I did not want to, I began to cry. Reaching down, I took hold of my hem and held it out to my stepmother, wishing to show her how carefully I had inserted the willow branch. But my grip was trembling and too tight, and with a loud cracking, the branch snapped in two.

Betsey glanced at my misshapen skirt, and then out at the carriage. "If we wait for you to change your dress," she told me, "we shall have to enter during the Benediction." She pulled again on Ann's curl. "No, I think the best thing is for the rest of us to go to church. And for you to remain behind to contemplate the sin of vanity."

I clutched at my stepmother's skirts. "Please let me come with you."

But with no further word, she shook off my grasp, grabbed hold of Ann's hand, and led her out the door.

I looked to Elizabeth, thinking she might go after her and defend me. But my sister had placed her fan over her mouth and was laughing behind it.

"You knew it would not make her glad," I accused her through tears. "You knew it when you said the idea."

My sister did not bother to respond to this. With not even a glance to acknowledge I had spoken, she gathered up her shimmering skirts and disappeared out the door. Frances, who had watched it all, put her fan before her mouth in just the same manner Elizabeth had done and followed her outside.

From my place in the foyer, I heard the carriage clatter down the drive and out onto the street. And once I knew that they had really left me, I let myself be overcome by a terrible rage.

Yanking at my hem, I grabbed at the branch caught between the folds of fabric and snapped it with a hundred cracks until it was in so many pieces, my skirt fell straight and childish. Once this was done, once my hem rattled with broken sticks, I pulled off the dress, scattering the buttons I did not take the time to unfasten, and threw it upon the floor, then raced up the steps to my sisters' room, dressed only in my slip.

I threw open the doors of the armoire and found Elizabeth's favorite dress – a pink gown with crape butterflies sewn by hand into the folds of the skirts. Gripping those skirts in both hands, I pulled the dress from the closet, then tore off every one of the butterflies, leaving them in a pile upon the floor so that it seemed as if death had come to them all at once. When that was accomplished, I grasped the sheer overskirt in my hands and ripped it from hem to waist. Pale pink fibers, like bits of skin, flew up around my head. Remembering my stepmother's needlepointing shears, I ran to fetch them, carrying them back to my sisters' room, and letting them bite into the lace at the dress's bodice, dismembered the ribboned sleeves. I worked at the dress until my rage was exhausted, until there was no more of it than bits of chiffon and crape.

I was still in the room when Elizabeth returned from church, sitting upon the floor with the needlepointing shears in my hand and pieces of pink fabric caught in my hair. My sister recognized the ruin of her dress at once and screamed with such volume, our stepmother flew up the steps.

"Look what she's done!" shrieked my sister. "Look what she's done to my gown!"

Betsey surveyed the mutilated dress, then turned to me, her face colorless with fury. "What depraved act is this?" she spat out.

Able to think of nothing else, I held out needlepointing scissors.

My stepmother slapped my face. "While we were at church," she exclaimed, "you have been committing savagery!" It was then she noticed the scissors in my hand. "And with my own needle-pointing shears!"

"I am sorry," I said. "I did not want to make you angry."

She grabbed the scissors out of my hand and with surprising strength, gripped my shoulder and spun me around. "Observe your sinful handiwork!" she demanded. Although she was shaking my body so violently, it was impossible to let my eyes rest on anything.

"Forgive me," I tried to tell her, but the shaking separated my words into short incomprehensible sounds.

"You are not a natural child!" she screamed. "You are too wicked to be natural!" Pinching the flesh of my shoulders, she spun me again, this time bringing my face very near to hers. "You are nothing but a limb of Satan!"

Her breath burned my cheek, and the needlepointing scissors were too near my eye. I opened my mouth to beg her, *Momma, Momma please, stop.* But I did not say it. For I had never been this near to my stepmother's face before, never looked so hard into her strange eyes. And what I saw was that there was nothing of my mother in them. Still, I searched that furious face, trying to see inside, trying to find the place where I had always believed my mother lived. But all I found was wrath and hatred. And I knew that all along, I had been wrong. Wrong about the hoodoo hand, and about Betsey's bavolet. Wrong about my mother coming back to me.

I felt then a pain so sharp at the side of my skull, I believed for a moment that my stepmother had stabbed me with the needlepointing scissors. But the pain came from headache which filled my mouth with the taste of metal and narrowed my vision to a tunnel. Headache which pulsed my brain so horribly that stabbing would have been easier to tolerate. The pain made me dizzy, made it seem as if the room were whirling about me. I turned my head and retched my breakfast over my stepmother's hands. With a shriek, Betsey let me go, and I fell to the floor.

"Get up," commanded my stepmother.

But I could not obey. If I moved at all, I was certain that my swollen brain would burst through my skull.

"You are acting the savage," she told me. "Retching and laying about upon the floor."

But still I remained curled up upon the tattered shreds of Elizabeth's gown, bits of chiffon scratching at my cheek.

Betsey did not stay to force me. Her hands were covered with my retching, and there was no water in my sisters' room.

"You cannot stay here," said my sister, prodding me with the toe of her boot. But Elizabeth might kick at me with all her strength and the discomfort would not be greater than having to lift my head from the floor. After one or two more proddings, she left me lying there and went out.

I remained upon the floor, breathing shallowly, as bigger breaths might feed the headache. The pain was terrible, but it was also a mercy. For it was overpowering enough to push away even grief. I had lost my mother a second time. And this time I could not convince myself it was not for good.

After a time, Jane, the slave woman who was as big as a man, was sent to carry me back to my room. When she lifted me, the pulsing within my skull made me whimper. But, at least, she did not speak.

It was a full day before I could lift my head from the pillow, two before I could tolerate any light. For nearly a week afterward, my brain felt as if bruised and I held my head very quiet upon my neck.

After the incident with Elizabeth's dress, I no longer sought my stepmother's company, no longer followed her from room to room, hoping for the opportunity to recite the dates of battles or declaim French verbs. And when again her body swelled with pregnancy – this time for a child which lived – I refused to touch the wine-soaked sponge.

For her part, my stepmother took pains to avoid my company. And shortly before I turned fourteen – the age at which I would finish my education at the Female Academy and, as my sisters had done, pass my days at home – my stepmother enrolled me in Madame Mentelle's Boarding School for Young Ladies.

"But why must Mary board?" my father asked his wife when informed of the plan. "The school is no more than a mile and a half from the house."

"I believe that Mary will be much improved if she is under the constant influence of Madame Mentelle," replied my stepmother, "who is so much the aristocrat, she was forced to flee France to keep her head."

So a compromise was reached. Every Monday morning, Nelson, the coachman, drove me the short distance to Madame Mentelle's Boarding School for Young Ladies, where I remained for the week, sleeping in a dormitory tucked beneath the gables of Madame and Monsieur Mentelle's cottage. The girls who shared my room came from more-distant places – Louisville and Frankfort – and at night some of them wept into their starched pillowcases with homesickness. But I felt sad only on Friday, the day that Nelson returned to carry me home.

(June 5) Mrs. Lincoln out walking to-day –
—Patient Progress Reports for Bellevue Place
Sanitarium

Mrs. Patterson has made an especial friend of me. Every day, she sends the matron to my room with an invitation to join her upon the asylum's side porch, so that "we might benefit from the wholesome air." Mrs. Patterson is an angular woman with browned and weathered skin, the result, I think, from too strictly following her husband's prescription for spending time in the open. However, the air which blows through the side porch does not seem so very wholesome to me. It is damp from the wind off the Fox River. And it has made the porch's wicker seats and chintz-covered cushions smell of mildew. Mrs. Patterson's company, too, does not feel beneficial. The doctor's wife talks too much of improving pursuits, such as female calisthenics and cold-water bathing. And conversing with her for even an hour leaves me exhausted from the constant effort to demonstrate myself cheerful and unlunatic.

Still, I never refuse any of Mrs. Patterson's invitations, for I do not wish Doctor Patterson to hear that I have been unaccommodating or unsocial. Indeed, I do not wish him to hear anything which might make him believe that I am anything but sane. Thus, every morning the doctor's wife and I sit upon moldy wicker, and I allow her to instruct me in the promotion of sound mental hygiene, and afterward ply me with questions about my time in the President's House. "Did you truly meet the Bonapartes?" she asks me. "Did you really entertain little Tom Thumb and his bride?" And once her questions are asked, she sits back in her mildewed chair, her hands busy with some form of stitching – Mrs. Patterson is a strong believer in the mental benefits of busy hands – and waits for me to tell her of all the famous people who came to Washington City.

I believe it is my celebrity which makes Mrs. Patterson wish to be my friend. If I had never been a president's wife, I think that she would ignore me as she does the other lunatics. And if a real Bonaparte lady were ever committed here, I suspect also that Mrs. Patterson would throw me over, as she did to poor Elvira Munger.

Mrs. Munger is the wife of a Chicago financier of no little renown, and until my arrival, the lady who was every day invited to sit upon the damp side porch with Mrs. Patterson. Mrs. Munger's particular lunacy takes the form of making her believe she can converse with inanimate objects; and I have more than once observed that lady loudly scolding her croquet ball for skittering beneath a bush rather than through a wicket. Mrs. Munger also suffers from an aversion to touching her own hair. When I first arrived at Bellevue Place, the financier's wife – a lady in her middle thirties, who is, perhaps, a bit too slender – appeared well-groomed. Her pale hair, which when unwound falls to her waist, was coiled into a neat chignon. However, once Mrs. Patterson decided that I, and not Mrs. Munger, should be invited onto the porch, that lady began to appear with her hair matted and wild about her head.

"Why is Mrs. Munger's hair undone?" I asked Mrs. Patterson on the day that I first observed it. We were sitting on the side porch near to where that lady was shouting at a wrought-iron bench, her hair falling into her eyes.

"Seeing to it daily required too much attention from the staff," she told me, "so I have decided to have it combed only on Saturdays. When Mr. Munger comes."

"Could it not be cut?"

"Mr. Munger will not hear of it."

I was sorry for Mrs. Munger. And I wished that it was she who had continued to be invited onto the porch and not myself. It was not that I did not long for female company at Bellevue Place. Indeed, I longed for it very much. But I could not be easy sitting with Mrs. Patterson. And I did not see which of the ladies who shared the asylum with me I might make a friend of.

Mrs. Wheeler, who pounded upon the walls at night, was too tired for friendship, and often fell asleep in the middle of her own conversation. Mrs. Sandefore, an elderly lady who was oft found sitting in the parlor, devoted the majority of her conversation to discussing which parts of her body – her right knee joint, left foot, the smallest fingers of both hands – had been taken from her and replaced by the parts of someone else. And Mrs. Munger, whose derangement kept her from knowing that croquet balls and garden benches were incapable of answering her, was at least clear upon the fact that I had taken her place with Mrs. Patterson – an understanding which caused her to snub me whenever I attempted to speak with her. The other ladies I had so far met at Bellevue Place were all so furiously mad, I developed neuralgia trying to follow their disorganized conversation. And I was made nervous by the possibility they might forget that I was only another of the ladies confined here and strike out at me, convinced I was one of the demons which tormented them.

This absence of a friend made my days at Bellevue Place lonely. Robert came only once a week, and his visits lasted barely an hour. Otherwise, the time that I did not spend with Mrs. Patterson proving my sanity, I spent alone, walking the grounds and trying not to think too much upon where I had been placed and whether I would ever leave.

I had been at Bellevue Place nearly two weeks when I was surprised on one of these walks by a young woman with very black hair, who was pacing the path which bordered the kitchen garden, the asylum Bible clutched to her chest. It was a warm day, and I had stopped to rest and watch Mrs. Wheeler, who was often set to working in the kitchen garden, weeding among the lettuces.

The young woman was rushing about so, her black hair had come a little loose in the wind; and she pressed the asylum Bible to her breast as if she longed to take in the words through her flesh. As I watched, she gazed down at the book, reading from it, although she read the Scriptures unlike anyone I had ever seen. She said the words aloud, shaping God's utterances with blood-swollen lips, as if she could taste them upon her tongue; and it seemed that what she read filled her with an ungovernable energy, one which sent her hurrying back and forth along the grass-edged path.

It was only a young woman reading a Bible, yet there was something in her manner which made me think that I should look away, remove my eyes for propriety's sake. But I did not look away. For such passion held me mesmerized.

I did not speak to the young woman, did not wish to disturb this reading which so consumed her. But the following morning, I asked Mrs. Patterson about her.

"That is Mrs. Judd," she told me. "Her husband is a reverend in the town of Geneva." She set aside her stitching for a moment – she was mending a flannelette nightdress – in order to cast her full attention upon her conversation. I had noticed that Mrs. Patterson had a fondness for gossip. "Mrs. Judd's parents, the Childs, are freethinkers from Boston," she continued.

"Freethinkers?"

"They are great believers in women's rights." The doctor's wife had uttered the words "women's rights," in a whisper, as if the notion of women voting was too indecent to be spoken at full volume. "Moreover," she continued, "a lady I know in Cambridge has heard it claimed in no small number of drawing rooms that both Mr. *and* Mrs. Childs are advocates of free love." The phrase "free love" was said in so low a tone, the damp wind off the Fox River nearly drowned it out.

"Mrs. Judd's parents are so well-known in Boston?" I said.

"They are acquainted with the Beechers and the Jameses," she told me. "I understand they are exceedingly wealthy."

The doctor's wife took up her stitching; and I gazed across the madhouse grounds at a lady lunatic who was pulling the leaves from Mrs. Patterson's rhododendrons.

"What do you know of Mr. Judd?" I asked.

Mrs. Patterson let the nightdress fall to her lap. I could not tell if it was a trick of the morning light, but her face appeared altered, as if it had grown softer. "The Reverend Judd is a beautiful man," she told me.

Although the doctor's wife had whispered no word of this sentence, the tone in which she'd uttered it made it sound the most indecent portion of her conversation.

"'Beautiful' is not a word one oft hears applied to a gentleman," I said.

Mrs. Patterson pulled up the nightdress. "I mean that he is beautiful in spirit," she amended. "Although I suppose his form might be thought pleasing."

"Mr. Judd has shown you this beauty of spirit?"

Mrs. Patterson's face resumed its usual tightness, and she sat straighter upon her wicker seat. "The Reverend Judd has demonstrated a wonderful forbearance with his wife."

"Mrs. Judd has behaved in some way which would require forbearance?" I asked in some surprise. The lady I had seen upon the path had seemed only passionate, not lunatic.

The doctor's wife focused upon the nightdress, taking up her stitching with an increased industry. "Mrs. Judd is possessed of an impulsive nature," she informed me.

I did not think this a quality which demanded tolerance, but

I was afraid to say so to Mrs. Patterson. "I have observed that Mrs. Judd spends a tremendous amount of time reading the Bible," I said instead.

"Mrs. Judd," replied the doctor's wife, frowning at her needle-work, "is attempting to memorize the Scriptures."

"You do not approve of memorizing Scriptures?"

Again, Mrs. Patterson set aside her stitching. "When it is done as a way to God," she said. "Mrs. Judd, however, is learning verses for her husband's sake."

"He has asked her to do such a thing?" Such a requirement did not to my mind demonstrate a husband's forbearance.

"Mrs. Judd has taken the task upon herself," replied Mrs. Patterson. "She believes the effort will prove to the reverend that she is sane."

"It would be an impressive accomplishment," I said.

Mrs. Patterson waved her hand dismissively. "She has begun with Psalms, which being poetry, is naturally easier."

I heard the lady in the rhododendrons singing a lullaby to herself. "Why is it that Mrs. Judd has been committed here?" I asked.

"Reverend Judd has been very discreet," she said. "All he would tell Doctor Patterson is that his wife is prey to unrestrained appetites."

I did not know what to make of Minnie Judd's diagnosis, for it did not seem much of a mania to me. Not enough to have confined her here. But I was relieved to hear that the young woman was not subject to fits or violence, or even to believing a croquet ball would benefit from her scolding, and I began to look out for her, hoping I might find her alone and not too consumed by Scripture.

Two days after my conversation with Mrs. Patterson, I saw my opportunity. I had only just come out upon the back porch to begin my walk when I spotted Mrs. Judd hurrying across the grass, carrying with her the asylum's leather-bound Bible. The weather had turned very warm, and the reverend's wife wore a linen dress with a low neckline, of the type one might wear at a watering place. I had noticed that Mrs. Judd possessed very fine clothes. Although I suspected they had been bought when she was still the unmarried daughter of wealthy free thinkers, for Mrs. Judd's dresses were too well-appointed to have been bought on a reverend's salary, and while elegant, were a few years out of fashion.

As usual, the young woman was walking quickly, and wishing to catch up with her, I rushed off the porch. But I had not gone very far when I heard Mrs. Patterson calling after me.

"I am so happy to have found you," she called out, forcing me to stop. "I have only just unpacked a sconce of smoked glass from Chicago and should like very much to show it to you."

Mrs. Patterson was fond of displaying for me the fixtures and furniture with which she decorated the private quarters of the asylum. Every day, it seemed, she had only just unpacked some lamp globe or upholstered footstool upon which she wished my opinion. I was certain that Mrs. Patterson would have read the newspaper stories of the sums I had overspent decorating the President's House, and though I suspected that the doctor's wife viewed such uncontrolled spending as a form of derangement, it did not appear to prevent her from considering me a lady of taste.

"I should very much like to see your sconce," I called up to the doctor's wife. "But I am just started upon my constitutional, and do not wish to forgo its soothing effects."

"I will delay you no more than a few minutes," Mrs. Patterson assured me. "And surely, it is equally calming to the mind to gaze upon a beautiful object?"

It was impossible to refuse the doctor's wife. Not without it being noted that I had been willful, which at Bellevue Place might be considered a symptom of insanity. Taking one last look across the lawn to know the direction in which Mrs. Judd was moving, I turned and hurried back up the porch steps, praying that Mrs. Patterson would have only one item from Chicago for me to admire.

It was some time before I was allowed back outside – Mrs. Patterson had wished to hear my opinion upon several alternate placements of the sconce. Standing on the porch steps, I could not see Mrs. Judd anyplace upon the madhouse grounds, but I recalled that she had been headed toward the greenhouse, so I took off in that direction.

The asylum greenhouse is only partially completed. No men come to work on it, and panes of glass lie in the dirt at its base, so I expect that the reason is lack of money. Some of its walls are glass, and some only air, and this half-done construction makes the building seem the delusion of a madwoman. I do not come here on my walks, for I have the feeling that the greenhouse is always attempting to prove to me that I am deranged. This day, however, I was seeking

Minnie Judd, and I hurried to the unfinished building and stepped inside through an opening made for a still-unhinged door.

Within the greenhouse, I was nearly overwhelmed by the thick perfume of flowering roses. Despite the building's unfinished state, Mrs. Patterson filled it with what seems a thousand winter roses, and the newly warm weather had coaxed them into bloom. Long tables arranged in rows were covered in roses, each of a different color – the deep pink of blushing, the white of a lady's throat, a yellow as warm as sunlight. They bloomed in great bunches, swelling upon branches and releasing a dense and dizzying perfume.

I found Minnie Judd by her hair, which was made blacker by the color of the roses. She was standing before a pot of scarlet blooms, and her hands were filled with red-colored petals. Before her on the table was what looked to be a daguerreotype, though I could not see whose likeness the photograph held. I could only see that she did not remove her eyes from it.

I stepped nearer, near enough to hear that the young woman was speaking to the picture, her voice rough with longing.

"My soul thirsteth for thee," she murmured. "My flesh longeth for thee in a dry and thirsty land where no water is." When the words were said, she put the scarlet petals to her mouth and rubbed them across her parted lips, touching their fleshy softness to her tongue.

I thought that I should back away. Back away up the row of roses and leave this hallucination of a greenhouse, and never say that I had come. For watching Minnie Judd press rose petals to her mouth felt as indecent as seeing her naked.

But I could not back away. Could not leave the place that I stood. For Minnie Judd's passion was too mesmerizing, and too recognizable in its heedless intensity.

The young woman pressed another handful of petals to her mouth. The scarlet blossoms clung to her lips, fell, and became trapped in the deep neckline of her muslin dress. Her eyes, which I now saw were as black as her hair, fixed upon the daguerreotype with a hard brightness I could only name desire; and she swallowed the perfumed air with uncurbed greediness. This was passion – a madness I understood. And after so very much of Mrs. Patterson's fettered sanity, it was a pleasure just to stand before it.

But as if I had conjured her up with my thinking, I saw through the glass walls of the greenhouse the doctor's wife striding toward us, a basket for collecting flowers over her arm and in her hands a pair of cutting shears.

I ran down the row of bursting roses. "Come!" I called out to the young woman. "Come before she sees you!"

Mrs. Judd seemed dazed, like one who has been suddenly woken. I caught hold of her hands, spilling scarlet petals over the floor.

"Mrs. Patterson is already on the path!" I said.

At the name of the doctor's wife, Minnie Judd's gaze lost some of its glassiness.

"We can leave by the back." I told her. "There is a place where the wall is open."

Mrs. Judd pulled one hand free to grab up the asylum Bible, which she had left upon the table, and allowed me to pull her toward the open wall. We had nearly reached it when she halted and made to turn back.

"My husband!" she cried out. "I have left my husband!"

At this, I was unsure whether Minnie Judd was as sane as I had believed her to be. "Your husband is not here," I said.

"His daguerreotype!" she told me. "I dropped it when you took my hand."

She dropped the Bible and began to run back, but I held fast to her hand. "Mrs. Patterson is nearly at the door! You must leave the likeness behind!"

"I cannot! I cannot let her take my husband!" And pulling herself free, she ran back along the roses.

Do not be caught with her! I said to myself. *Go out now!* But I did not move from my place until Mrs. Judd came running back, the daguerreotype of her husband held fast in her hand.

"We must go!" she told me. And this time, it was she who grabbed my hand.

We heard Mrs. Patterson's steps upon the flagstones outside, heard the knocking of her shears against the wooden framing of the doorway. And it is only that the doctor's wife stopped to see if she had caused any damage to the wood which gave us time to escape through the unfinished wall.

Together, Minnie Judd and I ran over the small rise behind the greenhouse, dipping down into a small depression in the land where we would not be seen. Beyond this depression was a wooded plot, which was dense and filled with darkness. And it must have frightened the ladies who lived at the madhouse, for though Doctor Patterson had had a little wooden bench set here, the spot was rarely visited. It was empty now, and Mrs. Judd and I sat beside each other upon the bench, gasping from running in corsets.

The young woman, by virtue of her youth and slenderness, regained her breath more quickly than I. But even after her breathing turned quiet, she did not speak, nor raise her eyes to look at me.

"I have your Bible," I said after a time. "I did not want Mrs. Patterson to find it." I waited for her to reach for it, and when she did not, I set it in her lap.

Mrs. Judd ran her fingers over the gilt letters which spelled out the name of the asylum. "You will not tell Mrs. Patterson how you found me?" she asked.

"Mrs. Patterson has no need to know things which she would not understand."

Minnie made an unhappy laugh. "I do not imagine that anyone would understand."

I put my hand upon hers. "That is not so," I told her.

She gazed at my older hand placed over her younger one, then lifted her face to me. Scarlet powder from the rose petals still dusted her mouth.

With a small cry, Minnie Judd leapt to her feet, dropping the Bible onto the grass. "You are Mrs. Lincoln!" she exclaimed. "Forgive me. I did not recognize you."

I smiled at her. "I suspect that protocol does not demand you rise to greet me when we are both inmates of the same asylum." Taking her hand, I drew her back upon the bench beside me.

"Your husband was a hero to my father," she said, a bit breathlessly. "To all of my family."

"My husband was a hero to a great many people," I told her. "But I expect he did not show so well in daguerreotypes as does this gentleman I assume is Mr. Judd." I nodded at the photograph still clutched in Minnie's hand.

The young woman gazed at her husband's likeness and for some moments appeared to forget that I sat beside her. Then with some small reluctance, she gave the portrait over to me.

It was not a well-made photograph. Either the subject had moved, or the camera, for the man in the picture was blurred about the edges, as if he were not entirely real – an impression reinforced by his unnatural beauty. Even in a blurred daguerreotype, Minnie's husband gave out a kind of radiance. His features – arched brows, unclouded eyes, straight nose – looked to have been set in place by a Divine Hand, for no Maker less righteous could have achieved such perfect symmetry; and his mouth was so sweetly shaped, I imagined that the words which issued from it could only be honey-flavored.

"If I possessed a husband who looked such as this," I said to Minnie Judd, "I should learn by heart any book which might please him."

Minnie took back the portrait from me and studied the beautiful man caught in it. "Do you imagine it will please him?" she asked me.

I was surprised by the uncertainty in her voice, for this seemed something one would know about a husband. "How could he not be pleased," I told her, "by something you do for him out of affection?"

She continued to gaze upon her husband's daguerreotype. "Yes," she said at last. "How could he not?"

Minnie Judd and I passed the whole of that afternoon sitting together on the little bench at the entrance to the dark woods. I let her talk to me a long time about her husband. And she let me talk to her of mine. And during the time that I spent in her company, I felt gladder and less alone than I had since coming to Bellevue Place.

Only afterward did I recall how uneasy I had been made by Minnie Judd's uncertainty of pleasing her husband. Something in her tone had made me think of cruelty meted out, some harshness that should not live in marriage. But I thought I would be wrong to give such fears much seriousness, for I had seen Reverend Judd's daguerreotype. And I could not believe that cruelty could exist in so beautiful a form.

Even I do admit that no beauty existed in my own husband's form. At least none that could be caught by a daguerreotyper. The first time that I spied him – standing near the doorway of my sister Elizabeth's Springfield house, his hands clutched together behind his back as if he were fearful they might take it upon themselves to fly about the room – I could not cease staring at him, held by his startling homeliness.

The night that he came to the house, I had only just turned twenty-one. Elizabeth was twenty-six, a securely married matron and a mother. It was Elizabeth's much-expressed opinion that she had made a good match. Her husband, Ninian Wirt Edwards, was the son of a governor and had served on the Illinois State Legislature.

It was my unexpressed opinion that my sister had been in too much of a hurry to escape our stepmother's house. For despite his socially correct attributes, Ninian Edwards possessed exceedingly bad teeth and the habit of sniffing whenever he encountered something which offended his finely tuned sensibilities – which by the number of times I heard that sniffing in the big house on Aristocrat's Hill, appeared to be remarkably often.

Once she herself was married, Elizabeth had turned into a diligent matchmaker – I expect out of her great fondness for directing the behavior of other people, particularly her sisters. Once settled into her big house in Springfield, Elizabeth invited Frances to come and stay with her. Within an impressively short time, she had married off Frances to William Wallace, a thirty-seven-year-old doctor with an easy disposition. In no less of a hurry to escape our stepmother's house, I moved into Elizabeth's spare bedroom within the hour of Frances removing her things from it. And before I had even unpacked my trunks, my eldest sister set to work upon finding a gentleman she could direct me to marry.

The notion of whom I might marry was much on my own mind. My most likely suitor was Stephen Douglas, who was short enough of stature to be an unawkward dancing partner – I was not much above five feet – and large enough of ambition for me to consider marrying. Mr. Douglas was a Yankee, though he knew how to be chivalrous. And he was not unlovely to look at. Still, the gentleman did possess an unsurmountable flaw. He was a Democrat. And as a young woman brought up amidst a family of lifelong Whigs, I could not imagine myself climbing into bed every night with a Democrat.

"For one dollar, Queen Ruby will say who you shall marry," my friend Mercy Levering told me, some weeks before the party at which I met Mr. Lincoln. Mercy, a lady with hair an almost scandalous shade of red, oft came to sit with me in Elizabeth's overdecorated family parlor – my sister had a fondness for landscape paintings and lace doilies. What we discussed, seated upon Elizabeth's tasseled chairs, was which gentlemen of Springfield might be considered marriageable, an assembly which had expanded somewhat now that we had both moved into our twenties.

"Do you believe she has such an ability?" I asked my friend.

"It is what she is known for," said Mercy.

Indeed, telling husbands was the profession of the one-legged colored woman who lived at the edge of Springfield. Queen Ruby was a mystery. She wore two dresses, one layered atop the other. And she had replaced her missing leg with a mahogany post that had the face of a demon carved upon it, which had become common knowledge due to Queen Ruby's habit of lifting her multiple skirts to frighten Springfield's children with the sight of it. Some claimed she was an escaped slave from Louisiana. Others said she was a conjure woman from a Caribbean isle. What had taken her leg was equally speculated upon. The stories ranged from an angry master to a hungry shark. What was known for certain was that for one dollar she would tell any lady about the man she was destined to marry. What was rumored was that she would assist any lady in ridding herself of what might become unwanted upon learning that a gentleman she had counted upon did not intend to marry her after all.

"Ninian will never give me a dollar for Queen Ruby," I told Mercy. "He believes her to be a blight upon the visage of Springfield." I imitated my brother-in-law's tight-mouthed way of speaking, which came from bad teeth and prissiness.

"I shall get the dollar from my brother," Mercy replied. "He has enough secrets of his own not to reveal ours."

"What about yourself?" I asked. "Do you not wish to know about your own husband?"

Mercy tugged at her bodice with a smug smile. "Queen Ruby has already predicted that I will marry James Conkling."

"That is not much recommendation for Queen Ruby's clairvoyant abilities," I told her. "She has only to have seen him following you about Springfield like an unhappy dog."

"Still, are you not a little curious what Queen Ruby will prophesy?" asked Mercy.

"What if she predicts someone terrible? Some old widower with a houseful of children? The drunkard who runs the feed store?" In truth, I was a little afraid of going to Queen Ruby. The way that my child's hoodoo hand had called up my stepmother had left me wary of Negro conjure women.

"I shall not let you marry anyone unsuitable," Mercy promised. She reached over a table protected by three doilies and took my hand. "Come, we will go together. If nothing else, it will be an outing." She smiled, and it seemed to make her hair burn brighter. "And it is unlikely that my brother will ask for his dollar back."

"Very well," I told her. "But we must tell Queen Ruby that I will consider no Democrats."

Within the week, Mercy had the dollar from her brother; and using the excuse that we were desperate to view the new gabardines which had arrived at Clark's store, we were on our way to Queen Ruby's house. It was a harsh day, and the November wind pulled at our skirts, as if wishing to rip them from our legs. In order not to be recognized, Mercy and I had wrapped ourselves in hooded cloaks, for though practically every Springfield lady over the age of fifteen had consulted with Queen Ruby, no one wished to be caught at it. It would be unmaidenly to display such unconcealed interest in whom one might marry.

Queen Ruby's house sat alone at the top of a steep rise. It was a small wooden structure, unpainted, save for the outline of a hand in blood red upon the side, which made it appear as if the little house had been slapped. Above the hand's fingertips, painted in black, were the words, "Palm Reeding $1." The very few windows the building possessed had been covered over with so many layers of oiled paper, they would have been impossible to see through. Yet the door was opened before Mercy and I had time to knock upon it.

Queen Ruby, wearing a dress of calico and a dress of plaid poplin, stood blocking the entrance.

"We have come to ask about a husband for Miss Todd," Mercy said. My friend's tone was more deferential than I had heard her use before.

"I know you have," replied Queen Ruby. The colored woman's voice carried the inflection of some island, which made it sound as if she was simultaneously scolding and singing to us.

"I have brought a dollar," Mercy assured her.

Queen Ruby looked at Mercy's reticule, as if she could see if the dollar were there. Then slowly, and with an uneven gait, she stepped out of the doorway and allowed us inside.

The interior of Queen Ruby's house was the strangest I had ever seen. Every surface was covered in cast-off clothing. Waistcoats were nailed to the walls, ball gowns tacked upon the ceiling, even the floor was covered with trousers and mourning dresses and little suits that had belonged to children. There was no order to the arrangement – striped overskirts butted against brocades, and disembodied bodices floated above my head. The room smelled of unwashed clothing, and the bitter scent of something Queen Ruby was burning in a little pot; I felt untethered, as if I had left behind all that was ordinary.

"The spirits of the people who belonged to these clothes stay in them," said Queen Ruby, following my gaze. "I keep them to guard me from the evil ones who are always trying to get at me."

Now, I know the reason in Queen Ruby's belief. But then, it seemed to me madness. And I thought I should tell Mercy to save her dollar, and to come with me out of this room filled with other people's clothing. But Queen Ruby's chastising voice and her eyes, pupil-less in their blackness, held me like the strongest conjure.

"You can give me the dollar now," she said to my friend.

Mercy did not hesitate, handing Queen Ruby a gold coin, which she slipped into the pocket of one of her skirts.

"You can sit," the colored woman told us.

We placed ourselves upon wooden chairs which had been set atop the wide taffeta skirts of someone's discarded wedding dress.

"Give me your hand," commanded Queen Ruby.

I put my hand upon hers, expecting it to feel rough like Mammy Sally's. But Queen Ruby's hand was smoother than that of any colored woman I had known, as smooth as my own, as if she had been able to magic away any work that would have been required of her.

Queen Ruby glanced at my hand for only a moment. "He is ugly," she announced. And rose from her seat.

I told myself that Queen Ruby's prediction was nothing more than rudeness. Certainly the one-legged colored woman, with her talk of evil ones and spirits which lived in old clothing, was lunatic, and nothing she might say about my future husband could be true. But Queen Ruby did not sound lunatic.

Mercy rose, but I kept to my seat, for I did not wish to leave this strange house until the conjure woman had told me more.

"My husband is ugly?" I said.

"Surprisingly so," replied Queen Ruby. She crossed the room, and I understood that social custom held no meaning for her, that even if I remained sitting here forever, she would return to whatever odd occupation had engaged her before we arrived.

Mercy took a step toward the door.

"Can you tell me nothing else about him?" I asked.

Queen Ruby turned back and regarded me with an expression which carried something of a dare. "How much do you want to know?" she said.

Everything! I was about to tell her. But the challenge upon her face halted me. "Is he at least kind?" I asked.

"He is."

"And ambitious?"

Again, Queen Ruby turned her back to me, and I feared she had decided this was all the information she would grant me for a dollar.

"Please only tell me this," I begged.

She did not look at me. But she did not walk away either. "I expect he is ambitious," she said, her eyes fixed upon a mourning dress tacked to the wall. "He will be president someday."

Mercy gasped. And indeed it was a startling thing which Queen Ruby had said. But for me, it was not the prediction which startled – it was how it spoke out what I had long believed.

"I shall one day be a president's wife," I had said to my stepmother, each time she took it upon herself to inform me that I was too willful and wicked to catch a husband. I had said the words out of spite, and a desire to make her see my worth. Still, each time I had spoken them, they had felt true. More true than even I had been able to believe. And only the logic of how very much this was to ask from the future made me forget my certainty when not in my stepmother's company.

"Can you give me his name?" I said to Queen Ruby. "So I will know him."

"I have told you enough for one dollar." She moved to a small, high table upon which sat the pot burning bitter smoke and began to murmur in a language so unfamiliar it did not sound natural.

"We should go," said Mercy. My friend's hair seemed less bright in this room.

Taking care not to step too heavily upon the wedding dress at my feet, I rose and gathered my cloak. Queen Ruby did not cease her strange chanting before the pot to open the door for us, so after a moment, I took the handle and let us out.

The wind blew hard atop Queen Ruby's hill, and Mercy and I hurried down it. We did not speak until we were some distance away.

"It is possible that Queen Ruby means Mr. Douglas," she told me. "He has ambition enough for president."

"Stephen Douglas is a handsome man," I reminded her.

"Perhaps she does not admire his looks," said my friend. "In any case, I believe Queen Ruby is more mad than when I went to her."

"Perhaps that is what makes her prophecies so accurate."

Mercy pulled back the hood of her cloak to see me better. "You do not wish to believe the truth of what Queen Ruby has told you?"

"I do not wish to marry an ugly man," I said to her. "But I do wish to be married to a president."

Over the next month, I studied all the unmarried gentlemen I encountered in Springfield drawing rooms, looking to find one sufficiently ugly to satisfy Queen Ruby's prediction. More than a few of these gentlemen possessed unlovely features – a nose which shadowed too much the mouth tucked beneath it, a chin so receded it could barely be said to exist. Still, every one possessed also some redeeming aspect which saved him from too much ugliness. And none showed either the ambition or charm of character necessary to be voted president.

We were near to Christmas and Elizabeth was hosting a tremendous fête. My sister was fond of parties; they gave her the opportunity to show off her big house and all of her lace doilies. For this occasion, she had decorated her parlor with an evergreen tall enough to brush the cornice of her twelve-foot ceiling, and had so covered it with candles, it seemed in danger of setting ablaze the whole of Aristocrat's Hill. Every marriageable lady was in attendance, dressed in satin and thick velvet, for Elizabeth always filled her drawing room with eligible gentlemen. The young matrons of Springfield were in attendance as well, dressed in gowns of dull-colored merino. These ladies sat together in groups, watching the ritual they had – more or less successfully – concluded. The gentlemen, wed or unwed, came to Elizabeth's parties for my sister's celebrated punch, which was laced with good Kentucky bourbon.

On the night of the fête, the big house filled with the crush of ladies' skirts and the scent of evergreen. Everyone glided across layers of carpet to the syrupy strains of waltzes, for my sister had engaged a small orchestra for the dancing; and before even an hour had passed, I had danced twice with Mr. Douglas, and once with the widower Mr. Webb, whom I suspected Elizabeth wished for me. Telling the widower I needed to collect my breath, I went to stand beside an opened window; the room had grown warm and I did not wish to risk my reputation by sweating. It was while I was attempting to will myself cooler that I spotted near the doorway the ugliest man upon which I had ever laid eyes.

His color was swarthy to the point of jaundice; and his ears were as large and fleshy as ham steaks. The crevasses at either side of his mouth were etched deeply enough to hide pennies, and he was tall – too tall to mitigate all that ugliness. Worse still, he was badly dressed – his swallowtail coat was too short and did not match the coarse cloth of his trousers – as if he believed that his unattractiveness was so great, it was useless to clothe it in anything fine.

This cannot be the man Queen Ruby means me to marry! I thought, no longer overwarm, but as chilled as if I had stepped out into the snow. *No amount of ambition or personal charm could turn this scarecrow into a president.*

It was then I noticed that the man in the doorway was staring at me, his look bearing too much frankness than was polite in the exchanges between unmarried ladies and gentlemen.

Avoid him. Stay dancing. He does not look capable of propelling those stretched legs into any motion resembling a waltz, and you cannot be made to marry any man you have never danced with. I turned away, searching my sister's drawing room for a partner. But before I could catch the eye of any suitable gentleman, the man, in the company of my cousin, John Todd Stuart, stood looming over me.

"I do not think you have met Mr. Lincoln," said my cousin. "He has recently come to work in my office as a lawyer."

"You know that I endeavor to spend as little time as possible in law offices," I replied. This was Mr. Lincoln's prompt to declare that my cousin's office would be much improved by my presence, but that gentleman stayed mute, only gripping his hands more tightly behind his back.

"It would brighten my day considerably if you graced the premises now and again," my cousin replied, displaying his Todd upbringing.

I was about to thank my relation for the compliment, when Mr. Lincoln bent abruptly at the waist in order to place his unhappy face nearer to mine.

"I want to dance with you in the worst way!" he declared. His voice was nearly as high-pitched as a girl's, and twanged with the accent of rural Kentucky.

I did not want to dance with Mr. Lincoln. He was a foot taller than I, and would make me look at best a child playing dress-up, and at worst squat. Moreover, dancing with the man felt too much the first step toward marrying him. But it would be ill-bred to refuse a man introduced to me by a relation. And my sister judged that any evidence of poor breeding upon my part should be dealt with by protracted lecturing.

"I shall dance with you, Mr. Lincoln," I told him, "if you promise it will not be in the worst way."

He made no reply to my witticism, allowing it to hang upon the air. With some trepidation, he released his hands – they were uncommonly large – and placed one upon my waist. Saying nothing, he pulled me out among the dancing couples.

Mr. Lincoln, I discovered, was incapable of small talk. As we waltzed – in what could have justly been described the worst way – he did not flatter my dancing, nor pay tribute to my eyes or my hair.

"Do you like poetry, Mr. Lincoln?" I asked, for even the most mute could quote some type of verse.

He proclaimed in his girl's voice:
Oh! Why should the spirit of mortal be proud?
Like a swift-fleeting meteor, a fast-flying cloud.
A flash of the lightning, a break of the wave,
He passeth from life to his rest in the grave.

"That is a rather melancholy poem to quote a lady whilst waltzing," I teased him.

"It is a favorite of mine," he replied. "It is called 'Mortality.'"

"I do not doubt it. But have you not memorized any love poems?"

He shook his head.

"Then you shall learn this one by Mr. Shakespeare," I told him.
Music to hear, why hear'st thou music sadly?
Sweets with sweets war not, joy delights in joy.

Mr. Lincoln was again watching me with too much frankness. "You have a bright spirit," he declared. "I would want it about me always."

I looked into his homely face, trying to see if there had been jest in the remark. But there had not. This was not the flattery doled out during dances – excessive and all upon the surface. Mr. Lincoln's remark had been too sincere – and too tinged with want. And none of the ready responses I employed when dancing seemed to fit it as reply.

"I should see if my sister requires me," I told him, though the waltz had not quite finished. "I am afraid I have neglected my duties as family."

Mr. Lincoln nodded and dropped his hand from my waist.

"It was a great pleasure to have been introduced to you," I said, backing away. And without hearing what type of response he would give this, I hurried off, leaving the unhandsome man alone among the dancers.

For the remainder of the evening, I kept myself engaged for every dance.

"I noticed that you were waltzing with your cousin's new lawyer," said Mr. Douglas, when it was his turn to take me around the floor.

"I do not know him, really."

"He holds a seat on the Illinois legislature."

"I would have thought him too unpolished for politics."

"Nevertheless, he possesses great political ambitions."

I did not like hearing that the ugly man possessed anything which might make him seem more the object of Queen Ruby's prophecy. Still, I assured myself, possessing ambitions does not guarantee they will come to anything. Desire alone will not make that man a president. Or my husband.

I saw Mr. Lincoln again two days later, at a breakfast given by the wife of a gentleman who had required the legal services of my cousin Mr. Stuart. The moment I entered the parlor, the gentleman hurried to me, and without the nicety of a greeting – or the patience to wait for me to remove my cloak – began to declaim:

If thou survive my well-contented day,
When that churl Death my bones with dust shall cover,
And shalt by fortune once more re-survey
These poor rude lines of thy deceased lover.

When he finished, he stood before me with such expectancy, I recalled myself, reciting a list of Revolutionary War battles for my stepmother.

"Did you scour poor Mr. Shakespeare's love sonnets in order to find one about death, Mr. Lincoln?" I asked him.

"No, Miss Todd," he replied. "It just found me."

On that morning, over the aspic and the tongue, I made Mr. Lincoln learn at least one sonnet that was not mournful. And as there was no dancing at the breakfast, I did not work so hard to avoid him.

Indeed, as the year progressed, it seemed I could attend no tea or reception without finding Mr. Lincoln seated uncomfortably upon a settee, or lurking in a corner with his large hands gripped behind his back, a posture which made him appear the penitent child of a giantess. The tall lawyer was not a success at these affairs. Whenever released, his big hands snapped the handles from Spode teacups and sent china plates of sandwiches crashing to the floor. And his conversation did not improve. At an afternoon tea, I overheard him talking to a young lady about suicide. And during one buffet supper, he entertained me with a humorous story which relied much upon the mating activities of barnyard animals – enough so that I was required to remind him I was an unmarried lady, and not an Illinois mountain man. Although the story had stirred me in a way which caused me to flush from more than genteel embarrassment.

None of this escaped the notice of my sister.

"What was it that Mr. Lincoln was speaking so animatedly to you about?" she inquired as we rode home after the supper.

"Livestock," I replied.

Elizabeth sniffed, an unfortunate habit she had picked up from her husband.

"It was most entertaining," I assured her. I knew that my sister did not like Mr. Lincoln, that she did not believe him suitable for marriage. But I would not give her the satisfaction of telling her I considered him equally unsuitable. And in truth, I found it impossible to dislike Mr. Lincoln. Certainly, he was too unhandsome and awkward and melancholy to make a husband. But unlike that of any person I had ever known, his character possessed no amount of unkindness. And by summer, I was no longer taking such pains to avoid him, although I never allowed him to carry anything china to me.

That was the summer the entire country became consumed by politics. The hero of the Indian wars, William Henry Harrison, was running for president against the Democrat Martin Van Buren, and no one, it seemed, held an opinion which was unfiery. Fistfights over which candidate was more deserving broke out on every corner. And it was impossible to travel anyplace in Springfield without hearing slander against either Harrison or Van Buren, sometimes both in the same argument.

It was on one very warm afternoon during this time that Elizabeth sent me to Joshua Speed's store to buy a length of muslin. Upon coming out of the store, I found myself in the middle of an impassioned recitation of the merits of Mr. Van Buren. The speaker, a rough-looking sort in boots which in the heat smelled strongly of bear grease, was sitting upon a crate of soda crackers in the shade of Mr. Speed's porch. His companions, all men, listened from their perches upon pickle barrels and bushels of feed. I knew that I should hurry home. Elizabeth wanted her muslin, and ladies did not loiter about Mr. Speed's store engaging in conversations about politics. But the man in the bear-greased boots was trumpeting the merits of Mr. Van Buren with such infuriating certainty, I could not make myself leave the porch.

"Harrison is trading upon nothing more than shooting at savages," declared the man, "when it is obvious Van Buren is the better choice!"

"That you would say so makes me wonder at your reasoning, sir." The words had come so suddenly, even I was surprised to understand that it was I who was speaking and waving Elizabeth's muslin for emphasis. "Indeed, I might well fear for your soundness of mind, that you would so loudly extol the virtues of Andrew Jackson's handpicked successor. For no one in possession of his full faculties could prefer Jackson's dimwitted lackey over the valiant and courageous General Harrison."

A great silence fell over the porch of Joshua Speed's general store. All the men present, including the one in the stinking boots, fixed their eyes upon the wooden flooring, too mortified by my unfeminine display to even look upon me. My face grew hot, hotter than even the heated day could be held responsible for, and if it would not have called more attention to myself, I would have thrown Elizabeth's muslin over my head and dashed down the steps.

"Miss Todd," drawled Mr. Lincoln, whom I had not noticed lounging on a sack of feed, "I dearly wish I could express the very same judgment at the courthouse next week. I have no doubt it would be a good deal more effective than anything more polite I might devise." Unfolding his legs, he rose and relieved me of my package. "Perhaps if you allow me to accompany you home, we might further discuss Mr. Van Buren's shortcomings?"

Gratefully, I let Mr. Lincoln take my arm and lead me from the porch.

"I sometimes forget that ladies should not speak of politics," I told him.

"If ladies can't talk about politics or mating," he replied, "they will have very little left to say."

"You came from town with Mr. Lincoln?" said my sister, when I had returned with the muslin. "I hope he did not talk to you of death."

"Mr. Lincoln may not be conversant in the language of chivalry," I said to her, "but he understands its practice."

"He is not handsome," Elizabeth reminded me. "His father is a farmer. His mother, I have heard, was illegitimate."

"Does that mean I should not allow him to carry home my package on a warm day?"

"So long as you do not think of marrying him."

"Even in your mind," I told my sister, "the carrying of muslin cannot be construed as a declaration of marital intention."

In early autumn, Mr. Lincoln invited me to hear him give a speech at the Springfield courthouse. Ambitious gentlemen oft made speeches in that place, hoping to catch the notice of the gentlemen who ran the state's political parties. I do not recall what the topic of Mr. Lincoln's speech was to be. And indeed, despite the announced topic, such talks were generally about government, and specifically about the speaker's notions regarding it.

The courthouse that day was half-filled – Mr. Lincoln was not as well-known as Mr. Douglas, whose speeches always claimed a full house. And I am afraid that some of the attendees appeared as if they had come into the building only to escape the heat, for though it was October, the sun was strong. Among these were some ladies of Elizabeth's circle, who sat in a side gallery, fanning themselves with linen handkerchiefs. Near the front of the auditorium was a group of men who seemed not quite sober, for they listed upon their seats and slapped each other's backs for what looked no reason at all.

At the appointed time, Mr. Lincoln came to stand upon the raised platform. At first sight of him, Elizabeth's friends ceased fanning themselves and began to titter behind their linen handkerchiefs. I thought it must be that the platform made Mr. Lincoln appear more giantlike which caused their laughter. Or perhaps it was that his trousers, for once pressed, ended six inches shy of his boot tops. Or possibly it was only Mr. Lincoln's startling homeliness which made the ladies snicker loud enough for the unsober men to take notice. I could not say for certain, for I had known Mr. Lincoln nearly a year and I supposed I had grown used to his strange looks. Indeed, to me, his odd face now seemed mostly kind, the features formed more by gentleness than dissymmetry.

It was the listing men at the front who laughed when Mr. Lincoln began to speak in his high-timbered voice. And unlike the ladies, these men were not well-bred enough – nor sufficiently clear headed – to cover their mouths. They slapped each other harder upon the back, their sniggering sending streams of tobacco juice over the floor-boards. And I wished very much that I was a man, one with a reputation for accurate shooting.

For his part, Mr. Lincoln only smiled at the men, calling one or two of them by name. He was not disturbed by their rudeness, but appeared as amused as they by the sound of his own voice, and the notion of him using it to deliver a speech in the courthouse.

"Perhaps because I myself do not drink," he told the men, "or worry overmuch about my clothes," he glanced at the ladies with such defenselessness they dropped their handkerchiefs and looked to be calculating how to present him with the name of their husbands' tailors, "I have had ample time to think about government, and those who are supposed to run it."

Again the ladies tittered and the unsober men laughed. But now no measure of it was directed against the ungainly man standing upon the platform.

Mr. Lincoln spoke then. And though his voice continued high and piping, and his large hands flew from his sides as if to make a point of their own, nobody left, or laughed. "Those who have come to be in government owe an uprightness to those who have put them there," he said. And his integrity made all who listened believe in their own goodness.

Made, too, the moving of his large hands seem not awkward, but sincere; not the practiced gestures of a politician, but the true-felt expressions of an undeceiving man. And I wondered what it might feel like to have those large hands upon me. They would span so much flesh. Cover the side of my face, the length of my throat. One of his hands could press upon the whole breadth of my heart, two could circle my waist, lift me into the air, and for as long as he desired, hold me in his possession.

My corset began to chafe distractingly against my sides, and the courtroom, which had seemed cool against the bright sun, grew overheated. As had happened on the night of Elizabeth's fête, I could not draw my eyes from Mr. Lincoln. But now, it was not his ugliness I watched. Nor his speech about government that I heard. It was not even his uncommon decency which drew me – indeed, what held me was nothing I would have described as decent. This time it was Mr. Lincoln's largeness, the lines etched about his mouth which held me. And the sight of them brought on a near-violent softening, a sensation which left me shaken and weak, and wanting very much more.

But it was improper to indulge in this sensation seated amidst the inebriated men and the ladies of Elizabeth's circle. It was scandal to sit in the courthouse in a state of fever over the speaker upon the platform. Hoping to fan myself cool, I retrieved my own handkerchief and turned my attention to the other people in the room – those whose hands I did not imagine upon my body.

The men at the front did not list so much as before. Indeed, they were focused – remarkably so for those who had drunk so freely – upon Mr. Lincoln, opening their mouths only to release a spray of tobacco juice toward the spittoon in the corner. The ladies of Elizabeth's circle did not distract themselves with rearranging the folds of their skirts, or whispering gossip to one another, but listened to Mr. Lincoln's speech with the attention they generally reserved for scandal.

They are all caught in an infatuation with him, I thought. *One less indecent than mine, but nearly as powerful.* And I knew, watching these men and these ladies who had come only to escape the heat, who had drunk too much to care about politics, that Mr. Lincoln could be president.

Knew, too, that he could be my husband. This awkward man with the fine heart and remarkable mind had been fated for me. And upon that Indian summer day in the Springfield courthouse, that seemed a thing of enormous fortune.

Afterward, I waited outside the courthouse for Mr. Lincoln to walk me home.

"Did I embarrass myself too badly?" he said, stuffing pages of his speech, now curled and damp-looking, into his pocket.

"You made them love you," I told him.

At this, he threw back his head and laughed into the golden-yellow leaves of a poplar tree. "I truly don't think I've ever made anybody love me by talking."

"Then you underestimate your ability."

He looked hard at me; then, as if fearful of the damage it might do, he lifted one large, awkward hand and put it to my cheek. "I am unused to inspiring love." His eyes, I saw, were the light gray of clouds which promise rain.

I leaned more strongly into that big hand. "That does not make you any less able at it."

Over the next weeks, it began to be gossiped in Springfield that "Miss Todd had formed an understanding with Mr. Lincoln." Indeed, it was said often enough to inspire Elizabeth to organize a remarkable number of small parties to which she invited marriageable gentlemen whose mothers were not rumored to be illegitimate. After these parties, my sister came immediately to my bedroom – not caring that I was dressed in no more than a half-buttoned chemise – so that she might enlighten me upon these gentlemen's very many virtues.

"I believe Mr. Douglas is destined for high political office," she informed me after one such gathering.

"Might we wait to discuss Mr. Douglas's political career until I am fully clothed?"

"I should not put senator beyond him."

"You recall that Mr. Douglas is a Democrat?"

Elizabeth looked about the room, filled with expensive furnishings and elegant china-based lamps. "A powerful husband is still a powerful husband."

I allowed my sister to press unmarried gentlemen upon me, flirting with them with all the excessiveness taught to Southern girls, in the hope that my frenzied eyelash-batting and overwrought fanning would persuade her the rumors regarding my engagement were false. But Elizabeth was difficult to deceive. And when she failed to interest me in one of the suitors who came to drink her tea, she turned over the task of improving my marital outlook to her husband.

"You are getting yourself talked about," my brother-in-law informed me.

It was the end of November, and though the weather had turned cold, no fire had been lit in the parlor to which Ninian summoned me.

"Perhaps that is because my sister is pushing me upon so many bachelors," I replied, seating myself upon a horsehide chair covered in lace doilies.

My brother-in-law's mouth drew tight, leaving me unsure whether it was reaction to my remark or only his unfortunate teeth paining him. "The talk is of Mr. Lincoln," he told me.

"I cannot help what people say."

"One can always help what people say," said Ninian. "One need only behave in an acceptable manner."

"And you believe marrying Mr. Lincoln would cause me to behave in an unacceptable manner?"

My brother-in-law's mouth grew tighter, and he crossed to a curio cabinet which held a doll collection belonging to Elizabeth. He stood gazing upon the china-faced dolls, as if they might be telling him his next words. "There are a great many differences between you and Mr. Lincoln," he said at last. "In education. In raising. In manner."

"Still, Mr. Lincoln possesses a great mind."

"A man's mind is not the concern of his wife," replied Ninian. "It is only breeding and social standing which affect the womanly sphere."

"And it is your opinion that Mr. Lincoln is deficient in these areas?"

Ninian sniffed so furiously, I imagined he had left no air in the room for me. "The man possesses no connections and is so impoverished, he lives free above Joshua Speed's store. It is no wonder that, at thirty-one, he has found no one to marry him."

"Perhaps he has not found the right lady."

Ninian laughed, the sound like the barking of a small, unpleasant dog. "It is more likely that none would have him. Without doubt, he is not adequately handsome to make a lady overlook his poverty."

I hated the tight-mouthed manner in which my brother-in-law spoke this. "Mr. Lincoln is a good and generous man," I declared. "And if he asks me to become his wife, I shall."

Before the last syllable of my defiant words had sounded, Ninian had crossed the room and put his hands upon the arms of my chair. I could detect the smell of rot which habitually came from his mouth.

"If Mr. Lincoln asks and you accept," he spat out, "I shall send you back to Lexington to live with your stepmother. If even the gossip about you and Mr. Lincoln does not cease, I will do the same thing."

I could not think what to say, overcome by surprise and by Ninian's breath.

"Further," my brother-in-law continued, "I am going to speak with Mr. Lincoln and inform him that your family disapproves of your match."

"He will not give me up so easily," I insisted.

Again came that dog's bark, filling my nostrils with the smell of decaying teeth. "I do not think you know your lover very well," Ninian said. "The man is subject to an overdeveloped sense of honor. He would never take you against your family's wishes."

I wanted to inform my brother-in-law that he was wrong, that Mr. Lincoln would take me despite any dishonor. But I did not know if such a thing were true.

I pushed at Ninian, sending him stumbling backward across the parlor. "You would not dare take such a liberty!" I shouted at him. But catching sight of Elizabeth's dolls in the curio cabinet, I knew that he would, and the thought made me rise from my seat and rush from the room. For a moment, I stood in the hallway, uncertain where to go. I suspected that my sister was waiting for me somewhere in the house, perhaps in my own room, and I threw myself at the door, pulling it open with such force, it banged against the wainscoting, leaving a dent in the shape of the knob.

The day had turned raw, and I was wearing nothing more than a cotton dress. Still, I would not risk going back for my cloak, but ran down the road, away from my sister's house, as if distance alone might eliminate her power over me. Stray pigs, which generally moved only for carriage wheels, fled from me. A man who had come out to repair a torn-away shutter stared as if I were an apparition.

I must see Queen Ruby! See her and ask her if I was wrong about Mr. Lincoln.

And then, as if I had conjured her up by my desire, the one-legged colored woman stood in the road not more than a few feet in front of me.

I had never before seen Queen Ruby on Aristocrat's Hill. Could not imagine what she was doing so far from her painted house, so far from town. But I did not think long upon it, only covered the distance between us in a few quick steps, not caring if everyone in Springfield saw me speaking to the conjure woman.

"I must ask you about my husband," I told her.

The colored woman looked me up and down. "I do not think you have a dollar," she said. "You do not even have a cloak." Irritably, she tugged at one of the numerous shawls tied round her shoulders. When it came loose, she removed it and wrapped it about my bare arms.

"Is it Mr. Lincoln?" I asked. "Mr. Lincoln I am supposed to marry?"

"I don't know any white men," she replied.

"He is tall and ambitious," I told her. "And, I expect, ugly."

"Then, that is probably him."

"My family will try to prevent it."

"If it's in your hand, they can't prevent it."

"I fear they shall."

Queen Ruby shook her head. "White ladies," she muttered. She backed away a step, and I worried she might leave me standing in the road.

"I believed what you told me."

"I did not tell you this would just come to you. I did not say it might not fall to you to make it true."

"But I am a woman. How can I hasten a marriage?"

The wind blew the layers of Queen Ruby's skirts, showing me the demon carved upon her leg. "You expect a lot for someone with no dollar."

"I want this marriage."

The colored woman pulled hard upon the knot of her shawl. "If a man is too decent," she said after a moment, "then maybe a woman should consider being less." Queen Ruby paused, as if making certain I had taken her meaning. Then she turned and began to walk down the Hill, although I had been certain that before she had been traveling up it. "Send back the shawl tomorrow," she called over her shoulder.

Despite the wind, which blew through the tatters of Queen Ruby's shawl, I remained standing in the road. The conjure woman's meaning had been most clear.

It was a plan which was perfect in its logic. If my proper sister and brother-in-law learned that I had been ruined, they would never allow me to go unmarried. And if I had lost my honor, who would have me, save the man who had taken it? Yes, there would be scandal – nothing happened in Springfield without someone gossiping about it. But such gossip would carry little weight once I was Mrs. Lincoln. And in the meantime, I could count upon Ninian to sniff out any rumors and quash them with his respectability. The only portion of the plan which seemed unsure was Mr. Lincoln. There was always the danger that the overdeveloped sense of honor of which Ninian had spoken might prevent him from taking my virtue.

I shall just have to convince him of the logic of my strategy, I decided. *And if that fails, I will rely upon the untamed carnality which*

I am told is lurking in all men. Clutching Queen Ruby's shawl tight about my shoulders, I hurried up Aristocrat's Hill, already plotting how I would persuade Mr. Lincoln to ruin me.

In the weeks before Christmas, as the rest of the household made ready to celebrate the birth of the Christ Child, I made ready to lose my virtue. But finding opportunity to accomplish the deed was no easy matter, for I lived beneath the respectable gaze of Mr. and Mrs. Ninian Edwards, and Mr. Lincoln shared his bed with the store owner Joshua Speed, an arrangement which saved him the expense of monthly rent. Moreover, as my brother-in-law had made good upon his threat to warn Mr. Lincoln away from me, that gentleman now went out of his way to avoid my company. Thus the Yuletide season, with its whirl of dancing parties and levees, came and went with my maidenhood unassailed, and as the New Year approached, I feared I would enter 1841 as chaste as I had entered 1840.

That season's New Year's party was given by Mercy's handsome brother, Lawrason. It was considered a great social occasion, and as I expected even the recently reclusive Mr. Lincoln would attend, I wore for it a gown which revealed so much of my bosom, Ninian was inches from apoplexy upon viewing it. Indeed, I believe he would have sent me back to change had he not been too correct to utter the word "bosom" in my presence. My sister and brother-in-law and myself were among the first to arrive at Lawrason's house – Ninian was always punctual, even for parties – and were led directly into the dining room. Lawrason's banqueting table had been laid with silver platters of stuffed quail and glazed goose, suckling pig covered in syrup, and piles of oysters.

Mr. Lincoln arrived late at the party and did not appear to notice my dress, or what it failed to cover. By the time the dancing began, he had disappeared.

"I have seen little of our friend Mr. Lincoln this evening," I said to Lawrason. I did not bother to pretend indifference; Mercy told her brother everything. "Is he off someplace with Mr. Speed?"

"Not unless he has decided to undertake a journey," replied Lawrason. "Joshua Speed has gone to Kentucky."

"Mr. Speed is away?"

"He is in Louisville with Miss Henning." Fanny Henning was Joshua Speed's intended.

"So Mr. Lincoln is entirely alone in his rooms?"

Lawrason, who possessed perfect teeth, showed them to me in a wicked smile. "You are very curious about our tall lawyer's sleeping arrangements."

"I only wonder that he did not stay longer at your party," I said, "as he will only have his own company at home." Lawrason did not always keep secrets as well as Mercy believed.

For the remainder of the evening, I could not cease thinking upon Mr. Lincoln's sleeping arrangements – and what could be accomplished now that they were so private. Near midnight, Lawrason called for a Bible so he might foretell the events of the next year.

"Is it not blasphemy to use God's Word in such pursuit?" asked a young lady from St. Louis, who was rumored to be pious.

"It is only a harmless parlor game," declared Lawrason. As he spoke, he raised the Bible above his head and let the pages fall open where they would.

"Where have we landed?" asked Mr. Douglas, who perhaps due to his lack of height had not failed to notice the flesh left bare by my gown.

"Ecclesiastes!" announced Mercy's brother.

Lawrason held a finger over the Bible, letting it circle over the thin page until his audience begged him to settle upon a verse before the New Year had run its course.

"It is unwise to hurry the prognostications of the Lord," he replied. And with much drama, he at last dropped his finger onto the page.

"Read it aloud," urged Mr. Douglas. It was well-known that in the coming year, Stephen Douglas was hoping to be appointed to the Illinois Supreme Court.

With a good deal of unnecessary throat-clearing, Lawrason read from Ecclesiastes. "*Two are better than one,*" he said in a solemn tone, "*for if two lie together, then they have heat, but how can one be warm alone?*"

The pious lady from St. Louis blushed. Mr. Douglas murmured something to me regarding the imprudence of ignoring any advice that originated with the Almighty. Lawrason again showed his teeth in that unchaste grin.

I had no doubt that Mercy's brother had searched the page for the most scandalous verse. Still, the very great coincidence between the prediction and my plan could not have been devised entirely by Lawrason. The Bible had naturally fallen open to the page, and the verse about two lying together had been upon it. What more evidence could I require to prove that God Himself approved of my scheme?

Now that I was certain this was the night I would forfeit my virtue, Lawrason's party took on a more vivid cast. I ate quail and the savory taste of the meat filled my mouth with wetness. I danced and the first contact of Mr. Douglas's hands upon my waist made me tremble. The air in Lawrason's rooms grew heavy with the scent of ladies' perfume and nutmeg and the roasted flesh of the birds, and I breathed it in greedily until I was near to panting. I allowed more hands to touch my waist, liking the feel of them. And in between, I went back to the table and swallowed oysters, their briny liquid sliding down my throat, put into my mouth pieces of the suckling pig, and coated my tongue with the sweet greasiness of the meat. I ate from all the silver dishes and wished for something more, although I could not have named what it was.

And through it all, I prayed for Ninian to come and say it was time for us to return home.

It was just past midnight when Ninian did come; and for once I made no protest, telling my sister and brother-in-law that I was much fatigued, although I nearly leapt into the carriage. Once home, I said my good-nights just inside the door, declaring that I would not stir until late morning. Then, I went into my room and waited for the rest of the house to fall to sleep.

I used this time to determine exactly what a lady might wear to entice a man into sin. While my corset pushed my flesh into its most alluring shape, I doubted whether Mr. Lincoln's hands, which had so much difficulty with teacups, would be able to undo the garment's complicated lacing. Nevertheless, without a corset I could not achieve the twenty-inch waist required for every one of my gowns. I shall just have to go to Mr. Lincoln without a dress, I told myself, thrilled by the wantonness of the idea.

Searching my closet, I found a silk pelisse overdress which opened at the front and was loose enough to fasten about my uncorseted body. I buttoned the pelisse over a nearly transparent chemise and stood before my glass. Without a corset, my unbound flesh swayed beneath the fabric, and the sensation of being so lightly held and the slide of silk over my skin caused me to shiver in a way that was independent of the chill of Ninian's house.

Listening to see that no one remained awake, I stepped into the hallway and hurried downstairs. At the door, I covered myself with a hooded cloak – no lady, even one on her way to willingly give up her virtue, could be discovered out alone after midnight – and grabbed up a small oil lantern, for though Aristocrat's Hill possessed fourteen gas lamps, Mr. Lincoln's neighborhood had very few. Careful to shut the door with no noise, I went out into the midwinter night.

Wind blew through the opening of my cloak and its chill bite inflamed my barely covered flesh. All was quiet on the Hill, where respectable gentlemen and ladies were asleep, but as I made my way into town, the frigid air was pierced by the screams and raucous laughter of those still celebrating the New Year.

Near the town square, I came upon a group of men firing guns at the façade of the capitol. I hid my lantern behind my skirts, hoping to get by them without being seen, for they appeared too drunk even to hit the building's side. But I did not get very far before one of them cried out.

"Stop!" he said. And I heard him fire his gun into the air.

"Who are you shouting at?" asked another voice.

"A woman!" exclaimed the first. "There's a woman there!"

I had come to be ruined by Mr. Lincoln and not a group of drunken louts with guns. I fled across the square, followed by the noise of feet clattering upon the wooden sidewalk. Once I thought they might catch me, for I stumbled and nearly fell, made dizzy by the volume of air I could draw into my uncorseted lungs. Still, I was sober and the men were not, and by the time I reached the block that held Joshua Speed's store, they were far behind me and seemed to have forgotten why they'd come that way.

The rooms which Mr. Lincoln shared with Mr. Speed were reached by a wooden staircase at the side of the store. Hearing the drunken men call to each other at the end of the street, I extinguished my light before beginning the climb. The steps were old and my pelisse, without hoops, was too long, and near the top, my hem caught upon a splintered board. Without warning, I was pulled backward. I lost my balance and I grabbed for the railing in the darkness. But my fingers clutched only empty air, and I was certain I would fall. *I have attempted to use God's Word to justify my debauchery and this is His punishment for it,* I thought. *The Almighty would rather have me break my body, than allow me to debase it.*

But perhaps the Lord was more merciful than I believed. Or perhaps, He had only wished me to stop and consider. For as I felt myself begin to fall, my fingers grazed the railing and I caught myself and only tumbled to the step below.

For some time, I sat upon the step, too shaken to stand. If God had almost thrown me to my death because He wished me to reflect upon my intention, He had succeeded. However, I did not think so much upon the act's sinfulness as its terrifying nature. Everything I knew about the marriage act I had learned from a little book I discovered at the back of Elizabeth's dresser drawer while searching for a darning needle. The book was titled "The Philosophical Fruits of Marriage" – although it contained very little that was philosophical and very much about preventing these marital fruits. The little book's precautionary information, which dealt at some length with pessaries and baking soda baths, did provide me with a basic knowledge of what to expect during the conjugal act. Information to which I reacted with equal amounts of dread and disgust, for the mechanics of it seemed awkward and embarrassing – certainly I could not conceive of my sister and brother-in-law engaged in such an untidy pursuit. What I had felt upon shutting the book and replacing it in Elizabeth's dresser drawer was the profound hope that I would never have to submit to anything so repellent.

You can still go home, said my less brave voice. *You can make God and Ninian happy and return to the house on Aristocrat's Hill.*

But if I do not go up, I told it, *Elizabeth will sooner or later marry me off to somebody else. And then I shall have to do with him the strange activity described in "The Philosophical Fruits of Marriage." Better to engage in it with Mr. Lincoln, whose large hands and what I imagine he can do with them will keep me from thinking too much upon the mechanics of the act.*

And pulling my hem free of the step, I rose and climbed to the top.

I knew that the door would be unlocked, as Mr. Lincoln often declared that he and Mr. Speed possessed nothing worth stealing. I pushed upon it, and it opened with a gentle click. Inside it was dark. I fumbled in my pocket for a lucifer to light my lamp.

The room was an unholy disarray. The floor was a sea of

unmated boots and crumpled newspaper, empty peanut shells and tin plates crusted with baked bean suppers. So much clothing was scattered upon the floor, I was reminded of Queen Ruby's house. In one corner, I spied a man's undergarment, and afraid that it might be in an unclean state, I yanked away the light.

I found Mr. Lincoln asleep in the bed he shared with Mr. Speed. He looked to have returned from Lawrason's party and done little before throwing himself on top of the bedclothes. He was still dressed in the long-tailed shirt he had worn to the party, though nothing else. I let my light travel the length of his body, over his hip which jutted sharply against the boiled cotton of the shirt, over his narrow-boned legs stretched across the bed. But it felt indecent to examine him this way, and I moved my light to his face, melancholy even in sleep. I noticed that his long fingers were curved about the plump edge of the pillow, and I felt again the slide of silk along my unbound flesh.

I set my lantern upon the floor and dropped my cloak beside it. Unbuttoning my pelisse, I slipped into the bed.

The linen upon which the bachelors slept felt oily and smelled of bay rum, of which Mr. Speed was very fond. What I had at first taken for shadows upon the coverlet, I now saw was boot blacking from men who did not always remove their shoes before getting into bed. Like most virgins, I had imagined the loss of my maidenhood. Yet in none of these imaginings did the event take place on bed linen that bore traces of street dirt and another bachelor's cologne.

Remember Mr. Lincoln's gentleness of nature and great good heart. Remember how much flesh can be covered by those hands. And stopping my breath against the odors of bay rum and sweat, I pressed my mouth to his.

I had never put my mouth upon a man's before and the sensation was odd and unexpected. Mr. Lincoln's lips were softer than I had anticipated, and the skin above them rougher. Still, it was not unpleasurable at all. I allowed my mouth to stay upon Mr. Lincoln's, and his own lips returned the kiss, with soft pressure at first, then with an insistence that pressed me back upon a pillow which smelled of Mr. Speed. Slowly, and with a deftness I had not believed they possessed, his hands moved along my uncorseted sides, lifting the hem of my pelisse.

I think that Mr. Lincoln was caught in a state between waking and dreaming, a state in which desire flowed unexamined. And I wished to keep him in this state, at least until he was so near to taking me, he could not turn back. But the drunken men celebrating the New Year with guns must have remained upon this street, for without warning came the loud snap of a bullet striking the wooden sign on Mr. Speed's store.

Mr. Lincoln's eyes flew open, and with a startled cry, he sprang from the bed. He stood gasping, the light from my lamp giving him the shadow of a giant upon the opposite wall. "Mary?" he said.

"I am glad that upon finding a lady in your bed, mine is the first name upon your lips."

"Why are you here?"

"Surely you will not make me describe my purpose. I am, after all, still a virgin."

Mr. Lincoln tugged at the hem of his boiled shirt, attempting to pull it lower over his legs.

"I should feel considerably more welcome if you did not keep staring at your bed as if you had awakened to find a snake in it."

"I don't know what to make of your being here."

I sat up, letting him see my unbuttoned pelisse, the sheer chemise beneath it. "I have come to let you ruin me."

"Why would you do such a thing?"

"For Ninian's sake."

At the mention of my brother-in-law's name, Mr. Lincoln seized a pair of trousers from the floor and tried to step into them. However, the trousers were too knotted up, half pulled inside out, and he could do no more than hold them in front of his naked legs. "Maybe it is the shock of finding a lady in my bed, but nothing you are saying makes sense."

"Ninian," I told him, "is far too respectable to allow his tarnished sister-in-law to remain unmarried."

Mr. Lincoln backed away from the bed. "I cannot ruin you."

I shifted so my pelisse would fall a little more open. "My pride will be severely wounded if you do not."

"But your reputation will be intact."

"I have no desire to be a virtuous spinster," I said.

"I believe Douglas is pretty willing to make sure you don't stay a spinster." He began to pull clothes from the floor, but found nothing wearable.

"Stephen Douglas is a Democrat!" I declared. In the dim light, I thought I saw Mr. Lincoln smile. "Come back to your bed." I patted the unclean linens.

He ceased searching for clothes, but remained at the other side of the room. "I think it best I stay where I am."

"I wish only to talk to you."

"I hear you fine."

I pulled shut the pelisse to show my good intent. "You recall that I am a woman who does not much exceed five feet in height?" I reminded him. "Even if I were to assail your virtue, you are more than capable of repelling me."

He waited a moment or two, and then he came and sat at the very edge of the mattress. "When I find my trousers," he told me, "I am going to walk you back to your sister's house."

"Perhaps we should wait a bit," I said, "as there are men outside attempting to murder Mr. Speed's store." I inched myself nearer to him.

He held his hands together in his lap. "I have promised to give you up."

"You cannot make that promise," I told him. I came very close to him, and when he did not move away, placed my lips nearly upon his and took his breath into my mouth.

A burst of gunfire rattled against the side of the building.

"I will make them stop." He made a motion, as if to rise.

"You shall be killed for it." I slid my hands under the hem of his shirt. The skin beneath his clothes was as soft as that of a child. "Put your hands upon me," I begged him. "Only once more."

His hands moved as if by their own resolve, the long fingers spanning the breadth of my collarbones, the thumbs pressing into the soft depression at the base of my throat. *He could snap my bones without effort,* I thought. And the notion of having such hands upon me produced an aching which almost made me wish for him to do it.

"You may use me any way you like." I showed him my throat, as though he might wish to put teeth to that flesh. "There is no thing I will stop you from doing."

I felt his breath upon my face, his fingers pressing my breastbone. With a sound I heard as equal part anguish and desire, he jerked me to him with such violence, my head flew back. Before I could raise it, his lips were upon mine.

This time his mouth was not soft. With his hands, with that

unsoft mouth, he pushed me back onto the soiled sheets. His weight fell upon me; he gripped my ribs, my hips, the long bones of my thighs so strongly, I was sure that indeed they would break. And I knew now for certain I would feel a kind of ecstasy in their snapping.

Mr. Lincoln took my maidenhood, and there was some pain. But even such rending – done roughly, for his desire would not let him slow – was incidental, overwhelmed by a sensation both profound and unexpected. For despite its detailed discussion of pessaries and baking soda baths, "The Philosophical Fruits of Marriage" had said not one word about pleasure. And pleasure is precisely what I experienced in the bed above Mr. Speed's store. Although pleasure does not go far enough to describe it.

Mr. Lincoln's large hands were everywhere upon me. His teeth grazed my most sensitive flesh. His skin, which possessed the uncommon scent of woodsmoke, slid over mine until my entire body shuddered. I had come to Mr. Lincoln's bed with the intent of corrupting myself enough to require marrying. However, once I had accomplished my intention, I wished only to be corrupted further and cared nothing about marriage.

When Mr. Lincoln fell upon the mattress, sated, I did not dress and return to my sister's house, but sat and let my unbound hair fall upon his chest and belly, tangling it in the coarse strands there. I teased his flesh with my fingers, pressed my tongue into the cleft that split his chin, until he moaned and took hold of my waist like the wickedest corset, lifting my hips and setting me upon him, so he might take me again. I was sore and aching, but the pain served only to cut the pleasure deeper; and I was so borne away by the shuddering swells that overtook my body, the exquisite sensation of weightless tumbling, that I feared for my reason; for I had heard it whispered that ladies who enjoyed the marriage act too strongly were in danger of losing their sanity.

The first morning of 1841 was dawning when I rose from Mr. Lincoln's bed. Some small amount of blood – red like the color of the hand painted upon Queen Ruby's house – stained the sheets. But they had been so soiled to begin with, I did not think Mr. Speed would notice it.

"Give me time to dress and I'll walk you back to Aristocrat's Hill," mumbled Mr. Lincoln. He barely glanced at me.

"It will be far more scandalous if I am seen walking home at this hour with you," I told him. "But come to the house once everyone is awake and tell Ninian what we have done."

I bent to kiss him, to feel again the soft hardness of his mouth, but he flinched and pulled away. *His mouth is only bruised. Like mine. I shall kiss it again, later, when he comes to the house.* And wrapping myself once more in my cloak, I went out into the cold dawn.

The men who had been firing at Joshua Speed's store were nowhere to be seen. Still, I kept my hood pulled over my face, raising it only enough to keep me from tripping over a slumbering pig or bumping into a hitching post. The air was so icy, it felt brittle. But I noticed it only upon my face, for beneath my cloak my flesh was heated by surplus desire and overuse.

Because of the unusually late hour of the party the night before, everyone at my sister's house was still in bed when I returned – even Ninian, who believed in the moral goodness of early rising. Once in my room, I undressed and washed with cold water left over from the night before. My pelisse and chemise were both torn at the seams, but I was reluctant to give them to the maid to mend – surely she would tell Elizabeth, and I did not wish my sister to know so much about Mr. Lincoln's lovemaking. I also did not wish to turn the garments over to be washed, for they held the scent of woodsmoke, as well as something unidentifiable which made me want to run back through the freezing streets to Mr. Speed's store. At last, I wrapped the torn clothing in paper and put them in the wooden chest which held my trousseau. Then I got into bed, slipping my still-thrumming body between sheets which appeared especially white and gave off the smell of lye.

Mr. Lincoln will come early, I determined. *Perhaps right after breakfast. By evening we will be engaged. In a month's time – it would be risky to wait any longer, too many in Springfield like to count the months between the wedding and the birth announcements – we shall be married and will spend the whole of every night repeating what we did this evening in that bachelors' bed.*

Although I had gone to bed at dawn, I woke with the rest of the household and was already dressed and at the breakfast table before Elizabeth came down. I ate two helpings of waffles – I possessed a remarkable hunger – and only half-listened to my sister's exclamations regarding Mr. Douglas's attentiveness to me at the party. *Before I swallow the last mouthful,* I told myself over and again, *the housemaid will come to announce Mr. Lincoln.* But even after I could eat no more and the dishes were cleared away, he had not come.

He did not come at midday, or by afternoon, and I began to fear he might not come at all. *Mr. Lincoln is too decent to desert me,* I reminded myself. *He is only working out what to say to Ninian.*

Not until it was nearly dark did the maid come to the sitting room to say that Mr. Lincoln had arrived. Ninian sniffed loudly upon hearing the name. For my part, I was so relieved, I thought how my brother-in-law would likely rupture something in his nose when he learned that Mr. Lincoln had (twice!) debased his wife's sister, and I was compelled to bend more closely over my needlework to hide my blushing.

But it was not Ninian whom Mr. Lincoln wanted to see.

"You are certain he said he wished to speak to me?" I asked the maid.

"He asked for Miss Todd, as usual," she replied, gazing at me as if I had lost my senses.

He must wish to rehearse his speech for me. To be certain he is saying the proper thing. And without meeting my sister's eyes, I hurried to the parlor.

My future husband looked to have passed an uneasy day. His face was drawn and his eyes were circled with shadows gray as ashes. I was startled to see that to come to speak with Ninian he had dressed himself in a suit of clothes which could not have appeared more creased had they been in his bed with us for all of last night. *This is only his nervousness at confessing our sin. Only his honor making him anxious.*

"Do not be afraid of Ninian," I said, trying for lightness. "He is far too well-bred to shoot you in his own home."

Mr. Lincoln remained where he was, standing beside a window at the other side of the room. "I did not come to speak with Ninian."

"But you must!" I hurried over to him. "If we try to marry against his wishes, he will send me to my father's house."

"I cannot marry you," he told me.

The words were the same as if he had taken one of his large hands and struck me. "I was certain you loved me," I said to him.

"If I did not love you so much, I would marry you."

I put my hand upon his sleeve. "You say this because you are poor?"

"And because you are a Todd and unused to poverty."

"Your poverty does not matter," I told him.

"Poverty always matters." He gazed about Elizabeth's parlor, crowded with furniture and gilt-framed landscapes. "I suggest you overcome your aversion to Democrats and marry Douglas."

Mr. Lincoln paced the room, stopping before the small table upon which Elizabeth still displayed a china crèche of painted figures. I saw his fingers reach for one of the figures – the Virgin – then fold themselves back into his palm before touching her.

"You took my virtue," I reminded him.

"I wish that I hadn't."

I went and took hold of those unsafe hands. "I do not. Moreover, I wish you would take it again. Here, upon every one of my sister's lace doilies."

An expression of fear came over Mr. Lincoln's face and with too much violence, he took back his hands. "That kind of desire is dangerous."

"It is only passion."

"And yours is too unrestrained."

"It did not appear too unrestrained for you last night."

"Last night I allowed it to overcome my reason. That will not happen again."

I wanted to take hold of his hands again, but he had clasped them behind his back.

"It can happen again," I told him. "If we are married, it can happen every night."

He turned away from me, rattling the china figures in the manger. "No!" he cried. He was shouting now. "It cannot ever happen!"

Stunned by his vehemence, and by his unwillingness to do again something which had been so very pleasurable, I followed him across the room. "You would not wish to repeat what occurred last night?"

Shaking his head furiously, he turned on me. "I regret what we did more than you can know."

"You regret it?" I asked in disbelief. "I gave you my honor and now you say you regret taking it?" It was this, even more than his refusal to marry me, which touched so hard upon my pride.

I looked about the parlor, afraid that someone – the housemaid, my sister – might have heard Mr. Lincoln say this to me. My eye fell upon the china Virgin and for an awful moment, I imagined that her face altered, the painted expression changing from saintly to scornful.

"I am the one who should regret what occurred last night," I declared. "For I have forfeited my virtue to a man who lacks the courage to accept it."

"I am afraid," he admitted.

"Of marrying me?" I said, incredulous.

"Of your desire."

"And it is that fear – more than my family's disapproval, more than your poverty – which allows you to leave me ruined and unmarriageable?"

Mr. Lincoln covered his face with his hands.

"You have done me the worst harm a man can inflict upon a woman," I told him.

"I would rather be dead than make you unhappy," he muttered into his hands.

"I do not ever wish to see your homely face again," I said to him. "Leave here, and never come back."

I thought he might argue, might make some fight for me. But Mr. Lincoln only nodded, and without showing me his face, exited the room.

I heard him ask the housemaid for his coat, heard the front door open. Already I wished to call him back and tell him that his face was as dear to me as any I had ever known. But anger and pride held me in Elizabeth's parlor.

I heard nothing of Mr. Lincoln for an entire week, until one evening at supper, when my brother-in-law brought news of him.

"I hear that Mr. Lincoln has not been seen in public since the New Year," Ninian said to Elizabeth and myself. "And that Doctor Henry has been called to his room every day."

"Do they say he is ill?" I asked.

Ninian did not answer right away, but fixed his attention upon cutting his beef into pieces sufficiently small for his teeth. He remained so long upon this task, I felt certain it was intentional. "Apparently," said my brother-in-law at last, "the man has fallen into an acute melancholy. It is so severe, only the doctor and Mr. Speed are allowed into the room."

It is the terrible things I have said to him, I thought, wringing my napkin in my lap. "Does Doctor Henry believe it is serious?" I said to my brother-in-law.

"Lincoln keeps the room in such darkness, one can barely make him out beneath the bedcovers. Mr. Speed has had to remove all the knives and razors from the room." Ninian stopped to cut more beef into tiny pieces. "They say the man is only inches from becoming a perfect lunatic for life."

I could not speak.

"You should count yourself lucky," declared my sister. "You have been spared becoming wife to a madman. Or a suicide."

Without thinking, without letting go of the napkin clutched in my hand, I leapt to my feet.

"You cannot go to his room," Elizabeth warned. "It would cause scandal."

"I must."

"He will not let anybody in," Ninian reminded me.

I opened my mouth to tell him that Mr. Lincoln would allow me in, but I did not know if that was true. Indeed I expected that it was not. "I shall go to Doctor Henry, then," I said. "To hear for myself how he is."

"If you go, people will talk," Elizabeth replied.

"I cannot care about that now," I told her. And stopping only to throw down the napkin and fetch a cloak, I hurried out the door.

I ran all the way to Doctor Henry's house, not feeling the weight of my skirts, or the hard wind which blew them tight about my legs.

"You must tell me about Mr. Lincoln," I begged the doctor when he opened the door to me. "For I fear his melancholy is my doing."

"I do not believe it would be correct for me to discuss Mr. Lincoln's case," replied Doctor Henry somewhat stiffly.

The man appeared cold, and I feared he would shut the door upon me. "Please," I said to him. "You must know that I am more than a disinterested bystander in matters concerning Mr. Lincoln." Although my words were formal, my voice was made unsteady by worry.

Doctor Henry looked hard into my face. "On the other hand," he said in a kinder tone, "I expect it would be even less correct to leave you out here in the wind. Come into the parlor and we will talk."

He led me to a room which held a museum's worth of artifacts. Every table was crowded with taxidermy animals caught leaping after prey or watching from branches. Small pedestals held the oversized eggs of ostriches and emus, and a glass cabinet in a corner was filled with fossils, the shapes of prehistoric creatures etched upon rock. Displayed upon the shelves of a large bookcase were the skulls of small mammals.

"I have an interest in animal biology," explained Doctor Henry. "It is less unpredictable than the practice of medicine."

He gestured me into a horsehair sofa and settled himself upon a wingback chair. Anson Henry was not much older than Mr. Lincoln, although he looked younger. At either side of his mouth he possessed fine lines which recalled the shape of his smile, even when his expression was serious.

"Please tell me what is wrong with Mr. Lincoln," I pleaded. "I cannot bear not to know."

"Mr. Lincoln is suffering from a case of hypochondriasis."

"I am a woman," I reminded him, "not a doctor."

"It is a severe form of melancholy."

"Can you say what has caused it?"

Doctor Henry glanced at his collection of fossils. "Mr. Lincoln has been subject to melancholic fits for some time. And it is difficult to determine their precise cause. I do believe, however, that they tend to come on when his mind is unbalanced."

"You are saying he is lunatic?" I asked, horror-struck.

The doctor shook his head. "Mr. Lincoln is not lunatic. But he is a man of high principles. Too high, perhaps. If something causes him to believe he has betrayed these high ideals, it creates a crisis of conscience – which unbalances his mind and sends him into melancholy."

"Then this hypochondriasis *is* my fault!" I exclaimed.

"You have caused Mr. Lincoln a crisis of conscience?" said the doctor in some surprise. "How?"

"I cannot say." I turned away so he would not notice me blush. "But you must let me see him."

"That would be unwise," said Doctor Henry.

"I may be able to make things right."

"This is a disease of the mind; only Mr. Lincoln can make things right. Meantime, if you are indeed the cause of his hypochondriasis, seeing you might only send him deeper into melancholy. And I fear for his ability to survive such a plummet."

No matter how fervently I pleaded, Doctor Henry would not

grant me permission to see Mr. Lincoln. And without the doctor's assistance, I did not think I would be let into his room. In the end, there was nothing for me to do, save heed Doctor Henry's advice and wait for Mr. Lincoln to make himself better. But I could not wait with only Ninian's repetition of rumor for information, so I began to call upon Doctor Henry several times a week.

At my first visit the doctor told me, "Mr. Lincoln does not eat and has not the strength to rise from his bed. His mind is consumed by morbid thoughts."

"He speaks of death?" I almost did not ask it.

"When he speaks at all."

At the visit after that, Doctor Henry said, "Mr. Lincoln is so thin as to cause alarm upon encountering him. He can barely push his voice above a whisper."

"Can you do nothing for him?"

"I have bled him and given him doses of castor oil, but they do not seem able to purge this melancholy."

Not until the beginning of February did the doctor have more-hopeful news. "He is frail, but now goes out in the world."

"Then I can see him?"

"If he has not sought you out, I would advise waiting. It would take very little to bring on another attack."

Once again, I resigned myself to following Doctor Henry's advice. But I began to wonder how long I might be asked to wait.

In March, Doctor Henry called Mr. Lincoln prone to bouts of distraction. In April, he said he was plagued by nightmares. In June, he told me he was worried that Mr. Lincoln might suffer a relapse, as he had taken to his bed and would not rise until the doctor administered a great amount of calomel for purging.

During these months, I was forced to rely upon Doctor Henry's reports because I saw Mr. Lincoln nowhere. He no longer snapped teacups in drawing rooms, or trod on ladies' feet at dances. I could not even count upon seeing him at Speed's store, for Joshua Speed had sold his business, and Mr. Lincoln had taken rooms with a family named Butler at the other end of town. He turned up nowhere I went, although I invented errands which would take me past the courthouse in the hope of encountering him. And even into the summer, Doctor Henry would not arrange a meeting between us, fearing that just the sight of me might send him into lunacy.

Meantime, I longed for Mr. Lincoln's company in a manner which was not ladylike. One Sunday in midsummer, I sat beside Elizabeth and Ninian in the pew at the Episcopal church and heard as if for the first time the story of Original Sin. *This is my story now,* I thought to myself. *I have eaten of the fruit and been made aware of my own nakedness.* And indeed, even in church I could not cease thinking of my bare flesh, trapped beneath the corset which held my ribs like a lover's hands.

"Do you require salts?" hissed Elizabeth, poking me with an elbow.

"No," I murmured. "Why do you ask it?"

"You appear as if you might swoon."

Certainly, I longed also for Mr. Lincoln's wit and his gentleness, the intricate working of his mind. But this new yearning was like appetite, more immediate and harder to suppress.

"I cannot wait any longer," I said to Doctor Henry at autumn's end. "You must give me permission to see Mr. Lincoln."

"It has been less than a year since his attack of hypochondriasis," he reminded me.

"Yes!" I exclaimed. "Nearly a year and I have not seen him! I hear that he has resumed his practice. That he argues cases and involves himself in politics. Do you believe that merely putting himself in the company of a lady will be enough to make him lose his hold on reason?"

Doctor Henry smiled. "From what Mr. Lincoln has said to me, putting himself in your company may well be more debilitating than a session in the legislature."

I stared at him, too shocked to be ashamed. "What has Mr. Lincoln said to you?"

The doctor let his smile fall, but kept his expression sympathetic. "Not so much to warrant such an expression of anxiety. But enough to make me wary of recommending he place himself in your presence."

"But I wish only to see him well."

"I know that." Doctor Henry rose and went to the bookshelves which held his collection of mammal skulls. I waited while he arranged them into a more-even line. "Like many men of great intelligence, Mr. Lincoln believes his mental state to be fragile," he told me. "And having seen how profound his slip into hypochondriasis, I cannot say I disagree with him."

"I do not see how this would make you wish to keep us apart."

Doctor Henry left the skulls and came to sit beside me upon the horsehair sofa. "Mr. Lincoln is convinced that any emotion which is too strong, which would cause him to lose control, will tip him into madness."

I knew that what Doctor Henry was telling me was as true as any fact of animal biology. I had already put my lover into hypochondriasis. How could I fault him for not wishing me to send him into lunacy as well?

"I appreciate your candor," I said to Doctor Henry. "Despite how much it has embarrassed me."

The doctor took my hands. "I would very much prefer to be advising you to go after Mr. Lincoln and get him to marry you."

"I would prefer it as well."

Then I rose and let him show me out.

The day which had begun warm had turned cold, and I did not have a shawl. *Perhaps I shall come upon Queen Ruby,* I thought bitterly, *and she will loan me one of hers. Then, I shall tell her that she was wrong about Mr. Lincoln and myself.* But only thinking upon Queen Ruby made me recall the warning she had given me along with her shawl. "I did not tell you this would just come to you," she had said about my marriage. "I did not say it might not fall to you to make it true."

But how might I make it true without learning to rein in my desire so that Mr. Lincoln and I could lie together in the marriage bed and he not rise a lunatic? To give up a wife's pleasure in order to be made a wife felt too much a Devil's bargain. Although in truth, the relinquishing of pleasure had never been the Devil's occupation. Such work was more the vocation of the Almighty.

If that is so, I thought, *perhaps I might count upon God to help me accomplish it. But could I count also upon God to help me persuade Mr. Lincoln I was capable of such sacrifice? Could I count upon Him to bring us together so I might plead my case?* I did not believe so. For in my mind, God was a man, and therefore too much like Doctor Henry. For this, I required someone who was willing to be deceitful in the name of love. For this, I required a woman.

The following day, I went to the house of Eliza Francis. Mrs. Francis's husband, Simeon, published the *Sangamo Journal,* for which Mr. Lincoln sometimes wrote, and the three were old friends. The first time I met Eliza Francis, at a dinner party in her home, she declared over dessert that the Democrats were "oppressors who would stifle every human freedom." I developed an immediate affection for her.

"I shall tell Mr. Lincoln that Simeon wishes to discuss his latest writing for the *Journal*." said Mrs. Francis when I made her my request. "I will say nothing about you being here."

"I am very grateful."

"Can you not tell what your quarrel was about?"

"I am afraid I may have behaved in a manner which was overeager."

Eliza Francis nodded. "Men do find that unsettling."

I wore for this meeting a dress which was so unappealing even Elizabeth noticed.

"I do not believe I have ever seen you in a dress which did not bare your bosom in some manner," she told me when I came downstairs. "You look like one of those New England spinsters who spend their time agitating for female suffrage."

"I am only going to pay a call on Mrs. Francis," I said, tugging upon the dress's collar, which did make me feel somewhat strangled. "No one in her parlor will be interested in viewing my bosom."

I arrived at the Francises' house before Mr. Lincoln. It was Eliza's plan that I be waiting for him in the parlor. "Like a spider?" I had asked. "Like a dutiful wife," she had replied. Taking note of my hideous dress, but being too well-bred to mention it, she showed me into the parlor, which was filled with an overwhelming number of books.

"You promise to remain behind the door to prevent Mr. Lincoln from fleeing at the sight of me?" I said.

"I shall station Simeon in the hallway with a shotgun."

She left me, and I sat upon a straight-backed settee with my knees pressed tight together. It did not of course, matter how my knees were positioned beneath my voluminous skirts, but the pose made my intention feel more attainable. After how long I did not know – it felt hours – the door again opened, and Eliza Francis entered with Mr. Lincoln.

Mr. Lincoln did not run at the sight of me, but his large hands did spring from his side like birds attempting an escape.

"I trust you will forgive my meddling," Eliza declared. "But it is the prerogative of the long-married to interfere in the romances of others." She gave Mr. Lincoln a small push to propel him into the room. "It is my very great wish that you be friends again."

She shut the door upon us.

Mr. Lincoln remained where Eliza's push had left him. It had been almost a year since his attack of hypochondriasis, yet his face and figure still bore traces of the melancholy disease. The lines at his mouth were now drawn with a harsher hand; and his gray eyes, the one feature of beauty he possessed, had sunk so deep beneath his brow they were entirely shadowed. I believed him thinner as well, for the wrists which showed from the cuffs of his shirt were more bone than flesh. The sight of them made me wish I were free to cover them with kisses.

"I have had a year to compose a pretty apology for the words I spoke to you at our last meeting," I told him, "and I fear I have devised nothing more poetic than that I wish I had never uttered them."

"You owe no poetic apologies to me," he said softly.

"I want you to know that there is not one moment of that night above Mr. Speed's store I would wish to erase."

At the mention of our encounter above Speed's store, Mr. Lincoln turned to one of the parlor's many bookcases and began to study what was shelved there, as if he intended to take something down and read it.

"There is also not a moment," I told him, "I will allow us to repeat if you do not wish it."

Still, he did not look at me.

"I understand better why you believe we cannot marry."

He put a hand upon the shelf as if he needed to steady himself to face me. "You have been talking with Doctor Henry."

"Yes. Though I am certain he would not approve of this meeting."

"Doctor Henry has been a great friend to me."

"If not an overprotective one."

"I believe I have need of his protection." He turned back to the books.

"Why is it you fear madness so much?" I asked him.

Mr. Lincoln stayed studying the volumes on the shelf for so long, I thought he had decided not to answer me.

"I have seen it," he said.

"Near to you?"

"Near enough." He turned to me now, and it seemed that his

melancholy-ravaged face had become more ravaged still. "Matthew Gentry," he said. "A boyhood friend. Probably the smartest boy I ever came upon. At sixteen he took a carving knife to his mother. Cut his own arm first, then turned on her. His father stopped him from murdering her, and he turned on him. The noise of their fighting brought the neighbors. They had to tie him up with the bedsheets to keep him from killing both his parents."

He leaned against the bookshelves and put a hand over his eyes. "I saw my friend when he was bound. He lay shrieking on the ground as if the madness had flayed him alive, as if it had locked him in a mental night that was worse than death. His eyes burned like a fiend's and he glared at those among whom he'd spent his entire life, looking as if he wished he might murder us all."

When Mr. Lincoln had finished, I went to him, took hold of those thin wrists and pulled him away from the bookcase. "You are not Matthew Gentry," I said, bringing him to sit upon the sofa.

"I have glimpsed my own mental night," he told me.

"During your melancholy?"

He nodded, and would not look at me.

"And so you believe yourself susceptible?" I said to him. "Especially if married to me?"

He touched no more than the edge of my sleeve. "I wish very much that I didn't think so."

At this, I rose and went myself to stand before the books, as if the rational arguments contained between their covers might color mine. "Suppose," I said firmly, "I endeavor to contain my passion? Suppose I learn to keep it in check so that yours does not overtake you?"

"You believe yourself capable of such action?" I heard doubt in his voice, but hope also.

"Does it not fall to women to establish restraints upon the carnal desires? Is it not in the female nature to limit pleasure?" I could not say if these maxims were true. But I had heard them spoken as true often enough to believe they might be. And I suspected I might count upon Mr. Lincoln having heard them as well.

And indeed, he said nothing against the argument.

I risked leaving the books to kneel before him. "I have been very unhappy away from you."

"I have been far worse than unhappy," he told me.

I lifted his hand from his lap and pressed my lips lightly to the back of it. For the briefest of moments, my nose filled with the woodsmoke scent of his skin. *I shall never be able to keep this bargain.* Then I raised my head and smelled only the potpourri Eliza Francis kept in a bowl, and the moment passed.

For the next ten months, Mr. Lincoln and I conducted our courtship in secret. We met sometimes at the Francises' home, although most often amidst the taxidermy animals and eggs of birds that cannot fly in Doctor Henry's parlor. This was at the doctor's insistence, for once he learned that Mr. Lincoln and I were keeping company – from Mr. Lincoln, and not myself – he insisted that every meeting between us be preceded by an examination of his former patient.

During this extended courtship, I was the picture of dispassionate decorum. I did not sit too near to Mr. Lincoln, and would not so much as take his hand except upon arriving and departing. And I never spoke of love. Our talk was of politics. For months, we discussed the future of the Whig party and the possible annexation of Texas, while I sat upon Doctor Henry's horsehair settee in a state of fevered excitement.

The promise I had made had been sworn by my mind, and not my body; and as the weeks passed, I discovered that it was no simple thing to acquire that entity's cooperation. There were afternoons I cared nothing for the Whig's political chances, so much did I wish to be kissed into obliviousness. Evenings I could not concentrate upon Texas because my mind was busy conjuring the sensation of flesh upon flesh.

For his part, Mr. Lincoln appeared to have no difficulty keeping his concentration. He sat among Doctor Henry's skulls and fossils, crossing his long legs (which I could not cease remembering naked), and granting the issue of annexation his full attention. *How can you remain so unpassionate?* I wished to shout at him. *Can you not recall how it felt to stretch over my unclothed body? How easy it was to take me?*

But he did not appear to recall it. Or if he did, it did not seem to distract his mind from an analysis of the Democrats' stand on expansion. And all this talk of politics did not move us any closer to marrying.

I had imagined that Mr. Lincoln would engage me within a month of our reconciliation at the Francises' house. Then I believed the offer would be made within two months. But as the months collected with no proposal, I wondered if Mr. Lincoln had been entirely convinced of my ability to keep my pledge, or if he had somehow learned of the dreams which left me damp and panting in my bed. And the longer I waited to be married, the more frequently came these dreams. So that by the end of ten months, I began to fear that if I were left to wait too long, even God would not be capable of keeping me to my agreement.

The season was autumn, and the weather had turned cold, but it was warm in Doctor Henry's parlor. Mr. Lincoln had gone first to be looked at by the doctor, and when he emerged from the examining room his cuffs were unbuttoned and his coat and vest were slung over his arm.

"Has Doctor Henry determined that you possess sufficient physical and mental vigor to court me?" I asked.

"Only barely," Mr. Lincoln replied. "For I have found that courting is enervating work."

I reached for his hand and pulled him to sit beside me upon the sofa. "Then let us do no more of it," I told him. "Let us be married. As quickly as possible."

"And all along I had heard it was the man who did the proposing." He smiled, taking my remark lightly.

"Nothing would give me more pleasure than to be spared the humiliation of asking you," I said.

He looked hard into my face. "You are in earnest."

"I will be twenty-four in two months' time. You have been thirty-three for almost a year. We are letting too much time pass."

I felt the cushion give as he moved away from me.

"You know my apprehension."

"And I have honored my pledge! For most of a year, I have sat beside you on courting couches and kept myself from touching your flesh – even when it was what I wanted most to do in the world."

"Keeping hold of passion in the parlor is easier work than keeping hold of it in the bedroom." He began to fasten the buttons at his cuffs.

I slid across the settee. "I possess the will to do it."

"A great many men – and women – have believed that about themselves."

"I shall prove it to you." I had not known until I uttered the words that this was my plan, but of course it was the only way. I might sit chastely beside Mr. Lincoln discussing politics until I was elderly, or lunatic from repressed desire, and still would not convince him. "Make this our bedroom," I told him.

"What are you saying?"

"Make this our *married* bedroom."

Mr. Lincoln leapt from the settee.

"That would be an outrage to Anson's hospitality!" he declared.

"Have you not noticed that the doctor never intrudes upon our privacy? Do you not suppose he imagines we are engaged in a courtship somewhat more amorous than discussing Whig politics?"

"I do not suppose he imagines, even in his most deranged fancies, that we are abusing his horsehair settee in the manner you are suggesting."

"I suggest it because I have no other course!" I told him. "After ten months, you refuse to accept my word."

"And so you make me an indecent proposition?"

"I cannot conceive of another way of persuading you. And if I cannot persuade you, I fear we shall never marry." And it did seem then that we never would. It seemed we would spend our lives discussing politics upon other people's sofas, and that I would never again know the plummeting pleasure of love. The thought was too much to be borne, and I fell to sobbing upon Doctor Henry's settee.

Mr. Lincoln was not a man who could stay unmoved by tears, and it was not very long before he came to sit beside me. "I'm sorry if I am making you miserable."

He pulled me into his lap and wiped at my face with his still-unbuttoned cuff. The fabric had a bitter smell, likely from some medicine Doctor Henry had given him, but beneath the bitterness I caught the scent of woodsmoke. I gazed up into his face, seeing apprehension, yes, but beneath it perhaps, desire.

"We will be reasonable," I promised him. "We will be calm and tender and reasonable."

I raised his hand to my face and brushed my lips lightly across the veins of his still too-thin wrist.

"We will do this," I swore, "and neither of us will lose control. Neither will be driven mad."

I thought his breath came quicker now, and I pressed my tongue to his palm. Then pressed his palm to my breast.

"Afterward," I vowed, "you will not be afraid to marry me. Or to have me in your bed."

I put my mouth upon his. But softly. So softly it was not like kissing. More like pretending to kiss.

He moaned lightly.

It was not necessary for me to undress, to compel him to help me with my complicated laces and stays. Beneath my hoop and petticoat, I wore split drawers to make it possible for me to relieve myself without the assistance of a maid. I needed only to bunch my skirts and sit upon his lap, shift the fabric to make myself available to him.

This was not the coming together which had heated my dreams. We were fully clothed, confined to the narrow seat of the horsehair settee, unpermitted to give up anything to passion. Yet what we did there stopped an ache which had tormented me for so very long, I could not stifle a small, rapturous moaning.

Mr. Lincoln went rigid at the noise. Fearing he would stop, would force me from his lap, I shut my mouth and turned my attention to Doctor Henry's specimens. Concentrate upon that taxidermy ferret, I urged myself. Think on how the glass in its eye was set wrongly, making it appear that the iris inclines toward the creature's nose. And by so doing, I lost myself to no more rapture.

It was an odd form of lovemaking – restrained, sparing of emotion. But when it was finished and again we sat side by side upon the settee, Mr. Lincoln was not lunatic. And I had proved my promise to him.

"Can we marry right away?" I said. "Within the week?"

"I don't suppose you will wait for me to ask you."

"I cannot risk it."

"All right," he told me. "No amount of time will make your relations hate me less."

It was good that he agreed, for I have long believed that the encounter upon Doctor Henry's settee was the making of Robert. A belief I have held since the day my son was born, and he showed me his eyes.

(June 17) Mr. Robt Lincoln came to see his mother –
He thought her not quite so cordial in her manner
toward him as at previous visits. He insisted on
taking her trunk back with him – and she finally got
it packed and he took it – she did not care to ride.
—Patient Progress Reports for Bellevue Place
Sanitarium

Robert made me a present of a clock today.

Until I came to the madhouse, my eldest son had not been a great giver of gifts. As a child, his younger brother Willie had brought me anything that was bright – glass buttons and shiny pieces of anthracite. Taddie had made me presents of what he most loved – arrowheads and insects he dug from the garden. And Eddie had come to me with the small dead creatures he found in the yard, believing that, like himself, I too would wish to feel the feathery softness of a house sparrow in my hands. But Robert had only brought me presents at Christmastime and on the anniversary of my birth, when it would have been improper not to do so.

However, since I have come to live at Bellevue Place, Robert has brought me a collection of small items meant to improve my asylum room – a delft plate painted with a blue windmill, a lace runner knotted by cloistered nuns. I tell myself that Robert brings these things because he has noticed the meagerness of my room, and because he wishes me to be comfortable and happy. I tell myself that like Willie's bright objects and Eddie's soft creatures, it is a gesture done out of love. And perhaps a little out of guilt.

Today the gift was a little scroll-worked mantle clock.

"I saw that you had no clock in your room," Robert said. He nodded at the clock held uncomfortably in his arms.

"It is uncommonly pretty," I replied. If he had been Willie or Tad, I would have thrown my arms about him, hugged him with the clock pressed between us like a third heart. Instead, I rose from the rocker which never seems to want me and waited for my son to enter the small room in which I am confined.

Robert looked about, as if searching for the mantle he had forgotten my room did not possess.

"It will look very well on the dresser," I told him.

"Yes!" he declared. "It will look excellent there." He placed the clock upon the bureau decorated with the ghostly outlines of its fallen acanthus leaves. "I shall set it for you."

Robert felt in his waistcoat pocket for his watch, a Swiss instrument cast in silver. My eldest son had inherited the gold watch his father had been wearing the night he was murdered, but I had never known him to carry it.

"This is a seven-day clock," he told me, positioning the filigreed hands to the correct time, then winding the mechanism with a small key. "Wind it next Thursday. The Thursday after that. And every one that follows."

Robert dropped the key into my hand. At once, I set it upon the scarred top of the bureau. "You expect that I shall live here so many Thursdays?" I asked him.

My son kept his eyes upon the clock. "I expect you to stay until you are completely well."

"I am completely well."

"You have been here less than a month."

"I was well when I arrived."

He gave me a hard look. "You were imagining men who lived in the walls. Filling closets with more possessions than you could ever use."

"I do not believe that was caused by madness."

"Do you believe it the behavior of a sane person?"

"Perhaps only a person who is distraught."

Robert made a sound of disbelief and turned back to the clock. He gave the pendulum a push. "For now," he told me, "only remember to wind the mechanism."

My son left his back to me. He straightened the delft plate in its stand, uncurled a corner of the lace runner. Neither of us spoke; and in the quiet, the clock's ticking grew louder, filling my ears with a hard knocking.

"For a small clock it is excessively loud," I said.

"You will grow used to it over time," he replied.

"Perhaps it is the size of my room which makes its ticking so noticeable. Perhaps it will be better when I am no longer in this place."

Robert moved the clock until it sat more centered upon the dresser. "I believe you will grow accustomed to it here," he said.

I did not know if it was still the clock we were speaking about, and I wondered how I might ask him. But the ticking noise seemed louder now. Too loud even to speak over. The relentlessness of it caught at me, made me believe that the mantle clock was marking the time I would be made to live in this room, increments which stretched longer with every pendulum swing.

"Let us go out," I said to my son. "Let us leave this room."

"It is very warm," he replied. "Could we not just sit on the porch?"

But the ticking of the clock had made my limbs too jittery for sitting. "Doctor Patterson encourages us to take exercise outdoors," I told him. And only by this was I able to convince my son to walk outside with me.

Robert was correct. The day was very close, the air full of heat and the buzzing of locusts. Every breath we drew was rank with the scent of the animals Mrs. Patterson kept in the stable and the smell of the pigs which roamed freely about the grounds, startling the madwomen on their daily walks. At a distance, I heard the smothered rumblings of thunder, a storm releasing some other place from the hot mugginess.

"Let us take the near path." I led my son past the kitchen garden where Mrs. Wheeler sat upon her knees in the dirt, pulling weeds with little energy.

"This is all very pleasant!" Robert declared.

"Do you believe so?"

My son gazed past the exhausted lady sitting among the weeds toward the wide green lawns. "I find it extraordinarily restful," he told me.

"Perhaps that is the tranquility of knowing you are free to leave it whenever you wish."

Robert frowned. "I believe it agreeable for its own sake," he insisted. Then before I might disagree, he walked ahead of me.

We followed the path which wound around the unfinished greenhouse. The heat made my corset stick to my flesh and turned the space beneath my skirts into an oven. Still, I could not return to my room and the ticking of that clock.

"Come this way," I said, when Robert made to return to the asylum. "I shall show you the croquet course."

I took him down another path and as we came over the small rise which bordered the course, I spotted Mrs. Munger playing croquet by herself, her hair wild about her head.

I turned toward my son. "I have been meaning to ask how I shall gain access to my money while I am here," I said to him.

"What could you want money for?"

"There is a dressmaker in Batavia who caters to the ladies of Bellevue Place."

Robert stopped so abruptly, I was a few steps ahead before I noticed he was not beside me. "Is something wrong?" I asked him. "Do you feel unwell?"

"You are ordering clothes?" His tone was severe.

"Only a lawn dress for the hot weather."

He tugged at the hem of his vest, a very fine one of a linen which matched his jacket. "I must see the bill."

"It is a lawn dress," I said. "Not lace curtains, or French perfume, or any purchase which might convince a jury I am deranged."

My son only appeared more determined. "I still must have the bill."

"Please," I told him. "It is sufficiently embarrassing to be driven to the dressmaker in a locked carriage belonging to a madhouse. I do not also wish to tell that lady that my bills must be sent to my son."

Robert shrugged. "If they are not sent to me, they cannot be paid."

"What do you mean?"

"I have been appointed conservator of your money."

The heated air felt too thick for breathing. I pulled it in through my mouth, but could not fit it down my throat.

"I cannot get my money?" I gasped.

"I must approve everything you spend," Robert told me.

I had not known until that moment that I had been counting so much upon escape; upon the notion that if I could not convince Doctor Patterson or my son of my sanity, I would find a way to leave Bellevue Place. Walk off the grounds with no one seeing.

But without money, there could be no escape.

"How could this happen?" I demanded. "How could my money be taken without my knowing?"

"You have been declared insane." He said this as if it was possible I had forgotten.

"But I am not insane!" I grabbed for my son's hands, and though I felt him try to pull them back, I would not release them. "I know you have become convinced that I am so. That my delusions of the past months have made you believe I belong in a madhouse. But I swear to you I have not lost my reason!"

Robert looked about as if fearing someone might have witnessed my outburst. "I cannot make that determination by your declaration only."

I let go his hands, thinking of Eddie, and of Will and Taddie, who would have believed me, who would never have committed me here. Robert wiped at his hands, as if I had soiled them.

"How can you be so certain of my madness?" I asked him.

"You have caused too much scandal."

"And that is what has made you think me lunatic?"

"It is some portion of it."

It was his sureness, his confidence in the wrongness of my behavior, which made me grab hold of his sleeve and drag him from the path. "Come!" I commanded. "Come with me and I shall show you lunatic!"

Robert pulled back, but I kept my grip, knowing he would not risk the sleeve of his linen jacket.

"I have learned very well these past weeks what mad truly is!" I told him.

"Stop this!" he cried. But I would not.

I pulled him across the wide lawn until we stood before Mrs. Munger, shrieking among the wickets of the croquet course.

It had been some days since Saturday and Mrs. Munger's hair, so long untended, had rubbed itself into knots upon her pillow, knots as big as birds' nests. The banker's wife was bent double at the waist, her flushed face very near her croquet ball.

"You have been exceedingly wicked!" she shouted at it. "You have disregarded my wishes entirely!" Saliva flew from her lips, and she clenched and unclenched her hands convulsively.

Beside me, Robert cringed.

"Are you having some difficulty?" I asked the lady.

Mrs. Munger did not unbend herself, only lifted her uncombed head, craning it at us like a wildly tufted bird. "This ball is willful!" she shrieked. "I have been extremely clear about not wishing it to bypass any of the wickets!" The banker's wife pounded her mallet upon the ground, leaving a deep depression in the earth.

"What would make you believe that a croquet ball can hear you?" I said.

"Am I not loud enough? Mr. Munger says I am very loud!" Mrs.

Munger drew back her chapped lips and screamed so loudly, birds flew from the trees above our heads.

With a jerk which threatened to tear his fine jacket, my son freed himself. "This is too much," he said. "Even for you." And leaving me with the shrieking lady, he hurried away across the lawn.

He was halfway to the asylum before I could catch him. And even then, I had to grab hold of his arm to make him stop.

"You see what you have confined me with?" I said. "The lunatics who now make up my society?"

Robert pulled away his arm. "You have only to avoid her."

"And risk Doctor Patterson thinking I am unsocial? Or that I neglect my daily exercise?"

"There must be other, quieter ladies here," Robert said. "Surely they are not all like that."

I put a hand to his collar, which had turned upon itself in his hurry. "What matters is that I am not," I told him. "I do not belong here."

Robert took a small step, leaving my hand with nothing beneath it. "I believe it is better for you in this place."

"When I am not mad?"

"Twelve jurors and five doctors say that you are."

I gazed into my son's handsome face. "What do you say?"

"I have seen no sign that your mind has turned rational."

"How can you make such a statement!" I exclaimed. "When I have weeded in Mrs. Patterson's kitchen garden until my spine is crippled. Soaked myself in so much salt my flesh is chafed raw."

"And still you want money for shopping."

"I want a dress for the heat!"

"You have come here with ten trunks. Is there nothing in them that is suitable?"

"Robert, you have been married long enough to know that ladies often wish for something new. It does not make them lunatic."

My son stared at the cool whiteness of the asylum and did not speak. I worried that I might have provoked him with the mention of his marriage, for it was a topic of discord between us.

"I promise there is nothing in my trunks suitable for summer in a madhouse," I assured him.

"Do you know Doctor Patterson considers those trunks a symptom of your lunacy?" Robert said.

"Every lady owns trunks," I told him.

"Doctor Patterson believes them to be a manifestation of your purchasing mania."

"I have no house," I reminded my son. "Where am I to keep my things except with me?"

Robert thought for a moment. "Send them to me," he said.

"What do you mean?"

"Demonstrate that your mania has abated. Send your trunks to me."

"But those trunks are filled with traveling clothes. Necklaces and brooches. Lengths of dress silk. Things I shall need when I go from here."

"You are a widow living in a sanitarium!" he declared. "You go nowhere, wear no jewelry, and dress in nothing but black."

"But when I leave Bellevue Place…"

"You shall never leave it!" he cried. "Not as long as Doctor Patterson and I believe you too attached to your possessions."

But without my possessions, said my disloyal voice, *without my money, you will be able to keep me here as long as you wish!* Then, beneath these terrible words, beneath the buzzing of the locusts, I heard – impossibly! – the ticking of the little mantle clock. I covered my ears, hoping to deaden the knock of the pendulum as it caught and held, caught and held. But the noise only grew more loud, until I could no longer think over it. Could not breathe over it. Until it no longer sounded like a clock ticking, but was instead the tumblers of a lock falling into place, shutting me up with mad women until I died.

I saw my son watching me; imagined how I must appear standing on the asylum path with my hands pressed to my ears. *Show that you are rational,* I instructed myself. *Show that you are entitled to be released. Or everything you fear will be true.*

Slowly, I let my hands fall to my sides. "Suppose that I pack one trunk?" I said to him. "Suppose that I fill it with what I will not want while I am here, and then send that to you? Would that not make you see me as reasonable?"

"It is only one trunk," he replied.

"But it is a start."

Robert appeared to think this over. "Then let us pack it now and I will take it with me."

"You wish to take it now?"

"I wish to not give your mania opportunity to override your reason."

It is only one trunk, I thought. And that will leave me nine more before I am out of means to escape from here.

"Very well," I told him. "We shall do it now. Although I am certain there are better ways to pass a hot day."

I returned to the asylum with my son and packed a trunk with things that did not seem too valuable.

"Remember to wind the clock," he instructed me before leaving with my trunk.

I watched him go, then sent word to Mrs. Patterson telling her that upon second thought, I did not wish to ride today. Once back in my room, I opened the little mantle clock and put my hand upon the pendulum, stopping it so it would not tick.

The summer I waited for Robert to be born was predicted to be the last of the world. Since not long after my wedding, all of Springfield – indeed all of the country – had begun to echo with the doomsday preachings of the Millerites. The Millerites were followers of a New York gentleman by the name of William Miller, who had studied the Scriptures and concluded that Armageddon would arrive upon the seventh of July, 1843. In preparation, his followers gathered in every large city in the country, where they stood on street corners urging the citizens to give away their earthly possessions, and then sold them muslin Ascension robes to wear upon the Day of Judgment.

I had much time to study the warnings of the Millerites, as I was already confined by my condition. It was lucky that Mr. Lincoln and I had been married in such haste. Although I do not think that Elizabeth and Ninian believed so at the time. I announced to my sister and brother-in-law over breakfast that my virtue had been taken by Mr. Lincoln, informing them that by nightfall we intended to be married. Elizabeth then forfeited so many hours attempting to convince me that I was throwing myself away upon a penniless man with no beauty and few prospects, she had little time to prepare for the wedding – of course I would be married in Elizabeth's house; it would have caused too much talk had I not. There was no time to have a dress made, so I borrowed the one in which my sister Frances had been married. There was no time to order wedding cakes, hardly time even for Elizabeth's cook to make them. And indeed, when my guests – mostly relations who could be summoned at the last minute without embarrassment – bit into them, the cakes were found to be uncooked at the center. Yet none of this mattered. For Mr. Lincoln had put upon my finger a ring which bore the engraved words "Love is eternal," and I believed in that eternity.

Because we could not afford to rent a house, Mr. Lincoln and I took up residence at the Globe Tavern. The Globe was a poor boardinghouse. Our wallpaper did not match at the joins and our planked floor was stained with small circles of tobacco juice spit by previous tenants. On warm days the furniture smelled of hairwax, and the bureau gave off the reek of bourbon, which clung to our clothes and made us smell like drunkards. My bedroom at the Globe bore so little resemblance to the chambers in which I'd slept in Lexington and the house on Aristocrat's Hill, some mornings after a pointed bit of straw in the mattress had poked me awake, I believed myself to have been kidnapped.

At first I went out as much as possible, attempting to disprove what wagging tongues had implied about my hasty wedding. But after only a few months, even the most rigid corset could not compress me presentable and I was forced to retreat to my boardinghouse room. I had little to do at the Globe. I had no kitchen – meals were prepared by a sullen cook, a widow who had fallen upon difficult times – and the cleaning, such as it was, was accomplished by an ever-changing staff of Irish girls. I had no company either. Elizabeth was in the midst of her own confinement. And Frances was kept busy tending to a sick husband or child, for her doctor husband too often carried home the illnesses of his patients. Yet, even had both my elder sisters come knocking at my door, I do not believe I would have allowed them in. My situation at the Globe was too much what they had predicted for me if I married Mr. Lincoln.

I felt my sisters' absence more keenly, for I did not have my husband for company. Mr. Lincoln's law practice – and our very great need of income – obliged him to ride the circuit, attending courts that were several days' journey from Springfield. The week of our wedding, he was away two nights. The following week, it was three. Within a month, it was not uncommon for my husband to be gone for a week at a time.

As an unmarried virgin, I had been warned about the bestial

appetites of men. As a wife, I was astonished by the number of nights I passed tossing upon the straw mattress while my husband slept serenely, his nightshirt buttoned to his neck. Indeed, for nearly six months of marriage, I remained, if not untouched, little-touched. At last, emboldened by my larger shape, as if my increased size entitled me to more privileges, I traveled the width of the crackling mattress and placed my lips upon those of my husband. Mr. Lincoln allowed my mouth to stay upon his, but did not press back.

"You do not wish to have me?" I asked, when he put no hand upon me.

"I do not think it wise to tempt fate too frequently."

"Certainly, two times in the space of a month could not be considered too frequent," I told him. "It seems to me barely frequent enough."

My husband raised himself to sit against the rusted bedstead and pulled me to rest beneath his arm. "You remind me of a child. A child who wants what she wants, when she wants it."

"And why not?" I said. "If she might have it."

I touched his mouth, still wet from mine.

"You have not often gotten what you wanted." He said it as if he had seen my whole life.

"Not before you."

"I do not believe I am much consolation," he replied. But as he said this, he put his fingers upon my mouth now, tracing the upward curve of my lip, and I knew that he was.

I slept that night nestled against his chest. And it was so sweet to be someone's child again, it was not until I woke with my own child bumping inside me that I realized my husband had refused to give me what I wanted, when I wanted it.

Even when my husband was with me, he could be absent; for Mr. Lincoln was never entirely free of melancholy. His fits came upon him with no warning and seemed as profound as death. Before the first month of our marriage was out, I returned to our room to discover my husband seated upon the edge of the bed, his muscles as rigid as those of a dead man.

I shouted his name over and again, until there came a knocking on our wall from the next room. But my husband did not stir, nor did he acknowledge me. I passed my hand before Mr. Lincoln's face. His eyes, which were fixed upon a point I could not determine, did not blink or shift their focus. I tugged upon his lifeless arm, making his stiffened body move all of a piece, but he made no motion of his own. At last, certain that my husband's mind had abandoned me, I fell to my knees and cried into his lap.

After what seemed a great long while, I felt the heavy weight of his hand upon my head.

"Are you ill?" I asked him. "Shall I call for Doctor Henry?"

But though he had managed to drop lids over those terrifying fixed eyes, he was not recovered enough for speech.

For nearly an hour, I sat at his feet, holding fast to him with all my strength, certain it was only my grip upon his leg which kept him tethered to the sane world. I did not draw a full breath until I felt the rigidity drain from his limbs.

"It is not necessary to keep such a tight hold on my trousers," he said. "They have already endured enough abuse."

At the sound of that soft – and sane – voice, I threw myself against his chest. "I could not make you see me," I cried. "I could not make you know I was here."

My husband lifted my wet face from his shirtfront. "You will have to grow used to these little spells. At least when I am seized by them, I shall be quiet and out of your way."

But I could not make myself used to them. For each time one occurred, I believed that my husband had abandoned me, and that no hoodoo hand would return him. And at such times when I could not reach my husband's mind, could not force his affection, I longed more strongly for my child to be born.

"You shall be tenderhearted," I told the swelling shape. "And we will be much devoted to one another."

Although if Mr. William Miller was to be believed, the world would end in fire before that day might come.

Being confined at the Globe had made me expert upon the predictions of the Millerites. One of these prophets, a fair young man with the face of a girl, had fashioned a pulpit from a crate which had once held tea and preached from a corner outside my window.

"The Almighty will cause the dead to rise from their graves and the righteous to fly into Heaven," he declared, making me recall Captain Postlewaite, who had died of the cholera and flown past my window. "But the corrupt shall perish in untold torment."

This fair young man who preached everlasting agony for those who were unrepentant was my only company, and I watched him from my boardinghouse window as if he were an entertainment. On the days that the young man did not take his place at the corner, I kept up with the prophecies of the world's end by reading the sermons of Mr. Miller, which were every day printed in the newspapers. "The wicked shall know castigation and defeat, and those who do evil shall feel the wrath of vengeful punishment." Mr. Miller was harsh upon sinners. I sometimes wondered if the actions which had sent me into confinement so swiftly after my wedding would place me in that category, but decided that as I had been obliged to do evil by my sister and brother-in-law, it could be argued that sin was theirs.

Such terrible prophecies were perhaps not the best reading for a lady in my condition. But there was little else in the papers – even politics were pushed aside by vivid descriptions of the cleansing which would be wrought by the fires of Armageddon. And thus for all that summer, I fed my unborn child retribution and righteousness.

On the day the Millerites predicted Armageddon – a day upon which my husband was a hundred miles away – the streets of Springfield grew more quiet than was usual. Even the child I carried, who generally spent much of the afternoon thudding about my insides, was so still I was forced to prod the growing mound to reassure myself that he continued to live. It was a scorching day, hot enough so that one could easily imagine the fires of the world's end, and I wondered if my mother might come to me, if she would seek me out in this boardinghouse where I waited to become a mother myself, for the fair young man outside the Globe had preached that on the day of Armageddon the dead would leave their graves. Before I had come to be carrying a child, I would have forfeited the world to flames to feel again her touch. But now I possessed too many hopes for the child in my womb. And I could not wish for one small portion of the Millerites' prophecy to be true, even to have my mother returned.

At dusk, a great line of people dressed in Ascension robes trudged back from the cemetery where they had gone to be reunited with their dead before flying to Heaven together. Some of these people were weeping. Others appeared stunned, as if from a terrible shock. The world had not ended. And though William Miller was quick to choose another date for Armageddon, his followers termed the weeks which followed "The Great Disappointment."

It was during this time that my son was born.

A boardinghouse is an uncomfortable – and unprivate – place to deliver a baby. To keep my respectability, I was obliged to time my screams to the clanging of the bell atop the Globe's roof, which was rung whenever a carriage arrived at the door; and it was lucky that the day saw many carriages. I did not fear death, for I knew that I was stronger in body and will than my mother had been. But I was so impatient to hold my child that I bore down even when Doctor Henry, who had come to assist my labor, instructed me against it.

When my son at last was born, I begged the doctor to give him to me.

"You cannot want him now," said Doctor Henry. "He is blood-soaked and covered with the fluids of your womb."

"I do want him now," I insisted.

But the doctor only frowned, as if he believed I might have contracted childbed fever, and gave my son to the midwife to be washed.

Once my child was brought to me, I held him as close as our now-separate flesh would allow and breathed upon his face. As if in response, he lifted his blue-veined lids, showing me his eyes. I could not hold back a cry.

"You are uncomfortable?" asked the doctor.

"It is just that his gaze is unusual."

The midwife, one of the Irish girls who worked at the Globe, leaned over the bed. "He is still a pretty baby," she said. "And perhaps the eye will straighten."

But I did not believe that it would straighten. My child's oddity of eye had been formed during a lovemaking marked by the constraint of its passion. It would stay canted, for it was intended – by God? the Devil? – to remind me of my promise of restraint.

"It's a great relief to see that he favors you in looks," said my husband, when he was called in to see his son.

"I am sorry for the imperfection of his eye."

Mr. Lincoln smiled down upon his child's face. "Mine does the very same thing," he said.

"Yours is the result of being kicked in the head by a horse."

"Well, at least we have spared him that."

I slept then, for the birthing had left me tired. Only once did I wake, and not until night was nearly over. I opened my eyes upon the shadowless light of dawn and saw my husband holding his small, swaddled son in his big hands – the same hands which had caused so much damage to teacups in ladies' parlor. However, I said nothing, only fell back into sleep, for the newly born child appeared utterly safe in them.

As we could not afford to hire a nurse, Adeline Bledsoe, a formidable lady of some girth who boarded at the Globe with her husband and daughter, offered to stop by every morning and help me with my son, whom I had named Robert, after my father.

"I have never witnessed a child so unhappy about nursing," declared Mrs. Bledsoe, watching me struggle to keep my son fixed to my breast. "Seems hardly any time before he's fighting to get free."

"Perhaps he has an excess of energy," I suggested. "My mammy claimed I was uncommonly lively when I was a child."

Mrs. Bledsoe wrung out a damp swaddling rag and looked skeptical.

"He might not possess much appetite," I offered.

She observed my small son attempt to arch himself away from me. "I believe he doesn't like to be held," she said.

"How can a child not wish to be held?" I asked. But in truth, I had come to the same belief. Robert remained at my breast so short a time, I did not know how he thrived. Still, the child was robust. For he pushed against me with strong fists, and if I did not set him free, he sent up such a howling, we were soon visited by Mrs. Beck, the widow lady who ran the Globe.

"You must keep your child from bellowing so," warned Mrs. Beck. "Both Mr. Broderick and Mr. Ward are threatening to move to the American House if they can get no peace here."

It was my desire to assure Mrs. Beck that both Mr. Broderick and Mr. Ward – as well as the rest of the house – would have their peace. However, the only way I could quiet my son was to set him down. And I did not wish to set him down. For during those brief moments that I did hold and nurse my son, I lost the separateness between his flesh and mine, and believed I would never again be entirely alone.

"A boardinghouse is not a congenial place to raise a child," I said to my husband. "If I economize, could we not afford to rent some little house?"

"Is there anything left to economize on?" he asked.

"I shall uncover something," I told him.

Mr. Lincoln found us a small cottage on Monroe Street, and we left the grateful Globe. The cottage was no larger than Queen Ruby's shack, and its clapboards were coated with even less paint. Inside, the wainscoting behind the hearth was sooty, as was the ceiling. But nobody shared our walls, and I hoped the neighbors were distant enough not to be disturbed by Robert's yelling.

Believing that my son needed only to grow used to my affection, I set out to accustom him. Each morning, I took my child into my lap and, brushing his soft cheeks with my fingertips, spoke endearments into his fine hair. My heart was overfilled with tenderness for this small creature, and I did not wish for anything but to remain exactly as we were. However, the clock, which rang every quarter hour, did not chime more than once before my son commenced to wave his small fists and whimper to be set free. Still convinced that I might accustom him to affection, I did not set him free, but kept him in my arms, pacing the tiny cottage and attempting to remember the Negro spirituals which Mammy Sally had used to comfort me. When that failed to quiet my unhappy son, I spoke to him as though he were a man and grown. "You do not have to show your affection yet," I assured him. "Only learn to rest in mine." But my pleadings were inaudible beneath his wailing and eventually I was forced to set my child back in his cradle before his howling brought a neighbor.

Although I wished to, I could not spend all day attempting to make my son used to affection, for now that we no longer lived at the Globe, the cleaning and cooking fell to me. And I had little experience with either. At my father's house, we had had Negroes to do everything for us. At my sister's, we had the two slaves Elizabeth brought with her from Lexington and an assortment of hired girls. On Monroe Street, there was only myself. And I had never cooked a breakfast, swept out a sitting room, or washed my own undergarments.

Hoping for some direction, I purchased a copy of Catherine Beecher's *A Treatise on Domestic Economy* – ordering the book by mail to keep the ladies in my sister's social circle from learning that Mrs. Lincoln needed to know how to clean out a chimney flue and make a bed.

Although Miss Beecher was a spinster and – having been born into an illustrious family; her father was the famous preacher Lyman Beecher – had never herself had to engage in the practice of housework, she possessed a considerable number of opinions upon the matter. Her *Treatise* gave instruction upon everything from the cleaning of gentlemen's coats and pantaloons to the proper airing of hair mattresses, from the modes of destroying vermin to the care of a cow – a chapter I was entitled to pass over, as we could not afford one. All of Miss Beecher's direction was delivered with the utmost clarity of expression and precision of detail. Yet no matter how much energy and mental concentration I put into the effort, I could not achieve the domestic perfection promised by the unmarried lady whom the newspapers referred to as the "Household Divinity."

When I made starch, I could not rub away all the lumps or seem to add enough spermaceti to keep the mixture from sticking to the iron. And when I attempted to prepare a concoction of beef's gall – ideal, according to Miss Beecher, for the removal of stains – the result reeked so terribly, I was obliged to burn one of Mr. Lincoln's shirts. My pasteboard flower basket, decorated, according to Miss Beecher's advice, with bits of unraveled yarn in green and brown meant to resemble moss, resembled something under attack by a terrible fungus. And my try at varnishing a little painting of a landscape – Miss Beecher believed all paintings to be improved by varnishing – resulted in my having to burn the picture along with Mr. Lincoln's shirt.

After some weeks of trying and failing at Miss Beecher's domestic economy, I visited my sister's house unannounced and passed several furtive hours questioning her Kentucky slaves. By this, I developed some little competence at household work. I also developed a great and abiding resentment toward Miss Beecher. A resentment which I nurtured, for the Household Divinity felt a safer object for it than my husband. Indeed, if I did not blame my difficulties with beef's gall and pasteboard baskets upon Miss Beecher, I might put the blame for them upon my husband for being poor, which he had been careful to warn me about, or upon his lack of ambition, which might make me believe he was not the husband prophesied for me. And so, I mixed starch and boiled shirts, and when the starch was lumpy and shirts scorched, I uttered curses upon the head of Miss Beecher.

In December, my father came to Springfield with the intention of visiting his daughters who now lived there. He had left the second Mrs.

Todd behind to tend to his youngest children – my father had now thirteen living sons and daughters – and put up at Elizabeth's house on Aristocrat's Hill. I had sent word that I would visit him there, for I did not wish him to see our unpainted clapboards – despite Miss Beecher's two recipes for whitewash, I had not attempted to paint the exterior of our cottage. Nor did I wish my elegant father to sit upon our chairs, which were secondhand and unreliable. My father's house had always been filled with French china and rosewood furniture, and had never gone unpainted. I feared very much that if he came to see me on Monroe Street, he might believe the things which Elizabeth told him about my marriage were true.

My father was a courteous man. I had never known him to turn up anyplace unannounced. So I was much surprised when I answered my bell and discovered his well-dressed figure standing upon my broken step.

"I know that I am unexpected," he said in the mouth-filling drawl of Kentucky. "However, I was anxious to meet my namesake."

I had been in the yard making soap, one of the economies which allowed us to afford the rent on the little cottage, and my hands were shiny with lard. "I would have been pleased to bring him to you," I replied.

"Then I would not have seen where you live."

I stood before him, damp and smelling of lye, and wished for a way to keep him out, to send him back to Elizabeth's big house without appearing unmannerly. But like my father, I was Southern and could no more send away someone uninvited and unfed than acquire the accent of the Yankees.

"Come and see it then," I said, attempting to sound as if I could imagine no happier prospect.

My father entered the house and allowed me to lead him into the parlor, which was also the sitting room and half of the dining room.

"Mr. Lincoln and I do not intend to remain in this cottage very long," I said. "My husband has been too much in demand on the circuit to attend to house-buying. And looking after Robert quite fills my time." I wiped my greasy hands upon the back of my skirt, leaving a mark there that only the Household Divinity would possess the skill to remove.

"It is not always a simple thing to find the right house," replied my father.

I settled him into our least undependable chair and went to fetch my son, who had been sleeping near the stove in the kitchen. Robert was now five months old, sturdy with a well-shaped head and close ears. His eyes looked to have settled into pale gray, and while the left still canted, even Elizabeth declared him handsome – although she had stated the opinion in a tone of amazement, as if she found it difficult to believe that Mr. Lincoln had had a hand in the making of such a pretty baby.

"Let me take him on my lap," said my father.

"I can put his cradle near your chair," I offered. I had never known my father to take any of his children upon his lap. His clothes were too fine, and he was far too careful with them.

"I wish to hold him." My father put out his hands, and I gave my son over to him.

"He is an energetic child," I said, "and will sometimes wish to be set free."

I feared that Robert would begin to squirm and howl and make his grandfather wish to be rid of him. However, my son appeared content to sit upon his grandfather's fawn-colored trousers, his eyes fixed on the watch chain my father dangled over his head.

He has never done that with me, I thought, then realized I had meant the remark to describe both Robert and my father, whom I could not recall ever taking me as a child upon his lap. For the instant, I felt jealous of them both.

"I shall make you some tea," I said.

"Yourself?" replied my father.

"It is very difficult to find help in Springfield," I told him.

While the water heated, I gazed out into the yard. The fire beneath the soap-making kettle was dying, and without a fire and constant stirring, the lye and fat would separate, undoing my morning's work. I told myself that I had time before the tea water boiled to run out and put more wood on the fire, time to stir the kettle once or twice. But I remained in the kitchen and let the soap be ruined. I could not risk that my father would catch me at a task Mammy Sally would have consigned to a lesser slave.

I brought out my best cups, the ones I did not allow Mr. Lincoln to handle; and served my father China tea which had come f   r   o   m Elizabeth's house. While we drank, he gave me all the news from

Lexington, telling me which little Todd Mammy Sally was frightening with tales of the "Debil," and of a border of heliotrope Betsey had had planted near the slave cabins. Not once while we talked did Robert shriek to be set down or beat his fists against his grandfather's mustard-colored vest. Instead he sat making contented chirps and watched his grandfather's waxed mustache appear and disappear into the teacup.

"You know that not one of my children, or other of my grand-children, is named for me," my father said. "None that are living." As he spoke, he wove his fingers into his grandson's hair, which was the same light brown as his own. "I am very grateful to you."

I had known little of my father's attention. I had been too young to travel with him to Frankfort and afterward had lived too much at boarding school. And then there had been all the new little Todds to claim him, the children produced by Betsey. But here in my plain house, I sensed the possibility of my father's affection for the first time. And it had come by way of the small creature upon his lap, to whom I had been unable to teach tenderness. *Perhaps they shall teach it to each other,* I thought. *And then direct some portion of it toward me.*

"I am glad that the naming has pleased you," I said. "I had hoped that it would."

My father rubbed a small amount of his sugared tea upon Robert's mouth, making the child smile. Then he rose and returned my son to me.

"I must return. Elizabeth has organized some sort of little fête in my honor."

I walked my father to the door. On the step, he stopped to look once more upon his grandson. "He is an exceedingly satisfactory child," he told me.

I was grateful to my father for not mentioning Robert's imperfect eye.

"I shall see you this evening at your sister's house," he said, "where I very much look forward to meeting my grandson's father."

He clasped my hands, which were still slippery, and took his leave. Not until he was gone around the corner did I notice that he had left a twenty-five-dollar gold piece in my slick palm.

Over the next months, my father referred several legal cases to Mr. Lincoln, and by April, these helped us to buy a small cottage on the corner of Eighth and Jackson Streets. The fence at the front of the house was missing pickets and some of its shutters hung drunkenly by one nail. The neighborhood itself was a far cry from Aristocrat's Hill. On warm afternoons the smell that passed between the yards made plain that most of my neighbors kept chickens. But I loved the little ramshackle house because it was mine, and because my husband had bought it for me.

I had hoped that settling in our own house might also work to settle my son's restless nature. However, as Robert grew older, he likewise grew more difficult to keep. Before he was a year, he had learned to walk – a precocity I believe sprang from his desire to propel himself away from me. Although we passed the entirety of each day together, I never had my son's company. If I were in the parlor, covering the sofa with sheets before sweeping, Robert was in the sitting room, playing about in the fireplace; if I were in the kitchen, cleaning the lamps with pearl ash, he was out in the yard, throwing rocks into my bluing water.

Only when he slept could I show him the tenderness which threatened to overwhelm me. During Robert's naps, I crept into his bed and curved myself to his back, breathing in the small boy scent of his head and not caring if the flannels were left too long in the washtub, or the bread swelled beyond usefulness. With my son asleep, I could lose myself in his scent, in the softness of his child's flesh, in the choking love I felt for him. But these afternoons were brief – and grew briefer still. For as the months passed, Robert seemed to require less napping, as if he were aware of the liberties I took when he was asleep.

I had continued to nurse my son, although he was approaching two years of age, past the time my sister considered well-bred.

"Only Negroes and immigrants nurse their children so long," she informed me one afternoon when she had come upstairs in her big house and caught me at it.

"But Robert is so fond of it," I replied. Although Elizabeth could plainly see that he was not.

In truth, I continued because I imagined that this feeding would work to soften my son's affections, the way that meat soaked in milk becomes more tender.

"If you are nursing him to avoid another child," my sister said, "there are other ways."

It had not occurred to me until Elizabeth spoke of it that I might have another child. I believe I had been too much focused upon Robert, and upon our lack of money, to consider the possibility. But Mr. Lincoln's income had improved. And if I gave up store-bought candles and burned lard in the lamps instead of oil, we might manage it. The more I thought upon it, the better an idea it seemed. With a second child, I would not count so much upon Robert. And a small sister or brother could very well teach my first son affection by example.

I weaned Robert that night, and when the timing seemed likely, approached my husband in the marriage bed with so much insistence, he could find no way to refuse me. Recalling the constrained circumstances of Robert's conception, I invested this child's making with all the tender passion I might without breaking my bargain. I kissed my husband upon the face and hands, brushed my cheek across his chest and along the bones of his arms. I never let him take his hands from me, and did not take mine from him, not until long after we were finished.

Within a month, I learned I was pregnant.

I fastened uncommon hopefulness upon this second child, and vowed to mold his nature before he – or she, for I wished very much for a daughter – emerged from the womb. During this second confinement, I read novels containing only the tenderest emotions, stories filled with constant love and unremitting affection. I even allowed myself to fall behind in my housekeeping – Mr. Lincoln was generally so distracted, he would hardly have noticed if I permitted swine in the parlor – and passed the better part of each day in my bed, reading these novels aloud to my burgeoning second child, repeating the most sentimental passages.

I tried to interest Robert in these stories of love and brought him into the bed with me each time that I read. But he could not be captured by tales that contained so many kisses and caresses, and before I had read very far, he would climb from the bed and go into another room.

In March of 1846, I became the mother of a second son. This child I named Edward Baker, after a friend of Mr. Lincoln who had been recently elected to Congress, for it was considered lucky to name children after those who were successful.

Eddie was a finely boned, slender child who was happiest beside me. When I held him against my shoulder, he nuzzled his tiny face so far into the curve of my neck, I feared for his ability to draw breath. If I left him in his cradle so I could roast the coffee or clean the flue, he waited for me to pass by, then flung out a small arm, as if trying to pull me toward him. On the day that I saw he could hold his head unsupported, I tied him to my back with a shawl, the way that our slave women had carried their babies.

"Is it not disgraceful enough that you air your own mattresses?" said Elizabeth, the first time she observed me like this. "But must you do it with your child tied to your back? Promise me you shall never leave the house in such a state."

My sister was wise to extract such a promise, for had I been permitted to indulge my desire, I would have attended the most elegant cotillion with my delicately boned son fastened to me by a shawl which matched my gown, so possessed was I by an uncontainable hunger for the company of this child.

It was a hunger made sharper by my second son's frequent illnesses. The first had come when he was three months old – a disease of the lungs. For six nights, my small son coughed with such ferocity, his already pallid skin took on a bluish cast which frightened me for its closeness to the flesh of the cholera victims of my childhood. When Eddie did not cough, he was left gasping for breath, drawing in only enough to produce a strangled mewling. Doctor Henry came, as did Doctor Wallace, Frances's kind-natured husband. Both recommended syrup of ipecac and prayer.

At the end of a week, Eddie began to recover.

"You must be careful of him," Doctor Henry told me when he came to see about my son. "He will always possess a weakness of the lungs."

"I shall do everything to safeguard his health," I said to the doctor. "No illness will take this child from me."

Doctor Henry looked at Eddie sleeping upon the bed. My son's cheeks were still rosy from fever. "It is best to remember that the illness of children too often pursues a course which is beyond our authority."

"Of course," I replied. But I did not truly attend him. I was thinking instead that perhaps the flush was not from fever, but from my son's restored good health.

In the autumn of 1846, five months after Eddie was born, my faith in my husband's ambition was restored: Mr. Lincoln was elected one of Illinois's seven congressmen. His winning had been no surprise. This was a seat which always went to a Whig, no matter who the party put up. And most recently, the party had decided to rotate the position among several aspiring politicians, two of whom were my cousins, and one, my husband.

No matter how it was accomplished, Mr. Lincoln was a congressman; and now Elizabeth could be heard informing the ladies of her coterie that her "brother-in-law Lincoln" would be taking office that winter, referring to my husband by that familial term for the first time since I married him. My sister was also full of plans for how I would manage in Springfield once my husband left for the capital.

"You shall have to hire a man to see to the chopping and other strenuous work," she told me. "I shall lend you mine." Elizabeth delivered this advice in the sitting room of her big house, which is where my sister delivered the majority of her advice to me, not being fond of the smell of chickens in my neighborhood.

"You shall have to lend him to the renters," I replied. "I am going to Washington City."

"What about your children?" Elizabeth exclaimed.

"Do you deem the renters might object to keeping them?" I asked, forgetting that my sister was immune to all forms of wit. "I shall take the boys with me," I assured her.

Elizabeth spent the better part of an hour attempting to convince me that wives of congressmen, particularly those with small children, did not travel to the capital with their husbands – not unless they could afford to rent a large house and employ at least one nurse. I allowed my sister to present her case, which she always did with a good deal of vigor and belief in her own rightness. However, there was nothing even she might say which would alter my decision. I expected Mr. Lincoln to be brilliant in Washington City, and I did not wish to miss it.

It was my opinion that in very short time, the entire Congress would recognize my husband's greatness of mind and honorable heart, and that even President Polk, a Democrat, would wish Mr. Lincoln a member of his own party. It was my opinion, too, that as the wife of such a man, I would be sought after by the ladies of Washington City. Ladies who knew much about politics and the intrigue of the capital, and who would invite the wife of the promising Congressman Lincoln to tea and tell her every bit of it – an afternoon of which would compensate greatly for a entire month of soap-making.

However, on the subject of my going to Washington City, Mr. Lincoln agreed with Elizabeth.

"I know of no other congressman who is bringing his wife," he said to me, after I had presented to him my plan. We were all of us in the parlor, my husband in a leather-covered rocker with a book of morbid poetry, Eddie crawling about his large feet, and Robert in a corner, pushing wooden blocks into straight lines.

"Perhaps those wives do not love their husbands sufficiently," I replied.

"Perhaps those husbands are able to exert more influence than I do." He shut the book and regarded me over its gloomy cover. "I take it you would bring the boys along?"

"I could not leave Eddie."

"We cannot afford to keep two houses."

"I have already found renters for this one. And we can make do in Washington City with two rooms.

Mr. Lincoln scooped up his youngest son, letting the child's feet rest upon the poems about death. "I don't know why you would want to come," he said to me. "Even with the rent we will have to live in one of the poorer boardinghouses."

"I want to see how they treat you in Washington City. Once they come to learn what you are."

"And what is that?" he asked, as Eddie tugged upon his ears.

"Noble," I told him.

My husband held up his youngest son. "And I am to refuse the heart's desire of someone who believes that of me?" he asked him.

We arrived in Washington City in December of 1847. Robert was four; Eddie, a year and a half; and I two weeks shy of my twenty-ninth birthday. My congressman husband was thirty-six.

It was a warm day for December, and we took an open carriage from the train depot so we would miss no detail of this new city. The men upon the streets all appeared distinguished, dressed from head to toe in somber broadcloth; while the women all were fashionable, transporting wide bells of ruffled skirts through the crowd, their hoops of such diameter no frugal lady in Springfield would have condoned the amount of material required to cover them. Small groups of free Negroes stood on street corners dressed in homespun versions of the white men's attire. Other Negroes, body servants to Southern politicians, trailed behind their masters, carrying umbrellas to hold over the gentlemen's heads in the event of rain. Grand houses of limestone and brick had been constructed on every corner, most of the streets were paved, and there were very few pigs.

Our boardinghouse, known only as Mrs. Sprigg's, for the landlady, was on Carroll Row, across from the Capitol building. Indeed, from the smudged windows of the front parlor, we could see the building's temporary wooden dome. The house itself was very much like the Globe; it even smelled like the Globe, though a little less like bourbon.

That evening at the supper table, I met our fellow boarders – ten Whig congressmen, none of whom had brought their wives – as well as Mrs. Sprigg, a widow of about thirty who chewed jaw-distorting wads of tobacco. Beside the landlady, I was the only woman in the house, excepting a young Negro servant named Almira who was working for wages to buy her freedom. When we settled ourselves at the table, the Whig congressmen regarded my children as if they might be a differing, and potentially unwelcome, species, although I had to believe some of them must have had their own offspring at home. I kept Eddie upon my lap, but Robert was not so easily controlled. My eldest son fled beneath the table, where he spent the meal banging upon the congressmen's shins with a spoon.

Mrs. Sprigg turned out to be a very acceptable cook. However, I could not entirely enjoy her lamb stew, for the politicians – perhaps as unused to ladies as to children – spewed tobacco juice across the table with such abundant regularity, it appeared we were dining in the midst of a brown rainstorm. Nevertheless, between the intake of lamb stew and the output of tobacco, the talk was of politics. The congressmen debated the annexation of Texas and whether President Polk was hoping for war with Mexico. And my own husband, although only arrived in the capital for twenty-four hours, gallantly argued the issues with them.

"Allow the president to invade another nation whenever he deems it necessary," declared Mr. Lincoln, "and you allow him to make war at pleasure!"

The other Whig gentlemen applauded my husband's assessment,

but I could not long enjoy his acclaim; for almost immediately, one of the other congressmen was prompted by Mr. Lincoln's speech to call President Polk by a vividly colorful epithet. I turned to the politician, expecting him to make me an apology, but the man seemed to have forgotten I was present. Further, several of his colleagues appeared to be working on forthright descriptions of their own. Gathering up Eddie in my arms and removing Robert from beneath the table, I hurried my children from the dining room. However, the damage had been done, as all the following week my eldest son felt compelled to repeat the colorful epithet to a good many surprised strangers he encountered in the park.

I soon learned that such frank assessments of the current president, as well as certain representatives of the opposing party, were commonplace at Mrs. Sprigg's supper table and decided it would be best to have Robert's meals, along with his brother's, served in our room. This I did, unless my eldest son's protests at being restricted reached an unmanageable volume. Indeed, the volume of Robert's protests – as well as many of his other pursuits – was the one topic our fellow boarders were always willing to discuss with me. If Robert ran in the corridor, or shouted up the stairwell, or brought barking dogs into the house, I would be certain to discover a red-faced congressman at my door, complaining that my child was making it impossible for him to focus upon the affairs of the nation. Even Mr. Giddings, the great abolitionist from Ohio, appeared as if he would be willing to moderate his views regarding the shackling of human beings when it came to my eldest son.

Unfortunately, Robert spent more time clattering up and down the hallways of Mrs. Sprigg's boardinghouse than I or the congressmen would have wished, for Eddie was often sickly and could not be taken out of doors. The damp cold of Washington City's winter was harsh upon my youngest child's lungs, and within a week of our arrival, Eddie developed a cough that was surprising in its hoarse depth. I knew no doctor in Washington City and was obliged to use one Mrs. Sprigg recommended, a small balding man who appeared always in a rush. Mrs. Sprigg's doctor prescribed mustard plasters, and our room was always filled with their sharp scent.

Robert did not like the plasters. He claimed the smell burned his nose. The moment I turned my back to apply one upon his younger brother's laboring lungs, he dashed from the room. Eddie did not like the plasters either. They left the flesh of his chest reddened and raw, and when I pressed a new one over the scraped skin, he flailed his arms about and was in so much distress, I could not leave him to go in search of his brother.

My husband was of little assistance during Eddie's illness. His work at the Capitol took all his time, and he did not come home until very late. Mr. Lincoln wished to make a name for himself in Washington City, and he had decided to accomplish this by confronting President Polk upon the subject of his war with Mexico.

The war had begun a year earlier, when American soldiers were killed on land near the Rio Grande, land which both the United States and Mexico claimed as theirs. President Polk had determined that the soil upon which the Mexican army had, as he decried, "shed the blood of our citizens" was indeed part of America, and had used this as excuse to declare war upon Mexico.

"Polk possessed no proof that the soldiers weren't on Mexican land," said my husband, "which makes this war unconstitutional. And an unconstitutional war begun by a Democratic president cannot go unremarked upon by a Whig politician."

Mr. Lincoln explained this to me on one of the uncommon nights I was able to remain awake until he returned to Mrs. Sprigg's.

"What are you planning to do?" I asked, handing him his nightshirt.

"Tomorrow I'll make a speech challenging Polk to prove that the soil where the American soldiers died was or wasn't ours."

"You've written it already?"

"Most of it."

"Practice it for me." I sat upon the bed, as our room did not possess any chairs.

My husband pulled on his nightshirt and stood at the end of the iron bedstead. Raising his voice, as if already in the House, he began to speak.

"In a whisper," I interrupted him. "We do not wish to have Robert wake and resume abusing Mrs. Sprigg's furniture."

Despite the whisper, the great logic and passion of my husband's speech filled our boardinghouse bedroom with a grandeur which the peeling dresser and smell of other people's hair tonic could not diminish. Mr. Lincoln accused President Polk of desiring only military glory, which he called "that attractive rainbow that rises in showers of blood, that serpent's eye that charms to destroy," and warned the president that "the blood of this war, like the blood of Abel, is crying to Heaven against you!"

"No one will hear this speech and not be convinced of its rightness," I told my husband.

"Particularly if I deliver it in something more decorous than a nightshirt."

"President Polk himself will be unable to suppress his admiration for your eloquence. And your bravery."

"Do you really think it so very fine?" he asked.

"I do," I said. "And if you would come around to the other side of that bedstead, I shall demonstrate my own unsuppressed admiration."

Mr. Lincoln smoothed the pages of his speech. "I think for now I'll stay on this side and work a bit more on the wording," he told me, "as I have a strong suspicion that you intend to demonstrate it in a manner more wifely than political."

The following morning, before he left for the Capitol, I flattened my husband's untamable hair with so great an amount of Macassar oil, the top of his head shone. I would have wished very much to accompany him, to see him deliver his challenge to President Polk before the Congress. However, I could not bring my sons into the House of Representatives, and Almira, the colored girl who worked for Mrs. Sprigg, could only be coaxed to stay alone with Robert once a day; and I had already arranged for her to watch my sons that evening so I could attend the presidential reception.

President and Mrs. Polk held several of these receptions each year, and although I was overcome with excitement at the prospect of going, I noticed that our fellow boarders did not share my enthusiasm.

"The president and his wife have outlawed liquor, dancing, and cards," warned the congressman who had so colorfully increased Robert's vocabulary. "Their receptions are like attending a Methodist camp meeting without the stimulation of a good sermon."

Nevertheless, I was anxious to go. Especially on this night, when I was certain my husband would have so distinguished himself before the Congress. All that day while I tended to Eddie's raw chest with a salve – my youngest son had only just recovered from one of his lung sicknesses – or chased Robert out of Mr. Giddings's room – the abolitionist had brought with him to Washington City an inordinate number of breakable items – I longed for it to be time to leave for the President's House. I wished the opportunity to observe the Whig gentlemen as they congratulated Mr. Lincoln upon his boldness and genius of mind, wished also to see how the Democrats would regard him with justifiable trepidation. Moreover, I very much wished to converse with a lady.

Since my arrival, the ladies of Washington City had been unanimous in taking no notice of me. It appeared that the wives of unknown congressmen possessed no social standing, particularly if they possessed no fashionable clothes. As a consequence, I received no invitations to tea or to luncheon, and my female companionship in the capital had so far been limited to the tobacco-spewing Mrs. Sprigg and the colored domestic I bribed to watch my sons. Tonight, however, I expected that the ladies of Washington City would overlook my social shortcomings and cluster about my too-narrow skirts in order to speak with the wife of the newly notable Mr. Lincoln.

I was dressed and the carriage already waiting when my husband returned from the Capitol. "What did the Congress think of your speech?" I asked, as he hurried into his evening clothes.

"They're politicians," he replied. "It's impossible to know what they thought."

This was the type of overly modest – and deeply trying – answer Mr. Lincoln was likely to give, but I had no time to press him further, as the carriage driver was charging us for every minute we made him wait. *I shall see what they thought for myself,* I decided. *See it when they fall upon themselves to shake his hand.*

While the frank-speaking congressman had prepared me for the lack of diversion to be found inside the President's House, I was entirely unprepared for the lack of elegance. The room in which we were received resembled nothing so much as Mrs. Sprigg's parlor – with perhaps a bit more attention paid to aiming for the spittoons. The carpet beneath my feet was worn through to the webbing, and the velvet edgings of the draperies looked as if industrious mice had been chewing on them.

"Did you not imagine it would be more grand?" I whispered to my husband, as we took our place in the receiving line.

Mr. Lincoln, who I sometimes thought would not notice the difference between a dirt floor and a Turkey carpet, glanced about. "It is at least very big."

"Still, possessing a settee which must be propped up by a wooden _cket does detract from the president's significance," I told him. "I _.iall never allow you to live in such a fashion."

My husband smiled and took my hand. "Anything you can do to enhance my significance will be much appreciated," he replied.

Near the front of the line, I spied the white-haired president and his wife. Mrs. Polk was plainly dressed in charcoal serge, like the wife of an unprosperous clergyman, although the bell of her skirt was wider than mine. I wondered how the man Mr. Lincoln had called "bewildered, confounded, and miserably perplexed" in his speech would greet us, and I let myself imagine that Mr. Polk was experiencing no small degree of unease about facing the fearless congressman who had demanded proof of the legitimacy of his unconstitutional war.

However, once Mr. Lincoln and I stood before the president, the sole issue about which he appeared perplexed was the identity of the tall man shaking his white-gloved hand.

"Lincoln, is it?" asked President Polk, with no hint of recognition that the man before him had only today declared the blood of his illegal war crying to Heaven against him. "And you are newly arrived?"

"Yes," replied Mr. Lincoln. "From Illinois."

"Then, welcome to Washington City," said the president. And we were propelled forward so that a Democratic congressman could be greeted.

"Could it be that the president has not yet heard about your speech?" I asked.

"Mr. Polk hears of everything that happens in the House as soon as it occurs."

"Then how could he say nothing?"

"Perhaps he is just being a good politician," said my husband. "Or perhaps I have made no impact on him."

Mr. Lincoln's speech appeared to have made little impact upon any of the gentlemen at the president's reception – Whig or Democrat. And it had made none at all upon their wives. For the entirety of the evening, no ladies sought me out. None even seemed to notice me, save for the few who glanced at the inadequate circumference of my hoops and then ignored me as completely as if I had turned up in a calico prairie dress.

Mr. Lincoln's challenge received no response from President

Polk. The president remained unconcerned about what an unknown congressman had said about a popular war which would add vast new territories – such as California – to the Union. Even the Congress paid little heed to my husband's speech, with the exception of a representative from Missouri who referred to Mr. Lincoln as "unpatriotic."

The newspapers, at least those from Illinois, whose citizens had sent Mr. Lincoln to Congress, were less quiet. "Congressman Lincoln has proved to be a Benedict Arnold," announced one. Another asked, with more self-righteousness than I believe the press deserved to possess, "How can Mr. Lincoln traitorously question the war that took the lives of so many gallant heroes?"

My husband remained largely undistressed by what the papers said of him. "It does seem a bit of a setback to be compared to Benedict Arnold during one's first month as a congressman" was all he would admit, before letting the subject drop. I, however, could not be so sanguine. I had come to Washington City to see my husband be brilliant, not proclaimed a traitor. And I had intended to find myself surrounded by ladies who talked of politics, not gentlemen who engaged in excessively frank language and spit tobacco juice across the dinner table.

It was to remedy this uncheerful mood that I set out on a January afternoon for the shops of Pennsylvania Avenue. Mr. Lincoln and I had plans to visit Carusi's saloon that evening to hear the Ethiopian Serenaders – minstrels who had twice performed for Queen Victoria – and I was in search of something new to wear.

"All the quality folk turn up at Carusi's," Mrs. Sprigg had informed me over breakfast. "Especially when there's anybody in blackface."

Her remark had sent me to my wardrobe, which I determined contained nothing adequate in which to appear before minstrels who had sung for the Queen of England. I counted the money my husband had left me for emergencies, but there was not enough of it to have one of my dresses made over. There was, however, enough for a shawl, which, if I uncovered a bargain, might be fine enough to draw attention away from the shortfallings of my dress. As I was obliged to forfeit one of my dollars – in gold – to Almira to keep my sons for me, I saved the money of a carriage by walking to the shops on foot.

Nothing I had seen before prepared me for the shops of

Pennsylvania Avenue. Unlike Springfield, where one's watered silk (when it was available) was measured and cut on the same counter as one's tallow, Pennsylvania Avenue was lined with entire shops that sold only dress silks, or ribbons for bonnets, or edgings of Maltese lace. Stunned by so much extravagance, I crisscrossed the broad street, stopping before windows in which great buntings of satin shimmered like sunlit pools, cameos made of jet perched upon velvet pillows like shiny pieces of night, and capes trimmed with the fur of rabbits promised the softest caress. I stood before shops selling waistbands of black *moiré d'antique* and sashes of taffeta, bonnets trimmed with peacock feathers and crape flowers which appeared so real, I imagined I could smell their heady fragrance through the glass. I gazed into glittering windows overflowing with yards of corded silk and French muslin, shawls trimmed with thick-piled ermine, and bracelets supporting entire rows of diamonds, and felt my whole body shiver with wanting.

It was necessary for me to walk the length of the avenue twice before my mind was calmed sufficiently to concentrate upon my own errand. It was in the window of P. H. Hood & Company that I spied a shawl of crocheted mohair which could be got for the sum I had in my pocket.

Outside the day was cold and darkly gray, but inside the shop it was warm and brightly lit. Gas sconces of etched glass hissed every few feet along the walls, and a chandelier shone brilliantly overhead. Every countertop was marble, every fitting polished brass. The floor had been overlaid with carpeting so deep, I stood still upon it, just to allow my boots to sink into its cushioning. I remained in that spot, surrounded by warmth and radiance, until a clerk approached me.

"Good afternoon, madame," said the man, making a very graceful bow. His hair was so well-tamed, it looked as if it had been painted upon his head. "How might I be of assistance?"

"I should like to see the crocheted shawl in the window," I told him. "The one of pale blue."

The clerk, whose name was Mr. Thurlow, fetched the mohair shawl for me. With another little bow and much flourishing of his small hands, he dropped it over my shoulders. The shawl was lovely and soft, and though it required all of the money Mr. Lincoln had left for me, seemed worth the price.

"That shawl is most becoming to madame," declared Mr.

Thurlow. He evened the folds of the mohair across my back. "The color is quite in keeping with—"

The clerk ceased speaking in midsentence and stared at my face with such intensity, I feared I had not sponged away all of the corn mush which Eddie had flung about during his breakfast.

"Please." Mr. Thurlow put up one elegant hand. "Remain as you are."

He removed himself from my side, and after some moments returned carrying a box covered in flowered paper more elegant than anything upon the walls of Mrs. Sprigg's boardinghouse.

"It is impertinent, I know," said the clerk. "But would you indulge me?"

With more flourishing, Mr. Thurlow opened the flowered box. Inside was a shawl of indigo blue, the exact color of evening sky just after the sun has set. Like a conjurer, he made the mohair wrap upon my shoulders disappear, replacing it with the indigo shawl.

The shawl was as light as breath and as soft as Eddie's skin.

"Cashmere," whispered Mr. Thurlow, as if even the word could only be spoken in the softest of tones. "With the color of your eyes, I could not allow you to leave until I had seen you wearing this." The small, neat clerk stepped back to admire me. "My instincts are always correct in these matters."

The indigo shawl wrapped me in an embrace as warm and yielding as love. Its price, however, was more than twice what I had to spend.

"I am flattered by your impertinence, Mr. Thurlow," I said. "But I believe the mohair will suit."

In an instant, Mr. Thurlow made the crocheted shawl reappear. "Very well." His voice was tinged with the slightest hint of regret. "I shall add this to madame's account."

"I do not have an account," I told him.

"But surely madame's husband is a senator?"

The clerk's elevation of my husband's status felt as soothing as the indigo shawl. "Mr. Lincoln is a congressman," I corrected him.

"Well, Madame Lincoln, you will discover that all the better shops in Washington City keep accounts for the wives of politicians."

"The shops extend credit?"

"Merely for the ease of the husbands," explained Mr. Thurlow, "who are assumed to be preoccupied with running the government."

He folded the mohair wrap into a plainer box. "Shall I begin your account with this?"

I ran my fingers over the indigo shawl. "Perhaps I should take your recommendation, Mr. Thurlow. No doubt, the cashmere is more suited to my complexion."

"And the divine blue of your eyes."

Although I attempted to pay some portion of the money that I did have against the account, Mr. Thurlow so elegantly insisted that it was not necessary, I felt it impolite to press the point. Instead, I spent my coins upon a lace collar and cuffs to complement the shawl.

That evening, as Mr. Lincoln and I were leaving for Carusi's saloon, my husband stopped upon Mrs. Sprigg's staircase in order to examine me.

"How did you manage to find a wrap to turn your eyes that tantalizing shade of blue?" he said.

I nearly had to clutch the banister to keep myself from tumbling down the steps. Generally Mr. Lincoln was so oblivious to clothes, I could have left the house wearing his and he would not have noticed.

"Washington City is filled with many remarkable things," I told him.

I kept the cashmere shawl wrapped about my shoulders during the length of the Ethiopian Serenaders' performance, despite the fact that Carusi's was stifling as an oven. The following day I returned to Pennsylvania Avenue and opened an account at Walter Harper & Company so I could buy a yard of bonnet ribbon the very same shade of indigo.

A week later, I was back at P. H. Hood & Company seeking something for the Washington's National Birth-Night Ball. This ball, held every year in February, was attended by all of Washington City society, and was an event which required more in the way of fashionable wardrobe than a cashmere shawl. As I could not afford the services of a Washington City dressmaker, I decided to widen the skirts of my best dress by sewing in contrasting lengths of satin cut from my second-best dress. Still, I needed something which would call the eye away from the alternating gores of satin, as I was not the most skilled of seamstresses.

"I am looking for a cloak," I said to Mr. Thurlow. "Something elegant for the Birth-Night Ball."

"I have exactly the thing," the clerk announced. He disappeared into whatever enchanted room he kept the items he showed me and brought out a pale green mantelet edged with pink roses of sheer crape. "I thought, 'This would be perfect for Madame Lincoln,' the moment I saw it."

The mantelet was made of silk so light it floated upon the slightest breath, and cost three times what the dress it was meant to cover had.

"I do not know if such a pale green is suited to my complexion," I told the clerk.

Mr. Thurlow draped the silken folds of the cape about me. "You are too modest," he said. "Your type of coloring appears well in any color."

The mantelet *was* lovely. And its full cut would cover the unevenness of my stitching.

"In that," declared Mr. Thurlow, "you shall be the belle of the Washington's National Birth-Night Ball."

I added the mantelet to my account and afterward stopped into Harper & Company to purchase bonnet ribbon the color of the cape's roses and a pair of pale green gloves, adding them to my account. As I walked back to Mrs. Sprigg's, I worried a little over how we might pay for these extravagances. But as the clerks in these elegant shops never mentioned payment, I convinced myself that perhaps it was not so rigorously enforced when one's husband was a politician.

Since the time of the first president, the Washington's Birth-Night Ball had been held at Gadsby's City Tavern & Hotel in Alexandria, Virginia. Gadsby's was a stately brick building which possessed marble lintels above every doorway. The ball was held on the second floor, and we were obliged to push our way up the crowded staircase; me all the while attempting to keep my pale green hem from becoming trapped beneath the soles of gentlemen's boots. The ballroom itself was an expansive hall with rows of molded cornices and velvet-draped windows. Still, it was full to overflowing with ladies in enormous hoops and gentlemen endeavoring to step around them. Even the orchestra had had to give up their space upon the floor. Their chairs had been moved to a raised gallery, an arrangement which lent them the aspect of a heavenly choir.

Once we had pushed our way in, Mr. Lincoln disappeared into the taproom, where the married men went to talk politics and escape the press of the ladies' crinolines. Left alone beneath the orchestra's gallery, I searched the room for a lady I knew – a futile pursuit, as it was unlikely I'd discover Mrs. Sprigg or Almira taking a spin about Gadsby's ballroom. As I did not wish to be seen standing alone in the midst of the ball – it would make me appear as friendless as I was – I began to work my way about the room, pretending that I was headed toward a dear acquaintance who would kiss me and admire my mantelet.

On my second pass around the ballroom, I spotted a lady who, if not a dear acquaintance, was at least an acquaintance. Martha Martin Douglas, the wife of my former beau Stephen Douglas. Mr. Douglas – who had proved Elizabeth correct and become a senator – had married the daughter of a North Carolina plantation owner, a man who had tested Mr. Douglas's anti-slavery principles by dying and leaving his new son-in-law two hundred slaves. I had met the new Mrs. Douglas in Springfield shortly after her marriage and found her to be well-bred, well-educated, and despite descending from a very Democratic family, entirely agreeable.

Here in Gadsby's ballroom, however, Mrs. Douglas appeared more than agreeable. She appeared like rescue.

"Mrs. Douglas!" I declared, "I cannot say how pleased I am to see you here!"

Mrs. Douglas employed her beautiful manners to introduce me to the circle of ladies standing with her. Mrs. Douglas's friends were dressed in gowns which had been copied – by dressmakers, for their stitches did not show – from the plates in the latest issue of *Godey's Lady's Book*. I had poured over the illustrations of evening dresses and costumes for watering places in those pages myself; however, I was as capable of stitching up one of them as I was of achieving Miss Beecher's domestic perfection.

"Where are you and Mr. Lincoln residing while you are in Washington City?" inquired a lady whose rosette-covered train I greatly admired when I had first come upon it in *Godey's*.

I wished to tell the lady that we were at Willard's, which was one of Washington City's best hotels. But I strongly suspected that these ladies knew exactly who was and was not staying at Willard's.

"For the time being," I replied, resettling my mantelet over my skirts, "we are at Mrs. Sprigg's."

"How pleasant," replied the lady. Upon her elegant features was an expression not unlike one she might have adopted had I informed her that Mr. Lincoln and I were bedding down in the cow shed on Capitol Hill.

"Your mantelet is charming!" exclaimed another of the ladies. Her own gown was trimmed with blonde lace and blue flowers. It had appeared on a plate of dresses suitable for bridesmaids.

"You are kind to say so," I told her. And then I began to describe for her – and for the rest of Mrs. Douglas's friends – every trimming and seam of the mantelet in detail.

I do not know what it was which overtook me. I can only say that it must have come because it had been so long since I had conversed with ladies, since I could talk about clothes, or anything which was not a complaint about my children or a plea to stay with them. Whatever the cause, I found that I could not stop. I talked about crape roses and green silk and the stitching which held them together until the lady in blonde lace was no longer listening and Mrs. Douglas was worrying the amber beads at her throat. And still I kept on. I believe I would have talked about the mantelet until the Washington's Birth-Night Ball was ended and the ladies' carriages came for them, had not the lady with the rosettes on her skirts interrupted me in a forceful tone to make some point about her own dressmaker.

Although I continued to stand at the edge of Mrs. Douglas's circle of friends, none of the ladies risked asking me another question. Instead, they fluttered fans trimmed with sparkling drops of crystal, which I knew had come from Newton & Brothers, and discussed the skills of their dressmakers and the dispositions of their maids. While I could not contribute to this conversation, I did not leave their circle; for if I did, I would have had to spend the rest of the evening going round the ballroom by myself. Thus I stayed and listened to Mrs. Douglas's friends talk of other ladies I did not know, and marveled at the ease of which my slightly plump figure had been rendered invisible.

The following day, I went to see Mr. Thurlow and purchased enough taffeta to make a hundred rosettes. I also visited Mr. Harkenson at Harper & Company and bought a set of pearl shirt buttons for Mr. Lincoln, as I had noticed on the night of the ball that his were badly chipped. Then I made the acquaintance of Mr. Beaumont at Newton & Brothers, where I acquired a sparkling fan for myself; and introduced myself to Monsieur Poulain at C. W. Berryman's, who kept in stock an ample supply of blonde lace.

Twice more that week and twice the following, I bribed Almira with a dollar and visited the shops of Pennsylvania Avenue. These shops were so bright and clean compared with our rooms at Mrs. Sprigg's; and inside them I could be in the company of other ladies, even if we said no more to each other than "Pardon me" when our skirts collided. In the shops, too, Messrs. Thurlow and Harkenson, Beaumont and Poulain treated me as if Mr. Lincoln were the most distinguished member of the Senate, and not a first-year congressman who had been called unpatriotic his first month in the House.

It was at the beginning of March that the bills began to arrive.

At first I sent back notes implying that my husband was so very consumed with the work of the government he might be a little while responding to these missives. When the bills came again, I sent cordial but firmly worded letters stating that it was my understanding that payment had already been tendered. When bills bearing a more insistent tone arrived, I burned them in the fireplace. By the start of April, I could no longer visit Mr. Thurlow or Mr. Beaumont, and both Mr. Harkenson and Monsieur Poulain had become considerably less friendly. Ultimately, the shops sent the bills directly to Mr. Lincoln's office.

"Can these be right?" My husband showed me a stack of bills which even in his big hand looked substantial.

I took the pages and spread them upon the bed, tallying the figures on a paper. The amount was so high, I thought at first it could not be correct. But there was nothing written there which I had not purchased.

"I did not realize it had become so very much," I told him.

His gray eyes were granite. "Who did you think you'd married?" he asked me. "*Senator* Douglas? Some well-off Todd relation?"

"You must not say it so loudly," I warned. "The boys are asleep."

My husband tried to pace our boardinghouse bedroom, but was stopped by a wall at every turn. "You married a poor man," he spat. "Could you not remember that?"

I glanced at a wallpaper seam picked open by some former tenant's nervous fingers. "Perhaps I wished to forget it," I murmured.

Mr. Lincoln grabbed up my bills in an angry fist. "By driving us further into poverty?"

"I am sorry. Washington City has not turned out as I expected."

He took himself to the farthest corner of the room. "I said that you would be better at home."

I leapt from the bed and went to him, tried to take hold of the hand which did not contain my bills. "I did not mean to spend so much. I could not stop myself."

My husband's mouth was set in a hard line which looked to me mocking and cruel. "Is it so impossible to rein yourself in?"

His question made me recall how much I had curbed myself, and what I had forfeited in pleasure and comfort and affection by doing so. "Perhaps I am being asked to rein in too much!" I exclaimed.

"Control yourself," he said. "Robert and Eddie are sleeping in the next room."

I put a hand over my mouth, but even to be quiet felt constraining.

"I think it would be best to remove you from temptation," he said, going to stand beside the fireplace.

"You are sending me away?"

"Maybe you should only have to rein in one passion at a time."

I flew across the room to him. "I will miss you too much." Again, I tried to take his hand, both of them this time, but he would not release the bills. "Suppose I promise to keep away from Pennsylvania Avenue?" I said. "Suppose I never again enter another shop?"

"Could you keep such a promise?"

I recalled the warm brightness of the shops, and Mr. Thurlow and Monsieur Poulain, who treated me as if I were a president's wife. Recalled, too, what little my husband would give me to compensate for practicing such restraint.

"No," I told him. "I could not."

"It will be for the best, then. Once it gets warm, Washington will be full of malaria."

"But where will I go? The house in Springfield is rented for the year."

He shifted his eyes away from me. "I was thinking of your father's house in Lexington."

"You would send me to my stepmother?" I asked in disbelief. "Who considers me to be a limb of Satan?"

"You're a grown woman with your own children. If you are a limb of Satan, she likely realizes that you're too old to be amputated."

I put myself in his gaze. "She has no affection for me."

"I know," he admitted.

Neither of us said anything for a time, then he began to spread my bills upon the mantle.

"If you and the boys go to your father," he explained, "it will cost us nothing for your board. And if it is only me here, I can give up one of these rooms."

I waited until he had smoothed every bill, shaped them into a thick pile. "Will it take us very long to pay these?" I asked.

"Yes," he told me.

A week later my sons and I, under the protection of a Kentucky congressman returning home, boarded the coach in front of Mrs. Sprigg's. Mr. Giddings, whose face I spied peering from an upper window, appeared much relieved to see my eldest son climb into the carriage.

My father's house in Lexington was crowded and lively. While my own brothers and sisters were no longer at home, seven of the children which Betsey had borne – from Samuel at eighteen to Katherin at seven – were always to be found dashing up and down the grand staircase and out through the flower garden which separated the main house from the slave cabins. My sons and I settled into the big house, and were soon seduced into the soft indolence of Southern life. We rose late, napped in the afternoon, and were cosseted by my father's Negroes – one for every white member of the family. For her part, Mammy Sally was outraged by the deprivations I was forced to endure in the uncivilized North.

"You mean to tell me none of that white help in Illinois knows how to make corn bread?"

"I do not know how either," I reminded her.

"You ain't supposed to," she huffed. And at every meal afterward, my place could be marked by the small mountain of yellow biscuits beside the plate.

"I don't know how you expect to be raisin' those boys without no colored nurse," she declared every time she caught me attempting to do something for my sons. And when I came to her asking for a basin in which to bathe Eddie, she insisted I turn him over to her for washing, then returned him to me so thickly dusted with cornstarch – Mammy Sally's remedy for prickly heat – I almost believed she intended to bake him.

At my father's house, I put my hand to neither water pump nor washtub, cooking skillet nor carpet beater, and I suspected I was in danger of forgetting the little Miss Beecher had been able to teach me. Within a week of my arrival, I did not even bother to retrieve the silk chemises I let fall to the floor while undressing.

Although I was apprehensive about sharing a house – no matter how spacious – with my stepmother, Betsey proved at least cordial. Not to mention that the constant correction and persistent instruction of her own children – who were so very many – prevented her from having time to practice them upon mine and me.

While it is true that I had been banished to Kentucky, it was not an altogether unpleasant banishment. April, which had been cold and damp in Washington City, was warm and saturated with the perfume of flowers in Lexington. And the well-bred – and well-enforced – gentility of my stepmother's supper table was considerably more appetizing than the great freedom of expression and tobacco juice displayed in Mrs. Sprigg's dining room. Indeed, my husband's company was the only thing for which I longed; for with slaves to do my housekeeping and my child-raising, I went to bed each night with an excess of energy and only a novel to spend it on – and the sultry nights of Kentucky, filled with the sticky scent of tuberoses, were far too stirring for novel-reading.

My sons also seemed to thrive at my father's house. The milder weather improved Eddie's lungs; he did not cough nearly as much. And Robert, with my father's property to roam over, was not always being returned to me by a red-faced adult. Most often in fact, my eldest son could be found at his grandfather's side, on his way to or from some excursion. The afternoon the local breeders raced their thoroughbreds down Main Street, my father took Robert to watch them, letting him stand so close to the pedigreed hooves, Mammy Sally needed two changes of water to wash the dust from his hair. When a traveling menagerie came to Lexington, both Robert and my father went to view the animals, returning with the pronouncement that the camel was an "uncouth and smelly beast," due to his fondness for spitting. And every Sunday after dinner, my son and his grandfather walked into town to visit Monsieur Giron's confectionery, from which Robert returned with meringue on his mouth.

The two were very much alike. They showed their affection for one another with small nods of the head and a light touching of the hands, like gentlemen greeting each other at a club. And Robert seemed to understand instinctively how much of such affection his grandfather would tolerate.

One particular Saturday, as my father and Robert made ready to leave for the music hall where they were to see a ventriloquist who had come all the way from Philadelphia, my father's nine-year-old son, Aleck, ran into the room and hurled himself against his father's legs.

"Momma says I can go," said the little red-haired boy. "If you say it's all right." While he spoke, he tugged upon the cream-colored fabric of his father's trousers.

Aleck, I had noticed, was always hurtling his warm little body into somebody's legs, or slipping fingers sticky with Mammy Sally's molasses candy into somebody's hand. Since coming to Lexington, I found him wrapped up in my skirts so often, I half-expected that when I shook them at night, my little half-brother would fall out.

My father looked down on the child at his knees. "My trousers," he told him.

Instantly, Aleck let go of the fabric, glancing away from the creases he had left there. "I am sorry, Papa," he said. He stood silent for a moment, then lifted his head. "But can I go?"

"Yes, you may," replied my father. "If—" But before he could finish, Aleck again threw himself against the trousers.

My father sighed and unwound his son's arms from his legs. "I was going to say, 'if you run and ask Pendleton to lay out another pair of trousers for me.'"

"Yes, Papa!" Aleck cried, and hurried away up the stairs.

My father stood examining the knees of his trousers.

"Aleck is an affectionate child," I observed.

"Yes," sighed my father. "You were very much like that. It took no small amount of training to teach you to contain yourself around my clothes."

"Perhaps I only wished for your attention," I told him.

My father looked up from his trousers with a slight look of bewilderment upon his fine features. Beside him, my own son, whom I had never seen disarrange his grandfather's clothes, mirrored the expression perfectly.

At the close of June, before Lexington could fill with the fevers and cholera of summer, we loaded the carriages with trunks and children and Negroes and traveled to Crab Orchard Springs. Crab Orchard was the most fashionable watering spot in all of Kentucky. Although it promoted itself as a health resort, ladies arrived at its wide doors with more ball dresses than wrappers; and gentlemen, unless they were very elderly or consumptive, filled their glasses more with bourbon than with the spring's sulfuric water. Meals at Crab Orchard were taken either on the shaded veranda or in the dining room, depending upon the weather and physical condition of the diner, and in both locations, Negro fiddlers entertained with light music meant to aid the digestion.

During the long afternoons at the Springs, unmarried ladies tortured their beaux by accepting and then refusing invitations to walk with them beneath the rows of flowering magnolia trees. Married ladies sat on the east porch discussing the indiscretions of those who were absent and childbearing, while sipping glasses of mineral-laden water. The married men congregated on the west porch, where the talk was of horses and politics, and the drink was either julep or whiskey, depending upon the time of day. And the children ran about the lawn without their shoes, inhaling so much of the lemon verbena that grew along the pathways, they were in a constant state of dizziness.

This summer, however, my father forfeited much of his west porch julep time to Robert. The two of them, sometimes in the company of Aleck, went riding together near the springs or swimming in a small pond heated by underground vapors. And most evenings, the boys followed my father and begged him to tell them stories about the Todd forbears which were bloody and filled with violence.

"My father, Levi Todd, saved Lexington from the Chickasaws," he told them one night, his voice full of drama and Southern drawl. "It happened at the Battle of Blue Licks, which he fought with his brothers, John and Robert."

It was a languid evening, the air warm and filled with the syrupy scent of the magnolias. The whole family had come out onto the veranda after supper and stayed sprawled over wicker chaises and rockers long enough for the sky to grow dark and the mosquitoes to be replaced by fireflies.

"It was during that battle that my Uncle John took a bullet in the chest," my father continued.

"Did he die?" asked Robert.

"Indeed he did," replied my father. "But gallantly. Still upon his white horse, although he had been killed."

"What happened then?" said Aleck.

"Uncle Robert, the courageous man for whom I was named, raised his rifle, took aim at the savage's war-painted chest, and shot," my father fired an imaginary rifle into a cluster of ladies in taffeta ball gowns, "killing that Chickasaw dead in an instant."

"He must have been brave," breathed Robert.

"He was your great-great-uncle, Robert Todd." My father paused. "And I possess the very rifle that slew that Chickasaw."

The two boys sprang from their places at either side of my father.

"Can we see it?" begged Robert.

"Please," said Aleck.

"The rifle is in Lexington," my father told them. "But upon our return I shall show it to you." He turned then to Robert. "And when you make ready to go back to Illinois, I shall give that rifle to you. For it has always belonged to a Robert Todd."

I heard Aleck make a small cry, as if he had been hit unexpectedly, and looked to see what expression had formed upon his heart-shaped face. But the light on the veranda was too dim.

"Come and sit with me, Aleck," I said. "For our father's stories have been much too grisly, and I feel the need of male protection."

My half-brother climbed into my lap and wrapped his arms around my neck. For the rest of the evening, until we all went inside, he stayed there, his weight warm and smelling of a boy who has spent the entire day out of doors. Robert remained beside his grandfather, begging more stories of Indians and killing.

The following morning, my father met me at breakfast. This was a rarity, for my father usually sat late with the gentlemen upon the west porch and did not generally rise before eleven. And when he did rise, he preferred to sit by himself with a pot of chicory-flavored coffee until he had read everything that those damnable Democrats had been up to.

"Did you not sleep well?" I asked him.

My father asked a waiter for his coffee, then gave me his attention. "Tell the truth, I had a good deal on my mind."

I watched a group of ladies dressed in summer frocks through the gingerbread fretwork of the veranda and waited to see if he would share his thoughts with me, for it often seemed as if I could only learn what my father was thinking by acting as if I were not so very interested in it.

"I believe young Robert should study Greek," he told me.

"That is the thought which kept you from sleep?" I smiled.

"And, perhaps, Latin."

"He has only just turned five years old," I reminded him.

"The child has a fine mind."

"That is the contribution of his father."

"I think he is very much a Todd," he said. "And for that we must credit you."

My father set down his coffee and rested his eyes – blue, like mine – upon my face. I could recall no other time that I had been held so long in his gaze, and I wished that, like my half-brother, I might fling myself across the table and crease the cream-colored linen of his suit. But I was kept back by the weight of my skirts, and my adulthood, and the remembrance of the way that my father had regarded his small, affectionate son.

"I would like Robert to remain in Lexington after the summer," said my father.

"You wish to keep my son?" I was surprised by the request, for my father's house seemed already overrun with his own offspring.

"For the winter. I understand that Mr. Lincoln will remain in Washington City and that you intend to return to Springfield alone. It is also apparent to me that Edward is something of a sickly child."

"It is only that I must be careful of his lungs," I said.

"Which will not be an easy task during the cold of an Illinois winter."

I did not want to agree with my father, for it seemed unlucky to speak about the delicacy of Eddie's health. However, I had already been made anxious by how I might protect my youngest son from the harshest weather when his brother would want so desperately to hurl himself into it.

"Leaving Robert in my house," continued my father, "will both assist you and profit him."

"Robert is indeed happy in your house," I admitted.

"It gives me great pleasure to have him there."

My father reached across the breakfast table and placed his hand over mine. I said nothing, afraid the disturbance of my words would cause him to remove it.

"Will you indulge me in this?" he asked.

My first impulse was to tell him yes; to say that he could keep my son for as long as he wished if he would only leave his hand on mine and rest his eyes again upon my face. But I wondered if my father was correct, if a season in his house would profit my son. For since we had come to Lexington, Robert had acquired a new reserve; one which stiffened his small frame into straightness and made him speak to me in tones too formal for affection; one which reminded me of his grandfather.

"I shall need to write to my husband and get his opinion," I told him.

My father lifted his hand from mine. "I trust you to present the case convincingly."

As our time at Crab Orchard passed, I wrestled with the decision of whether to leave Robert at my father's house. Each afternoon when the mail came, my father asked if I had heard from Mr. Lincoln. "I expect that the press of his work for the government prevents him from writing," I said. "I imagine the candidacy of General Taylor for president has claimed all his time."

In truth, I had not written to my husband. Mr. Lincoln gave me unbounded liberty when it came to the raising of our children, and if I had wished to leave his eldest son with my father, he would make no protest. I was only unsure whether I wished it. Leaving Robert would certainly make my father happy, and make him perhaps more affectionate toward me. But I could not be easy about giving my already untender son to a grandfather who did not care for emotions which might disorder his clothes.

Too quickly, our last full day at Crab Orchard was upon us. As was our custom when the weather was fine, the ladies of our party embarked on a morning constitutional – led by my stepmother – around the grounds. We were just returning when Betsey stopped us before a large cereus bush planted behind the grand ballroom.

"That bud has been pointing upward for two days," she said. She dipped the brim of her English straw bonnet at a swollen bud which showed white at the tip. "I am certain it will bloom tonight."

"But the cereus is said to bloom only once every hundred years," protested a lady from Baltimore who had joined us and was unaware that Betsey Todd was considered by all – including herself – to be expert upon the subject of flowers.

"Yes," my stepmother told the lady from Baltimore. "And this will be the night." She turned to Jane, the slave who had been her wedding present. "Arrange to have some chairs brought here after supper. We shall gather and watch it open."

"May we stay up too?" asked one of my little half-sisters.

"All the children may remain awake for the blooming," declared Betsey. "An appreciation of flowers is the mark of a finely reared character."

That evening after supper the family made its way to the wide lawn behind the ballroom, upon which white chairs had been arranged in a half-circle about the bush. There was dancing that night, and the ladies of our party sat in the white chairs and watched the whirling skirts of the unmarried girls through the ballroom window – skirts of pale chiffon in shades of pink and lavender, so like night-blooming flowers themselves. Our gentlemen stood a little way off so they might smoke, tempering our soft femininity with the masculine scent of tobacco. Out upon the lawn, the children ran about catching fireflies in their hands and calling to each other in high voices that grew fainter as the sky darkened.

"What do we do?" asked my half-sister Emilie, who at twelve believed she should sit with the ladies, although her slipper-clad feet moved as if they were propelling her across the lawn with the younger children.

"Just watch," instructed Betsey. "And be patient."

It grew late. The spinning of the flowerlike skirts through the window slowed as the Negro musicians switched to waltzes. The children wandered across the lawn, drifting to their mothers' sides. The air turned cool, and the ladies covered their shoulders with shawls light as a breeze. Eddie fell asleep in my lap. Robert sat at my feet.

"It must be near midnight," said my father, who had come to sit between Betsey and myself.

"It will happen very soon," my stepmother told him.

And as if the bud had only been waiting for her consent, one thin white petal started to uncurl.

"I saw it!" declared Emilie in a whisper. "I saw it move!"

"I saw it too," whispered Aleck.

We were all whispering, as if we believed the harsh sound of our voices might cause the bud to close for another hundred years.

The blossom opened so gradually, it was like a trick of the eye and could be noticed only if one looked away and then looked back again. But it was happening, for before very long a delicate white petal stood trembling with our collective breath. It was then that the air filled with the scent of vanilla, the scent of the hundred-year blossom: and quicker now the rounded inner petals began to open, so white they glowed in the darkness which had fallen upon the lawn.

The younger children sat cross-legged before the night-blooming bush like India mystics – Betsey's youngest girls Elodie and Katherin in sprigged muslin dresses that pooled about their legs, Aleck and Robert so near to each other their shoulders touched – children up too late on a summer night, their eyes fixed upon a hundred-year miracle.

"Is it not like magic?" whispered Aleck to his half-nephew, so near to his own age. As he spoke the question, he threw his arm about Robert's neck; and Robert did not shrug it off.

That is when the recognition came to me. If I were to leave my eldest son with my father, I would be leaving him with his small half-uncle as well. Leaving him in the company of the child who could not be trained to control his emotions around fine clothes, who of everyone was permitted to touch Robert out of affection, who might work upon my son a hundred-year miracle.

I kept this thought, and when the cereus blossom had opened and everyone went to their beds, I remained upon the lawn, turning it over until the Negro porters had extinguished the candles in the empty ballroom and the only light came from stars and the white flower.

The next afternoon after the mail came, I informed my father that I had heard from Mr. Lincoln.

"And what does our rising young congressman say about relinquishing his firstborn son to an old Kentucky gentleman?"

"He says he reckons the boy will be much improved by the experience," I said, praying that I had not just sacrificed my son's affections upon the altar of my father's.

When autumn came, I left Robert with my father in Lexington and Eddie and I returned to Springfield. Because the house on Eighth

Street was rented for the year, and because the payment of my Washington City debts took so much of Mr. Lincoln's salary, Eddie and I stayed at the Globe Tavern.

That winter alone with my youngest son was a dreamy time. I had no house or husband to look after, no older child to worry over. Nothing required my attention, and nothing received it, save for Eddie. We passed the long winter mornings beneath the bedclothes, dozing and waking, while the gray sky turned to snow and back again. When the short winter afternoons turned to darkness, I sat before the fire with Eddie upon my lap and read the novels of Sir Walter Scott, tales of romance and gallantry told in language too rich for my two-year-old son's ears, but to which he listened with widened eyes and a small hand clasped around my wrist.

We rarely left the Globe. The cold was not good for Eddie's lungs, and in our undivided affection, I had no need of other company. Elizabeth sent invitations to fêtes and supper parties, but I declined most of them. The society of my sister's coterie and my Springfield relations held no charm compared to an evening spent sharing a child's supper of porridge and honey, my dining companion propped up on bed pillows in order to reach the table.

I did not leave the Globe even to visit the shops of Springfield. Elizabeth's servant delivered notes saying, "Accompany me to Courthouse Square tomorrow. Mr. Smith is expecting some fine wool gabardine from St. Louis." Clark Smith had married my younger sister Ann, and I suspected that, as Elizabeth had arranged the match, she was anxious to see Mr. Smith's shop succeed. "I fear I am suffering from chills," I wrote back, though I had rarely felt better. For even had Mr. Smith been expecting watered silk from France, and even had he offered to give me it for free, I did not wish to leave the warm nest Eddie and I had made of the bed.

This soothing time continued until spring, when the warmed weather and Mr. Lincoln's return coaxed us out. My husband's term in Congress, which had passed largely undistinguished – although at least he had not again been compared to Benedict Arnold – was at an end. The seat would now pass to another prominent Whig, and my husband would return to Springfield, stopping first in Lexington to fetch home his eldest son.

I was eager to see my husband. Eager also to see my son and know if my young half-brother had worked a change upon him. The day they were to arrive, Eddie and I went early to the depot so we would not miss their train.

It was early April, that unsettled month, and though the sun was warm, the wind promised frost; and I fastened shut the top buttons of Eddie's woolen jacket to protect his chest. Few people were at the depot – the season was still too early for travel – and the two of us waited alone upon the platform, save for an elderly porter who seemed soured by the lack of customers.

"Do you remember Robert?" I asked my son.

"Robert!" he shouted with enthusiasm. But it was impossible to tell from this whether he remembered his elder brother, for Eddie showed enthusiasm for all creatures equally, from his doting aunts to the neighbor's turkey.

"He may have changed," I told him. "It is possible he may be different." And as I had done all winter, I prayed that such difference would be for the better.

The train arrived in a cloud of steam, which Eddie purposefully inhaled, so used was he to breathing in bowls of steam at the times his lungs closed. I saw Mr. Lincoln open the compartment door, then turn to help his eldest son from the train, and I raised an arm, ready to call out. But as my husband and eldest son came toward me, my bright greeting stuck in my throat.

It appeared that the tall man and the small boy did not belong together. Robert looked every bit the Southern gentleman in cream-colored trousers and a little waistcoat of brown wool. These rich clothes were clean and unrumpled, remarkably so, as they had been on the back of a five-year-old boy since the train had left Chicago. Mr. Lincoln's jacket, on the other hand, needed brushing as well as matching to his trousers. The trousers themselves called for burning, as they were worn through at the knees. Moreover, while Robert walked with a straight spine and his head high, his taller father was obliged to slouch in order to reach his son's hand, which lent him a beggarly aspect. Rather than a returning congressman, Mr. Lincoln resembled nothing so much as a shambling vagrant which the little gentleman at his side had dragged home for a charity meal.

My husband did not know and did not care about the impression he made stepping off the train with his eldest son. He reached us in two long strides and took Eddie from my arms, holding the boy high above his head in order to "take the measure of the rascal." Eddie showed no difficulty recognizing his father, for he shouted, "Pa! Pa!" without being prompted – and with more enthusiasm than he had ever showed for the neighbor's turkey. For myself, I was so happy to have my husband with me, I buried my face in his rumpled shirtfront and did not lift it until he warned that I was in danger of giving the porter apoplexy.

I then turned my attention to my eldest son. "I have missed you more than I can say." I pressed my lips to his hair, which had darkened a little, and gathered him into an embrace. But my son's body was unyielding, as if lengths of wire had been hidden in his fine clothes.

It is the clothes, I told myself. *My father must have cautioned him to keep them orderly.*

"Tell me about Grandfather Todd," I said quickly. "And Mammy Sally. Did you like staying in Lexington? Was Grandmother Betsey good to you?" I flooded my son with questions, as if their onrush might break the enchantment which had turned him into a stiff little gentleman.

"Everyone is well," he told me, his words echoing his grandfather's drawl.

"Do you miss your half-uncle?" I asked him. "Do you miss Aleck?"

"I shall miss Aleck as much as is expected," he said. Then he turned and walked toward an enclosed carriage, the nicest of the three waiting at the depot, as if assuming we had hired it.

We were done with the renting of our house and were back living on Eighth Street. I imagined it might require some days before Robert grew used to being at home, some time before he lost the formality of a visitor. For a week or more after his homecoming, I resisted putting my hands upon him and did not ask for his company, trusting such restraint might make him come to me.

Robert did come, on a day too full of rain for even him to go out, wandering into the kitchen where I was seated at the pine table refilling the astral lamps with lard. For a long time, he stood at my side watching me; and I did not speak, or push back the hair that had fallen into his eyes, or even acknowledge he was there, for fear even that would make him go.

"Why are you doing that?" he said at last.

"The lard is what fuels the light."

"I already know that," he told me. "Why are *you* doing it?"

"What do you mean?"

"Grandmother Betsey has a servant to fill the lamps."

"I find it is not so very difficult to do myself." I did push back the hair then, just to feel some part of him beneath my fingers.

"We're poor, aren't we?" he said.

"We are not poor."

"We don't keep ponies or hunting dogs or slaves."

"Your father does not believe in keeping slaves. And neither do I."

Robert twisted a length of the yarn I was using for wicks. "What about Mammy Sally?"

"Your grandfather inherited Mammy Sally, and I cannot tell him what to do with his property. But Mammy Sally has lived in the house in Lexington so long, I think she would be sad to leave it."

He watched me pour melted lard into the lamp-filler.

"Aleck has his own horse. And clothes just for riding."

"Lexington is full of horses."

"Grandfather Todd is richer than we are."

I set down the filler so I would not burn myself on the fat. "It is true that we do not have as much money as Grandfather Todd," I began, not entirely certain how I would complete the sentence.

"Why not?" interrupted my son. "*You're* a Todd."

"I am a Lincoln now. Just as you are."

He drew himself up. "My name is Robert Todd."

"Robert Todd Lincoln," I reminded him. I wiped my hands, shiny and pork-smelling from the lard, upon a cloth and took hold of his face before he might move away. "You have the best of all possible fathers," I told him. "I think that one day he will take you to live in a much bigger house than even Grandfather Todd's."

Robert regarded me with his skewed gaze, as if suspicious of my authority to make such a prediction.

From that time onward, I noticed that Robert looked upon his father's denim trousers and unshined boots with a judging eye. And when Mr. Lincoln went to his knees to speak to his son more easily, the boy narrowed his eyes at the coarse hair standing in tufts upon the man's head, and did not hear a word of his father's gentle discourse.

"Great-grandfather Levi Todd captured a Creole general," Robert told his father one evening over supper. "What did Great-grandfather Lincoln do?"

"My grandfather was killed by an Indian while working in a cornfield."

"The Indian killed *him*?" said Robert incredulously.

"Yes," admitted his father. "But my Uncle Mordecai did shoot the Indian dead."

"What else?" prompted his son.

My husband studied his plate, as if heroic stories of his forbears, all of whom were unknown or unillustrious, might be discovered in the stew. "Nothing else to tell," he said after a bit. "Though if it would please you, I'll go out into the yard and see if I can capture any Creole generals."

"My father's stories tend to be improved by embellishment," I told my husband, after Robert had left the table. But I could hardly bear to look into his melancholy face.

It was my doing that Robert had been made aware of our poverty, my fault that he gazed upon his father with measuring eyes. I had left my son to be influenced by the big house in Lexington, and my father's ponies, and the tales of the Todd ancestors, all of whom were distinguished and brave, and spoken about continually. And for all of that, he had remained entirely uninfluenced by the small boy who could not contain his affection. I was more than sorry I had left Robert behind in Lexington. And now that he had returned, I was happy Mr. Lincoln had taken him away.

I was made more happy when we received word a month later that Lexington had been seized by the worst epidemic of cholera it had ever known. "Every hour," my father wrote to me, "whole batteries of field artillery are fired, in hope the bullets and noise will rend the clouds of disease that fill the air. Still as many as forty people perish over the course of a single day. The death carts can barely contain them."

"I pray that you and all the little Todds are away from the city," I wrote back, "and have gone someplace where you will be safe."

"I have moved the children and your stepmother to the house in the country," he replied. "However, as I am attempting a try at senator, I must remain."

"Politics are not worth your life," I told him. "Please write to tell me you have left Lexington."

But the next letter that arrived from Kentucky was from my brother Levi.

I had never before received a letter from my brother. Levi was not given to writing, and I did not believe he possessed any fondness for his siblings. If it was he who had penned the letter, I knew the news inside it could not be lucky. I brought the letter into the parlor to read, a parlor in a house which my father had helped us buy but never seen.

"On July seventh," wrote my brother in a hand with no flourishes, "after delivering a lengthy speech, our father was stricken with cholera. He was removed to the country, where he was attended to by several doctors. After one week, as he had not improved, he dictated his will. Two days later, he died."

This was all my brother had written, but it was enough to make me imagine my father's handsome flesh gone blue with cholera. Enough to make me think of the children, nearly as young as my own, he had left behind. Clutching Levi's uneffusive letter in my hand, I fell upon a brocade settee meant for company and wept.

I brought Robert into the kitchen to tell him this news, because it seemed to me the most comforting room – perhaps because I had been raised with a kitchen which always had Mammy Sally in it. And I was certain that my son would need comforting, for he had loved – no matter how reserved he had been about its demonstration – the courtly gentleman who had taken him to see thoroughbreds and ventriloquists.

"Your grandfather has been called to God," I said to him.

"Grandfather Todd is dead?"

"Yes," I told him.

I was seated upon a wooden kitchen stool, and from that vantage could see directly into the face of my son; see perfectly the eye, which we had not been able to straighten by making Robert look through keyholes, tug toward his nose. *It is the force of his emotions which shifts the eye,* I thought for the first time. *Or perhaps the force of holding them back.*

"Did an Indian kill him?" he asked me.

"The cholera took him."

My son's finely curved lip trembled, and in that skewed eye I saw the shine of tears.

"It is all right to cry for Grandfather Todd if you wish," I told him.

Robert looked away, but I saw two tears fall from my son's inclined left eye, saw, too, more pooling behind his lashes. But as if in defiance of gravity, they did not fall.

"Grandfather Todd would not wish me to cry," he said.

I put fingers upon his chin to turn his face back to me. "Grandfather Todd would not wish you to be unhappy."

"Crying isn't seemly," he replied.

I touched the wet left by the escaped tears. I had never known my eldest son to cry out of anything save frustration at not getting his way, and these tears seemed a kind of miracle. "Grief is excused from all forms of seemliness," I told him.

His small boy's face was sorrowful, with one gray eye inclined to his nose. I put out my hands, intending to pull him into my lap, kiss his head, and let him weep those miraculous tears. But as I reached for him, I was checked by an unnatural sight. The tears which had pooled in my son's eyes were lessening, shrinking into nothing, as if Robert was absorbing his sorrow back into his body.

I watched Robert from that time, watched him to see if any of the grief at his grandfather's death would show itself. But it did not. And then I could not watch him any longer. For the weather turned cold, and Eddie fell sick with an illness which made it difficult for him to draw breath.

My brother-in-law Doctor Wallace prescribed salts to purge the poison in Eddie's system and steam to loosen his lungs. Upon his instructions, I fed my son tea made from slippery elm bark which was meant to soothe his throat and laudanum to stop the ache the fever put in his limbs. On the worst days, my three-year-old son lay upon his mattress and gasped like a fish on land.

After a week, Eddie's fever subsided and his breath came easier.

"He is better now, is he not?" I said to my brother-in-law.

"We will hope so," he replied. "We will very much hope so."

But that evening, the coughing began.

I do not know how Eddie did not become light-headed, how he did not swoon from lack of breath, for the coughing was ceaseless and so violent it was difficult to fathom how my son's small frame possessed the strength for such wracking. With the cough, Eddie's fever rose so high he became lost in delirium. Doctor Wallace brought leeches, a remedy with which Eddie was so familiar, he did not twitch when the black creatures were attached to his throat.

"What is it you believe he has?" I asked him.

The doctor kept his eyes upon the leeches. "Eddie has had much sickness of the lungs, has he not?"

"Yes," I said, though my brother-in-law knew this to be true as well as I.

He sighed and put his hand upon my son's forehead, brushing back the fine hair. And it was these – the sigh and the light, regretful touch – which frightened me more than all of Eddie's coughing.

"You think it is very bad," I said.

"I think it is consumption," he replied.

The word choked off my own breath as absolutely as if I suffered from the same sickness. I had known many who had been stricken with consumption. Very few who had survived it. And none of those had been children.

I grabbed for my brother-in-law's hands, though they were spotted with Eddie's blood dripped from the leeches. "We must try everything," I told him. "Every cathartic and herb you know. Every patent medicine in your apothecary. Every folk remedy and piece of slave voodoo of which you have ever heard."

Doctor Wallace shook his head. "I am a physician, not a Negro conjurer."

"You must be what will make Eddie well." I gripped his hands more tightly. *I cannot let consumption take my best son.*

When he had gone, I arranged for Robert to stay at Elizabeth's house on Aristocrat's Hill. Then I sent for my husband, who was attending court some distance away. "Eddie is dangerously ill," I wrote, for I could not set down the word "consumption" in ink. Mr. Lincoln arrived the next afternoon, his horse lathered and panting for lack of water.

Doctor Wallace did as I requested, and each day I had a new remedy to try upon my son. We experimented with poultices made of mustard and balsam, teas brewed from hot peppers and roots I had never before seen, and every type of patent medicine, particularly Wistor's Wildcherry, which contained a large amount of opium. On one of his visits, my brother-in-law brought me a little figure made of twigs.

"I have a patient who employs a mammy from New Orleans." he explained. "She is said to know some conjure."

I took the figure from him. Over the place where its chest would be was tied a small pillow of burlap filled with something bitter-smelling.

"You are to keep it beneath the bed until the patient is made better, or . . ." He did not finish the thought. "There seemed no point in not trying it."

I put the figure under Eddie's mattress, beneath the place where his own chest lay.

Weeks passed and Eddie's sickness established a pattern. For the space of three days, his fever climbed and he was stricken with a cough which robbed him of all breath. When his struggling for air grew panicked, I sat upon his bed, took hold of his hands and drew large draughts of breath into my own lungs, as if his battered ones would somehow benefit from it. When the coughing did not cease, I fed him massive doses of the Wistor's Wildcherry.

After the days of coughing and fever, Eddie fell into an exhaustion so profound I could barely rouse him to eat even a small portion of rice jelly. On these days, my youngest son's flesh turned pale and cold as marble, and once an hour I put an ear to his mouth to assure myself that his wheezing breath continued. I woke Eddie to feed him, hoping to restore his strength to battle the consumption. But my beef tea and thinned oatmeal only fortified him enough to resume coughing.

No matter which form the consumption took, I concentrated only upon my nursing. For if I ceased thinking about poultices and patent medicines, I would recall how Eddie could not enter a room without coming first to touch me, to place his hand upon my bare arm or upon my face. And such recollection would only put forward the possibility that my son might not be present to do such a thing; that he might not be present with me in any room again. And such a possibility pressed upon my chest with premature grief.

My days took on the shape of Eddie's illness, and I lost all sense of other time. One evening, my brother-in-law arrived at the house carrying a small evergreen tree, which I believed he had brought to make an infusion.

"Should it be drunk or inhaled?" I asked him.

"I'd suggest that you decorate it," he replied. "And set it in the parlor."

I sank onto the mattress where Eddie lay in exhaustion. "It is that near to Christmas?"

"Near enough so that your sisters have been scurrying about filling stockings for your boys."

The night before the holiday, I threw a length of cranberry garland over the tree and sent Mr. Lincoln to bring home Robert.

"Aunt Elizabeth and Uncle Ninian have a much bigger tree," he declared upon viewing the little evergreen. "And more decorations."

Because Eddie could not leave his bed – Christmas had come during one of his times of exhaustion – I had Robert bring his stocking into his brother's room so the boys could empty them together.

"This is what Saint Nicolas brought you," I said to Eddie, giving him the stocking which had been filled by my sisters.

"You do it, Mama," Eddie told me.

"But it is your Christmas," I protested, thinking, *Not your last. Please, not your last.*

"I'm too tired."

I sat upon the mattress and emptied each item from Eddie's stocking, exclaiming over every piece of hard candy, every small toy, providing the eagerness which he could not. "A whistle!" I cried. "Peppermints!" I arranged these prizes over Eddie's quilt, handling each as if it merited long examination, attempting to stretch out my youngest son's Christmas.

In much less time, Robert emptied his stocking onto the foot of Eddie's bed, then waited to be taken back to a house possessed of more cheer.

Our house grew even less cheerful after the New Year when we received word that Grandmother Parker had died. My grandmother's death was expected; she had over the last years grown elderly. But her death had come hard upon my father's, and the two together made me think of something which Mammy Sally had claimed. "Deaths allus come in threes," she would tell me whenever word came of any dying. "Three must be the Reaper's favorite number."

This is only colored superstition, I told myself. *It does not mean that my son is required to make up death's threesome.* But after the news of my grandmother, my nursing become more vigilant. I changed Eddie's plasters twice as often as Dr. Wallace instructed me and kept so many bowls of steaming water about my son's room, the windows dripped and his bedclothes had to be changed three times a day. I burned bundles of bitter-smelling herbs that had been sent over by one of Elizabeth's slave women; herbs which filled the room with so much smoke, my eyes teared as though my son were already dead. And while I labored to save Eddie, I prayed for the death of another soul, somebody else who would satisfy the Reaper's fondness for three.

I came to believe that I could keep my son alive if I remained awake, and so I did not sleep – save for the times I fell into an exhausted oblivion that was more like the failing of consciousness than anything resembling rest. I woke from this state with the sharp taste of panic in my mouth, certain that during my inattention – because of it – Eddie had died.

"You must promise to wake me," I told my husband. "No matter how much you believe I require the rest." And from that time onward, I was awakened from this unconsciousness by Mr. Lincoln's hand upon my uncombed hair and his whispered assurance that, "The little fellow is only sleeping."

During this time, Mr. Lincoln did not leave for the circuit. Indeed, he rarely left the house, except to go to the yard to pump water for Eddie's steam or run to Corneau and Diller's for more patent medicine. And my husband *did* run to the apothecary, for I watched him from the window of the sick room, his long legs flying down Jackson Street. If I needed to prepare a fresh batch of rice jelly or change the dress I had been wearing for more days than I could remember, my husband stayed in Eddie's room; I believe that neither of us wished Eddie to be alone, for fear he might die with no one beside him. When I returned with the jelly or the clean dress, I found Mr. Lincoln sitting upon the bed, his son's head cradled in his lap.

Doctor Wallace came to us two and three times a day, bringing concoctions of herbs to be drunk or spread over the chest, bags of charms made up by people's servants. Because my brother-in-law had been so often ill himself, he seemed to understand what Eddie suffered and how to comfort him; and when my son's coughing became so fierce it raised him from the bed, Doctor Wallace picked up his sick nephew and carried him about the room.

Despite the herbs and the charms and the patent medicines, Eddie grew no better. By the end of January, my son's intervals of exhaustion, the times when he lay upon his bed in imitation of death, had become so extended, I almost prayed for the bouts of coughing. Doctor Wallace, however, warned us that Eddie had not the strength to survive another episode.

"I am not certain he has strength to survive another day," he said, brushing the hair from Eddie's forehead the way he had when he first spoke the word "consumption."

Mr. Lincoln and I took up vigil at either side of our son, each of us holding a small hand which, I could not keep myself from thinking, would grow no bigger. Once it became dark and we could not see the other, my husband and I recited every memory we possessed of him, as if his not-quite-four years required reviewing before we could let him go. We spoke this way throughout the night, recalling for each other every small portion of our dying son's character. How he brought into the house unclaimed kittens which were thin to the point of painfulness and tried to rescue them. How he smelled of spearmint, so that you always thought he was chewing some when it was only him.

As the room lightened with the weak dawn of winter, Eddie's eyes fluttered open. The irises were a darker blue than they had been before, as dark as the circles burnt into his skin by fever. I clasped my son's hand as if I could hold his soul to his body; and Eddie looked upon me with those newly dark eyes, his fingers tightening upon mine. I think he wished to tell me something. His lips, cracked from fever, parted, then closed. And then the pressure of his fingers lessened. I searched for his breath, but it was not there.

It was the first of February. Eddie had been sick for fifty-two days.

At first, I was too wearied for real grieving. Too wearied and too distracted by the tasks of death, which I think now have been designed for that function. I sent my husband – stunned, and in need of some distracting purpose himself – for my sisters, and within the hour, Elizabeth, Frances, and Ann arrived to help me prepare my youngest son's body for the grave.

We washed Eddie's slack limbs with water that had been scented with oil of peppermint – the same oil with which I had attempted to cut his fever. Then we trimmed his fingernails and toenails, and cut locks of his pale hair for keepsakes.

"He must have white clothes for burying in," said Elizabeth.

"I have only his christening robe," I replied. "And he has outgrown that."

"He owns nothing white?"

"I did not expect him to die."

Elizabeth sent word to her house to have a white suit which belonged to her son Charles – the same age as Eddie – brought down to us. Although too long in the sleeves and trouser legs, the suit looked handsome on him, and I came close to assuring my sister that Eddie would grow into it.

"You must change out of that dress," Elizabeth told me.

I looked down to check what was on me and saw that I was wearing a faded calico, stained with Wistor's Wildcherry and something brown I took for root tea.

"Do you have something suitable for mourning?" she asked.

I nodded, for every lady possessed at least one dress of black bombazine kept ready for death.

"Then go and put it on," she instructed.

I did not want to leave Eddie, but I possessed no strength to resist my sister's command. I went into my room and removed the filthy dress, wondering that Elizabeth should be so insistent I go immediately to change. But as I buttoned myself into the bombazine, which was made of fabric so stiff, I had often suspected its intent was to keep a lady upright despite her grief, I heard my husband's footfall outside the door. Mr. Lincoln's step was heavier than normal, and it came from the direction of Eddie's room, and by that I knew my sister had sent me to change clothes to spare me the sight of my son's lifeless body being carried to the parlor by his father.

A bier had been put in that room and Eddie laid upon it. About the bier were arranged my few parlor chairs, and once I was dressed in the black, I joined my sisters upon them. For the rest of that day and all of the night, my sisters and I sat in those chairs keeping company with Eddie, as if he should not be left alone, as if the following afternoon he would not be set beneath the ground in eternal isolation. Elizabeth's servant brought in coffee, which all drank, and meat sandwiches, which no one touched. During these hours, we talked little. I believe we were all listening to the thudding overhead which was Mr. Lincoln pacing his son's room.

In the morning, Ninian brought Robert home from Aristocrat's Hill.

"Come and say farewell to your brother," Elizabeth directed him.

My eldest son stood very straight before his younger brother's bier. "Is he dead?" he asked.

"Yes," Elizabeth told him.

I believe that Robert had been fond of Eddie. He had sometimes knocked the smaller boy to the ground when Eddie, out of affection, had grabbed his older brother about the waist. But he had also lent the younger boy his leaded soldiers, and arranged them in a straight line for him when his brother could not.

"We will miss him very much," I said to Robert. And then I watched my eldest – and now, only – son's face.

Robert touched his brother's hand, which had been placed upon the buttons of his cousin's white suit, and his imperfect eye inclined toward his nose. Tears came and sharpened the grayness of that eye, but none fell. A moment passed, and then Robert retrieved his hand, wiping it upon his trousers as if death had left residue he wished to be rid of. I looked hard, but my eldest son's eyes were now entirely dry, and I was struck by additional grief at the uncommon mastery he had achieved over his sentiments since the death of his grandfather.

When the bearers carried my youngest son's body from the house, fifty-two days of sleepless nursing and inconsolable grief fell upon me like a hammer. Despite the rigid fabric of the dress, I dropped to the floor as if struck and commenced a terrible sobbing. My sorrow tore from my breast, and my mouth filled with the metallic flavoring of headache, the throbbing of which made it impossible for me even to lift my head from the floor. Mr. Lincoln had gone with Eddie to the cemetery, so it was my sisters who carried me to my bed and removed my stiff dress, unlacing the stays to help me draw the breath necessary for weeping.

For a week, I remained upon my bed in imitation of Eddie as he had been during his times of exhaustion. Like him, I could not eat, not even the invalid's food which was brought to me, not even the milk-soaked bread which my husband tried to feed me with his own hands. When I did not sleep, I wept. And I think that I sometimes wept in my sleep, for my hair and pillow were soaking when I woke.

During this time, the door to my room was always kept shut, for Elizabeth, who had come to tend to me, believed that grieving should be conducted in private. However, one afternoon, Mr. Lincoln, who had entered in hope of encouraging me to eat some thinned porridge, left the room with the door standing open. I always wept more after my husband's visits – the sorrow upon his face tended to increase my own – and it was some little time before I felt the unaccustomed breeze and turned my head toward the open door. My vision, blurred by so many days' worth of tears, could not at first hold focus. And it was only after a minute that I saw my eldest son standing in the opening, his face half-hidden behind the door.

Robert's face was white as that of his brother's when he lay upon the bier, and the single gray eye – the uncanted one – which peered around the door was filled with what even my unclear vision could see was horror. For the briefest instant, I wondered what had so distressed my son, but even in the midst of my uncoherent mourning, I knew that it was me. My grief-wracked body, unwashed, unfed, and given over to uncontrolled sobbing, was the manifestation of all which Robert believed unseemly, all which he worked so hard to contain.

Say something to him, I commanded myself. *Say something which will assure him you have not gone mad.*

But when Robert saw that I had noticed him, he fled from the doorway as if fearing the infection of my unrestrained tears.

That evening, I made myself drink the beef tea which Mr. Lincoln brought me. The following morning, I took some milky oatmeal; and that evening, I ate a broth which Elizabeth sent down. I swallowed these meals with tears coursing down my face, but by keeping my son's horrorstruck expression before my eyes, those of the afternoon were fewer than the ones of the morning, and by suppertime, they were not much more than a trickling.

It was two days more before I possessed the strength to leave my bed. It required an entire week before I could make myself enter the room in which Eddie had died.

Elizabeth's servant girl had distempered the walls and soaked the linens in lye, yet beneath those smells of cleanliness I caught the sticky scent of Wistor's Wildcherry and the sharpness of mustard. And there was something else. Something I did not at first recognize. I breathed it in, hoping, I think, that it was some remnant of the scent of Eddie's skin, but finally recalling that it was the figure made of twigs which had come from somebody's New Orleans mammy. Elizabeth's servant must have missed it when she had cleaned the room, and now I fell upon my knees and retrieved the figure from beneath the bed.

I had not noticed before how much the thing resembled a child. Untying the bundle of herbs from its chest – as if I were a more benevolent God granting it health – I cradled the small figure in my lap. With Eddie's death it seemed that I had forfeited not only my youngest son, but also my claim upon motherhood. My other son felt as lost to me as Eddie, made distant by his nature, and his time in my father's house, and now by my own unrestrained grieving. I did not imagine that Robert could learn to be tender toward me, no more than could the figure made of twigs, and the thought left me feeling childless.

Still, I thought, rubbing my finger over the walnut shell the New Orleans mammy had used for the small figure's head, *I have only just passed my thirty-first birthday. That is not too old to bear another child. One whose temperament might be formed more like Eddie's. Or even just a little less like Robert's.*

That night I came to the bed dressed only in a sheer chemise, though it was winter and the room was chill.

"I need to be mother to another child," I told my husband.

"I think that is so," he replied.

We said nothing more about what it was we set out to do, only came together in a passion which was tempered by grief and purpose.

*(June 27) Mrs. Lincoln as usual today – Did not
ride or go out though asked to do so –
—Patient Progress Reports for Bellevue Place
Sanitarium*

I have finally met the beautiful Reverend Judd.

Since the day I came upon Minnie Judd in the greenhouse with the daguerreotype, a friendship has developed between us. Minnie's parents, the freethinking Childs, had educated their daughter as fully as any son, and the young reverend's wife is capable of speaking equally well of politics and poetry. Moreover, unlike the high-minded Mrs. Patterson, Mrs. Judd does not ever wish to discuss female calisthenics or the benefits of cold bathing.

Minnie and I meet every afternoon at the little bench near the dark woods where no other ladies of the asylum ever go. My friend asks me for stories of Mr. Lincoln and lets me talk as much as I wish about my sons, about Eddie's fondness for unclaimed cats and Willie's for railroad schedules; about the way that Taddie dressed himself in the uniform of a Union soldier, borrowed a musket, and searched beneath the furniture of the President's House for rebel spies. I have talked to Minnie very little about Robert. There do not seem so many stories of him as a child I wish to share, and even fewer of him as a man.

For her part, Minnie talks a great deal about Reverend Judd, and only mentioning her husband makes the young woman's eyes go more black and her lips turn scarlet. "When the Reverend Judd preaches from the pulpit," she has told me, "it is so like an angel talking, I can see how it was that Mary was made pregnant by only a whisper." Once she had confided this, my friend turned her face toward the dark wood, but I could see that her cheeks were flushed and that beneath her lawn dress her legs trembled.

It is this passion, larger than her command, which most makes me love Minnie. Such desire recalls for me myself, and perhaps that is the reason the remembrance of Minnie Judd crushing rose petals to her throat stirs something in me so recognizable, I believe I possess my own memory of the soft petal flesh against my skin.

I have come also to love Minnie for the time she spends with Blanche. Beside myself, and occasionally, her own mother, Minnie is the only lady at Bellevue Place who pays any notice to the retarded girl. Nearly every morning, I find them sitting together upon the limestone steps of the rear porch. When Mrs. Patterson is not near, Minnie unplaits the child's overwound braids, and smoothes her fingers over the girl's small head, rubbing away the tension the braids have put there. Afterward, Minnie allows Blanche to unwind her own black hair and bury her Asiatic face in it.

On some days, Minnie practices her verses for the retarded child. I have heard no one say the Bible the way that Minnie does, holding each word of Scripture an extra time in her mouth, as if reluctant to part with the feel of the letters upon her tongue. Hearing her, I have sometimes wondered at my friend's relationship with God. Even Blanche, I think, can feel the emotion with which Minnie says her verses, for the weak-minded girl keeps herself beside the reverend's wife, listening intently to every word.

Practicing her verses for Blanche was what I assumed Minnie to be doing in the lunatics' parlor on the morning that I met Reverend Judd. While the girl and the reverend's wife generally met upon the porch, the day was cool and unsunny, and I imagined they had become chilled on the stone steps. However, as I stood listening in the corridor outside the parlor, I heard an additional warmth and a thickness like syrup in my friend's voice. On this morning, she lingered longer over every syllable, allowing each sacred word to swell in her mouth before releasing it. This was not the way which Minnie Judd recited Psalms for the retarded girl, or for me, and I could not keep myself from following her voice into the parlor.

The parlor reserved for the ladies of the asylum contains no breakable items, save for the glass globes of a chandelier, which are fixed too high for any to grab at. The small tables beside the settees hold no objects, no landscapes hang from the picture railings, and the shelves of the corner curio cabinet are empty, which gives the piece an air of bereavement. Despite Mrs. Patterson's watchfulness, the madwomen who use the parlor have left their marks upon it. The upholstered arms of a sofa have been so shredded by the ceaselessly plucking fingers of Mrs. Bartholomew, it looks to have been abused by a cat. Long strips of wallpaper have been ripped from a corner by Mrs. Ogden, who was convinced that the sound of her deceased child's crying could be heard from behind its floral pattern. And Miss Price, the daughter of a minister, has scratched the word "redemption" a hundred times into the surface of a maple sideboard with a hairpin. But on this day, it was Minnie Judd which drew my attention.

"*I speak of the things which I have made touching the king,*" she declared. "*My tongue is the pen of a ready writer.*"

My friend stood very straight beside the maple sideboard, dressed in one of her loveliest gowns, one which was made of silk organza and delicately pleated at the waist. As she recited her verse, she kept her eyes upon the man seated before her in a high-backed chair, the man whose image had been caught in Minnie's daguerreotype.

It might have been the shabbiness of the lunatics' parlor which so made my friend's husband appear like an angel, but I do not believe so. I think instead that Reverend Judd was made more beautiful than God intended any mortal man to be. His nose was straight and fine, his brows arched in perfect symmetry, and his eyes were the color of a heart-wrenching sea. The Reverend Judd wore his hair longer than was customary, so that it touched upon his shoulders. Yet it was impossible to desire it cut, for it would have been sacrilege to take scissors to curls so filled with light.

The effect of the reverend's beauty was so incapacitating, I stood wordless before it.

However, Reverend Judd had heard me enter, and he rose from his chair and turned toward me. "Mrs. Lincoln," he said. His voice, soft and melodious, wound itself about my name, making it sound as lovely as the mouth which had uttered it. "I had heard from my wife that she has formed such a distinguished friendship."

I knew that I was required by politeness to answer him. To make some reply that would show me capable of social discourse. But nothing issued from my mouth save air.

The reverend appeared accustomed to ladies standing dumb in his presence. "I'm pleased that Mrs. Judd has made a friend here," he continued in that caressing voice. "It will make her stay at Bellevue Place easier."

"I hope that we can continue the connection," I replied, finding my speech, "when we are both away from here."

Reverend Judd allowed his flawless mouth to take the shape of a frown. "It was my impression that Doctor Patterson discouraged too much thinking upon release."

"But how can we not contemplate our liberty?" I said.

"As long as it does not come before you are ready for it," replied the reverend, glancing at his wife.

I looked to Minnie too and saw from the darkness of her eyes and the scarlet of her mouth that she wished to be left alone with her husband. "I have interrupted you and Mrs. Judd." I moved nearer the door. "I shall let you resume your visit."

But the reverend stopped me with his embracing voice. "You do not find the Bible agreeable?" he asked.

"I am very fond of Psalms," I told him. "Particularly when Mrs. Judd is reciting them. But she has learned the verses for you, and I am certain you do not wish to hear them said in the company of a middle-aged widow." Again, I attempted to make my way toward the door.

"I should be happy for your company," said Reverend Judd, making me a bow which for all its grace seemed tinged with irony. "It is not every day I have the honor of meeting a president's wife. You would not deprive me of the pleasure so quickly?"

"I am afraid I must," I replied. "Mrs. Patterson is expecting me to use the carriage."

Ignoring my remark, the reverend lifted a heavy-legged parlor chair with observable ease and set it down firmly beside his own. "Come. Or I will believe you have taken a dislike to me."

I heard now something rough in Reverend Judd's speech, something truer to his nature, as if the melodious voice in which he'd spoken until now had been the showmanship of preaching. However, the man's beauty possessed the power of a mesmerist, which can command one to sing before an audience or dance against one's will. And against my will, it commanded me back into the room and into the chair.

"I am gratified by your acquiescence," declared Reverend Judd, his harmonious voice restored.

I sought to send some message of apology to my friend, although I expected she understood the mesmerizing power of her husband's beauty. I knew very well why Minnie would wish to be alone with her beautiful husband. I only did not know why he did not want to be left alone with her.

Reverend Judd resumed his seat. "You may begin at the place where you left off," he told his wife.

Minnie smoothed the pleats of her dress and gathered her breath.

Speak the verses, I urged my friend. *Say them as beautifully and as sanely as you say them for Blanche and me. Recite every word of petition and praise that David wrote, and prove to your husband that you do not belong in a madhouse.*

My friend stood before the sideboard which bore the word "redemption" scratched upon its surface. As Minnie let her eyes go blank, recalling her place, I repeated my plea over and again. Minnie Judd and I were alike. Both of us put here by desire we could not control; desire which was seen as insanity by the ones we most loved. I had come to believe that our fates were entwined, that what happened to one also happened to the other. And if Minnie might persuade her husband of her reason, then I could persuade my son.

I watched my friend again fix her gaze upon her beautiful husband. With a subtle shifting, as if her form had filled with an emotion so great it was made visible, she began to recite.

As a child, my cousin Emily Todd had memorized over one thousand Bible verses, an accomplishment she displayed at family gatherings, standing like a small soldier as she repeated Scriptures for the relations who had not thought to escape to the veranda. Emily's method of delivering the Word of God was to speak her memorized verses in an inflectionless tone, as quickly as possible, so that it sounded as if she were uttering one long and vaguely devout word.

Minnie Judd, however, spoke the songs of David as if she herself had been inspired by God. Her low voice throbbed, her dark eyes burned like those upon the faces of frescoed saints, and the vein which pulsed at the side of her throat revealed the workings of her heart. I had watched my friend recite her verses to Mrs. Patterson's weak-minded daughter and to the blurred daguerreotype. But I had not seen her say them to their true object.

"*Thou art fairer than the children of men,*" she told her husband, "*grace is poured into thy lips; All thy garments smell of myrrh and aloes and cassia out of the ivory palaces.*"

The very air of the lunatics' parlor pulsed with Minnie's desire, and my own body grew taut with a craving I had spent the past ten years attempting to quiet. It would be unseemly to look now upon Reverend Judd, I thought. Unseemly to observe the way which Minnie's passion affected him. But I could not help but look. For it had been so long since I had seen the signs of a man's affection.

What I saw upon Reverend Judd's face and form was not

affection. Nor desire. But something very much like fear. The reverend's indescribable face had paled and his breathing possessed the shallow quickness of the panicked. I glanced again at Minnie, to see if she had noticed her husband's response to her verse-saying, but my friend was too consumed by her own ardency.

"*Hearken O daughter forget thine own people and thy father's house. The king shall greatly desire thy beauty.*" Minnie's eyes were glazed and her face flushed, as if it were she who had stolen the blood from her husband's.

"*She shall be brought unto the king in raiment of needlework. The virgins her companions that follow her shall be brought unto thee.*" The young woman's breast rose with the air she drew into her body, air she released reluctantly, in an exhalation from which her husband shrank.

You must stop, I begged my friend. *Can you not see how your husband is pressing himself into the back of his chair? Do you not notice that he has wound together his graceful legs and turned them away from you?*

But Minnie saw nothing beyond the passion she possessed for her too-beautiful husband.

"*With gladness and rejoicing shall they be brought: they shall enter into the king's palace. Instead of thy fathers shall be thy children.*"

Stop before you convince him more surely of your madness, I pleaded. *Stop before you condemn us both to living forever with lunatics.*

With the supple lunging of a panther, Reverend Judd leapt from his seat and grabbed hold of his wife's wrists. "It is blasphemy!" he shouted, his voice containing only roughness now. "Blasphemy, these verses!"

Minnie ceased speaking. They were standing close, only the distance of the reverend's arms. She stepped closer. "How can it be blasphemy to learn the Bible?" she said to him. She asked the question, but did not appear to seek an answer. Instead, she turned up her face, brought her mouth nearer to her husband's delectable one, and waited for it to fall upon hers.

Reverend Judd pulled hard upon his wife's wrist to distract her from his mouth. "It is not the learning which is sacrilege," he declared, "but your appetite for it."

Minnie looked at him, bewildered. "I only wished to memorize the Psalms."

"You want to memorize *all* of them!" The reverend shook off his wife's wrists, as if it had been she who had taken hold of him. "You want to consume every one of God's words!"

"But only so I might give them back to you." She put out her wrists, in the event he might want to take them again.

Reverend Judd backed away from his wife. "Such ambition is too voracious! Too insatiable!"

Minnie gazed at him, her black eyes stricken. "You believe me insatiable?"

The reverend's radiant features burned darkly. "We both of us know that it is your own appetite which has put you here."

It was Minnie now who went white. I saw her waver and put a hand to the sideboard, covering some of the scratched words. I rose from my seat.

"Do you not think that the great number of Psalms Mrs. Judd has learned proves her steadiness of mind?" I said to the reverend.

"I believe that Doctor Patterson and I possess a clearer understanding of my wife's mania than do you," he informed me.

"But surely so much memorization demonstrates that Mrs. Judd is unlunatic," I insisted.

"What it demonstrates," he replied, "is that I was correct to commit her to Bellevue Place in the first instance."

I put out my hand, thinking to place it upon his arm to make him hear me better, but Reverend Judd's beauty was such that it felt heretical to touch him. "I have passed many hours in Mrs. Judd's company," I said, "and I am certain she is entirely sane."

The reverend gave me a cruel but exquisite smile. "And how is it that you, who have been committed here by a jury, are now considered a judge of sanity?"

I made a small cry, as if he had taken one well-formed hand and struck me. I wanted to run from the lunatics' parlor, hide myself in my room so I would not have to stand before Reverend Judd's brutally dazzling face. Yet, as eager as I had been before to leave, I was now equally eager to stay; for though I could not have said why, I feared leaving Minnie alone with this beautiful man.

"Mrs. Lincoln is my friend," Minnie said to her husband. "And I am afraid you have insulted her." The remark was chastising, but her tone was that in which she would have spoken to him of love.

"In that case," he told her, "perhaps it is you who should ask your friend to leave us."

"I have already overstayed," I announced. But I did not move toward the door until I had given Minnie opportunity to contradict me.

"It is best this way," she said to me.

And there was nothing to do save leave Minnie Judd with her husband in the lunatics' parlor.

For two days following Reverend Judd's visit I did not find my friend upon the porch steps with Blanche or on the bench which faced the dark wood.

"Is Mrs. Judd unwell?" I asked Mrs. Ruggles. I had come upon the matron, who without her bun and skirts could have been mistaken for a man, lurking about in the corridor outside my room.

"Unwellness is what she is claiming," Mrs. Ruggles replied.

"But she is recovering?" I asked.

Mrs. Ruggles made her small eyes smaller. "Why is it you have such uncommon interest in Mrs. Judd?"

Finding myself beneath the scrutiny of Mrs. Ruggles, I wondered if it was the matron's task to report to Mrs. Patterson which of the lunatic ladies befriended one another. "I was brought up to show interest in the well-being of all the ladies with whom I share my society," I replied, with as much haughtiness as I could call upon. "I also intended to inquire after Mrs. Munger's skin irritation."

Mrs. Ruggles regarded me with suspicion. "Mrs. Munger has been given a salve," she told me. "I don't know what the doctor makes of Mrs. Judd's complaint." Then she turned and clopped down the corridor with the weight of a dray horse.

When Minnie did not appear at lunch, I went to her room.

Mrs. Patterson had spoken truthfully when she told me that I had been given one of the best rooms at Bellevue Place. For worn as my chamber was, it was superior to the one in which Minnie Judd lived, and I suspected that the reverend did not pay Doctor Patterson as much for it as I did for mine. Minnie's room was dark, its single window shadowed by an overhanging roof, and it was barely larger than her iron bedstead and pressed-wood dresser. The only object of any richness was a tall trunk with gold hinges, which Minnie must have brought to the asylum with her and from which spilled the skirts of her lovely dresses, so bright and fragile in the dismal room, I almost feared for them.

My friend was sitting upon the only chair, a four-legged seat made of wood, probably taken from the kitchen. She appeared oddly still.

"I have heard you are unwell," I said, sitting upon her mattress, which gave like straw.

Minnie turned her eyes upon me. In the dim light of her room they were black as mourning stones. "I am not truly unwell," she replied. "It is only the best way I know not to be made to eat."

"Why would you wish that?"

"For my husband's sake."

I took her hand and was surprised to find her wedding ring tucked in the palm. "It is true your husband was not pleased by the verses," I said, "but he would not wish you to punish yourself for them."

"I was wrong to learn the Psalms."

I tucked up some strands of her black hair which had fallen loose from the knot at her neck. "I have done many wrong things thinking to please my husband. And he has always overlooked them."

Minnie turned to look out the dark little window. "The reverend believes that my appetite is insatiable."

I was about to offer her some further observation about marriage, some piece of advice of the type which women of my age recommend to women of hers, when the import of what my friend was saying struck me.

"This is the reason you do not wish to be made to eat?" I asked her.

"I must prove to my husband that I can contain my appetite."

"Minnie, that is wrong!" I tugged upon her hand, knocking the ring to the floor. "You will make yourself ill."

She bent to retrieve the wedding ring. When she rose, I saw upon her features the determined cast with which she had set about learning a new set of verses.

"You have seen him," she said. "You must know I would do anything which might win me his affection." Minnie replaced the ring upon her finger and took hold of my hands. "I believe that you of everyone must understand such love."

I looked hard then into my friend's face, which after two days without eating already seemed drawn. "I am worried for you," I said, for I did understand such love. Understood it better than Minnie knew.

* * *

The child Mr. Lincoln and I made out of our grief for Eddie was born on the twenty-first of December, 1850. We named him William, for my brother-in-law Doctor Wallace, who had carried Eddie about the room when his coughing lifted him from the bed. From an early age, Willie possessed Mr. Lincoln's qualities of mind, and mine of affection, as well as a compassion of spirit I believe had been woven into his nature by being created from his parents' grief.

I would have been happy with only Willie, but I had seen how quickly and irrevocably a child could be taken away. After a year of nursing, I weaned Willie and shortly thereafter became pregnant with my fourth child.

This last child's birth was uncommonly difficult. When half a day had passed without the child being delivered, Doctor Wallace sent for Doctor Flagler, who specialized in diseases of the womb. This doctor brought with him a set of obstetrical forceps which, he informed me, "have come direct from France," as if the shiny instrument were a new bonnet, as he had been told by Doctor Wallace that my partially born child's head was abnormally large.

Mr. Lincoln and I had hoped for this child to be a daughter, had hoped it so strongly, I had chosen only one name, Eliza, after my dead mother. Thus, when this new baby turned out to be my fourth son, I had to cast about my birthing-addled brain for something more masculine to offer my husband, who could not name a cat.

"Thomas," I told him, "after your father." Then I fell into an exhausted sleep and never did devise a middle name for him.

As it turned out, I could have named my new son Eliza, for all that he was called by his given name. When he was no more than three months old, Mr. Lincoln came upon me bathing him, and noting the contrast between his large – though not, in my opinion, abnormally so – head and his small body, my husband remarked, "It seems that rather than a little girl, we have produced a little tadpole." And from that time forward, my youngest son was known as Taddie.

During this period, these years after Eddie died, I lost myself in the milk-sotted world of babies. To keep my body from being consumed by grief, I surrendered it to the making and feeding of children. I ate and slept in the rhythm of the newly born, and let the soft flesh of the sons I had made to replace the one I had lost insulate me from my sorrow. My days and nights ran together. Oft times, when

Mr. Lincoln was out on the circuit, I did not leave my bed for more than an hour at a stretch. Instead I remained nested in the bedclothes, feeding my children and then feeding myself with the same food I gave them – biscuits softened in milk and vegetables mashed to paste.

My eldest son rarely joined us in the bed. Robert was seven years older than his nearest brother, and though I used that as excuse, I knew that no matter his age, he would not have climbed into the crowded bed for softened food and stories. Instead, he ran away to Elizabeth's house on Aristocrat's Hill, which seemed to suit him better.

It was my opinion that Mr. Lincoln tempered his grief during this time with lawyering. But when I woke from my dream of childbearing – stunned, like one who has slept for too long, and plumper than when I had gone in – I found my husband subject to a deep and terrible melancholy, the hypochondriasis striking as often as three times a week, leaving Mr. Lincoln fixed upon the mattress, scarcely willing to draw breath. His gaze on such occasions remained dull and unblinking, and for all that he heard or saw or spoke, he might have become deceased. This imitation of death so frightened me that I attempted to harry him from the bed by shouting in his ear and pulling upon his wrists. Some days, if I was especially forceful or the melancholy was not too deep, I was able to propel him as far as the rocker in the bedroom. But I could not coax him to dress and had to leave him sitting there in nothing more than a tattered nightshirt, with nothing more to do to make him presentable than wrap a shawl about his shoulders and work a pair of carpet slippers onto his wide, flat feet.

Robert, who was ten the winter that I rose from the childbed, spent much of the day out of the house, attending Mr. Esterbrook's academy, and was spared the sight of his father's fits of melancholia. One time, however, he returned home early and spied Mr. Lincoln sitting upon the rocker like a large, lifeless doll. Uttering a small, startled cry, my eldest son averted his eyes and hurried past the door, as embarrassed as if he had chanced upon his father using the privy. It pained me to have Robert see his father as less than he was, and afterward I always remembered to shut the bedroom door.

Robert's younger brothers reacted differently. Willie, who had just turned three, attempted to beguile his father into happiness by bringing into the bedroom objects connected with Mr. Lincoln's hobbies – a whittling knife or a book of Euclid's geometry. These objects, however, did not release my husband from his melancholy; he never seemed to notice they were there. Still, Willie continued to leave them piled upon the bedclothes like tokens of a brighter world. Taddie, who was three-quarters of a year old, seemed always happy to find his father still in bed. Despite the fact that Mr. Lincoln responded no more than a statue might, his youngest son pulled himself upon the mattress and spent an hour or more filling his father's deaf ears with sibilant babbling. Taddie had been born with an improperly formed palate, and all his talking issued mushy as overripe fruit.

Sometimes my husband's fits lasted past nightfall, and although when in them he possessed no awareness of his surroundings, I still came to light the lamps in the bedroom, for it felt too unhappy to leave him sitting in the darkness. One such evening, as I raised the wick on the bedside lamp, I heard the shuddering sigh which signaled my husband's return from the hypochondriasis. Mr. Lincoln had passed the entirety of that day in the rocker, in nightshirt and shawl and carpet slippers, and as he woke from his melancholia, he sank his large hands into his hair and pulled at the roots, as if the pain might anchor his wandering brain. Observing this, I sat at his feet and, putting my hands upon his, loosened the fingers from his hair to stop him from pulling on it.

"Was it very bad?" I said.

"I'm always astonished that they can get worse."

I noticed that the slippers had been knocked from his feet – at times my husband came out of his fits with a sudden jerking – and bent to slide them back, for the room was chilled. "Perhaps more of the valerian root tea?"

Mr. Lincoln looked down upon me with his face full of a bitterness I suspected he oft times hid. "I have drunk valerian and black hellebore and swallowed camphor until I believe I will retch them up," he said. "And I get no better. I fear very much that next time I sink into that pit, I won't come up again."

"The melancholy is that strong?"

"It is so black, I don't believe it can be endured save by death, or loss of reason."

The despair in these words, coupled with the words themselves, froze me, and I tugged the shawl so tight around my husband's shoulders, he was pulled into a slight hunch.

"I have worked too hard to help you keep your reason," I told him. "And I would not wish to live if you should die."

I dropped my head into his lap and after a moment felt the heavy weight of his hand upon my hair.

"I will find something to cure your melancholy," I promised him.

The following day, I left my youngest sons with one of Elizabeth's servants and went to see my brother-in-law Wallace at his apothecary. I rarely visited this little shop – no more than a tiny storefront really – because only entering it made my eyes water and my stomach queasy. The atmosphere of it, which was never changed, for the place had no window, was thick with the bitter scent of the herbs Doctor Wallace used for medicinal tea, as well as the tang of the powders – quinine and morphine – he formed into pills. I also was always made uneasy by the rendering my brother-in-law kept upon his wall, an illustration of a man with his flesh cut away in order to expose his organs.

I found Doctor Wallace seated below this illustration, studying a medical text. In the time since he had attended Eddie, my brother-in-law had grown the pointed beard of a satyr, although it could not disguise the openheartedness of his face. I was fond of the man for whom I had named my middle son, and would have stayed talking with him for some time, but today I wanted only to hurry home with whatever would save my husband.

"You are aware that Mr. Lincoln suffers from melancholia," I said, bringing into the open what I suspected my brother-in-law already knew. I had been careful to hide my husband's condition from the family, but Frances's husband had been called to our house to attend to every illness of my sons, and the doctor possessed a keen observance of the condition of others.

"I have suspected as much," he replied.

"I wish you to cure him."

My brother-in-law let a hand rest upon the medical text he had been reading. "Even the best Boston doctor does not promise to cure melancholia."

"Then at least make him better."

Doctor Wallace gazed at the wall which held the hundreds of small wooden drawers in which he stored the ingredients to make his potions. "I have heard of some success in alleviating hypochondriasis with Blue Mass," he said after a bit. "But I do not know if it will cause other, more extreme behaviors."

"If they are not more extreme than death or lunacy," I told him, "make it up for us."

My brother-in-law scratched at his beard, disarranging the point. "And Mr. Lincoln will consent to take the Blue Mass?"

"I will see to it."

Working from a formula written in a small spidery hand, Doctor Wallace made up the pills, a mixture of licorice root, rose water, honey, desiccated rose petals, and mercury.

"I have put in an extra amount of the mercury," said my brother-in-law. "As it is the most effective of the ingredients."

That evening, as we were preparing for bed, I showed my husband the case of blue pills.

"Doctor Henry doesn't put too much faith in Blue Mass," he said, eyeing them.

"I do not wish to contradict Doctor Henry, to whose discretion we owe a debt, but Doctor Wallace believes you might have some success with these."

My husband sat heavily upon the mattress beside me. "You find my spells so troubling?"

"Do they not trouble you?"

"They make me wish for death."

"Then Doctor Wallace's Blue Mass cannot make you worse. And may well make you better."

Mr. Lincoln began to take the Blue Mass and I began to watch him, searching for signs that he was better, and for any symptom that showed he had been made worse. Within only a few weeks, it did seem that I woke less often beside a husband locked in impersonation of a corpse. However, the Blue Mass caused Mr. Lincoln's hands to develop an uncontrollable tremor, and he broke six Chelsea-patterned cups before I had the plan of serving him his coffee in a pottery mug.

"It is fairly embarrassing to be forced to drink from the same crockery as my littlest sons," he told me, shaking a large portion of the coffee out upon the tablecloth.

"I find your propensity to shatter china romantic," I replied. "It reminds me of our courting days."

The Blue Mass also subjected Mr. Lincoln to nightmares; dreams which made him cry out in sentences formed of no known language. Always it was his own shouting which woke him, causing him to spring from the mattress as he wished to distance himself from the very spot where he'd dreamt the dream.

"Can you recall anything of the dream?" I asked him, each time I woke to find him cowering in the darkened corner.

"Only a deep sense of dread," he would tell me.

The most extreme side effect of the Blue Mass was the effect it had upon my husband's temperament. The first time that I noticed it, he had arrived home from his office in a fury over a letter he had received from my brother Levi. Mr. Lincoln was lawyer for my father's estate, a position which put him in frequent contact with my brother, who was, it must be admitted, adept at being infuriating. For the better part of an hour, Mr. Lincoln followed me about the house, raging over Levi's rascality. No amount of recalling for him that Levi was in Lexington and "unlikely to benefit from any remarks you make here in Springfield" worked to soften my husband's anger. Finally, when the doorbell rang, I sent Mr. Lincoln to answer it, imagining he would feel obliged to calm his temper before a visitor.

When only some few seconds later I heard the sound of someone being strangled, I feared that my brother had been so misguided as to journey to Springfield and ring our bell. Once I reached the door, however, I saw that it was not Levi whom Mr. Lincoln held by the throat, but a button seller, for as my husband shook the small bearded man, cards of buttons flew from his coat pockets and clattered upon the ground.

"Mr. Lincoln!" I shouted. "You are choking the button seller!"

My shout recalled my husband from his hypnotic state, and he gazed down upon the terrified button seller, as if unsure how the little man had inserted himself into his grasp. Immediately, Mr. Lincoln loosened his hands from the peddler's throat. The man fell to the ground and began stuffing the spilled cards of buttons into his pockets.

"I am distraught over a legal matter," my husband apologized. "My wife will choose some buttons."

But, the button seller fled our house the moment the last card was in his pocket.

"Why did you put your hands upon the button seller?" I asked my husband. "Did he threaten us?"

"I had no reason," he replied, all the fury gone from him now. "Save that I wanted to throttle him." Then he went to his desk to write to Levi, and refused to talk of it any further.

Mr. Lincoln's tempers continued into the spring, brought on by incidents of small significance: a broken bridle strap or missing legal document. I found my husband's furies unsettling; however, I was sometimes subject to fits of temper myself and knew that such moods could dissipate as swiftly as they had come on. Mr. Lincoln's littlest sons also seemed to understand this and learned to absent themselves when they heard their father ranting in his soft-pitched voice. It was Robert who was most disconcerted by these rages. The uncontrol with which they showed themselves never failed to send my eldest son running from the house, as if he, like the button seller, had been badly frightened by his father.

It was this which sent me back to Doctor Wallace.

"How is it the Blue Mass can cause such symptoms?" I asked my brother-in-law. I imagined that if I could understand their origin, I might understand how to make them cease.

"The Blue Mass has created an increase in Mr. Lincoln's energetic force." He glanced up at the illustrated man with his organs exposed as if conferring with a colleague. "Tremors, disturbances of the sleep, increased agitation – these are all symptoms of excessive energy."

"And if I were to find Mr. Lincoln an outlet for this energy?"

My brother-in-law smiled behind the satyr's beard. "Then button sellers who turn up at your door will no longer be in any danger."

I did not take a carriage back from Doctor Wallace's apothecary, but walked instead, for I thought better when I was in motion. I knew of only one thing which would be outlet enough to consume Mr. Lincoln's energy of the Blue Mass – politics. But my husband's political ambition had died when Eddie had, and in the five years since his return from Washington City, Mr. Lincoln had not sought political office. Once or twice, I suggested another try for Congress or perhaps the Illinois legislature. "I don't think I have much chance of being elected to anything," said my husband. "It turns out to be an unwise idea to question the legality of a popular war."

It would be unaccurate to say that I remained undistressed by my husband's lack of political ambition. Although I was past thirty and should have no longer believed in the marital predictions of colored ladies, I still possessed faith that I had married a man who would be president. But grief and melancholy – and perhaps the responsibility of keeping the children I had needed to replace Eddie – had worked to push him further from such ambition. And I did not know how to push him back.

Unless, I thought, *he was moved back by a cause.* I ceased walking to better recall an incident which had occurred during a visit Mr. Lincoln and I made together to Lexington. While there, my husband had passed a day in the gallery of the crumbling theater, watching white men buy black from the same stage upon which actors once declaimed Shakespeare. Mr. Lincoln had been so affected by this cruelty that for days afterward he forbid me to tease Mammy Sally, until my old nurse decided I was "feeling poorly" and dosed me with salts.

Only a cause as monumental as slavery could push Mr. Lincoln back into politics. And all it would require was for me to make him recall the moral outrage which had gotten me dosed with salts, for me to remind my husband of the unrighteousness of the institution. And as long as I stopped short of turning him abolitionist – for abolitionists were never elected to office unless they were running in New England – he might have some success.

From that time forward, my domestic conversation centered upon nothing save the politics of slavery. I discussed the Fugitive Slave Act over breakfast and the Kansas-Nebraska Act at dinner. I subscribed to abolitionist newspapers – the *Emancipator* and *The True American* – and read them to my husband after supper. I became so obsessed with the topic, one night I sat up in bed and asked Mr. Lincoln if he believed Senator Douglas was truly planning to repeal the Missouri Compromise.

"This is an interesting time to debate whether your former suitor is going to allow slaves in the territories," he replied.

"But does not the very notion incense you?" I asked.

"I do not like it," he admitted. "But since, as far as I'm aware, your old beau is not in the bedroom with us, there's little purpose giving up the sleep to debate it now."

For all these efforts, I was unable to direct my husband's energy in the direction of anything political. At the close of spring, the Kansas-Nebraska Act, which permitted those territories to join the Union as slave states, became law. I waited for Mr. Lincoln to show some public opposition, but he only vented his outrage upon a loosened picket and a legal client who had neglected to pay his bill. I had nearly run out of fresh invective against human bondage to serve up to my husband with his batter cakes, when I read in the

Emancipator that Cassius Marcellus Clay was coming to Springfield.

Mr. Clay was the cousin of the eminent Kentucky statesman Henry Clay, and had been a friend of my father. When I was eleven years of age, Mr. Clay had come to stay with us while he attended university in Lexington, and I recalled that the young gentleman had possessed the black hair and eyes of a pirate, and that I had found him dashing and dangerous in a most pleasurable way. Now Mr. Clay was grown and quite outspoken upon the issue of slavery; indeed, the majority of Kentucky newspapers referred to my father's friend as an "abolitionist madman." Only *The True American* did not slander him, and that is likely because Cassius Clay was its editor and publisher. However, the abolitionist newspaper did daily receive letters calling for his death. One such missive, I had been told, was written entirely in blood and was of such length it was a marvel the writer had retained the energy to post it.

As a speaker against human bondage, Cassius Marcellus Clay was expert at inciting emotion. At a political rally in Kentucky, he debated an advocate of slavery named Squire Turner with such ruthlessness, the man's son Cyrus called him a liar; and Cyrus's brother, Thomas, put a revolver to Mr. Clay's head and pulled the trigger. Luckily for Mr. Clay, Thomas Turner was careless about maintaining his weaponry. Unluckily for the liar-calling Cyrus, Mr. Clay always carried with him a bowie knife.

I was exceedingly glad to learn that this abolitionist gentleman, who could so excite the passions of those who heard him that slave-holders wished to shoot him in the head, was going to speak in Springfield.

"We should attend Mr. Clay's speech," I said to my husband. "He talks most forcefully against slavery."

"All right," he replied, "I reckon we shouldn't deny the boys the opportunity to see somebody killed with a bowie knife."

Not wishing to be party to a knifing, the Springfield City Council refused Mr. Clay permission to speak at the statehouse, or in any public building, for that matter. Not caring overmuch about permission, Cassius Clay announced that he would speak in the open air, and had a small platform built in Mather's Grove at the west end of town.

It was summer now, and the day of Mr. Clay's appearance dawned hot. By midday the blinding prairie light had entirely bleached the blue from the sky. Despite the heat, Mather's Grove began filling with the wagons of spectators long before noon – so many that the following day, the *Illinois Journal* would report that there was "full fifteen hundred assembled." And within a very short time, the crowd had grown restive – from the heat, and from the ale and whiskey many were drinking to kill the thirst it produced.

We had arrived early ourselves, for I wished my husband to be as near to Mr. Clay's inspiring righteousness as possible. But before my father's friend made his appearance, Mr. Lincoln declared to Taddie that "only someone with legs as short as your mother's would be comfortable sitting in this wagon," then scooped up his youngest son and took him to sit in the grass a little way off.

"Standing here in this grove," declared the abolitionist, leaping to his platform, "I feel much like John the Baptist preaching in the wilderness."

"Take him down!" shouted a crimson-faced man at the front of the crowd. There was a scuffling, and Mr. Clay's platform, which had been hastily constructed, began to wobble.

"I see that some of you take exception to my right to speak against human bondage," said the abolitionist. "Allow me then to present you with three arguments which support my right." He reached into a worn carpetbag at his feet. "For those who follow the laws of this country, I give you my first argument." From the bag, Mr. Clay removed a rolled parchment. "A copy of the United States Constitution!"

Some few of the sweaty crowd cheered the document.

"For those who profess to believe in the Word of God – my second argument." Again he reached into the carpetbag, this time pulling out a leather-bound Bible.

A larger portion of those in the Grove shouted their approval.

"And for those who disregard both the laws of God and of man – my third argument." Thrusting both hands into the carpetbag, Mr. Clay took out two long-barreled pistols.

With the appearance of the pistols, what seemed the entire fifteen hundred sent up a great cheering. For all, no matter their opinion of human bondage, possessed an appreciation for expensive firearms.

When the noise had ceased, Mr. Clay placed all of these items upon a small table, keeping the pistols within easy reach, and began to speak.

My father's friend possessed a charismatic presence, and when he spoke with the full force of his righteousness, even those whose slippers were carried to them each night by Negroes found themselves calling wrath upon that "unconstitutional practice which will lead us back to barbarism." Hearing Mr. Clay speak, I forgot the corset stuck to my sweat-dampened flesh and the small flies which buzzed about my mouth.

It is impossible for Mr. Lincoln to hear this and not be moved to action, I thought. *Impossible for him not to turn the energy caused by the Blue Mass against this wrong.* But when I searched the crowd for my husband, I found him stretched upon the grass, whittling branches with a tremoring hand.

I felt the heat then, felt the weight of its oppressive air fall upon me. If Mr. Clay's fiery eloquence, which caused slave-owners to threaten him in blood, could not set fire to Mr. Lincoln's ambition, what hope had a wife who possessed nothing more inflammatory than subscriptions to abolitionist newspapers?

For the remainder of that summer, my mood echoed my husband's. I lost my temper over biscuits that did not rise, and became furious at milk which soured. Like him, I seemed also to be filled with an excess of energy I could not direct. An energy which caused me to seek out my volume of Miss Beecher's *Treatise on Domestic Economy* and follow the direction inside it with new scrupulousness. If the Household Divinity suggested sweeping the parlor once a week, I swept it twice. If she prescribed taking apart the astral lamps and washing them with pearl ash water every month, I accomplished the task every second week. Every afternoon, save the Sabbath, I dragged a carpet into the sun and beat it with a dedication meant to make me forget I had married a man who could be president, but did not wish to be.

Mr. Lincoln was never the direct recipient of my frustration. However, it was true that I often found it necessary to take a dust brush to the chair upon which he was seated at the time, or to replace the wick in the lamp he was reading by. Neither did I badger him again about slavery, stopping the subscriptions to abolitionist newspapers so I would not have to see them. I did, however, continue to feed Mr. Lincoln the Blue Mass, for I did not wish to have a husband who was both melancholic and unambitious.

At the beginning of autumn, Mr. Lincoln and I took our sons to the Illinois State Fair, an event at which livestock were judged by their height and weight, and ladies by their pies and preserves. The day one of Indian summer – hot, though the maples and elms had already turned crimson and gold. My husband went off to the tent which held the latest inventions – machines which sewed by means of a foot pedal and artificial limbs. Robert merely went off, not saying where he was headed, just leaving us the moment we entered the fairgrounds. My youngest sons I set free to terrorize the penned rabbits and geese. I was brushing the hay from my skirts when Elizabeth arrived. My sister was dressed in cream linen – unsoiled by hay – and wore an exceedingly fashionable split straw hat.

"Are you and Mr. Lincoln going to hear Senator Douglas?" she asked. The state election was the following month, and my old beau had come to garner votes for the Democrats.

"Why is it you are always so scrupulous to refer to Mr. Douglas as Senator?" I replied.

"That is his title," my sister said airily. "When Mr. Lincoln was in Congress, I always referred to him as *Congressman* Lincoln."

I imagined my sister sprawled in the mud of the goose pen, her cream-colored skirts covered in droppings and her split straw hat plucked from her head. It was an unkind – yet satisfying – image, the kind to which Elizabeth oft inspired me.

"I did marry the better man," I informed her. "Despite what you believe."

Before she might reply, I turned away, dislodging my own bonnet, which was not nearly as fashionable as hers. Leaving Elizabeth standing outside the pen, I stalked off to deliver a terrified rabbit from Taddie's enthusiastic affections, swishing my skirts in a show of resentment, which, in truth, was directed as much at the man I had just defended as at my sister. As if the weather had become infected by my mood, the air was suddenly rent by a cracking of thunder, and within a moment a torrential rain fell upon the animals and the prizewinning pies.

The rain forced Mr. Douglas's open-air meeting to be moved to the statehouse, and there was much scurrying for carriages and ladies running with copies of the *Illinois Journal* over their heads to prevent their straw bonnets from turning to paste. Within a short time, the statehouse hall was filled with fairgoers shaking out wet skirts and sopping waistcoats, all eager to grant Senator Douglas the same attention they'd bestowed upon the judging of hogs. I lost my

crush, and Taddie, who, though already adequately
ιecessary to run back into the rain at regular intervals.
Douglas's short stature and booming voice had earned
ε of Little Giant, and it had to be admitted that he was
His defense of the Kansas-Nebraska Act was met with
clamι s support from the same citizens who had been equally
enthusiastic of Mr. Clay's condemnation of it. While the senator
spoke, and I attempted to prevent my youngest son from wiping
his wet head upon strange ladies' skirts, I searched the hall for my
husband. But Mr. Lincoln, who was easy to spot because of his height,
was not inside. *Elizabeth may be right*, said my traitorous voice.
Perhaps I should have married Stephen Douglas. But Mr. Douglas was
a Democrat, and did not mind slavery so much as to stop its spread.
And of course, I did not love him. *No*, I thought bitterly, *I love the man
who would not even come out of the rain to listen to politics.*

When Mr. Douglas finished his speech – which was met by
gentlemen's foot-stomping and the waving of ladies' handkerchiefs –
I collected my youngest sons and joined the throng of people
attempting to exit the hall. But we could get no further than the lobby,
for a great crowd had stopped there and was looking up the marble
staircase which led to the second floor. I followed their gaze and to my
astonishment saw my own husband, his waistcoat dripping and his
hair flattened by rain. Mr. Lincoln was grinning in a way which I had
not seen since long before the Blue Mass.

"Senator Douglas has just expended considerable breath in the
attempt to prove that the Kansas-Nebraska Act won't add any slave
states to the Union," my husband declared to the assembly. "Well,
if you will come back here tomorrow afternoon, you will hear me
challenge that contention."

The crowd cheered and gentlemen threw dripping boaters into
the air.

"And," continued Mr. Lincoln, "as it would be unsporting to
rebut a man's speech without granting him the opportunity to call
you a liar, the senator is welcome to return and direct his eloquence
against me."

There were shouts of "Where's Douglas?" and "What say you,
Senator?" The crowd swiveled their heads searching for Mr. Douglas.

"He has agreed!" called out a gentleman near the doorway. "The
senator says yes!"

The prospect of debate set the crowd to more cheering and hat-throwing. I looked about at the dampened fairgoers gazing at my husband, their hands full of prizewinning jellies and livestock ribbons. Then I looked myself upon the wet and homely man standing at the top of the steps, and knew without doubting that I had married correctly, by both the definition of Queen Ruby and my own heart.

The following afternoon was hot as midsummer, yet when Elizabeth and I arrived at the statehouse, we found it more filled with spectators than it had been for Mr. Douglas's speech the day before. I pointed out this fact to my sister as we waited for the reluctant chivalry of two gentlemen to earn us our seats.

"I am surprised the senator would agree to debate a man who holds no political office," Elizabeth replied.

"Mr. Lincoln only holds no office at the present time," I said to her. For it did seem to me that was a circumstance certain to change.

We settled into chairs still warm from the gentlemen who had vacated them. *All these people have come out to hear my husband,* I thought to myself. *And Mr. Douglas, I expect. Although they have heard him yesterday, and so it is mostly for Mr. Lincoln they have come.* This notion made me flush with pride, and with something less defined which caused the overheated hall to feel warmer.

Mr. Douglas entered the hall to considerable applause. Despite the hotness of the day, he was dressed in a black waistcoat of such rich wool, I knew it must have come from one of the glittering shops on Pennsylvania Avenue. Once he had settled himself into his seat, placed right at the front of the stage, Mr. Lincoln entered – to an equal, at least to my ears, volume of applause.

"Where is Mr. Lincoln's waistcoat?" hissed Elizabeth.

I had used up an hour brushing and pressing my husband's waistcoat, which was now likely thrown over some chair in the corridor because of the heat.

"It is Mr. Lincoln's intention to convey that he is a man of the people," I told my sister.

"Whatever for?" she replied.

My husband bantered a bit with those assembled, to make them used to his looks and the high timbre of his voice. Although his posture was relaxed, he kept his hands clasped behind his back, a trick to hide the Blue Mass tremor of his hands. The crowd did not notice when

Mr. Lincoln shifted from jokes against himself into the substance of his speech, so gracefully did he take them. They only noticed that when he spoke of slavery, he became moved by a moral outrage, and that they were moved with him.

"There can be no moral right in connection with one man's making a slave of another," my husband declared to the overfilled statehouse. "Yet Senator Douglas, who is in favor of the Kansas-Nebraska Act, has no thought that there can be any moral question in legislating about the Negro's enslavement." Mr. Lincoln brought his hands forward, and they did not shake. "Mr. Douglas has no very vivid impression that the Negro is a human. But the Negro *is* a man. And human slavery the most monstrous evil."

There was much applause, from those who agreed and those who had only been carried along by my husband's ardency, and it made me recall the first time I had come to hear Mr. Lincoln speak, in this very statehouse, upon a day equally as overheated. Then I had sat imagining how it would feel to have those large unshaking hands upon me, imagined it until my corset chafed and I could not concentrate on Mr. Lincoln's words about government. I now knew very well how those hands would feel, and the response they could call up; and as my husband spoke to the crowd of morality, I went taut with a desire which turned my flesh susceptible to every stitch of my clothing, so that I was forced to shallow my breathing to prevent my breast from moving against the muslin covering it. I shifted my eyes to the gentlemen and ladies seated about me, but they were fanning themselves with a motion almost too rhythmic to bear.

Mr. Lincoln spoke for three hours. The heat in the hall grew overwhelming. A lady near the stage swooned, and the gentleman beside her propped her up with his shoulder and carried on listening. Indeed, for the length of Mr. Lincoln's speech, no one uttered a sound or stirred from the hall. Finally, when he had finished speaking, when the final syllable – not seeming so high-timbred after all – fell to silence, the gentlemen took up a thunderous foot-stomping which shuddered the painting of President Washington hung upon the wall. The ladies showed their approval by the waving of handkerchiefs, and it seemed that a snowstorm of white linen descended in the overheated room.

Although Mr. Douglas rebutted my husband's arguments for two hours, I apprehended little of it, for I was thinking only of

Mr. Lincoln's success – and of my own, for had not I been a little responsible for bringing him here? It was I who had forced him from his melancholic bed by feeding him the Blue Mass. I who had given him no conversation save the politics of slavery and took him to Mather's Grove to hear the abolitionist madman. Now that Mr. Lincoln stood before this crowd, debating a senator and besting him, it felt that some portion of the foot-stomping and handkerchief-waving belonged to me.

The day following the debate with Mr. Douglas, we were visited by several gentlemen of the Whig party. It was their desire that Mr. Lincoln follow Mr. Douglas about the state, criticizing him for his support of the Kansas-Nebraska Act until he "ran him into his hole and made him holler." My husband told the gentlemen that such an activity would give him no end of pleasure, "particularly the hollering," and Mr. Lincoln spent the rest of that autumn debating my former beau in Peoria, Urbana, even in Chicago, where the local newspaper described him as "an honest man and a powerful speaker" – a description I quoted to my eldest sister so frequently, she eventually forbade me to mention the city's name in her presence.

That November, a majority of representatives who opposed the Kansas-Nebraska Act were elected to the state legislature, which caused those same Whig gentlemen to return to our house and remind Mr. Lincoln that, come January, these representatives would choose a new senator to join Mr. Douglas in Washington City, and that this time, the man might very likely be a Whig.

From that day forward my husband campaigned for the position of senator from Illinois. He approached every political gentleman he knew and worked to enlist his support. And it would require work, for the legislature which would choose the new senator was divided between anti-Nebraska Whigs and anti-Nebraska Republicans, pro-slavery Democrats and Democrats with abolitionist leanings, as well as the Know-Nothings, who were such a secret society nobody quite knew who belonged.

A week before the legislature was to vote, Springfield was struck by a blizzard. Snow blew fiercely from every direction, blinding those senseless enough to venture out and frightening horses into breaking their traces. The storm isolated Springfield from the rest of the state; neither riders nor the telegraph could travel in the heavy snowfall, and no business was conducted. Even the election of the new senator was postponed.

We were confined to the house on Eighth Street, insulated by the snow which fell thick as cotton batting. My sons passed the time by reenacting the fatal encounter between Cassius Clay and Cyrus Turner, employing the use of wooden daggers. Mr. Lincoln occasionally joined them as the slave-holder Squire Turner, because "it's good practice to argue the other side of an issue from time to time."

After we had been kept to the house for two days, I came one evening upon my husband sitting before the parlor fire, staring fixedly at an astral lamp as if it were communicating with him.

"What is it you are doing?" I asked in an overloud voice, for whenever I found Mr. Lincoln so concentrated upon something, I feared he had been taken by a spell of hypochondriasis.

"There's no need for more than ordinary alarm," he replied, "I am only thinking."

"Of the balloting?"

"I was running through the legislators to see which ones were likely to vote for me."

I set down a basket of root-cellar potatoes I'd been taking into the kitchen to make soup. "How many have you come up with?"

"I think I can feel certain of twenty-six. But I'll need to find twenty-five more if I want to be senator."

I sat across from him. "Have you counted the vote of Mr. Ogden?"

"I fear that after my rebuttal of Mr. Douglas, Ogden is very much of the mind that I wish to emancipate his slaves."

"In that case, you should be able to depend upon the vote of Mr. Eastman, for he is a fervent abolitionist."

"Eastman has made it known that he believes my having married into a slave-holding family has tempered my views upon the matter of human bondage."

"Perhaps we should put the two men together and see if one can convince the other of your suitability."

My husband smiled. "There's merit in the suggestion, as neither wishes to vote in accord with the other."

I settled more firmly into my chair and mentioned the names of several other gentlemen of the legislature, seeking Mr. Lincoln's determination upon how they might vote. As the snow blew across the window, cutting off the sight of the Gourleys' house next door, we sat before the fire and discussed the loyalties of each of the one hundred representatives who made up the legislature, being obliged on occasion to shout our opinion over the death cries of the slaughtered Cyrus Turner. At one point, unsure if we had determined a Mr. Branch's allegiance to the Democratic party lightly held, my husband retrieved the leather satchel he carried to the courthouse each day and took from it a small notebook. "Let's put these slippery fellows someplace where we can keep track of them," he suggested.

I went for pen and ink, and together we inscribed the names of all one hundred legislators into the notebook. After each name, we wrote whether the man was a member of the Whig, Democratic, or Republican party; if we suspected he belonged to the Know-Nothings, which objected to the presence of immigrants; or if he was Temperance Society, which felt the same way about drink. We recorded each representative's opinion regarding slavery, and whether he had shown support for the Kansas-Nebraska Act or the Fugitive Slave Act. Then we deliberated over the likelihood that each might be persuaded to vote for Mr. Lincoln.

Halfway through the list, we were interrupted by Willie and Tad, who came running into the parlor to complain that Robert insisted upon acting the role of Mr. Clay and "will only let us be Cyrus and Thomas Turner."

"Why don't you sit by the fire and exhaust your love of bloodshed with leaded soldiers?" I said to them. With loudly voiced battle cries, my youngest sons ran off to collect their armies, while Mr. Lincoln and I returned to debating a certain representative's attitude toward those who practiced law.

When it grew so dark outside the window we could no longer see the falling snow, Robert came into the parlor with his own army of leaded soldiers.

"Why haven't we had supper?" he said to me. "It's long past the time."

"I have been talking over with your father whether the gentlemen of the legislature will vote for him."

"You should be making supper," he replied, sounding older than his eleven years.

"Your brothers have been wishing for another army to join their war," I said. And while Robert dealt his younger brothers a series of ignoble defeats, Mr. Lincoln and I continued our speculation upon whether a particular Temperance Democrat would continue to favor one of Mr. Lincoln's opponents if he learned that the gentleman was an imbiber.

Hours passed. Taddie fell asleep upon the hearth rug with the barrel of a metal cannon pointed at his cheek. Not long afterward, Robert and Willie also drifted off, stretched out across their soldier-strewn battlefield. It was now past midnight, and my basket of root-cellar potatoes was still upon the carpet, as far from being soup as when I had brought it up.

"I expect we ought to carry these generals up to bed," said my husband.

"But we have yet to decide upon Mr. Morrison," I protested. "I worry that his marriage to a Catholic lady may cause him to favor the Irishman Mr. Shields."

Mr. Lincoln scooped Taddie into his arms. "I suspect Mr. Morrison will still be married to the Catholic lady in the morning. We can calculate her political influence then."

We returned to the topic of the Papist Mrs. Morrison at breakfast, then took on the question of several possible Know-Nothings over lunch – the potato soup I had neglected the night before. Throughout the day, as snow fell and my sons murdered each other above our heads, my husband and I turned our attention to the notebook, revising our judgment about one or another of the legislators, then recounting the votes we believed would go to Mr. Lincoln.

By the time the blizzard cleared and a date for the balloting was set, we both believed that Mr. Lincoln stood the best chance of any of the candidates. I felt so certain of my husband's success, I induced Elizabeth, who had never lost her taste for showing off her house, to host a party afterward in his honor.

The day of the balloting was clear and so cold the air felt it had been thinned. Sunlight reflected from the stacks of snow piled along the curb, turning everything so bright that ladies were obliged to wear their bonnets much farther forward than was fashionable. I had persuaded Elizabeth to come with me, coaxing her away from the preparations for Mr. Lincoln's victory party – which largely consisted of hovering about making the servants nervous – as I wished my sister to witness for herself that no less a body than the Illinois State Legislature believed my husband the equal of Stephen Douglas.

Although we had come early, we were obliged to push our way into the statehouse lobby through tight-packed groupings of gentlemen in knitted shawls and ladies shaking slush from their hems. I hurried my sister up the marble staircase to the gallery as quickly as the woolen weight of our winter skirts would allow, and we captured the last seats at the railing – the only place we could see what was happening on the floor below – only by way of Elizabeth's manner, which halted two young ladies in their tracks.

"You are very certain Mr. Lincoln will win?" my sister asked, ignoring the glare she was receiving from one of the thwarted ladies. "I have already instructed the cook to prepare a white cake with the words 'Senator Lincoln' written in boiled frosting, and I would not wish to have it iced over."

"He shall win," I assured her. "We have calculated his chances with some accuracy."

The tautening of Elizabeth's lips reminded me of our stepmother. "You have involved yourself in Mr. Lincoln's campaign?" she asked.

"I have given him the benefit of my intuition as to the loyalties of certain legislators," I replied. Then I turned my attention to the floor below.

The legislators arrived one by one, as if their eminence required each to make an entrance without the others. They removed their stovepipe hats and tucked them into the crook of their arms like tall cakes, rocking upon their feet and from time to time spitting into a brass urn, feigning ignorance of the great crowd looking down upon them from the gallery. When Mr. Lincoln entered the hall a small group gathered around him, no man taller than my husband's shoulder. I watched him tell the representatives a story which made them laugh – even the Democrats – and attempted to calculate whether such a showing of goodwill might mean a vote. But it was an exercise in uselessness, for in politics, showings of goodwill are far easier to come by than votes.

At last, the bell was rung and the representatives moved to take their seats. As was customary, my husband would pass the day in the lawyers' offices on the second floor, pretending to be disinterested in the outcome of the voting, although his supporters would make the journey up and down the stairs many times. As he was exiting the hall, Mr. Lincoln glanced up into the gallery and made a slight movement of his hand which resembled a tremor, but I knew for a wave.

During the first ballot, I kept count of each time a representative spoke my husband's name and before the tallying was returned, I knew that we led with forty-five votes. James Shields, a Democrat, was second with forty-one. Third place belonged to Lyman Trumbull, a colleague of Mr. Lincoln, whose anti-slavery stance had recently pushed him from Democrat to Whig.

"Mr. Lincoln requires only six more votes to become senator," I confided to my sister.

"Do you imagine he will receive them on the second ballot?" she asked.

"There is a very good chance you will be able to return home to badger your cook about the cake before lunch," I replied.

However, on the second ballot, Mr. Lincoln's tally went no higher. Neither did that of Mr. Shields. But a number of votes which had been scattered among other candidates had come to settle upon Mr. Trumbull.

"Is not Mr. Trumbull married to *your* old friend, Julia Jayne?" Elizabeth said.

"He is."

"I always thought his manners exceptional."

"I always thought he possessed the demeanor of a Massachusetts schoolmistress."

There was little change in the third, fourth, fifth, and sixth ballots. As the hours passed, the gallery grew hot and filled with the reek of unwashed winter bodies encased in too many layers of woolen clothing. Elizabeth, who prepared for any emergency, removed a perfumed hankie from her reticule and pressed it against her nose. I kept rearranging my skirts, hoping to encourage a breeze to find its way beneath them.

We must have calculated wrongly, I thought. *Must have imagined that this Republican was less set against Kansas-Nebraska than we had thought, that that Whig more in favor of enslaving Negroes than we realized.* I wanted nothing more than to fly up to the lawyers' offices, where no lady ever went, and confer with my husband. Surely if the two of us went through the notebook together we would uncover those needed votes. But my sex kept me trapped in the gallery.

On the seventh ballot, without warning, all of Mr. Shields's supporters changed their votes to Joel Matteson, the governor of Illinois and a Democrat.

"What has happened?" asked Elizabeth.

"The Democrats have come to the conclusion that they cannot elect Mr. Shields and are looking for another candidate," I explained.

"You know an uncommon amount about politics." My sister's tone did not imply admiration.

"You were the one who asked me the question," I reminded her.

Governor Matteson gained more votes on the eighth ballot; and by the ninth, his total had been raised to forty-eight.

"Mr. Matteson is only three votes shy of beating Mr. Lincoln," declared Elizabeth. "What am I going to do about my white cake?"

Feed it to the hogs, I wished to tell her, for all my hopes of seeing my husband be brilliant in politics were vanishing as surely as the snow outside. What was Mr. Lincoln doing? Mr. Matteson was governor – a position which allowed him to grant profitable favors. He would have no difficulty finding those three votes – possibly before the next balloting. Clearly, unless something was done now, Mr. Lincoln would lose and Elizabeth could very well feed her cake to the hogs.

I sprang from my seat. "Defend my place," I told my sister. And before she could inquire where I was headed, I forced my way out of the aisle.

I had recalled seeing Julia Trumbull at the back of gallery, her pale hair swept very high beneath a velvet winter bonnet, and now I hurried to her row, motioning to her until she understood that I wished her to come out. Julia took so long to maneuver her skirts past the gentlemen and ladies seated between her and the aisle, I feared the balloting would be called before she reached me; and as soon as I could take hold of her elbow, I dragged her in the corridor.

"I am extraordinarily grateful to you for taking me out of there," Julia sighed. "I believe I was near to expiring from the heat and the tediousness."

"I fear I am obliged to presume upon our long-standing friendship," I said to her.

"You know you always have my leave to request a favor."

I grabbed hold of her hands, gloved in velvet despite the heat. "You must persuade your husband to release his votes to Mr. Lincoln."

Julia looked as shocked as if I had requested she descend to the floor and cast the ballots herself.

"Mr. Trumbull cannot win," I continued. "His votes are too

few. And if he continues to hold them, we shall have Governor Matteson – a Democrat – as senator."

Julia took her hands away. "I cannot advise my husband," she declared. "Not about politics."

"I am only suggesting that you help him to see that the cause against slavery would be better served if he told his supporters to switch their votes to Mr. Lincoln."

Julia gazed at me in horror. "It would be unnatural for me to do such a thing."

"I am merely asking that you speak to your husband about politics."

Julia straightened her velvet bonnet, which had not been in the least crooked. "For whom Mr. Trumbull's supporters cast their votes is not my concern. Neither is the selection of a senator."

It was myself now, who gazed at her in disbelief. "You do not care if your husband is elected?"

"Politics should be left to those for whom God intended it," she informed me. "You may be willing to unsex yourself for ambition. I, however, am not." With that, Julia raised the hem of her woolen skirt as regally as if it were taffeta, and executing a sharp little turn, returned to the gallery.

I wished to call back my friend, explain that this was not ambition, not a thing which might unsex me; and I almost ran after her. But instead, I remained in the corridor, surrounded by the swirl of ladies' skirts and the half-glimpses of rushing gentlemen, uncertain I would be able to make the case.

The bell rang for the tenth balloting, and I hurried back to my seat.

Elizabeth regarded my return with narrowed eyes. "I saw you leave with Julia Trumbull," she told me.

"I wished to ask after her mother."

"She returned to her seat looking distraught," she observed.

"Perhaps she is apprehensive over Mr. Trumbull's chances to be senator," I replied.

Again my sister copied our stepmother's mouth. "Julia Trumbull is too much a lady to allow herself to be stimulated by politics."

"Do not say any more," I told her. "I must keep track of the balloting."

In addition to keeping track of Mr. Lincoln's votes, I also tallied up those cast for Governor Matteson, fearing he might have gotten his three. I did not at first count the votes for Lyman Trumbull. Not until the hall began ringing with men declaring, "I am for Trumbull" and "My vote for Trumbull," many of them the same gentlemen who on the previous balloting had proclaimed, "Put me down for Lincoln."

"What is happening?" Elizabeth asked me.

"Mr. Lincoln has done the honorable thing," I said bitterly.

"Whatever are you talking about?"

"He has prevented the election of a Democratic senator."

When the tenth ballot was tallied, Mr. Lincoln, who had begun the day with forty-five votes, did not possess one; and Lyman Trumbull, who had started with five, was senator.

The balloting had gone past suppertime and now that the results were announced, the gentlemen and ladies crowded into the gallery began to push their way up the aisle. I remained in my seat, cursing Julia Trumbull's propriety, Lyman Trumbull's treachery, and my own husband's damnable honor.

"Come!" commanded Elizabeth. "Or we shall never get a carriage."

"I will stay behind," I replied. "There are things I wish to say to Mr. Lincoln."

My sister yanked me from my chair. "I have no plan to allow you to remain in the statehouse and discuss politics like a man," she declared.

I fought against her grip, but Elizabeth had always possessed uncommon strength for a lean woman. "I only wish to speak with my husband."

"You will speak with him at home, where wives are expected to speak to their husbands." Not releasing her hold upon me, my sister guided me up the aisle, all the time whispering fiercely in my ear. "This hall is filled with our neighbors," she hissed. "Before them you must smile and appear as if you are indifferent to politics."

"How can I be indifferent?" I said to her.

Elizabeth's grip grew more viselike. "Because you are a lady."

My sister propelled me down the steps and through the state-house lobby. And while I allowed her to do it – I had never been equal to Elizabeth's strength – I could not compel myself to smile into the faces of my neighbors. Outside, a great gathering of shivering ladies and impatient gentlemen waited for carriages, but my sister did not heed them, only pushed me forward through the snow banked along the curb and into the first closed brougham in the line.

"I think I know what you were doing with Julia Trumbull in the corridor," she said, the moment the carriage door was closed behind us.

"As you can see, I was unsuccessful," I replied.

Elizabeth's indignation at this was so great, it filled the dark little carriage, making the closed space feel more confined. "I am not concerned with whether you were successful," she spat out. "I am concerned with how completely you have unsexed yourself."

"I have not unsexed myself," I insisted, angry to hear the word which Julia Trumbull had used come from her mouth.

"You are involving yourself in politics."

"I am helping my husband into political office," I said. "Is that not a wife's duty?"

Elizabeth wrapped her shawl more tightly about her. "A wife's duty is her home and her children."

"But I wish Mr. Lincoln to be senator."

My sister drew away from me, as if I had confessed to smallpox or typhoid. "That is ambition," she said. "Which renders it worse."

"I am not ambitious!" I cried. No lady was ambitious. Only suffragists and spinster abolitionists and believers in female rights who walked the streets in Turkish pantaloons were ambitious. And they were not considered ladies.

"You have given political advice to your husband, most likely to the neglect of your children," said my sister. "You have held scheming conversations in the corridor of the statehouse and attempted to persuade another lady into following your scandalous behavior. You have not accepted your husband's defeat with the tranquility and impassiveness toward the affairs of men required of a well-bred wife." Elizabeth's back was pressed firmly against the leather seat of the carriage. "Not only do you possess an unwomanly ambition, you practice no hold upon it."

I knew that Elizabeth was correct. It was the reason I had not chased after Julia to explain myself. Because there was no explanation. Even my eldest son had recognized the wrongness of my actions, seen it in the forgotten basket of potatoes and the unfixed supper. My husband's political success had become my own desire, and it had made me what I had been taught ladies should never be.

Over the following months, I attempted to smother my ambition beneath a soft cushion of womanly pursuits. I put up my own preserves, although for all the sticky work, they did not taste as well as the ones sold at Irwin's General Store. I tried my hand at watercolor, transforming a bowl of winter squash into something so unlifelike, I told my husband it had been painted by Taddie. I even allowed my younger sister, Ann, to give me lessons in embroidery, until I became too discouraged by her pedantic manner and the very tediousness of cross-stitching.

During this time, I watched my husband for signs of melancholy and kept him supplied with the Blue Mass. But Mr. Lincoln's own political ambition had been aroused, and though he remained unsafe around crockery, he did not try to choke any button sellers, nor sink so deep into hypochondriasis he imitated the dead.

We continued this way for two years; me devoted – no matter how inexpertly – to the pursuits of domestic economy, and Mr. Lincoln concentrated upon politics. During this period, the Whig Party dissolved over the issue of slavery, and my husband joined the newly formed Republicans. "There are a great many abolitionists in that party," Elizabeth warned, when she was informed of the news. However, the Republicans were happy to have Mr. Lincoln, and in June of 1858, at their state convention in Springfield, they nominated him to run for senator against Stephen Douglas.

My husband's acceptance speech was to be given that evening at the statehouse, and after supper, I dressed all three of my sons in the clothes I saved for church and brought them to hear their father. To five-year-old Taddie, this donning of Sunday trousers and jacket only reinforced his currently held notion that his father was God. To Willie, who was seven, these formal clothes made him believe that while not the Almighty Himself, his father was doing the Almighty's work, for already my middle son had developed a terrific dislike of slavery. As for Robert, who was about to turn fifteen that summer, and who I most wished would come to see his father in a Godlike light, I knew only that he thought his best clothes shabby and wished to know why we could not buy new ones.

The night of the speech was the first soft one of June, still warm after dark, the air thick with all the summer roses which had bloomed that week. The lobby and staircase of the statehouse thronged with gentlemen in straw boaters, which their wives had taken from trunks only days before, and ladies in summer frocks of eyelet, which left their arms bare. Seats had been saved for us at the front of the gallery, so near to the speaker's platform that when Mr. Lincoln entered the hall, Taddie attempted to vault over the railing into his father's arms. I was the one who had dressed my husband for this appearance, and for once his coat and trousers matched and the ankles of his boots were covered.

I knew nothing of my husband's speech, only that he had taken some portion of it from Scripture. After Eddie's death, Mr. Lincoln had begun reading the Bible, working his way through all the books until he reached Revelations, then beginning over again with Genesis. "You will know the speech when I deliver it," he had told me. And so I could not spy, he tucked the bits of paper he was memorizing into the lining of his hat.

Now my husband stood in the statehouse before all of Springfield, his clothes brushed and fitting as well as they could, his unstill hands caught behind his back. "A House divided against itself cannot stand," he declared into that soft June night.

The phrase was from the Gospels – Matthew, I believe – and the elderly lady seated beside me met it with a whispered "Amen."

"This government cannot endure permanently half slave and half free," he continued.

Some of those assembled spoke "Amen" to this. Some others, gentlemen mostly, shifted about in their seats and seemed to more tightly grip their summer hats.

"I do not expect the Union to be dissolved," said my husband. "I do not expect the house to fall. But I do expect it will cease to be divided. It will become all one thing, or all the other."

There was no doubting that the all one thing Mr. Lincoln believed the Union should become was free, and the manner in which he had spoken this made it the strongest statement uttered against slavery by any politician – any who was not branded complete abolitionist. For some, such as those who continued to grip their straw boaters, this could be heard as a promise of war against those states where it was lawful for white to own black. But in my husband's mouth, the words sounded reasonable, inspired by the logic of his mind and the nobleness of his heart.

Mr. Lincoln spoke of the wrongness of slavery, releasing his large

hands from behind his back. They moved about in the warm air,
I saw that the force of his purpose had taken away their tremoring,
made them appear nearly graceful – as graceful as they became when
he put them upon me.

Look at the elderly lady beside you, I commanded myself. *She is so
caught up in Mr. Lincoln's speech, she has forgotten that her handkerchief is halfway to her face. Look at Taddie, watching his father with the
same awestruck gaze Moses turned upon the Burning Bush; and Willie,
hands folded in case he is called upon to pray. Look at Robert, for you
shall see that he now recognizes the worth of this man whose mind is
greater than that of any Todd ancestor who became legend by shooting
at Indians.*

However, when I cast my eyes upon my eldest son, I saw that he
was not looking at his father, but staring instead at me – at the way
that my breath came too fast, the flush I knew was upon my throat.

The audience in Springfield seemed to sense that what they were
hearing was an uncommon speech, one which would be quoted in
newspapers, both Northern and Southern. And when Mr. Lincoln finished speaking, there was great uproar – so boisterous it sounded as if
the war he had predicted had begun – and one or two gentlemen
found it necessary to fire their guns out the statehouse window to
demonstrate their approval.

My Southern relations also showed strong reaction to my
husband's speech. "Some of your family are declaring Mr. Lincoln a
nigger lover," wrote my half-sister Emilie, who since our time at Crab
Orchard had grown into a young woman and married the son of a
Kentucky governor. "If I wished to be truthful, I would tell you that
your half-brothers and sisters are saying the same."

I was incensed that my family should so misjudge my husband,
and I hurried to the leather-topped desk in the sitting room where my
husband often worked and immediately began a letter to my half-
sister. When I had finished, I decided to write to all my Southern
relations, explaining Mr. Lincoln's position upon slave-holding, for
the Southern Todds possessed no little political influence.

"Although Mr. Lincoln is a Republican," I told them all, "he is not
an abolitionist. All he desires is that slavery should not be extended
beyond where it already exists."

For the better part of the morning, I remained at Mr. Lincoln's
desk, becoming translator for my husband's politics. And I did not

children's dinnertime had passed, until Taddie turned
with lemon custard on his face.

gave me my dinner," announced my youngest son,
mouth upon my skirts.

at did he give you?"

ie."

I set down my pen and took Taddie's hand, leading him out to
the water pump, where I gently cleaned his face with the edge of my
petticoat. *It had been necessary for me to write the letters,* I told myself.
*For Mr. Lincoln's political career. And lemon custard for dinner one time
is not so very terrible.* But I did not return to my husband's desk that
afternoon, going instead to the kitchen where I set to work upon roast
chicken and boiled potatoes and a burnt-sugar cake.

"Are you going to cook for us now?" asked Robert. We had just sat
down to supper, a little past our time due to the late hour that the
chicken had gone into the oven.

"Of course," I said. "What would make you think otherwise?"

"You were at father's desk," he accused. "Writing."

I put upon his plate the largest piece of chicken, only smaller
than the one I was saving for his father. "I have cooked for you now,
haven't I?"

Robert pushed about his boiled potatoes as if unconvinced of
their cooked state, and I resolved to do my letter-writing at night,
after my son was asleep, and after I had prepared something for his
breakfast.

In July, Mr. Lincoln challenged Senator Douglas to debate him in no
less than fifty cities throughout Illinois. Mr. Douglas, who was too
aware of how my husband's speaking affected even those who were
not married to him, agreed to seven. The first debate would be held
in the northern city of Ottawa and was scheduled for August the
twenty-first.

Immediately, my husband began to prepare, not only what he
would say, but also how he would say it. I discovered him muttering
over his morning buttermilk and gesturing broadly while shaving;
and one night as I lay in bed cutting apart the pages of a novel, I
overheard him in the room next to mine, the one he used for his
bedroom, speaking his entire speech. I had grown used to my
husband's high-tenored voice. But I knew that those who would hear

him for the first time would be startled by that soft, nearly feminine tone issuing from such a giant. Mr. Douglas, on the other hand, had always possessed a rich baritone, which emanated from his short frame like the utterance of the Almighty.

Hearing my husband speak the weighty words of his speech with such lightness of tone recalled for me my time at Madame Mentelle's boarding school and the amateur theatricals we had performed there. Madame had required us to practice our French by acting in Gallic tragedies, and during my final year, Madame chose for us a play entitled *Andromaque*, casting me as the title character, the embodiment of maternal love. Although I would have much preferred to play Hermione, the embodiment of passionate love, a role which was given to an excessively slender girl from Louisville.

While my less-willowy figure may have been more suited to the portrayal of motherly love, my voice was not. Trained from my earliest babble to affect the Southern girl's flirtatious trilling, I could not deliver a single one of Andromaque's lines to Madame's satisfaction.

"*Comme une mere!*" my instructor commanded from her place in the audience. "*Pas comme une coquette!*"

At last, frustrated by my inability to pitch my voice into a motherly register, Madame ascended the stage, spun me around with some force, and proceeded to unfasten the buttons at the back of my dress.

I was too startled to utter a word – not that I would have questioned Madame's actions. Madame Mentelle was so very much in charge, she could have stripped us all naked and we would have remained silent, convinced the removal of our garments was necessary for the furtherance of our education.

Once Madame had unfastened my dress, she undid the laces of my corset. "*Maintenant,*" she said, poking me beneath the ribs. "Breathe from here. Then speak."

I did as Madame instructed, and with the force of this unaccustomed breath, I spoke the dialogue of Andromaque in the resounding tones of a matriarch.

I set aside my knife and my novel. *There is no reason I cannot teach Madame's trick to Mr. Lincoln,* I thought, making to rise. *Especially as he already wears clothing which permits full breathing. No reason save that doing so will unsex me.* I sank back upon the bed. *As well as earn me a lecture from Elizabeth and a disapproving look from my eldest son.* I tried to take up the novel again, but could not keep from hearing my husband's unsubstantial voice through the door. *Then again, Robert is sleeping. And Elizabeth is unlikely to turn up in Mr. Lincoln's bedroom. Moreover, I cannot allow my husband to debate my deep-voiced former suitor in a piping tone.*

I leapt from my bed and hurried into my husband's room. "If you wish to convince an audience to extend the liberties of the founding fathers to Negroes," I said to him, "you shall have to do so in a stronger tone of voice."

My husband, who had been practicing his speech in a muslin nightshirt, did not appear startled to see me. "I'm afraid that, like my unhappy appearance, this squeak is all the voice the Almighty gave me," he replied.

With all the purpose of Madame Mentelle, I crossed the room and pressed a palm to my husband's nightshirt, fitting my hand into the space beneath his ribs, felt the warmth of his flesh cross into my palm.

"Breathe until my hand rises," I instructed him. "And then tell me about the Negroes' inalienable rights."

I felt my husband's breathing push against my palm, and did not let myself dwell upon how it would be to feel this rising against my own ribs. When next he spoke the lines of his speech, his voice issued forth in a deeper register.

"I sound nearly as good as your former beau," he declared.

"You sound better," I told him.

The following day, recalling how I had invited myself into my husband's bedroom to give him direction upon the delivery of a political speech, I spent several hours making a spun-sugar cake of great elaborateness. That night, however, I went to him again so I might demonstrate Madame Mentelle's advice regarding dramatic gesture. Indeed from that time onward, I came every night into my husband's bedroom in order to share some portion of Madame's theatrical instruction. And every day following, I prepared a cake which required no fewer than twelve steps, and then swept and scrubbed some long-neglected portion of my house.

All this baking and cleaning – performed with a vigor which would have impressed even the Household Divinity – left me exhausted. But the hours it permitted me to pass in my husband's bedroom were worth the hair made sticky from batter and the fingers cracked from lye. For what Mr. Lincoln and I did together before the glass – my hands moving his in a gesture, or pressing against his breathing flesh – was nearly as pleasurable as what we did upon the mattress. And this he did not ask me to rein in.

My husband left for Ottawa on the nineteenth of August, 1858. Immediately after bidding him good-bye, I wrapped my head in muslin and put to good use Miss Beecher's instructions involving the cleaning of flues and chimneys. For the next three days, though the weather was stifling, I practiced the most rigorous domestic economy to keep myself from thinking upon the debate. However, it was no difference how weary I made myself scrubbing glass chimneys and scouring bricks; still, I tossed upon the mattress until nearly dawn, imagining – in much detail – Mr. Lincoln both triumphing and failing horribly. Indeed I was so anxious, the morning after the debate I rose early and hurried to the depot so I might buy the Chicago papers directly from the train.

The debates between Mr. Lincoln and Mr. Douglas were of such interest, the *Chicago Press and Tribune* and the *Chicago Times* had each sent a writer expert in phonographic reporting to cover the event. It was the task of these reporters – Robert Hitt for the *Press and Tribune*, and Henry Binmore for the *Times* – to record every detail of the encounter between Mr. Lincoln and Mr. Douglas, including a word-by-word transcript of each man's speech. However, as I stood reading their accounts upon the platform, I wondered if Mr. Hitt and Mr. Binmore had been dispatched to the same location, as all the journalists appeared to agree upon was that the day had been scorchingly hot.

Writing in the *Press and Tribune*, which was known to be a newspaper of Republican leanings, Mr. Hitt had reported that following Mr. Lincoln's "high toned and powerful" performance, my husband had been borne away upon his supporters' shoulders "in glorious triumph." Conversely, in the *Times*, which was considered a newspaper of Democratic sympathies, Mr. Binmore had reported that the power of Mr. Douglas's verbal attacks had left Mr. Lincoln with his "limbs cold and his respiratory organs obstructed," such that he required carrying from the stage in a "funeral procession."

Folding both newspapers beneath my arm, I pushed through the morning passengers bound for Chicago, then spent the money on a carriage which would get me home quicker. While the Democratic reporter's story was certainly prejudiced against Mr. Lincoln,

Mr. Binmore was more likely to point out any flaws in his performance than the Republican Mr. Hitt. And though I did not believe that my husband's respiratory organs had undergone obstruction, there was probably some element of truth in the Democratic reporter's account. Enough to warrant me making to Mr. Lincoln a few suggestions which would result in Mr. Binmore having that much less to write about after the next debate.

The moment I arrived home, I sat myself at my husband's desk and began a letter to Mr. Lincoln filled with more of Madame Mentelle's dramatic advice – emphasizing especially how to give the impression of robust breath. I was so very intent upon my work, I did not notice that my eldest son had entered the room until he spoke.

"It is almost time for dinner," he told me.

"I am nearly finished."

"You should be in the kitchen. Both Tad and Willie have not eaten."

He gave me then such a fully formed look of disapproval, I almost believed that rather than turning fifteen the week before, he had reached twice that age. I studied my son's face, the fine features which had already begun their hardening into those of a man, and wished I could pull him into my lap like a child – though not the child he had been – and soften just the edges of that look. *Still*, I thought, *he is correct. I should be feeding my children, not writing advice to my husband.* I folded the letter and pushed it into one of the pigeonholes at the back of the desk.

"I found myself distracted," I told my son. "I am grateful to you for recalling me."

It was during this time, when my husband was traveling between the cities where he would debate, that we were visited by the appearance of Donati's Comet. The comet, named for the Italian professor who had found it, came upon an early-autumn night which was perfectly clear; and at the first fiery sighting I woke my sons to come and see. We crept down the back stairs, whispering to each other as if trying not to wake an unseen sleeper; and once outside, we sat together upon the steps of the back porch, all of us wrapped against the first chill of autumn in a quilt stitched for me by a Kentucky aunt.

As we watched the comet trail light across the sky, Robert, who was wearing a silk dressing gown which had once belonged to Ninian, inaccurately named all the constellations for his younger brothers. Taddie chattered to me in his soft lisp, putting everything we were seeing into his misshapen words. Willie was silent, staring open-mouthed at the sky, as if attempting to swallow the comet's brightness.

"Where does a comet come from?" Taddie asked.

"From God," said Willie.

"A comet is nothing more than dust," Robert informed him.

"I think it is your father's comet," I said. "I think it is his future written in light."

The thought had streaked into my mind in the way it was said the comet streaked across the heavens, surprising even myself. Yet once I had uttered the words, the truth of them was bright as the object's blazing tail.

"Does the comet mean God wants Pa to win?" asked Taddie.

"I believe it does," I told him. "For your father opposes a genuine evil."

"I will pray that Pa beats Mr. Douglas, then," said Willie.

"That is blasphemy," declared Robert.

"No," I told him. "It can never be blasphemy to pray for the success of one who is destined to fulfill the wishes of the Almighty."

"You are saying it is God's will that Father defeat Senator Douglas?" Robert tugged upon the belt of Ninian's robe, his voice pitched to the tone of aggrieved condescension which had arrived with his fifteenth birthday.

"Yes," I replied. "I think that it is." And it seemed to me then, in the glow of Donati's Comet, that if what Mr. Lincoln was doing in politics was the will of the Almighty, then anything I might do to aid him could not be thought wrong. Or unwomanly. It might even be argued that I possessed a *Christian* obligation to assist my husband. Even if that assistance fell outside the domesticity prescribed by Miss Beecher, or my sister. For certainly God was a higher authority upon what constituted female behavior than either of these models of Household Divinity.

Beneath the lit heavens, I wrapped my smaller sons more tightly within the Kentucky aunt's quilt and determined that no longer would I be like the "House divided" of Mr. Lincoln's speech – half wishing to exercise my ambition for my husband, and half wishing to be content with intricate cakes and cleaned chimneys. And when the last glowing bands of the comet had faded and I had returned my sons to bed, I went to Mr. Lincoln's desk and removed my unsent letter from the pigeonhole, marking it for the morning post.

After the coming of Donati's Comet, my "House divided" became all one thing, that which allowed me to be my husband's partner in politics. Allowing my sons to breakfast upon cold biscuits from the night before, I penned letters advising the elimination of a little bow which Mr. Binmore had deemed ungainly, or suggesting my husband cease permitting his supporters to bear him upon their shoulders, as it had caused the Democratic newspaperman to report that Mr. Lincoln's "pantaloons were pulled up so as to expose his underwear almost to the knee."

I did not attend any of these debates myself. In the northern half of the state, I would have been perceived by those in the crowd as one of the slave-owning Todds. And in the southern half, after Mr. Lincoln's "House divided" speech, I might trail after him with an entire troupe of darkies, and they would still believe my husband an abolitionist. Moreover, with Mr. Lincoln campaigning instead of lawyering, we could not spare the extra traveling expenses.

Not until the final debate, which was to be held in Alton. For this event, the Sangamon Railroad ran a half-price train from Springfield to Alton, and that seemed economy enough to buy a ticket for Robert and myself. It was my eldest son I wished most to see his father in these debates. For if only half of what the Republican reporter wrote of Mr. Lincoln were true – and half was likely the accurate portion – then Robert might at last see better what his father was worth.

Robert and I shared a compartment down to Alton; and as we left the depot – amidst an impressive number of marching bands and banners in light of the fact that nothing more momentous would occur in Springfield than the departure of a train – I thought how very handsome my son looked in his gold-braided cadet's jacket. That summer, Robert had joined the Springfield Cadets and spent every Saturday drilling behind the feed store with a real sword – to the great rapture of his younger brothers.

I was happy for the compartment, as the train was overflowing with merry-makers, few who appeared to be Temperance Society. One gentleman, wearing an American flag in every buttonhole of his waistcoat, thrust his head in the doorway, shouted, "Lincoln is a Giant-killer," and then without waiting for a reply, went on his way.

An hour out of Springfield, I spied Josiah Riley passing by our compartment. Mr. Riley was a reporter for the *Illinois State Register*, a Democratic newspaper.

"Mr. Riley," I called out. "Would it be against your principles to come and speak to the wife of the Republican candidate?"

The reporter angled a hairless head into the compartment. "It would be impossible to refuse," he replied, "when she has a reputation for being the prettiest talker in Springfield."

Nodding to Robert, the reporter entered and perched himself upon the seat across from me. Mr. Riley was an egg-shaped man with uncommonly short legs. Only the tips of his boots touched the floor.

"You are going to Alton to write about Mr. Lincoln's speech?" I inquired.

"And that of Mr. Douglas," he reminded me.

I smiled at the newspaperman. "You would not fault a wife for attending only to her husband's words."

"On the contrary," he replied, "it is a praiseworthy trait."

"I am pleased that you feel thus," I continued, "as it is my faithful attention to Mr. Lincoln's words which prompts my speaking with you."

"Whatever the cause, I am delighted," Mr. Riley assured me. He turned to share his good breeding with Robert, but my son was preoccupied with scowling out the window.

"I have had the pleasure of reading your account of the debate at Galesburg," I said to the journalist. "For I do read you, sir, even though you *are* a Democrat."

The newspaperman bowed his acknowledgment of my compliment with such energy, I feared his egg-shaped body would topple onto the compartment floor.

"However, there is one point regarding Mr. Lincoln's position upon which I might offer revisal."

"My dear Mrs. Lincoln," said the reporter, "I would be most indebted for your revision. Accuracy is my loftiest aspiration."

"I knew you would feel thus." I reached over and touched Mr. Riley's ink-stained fingers, a gesture which caused my son to shift about in his seat. "It is evidenced by the elevated tone of your journalism."

The newspaperman attempted another of his perilous bows.

"In your commendable story of the Galesburg debate, you wrote that Mr. Lincoln's opposition to the Dred Scott decision was based upon my husband's desire to bestow full equality upon Negroes."

Mr. Riley nodded. "I believe I recall making mention of such a statement."

"Now here is where I offer my small correction," I said to him. "For it is not merely the fact that the court denied Negroes equality under the Constitution which has prompted Mr. Lincoln's opposition, but that such a decision represents the first step toward making slavery a national institution." Again I smiled at the newspaperman. "Do you see the difference, Mr. Riley?"

The reporter nodded, though with far less eagerness than he had displayed for my compliments.

"I have taken the liberty of pointing out this inaccuracy now," I continued, "as I am confident that Mr. Lincoln will once again address the matter of the Dred Scott decision in Alton, and I was certain you would not wish to make the mistake a second time."

"But…" replied Mr. Riley.

Once again I stroked his black-tipped fingers. "Moreover, I believe you to be too scrupulous a writer to wish to fall short of your loftiest aspiration."

The egg-shaped newspaperman did not seem certain what type of reply was called for. "Thank you," he mumbled, after a few moment's time.

"It is I who am indebted to you for stopping by to entertain me," I replied. "I do hope you have a pleasurable time in Alton."

Seeing that he had been dismissed, Mr. Riley stood upon his little legs.

"I look forward to reading your vigorously written – and accurate – account of the Alton debate," I told him.

"Yes," he said. "Well." And in some confusion, Mr. Riley exited the compartment.

The reporter had barely disappeared down the corridor when my son turned to me, white-lipped with rage.

"I cannot convey to you the measure of my humiliation," he told me.

"Surely it cannot exceed mine on the occasion of our last train trip together, when you deemed it necessary to fashion a fort from several pairs of my underdrawers," I said, forgetting that my son could not be coaxed out of a temper by wit.

"I was ten years of age when that occurred," he spat out. "You are nearly forty."

"If you wish to make my humiliation equal yours," I replied, "you shall accomplish it by trumpeting my age in a train filled with half the citizenry of Springfield."

Rage propelled Robert from his seat. "I merely mention your age to remind you that you are too old to pretend ignorance of social custom! And too old to play the Southern belle with newspaper reporters!"

My son had spoken with the pitilessness of one who is fifteen, and I worked to remind myself that it was his age which made him so heartless against me.

"That is a cruel observation," I told him.

"You have invited it!" he responded. "What you have done is scandal."

"What I have done," I said evenly, "is act to put an honorable man in office."

With a harsh noise I could not convince myself was anything save revulsion, Robert threw himself into his seat. "You are becoming an embarrassment," he told me.

I looked at him, a boy in a military jacket, and thought of what I might use to defend myself, the revelation which had come with Donati's Comet, and my own divided house. But I did not think that any revelation of mine would alter my son's mind. That would come only by a revelation of his own. Only by Robert seeing what I had – that his father was noble and good. And that nothing which might put him into office could be scandal.

"Watch your father at the debate," I said to my son. "Hear what it is he believes."

"That is only politics," he sneered.

"Not all of it," I told him. But Robert had already turned away, leaving me the view of his set shoulders, boy-narrow beneath the gold-braided jacket.

When we reached Alton, Robert left me to join the others of the Springfield Cadets, while I went into town by carriage. The newspaper accounts I had read did not prepare me for the atmosphere of carnival which seized Alton upon the day of this final debate. It seemed that every saloon sent out a stream of whiskey-soaked men ready to debate the question of slavery with swinging blows that rarely connected with anything more substantial than air; and at every corner the sellers of patent medicines stood upon upended crates and hawked bottles of opium and painkillers in voices made hoarse with shouting. In the side streets, marching bands, both Democrat and Republican, played competing anthems as if their candidate would win by loudness. And in the town square, cannon fire sent pigs squealing and made elderly ladies clutch their bosoms.

An open-air stage had been constructed near the town hall, flanked by a raised platform meant for local politicians and their friends. As the wife of the Republican candidate, I was allowed a seat on this platform, and from this spot I could observe the great crowds moving through the city streets, a swarming sea of black stovepipe hats and autumn bonnets topped with stuffed birds. Perhaps because it was the final debate, or perhaps because no one did not have an opinion about slavery, all of Illinois, it seemed, had turned out. I felt nervous for Mr. Lincoln, and I wished I could have waited with him, letting him breathe against my hand.

"You still appear to me the belle of Springfield," said a voice.

I turned to see Stephen Douglas standing beside my chair.

"I appear the over-plump mother of a nearly grown Springfield Cadet," I replied. "But it is chivalrous of you to claim otherwise."

"I trust you will not consider it unchivalrous of me when I am forced to reveal Mr. Lincoln's arguments as unsound," he smiled.

"And I trust you will not cease to flatter me after Mr. Lincoln has demonstrated that your own are faulty," I replied.

Mr. Douglas spoke first at Alton. He did not appear entirely well, and I recalled that his health was often uncertain. Even his booming voice had been rendered less booming by so much open-air speaking, and I could not help but worry for my old beau. In truth, it was to make a point with Elizabeth that I was happy it was Mr. Douglas my husband was running against. For myself, I would have wished it somebody else. Still, Alton was pro-slavery – not so long before, its inhabitants had murdered a newspaper editor named Elijah Lovejoy for his abolitionist leanings – and Mr. Douglas's speech was met with cheering and music.

It was the story of Elijah Lovejoy which prompted the last advice I had sent off to Mr. Lincoln before traveling to Alton. "When you speak of the moral outrage of human bondage," I had written him, "an exaggeration of your Kentucky drawl might be heard as soothing." And now that my husband stood upon the Alton stage, challenging the citizens of Illinois to determine whether they looked upon slavery as a right or a wrong, I heard the slow, rounded intonations of the South in his mouth.

I saw as well, much of my advice printed upon his body – in the nearly graceful sweep of his arm, the outward leaning of his broad shoulders. These gestures, this altering of his accent, felt to me a communication between us; an intercourse unknown by any other person in the great crowd; private as the things which occur in the marriage bed. And as I watched the hands which moved as surely as if I still held them, the mouth forming words to please me, I was made aware of how the October wind was blowing strands of my loosened hair across my mouth, and how the delicate feel of it was wonderfully tormenting.

Do not succumb too much to this, I warned myself. *For you are seated in view of all of Alton and you do not want it said that Mrs. Lincoln cannot control her desire for her husband.* I fixed, then, my fevered attention upon my husband's words, his reasoned arguments against the spread of slave-holding, and tried to recall that his charter came from God.

And indeed, my husband did seem inspired by God that day. Though the audience at Alton possessed, as Mr. Lincoln acceded, "strong sympathies with the South," when he came to define the principles of those who held slaves as "you work, you toil, you earn bread, and I will eat it," there was applause and shouted approval, and only one or two who called Mr. Lincoln "Black Republican."

When my husband finished speaking, the uproar which rose from the crowd shook the platform upon which I was seated, and it seemed that my husband had called forth a tumult which would change the course of the country. *Surely after this,* I thought, *they will see my husband's greatness and shall make him senator. Surely after this, Robert will know the rightness of his father's purpose and forgive me everything.*

(July 19) Mrs. Lincoln moved temporarily to the East side of house. She admired the new rooms very much and wished to keep them – cheerful and pleasant –
—Patient Progress Reports for Bellevue Place Sanitarium

I have been moved to the East Wing of the asylum, where are kept the most furiously mad at Bellevue Place. Most of these ladies live upon the third floor, the one above my own, but they wander about the wing so freely, I oft do not know what I shall encounter in the dark and narrow corridor outside my room. Here, I have come to know Mrs. Norris, who, when she lived in the West Wing with the saner ladies, stole a carving knife from the kitchen and used it to stab herself in the abdomen. Only her habit of wearing whalebone corseting prevented her dying. Here, I have also met Mrs. Teagarden, who has gone completely bald from a nervous disorder. This poor lady has so worried her scalp, it has become covered with sores which she cannot keep herself from scratching open.

I cannot always tell which of the ladies here are the furiously mad. Some seem, for the most part, perfectly sane. Not long after I had been moved, I encountered Mrs. Johnston, the wife of an Episcopalian minister. This lady so impressed me with her composed demeanor and neat appearance, I determined that, like myself, she had been relocated because of the repair work going on in the West Wing. I believed this until the afternoon I came upon the minister's wife standing in the corridor, her skirts lifted and a puddle forming between her shined and buttoned boots.

"Mrs. Johnston!" I cried out. "That is not suitable."

"Nothing is not suitable which comes from God," the lady replied.

"But it is unclean."

"God," the lady countered, "imposes higher duties than cleanliness."

Mrs. Matthiessen, a finely boned lady of middle years, seemed also sane to me. Her only oddity was an uncommon shyness, evidenced in the manner in which she walked about the East Wing with her head lowered and in the way she returned my greetings in the softest of voices. I had been entirely astonished one afternoon when this retiring lady without warning threw herself against the window at the end of the corridor, hurling her frail body against the bars as if she thought she might break them. It had required two attendants, Mrs. Ruggles, and a good dose of chloral hydrate poured into Mrs. Matthiessen's shrieking mouth to pull her away from the window.

It is these ladies, these ones who appear sane though they are consumed with madness, which unsettle me most. I cannot help but think that their derangement hides within them like sickness – like smallpox or consumption – waiting for an unexpected moment to show itself. And like such illnesses, I have sometimes believed that the madness of these ladies is contagious. That, like cholera, it is borne upon a miasma, ready to infect all who breathe it in.

I know that this belief is a form of madness. That lunacy can no more be caught from a madwoman than it can from the moon. Yet I have lived nearly two months in this place where ladies claim their body parts are stolen in the night, and it is becoming more difficult to know which beliefs might be considered unreasoned. Despite my logical surety that insanity cannot be contagious, I hold my breath whenever I pass Mrs. Munger on my walks, as if each time the lady shouts at her croquet ball, spores of madness float from her mouth.

Even the East Wing night attendant could be described as mad – at least by some. She is a widow of forty named Sarah Bunker, who bears the pitted scars of smallpox upon her cheeks.

"I have communicated with my dead husband," Mrs. Bunker told me the first night that she came to lock me in. "Through séance."

"Are you not afraid that admitting it will result in you being put on the other side of this lock?" I asked her.

"I have never told the matron," she said hurriedly. "Or Mrs. Patterson. I am only saying it to you because I know you have contacted your dead sons and martyred husband through mediumship."

"And you see where it has gotten me," I replied.

Minnie Judd is here in the East Wing as well. Not on the second floor where I stay. And not because the workmen were hammering outside her door. Minnie has been moved to the third floor because she will not eat.

I learned of Minnie's moving from Mrs. Patterson. As was usual, the doctor's wife and I were seated upon the damp side porch, profiting from the benefits of the mildewed air.

"Doctor Patterson has diagnosed Mrs. Judd with hysterical anorexia," Mrs. Patterson told me. "Which he attributes to her attempt to memorize the Scriptures."

"Learning Scriptures has given Mrs. Judd a mental condition?"

The doctor's wife took up a shirt from her sewing basket and began stitching a tear at its cuff. "It is well-known that too-ambitious intellectual activity is draining upon the female nervous system."

"But Mrs. Judd has ceased her learning of the Bible."

"The damage to her nerves has already been done."

I sat forward in my seat, making creak the soggy wicker. "Was it necessary to place her with the most deranged?"

Mrs. Patterson narrowed her lips. "Doctor Patterson wished Mrs. Judd placed where she might be more easily subject to Mrs. Ruggles's persuasive encouragement."

My friend is not the only food-refuser who has been placed where she might be more easily subject to Mrs. Ruggles's encouragement. The East Wing is home to a great many ladies who are starving themselves. I have seen there one lady whose unfleshed face has fallen into such deep crevices, I believed her to be approaching sixty years of age, until Mrs. Bunker informed me that she is only thirty-six. I have seen also another lady of three-and-twenty whose starvation has so eaten away at her womanly attributes, she appears a child of no more than twelve. These undernourished ladies, gaunt and brittle in their flapping clothes, spend their day rushing up and down the East Wing staircase. Indeed, they seem always in motion, as if the flesh their bodies are consuming produces more energy than food might.

As to Mrs. Ruggles's methods of encouragement, I believe I nearly got a glimpse of them upon one of my first visits to my friend. I had just arrived at Minnie's door, which, unexpectedly, was shut, and was stopped from entering by the sound of the matron's low-toned voice coming from the other side.

"You have drunk only a little of the eggnog and whiskey," Mrs. Ruggles accused, "and eaten nothing of breakfast."

"It is too much," replied Minnie. Her voice sounded muffled, as if by more than the door.

"It is no more than an egg and toast," declared Mrs. Ruggles.

"I could never consume all of it," said my friend. "I would not wish to."

I heard a scraping sound.

"If you do not eat of your own will," the matron replied. "I shall be obliged to make you eat."

"Leave the tray," Minnie told her. "And if I develop some little appetite, I shall eat something."

"I left the tray yesterday," Mrs. Ruggles reminded her. "And the day before. And it remained untouched."

The matron's voice had turned menacing. I felt through the wood of the door the vibration of Mrs. Ruggles's heavy footfall as she crossed the room.

"I cannot go to Doctor Patterson and report that you have eaten nothing," the matron continued.

I heard again the sound of scraping, and imagined Mrs. Ruggles's mannish forearms pressed against Minnie's throat, her large-knuckled hands forcing my friend's mouth to open so she could fill it with egg and toast. I pushed against the wood with enough force to send it slamming into the wall, startling Mrs. Ruggles.

I could not tell if my imagining had been correct, if the matron had truly had her arms about Minnie's throat, for before my eyes could register the scene, Mrs. Ruggles, who was holding a spoon in her hand, turned abruptly to see who had entered, leaving Minnie coughing in a chair.

"Leave the tray." I said. "Leave it, and I shall see that Mrs. Judd eats."

The matron fixed her small eyes upon me, determining, I suspect, the weight of my status as president's wife.

"I promise to report my progress to Mrs. Patterson," I continued, "when next we are together upon the porch."

Mrs. Ruggles mulled this over for some moments, like a large and slow-moving animal. At length, she let the spoon drop onto the tin tray, making a loud clatter. "I will return within a quarter of an hour," she announced. "And if you have been unpersuasive, I will resume my work." Then, casting upon Minnie a scowl which seemed full of regret, the matron lumbered from the room.

Minnie pushed away the tray and straightened her bodice, which had been pulled crooked. My friend had lost so much flesh that her elegant dress gaped at her bosom, and inches of extra fabric at her waist had to be folded and tied flat with a sash.

"I see that the influence of a First Lady does not diminish outside of Washington City," Minnie said, managing a smile.

"Perhaps I have at last found where it is most likely to be recognized."

I entered the room, which was smaller and more plain than the one in which my friend had been put before. This little chamber contained a bed, a table barely bigger than the meal tray, and the wooden chair upon which Minnie sat. There was not even room for a washstand, and her pitcher and bowl took up much of the top of a battered dresser. I wondered what had happened to the trunk with all of Minnie's lovely dresses.

"Have only a small amount of the egg and a bit of toast," I coaxed. "And I shall eat the rest for you."

Minnie put her hand over her mouth. "Do not do that, please. Or Doctor Patterson will tell my husband that I have been eating."

"Drink the eggnog then," I said. "That is not really eating."

Minnie allowed me to give her small sips of the eggnog, which by the smell contained a large quantity of whiskey. When she turned away to cough a bit upon it, I ate half her egg.

I did this once or twice more, eating bits of beef broth with egg and porridge laced with cream from the tray in Minnie's room whenever my friend's attention was elsewhere. But I do not believe the matron was tricked by this; and when only a few days had passed, I came upon Mrs. Ruggles leaving Minnie's room with a rectangular case made of mahogany wood clutched in her hands.

"What is that you have taken in to Minnie?" I asked her.

"It is the method by which we convince many of our ladies to begin eating." With a show of self-satisfaction, the matron opened the case.

The lining of the mahogany case was velvet, and upon that plush lining was a cylinder made of brass, a coiled length of tubing, and a small black object shaped like an eye.

"I do not know what this is," I said.

"It is a stomach pump," replied the matron. "The best that can be bought." With great care, she lifted out the eye-shaped object. "The mouth gag is made of pure ebony."

My throat convulsed only looking at it. "You do not intend to use this upon Mrs. Judd?"

"In most instances," Mrs. Ruggles responded, "only bringing the instrument into the room is enough to frighten a food-refuser into eating. It is apparent that Mrs. Judd requires more to force her out of her obstinacy."

I looked again into the mahogany case. I did not want to think of that ebony eye being fixed to my friend's mouth, the tubing being forced down her slender throat. Pushing past the matron, I hurried into Minnie's room.

My friend was sitting in her one chair, scratching at bits of egg yolk splattered upon the slack bodice of her dress.

"You must eat something," I said to her. "Or Mrs. Ruggles will force food into you with that terrible instrument."

Minnie gazed up at me, her face sharp with starvation. "As long as I do not consume anything of my own accord, it is of no matter."

I saw the determination in my friend's expression and turned away from it. Instead, I crossed the room and wet my handkerchief in Minnie's water basin, then took hold of her nervous fingers, pulling them away from her bodice. I wiped away the bits of egg upon her dress.

"You are my friend and I love you," I said. "But this is insanity."

"No," she told me. "It is love."

"For the reverend?"

Minnie's sunken cheeks flushed with the reference to her husband.

"You are wasting to nothingness," I said to her. "How is that love?"

She met my eyes. I saw how her own, made large by her loss of flesh, burned with the fevered rapture of a martyr.

"When Reverend Judd sees how well I can control my appetite, he will allow me back home."

I tugged upon the loose bodice of her dress. "Mrs. Patterson says you have lost forty-seven pounds. Is that not demonstration enough?"

My friend stared down at her gaping dress as if it belonged to someone else, someone larger, and had been slipped onto her without her noticing. She lapped over the spare fabric, as if gauging how much of it there was.

"It must not be," she told me. "For I am still confined."

It was after this that I began to be afraid for Minnie. For my friend brought to her starvation the single-minded purpose she had shown for her Psalms, and I feared where such resolve might take her.

When next I sat with Mrs. Patterson upon the side porch, I took up Minnie's case.

"I believe if Reverend Judd would bring his wife home," I said to the doctor's wife, "Mrs. Judd would eat."

Mrs. Patterson regarded me as if my remark were further proof of my lunacy. "Mrs. Judd is not in control of her reason," she declared. "And the reverend should not be made to live with a madwoman."

"But she is starving herself!" I said. "She will die."

"We do not allow ladies to die at Bellevue Place," Mrs. Patterson replied. "The doctor has convinced Reverend Judd to allow us to use the pump."

"He had not wished it?" I was surprised by what seemed the reverend's reluctance. For while I could not want to see the instrument used upon my friend, I also could not want to forbid any procedure which would let nourishment into her wasting body.

"I am certain it was out of Reverend Judd's great kindness," Mrs. Patterson replied.

"The pump is a painful process?"

The doctor's wife shook her head. "I am made to understand it produces nothing worse than some scraping of the throat and the lethargy of shock."

"When will this be done?" I asked, hoping it would be the next day, or the one after that, time enough for me to convince my friend to swallow just enough to save her from the instruments in Mrs. Ruggles's mahogany case.

"Tonight," replied Mrs. Patterson. "After supper."

When I left the porch, I went directly to Minnie's room and described again for her the brass pump and ebony mouthpiece, repeating what Mrs. Patterson had said about the scraping and the shock. But none of it would persuade her to eat.

"I only do not want to be alone," she told me, "when it is over."

"I shall find a way to come to you," I promised. "For the whole of the night."

All of the inmates of Bellevue Place were locked into their rooms at the coming of dark, and on the night which Minnie Judd would be fed with the stomach pump, I appealed to Sarah Bunker to leave my door unbolted. When the night attendant showed hesitation, I reminded her that the topic of the conversations she had conducted with her dead husband might be of interest to Mrs. Patterson, and she became more amenable. "Only pretend to throw the bolt," I instructed her. "And when they are finished with Mrs. Judd, knock upon my door." And shortly after nine, I heard the knock.

Waiting until Mrs. Bunker had passed out of the corridor, I slipped from my room and up the stairs to the third floor. It was quiet along the corridor's dark length, unusually so, as if the ladies who lived there had fallen into shock at what had been done to Minnie Judd. With no random shrieking or muttered gibberish to cover my noise, I crept to Minnie's door.

Minnie's little room smelled of bile and the bitter tang of sweat. A small lamp had been left burning upon the dresser, and by its faint light I saw my friend in her bed. Minnie's eyes were shut and her lips pale and peeling. Something white was crusted over the front of her nightdress. She appeared so deeply asleep, I wondered if after the matron had finished pumping supper into her, she had followed it with a dose of laudanum.

"I shall stay with you," I assured my friend, though I did not think she heard. Dragging the single chair nearer the bed, I sat upon it.

Minnie's black hair had become disheveled – how, I did not wish to dwell upon. I smoothed the knotted strands from her forehead, unsettled by the coolness of her flesh. The strange silence of the third floor remained unbroken, and I must have fallen into slumber sitting in Minnie's chair, for the next sound I heard was Mrs. Matthiessen's shrieking.

I had heard this shrieking enough to know that it came from the shy, finely boned lady. Moreover, I knew that Mrs. Matthiessen was kept in the room next to Minnie's. Her terrible screaming penetrated the wall between the chambers, filling my friend's room with the mad lady's raving. But tonight, it was not only shrieks Mrs. Matthiessen sent out into the asylum, but words as well. She called down curses upon something she did not name – her room? her mattress? herself? – wanting whatever it was to be harmed in unimaginable ways. Her tirade contained such invective, it was violence to listen to it.

Minnie did not stir. But I could barely breathe in the noise. I pressed my hands to my ears, hoping to shut it out, but Mrs. Matthiessen's shrieking cut through my very flesh.

It seemed hours before anybody came to see about the mad screaming, but perhaps it only felt so. Finally, I heard the sound of footfalls in the corridor – one set heavy enough to belong only to Mrs. Ruggles. Fearing the matron might decide to look in on Minnie and discover me, I ran to hide behind the door. But no one was anxious over the force-fed reverend's wife. Not when Mrs. Matthiessen had begun ripping something – her bed linens? her clothes? – with a savage-sounding fury.

"Give her thirty-five grains of chloral hydrate," came the matron's voice from the next room. "And make certain she swallows all of it."

I heard thumping then, as if something dense – Mrs. Matthiessen? – had been hurled against the wall. Then I heard the sound of a choked coughing.

It required a quarter of an hour for the dose of chloral – a larger amount than I had ever swallowed myself – to quiet Mrs. Matthiessen. Not until I heard the footsteps, one heavier than the others, pass down the corridor, did I return to Minnie's side. In the time I had been away, a purplish bruise with the same eye-shaped outline as the ebony gag had come up around her mouth.

Though the dosage of chloral had been large, it had not completely sedated Mrs. Matthiessen. Before an hour had gone by, she began again to shriek. I could hear the drug in her blood. Her curses came forth slurred and containing little sense, but none of it was less terrible to listen to.

The matron came quicker this time. "Give her another forty grains," she commanded. But after half an hour, Mrs. Matthiessen was still raving.

"You must have allowed her to spit some of it out," accused Mrs. Ruggles.

"There was none on her dress," came the voice of the attendant who had been made to accompany her. "Or on the floor."

"You only did not see it," said the matron. "Dose her with another thirty-five grains. And hold her still until she has drunk it."

Something thumped against the wall, very near to where I hid behind the door, and I started, as if the mad lady in the next room had come after me. Again, I heard coughing, this time a ragged sound made by an overused throat. When it ceased, there was nothing more, save the creaking of the mattress springs and the departing footsteps of Mrs. Ruggles and her assistant.

I returned to Minnie's side, wondering how much of the laudanum the matron had administered to keep her sleeping through Mrs. Matthiessen's screaming. But my friend's breathing was only a little shallow and I could see by the early light coming through the window that she was not so very pale.

I sat again beside her, hoping she might wake and know that I had come, know it before it was fully dawn and I would have to return to my room. I placed my hand upon Minnie's black hair, duller and more sparse since she had begun her starving.

Without warning there came from Mrs. Matthiessen's room a frenzied beating, a sound like fists upon the locked door, and the noise made me turn to the wall behind which she pounded, my breath caught in my throat. This sound was not like the unbroken pounding of Mrs. Wheeler – which was so constant and methodical, it had no purpose other than its own making. This was the noise made by the frantic wings of a trapped bird so filled with intention, it will break itself in an effort to escape. It was so terrible to hear, I determined to call for Mrs. Ruggles myself – no matter that she would discover me unlocked and in Minnie's room – for no punishment was worse than the sound of this beating.

I ran to the door and flung it open, intending to shout for the matron. But before I could utter a sound, the pounding stopped.

I did not like the suddenness of this stopping, and I stepped nearer Mrs. Matthiessen's bolted door, hoping to hear that lady moving about, or perhaps muttering to herself. But all was silence on the other side. I looked at the space at the bottom of the door, and noticed that none of the colorless dawn light shined through, as if something bulky lay upon the floor blocking it. The fact of this light reminded me that it was late, and one of the day attendants would be coming to unlock me.

Leaving Mrs. Matthiessen's door, I hurried back to Minnie's room, staying only long enough to place a handkerchief embroidered with my initials upon the dresser so she would know I had been there. Then making certain the corridor was empty, I hurried down the stairs to my own room.

I went to Minnie after breakfast. My friend was awake, but frail and too chafed of throat to speak. I gave her water and drank some of the broth on her tray myself, for she was too weakened to make much protest. Once I had settled her more comfortably in her bed, I went into the hallway to try Mrs. Matthiessen's door. This time, it was unlocked. However, when I pushed it open and glanced into the room, I saw nothing save a bed without linens and a dresser which held not one personal item.

Although I tried when we were together upon the side porch, I could not compel the doctor's wife to speak about Mrs. Matthiessen. Mrs. Patterson would only say that the lady had left, and would not acknowledge the suddenness of it. I knew I would learn nothing from Mrs. Ruggles, or from the attendants who were so fearful of her. I was forced to wait until just before supper for information, the time that Sarah Bunker arrived at the asylum.

"You must tell me what has happened to Mrs. Matthiessen," I said to her.

Mrs. Bunker put a chapped finger to her lips, then pulled me away from the carriage entrance where I had been waiting for her, propelling me into the kitchen. She did not speak until she had made certain that our only company was the Negro cook, a young woman who possessed a clouded, wandering eye, and that she was occupied with stirring a large cauldron.

"Mrs. Matthiessen has died," she told me in a whisper.

"I heard her shrieking and pounding at her door," I insisted. "How could she die?"

Sarah Bunker glanced again at the colored cook. "Mrs. Patterson has written in the log that it was Mrs. Matthiessen's mania which exhausted her life force."

"Her insanity killed her?"

"That is the conclusion."

"Is such a thing possible?"

The night attendant put her pocked face close to mine. "Mrs. Patterson says that it is. Though I have never known it to happen without also a substantial dose of chloral hydrate."

They have killed Mrs. Matthiessen! I thought. And it seemed then that the asylum kitchen became too filled with steam. I glanced at the colored cook to see what it was she was doing that was making it so difficult to breathe. The woman's wandering eye possessed a tendency to roam in its socket before fixing upon something only it could perceive, and now I felt that that eye had fixed upon me. It held me in place as its owner emptied a fine powder from an unlabeled box into the cauldron, making me wonder what it was she was putting into our supper.

I stood in the suffocating steam of the asylum kitchen and did not know what to fear most. That the colored cook would poison me. Or that I would believe it so. Either way, it was derangement, the contagion of lunacy infecting my own mind. A great cloud of steam rose from the cauldron, a sickness-carrying miasma made visible, and I knew that the colored cook was brewing up madness.

"Are you well?" asked Mrs. Bunker.

"It is too close for me here."

I pushed past the night attendant into the corridor. At the far end I saw the lighted windows of the door to the back porch, and I ran toward it, seeking escape. My lungs burned, seared by the steam and by the fact that I would not breathe. For it seemed to me that no matter how many times the asylum's limestone walls had been distempered with paint, they still gave off a lunatic contamination.

At last I burst through the door and into the air, breathing now, but not halting until I had reached the bench near the dark woods, the place where none of the mad ladies came.

Even if the madness of Bellevue Place is not contagious, I told myself, *your fear that it is will drive you mad. Your own terror of becoming like Mrs. Munger or Mrs. Matthiessen will turn you like them, make you shriek and pound for release upon your door, rant until Mrs. Ruggles comes with enough chloral hydrate to silence you forever.*

Writing of this now in my room in the East Wing, where I cannot hear Mrs. Wheeler but still cannot sleep, my thoughts upon the bench show me but one course. I can no longer wait to prove my sanity to Robert. For if I do, there may be no portion of it left to prove. No, I must work to find my own way out of Bellevue Place. And I must find it soon. Before I am mad. Mad, or dead.

Despite the uproar in Alton, my husband was not made senator. In November of 1858, the voting citizens of Illinois chose a Democratic legislature. The following January, they voted – by a tally of fifty-four to forty-six – to send Stephen Douglas back to the United States Senate.

We were all sorry for the loss. Mr. Lincoln required extra doses of Blue Mass for some weeks, and I was obliged to explain to my younger sons the mysteriousness of God's ways. Willie accepted the explanation with solemn nodding. Taddie, who since the night of Donati's Comet had come to view the Almighty as primarily one of his father's political supporters, was more difficult to convince; and I could not say that I found the Divine's reasoning any easier to comprehend. For his part, my eldest son did not seem so much affected, and I used for excuse his preoccupation with his education. Robert wished to go to Harvard; however, having taken and failed the entrance exam, he was first obliged to complete a year at Exeter. Nevertheless, my eldest was made excited by the prospect of an Eastern education, and in the weeks before he left for New Hampshire talked so often – and proprietarily – of his school, Taddie once asked him if he had been elected president of it.

After the election, my husband returned to his law practice. This he was compelled to do by the fact that during the months he had campaigned against Mr. Douglas, he had earned nothing, and we were now living upon our shop accounts.

"Politics is a hobby better suited to men richer than me," said Mr. Lincoln, examining the bills which filled the pigeonholes of his desk.

"Politics is not your hobby," I told him. "It is your calling."

"That's an unhappy observation," he replied, "when you consider how I keep losing."

In addition to his law practice, my husband earned income by accepting the invitations which came for him to speak at political rallies. Despite his loss, the debates had placed Mr. Lincoln in the minds of Republican gentlemen across the country, and such requests came frequently – including one which arrived in the winter of 1860, inviting him to speak at the Cooper Union in New York City.

"It would be good to give the Republicans in the East the opportunity to take your measure," I said to him.

He examined the invitation, printed upon paper more richly embossed than even Elizabeth's. "Only you could believe me capable of impressing an Easterner."

Notwithstanding his doubts about impressing Easterners, my husband appeared determined to try. I discovered scraps of his speech tucked beneath his dinner plate and wound into his bedclothes, papers covered with sentences which seemed to me both reasoned and poetical, but through which he had drawn lines. We stayed awake late together, working upon gesture and intonation; and I dedicated so many hours to coaxing my husband to imitate the Yankee accent of Mr. Douglas, he was at last compelled to inform me that, "Unless you are capable of altering my place of birth – an accomplishment I would not entirely rule beyond your powers – this is as Northern as I'm going to sound."

To ease the expenses of the journey, not all of which were covered by the New York Republicans, Mr. Lincoln accepted invitations to speak in a number of Eastern cities, including Exeter, New Hampshire. The day I learned of this, I took myself to Woods & Henckle, the same shop from which Ninian purchased his clothing. I did not bring Mr. Lincoln with me, for I knew he would not readily stand still for measuring; and I did not believe he would approve the purchase of a hundred-dollar suit, even for political reasons. Instead, I brought the tailors the least ill-fitting of my husband's clothes and had them make up the suit from these, explaining where the length might be too short or the closing too wide.

"This suit is so fine," declared Mr. Lincoln, when I fitted him into it, "I expect it cost me more than fifty dollars."

"Not very much more," I replied.

In truth, even a hundred-dollar suit could not turn my husband's gangling limbs graceful, and as I observed him in the glass, wishing I had been a little clearer with Woods & Henckle about the length of the trousers, I prayed that rather than the inadequacy of the suit, Robert – and the New York Republicans – would see instead Mr. Lincoln's goodness and intelligence of mind.

The morning of Mr. Lincoln's departure, I presented him with a large bottle of Macassar oil and instructions upon disciplining his hair. After he left for the train station, there was nothing more for me to do save fret about the suit, and wonder whether I had sufficiently made the point that sophisticated Yankees rarely say "reckon."

First word of how my husband's speech was received came by way of his own telegram. "Talk went tolerably well," he wrote to me. "I don't believe I embarrassed myself more than once or twice." This assessment ruined my sleep and sent me out early next morning for the New York newspapers, which came down on the train from Chicago. These I read at the depot, despite the icy wind which blew off the prairie, for what was in them was warming.

"Mr. Lincoln is one of Nature's great orators," was the opinion of the *New York Tribune*. "He possesses rare powers," declared the *New York Evening Post*.

After I had read them all, I went to the telegraph office and sent a message to my son. "Did you read of your father's appearance at the Cooper Union?" I asked him. "Did you know that four Eastern newspapers have printed the text of his speech?" And I hoped that by this information Robert would know what to feel.

A week later, the newspapers from New Hampshire hailed Mr. Lincoln as "the greatest man since Saint Paul." My husband wrote to me only about Robert's academy. "They've got some mighty cultivated boys in the East," he declared. "And every one of them has got a nicer suit than I."

When Robert's letter came, I read it over several times, as if I believed I would discover something more among the neatly penned lines, the way that looking harder at a complicated painting uncovers new meaning. But I could find no meaning beyond what Robert had stated upon the page, and nothing of what appeared there was about his father.

The speech at the Cooper Union put Mr. Lincoln more in the notice of those Republican gentlemen who were just then contemplating who might best represent the party in the presidential election which would take place in the fall. Of course, Mr. Lincoln was not the only man to gain the Republican gentlemen's notice. Indeed, at the start of the spring, only some weeks before the nominating convention, *Harper's Weekly* published an illustration of eleven possible candidates.

In the journal, the gentlemen had been drawn all together upon one page, surrounded by inked scrollwork and laurel leaves. William Seward, the current governor of New York, and the front-runner, occupied the center position, and was the only candidate to be drawn all the way to his shoulders. Mr. Lincoln's illustration – which looked little like him – was at the bottom left. Upon the page following, my husband's biography was listed last. It informed readers that Mr. Lincoln was "intimately acquainted with the industrial classes," which made it sound as if our house was filled day and night with ironwrights and stevedores.

Being so little known, my husband was aware that he would not be the first choice of very many of the delegates. However, with so many possible candidates, it was likely that no one would capture enough votes to be nominated, and the gentlemen would have to turn to a compromise candidate. Thus, Mr. Lincoln determined to be the second choice of as many of them as possible.

"But to do that," I protested, "you must give offense to no one."

"That is why from now until the convention, I intend to express no actual opinions."

A month before the convention, Judge David Davis arrived in our parlor to show us the image of Mr. Lincoln which the Republican gentlemen of Illinois believed would win the nomination – the gentlemen possessing little confidence in the electability of one "intimately acquainted with the industrial classes." At no less than three hundred pounds, Judge Davis seemed more a structure designed by man – a moveable wall or immense battleship – than a breathing being made by God. His body gave the impression of no shape, only mass; his limbs were thick and round, and his eyes were squeezed by the flesh of his cheeks into half-moons. Only to have him in my parlor turned my upholstered chairs and triple-cushioned settee into furniture meant for children; and upon this night the impression of the judge's largeness was made more so by the enormous banner furled in his arms.

"This is the standard we shall carry with us into the convention," the judge declared, when all of us – even Willie and Tad – were assembled in the parlor. "Upon it is painted the Abraham Lincoln who will rouse into action the voting gentlemen of the Republican Party."

"That must be some considerable piece of portraiture," said my husband.

"Behold!" cried the judge. With a snap of his swelled-looking arms, he unfurled the banner. A corner of it knocked against a table leg, topping a figurine of a shepherdess. "Abe Lincoln, the Railsplitter Candidate!"

Upon the length of canvas was painted a portrait of my husband which was at least his own size, perhaps larger. At his feet was a stack of wooden rails, and in his hand was a rail-splitting mallet, which he held high above his head. In order, I supposed, to facilitate this arduous labor, Mr. Lincoln's shirt was shown unbuttoned nearly to his waist, revealing a scandalous expanse of inaccurately portrayed hairless chest.

Once they had taken in this depiction of their father, Willie and Tad fell down laughing.

"There is the matter," said my husband to Judge Davis, "that I have never willingly split a rail in my life."

"Such scrupulous honesty has no place in a political campaign," I declared. "Especially as the country's voters are partial to a candidate who can be proved to be a man of the people."

I imagined that the judge would make some agreement, for certainly this was what the Republican gentlemen had been thinking when they fashioned this image for my husband. But Judge Davis said nothing; and it seemed, even to myself, that I had not spoken.

"You *have* split rails?" the judge asked Mr. Lincoln.

"I've mauled a few," he answered.

"Then there is no falsehood in the banner."

"Except for his chest," Taddie pointed out.

The judge also did not acknowledge this.

The morning the Republicans would choose a candidate, I woke at dawn. The sky outside my window was as pink as the blooms upon Mrs. Dubois's plum tree next door, and the air was thick with song from birds half-crazed with spring. My sleeping had been filled with strange dreams, caused, I expected, by the muslin bag holding a chicken claw which lay beneath my pillow, a charm of good fortune bought from Elizabeth's slave Ophelia, who was known – by all, save by my sister – to deal in conjure. In some of my dreams, Mr. Lincoln had received the nomination; and in some of them, he had not. And I did not know which I might call prophetic.

I rose from my bed and went looking for my husband. Although Mr. Lincoln had wished to attend the convention, he had been talked away from it; for it would have looked unseemly for him to appear to want the position too badly, it being believed that elected office was an honor bestowed by the people upon a politician who possessed no self-interest. Despite the early hour, I did not find my husband in his bedroom, nor in the kitchen, and I guessed that he had gone to wait for news at the offices of the *Illinois State Journal*, where they had just acquired a telegraph machine.

To keep from thinking too hard upon my hopes, I fixed Willie and Tad waffles and porridge and platters of cured bacon, a breakfast bigger than the one we ate at Christmas; then I scrubbed every inch of my kitchen so it looked as if no one had eaten in it for weeks. Afterward, I undertook tasks which Miss Beecher prescribed attending to once a week – scouring the oil lamp chimneys and polishing the picture glass with whiting and silk – and which I had not approached for months. But after an hour, I left off sweeping or scrubbing and went to find my sons, so I might touch their heads for luck – a superstition I invented, but which felt no less powerful for it.

"Is something not right with my hair?" Willie asked me.

"No," I told him. "It is perfect." Then I placed my lips upon the smooth strands at the top of his head, for that felt lucky as well.

As the morning wore on, I began projects, and forgetting them, started others, all the while forming prayers which were more political than pious.

At shortly after two, every church bell in Springfield began to ring. Dropping my lye-soaked rag, I ran outside to listen. The sound of the bells was dazzling, too dazzling to be coming from the clapboard and brick churches of the city. Rather, it seemed that this bright ringing issued from the blossoming trees, the sweetened spring air, from the very heavens.

This means he has won the nomination! For only that and the Second Coming would prompt all the churches to ring their bells at once. And indeed, would not the eventual election of such a man as president be a Second Coming for the country? I smiled at my blasphemy. *You think too much of your husband,* I told myself. But I did not truly believe it so.

Willie and Tad ran to the offices of the *Illinois State Journal* to find their father, but I was dressed in my housekeeping clothes and knew that my husband would be surrounded by well-wishers, and by gentlemen who were already thinking of the political favors Mr. Lincoln might be able to grant them. *I shall scrub out the stove,* I thought. *That will use up a good portion of time, and by then he may be back.* And wrapping my head in a rag, I got out the pearl ash and set to work.

"It's lucky I didn't bring home any newspapermen interested in seeing how the wife of the Republican candidate comports herself in a life of comfort and ease."

Looking up from a blackened cooking ring, I saw that my husband stood in the doorway.

"Did no one come to congratulate you?" I asked, unable to imagine that was true.

"They came," he assured me. "So many I had to fight my way down the stairs of the *Journal* offices."

"Then why are you here?"

"I wanted to bring you the news myself."

I left the stove then and went into his arms, though I smelled of grease and he of the sweat of worry. *They have put this man breathing against my heart up for president,* I said to myself. *And proved that I was never wrong about him.*

"The Republicans have done a good and noble thing," I told him.

The exhalation, deep as a sigh, left his body as if it were the last one. "Let us pray that none of us regrets it."

It took little time for the newspapermen with which my husband had threatened me to descend upon our house. Once Mr. Lincoln's nomination was made public, reporters from as far distant as Baltimore and New York arrived at our door – sometimes as many as five or six a day. They came seeking my husband, but as he was so often shut up with Judge Davis and the other political gentlemen, I invited them into the family sitting room, and even into the kitchen for refreshments, for newspapermen, it appeared, were always eager for refreshments.

Without Mr. Lincoln to write about, the reporters turned their pens to me. Inside of a week, a New York paper had declared me a "sparkling talker," while one out of Pennsylvania claimed that I "conversed with freedom and grace, and was much accomplished." A Massachusetts daily passed this judgment upon me, "Without doubt," it announced, "Mrs. Lincoln is a true type of the American lady."

"Ladies should not be written about in newspapers unless they are dead," Elizabeth reminded me the day that I carried these stories up to her big house.

"I cannot help it if the newspapermen wish to practice their literary skills upon me," I told her. "Moreover, I am beginning to believe that the rules regarding the proper behavior of ladies do not entirely apply to political wives."

Over time, I noticed that the newspapers in Kentucky and Baltimore made much of my Southerness, while those in New York and Boston always mentioned that I spoke French. This regional peculiarity gave me the notion that I might accomplish more in my kitchen than keeping the newspapermen fed. A notion which I presented to my husband and Judge Davis one night, after I had taken into the parlor the tongue sandwiches with which the judge was partial to ending his evenings at our house.

"Do you not think stories of my upbringing with a colored mammy might reassure Southern voters who believe Mr. Lincoln too much against the practice of human bondage?" I suggested. "While descriptions of my European education would ease the minds of Easterners who find 'Abe Lincoln, the Railsplitter' somewhat too rustic?"

My husband, who as usual was seated in his rocker, glanced at Judge Davis. The judge bit into his sandwich, sending crumbs tumbling down his mountainous front onto my carpet.

"Perhaps," I continued, directing my words toward Judge Davis's bulk, "there would be some advantage in encouraging *all* the newspapermen to speak with me, not just those who are hungry."

The judge finished chewing before answering. "There would be no advantage at all."

"You do not think a wife might influence a voter's estimation of a candidate?"

He shook his fleshy head. "I do not think a wife possesses any influence."

"That's because you don't live at my house," replied Mr. Lincoln.

But I would not let my husband's joking give Judge Davis opportunity to dismiss me. "You see no political worth in what the newspapers write about me?" I said to him.

"I do not," replied the judge. "Moreover, I do not approve of women putting themselves forward in any way."

The rebuke sent me from my chair, my limbs quivering with an anger I did not want to show before the judge.

"No one wishes Mr. Lincoln to become president more than I," I declared. "So it would be advisable to cease treating me as if I were a Democrat."

The judge made no reply to this, only fixed upon me eyes which were opaque with loathing. I turned away from them.

"What is your opinion?" I said to my husband.

Mr. Lincoln sat back in his rocker and addressed the judge. "I don't guess you want to discount the value of a wife who believes the worst insult is to be called a Democrat," he said.

Later, as I stood in the kitchen washing the plate which had been emptied of tongue, I determined that I would continue talking to the newspapermen, telling each what he most wanted to hear. Then I thought upon my husband's defense of me, and while I was happy to know that he did not agree with Judge Davis about the valuelessness of wives, I would have been happier if it had not been so lightly done.

The August before the presidential election, the Republican Party held a great rally in Springfield. The day of the event was one of terrific heat, as if the considerable number of people who had gathered in the town – some said four times the city's population – had raised the temperature only by their breath and their excitement. Out at the fairgrounds, where there were to be speeches and drinking, entire steers had been set to roasting in pits dug into the earth; and near the courthouse, parade carriages decorated with bunting and banners were gathering, including a flower-draped wagon which would carry thirty-three unmarried ladies dressed in white, representing all the states of the Union. "There are so many marching bands and carriages," declared Taddie, who had spent the morning running to and from the fairgrounds, "they say it will take eight hours just to pass by our house."

A photographer had come down from Chicago and persuaded Mrs. Dean, whose house stood across from ours, to permit him to set up his daguerreotype equipment at her second-floor window. Knowing that daguerreotypist's image would likely appear in the country's newspapers, I chose for the occasion a deep blue silk dress with full sleeves, which I believed projected the proper balance of Southern sympathy and Eastern refinement. It had been no simple matter to devise an ensemble which displayed such political acuity, and though the silk was heavy and the neck high, I could not consider setting it aside only because the thermometer told the temperature to be over ninety.

The singing began an hour before the parade was due – the party anthem, "Ain't You Glad You Joined the Republicans," and another song which began, "Old Abe Lincoln came out of the wilderness." This last made it sound as if my husband had been raised by wolves, and to counter that impression, I intended to wear a bonnet of white Cluny lace, which, if not precisely from Paris, was very much in the Parisian style.

Although I was ready hours early, I did not want to miss a single dog cart or band of Mexican War soldiers, and I hurried down the stairs, thinking I would go to the fence and look out for the parade. However, when I reached the foyer, my way was blocked by the mammoth figure of Judge Davis.

"I have removed your doors from their hinges," he said, when he spotted me.

And indeed, the doors which normally hung over the front entrance were now lying upon the floor of the parlor, their rusted hinges resting against the wallpaper.

"Was that required?" I asked him.

"There are a good many friends of the party we wish to have stand with Mr. Lincoln," he replied.

"I hope you have left a place for me." I delivered the remark lightly, the way a Southern lady does when seeking a compliment and certain of finding one.

Judge Davis squinted his flesh-compressed eyes at my dress and bonnet, too hot for the day and too formal for the house. "You were not thinking to stand in the doorway?"

"It is my house," I reminded him. "Despite the fact that you have gone removing the doors."

"This is a political rally, Mrs. Lincoln," he informed me. "Not a strawberry party."

As he uttered this remark, the judge seemed to swell, and I suddenly had the impression that he was becoming more massive, and that his enormity would begin to overfill my house, crowding me into smaller portions of it.

"I know you do not acknowledge the political value of wives," I said to Judge Davis. "But there is only good to be gained by letting me stand with my husband."

"What is that you are saying?" My eldest son stood at the bottom of the steps.

Robert was only lately returned from his year at Exeter, and I was happy he was home; although he had acquired a set of Eastern manners which made it seem we were being visited by a well-bred stranger, a distant relation who had never entirely approved of us.

"I am only making the point that it might improve your father's political chances if I stood in the doorway with him."

Judge Davis shifted his bulk impatiently. "What would most

improve Mr. Lincoln's political chances," he replied, "would be for him to stand surrounded by prominent Republicans – particularly those who would take affront at not being included."

"But it is a large entryway," I told him, "especially now that the doors have been removed."

"I think it would be better if you listened to the judge," said my son.

I turned toward Robert, intending to explain to him my conjecture about the newspapers, but was struck into speechlessness by what I saw upon his face, for there in my eldest son's eyes was the same opacity of dislike I had encountered in those of Judge Davis.

There exists still the Chicago photographer's daguerreotype of that day, the one made from Mrs. Dean's second floor. Mr. Lincoln is standing in the doorway in a white suit, towering over the throng of gentlemen who appear to press upon him, as he gazes upon the wagon of white-dressed ladies representing the Union. Taddie is watching from an upper-storey window, leaning too far out over the sill. Willie, dressed in a nightshirt, for he was recovering from an episode of scarlet fever at the time, watches also from the second floor. Robert is nowhere in the picture.

If one looks closely, I can be spotted at the corner of a ground-floor window. A figure in a dark dress wearing a bonnet of Cluny lace inside her house.

As Election Day drew near, we had reason to believe that Mr. Lincoln's chances were good. The Democrats, who could not agree upon the issue of slavery, had split their party and nominated two candidates: Stephen Douglas, who did not like the practice but would not stand in its way, and a Kentuckian, John Breckinridge, who possessed no objection to seeing it spread. Meantime, Mr. Lincoln had been so careful to express no opinion upon any subject, voting gentlemen of all convictions could find little for which to dislike him. Nevertheless, during that October, I visited Ophelia and obtained a fresh chicken claw, for I knew that the minds of voting gentlemen tended toward unpredictability.

On the eve of the election, I left Mr. Lincoln at the offices of the *Illinois State Journal*, where he and a great crowd of other gentlemen waited for the results of the balloting to come through the telegraph machine. It was my plan to distract myself with a novel which contained a good deal of romance, although I do not expect that even the actual experience would have distracted me. Indeed, the heroine's turbulent passion was no match for the electoral process, and as I lay upon my bed, I found I was reading the same highly strung paragraph three and four times over.

All I had believed about myself and my future was riding upon this night. Mr. Lincoln had already lost two times. If this became three, it was impossible to imagine he could be made to try again. And what of afterward? Would the hypochondriasis overtake him? Would I be forced to feed him so much of the Blue Mass he would never cease shaking?

Do not think of him losing, I told myself. *It is unlucky.* And then it felt equally unlucky to be reading a novel of such arguable wholesomeness, and I cast the book aside and took up the Bible, praying to the Almighty to make my husband president.

Again the news was told by the ringing of church bells – a pealing so bright and unbounded, it seemed in the darkness even more that it was God's music.

He has won! I let the Scriptures fall from my hands.

Then in counterpoint to the bells, I heard my husband's footfall upon the plank sidewalk outside our house, heard him shouting into the darkness of the slumbering neighborhood. "We are elected!" he cried out. And that, too, was God's music.

As Mr. Lincoln was so little known to the country which had elected him, it was decided he would travel to his inauguration by special train, which would journey through Ohio and Indiana, Pennsylvania and New York. Along the way, the presidential train would stop in the bigger cities, so the population would, as my husband phrased it, "have opportunity to observe my interesting countenance."

I wished very much to be upon this train; however, Judge Davis had little difficulty persuading my husband that such a plan was too unsafe. From almost the day Mr. Lincoln was elected, threats against his life began to arrive at our house, letters containing rough drawings of skull and crossbones, angry scrawlings condemning my husband to Hell. Those who feared that Mr. Lincoln would remove their slaves, or those who believed he would give the Negro the vote, sent daily missives promising assassination in a hundred different ways, from gunshot to knifing to poisoning by spiders. Not all of these threats came by letter, or addressed to my husband. A package with Taddie's name upon it contained a monstrously made rag doll of a colored man choked by a noose. One which came for me was revealed to be a portrait in oil of Mr. Lincoln's death-limp body hanging from a rope, his feet and wrists bound in shackles, a blackened tongue lolling hideously from his mouth. In the weeks before the inauguration, we received so many letters which threatened to explode Mr. Lincoln's train, the country's finest detective, Allan Pinkerton, determined to station flagmen along the track at every half mile.

Although I was kept off the train, Judge Davis permitted Robert to be on it, as my eldest son was "nearly a man." Thus, in the early morning of February eleventh, 1861, when Mr. Lincoln's train left Springfield for Washington City, I remained behind with my younger sons. The train had not been gone many hours when I received a telegram from General Winfield Scott, my husband's newly appointed Secretary of War. "*I believe the president-elect would be in less danger in the company of his family,*" the general had written. "*For no Southerner, no matter how strongly in favor of secession, would be unchivalrous enough to murder a man before his wife and children.*" I promised my sons a half-dime each if they could get their trunks packed within an hour, and we caught up with the presidential train the following morning in Indianapolis.

My husband appeared pleased to have me aboard the train. "If General Scott believes that your presence will preserve me from death by high-minded assassins," he said, "then I am happy to have you here."

Judge Davis declared the general an old fool.

The train carrying us to Washington City was made up of three cars: one at the back, which was designated for Mr. Lincoln and his family; a middle car reserved for the various political gentlemen who rode with us between cities; and one which was placed just behind the cinders and steam of the engine where the newspapermen were kept. Each of these railroad cars, inside and out, were decorated with red-white-and-blue bunting, and so many flags had been attached to the backs of the seats and set above the windows, it was impossible to walk a single aisle without committing the unpatriotic act of stepping upon one.

It was to be a journey of twelve days, over eighteen railroads, and for the first portion of it, we moved slowly through Indiana and then into Ohio. The weather was frigid, even for February, and the day we approached the small Ohio town of Loveland, a covering of ice had crept up the window glass. Despite the cold, for as much as half a mile from the station, the railroad track was lined six and seven deep with people who had come to see the new president, some wrapped in so many woolen blankets, they resembled Plains Indians. As we passed, the men and women along the track cheered Mr. Lincoln's train, their breath making puffs of steam, as if in imitation of our locomotive.

When we arrived at the station, Mr. Lincoln went out to the platform at the back of the train to greet the crowd. Through my iced-over window, I watched him wave and nod to them, and when he spoke, I imagined that, as he had done at other stops, he flattered Loveland's ladies upon their attractiveness and congratulated its men upon their patriotism. Mr. Lincoln remained outside only long enough to hear the Loveland Republican Marching Band, shivering behind their instruments, perform one tune, and to give all opportunity to admire his new whiskers, before he hurried back into the warmth of the railroad car.

Once he was inside, a cry went up from the crowd.

"Where's Mrs. Abe? Give us the Old Lady!"

To be called by so many people made me less brave, and I hid behind the covering of ice over my window. But the crowd did not cease their calling.

"What should I do?" I said to my husband.

"Stand up and show them you're not so very old."

I rose from my seat and stood before the little window.

"We want to see her!" shouted the crowd.

"I don't think they'll be satisfied until you go out on the platform," Mr. Lincoln told me.

"I could not do such a thing," I said to him, recalling that Judge Davis was upon the train, that Robert was there.

"I believe they have stood too long in the cold to deprive them." And taking hold of my arm, my husband pulled me toward the door at the back of the compartment.

He stopped only long enough to wrap me in a heavy woolen cloak, then opened the door, letting in a chill wind which blew through the car, and led me out onto the bunting-draped platform.

The cold was a shock, as was the sight of upturned faces

stretching as far as I could see. The crowd was so great it looked as if the prairie had disappeared beneath a flooding of human beings. At the first glimpse of me shaking in my unfastened cloak – as much, I believe, from fear as from the frigid air – the crowd sent up a cheering which trembled the platform beneath my feet.

"Hooray for Mrs. Abe!" they shouted.

"Wave and smile, and don't say anything about secession," instructed Mr. Lincoln.

But the advice was unnecessary, as I was already doing what he asked. Moreover, despite the wind which blew bits of ice into my face, I had ceased to shake, for I no longer felt cold, or afraid. Indeed, as I gazed upon the steam-breathing faces of the crowd, all of them turned up to me, I felt full of a suffusing warmth.

In the towns of Milford and Xenia the people called for me and I went out. In Columbus, the Republican Ladies Club presented me with a bouquet of winter roses. In Poughkeepsie, I was greeted by cannon fire. In Buffalo, I was cheered for so long, my uncovered fingers grew numb waiting for the sound to stop, although I did not notice this until I had come back inside and they began to burn.

The newspapermen in the first car reported upon my every appearance, writing that "the gracious Mrs. President Lincoln braved a dangerous chill in order to greet admirers," and referring to me – without any irony I could discover – as the "Illinois Queen." Halfway through our journey, an English newspaperman gave me the title of "First Lady," and before long all of the reporters were referring to me in this way.

I relished the name, and took to calling myself by it, prefacing all my opinions with the phrase "as First Lady." To my ears, the title sounded as legitimate as Secretary of State, or of War. It described a position which carried standing and influence, which was nearer to the president than any gentleman of the cabinet might come. I was First Lady and would have a role in my husband's government. And as our train drew closer to Washington City, I did not doubt this would be true.

On March fourth, 1861, my husband was sworn into office beneath the watchful gaze of sharpshooters, who had been stationed upon the rooftops by General Scott. His inaugural address was delivered to a crowd shipped in from the North – Washington City being more full of secessionists than otherwise. In that speech, Mr. Lincoln assured the Southern states that "we must not be enemies" and spoke of "the better angels of our nature." I sat upon the platform in the cold March wind, eyeing the sharpshooters and praying that those better angels would prevent anyone in the crowd from requiring them to fire.

During the ten days we had been in Washington City, we had been living at the Willard Hotel – an opulent place of thick carpets and hand-brocaded chairs, where we had run up a bill of nearly eight hundred dollars, an amount we would not possess funds to pay until Mr. Lincoln received a presidential paycheck. As soon as the inauguration was concluded, we returned there for our trunks, and then took carriages to the President's House.

Mr. Lincoln went immediately to the second-floor office which would be his own, and while Willie and Tad ran up and down the marble hallways, startling the servants, who were unused to children, I took stock of our new home. The first floor consisted mainly of reception rooms – the State Dining Room, the Crimson and Blue Rooms, and the enormous East Room, which ran the entire length of the house. We would live mostly upon the second floor. I chose for my husband the most southern-facing bedroom, which possessed its own dressing room, in the hope he might come to see dressing as an activity requiring some amount of conscious thought. I took for myself the adjacent bedroom, as it connected onto his by private entry, thus preventing the possibility I would be caught in some state of undress in the more-public corridor. Willie and Tad I put in a bedroom across from my own. The nicest of the guest bedrooms I reserved for Robert, as encouragement for him to visit us during his breaks from Harvard.

The condition of the house had improved little since I had visited it during the time of President Polk. Mr. Pierce, who had come after him, had installed hot-air heating, although it only warmed you if you stood in its blast; and then it also parched your throat. Mr. Buchanan, who had lived here before us, had fitted the bedrooms with sinks intended to be fed by water from the Potomac. However, the former president had not gotten round to having the pipes put in, so they only sat there trapping spiders. Indeed, the sink in my own bedroom contained one of tropical proportion, and I stood before it, contemplating its abolishment, when Taddie ran past, brandishing what appeared to be the carved oak leg of a footstool.

"Where did you discover that?" I asked.

"I only sat upon the thing," he told me. "I swear it."

Taking the leg from him, I saw that this was likely true, as the wood at the top was wormy.

When I asked about the poor upkeep of the house, Mr. Nicolay, my husband's secretary, informed me that every president received a twenty-thousand-dollar appropriation to spend upon the upkeep of the house. Mr. Nicolay was a Bavarian gentleman whose sharply pointed beard told him as European before his accent did. "Thus far," said the secretary, "I am unable to discover what they have done with it."

"Whatever it was," I told him, "they have not spent it on footstools or furnishings. For what is here looks to have been brought in by the *first* president."

My first day's inspection revealed that all of the bedsteads were splintered at the legs and cracked in the headboard, mice had nested in the cushions of the sofas, and something with sharp teeth had nibbled at the baseboards. The ceilings were sooty, the draperies full of moths' wings, and there was evidence of rats in the pantry. Moreover, souvenir hunters, believing that, as the country was a democracy, the President's House was as much theirs as the president's, had snipped tassels from the footstools and swatches from the curtains, so that nothing had been left whole.

The deteriorating condition of the house seemed metaphor for the country. By the time of my husband's inauguration, seven states – South Carolina, Florida, Mississippi, Alabama, Georgia, Louisiana, and Texas – had seceded from the Union, and four more were threatening to join the new Confederate States. Everyone in Washington City seemed certain there would be a civil war. Even the shops on Pennsylvania Avenue, which generally noticed nothing save the latest fashions from New York and Paris, displayed in their windows gilt-lettered signs which proclaimed, "The Union is in danger, but you may save it by buying at our store!"

But no matter how many bonnets or shawls the ladies of Washington City purchased, it seemed inevitable that war would come, and that it would come over Fort Sumter. In the days before Mr. Lincoln's inauguration, rebels in South Carolina surrounded the island fort, trapping the Union soldiers inside. Now the rebels were threatening to fire upon any ship attempting to bring in supplies, leaving my husband little option. If he sent food and water to the Union soldiers, it would mean war. If he did not, the men at Sumter would eventually be forced to surrender or starve.

Each gentleman in my husband's cabinet held his own opinion regarding the course of action the president should take. For long hours each day, these gentlemen stayed locked in Mr. Lincoln's office, each working to persuade him to adopt his own plan. Passing by, I heard them arguing in loud and rancorous tones, and only occasionally would I catch the soft voice of my husband.

Mr. Lincoln made no decision swiftly. And as the weeks passed without any action taken upon Sumter, the newspapers had much to say about my husband's indecisiveness. "The president is abandoning our brave Union forces to the traitorous rebels," declared the papers in the North. While those in the South argued, "He is keeping by force a state which, following the worthy example of the Country's Forefathers, has declared its independence from the Union." The papers agreed only upon one thing: no one believed Mr. Lincoln competent to run the country.

I worried for my husband, and began to fear that the situation over Sumter would accomplish what those who had sent him the letters decorated with skull and crossbones had not. Mr. Lincoln looked sick and worn, and he did not eat, losing flesh where there was none to spare, until I could not find a soft place upon him. One morning, he rose from the breakfast table and quietly fell to the carpet. He had gone down so silently, almost gracefully, that I thought at first he had only stooped to retrieve something dropped. Only when he did not rise again, did I know he had fainted dead away. I had never known my husband to swoon, and the sight of his limp body upon the floor, his homely face slack in unconsciousness, chilled me the way no woman's faint had ever done.

I wished that I might help my husband. For while I knew little about military strategy, I knew much about men's ambition, and it seemed that if Mr. Lincoln would describe for me the plan of each of the gentlemen of his cabinet, I might help him discover which course served the country more and the politician less. However, my husband rarely left his office, save to sleep, and even First Ladies were not welcome at cabinet meetings.

Indeed, it began to appear to me that First Ladies possessed no actual function, beyond abolishing spiders and attempting to keep the furniture upright. Thus, when it became time to arrange the State Dinner which would be given for Mr. Lincoln's cabinet, as well as other distinguished guests – chosen by a protocol which only Mr. Nicolay understood, I threw myself into the planning of the affair as if the Sumter situation might be resolved by whether we began with mock turtle soup or curried crab.

Fortunately, the fate of Sumter did not rest upon the condition of the house, as there was little I could do to improve it in the time before the dinner, save hire an army of domestics to attack the public rooms with lye and distemper. Once the carpet in the dining room had been cleaned, I observed that a large section of it was water-stained, and arranged for the Marine Band, which boasted many members, to stand upon the spot and play for the entirety of the dinner. I thought to divert the ladies' notice by having made for myself a gown of such elegance and style, it would call attention away from the chipped china and termite-eaten chairs. To accomplish this, I engaged the services of Washington City's most highly regarded mantua-maker – a mulatto seamstress named Elizabeth Keckly.

Mrs. Keckly had skin the color of butternut-dyed wool and strong teeth, which she rarely showed. Despite having been born a slave, the mulatto dressmaker could readily have been termed a lady, as her former master – who had also been her father – had seen to it that she be taught to read and make her letters; and her years spent sewing dresses for the ladies of the Southern aristocracy had given her a speech and manner as refined as that of any Virginia-bred belle. Mrs. Keckly had made dresses for the South's most distinguished ladies, including the wife of Jefferson Davis, the recently chosen president of the Confederacy, and it was through her needle that she had bought her freedom.

I had few friends in Washington City; for society there was dictated by Southern ladies, and their belief that my husband intended to steal away their house slaves made them reluctant to invite me to teas and afternoons of shopping. I looked forward to my fittings with Mrs. Keckly, who was a widow and near my own age, and the dressmaker spent long afternoons in my room, draping me in shimmering fabrics, as we talked of the South and how it was to be raised there. After we had known each other longer, we spoke also of our regret over its practice of human bondage, and upon these afternoons, I would have, at parting, embraced her if I believed she would have tolerated it.

The dress Mrs. Keckly made for me was a success, with a wide skirt fashioned from changeable silk and a bodice trimmed in swansdown. The night of the State Dinner, I dressed in it early, then went to my husband's room to see if he had made himself ready; for I had heard him go in some time ago, but had detected little else afterward.

I found Mr. Lincoln dressed in the clothes I had laid out for him – except for his white gloves, which he always put on at the last moment, as he did not like how they made his hands appear overlarge. However, rather than standing before the glass, or sitting in a chair reading, my husband was lying upon the bed in a state so like the death-impersonation of hypochondriasis, my flesh contracted beneath the cool silk of my dress.

"I have had to send a ship with provisions to Fort Sumter," he muttered.

I did not like the dullness of his voice and came nearer the bed, noticing how it was too small for his height, and how his boots pressed against the termite-weakened footboard.

"Do you believe the rebels will try to stop it?" I asked him.

"It is what they have been waiting for." He studied his ungloved hands. "I don't know if I have done right."

"If you had not sent the ship, hunger would have forced the surrender of the fort."

"I could not let that happen," he said, his face altered by a dark determination. "If we lose Sumter, we lose the Union."

"Then you have done right," I told him, cursing the rebels who had wanted war.

I cannot recall whether the dinner began with the mock turtle soup or the crab, or if it seemed that the ladies concentrated more upon Mrs. Keckly's dress than the battered china. I do remember that the Marine Band stood upon the water stain and played patriotic tunes more suited to marching than eating, and that they played too loudly for a dining room. I remember also that I was happy for the loudness, as it kept me from having to invent any conversation, for my thoughts were too much upon this war the country would have with itself. I feared for my half-brothers, particularly for Aleck, now grown enough to fight for the other side. I feared, too, for Robert, too near of age and too duty-bound to remain long out of war. *Would these two boys who had passed a Kentucky summer together now take up arms against the other? Would they be killed and the war come looking for my younger sons?*

These questions repeated themselves with the measured regularity of the Marine Band's marches, and I am certain that if the band had not played so loudly, and if I were not First Lady and constrained by obligation, I would have risen from the table and told my guests, "The ship which will start war is already on its way to the South, and now we will begin to kill each other. Leave here. Go home and pray. Pray to the Almighty for men to give up their inclination to violence."

As soon as news of the war became known, Southerners packed up their slaves and went home to the Confederacy, their wagons loaded with trunks containing all the lovely dresses which had been worn at the capital's important social events. Four more states – Virginia, Arkansas, North Carolina, and Tennessee – seceded from the Union; and the Confederacy established its own capital in Richmond, just across the narrow Potomac from Washington City. A Confederate flag was raised on the rooftop of the Marshall Hotel in nearby Alexandria, which we could see on clear days. Every afternoon my younger sons went to the roof of the President's House and fired upon it with a rotting log they pretended was a cannon. Taddie swore in his imperfect speech that he intended to "murder every dirty rebel who crossed the river." Willie assured me that he was not afraid to have the enemy so close. But I had come of age in the South and knew how violent men raised upon honor could be in its defense.

At the times that I stood up there with them, I was certain I could see the rebel soldiers across the river stockpiling rifles and long-bladed knives. Just the knowledge they were so near made me more cold than the stinging wind of early spring which pierced my cloak, more cold than I imagined the sharpened steel of their bayonets to be.

It is my family they will come for. They will like the symbol of it. Myself they will consider a traitor to the Glorious Cause, and no notions of Southern chivalry will be protection against any degradation they wish to inflict upon me. My husband is the Great Enemy, and they will make true that terrible portrait in oil, shackling him and hanging him, and leaving him with blackened tongue. And my sons, I thought, as I watched them do battle in the hard spring sunshine, two small boys firing pretend rounds from a log. *My sons they will not see as different from their parents.* And this thought so froze me, I knew I would shatter like ice if either were ever harmed.

All Washington City feared attack from the rebels across the river. Within days the glittering shops of Pennsylvania Avenue had boarded their windows, and barricades were constructed over the doors of all the buildings of government. Those who did not flee the city shut themselves inside their houses, and the streets of the capital were empty, save for the petals blown from the trees no one had noticed were blooming.

General Scott came and talked about sending myself and my sons north, but Maryland was full of secessionists, and it seemed less safe to go than to remain. To protect us until soldiers from the Union could arrive, a troop of Frontier Guards were moved into the enormous East Room, where they set up tents over the threadbare carpets and boiled coffee in the fireplace. These guards were no more than farmhands made soldiers, recruited by a senator from Kansas whose office had grown overfilled with too many of his unemployed fellow statesmen.

Taddie was glad to have men in the house who carried upon their person every type of weaponry from shotgun to bowie knife; and despite his odd-formed speech, he was able to coax a few of them into letting him fire their rifles into the plaster walls. I also liked these Frontier Guards for their plain manners and how they waited patiently for Taddie to make himself understood. Still, I possessed little faith in their ability to defend us against the Confederates, many of whom had trained at West Point, and all of whom were fighting for a Cause.

The first battalion which was dispatched to us was the Sixth Massachusetts Regiment. These soldiers came as close to us as Baltimore, where they were halted by a secessionist mob brandishing knives and pistols. Many of the Sixth Massachusetts were gravely injured, a few were killed, and the War Between the States, as the newspapers had termed it, acquired its first casualties. The news of this assault upon the Union soldiers was the last word from the North to reach us, for after the mob attacked the Sixth Massachusetts, they tore down the telegraph wires and destroyed the railroad bridges which connected Washington City with the rest of the country.

Once we were cut off from the North, I ceased to sleep. That cold which had come for me upon the roof now found me in my bed, slipping under my flesh until no matter how many shawls I wrapped about myself, I never warmed. I took up wandering the second floor of the President's House, going over and again into Willie and Tad's room to watch them sleeping untouched by Confederates, then crossing to my husband's bedroom – if he had even come to it – to make certain he had not been strung up by rebels.

One week after the mobs in Baltimore cut the telegraph lines and tore up the rail tracks, the second battalion which was dispatched to us, the Seventh Regiment of New York, arrived in Washington City. We heard them first, a noise like the rumbling of unceasing thunder; and only when I was certain that the sound came from the north did I grab my sons and run to the roof to see them. The troop was still at some distance, a sea of blue moving through the empty streets of the capital. But as more of those who had shut themselves into their houses heard the direction of the marching, they threw open their windows and climbed upon their rooftops to cheer the soldiers who had come to protect us.

This war is not over, I told myself. *It is only beginning.* But the sea which swept through the streets of Washington City like evidence of thaw drove away the sharpest edge of my body's cold.

In the days which followed the arrival of the Seventh New York, more regiments from the North arrived in Washington City. Whole battalions of soldiers set up camp on the grassy hills around the President's House and the Capitol building. Within the week, the broad avenues and tree-shaded parks where elegant ladies had taken their walks were crowded with soldiers who spat upon the pavement and shot the blossoms from the trees. And those of us who remained in Washington City were grateful to have them.

Mr. Lincoln was grateful as well, and wishing to personally thank the soldiers of the Seventh New York who had been the first to reach us, asked to have a delegation brought to the President's House.

We received these soldiers, many of whom had also been wounded in Baltimore, in the Blue Room. At the direction of their commander, Major Ethan Broderick, they lined themselves at attention – save for those whose injuries forced them into wheeled chairs – beneath a chandelier which was cracked and broken and missing too many of its pieces, as if in cruel imitation of the men who stood under it. Mr. Nicolay had warned me that I might find the sight of these soldiers' injuries distressing. "You forget that I was brought up in a state full of combative gentlemen," I had assured him. "I have seen wounds before." However, the dashing scars of dueling swords I had seen during my Kentucky girlhood were no preparation for the wounds carried by the soldiers who came to the Blue Room. These men had been beaten by a mob which had employed bricks and staves, and such weapons had left the injured with wounds which were ugly and ragged; to look upon them made my own skin feel as if it were ripping.

Major Broderick made the introductions. The major's voice was cultured, and his uniform perfectly pressed. He had given up an eye in the fighting, and wore a patch over the place where it had been to spare us the sight of the empty socket.

"Your soldiers were the first we saw or heard from the North since the riots in Baltimore," Mr. Lincoln told him. "Until you came, I had almost convinced myself the North no longer existed."

"When there was no word from Washington City, I feared the same of the capital," replied the major. "All the time we were marching from Annapolis, I kept watch for a sight of the President's House. For it seemed to me that if it was gone, then the country itself was gone." He rubbed his face, disarranging the patch to which he had not yet had time to grow used. "When we arrived and I saw that it stood, I fell to my knees and thanked the Almighty. For by that sign, I knew the Union still existed." Tears fell from Major Broderick's remaining eye.

My husband touched the major upon the shoulder. "We stand," he told him. "And we shall continue to stand."

Mr. Lincoln greeted the soldiers in turn, shaking the hands of those whose arms were undamaged. I followed behind, smiling and making conversation with each, as if there were no crushed bones in any face, no wounds which seeped dark upon any uniform. Yet all the while I thought upon Major Broderick's story.

I had forgotten that the President's House was a symbol. Although I supposed it was a poor one now, with its worm-ruined furniture and snipped drapery. *Still, who was to say that it was required to remain so? Who was to say that it could not be cleared of all which made it appear that the Union for which it stood was crumbling and furnished with fittings which were elegant and fine?*

For did I not possess a twenty-thousand-dollar appropriation?

I bent to clasp the hand of a soldier in a wheeled chair, and worried I might have squeezed it too strongly from my own exhilaration. *This,* I was thinking, *this is the way I might help my husband. In a pursuit which falls so solidly into the realm of feminine endeavor, no one – not Judge Davis, not my eldest son – can criticize me for it.*

As soon as the rail lines were open, the moment it was safe to travel north, I would go to New York and buy all that was required to turn the President's House into a true symbol of the Union. I would replace everything, for nothing here was fine enough. I would spend the entire allotment if necessary. And when all was completed, every length of flocked wallpaper hung, every inch of floor covered with silk and wool, I would throw open the doors and invite all who had stayed in Washington City to a grand reception – including the newspapermen, who would write about it; write about it and deliver the message to the entire country, North and South, that the nation was not falling to pieces, but stood more splendid than ever.

(July 28) Mr. Robt Lincoln and daughter came to see Mrs. Lincoln. She was very glad to see them. Aft(ter) they had gone she asked to ride to the post office to deposit a letter which she had written to a sister in Springfield – At the P.O. she got out and deposited her letter herself – spoke of the ride as a very pleasant one.
—Patient Progress Reports for Bellevue Place Sanitarium

I am haunted by Mrs. Matthiessen. When I sleep, I dream that I am back in Minnie's room, that the sound of the lady comes so thickly through the walls that it becomes my own voice. When I go outdoors, I imagine I hear Mrs. Matthiessen's shrieking beneath the splashing of the river; and when I am in the asylum carriage, I can detect her terrible curses in the rumbling of the wheels. These sounds, the noise of a lady's madness, make me cover my ears and sing hymns to myself in order to drown them out. And I sometimes fear that I seem no different from any of the other lunatic ladies who live here, no different from Mrs. Munger shouting at a rose bush.

Still, the shrieking and the curses do not haunt me as much as the remembrance of that frail lady's frantic beating upon the door. That sound, which can be recalled for me by any knocking – the dropping of the coal scuttle, the colored cook bumping her cauldron against the washing basin – makes me too short-winded to cover it with hymn-singing. I suspect I am most distressed by this because I know what was behind the frantic quality of Mrs. Matthiessen's beating. I recognize that recklessly single-minded desire for release.

Today when my son came to visit me, I had to work not to hear again the pounding of Mrs. Matthiessen upon her door; for a group of the ladies of Bellevue Place was playing croquet not far from the covered porch upon which we sat, and the sound of their balls knocking together had a quality which was much too similar to that which haunts me. I would have been safer from the noise if I had taken my son to my room. However, Robert cannot go there without noticing that the mantle clock he gave me has stopped, and he cannot resist winding its mechanism so tightly, I fear it will run forever.

As he does on occasion, Robert today brought me my granddaughter. I think my son does this to keep me more content at the madhouse, but I worry sometimes over how the sight of Bellevue Place's mad ladies will affect the child. Mamie is just shy of her sixth birthday, and has the same bright hair as her mother, whom I have not seen in many years, not since Taddie died.

The day was warm, and Robert and I sat upon wicker chairs – my son being first careful not to catch his light-colored linen trousers upon any unwound branches – beneath a trellis of clematis which has had all its flowers pulled off by one of Bellevue Place's madwomen. Mamie placed herself upon the steps with Blanche, where the two of them sat cutting silhouettes of ladies from Doctor Patterson's old newspapers. Mamie and the doctor's daughter have become friends, for though my granddaughter is half Blanche's age, the two are much the same in their thinking.

"I had not noticed before how very picturesque that river is!" Robert declared with as much enthusiasm as if he had not observed the same river's picturesqueness only the week before.

"I am afraid the river is best at a distance," I said to him. "For there is a paper mill along it which turns the water cloudy."

He let go no measure of his enthusiasm. "Still, I do not believe I would ever tire of this vista."

"Perhaps that is because no one is obliging you to test the theory," I replied. I had meant to speak the words teasingly, but they issued from my mouth sharp-edged and harsh, as if they had decided their own tone. Of late, harshness had become commonplace in my conversations with Robert. It was a severity which came without intention and made me reprove myself once his carriage had driven away, yet it left a hard satisfaction upon my tongue.

My son made no reply to this last remark, only continued to sit and regard the river he insisted was so picturesque. I did not wish things to be uneasy between us, but I could not make myself concede the loveliness of any portion of Bellevue Place.

"Let me see what you have made," I said to my grand-daughter.

Mamie came and put into my hand a newspaper lady cut with a wide skirt. "I have cut her to decorate your room."

Like her father, Mamie gives me presents meant to make me feel at home in my madhouse room – a practice, I suspect, encouraged by my son. I receive several newly cut paper ladies upon every visit, and although I possess a grandmother's affection for anything my grand-daughter might give me, each newsprint lady has begun to feel like a houseguest I shall have to evict before I can leave Bellevue Place myself.

"Now I shall make you another one," declared Mamie, gathering up her white eyelet skirts to retake her place upon the step beside Blanche. "One with a hat."

I watched my granddaughter cut another figure from the newspaper I was not permitted to read, using shears I was not allowed to handle. Carried across the lawn came again the knocking of croquet balls. The clacking of them was quick and frenzied, for the mad ladies did not always wait their turn; and I felt an entrapment in my chest, constricting my breath and tightening my grip upon the paper lady in my hand until her head began to tear away from her body.

"Do you know I have lived here more than two months," I said to my son, working to make myself sound unfrantic.

Robert's voice was pitched to casualness. "That seems not very long."

"It is long enough for me to have grown anxious about keeping hold of my reason."

My son shook his head. "Everything at Bellevue Place is calculated to restore reason."

"It is not a soothing place."

"Look about you. All is calm and orderly." He raised his linen-clad arm in the direction of the mad ladies playing croquet. As if he had accomplished it only by this gesture, the knocking together of the balls began again.

"They have killed a lady." I had not intended to tell him this – not before Mamie, and not so irrationally.

Robert stared at me, and I imagined he was deciding between belief in my judgment or my madness. After a moment he sat back in his chair. "Nobody is killing ladies at Bellevue Place," he said confidently.

I kept my voice lowered. "The matron fed her too large a dose of chloral hydrate."

"It is only your hallucinations which make you think so," he informed me.

"I promise you, I have seen no hallucinations since I have come here."

"Then that only proves my point," my son declared. "Bellevue Place is favorable for you." He looked out again over the river, then slipped a hand into the pocket of his jacket where he kept, I expected, his train ticket back to Chicago.

Seeing that Mamie was absorbed in showing Blanche how to cut a properly formed profile, I leaned nearer my son and, before he might move them away, took hold of his hands. "I am fearful to stay here."

Robert looked at me hard. "I am fearful to let you leave."

In surprise, I released him. "Of what are you afraid?"

"That you will commit some new scandal," he said, something of harshness in his voice now. "Some action which will put your name in the newspaper, make you talked about by everybody."

It seemed so little of which to be afraid. "For that you would leave me where I might come to harm?"

Robert cast his eyes about the asylum grounds, as if searching for the thing he would say next. "I am fearful also that you will come to harm if you are let out to live upon your own."

I wondered if that was true – if it was fear for my safety which caused him to keep me here. But I would not consider the question for too long a time. *I must believe it genuine,* I told myself. *For Robert is my son and it would be too unhappy to think otherwise. No, it is my protection for which he worries, for which he has put me here.* I repeated this to myself, let it cover the noise of the mad ladies' croquet balls. And when I had persuaded myself of it, there came another notion, another way I might convince my son to let me out of Bellevue Place.

"What if I did not have to live upon my own?" I asked. "What if I were to find a place where there was someone to look after me?"

Robert narrowed his eyes. "You have such a place?"

I did not have it yet, but I had an idea where I might find it. Robert had always been fond of his aunt Elizabeth. What I thought my sister's snobbishness, he considered good breeding. Where I believed her stiff-necked and conventional, he found her proper and well-mannered. My son had never objected to Elizabeth, not when she suggested Taddie should be beaten into obedience, not when she made ill remarks about his father. And now, perhaps, he would continue to have no objection to her, even if she were willing to take me in.

I almost said this to my son, almost told him of my plan. But then I noticed that Robert's imperfect eye was pulling toward his nose. *I shall say nothing until it is sure,* I decided. *Until I have written to Elizabeth myself.*

"I am only speculating," I said to him.

Robert tilted his head so I could not see the defective eye. "Doctor Patterson would have to approve of the situation."

"I understand that."

"And myself."

"Yes."

"And the person would have to be willing to live with you."

"Of course."

Robert nodded and relaxed back into his chair; and for an uncharitable moment I believed my son had soothed himself with the impossibility that all this could be arranged.

We sat and watched Mamie correct the shapes of all of Blanche's paper ladies. Every few minutes, Robert opened his watchcase to check the time, making me suspect that he had memorized the schedule of trains which would take him back to Chicago. I thought of Willie then, and how he had learned the railroad timetable so we might imagine where and when we could travel together.

After not very long, and with a final-sounding snap of his watchcase, Robert rose from his wicker seat. "Thank Blanche for the use of her scissors," he said to his daughter. "And then wish your grandmother a proper good-bye."

Mamie returned the shears into Blanche's graceless fingers and rose from the step to make me a very pretty curtsey. "Good-bye, Grandmama," she said.

"You are leaving, Abraham's Widow?" shouted Blanche in her overemphatic voice.

"No," I told the girl. "I am staying. For the time at least." I glanced at Robert, who appeared fixed upon a snag the wicker had put into his linen trousers. "But Mamie is leaving and must come and sit in my lap. For that is the only proper way to bid good-bye to a grandmama."

Mamie, who, like her father, believed in doing things in the proper manner, gathered her eyelet skirts before climbing into my lap. Her weight was light and sweet smelling.

"Shall we have a hug?" I asked her.

Nodding with much seriousness, she circled her arms about my neck and lightly pressed her cheek upon mine. I had only ever known the rough, self-conscious love of boys, and I was always startled into gladness by the gentle affection of my small, neat granddaughter.

"I shall draw something for your room," she offered. "I am quite good at cows."

"That would make me glad," I told her. "For I am exceptionally fond of them."

She was very pleased by this and sat for some minutes in my lap, smoothing the edges of the sash tied at my waist over her skirt, the black of my mourning trimming the white of her girlhood. I wound my fingers into her bright curls, taking pleasure in the slight tugging she made at my waist, and did not at first notice the small figure dancing at the edge of the croquet lawn. Not until the movement of it caught my eye. Then I saw that the figure leapt and waved its arms, and immediately I knew it to be Miss Crawford, a church organist and thirty-year-old spinster, who had recently come to stay at Bellevue Place.

Miss Crawford's mania exercised itself in dancing, though not the kind of dancing witnessed in any ballroom, as it was performed alone and to music only Miss Crawford heard. From a distance, the mad organist's motions were no more alarming than the fluttering of leaves upon a tree. But close by, they contained nothing of grace – and everything of a great and disjointed anxiety.

Holding my granddaughter tight upon my lap, I watched Miss Crawford travel across the croquet field until she was upon us with unnatural suddenness. The organist's performance commanded our attention. Even Mamie watched Miss Crawford dance, her eyes round and fixed.

I should take her away, I thought. *For the dancing of this mad spinster will spoil her dreams.* I lifted Mamie from my lap, intending to bring her inside. But I had barely risen from my own seat when my granddaughter gazed up with Robert's pale eyes.

"Is that how you behave, Grandmama?" she asked. "When we are not here?"

The question, delivered in the sweetest of voices, held the force of a blow. I went down to my knees – only in part to see more closely into my granddaughter's face.

"Why do you think that?" I said.

Mamie's gaze was full of the logic of her argument. "You live here with her."

Her words – and the clarity of that gaze – called up a hatred for my son which was entirely unresistible. A hatred which lifted me from my knees to stand before him.

"It is you who have done this," I said in a voice fiercely quiet. "You who have made my granddaughter believe I am the same as a lady who dances by herself in a madhouse."

"You have done it yourself," he replied.

I could hardly bear to see him, handsome and eager to be away from here. "I can overlook that you have made the entire country believe that I am lunatic," I told him. "But it may be beyond any forgiveness I can devise that you have persuaded my granddaughter of it."

I turned away before he might reply – before I might speak more – and again went to my knees. "I do no dancing without music," I said to my granddaughter. "Nor do I do it without a partner. The last time that I danced was at your papa and mama's wedding. And it was with your uncle Taddie, whom I do not think you remember."

Mamie nodded, taking in this new information.

"We must call for the carriage if we are to catch our train," announced Robert.

I rose to my feet. "You do agree about another place?" I said to him. "If there is someone to stay with me?"

"*If* you can persuade someone," he replied. "And *if* I believe them suitable."

I nodded, and with no more farewell made by either of us, he went inside to arrange for his carriage.

I did not see them off, but went directly to my room in order to write to my sister. It would be necessary to persuade Elizabeth to issue me a formal invitation to come to her, for that would be the only thing which would suit Robert. And for my sister to do such a thing, she would have to feel very certain that she wanted me. With this circumstance firmly in mind, I dipped my pen deeply into the ink – Elizabeth liked letters where the ink was dark – and wrote at the top of the page, *Dearest Elizabeth*. Then, employing my most careful hand, I promised my sister that while beneath her roof, I would provoke neither gossip nor scandal, and swore that I would refrain from agitating her husband. To render the prospect of taking me in more appealing, I offered Elizabeth one hundred and fifty dollars each month for my board.

As I blotted the letter dry, I thought upon how much I did not want to live with my sister. I did not want to be beneath her inspection at fifty-six as I had been at twenty-three. I did not want especially to live again with Ninian, who even after my husband was made president, never considered him much improved and had even gone so far as to turn Democrat to demonstrate the point. However, if I did not convince my sister to take me in, I knew that I would continue to hear Mrs. Matthiessen's frantic beating in the knocking of mad ladies' croquet balls, or the ticking of Robert's mantle clock, or the noise of my own heart.

When the ink was fully dry – Elizabeth did not like her correspondence to be smudged – I carried my sister's letter to Mrs. Patterson's office to be mailed. Then I went to the third floor to visit Minnie Judd.

I go to Minnie every day, despite the harm I think it does my association with Mrs. Patterson. My friend has still not eaten, not of her own accord, though she has been fed twice more by the pump. But the nourishment which Mrs. Ruggles forces into her is not enough, and Minnie's complexion is pale and dusty as chalk, and her black hair, which Blanche so loves to unwind, has begun to come out. Even my friend's breath has altered, turned sour by whatever harm her starving body is carrying out upon itself.

I must go to Minnie because she does not ever come to the bench beside the dark woods. Indeed, she does not leave her room, and I think that contributes to her unwellness. *I shall try and persuade her to walk the grounds with me,* I thought today, as I climbed the stairs to the third floor. *Perhaps the air will stimulate some little appetite.*

I found my friend standing in the gloom before her shadowed window.

"Come outside with me, Minnie," I urged. "I will support you if you are feeling weak."

As my eyes adjusted to the dimness of her room, I saw that Minnie appeared flushed as if she carried fever, and by that I knew that her husband had visited her.

The Reverend Judd's visits worked an odd spell upon his wife. While my friend was generally possessed of fatigue so profound that even drawing breath or blinking seemed to require too much of her strength, for an hour or more after her husband's visits, Minnie's frame was like a spring overwound. Consumed by an energy I imagined as the starving remains of her passion, she could not keep still, but darted about her tiny room, her hands waving around her face, her mouth twitching as if in silent conversation. At such times, I believed that if I touched her, she would be vibrating.

"The reverend has been here?" I said to her.

"He has only just left." As she spoke, she twisted the curtain pull around and around her nervous fingers.

"Has he instructed you to eat?"

"He has said that Doctor Patterson is causing him to be worried for my health. But I believe that Reverend Judd admires my restraint." Her voice, which had thinned along with her frame, sounded unusually sure.

I went to her and took her hands, felt something in them which was like trembling. "I believe you wrong," I told her. "Your husband could not wish for you to starve yourself."

Minnie smiled, and that too was thin. "Have we not already had this disagreement?"

"I would be pleased to have it again if I believed it would convince you to take food," I replied. "But I do not believe it. And I do not want to tire you too much, for I wish to take you outside."

My friend hesitated.

"If you let me take you to the bench behind the greenhouse, I promise not to speak about eating." I smiled at her. "Although it is one of my favorite topics."

Minnie returned the smile. But the effect of it was disquieting, for the flesh which had been stolen from my friend's face now caused her teeth to appear too large.

"All right," she told me. "If we go for a short time. And if you say nothing about broth."

I led her out by way of the portico, as that would take us nearer the path to the greenhouse, for I was worried for when Minnie's strength would falter. And indeed, we had only reached the portico door, when my friend began to lose much of the frantic energy which attended her husband's visits. However, as we stepped outside, Minnie gave a small cry and pulled me to a halt across from a black-sided barouche with more force than I would have believed her capable.

"That is the Reverend Judd's carriage!" she exclaimed. "He is still here!"

"I expect he has gone to speak with Doctor Patterson," I said.

"Yes! That is it!" She gripped my arm more fiercely. "He has gone to tell him I am ready to come home."

I made no reply, for I did not wish to say to Minnie that I knew of no one of Bellevue Place's starving ladies who had been released before they had resumed eating.

"I am certain that is the truth of it!" Minnie continued, heedless of my silence. "Did I not say that he had come to admire my restraint?" Her white face glowed in the shadow beneath the covered portico. "Let us wait by his carriage. He will surely wish to give me the news when he comes out."

She took some steps toward the black barouche, but had not gone far before she pulled herself to a stop. "Oh!" my friend cried out, as if she had stepped upon a sharp rock.

"What is it?" I asked. "Has something hurt you?"

Minnie made no reply, but kept her gaze upon her husband's carriage. I followed her glance and saw inside what appeared to be a lady.

"Do you know who that is?" I asked my friend.

"It is Mrs. Gill." I heard something spiritless and resigned in Minnie's voice.

"What is she to you?" I asked.

"She is a lady of my husband's congregation."

Standing together, we watched Mrs. Gill bustle about the reverend's barouche, too busy to notice us in the shadow of the portico. The lady rearranged her skirts over the seat, then settled her bonnet more securely upon her hair. Then she lifted the lid of something which looked very much like a picnic basket.

I felt Minnie sway beside me.

"Has that lady been unkind to you?" I said.

"She shall be," Minnie replied. "After she has become my replacement."

"What do you mean?"

"Mrs. Gill will marry Reverend Judd when I am committed here for life." My friend's voice came as sour as her breath. "Or when I die."

"You cannot be right about such a thing," I told her. "It is only how you think because you have not eaten." But though I said the words with confidence, I had no ready explanation for Mrs. Gill and her picnic basket.

I do not know how long Minnie would have stood watching the lady in her husband's carriage; all the strength in her underfed frame was set upon keeping her rooted to the spot. But before many minutes had passed, before Mrs. Gill had opportunity to see us, there came the sound of footsteps upon the gravel and I caught the too-beautiful form of Reverend Judd coming round the corner of the asylum.

"Come!" I tugged upon my friend's arm. "You need quiet," I told her, for I saw that in an instant the reverend would spot us, and I feared that Minnie had neither strength nor mind to face him.

As I pulled her toward the door, Minnie made little protest. I did not think she had seen her husband, for she had not once removed her gaze from Mrs. Gill. But the moment she was inside, she began to sway, as if all that had been bearing her up had been the hard stare she had fixed upon the lady in her husband's carriage.

It was plain that Minnie did not possess the strength to climb the stairs to her room, or to mine. Even the lunatics' parlor, only some little way down the corridor, would be too far for her. I felt my friend's slight weight fall more upon me, and I knew I had to find her a place at once, or she would crumple to the floor where we stood.

"In here," I told her, pushing open the nearest door. It led into Mrs. Patterson's private parlor, the room which we lunatic ladies were forbidden to enter, the one I came to when the doctor's wife wished to show me a new sconce or curtain pull, and never at another time. I did not know where Mrs. Patterson might be at that moment. But I could not spare the worry she would find us in her parlor, for Minnie was already losing all facility to stay upon her feet.

I settled my friend upon a sofa too covered with needlepoint pillows and then shut the door. *If Mrs. Patterson discovers us,* I thought, *I shall tell her Mrs. Judd was about to swoon, and I imagined it would disturb the other ladies to find her fainted upon the floor. If I am lucky, she will see such conduct as rational, and not the disobedient behavior of the mad.*

I seated myself beside my friend and waited for her face to lose its limestone cast before I spoke.

"You say that Mrs. Gill is a member of Reverend Judd's congregation?"

Minnie's words came faint, but not without venom. "She does not miss a Sabbath – and always takes great pains to seat herself near the pulpit."

"None of this indicates the Reverend Judd intends her to be your replacement."

My friend made a kind of grimace, which her large teeth turned wolfish. "He could apply for no more ideal wife."

I touched the place on her fingers where her wedding band, too large now, knocked against the bone. "He already has a wife."

"A difficult one."

"And Mrs. Gill is ideal?"

"She has grown sons from her dead husband, so she will not press him for children. And she possesses a cold character, so she will not press him for anything else."

"What do you mean?"

Minnie turned her black eyes upon my face. "In all your conversations with Mrs. Patterson has she not told you how I came to be here?" Before I could answer, my friend shook her head. "No, she could not have. She does not know the reason. Neither does Doctor Patterson. My husband would not have told him." She gazed down at her fleshless lap. "He has not told it to anyone. And neither have I."

I kept my hand pressed upon hers. "You can tell it to me. I promise it will make me feel no differently toward you."

Minnie curled her fingers about mine and showed me her starving face. I watched her draw breath and then release it. And then she spoke.

"I committed adultery against Reverend Judd."

She paused. I nodded to show her she might continue.

"It was with the son of one of my husband's deacons," she told me. "He was young. Younger than I. And handsome. Although not as beautiful as my husband."

"He tempted you," I said.

She shook her head. "I tempted him."

Again she ceased speaking.

"That is not something for which I feel entitled to fault you," I told her.

Again Minnie turned her night-colored eyes upon me. "His father sent him to the church to help keep it in repair. He was skilled at such labor, where the reverend is not. I put myself in his way. Made it obvious I would not refuse him. Talked to him of free love. Opinions which belonged to my father's friends.

"The first time I gave myself to him was the night before Easter. The night Christ spent in his tomb. The night my husband locked himself in his study to make ready the next day's sermon. I led the deacon's son into the sacristy – a small room which locked from the inside. A room with no windows. I did not even pretend to protest."

She glanced at our clasped hands, as if making certain they remained twined.

"I took him there again the Monday after Easter. The day we were supposed to be ridding the church of the lilies which had died. Then again the following Thursday. Indeed, the sacristy became where we most generally went to commit our sin. Although I also let him take me in the choir box. And in the alcove where we stored the hymnals."

"And Reverend Judd learned of it?"

"He discovered us. He returned to the chapel unexpectedly, seeking a book of sermons he had left on the pulpit. The deacon's son and I were behind it, making use of the floor."

Minnie's hair, which was thin and difficult to keep pinned, had fallen too far over her eyes. I smoothed it back and some strands came away in my fingers.

"Was your husband very angry?"

"I cannot say. But it is the nature of his outcry which most remains with me, the oddity of it. It was not the cry of outrage. Nor of vengeance. But the sound one might make if one were to come upon some perversion – something too vile to be thought of, much less witnessed.

"I tried to rise and go to him. But the deacon's son was heavy to move, and before I could shift him, my husband had run from the church. I found him in the side garden, retching into the bushes." Again she cast her eyes into her lap.

"He could not forgive you?"

"He said that my passion was an unholy thing. And that he could take no chance of the congregation learning how I had betrayed him. The deacon's son was sent west. And I was committed here."

Minnie sat silent for a moment, then gripped my hand with unimagined strength. "You must believe that despite what I did with the deacon's son, I never loved my husband one small part less. Never ceased wishing it was he who lay atop me in the sacristy. Never ceased wishing it was his beautiful mouth pressed upon my own." She stared off into Mrs. Patterson's overdecorated parlor. "But I did not know how to even imagine it."

I gazed at her in some confusion. "You could not put the reverend in the place of the deacon's son?"

Her eyes became onyx from the tears which filled them. "I had no reference from which to work. No remembrance of the feel of my husband's flesh. No recollection of the sound of his passion."

"What are you telling me?"

"The Reverend Judd and I have never shared a bed. Not one night since we were married."

I gaped at her, understanding but not believing. "He has never touched you?"

"Never more than is required to guide me across the street. Or to my pew in his church."

"If he does not want you, why did he marry you?"

Minnie glanced again about Mrs. Patterson's parlor, at the great many china figurines and the collection of damask-covered footstools. "I expect Mrs. Patterson has made mention that my family is well-off."

"Reverend Judd was poor?"

"And he required a wife. Congregations prefer their ministers married." With a shuddering exhalation, she sank back against the needlepoint pillows. "That is why my husband will marry Mrs. Gill."

"The churchwoman may have placed herself in his way," I said to my friend. "But I am certain he would rather that you leave here."

Minnie sighed, a whispering with more sorrow in it than energy. "I think I have become too inconvenient to be let go."

Minnie's words froze me upon the pillow-crowded sofa as surely as if I had been struck by a paralysis. I had created scandal, had my name put into newspapers, gotten talked about by everybody. I had cast the world's attention upon myself – and my son, who did not want it. And admitting this, I could not make myself believe other than that I had made it more convenient for Robert to believe me mad.

I studied my friend, her head sunk so deep into a pillow stitched with a landscape, it seemed she was being swallowed up in it. Minnie was certain her husband would never allow her to leave the madhouse, certain she would die at Bellevue Place. And her surety threw a shadow upon Robert's approval of my plan to live with Elizabeth.

My son will have no faith in Elizabeth's ability to keep me from becoming inconvenient, I thought. *For he knows that I married while beneath her scrutiny. And though I may persuade my sister to make me the invitation, he will find some excuse to refuse it. He will say Doctor*

Patterson is against the idea, or that the law disallows it. And I will not be able to convince him otherwise. Not by myself.

I must have help. Others who will attest to my sanity. To my capacity to create no scandal. And these others must be gentlemen. Gentlemen of influence. Gentlemen to whom my son will pay mind. What I must do is write to every important gentleman I have known, write and beg each one to come to the madhouse. Come and see for himself that I am not insane. And once each has come, I will plead with him to go to my son and say that I have been wrongly committed, and that the only just course is to release me.

This scheme made me feel as full of energy as those in the early stages of food-refusing. Filled with resolve, I turned back to my friend. "Reverend Judd will not marry the churchwoman," I told her. "Not if you can make him know you do not belong here."

Minnie did not bother to open her eyes. "I have already done all that he wished. I have ceased learning the Bible. I have demonstrated control over my appetite. And still there is Mrs. Gill sitting in his carriage with a picnic basket."

"Starving yourself is not the way."

Minnie opened her eyes then, and her gaze was hard as the bones which showed too much beneath her skin. "What else do I have? Here there are no deacons' sons upon which I can prove my restraint. No marriage bed into which I might refrain from begging my husband to come. Here there is nothing I can deny myself save Doctor Patterson's tasteless food."

The promise of my own release had made me more hopeful of my friend's, and I searched for the phrase which would keep Minnie from dying of her powerful restraint. But before I might discover it, the door to the parlor banged open and we were assaulted by the manlike voice of Mrs. Ruggles.

"This is Mrs. Patterson's parlor."

I believed that as with any large and threatening beast, it was best not to permit Mrs. Ruggles to know you were afraid. I turned to the matron standing in the doorway, but did not rise. "I am very much aware of that," I said calmly. "The doctor's wife has brought me here upon many occasions."

Mrs. Ruggles began to take a step into the room, but then seemed to think better of it. "You are forbidden to be here on your own," she told us.

"Mrs. Judd was unwell, and this was the nearest place I could bring her," I explained, as if it would be impossible to make objection.

The matron stood breathing hard in the doorway.

Minnie lifted her head from the pillows. "If you will help me," she murmured, "I believe I can walk to my room."

"Mrs. Judd is well enough to return to the third floor," I announced to the matron. I clasped my friend's elbow and helped her from the sofa, and together we crossed the room in small steps, coming to halt before the doorway, which was blocked by Mrs. Ruggles's broad frame.

"I am going to tell Mrs. Patterson that you were here," she threatened.

"That is a good plan," I replied. "She should know that a lady who is beneath your care is in danger of collapsing in the corridor."

This comment caused the matron to fix her smallish eyes upon me in a slow, dumb fear. I led Minnie a step nearer the door, so near we could smell Mrs. Ruggles's sweat, and something else which was bitter, like chloral. The fear still working, the matron moved out of our way and I helped my friend out of Mrs. Patterson's parlor.

It took some time to return Minnie Judd to her room, for there were two flights of stairs and she was required to rest after only four or five steps. I said nothing more to her about eating, for I feared she would use up too much energy upon refusal. *I shall wait until she feels stronger,* I decided. *When she has gotten more over the shock of Mrs. Gill.*

Once Minnie was settled, I went to my room to write the letters. I had only a little time to pen them, for I would need to mail these pleas myself. I was not permitted to write to anyone who did not appear upon a list which Robert had given Mrs. Patterson – a list which consisted mostly of relations and a small number of my unscandalous friends. Robert believed that "gangs of Spiritualists" were after my money. He believed also, I suppose, that I was unreasoned enough to oblige them.

I wrote five letters, hurried, scrawling things I hoped for all their rush would give the impression of sanity. After I had hid them in my reticule, I returned to Mrs. Patterson's office – mercifully, still unoccupied, and retrieved my letter to Elizabeth.

Mercifully also, the asylum carriage was available. I asked the driver, a man named Paddleford, who was large enough to restrain even the most energetically violent lady, to take me into Batavia. Mr. Paddleford was fond of procedure, and though he obliged when I asked him to stop in front of Batavia's limestone post office, he was reluctant to grant the rest of my request.

"I'm not supposed to unlock ladies in town," he told me, leaning his bulk against the bolted carriage door.

"I give you my word as the former First Lady of the land that I will not try to outrun you through Batavia," I assured him.

"But doesn't Mrs. Patterson have to inspect all your letters?"

"It is only a note to my sister. She can have no quarrel with that."

Mr. Paddleford thrust a thick hand into the carriage. "Let me see the letter."

Reaching carefully into my reticule, I removed the envelope bearing Elizabeth's address. The driver took it from me and examined both sides.

"This is the only one?" he asked.

"I fear I am a poor correspondent."

He pressed his big fingers the length of the envelope, smudging the address, then returned Elizabeth's letter to me. "Come right back," he commanded, at last unlocking the door.

"I shall," I promised. I stepped out of the asylum carriage and hurried into the post office, grateful to have been correct about Mr. Paddleford. For while the carriage driver possessed sufficient fondness for procedure to inspect one's letter, he – like most gentlemen – did not want to know what was in a lady's reticule.

I took with me to New York William Wood, who was being considered for the position of Commissioner of Public Buildings. My husband and I had met Mr. Wood on the train from Springfield to Washington City; the gentleman worked for the railroad, and it was he who had made our arrangements.

Mr. Wood was handsome, though not as beautiful as Reverend Judd; and his looks were certainly not formed in an angelic manner. Mr. Wood's attractiveness was shaped more by decadence, as if his gold-colored eyes and slightly flaring nostrils were the outward sign of indulgences devised and satisfied; and there was something in the gentleman's appearance which was both feline and unsettling, perhaps because it contained nothing domesticated in it.

As it would have been improper for me to travel alone with a gentleman, even a gentleman who was a government official, I took also one of my Todd cousins, Lizzie Grimsley. Lizzie, who was near to my own age, had never – not even when she was young – possessed any beauty. Her eyes were more horizontal than can be called pretty, and her upper lip was too long and flat; and as consequence she had ended up with a husband as dour as his surname. Still, my cousin Lizzie owned a sharp wit, which was scandalously agreeable to hear, and a soft heart. And unlike most of my Todd relations, she loved Mr. Lincoln – a trait for which I could not help but love her.

The three of us traveled north at the beginning of May, two weeks after the arrival of the Seventh New York Regiment in Washington City, and as quickly as General Scott deemed it safe. Mr. Wood, who had lived in New York, arranged rooms for us at the Metropolitan, a sumptuous hotel in which everything was done to luxurious excess. The lobby contained a jungle's worth of potted ferns, and every room boasted an enormous bed topped with a real horsehair mattresses, so high a velvet footstool was required to climb into it. Lizzie and I settled in adjoining suites upon the third floor. Mr. Wood took a smaller room a proper distance away upon the fourth.

Upon our first morning in New York, we stepped from our comfortable hotel into a warm, intoxicating day in which the breeze blew like soft hands upon our faces. Mr. Wood hired us a hackney and instructed the driver to carry us along the stretch of Broadway between Eighth Street and Twenty-third, known as the Ladies' Mile for all the shops which were upon it. The glittering stores of Pennsylvania Avenue which had been so capable of seducing me into financial indiscretion did not compare to what could be found on this stretch of street. In New York, every store was a palace of marble or scrolled ironwork, every window filled with real *chinois* silk, carpeting from Arabia.

"Might we visit them all?" I asked Mr. Wood.

"It is not my position to limit you in any manner," he assured me.

"You have not seen my cousin shop," warned Lizzie. "She is one of nature's own forces."

"I look forward to the pleasure," the gentleman replied. The hackney was small and we were obliged to sit very near the other, and when Mr. Wood smiled, I saw that his teeth were startlingly white.

Mr. Wood took us first to the department store of A. T. Stewart & Company, which occupied the entire block at Ninth Street and

Broadway. The façade of Mr. Stewart's establishment had been fashioned of Italianate ironwork painted white to resemble marble; and the shop itself was considered remarkably advanced, being equipped with a ladies' parlor which contained the latest Parisian mirrors – looking glasses made large enough to reveal one entirely from head to foot. All the counters at A. T. Stewart were made of a marble which was cool and smooth, and upon these alabaster altars were displayed only the most lavish goods – draperies of the plushest velvet, small rugs woven wholly out of silk. Behind these marbled counters stood another of Mr. Stewart's advancements, the well-dressed "Stewart's Nice Young Men" – more gentlemen than shop assistants, the Nice Young Men were uncommonly adept at ministering to female desires.

Mr. Stewart attended to me himself.

"It is a very great honor to have you here, Mrs. President Lincoln!" he exclaimed, hurrying along the marble-tiled floor toward me. Mr. Stewart, who was known in New York as the Gentleman Merchant, possessed an unlikely accent, one in which the lilt of an Irish tongue knocked against the roughened edges of a Scottish one.

"The First Lady is seeking new furnishings for the President's House," explained Mr. Wood. "Fittings intended to make the Confederacy lose heart."

Mr. Stewart bowed to me so deeply, I saw the short, reddish hairs which grew at the back of his neck. "Rest assured that I am the most resolute of Union men," he declared. "And as such, shall commit all the resources of A. T. Stewart & Company to your sacred duty to the Republic."

He clapped his hands before his face like an Eastern sultan, and a clutch of the Nice Young Men appeared at his side.

"Fetch chairs for Mrs. President Lincoln and her companion, in the event they become fatigued," he commanded them.

The Nice Young Men hurried off to retrieve a pair of upholstered chairs, which two of them carried behind us as the Gentleman Merchant led us through his fabulous store.

Mr. Stewart showed me only goods which were of the loftiest quality. The Nice Young Men fetched brocade stitched in France and china fired in England, porcelain teacups so fine, the shadow of one's fingers could be seen through the sides, and thick wallpaper painted entirely by hand. Mr. Stewart talked of the fineness of each object, the care which had been taken in its manufacture – and never once told me the prices of these luxuries. And I never asked. For what was of significance was the richness of the materials, the exquisite craftsmanship of their making, for neither the rebels nor the Unionists would be convinced by a President's House which appeared thrift-conscious and penny-pinching.

I bought nearly everything Mr. Stewart showed me. And each time I told the Gentleman Merchant that, yes, I would have the silken bell pulls, the beaten gold pitchers, I felt such a pleasurable excitement, I asked him to fetch me more, just so I might experience it again.

As we moved through the brilliant halls, Mr. Wood kept close beside me, sending for tea before I requested it, and keeping count of the number of tasseled ottomans and mahogany tables I ordered. Each time he brought himself near to me, I caught the scent of bergamot which he wore upon his skin. It was a scent like an orange peeled and left open in the sun; and to smell it called up a desire which made me command the Nice Young Men to bring more cashmere bedcoverings, more silk-covered pillows.

We passed the entire day at A. T. Stewart's and left with a promise to return the next morning to view a shipment of serpentine-backed sofas. Outside, Mr. Wood hailed us another hackney for the journey back to the Metropolitan Hotel. This carriage was smaller than the first, and possessed an uneven wheel which rocked me into Mr. Wood's legs no matter how much I worked to stay away.

"You appear wonderfully fresh after your exertions at Mr. Stewart's," he said to me.

"I confess that I find the act of spending money stimulating."

"I believe you should remind my cousin that profligacy is a vice, Mr. Wood," teased my cousin.

"Might you forgive me if I don't," he said to her. "For I confess that I find it immeasurably agreeable to watch a woman take her pleasure."

I should reprove him for the impertinence, I thought. But the afternoon sunlight which came low through the carriage window had turned Mr. Wood's eyes to amber, and I could concentrate upon nothing which was reproving. Indeed, all my attention was focused upon how very soft the gentleman's mouth seemed, and how such softness made me wish to run back to A. T. Stewart & Company and have something else.

My time in New York passed in a warm, bergamot-scented haze. Each day Mr. Wood took Lizzie and me to the dazzling shops along the Ladies' Mile; shops which displayed goods so excessively opulent, they seemed at once both graceful and decadent, much like Mr. Wood himself. Riding about in close hackneys, we returned to A. T. Stewart's to view the serpentine sofas, then moved on to Brewster's carriage shop, and to Haughwout & Company for china, and to Lord & Taylor for draperies. My head swam and each time I shut my eyes, I saw endless swaths of satin DeLaine, immense piles of dinner china rimmed with Solferino and gold. I felt in a constant state of agitation, a fever of longing never entirely satiated by the polished wood and sparkling glassware. Holding fast to Mr. Wood, I moved from shop to shop in a daze, flushed and breathless, and saying no to nothing.

By the end of a week, my craving was such that I did not want to wait to have the velvet draperies and lace-edge linens sent on to Washington City. I wanted instead to have everything brought to me immediately, so that I could place my hands upon these ravishing objects whenever I desired. Most of what I purchased was too large or cumbersome to be sent to my hotel; however, at Haughwout & Company, I bought a set of Dorflinger water glasses which would fit into a small box.

"Could I not take these with me?" I asked Mr. Wood, who was standing very near, surrounding me with his scent of bergamot. "I cannot wait to drink from them." And indeed, I was made almost light-headed from the longing to put my lips against the glasses' fine-edged hardness.

"I know that our Southern relations believe Mr. Lincoln wishes to make the Negro equal in all things," said my cousin slyly. "But I have never known a white woman to carry home her own purchases."

I could not say why, but this mention of my husband's name caused me to reconsider my desire, making me suspect that it would be unwise to succumb to the impulse to drink from the new glasses; for who could say what damage might occur?

However, Mr. Wood was already translating my wish.

"Wrap the glasses carefully," he instructed the clerk. "But not so carefully they cannot be laid bare and drunk from tonight."

That night was to be our last in New York; the following morning we would board a boat for Boston where I planned to visit with Robert. To celebrate the success of our enterprise – for if wallpaper and ottomans could turn the tide of war, I had certainly purchased enough to assure Union victory – Mr. Wood suggested the three of us dine together at the Metropolitan.

"I hope very much you do not have occasion to bend," said my cousin, when she came to my room to collect me. "Or there will be nothing the country does not know about you."

I leaned a little before the glass, gauging the integrity of my dress, a gown of green silk which dipped deeply at the bosom. "I shall endeavor to remain upright," I promised her.

The dining room at the Metropolitan was lit by gas lamps covered by pink glass which made the room glow like the flush of blood beneath a porcelain cheek. The carpeting was soft, the seat cushions softer, and all conversation turned to gentle murmurings by the layers of velvet curtains draped over the walls. It was an atmosphere meant to coax one into indulgence, and beneath its influence I ordered the most sumptuous dishes upon the menu: curried oysters and a plate of small roasted quail, followed by a sage-stuffed bullock's heart. For dessert I was unable to decide between chocolate Bavarian and an assortment of perfectly formed meringues, and upon the urging of Mr. Wood, ordered both. I ate everything in a rush, nearly swooning from the richness – and perhaps the increasing tightness of my corset.

"I am afraid I have been unforgivably greedy tonight," I declared, my tongue swollen from the sweetness of the meringue.

"That is one of the most appealing things about you," said Mr. Wood. "Your greedy desire." In the warming light of the room, his skin looked the color of the caramel the waiters were pouring over vanilla-scented baby cakes I was suddenly sorry not to have ordered.

"You have just invested my poor cousin with two of the deadliest sins," declared Lizzie.

"But certainly the most interesting of the seven," replied Mr. Wood.

"Do you not find the virtues equally interesting?" she asked lightly. "What of piety? Or charity?"

"They are certainly commendable," he told her. "But not, in my opinion, interesting. I am afraid that for me, the only interesting human beings are the ones in whom passion runs strong."

"You do not think it can run too strongly?" I teased.

Mr. Wood leaned across the table. "Not everyone is granted a large passion," he replied. "Suppressing it would be like curbing a rare talent for the piano or a great facility with paint."

My blood, full of the flesh of animals and the heat of exotic spices, pulsed at my throat. I saw nothing but Mr. Wood's soft mouth, smelled nothing save the bergamot which surrounded him like a warmer season. Not until the waiter came to retrieve the plate with my leavings of meringue did I remember that I was in the dining room of the Metropolitan Hotel, did I notice that my cousin had gone unnaturally quiet.

From behind her dish of melting glacé, Lizzie regarded Mr. Wood with a face so white, it looked as if she feared the handsome gentleman.

"Are you well, Lizzie?" I asked. "Has any of the dinner upset you?"

"I think it would be best if we returned to our rooms," she replied.

"It is not so very late," I told her, though I had no notion of the time, only that I still possessed some appetite which felt unsatisfied.

"We are leaving early for Boston," she reminded me. "To see your son."

"Mrs. Grimsley is quite correct," said Mr. Wood. "We might all be better in bed."

The gentleman escorted Lizzie and myself to the third floor, waiting outside my cousin's door until she was safely inside, before accompanying me to my own.

"I trust the day has not been so arousing that it will disturb your rest," he said to me.

I gave Mr. Wood my hand in farewell, and with surprising speed, he turned it over and put his soft mouth to the palm. The feel of that mouth upon my flesh pulled tight upon a chord which resided deep within my body, and the sensation was so sharply pleasurable, I cried out. Mr. Wood raised his eyes to my face and held me in his gold-flecked gaze. With tormenting slowness, he slid his fingers along my wrist before releasing my hand.

With a great urgency, I let myself into my room, shutting the door and pushing myself against it as firmly as if Mr. Wood were attempting to batter it down. How could I not have recognized the nature of the craving which had driven me to purchase so many extravagances? Pushed me to stuff myself with the lush organs of animals and fill my mouth with sweetened cream? How could I have been turned so breathless by Mr. Wood's nearness, so willing to bare myself for him, and not seen what it was which compelled me?

My flesh burned – with shame, I told myself – and spotting the box from Haughwout & Company upon a table covered in scarlet baize, I rushed to it, tearing open the wrapping and uncovering the drinking glasses. I carried one to the carafe at the side of the bed, filled it with water, and drank it all without stopping for breath. The moment it was emptied, I filled it again and drank it down with such desperation, water fell out of my mouth, wetting the flesh exposed by my dress. Gulping water until it nearly choked me, I worked to dampen the fire which licked at the underside of my skin.

As I sat there drinking, the door which connected my room to Lizzie's opened. My cousin was still in dinner clothes. In her hand she clutched a bottle made of blue glass.

"I have brought laudanum to help you sleep," she told me.

Take it! I commanded myself. *Take Lizzie's opium and drug yourself into chasteness.*

"I do not think I will require it." It was not me who had answered my cousin.

"You are very certain?" asked Lizzie.

"I have been made tired by the shopping, and the dinner."

My cousin hesitated. "I am just on the other side of that door, if you want me," she said. "If anything makes you restless."

"I am going directly to bed," I assured her.

Lizzie nodded, and too quickly for me to call her back, shut the door between us.

Think of your husband, I said to myself. *Think of his kind and homely face, and how it will be to live beneath the goodness of his gaze if you do this thing.* But all I could think of were Mr. Lincoln's hands, how infrequently they were upon me, and how very much I was required to hold back, even when they were.

I leapt from the bed and began to pace, attempting to exhaust the desire which wanted to drive me from the room. But the slipperiness of my petticoat was a torment where it touched upon my legs. *All that I crave is one floor above me,* I told myself. *And I can possess it as absolutely – and immediately – as that box of Dorflinger crystal.*

Perhaps it was that, the ease with which I could have what I wanted. Or perhaps it was the consequence of desire too long suppressed. But it seemed then that my passion was a madness which removed reason from my thinking. *Leave this room and take the stairs,* it told me. *You know he will not turn you away.* And I did as it commanded, not even stopping for a cloak to hide myself.

Mr. Wood's door opened before I put hand to it. He uttered no word as he pulled me inside, only made a sound which was feline and feral. Keeping one arm wrapped tight about my waist, as if to hold me should I try to leave, he pushed shut the door and pressed me against it, fixing me there with his mouth upon mine. Every nerve in my body, even those which ran most deeply, rose to him, and I knew I would not try to leave until he was done with me.

Mr. Wood removed my dress so quickly and capably, I could only think he had much practice with the hooks and buttons of ladies' clothing – an idea which thrilled and disgusted me in equal measure. Everything I wore, the hoops and petticoats, was removed with the same subtlety, until I stood clad only in a sheer chemise which clung so closely to my flesh I was good as naked.

Mr. Wood held me against the door with his body. His mouth fell upon my face and neck, traveled to the bosom I had been so willing to show to him. I licked at his throat, which tasted of the orange of his bergamot, and which made me believe I was in a foreign place, where what I did would have no consequence in the ordinary world.

I had not known it was possible to accomplish all we did standing against that door – or the sweet depravity to be found in it. With the green silk of my dress foaming at our feet like the sea, our salt-soaked flesh came together and would not be separated until we had wrung out every last pleasure. And even then, we did not cease, only took ourselves to sofa, to mattress, to the intoxicating debasement of the floor.

"Cry out," murmured Mr. Wood, when I attempted to stifle my mouth against the hard muscle of his shoulder. "I want to hear how your passion sounds."

I raved and pleaded, and held nothing back. There was no propriety, no decency or virtue; only the ecstasy I could wrest from my flesh and his.

When light began to show beneath the window curtains, Mr. Wood covered himself with a silk dressing gown the amber color of his eyes, and helped me with my hooks and laces. I slid my dress over flesh inflamed like infection, then held on to the back of the sofa we had abused while he buttoned the back with provokingly adept fingers. Before I left him, he lightly touched my hand, and I knew it would have taken only the lightest tugging upon my wrist to induce me to tear open all the just-fastened hooks and buttons. With barely a glance to see if anyone lingered outside, I hurried down the hallway, my step weaving and unsteady.

My cousin waited for me in my room. She was dressed in a brown wool wrapper and seated so deeply in a wingback chair, I suspected she had been there all night. Beside her upon a marble-topped table was the blue bottle of laudanum.

"You possess the best and most tender of husbands," she said.

Lizzie did not utter these words as accusation, but as if she believed I required reminding. And being reminded, my shame came upon me in a rush. I dropped to the floor at her feet.

"My stepmother was correct about me," I told her. "I am wicked."

Lizzie put her fingers in my hair, working to unknot the tangles put there by the rough cushions of Mr. Wood's sofa. "Betsey Todd is a hard woman," she said. "And you are not wicked. But Mr. Wood is dangerous."

I took her hand from my hair, too ashamed to have her fingers entwined in the result of my debasement.

"I did not see it at first," she continued. "His manners are so polished, and he is so very charming. I expect that is what turns him dangerous."

I looked up at my cousin. "You will not tell Mr. Lincoln?"

Lizzie shook her head. "I love him too much. But you cannot allow it to happen again." She rose from the chair, and I could see by the time it took how wearied she was. "You are no longer just any lady," she reminded me. "You are the First Lady. And there are more who will watch what you do and be pleased to pass on any indiscretions to Mr. Lincoln. Or his political rivals."

Her words stole the heat still caught in my flesh.

"I shall stay away from Mr. Wood," I promised my cousin. And I vowed to swallow the entire bottle of laudanum if my desire again threatened to send me to him.

For the length of the boat ride to Boston, I avoided the company of Mr. Wood, staying close to my cousin's side, making Lizzie the mast upon which I tied myself to escape the siren's song. For his part, Mr.

Wood was discreet and courteous. He behaved solicitously toward Lizzie, bringing her a shawl from her trunks when he imagined she looked chilled, and carefully with me, speaking only of our travel arrangements and indicating by neither word nor look what had passed between us. He was so circumspect, I might have convinced myself that none of it had happened, save for the proof of a cut upon his bottom lip, put there by my teeth.

Once arrived in the city, we took a carriage to the Revere House, a hotel of prim furnishings – horsehide chairs with straightened backs, and beds covered by hard mattresses which did not require footstools to climb upon. I believed the Revere House precisely suited my mood, or the mood I wished to possess.

Mr. Wood arranged to have my eldest son collected from his rooms in Cambridge and escorted him to my suite shortly before supper. Even beside the well-turned-out Mr. Wood, Robert was handsome, dressed in a coat of dove gray with velveteen banding which matched exactly the color of his eyes.

"I have missed you awfully," I said to my son.

I crossed the room to kiss him, but once I stood before his upright figure did no more than take his hand, for the nearness of Mr. Wood turned all kissing wanton.

"Now that young Mr. Lincoln has come to be chaperone," said Mr. Wood. "I shall absent myself, and leave you to the privacy of a family supper."

Lizzie also did not join us for supper, saying for excuse that she had not slept well the night before. Although my cousin was fond of Willie and Tad, she seemed always to find reason to remove herself from Robert's company.

The dining room of the Revere House was as puritanically decorated as my suite. There were not so many curtains on the walls here as at the Metropolitan, and the light was brighter and less illusory. The chairs were uncushioned, the china an unsullied white, and the table linen carried the faint odor of lye. I ordered only a little clear broth followed by beef without gravy. The food possessed no flavor – the broth was little more than boiled water. However, highly spiced food was purported to inflame the senses, and I regarded this meal as both penance and prescription.

My son's company was no more stimulating than my dinner. Robert consumed spring lamb with rosemary without enthusiasm, and answered my questions with few words, as if he expected to be asked to pay for each of them.

"Harvard has taught you a great economy of speech," I told him.

"Economy," he repeated, setting down his fork with a clatter which echoed in the unsoftened room. "That is a rare word coming from you."

I gazed at him, perplexed. "You find it rare that I should use the word?"

"As it is a virtue to which you do not subscribe." In the unconcealing light of the Revere House's dining room, Robert's face was hard with dislike.

"I am only your mother," I said, wearily, "and not a Harvard scholar. If you wish to insult me, you will have to explain your meaning."

My son removed from the breast pocket of his coat a folded newspaper. "This was left at my rooms," he said. "Probably by one of my Harvard schoolfellows."

For an irrational moment, I believed the newspaper had printed the information that I had passed the night in Mr. Wood's hotel room. *This is only the effect of Lizzie's warning,* I said to myself. For no news could travel to Boston that quickly. And I was almost certain I had not been seen.

Rather than showing the paper to me, Robert unfolded it and began to read aloud. *"Mrs. President Lincoln – as the ladies call her – has been shopping to a considerable extent in New York. Evidently that lady has no comprehension that Jefferson Davis intends to make good his threat to occupy the President's House by July, for she is expending thousands and thousands of Union dollars upon furnishings of luxurious taste."*

I sat stunned by how quickly the newspapers had traveled from the "gracious Mrs. Lincoln" and the "Illinois Queen" to this.

"I think they have exaggerated the amount," I said to my son.

Robert shoved the newspaper back into his pocket. "Can you not imagine how it is for me to have this printed?"

"But the story is about myself and not you."

"You do not think that every time my father appears in a cartoon as a rustic or an ape, every time he is drawn embracing Negroes, my schoolfellows do not look at me a little harder?" he asked. "Can you not believe that is enough to bear without having your faults described there as well?"

"I am sorry," I told him. "But it is to be expected that newspapermen will write stories about our family."

"Only if you persist in giving them something scandalous to write about!"

"I have only been shopping," I protested, saying it as strongly as if it were true.

Robert pushed his chair from the table and signaled the waiter to fetch away his lamb. I reached for him, intending to touch the back of his hand, his cheek if he would allow it. But the motion caused my skin, abraded from the carpet in Mr. Wood's room, to scratch against my stays. I let my arm fall upon the bleached-white cloth.

"I think such attention is something to which we must become accustomed," I said to him, "at least for the time your father is president."

Robert regarded me as if I were slow-witted. "Being the son of a president is nothing that I wished."

The following day, we left Boston to return to New York. Although we passed another night at the Metropolitan, I did not go to Mr. Wood. Instead, I skipped supper, as if denying one appetite might make it easier to deny another, and allowed my cousin to drug me into virtuousness.

We journeyed by railroad to Washington City, our train arriving late, as rebels in Baltimore had tried again to tear up the tracks. Despite the hour and the darkness, when my carriage at last clattered to the door of the President's House, I saw that my husband was waiting for me. Mr. Lincoln stood beneath the rounded portico, wearing an old gray shawl, and the sight of him looking older by more than the two weeks I had been away filled me with a remorse which turned my breathing bitter.

"I am happy to have you here and safe," he said, helping me from the carriage.

I wished to put my arms around him, feel if he had grown too thin, know if he was entirely well. But I was too fearful that my flesh might transmit to him all that had so recently been impressed upon it.

"Now that I have seen you," he said, "I must go back to my office."

"But it is after midnight," I protested.

"Turns out war is no great respecter of a man's sleep."

I slept little myself that night. For hours, I lay upon the mattress, filled with loathing for my own flesh, which was tender from all that I had done with Mr. Wood. Flesh made more tender from the desire to do all of it again. When I did sleep, I dreamt over every act of depravity. When I woke, I tortured myself with every kindness my husband ever granted me.

Mr. Wood sent a note the next day asking me to meet with him to decide some matters of wallpaper. "I am indisposed from travel," I responded, "and cannot come." The following day, arrived a request to review "certain expenses concerning the cleaning of chimney soot." I pleaded headache, advising Mr. Wood to settle the bill on his own authority. Although the gentleman sent a note every day wishing to see me about some piece of business, I declined him. I did not trust myself in his company – not in the rooms of Willard's Hotel where he lived, not even in the unprivate spaces of the President's House. For I doubted my ability to talk calmly of bills and appropriations when all I desired was to be unclothed by his cool competence.

When the markings left by Mr. Wood faded from my skin, I attempted to free myself of the craving for those unblessed acts with the permissible pleasures of the marriage bed. Since the war, Mr. Lincoln had taken to sleeping upon a sofa in the small room adjacent to his office, and I was obliged to pass five nights waiting in his bed before he came to it. Once he did come, I was so fearful I would betray myself with some new pliancy of body or wantonness of touch, I did no more than lie rigid with my arms at my sides, until my husband was prompted to ask if he was injuring me in some way.

"I am only chilled," I told him, although it was nearly summer and the night a warm one.

I clung to him then, attempting to forget all that had been done to my flesh since we last lay together. But it seemed that my time with Mr. Wood had rendered my passion more accessible, bringing it nearer the surface so I had to work more strongly than ever to keep myself in check. I tightened my throat so I would not moan and kept my mouth from my husband's skin, knowing the warmth of it upon my lips would have made the rest impossible. When at last it was done, and he lay sleeping with his face in my hair, I wept at how freely I had been allowed to spend my passion upon Mr. Wood, whom I did not love.

Summer came, and Washington City filled with damp heat and the barnyard smell of the hundreds of soldiers who camped over every green place. Most of these soldiers were untried: immigrants from the cities of the North who had enlisted for the pay, farm laborers from the territories who had done the same. General Scott wished more time to train these men, but Mr. Lincoln did not wish to give the Confederacy opportunity to train its soldiers. So on July twenty-first, the Union regiments marched upon the Virginia city of Manassas. But the Federals were unprepared for battle, and the Confederates turned them back at Bull Run. Eight hundred and forty-eight soldiers were killed, two thousand more wounded.

I believe Mr. Lincoln took each of these deaths upon himself, that he bore the responsibility of every maimed limb and broken spine. But I could not know for certain, for I saw little of my husband that summer.

I saw so very little of him, that when Mr. Hay, a young gentleman with a large mustache who had been hired as Mr. Nicolay's assistant, came to tell me I was wanted in Mr. Lincoln's office, I sprang up from the breakfast table, fearing that my husband had fallen ill. However, I knew otherwise when I saw the cast of his face, for Mr. Lincoln's features were turned brutal by rage.

"You can go," my husband said to Mr. Hay. "And you can sit," he told me.

Mr. Lincoln's office possessed both walls and carpeting of a dark shade of green, which on this day, made me feel as if I had wandered too far into dense woods. My husband was seated behind his desk – he had not bothered to stand for me, not even before the young secretary. I took the chair opposite, a large, high-backed thing meant for the proportions of men rather than ladies.

"I have received a letter," he said.

"Is it another threat?" I asked, hoping that his rage was for some rebel who meant us harm.

"In a sense." He placed a folded paper upon the green baize top of his desk. "Perhaps you should read it for yourself."

"If it is ugly, I do not wish to see it."

"It is not ugly," he replied. "Not in the manner you mean."

He pushed the letter across the desktop toward me.

"Read it," he repeated.

I took up the paper, slowly unfolding it. The hand was careful, the ink unblotted.

"*Dear President Lincoln,*" went the well-formed words. "*It appears that the appointment of Mr. Wood as Commissioner of Public Buildings has given great dissatisfactions to the citizens of this District, and some dastardly politicians are only waiting the action of the Senate. If Mr. W is confirmed, they will attempt to stab you in the most vital part by circulating scandal about your estimable Lady and Mr. W. They say the papers of this country and Europe will teem with it.*" The letter was signed, "*Union.*"

"Should I believe it?" my husband asked.

I cast about for an answer which would injure neither of us.

"Remembering," he said, "that we have promised to be truthful toward each other."

I set the letter upon the desk. "There is scandal between me and Mr. Wood."

My husband's mouth twisted. "Scandal of what kind?"

"The lowest kind."

On the day Mr. Lincoln came to tell me of the soldiers dead at Bull Run, he had said the number, and then pressed his hands against his temples, perhaps to force the information from his brain. Now I watched him repeat the gesture, his elbows pushing into the desktop, his fists pressing against his head.

"Did you not think of me at all?" he asked.

"I did," I told him.

"Apparently, it was not enough."

I wished to touch him, but the massive desk had placed him beyond my reach. "Could you not forgive me?" I asked. "I have heard you say that a woman has as much right as a man to break the bonds of marriage."

My husband raised his face to me, and I saw that it was marked by an awful melancholy. "I have never considered breaking them," he said.

I nearly choked then, upon a shame which seemed too big to hold, which pushed me to find some excuse to diminish it. "I expect it is easier for you to keep such promises," I replied.

Mr. Lincoln was up and around the desk before I could draw breath. With a jerk, he pulled me from the chair, gripping my shoulders with fingers ungiving as steel bands. His sallow face was flushed with blood, his breath fell acrid upon my cheek.

"You think I have no passion? You who should know better?"

With each word he shook me, loosening my hair and scattering my hairpins across the desktop. I feared he would harm me. And feared he would not.

"I have enough passion to drive us both into madness!" he declared.

"Then show it to me," I begged. "For there are times I believe it is the withholding of my desire which will drive *me* into madness."

"Is that what you do with Wood?" he spat. "Remove all hold from your desire?"

His question – which I would never have answered with words – called up an image of what I did do with Mr. Wood. My husband saw the blood rise to my face, and knowing it for my response, shoved me back into the chair.

"You have no honor," he said.

"I have never pretended to it," I told him. "My only admirable quality has been my love for you."

"And yet you debase it with what you have done with Wood."

"Nothing about what I have done with Mr. Wood has been about love."

He turned his face from me. "That makes it all the more disgusting."

I fell upon my knees. "It is disgusting," I said. "And I have done nothing except reproach myself for it." I pressed my face against his trouser legs, but his shins were so fleshless, his muscles so rigid, I might have been seeking comfort from a fencepost. "Can you not forgive my weakness?"

"I can forgive weakness," he replied. "But I cannot convince myself to love it."

I clutched at the fabric of his trousers, for I felt in danger of flying apart. "You do not love me?"

"It is better if you don't ask me that question," he said. "For I will only want to give you an honest answer."

I felt a terrible stabbing behind my eye. My vision narrowed and turned tunnel-like, making my husband's figure appear more distant. I pulled myself upright, but the effort of rising made the blood overfill my brain, and I was forced to take hold of my husband's waist to keep from falling to the floor.

Mr. Lincoln removed my hands from his sides. "It may be my

own weakness," he told me, "but I do not want to be made to touch your flesh."

The pain behind my eye was so great, I could not see with it. "You will not let me in your bed?"

"I couldn't put my hand to you without thinking how you'd been misused."

I shall retch, I thought. *Here in this office where gentlemen come to beg my husband for their own favors.* I took a stumbling step to the massive desk, still covered in hairpins, and laid my head upon it. For some time, I remained upon the green baize taking shallow breaths meant to put down my sickness, while Mr. Lincoln waited, silent and less solicitous than a stranger might be had I collapsed in the street.

By small degrees, I raised my head, testing to see if I would retch, if I might remain upright. "I shall not cease to hope you will forgive me," I said to my husband.

Then, I went out, leaving behind the hairpins like small objects of conjure.

As summer moved into autumn, the bills from my shopping trip to New York began to arrive. The amounts written upon these state-ments were high, much higher than I had imagined; and though I had kept myself out of Mr. Wood's company since my return, I knew that if I wished to prevent any of these being sent to my husband, I would need to see that gentleman another time.

I arranged to meet Mr. Wood in the tearoom of Willard's Hotel. This little parlor, outfitted in an abundance of ruffled table linens, was inhabited at all hours by elderly ladies. As further protection, I clothed myself in a gray dress with a high neck, which possessed a great many buttons. The dress was chaste to the point of spinsterish; still, as I stood before the glass fastening myself into it, I could not keep from imagining the exquisitely long time it would require to be unbuttoned from it.

I arrived early, for I did not trust myself to walk with steadiness into any room which already had Mr. Wood in it. Mr. Wood arrived some minutes late, seeming in this little parlor precariously masculine. He ordered black tea spiced with bergamot, as if he knew how it would affect me. I asked for a tea from China which smelled strongly of coal fire in order to keep away the scent of his. Once our tea was served – in cups almost as fine as those for which I now possessed the bill – I took from my reticule a collection of notices and placed them upon the table between us.

"I have just received these from A. T. Stewart's," I informed him.

Mr. Wood glanced at the bills, but did not touch them. "Mr. Stewart is admirably prompt."

"And the sum is excessively high," I added.

The gentleman nodded, as if this did not surprise him. "Alexander carries quality. And you have a talent for recognizing it."

"What is more," I continued, ignoring the suggestion in his remark, "these bills have come to the President's House because they have remained unpaid."

Mr. Wood shrugged – a languid, sensuous gesture. "That is because I have run out of money."

"What about the appropriation?"

"Gone."

"Gone where?"

"To Lord & Taylor and Haughwout & Company, and to the prompt Mr. Stewart."

"But there was twenty thousand!"

"The French wallpaper was six thousand eight hundred, the Solferino china three thousand two hundred, the East Room carpeting two thousand five hundred."

"You have developed quite a competent head for figures," I told him. "Much more than you demonstrated in New York."

"Your dress today is far less distracting." He nodded at my gown.

"Was it not your task to keep track of the spending?" I asked.

"It was difficult keeping pace with you." A corner of his mouth lifted. "In all respects."

I forced myself to think only upon the bills. "If the appropriation is already gone," I said, calculating quickly, "then we have spent nearly half again as much as the original figure."

"That would coincide with my estimation," he replied.

The coal smell of my tea had begun to make me ill. "I cannot allow Mr. Lincoln to discover this."

Mr. Wood leaned back upon a ruffled chair which only made him appear more undomesticated. "I imagine that with all your husband has discovered, a few bills for china and carpeting will only prove a minor indiscretion."

"What are you talking of?"

"Most of Washington City knows about the letter threatening to expose us if I am confirmed as commissioner."

"How can that be?"

"It appears that young Mr. Hay is something of a gossip."

I felt as exposed as if Mr. Wood *had* unfastened all my buttons. "We must pay every bill," I told him.

"With what?" he said. "I cannot put my hands on any more money unless I go to the president. And I do not imagine he would enjoy seeing me in his office."

"We shall have to find it!" I insisted.

Mr. Wood laughed, and a young lady in a feathered hat turned to look at his flashing teeth. "And what do you propose?" he asked. "Shall I enlist for soldier's pay, since it is very unlikely I will be confirmed as commissioner? Or do you intend to barter your creditable charms upon the open market?"

"Please," I begged him. "I need your help."

"And I have no help to give you." His eyes were unsympathetic as a cat's.

Mr. Wood raised the bergamot-flavored tea to his mouth, breathing in the scent, so like that of his own skin, with unsuppressed pleasure. "You know that I live here," he said. "I have a room on the second floor."

I placed both hands upon the stack of bills, and kept hold of them as I got to my feet. "Good day, Mr. Wood."

Mr. Wood rose gracefully from the table. "Good day, Mrs. President." With swiftness I could not counter, he took my hand and put his lips to it.

My legs trembled so, I did not know how I would walk out of Willard's. I gazed about at the elderly ladies sipping tea, the sentinels I had imagined would protect me, and knew that they were powerless. For if Mr. Wood had wished to take me here in Willard's tearoom, I would have lifted my skirts to render it easier.

Over the following weeks more bills arrived from New York, and I thought of nothing but how I might raise the money to pay them. My first idea was to sell the old furniture I had spent so much replacing, and I had the mouse-gnawed settees and sofas set out upon lawn, hoping the fact that they had been sat upon by presidents might lend them some historic value. Many people came to examine the broken-down pieces – including a newspaper reporter, who the following day pronounced my economy to be an "embarrassment to the country." However, it appeared that that country suffered this embarrassment for no good cause, as the furniture sold for very little more than it would have cost to cart it away.

Next, I attempted to sell the manure from the stables of the President's House. "When one considers the horses, and Willie's pony, and the goats sent to Taddie," I explained to the groundskeeper, a red-faced man named John Watt, "we must be generating more manure than we can use in the gardens."

Mr. Watt, who had been spreading fertilizer around the roots of the azaleas when I came to tell him this plan, studied me through watery green eyes.

"Do you not think we might be paid ten cents a cartload for it?" I asked him.

"Ten cents is rather costly, madam," he replied. "Even for presidential manure."

Nevertheless, I instructed Mr. Watt to make up a sign offering our excess fertilizer for ten cents a cartload. This time, the newspaperman wrote that "Mrs. Lincoln must certainly be a monarchist, for under a democracy, the manure of the President's House rightfully belongs to all the people."

"Perhaps if we lowered the price," I said to Mr. Watt some days later. "Or made a larger sign?"

The groundskeeper, whom I had followed into the kitchen garden, rose from his work staking the small wild strawberries called *fraises du bois*, which we distributed at state dinners like gems. "Are we trying to finance the war with manure?" he asked. Mr. Watt was Scottish-born, and the rolling cadence of his accent oft kept me from knowing whether he was serious or mocking.

"I am trying to pay the bills for refurbishing the President's House," I told him.

The groundskeeper regarded me closely, perhaps to learn if I was serious or mocking.

"Was there not a large appropriation?" he said.

"Twenty thousand."

"And it is used up?"

I nodded. "The bills, however, continue to arrive."

Mr. Watt squinted at the house through the low autumn sunlight. "Does the president know?" he asked.

"Mr. Lincoln cannot learn of it."

The groundskeeper shifted his gaze back to me. "Any idea how much is needed?"

"Only today I received a bill tallying one hundred and ninety-six dollars for window washing."

Mr. Watt rubbed his cheek, leaving a smear of dirt upon it. "That is an amount which would be easy to add to my own expenses," he said. "And after it is paid to me, I could let you have it for the windows."

"That is very kind," I told him. "But one hundred and ninety-six dollars is only a fraction of what I require."

"Of course." He glanced about the grounds, as if the money were to be found among the plantings. "Let us say, then, that the next time I place an order for roses, the voucher I turn in for payment includes one thousand dollars' worth of camellias that did not appear on my actual order. Might that go a longer way toward solving your dilemma?"

"Would that not be dishonest, Mr. Watt?"

The groundskeeper bent to the vines he had been staking and pulled off a few of the small *fraises*, dropping them into my palm. "I don't know if it would rightly be called dishonest," he replied. "All we are doing is taking one thousand dollars which has been approved for camellias that the President's House does not need, and reappropriating it for new draperies, which it does."

I put the berries upon my tongue. They were warm from the sun and remarkably sweet. "Seen in such a light," I said, "I expect there would be no harm."

"Just as there would be no harm," continued Mr. Watt, his eyes becoming more focused, "if I were to come to you with the name of a man who might wish a postmastership or a clerk's position, and you were to repeat that name to the president."

The *fraises* had left a stain upon my palm, and I rubbed my hand against my skirt. "You are speaking about patronage."

"I would call it more of a suggestion," said the groundskeeper.

But I knew that Mr. Lincoln would call it patronage and think it dishonorable.

I was about to inform Mr. Watt that I must turn down his offer, no matter how generously made, but I recalled the bills which had come for the windows, and the French wallpaper, and the miles of carpeting. If none of these were paid, sooner or later newspapermen would hear of it. If not from the merchants themselves, then from young Mr. Hay. And such stories, printed in the papers, would do more harm to my husband than the giving of a postmastership to a friend of Mr. Watt.

"When were you planning to order the roses?" I asked the groundskeeper.

"I will do it today," he assured me.

Throughout the autumn, I conspired with Mr. Watt to pay the most insistent of my creditors – sending money approved for hothouse flowers and a plantation's worth of vegetable seedlings to the merchants of New York. Two or three times, the groundskeeper came to me with a name, and these I dutifully put in a note to Mr. Lincoln; for during this time, my husband stayed out of my company. I made no effort to learn if any of Mr. Watt's friends were given appointments, convincing myself that ignorance was equal to innocence. Nevertheless, despite the ingenuity of Mr. Watt, who was as skilled at padding accounts as at raising French strawberries, the great majority of my bills remained unpaid; and by the time the cold weather arrived and the garden did not create so many expenses, Mr. Watt's accounting could not cover even the smallest portion of my debts.

As he had predicted, Mr. Wood was not confirmed for the position of Commissioner of Public Buildings. The job went instead to Major Benjamin French, an elderly gentleman of above sixty, who possessed a white beard and a thin-lipped mouth which could present no temptation. I sent a few of my bills on to Major French, but only the lesser ones. The rest I replied to by way of notes which begged more time, arguing that "it would be unpatriotic to press the president upon the topic of wallpaper, when he is so distracted by matters of war."

The rich things I had bought in New York continued to arrive at the President's House, and I concentrated upon transforming the neglected residence into a splendid symbol of the Union. I oversaw the laying of carpets and the replacement of chandeliers, filled the public rooms with silk-covered chairs, and the private ones with rosewood bedsteads. The oddly shaped oval room upon the second floor, I lined with books and made into a family library, fitting it with thickly pillowed window seats and deep chairs for reading, and placing upon every table an astral lamp which could be turned up bright.

This library became my favorite room in the house. During the beginning of that winter, I went to it every day, passing the time before supper there with Willie, who was about to turn eleven, and liked to read the volumes of poetry which belonged to his father. Poetry which was morbid, but did not ever make Willie so. When he had had enough of poems, he would sit upon the arm of my chair and recite for me the train schedules of the Great Western and the Baltimore & Ohio Railroads.

Such conversation would have been tedious delivered by anybody else, but Willie possessed a passion for the subject of trains, and viewed the intricate timing of arrivals and departures as if such a feat of orchestration was as remarkable as the working of the heavens. He described the comings and goings of trains bound for distant cities with such unreserved eagerness, I grew lost in contemplation of tight-scheduled connections and the particulars of track switching in Albany.

It was upon one such afternoon, a day in mid-December when the tall windows of the library showed a sky smothered in snow clouds, that I glanced up from Willie's explanation of how a train might travel from Chicago to New York in the space of a single day, and noticed Mr. Lincoln standing in the doorway. Seeing my husband so little, I perceived more the changes in his appearance, and on this day noticed how his skin looked as if it had been covered with dulling powder.

Mr. Lincoln did not speak until his son had finished describing his invented journey. "I wonder if I might talk with your mother," he said to him.

"All right, Pa." Willie slipped off the arm of my chair.

"Come see me later," his father told him, "and we'll plot your route on one of my general's maps. Might be the best use anyone's made of them so far."

Willie went out, and Mr. Lincoln stepped into the room.

I imagined all the phrases of forgiveness he might utter, as if to plant them in his mind, compel them from his mouth. But in truth, I did not wish my husband to say anything, I only wished for him to touch me.

"I have been sent some of your bills from New York." He fell into one of the deep chairs as if falling into drowning. "How much more than the appropriation have you spent?"

In the light, his face was sallow with exhaustion, and it made me wish to lie to him. But in time, I knew that he would learn the amount, and it felt unkind to make him come to me twice.

"At least another ten thousand," I told him.

He scraped at his face. "We will have to pay everything you have overspent ourselves."

"If we had the money, do you not think I would have used it to pay these bills before you had seen them?" I asked. "We have spent everything we had making you president."

He sank deeper into the chair. "Nevertheless," he told me, "I cannot allow the country to take responsibility for your indiscretion."

This felt a cruel word to use for it, but I was not blameless enough to complain. "We cannot pay bills with money we do not have," I replied.

For some time he sat without speaking, so long that I found myself studying his face for signs of hypochondriasis. But rather than dead, he looked only sorrowful. With what seemed too much effort, he pulled himself out of the chair.

"You will force me to go to Congress and ask for money for decorating when we are at war," he told me, moving to the door. "The newspapers will savage me for it, and rightly so." Then he left me sitting alone in the room I had fixed up for our family.

I expected I would weep, but though I was very near to it, I was taken instead by a stronger desire which did not allow for weeping. Getting to my feet, I hurried out of the library and down the corridor to the wide staircase which led to the first floor. All at once, I had to see the newly hung wallpaper, the just-laid carpeting, the dining chairs cushioned in silk. I had to see that there was something good and beautiful in what I had done.

Going from room to room, I opened cabinets, placing my hands upon the bone-smooth china, lifted the furled lengths of velvet draperies to feel the weight of them. There was nothing left in any of the rooms which was tattered or broken. Nothing left which would make anyone believe that the Union's soldiers could not move the rebels from within a river's breadth of its capital. And that knowledge alone was more soothing than weeping.

* * *

The reception to show off the refurbished President's House was planned for the beginning of February. I sent out eight hundred invitations and then consumed myself with the preparations, hiring caterers from as far as New York and consulting with florists who could produce flowers in the dead of winter. But three days before the reception was to take place, Willie was stricken with a terrible dysentery accompanied by a cramping which made him fold upon himself in wordless agony.

"We cannot have the reception while Willie is so ill," I told Doctor Stone, who had recently become our Washington City physician. Doctor Stone was a gentleman of not quite forty, who, like all doctors, equipped himself with an ample beard and a firm conviction in the rightness of his opinions.

"You have half of Washington City rapturous over the fact that they have been invited," he replied, "and half sunk in invidious despair that they have not. One of my lady patients has informed me that if I do not cure her catarrh by the night of the reception, she will come anyway and infect all of your guests."

"But Willie cannot lie straight for the cramping of his bowels." I kept my voice lowered, for we stood speaking in the corridor outside my sons' bedroom which led to Mr. Lincoln's office, and seemed always to be crowded with a steady current of gentlemen come to petition the president for some favor.

"I shall dose Willie strongly with calomel to purge the disease," Doctor Stone assured me. "He should be quite recovered by the reception."

At first it appeared the doctor's assessment was correct. By the following day, Willie was able to drink the blackberry cordial Doctor Stone had prescribed, and the dysentery came only in the morning. By evening, however, a rash the color of roses had come up over Willie's chest.

"It is typhoid, is it not?" I said to Doctor Stone. I uttered the name of the sickness in a whisper.

"There is a great deal of typhoid in Washington City since the soldiers have set up camp," replied the doctor. "But this may yet be a case of malarial fever. Make up a tea of Peruvian bark and get him to drink it every hour."

Willie did not like the tea, which coated his tongue and caused him to gag. Only my promise that drinking it would halt the spasms which roiled his intestines persuaded him to sip at it. But though I forced the tea upon him for an entire day, the cramping did not cease, and I imagined it was only my son's gentle nature which kept him from accusing me of telling lies.

When I reported to Doctor Stone that Willie was no better, he instructed me to increase the amount of bark to water. But my son retched up half of what I urged down his throat, and by nightfall, his fever had risen so, Mr. Lincoln came and carried him out so his unhinged ranting would not frighten Taddie.

We put Willie in the Prince of Wales Room, which had been intended for guests, and which I had outfitted with an enormous rosewood bed eight feet in length. The bed possessed a carved headboard of nearly equal height, and lying upon the mattress beneath it, my sick son seemed smaller and more vulnerable. I tied back the gold-edged curtains which surrounded the bed so that I could dose Willie with calomel and bring him the chamber pot for the dysentery which would not cease. For the length of that night, I sat upon a chair upholstered in Morris velvet and watched my son in uneasy sleep.

I stayed with Willie the morning of the reception, waking him to drink the bark tea and praying he would fall to sleep before he retched it up. I left him only when a servant came to tell me that the catering gentlemen from Maillard's had insisted upon speaking with me regarding matters of utmost importance.

Until this summons, I had come near to forgetting the reception, and when I entered the dining room, still wearing my calomel-stained dress from the day before, I was surprised by the sight of the elaborate confections upon which I had devoted weeks deciding. At regular intervals along the linen-covered table, catering gentlemen in white jackets hovered about centerpieces, each more elaborate than the next – a candelabra supported by a pair of kneeling Cupids, a shell of tropical fruit held aloft by mermaids, a cake in the shape of Fort Pickens filled with candied quail. Although I had memory of ordering such extravagances, Willie's sickness had clouded it; to have these fancies suddenly appear made them seem the products of my own fevered dream.

"Where would madam like the Goddess of Liberty?" One of the catering gentlemen stood before me, his jacket too white for my sleep-starved eyes. I knew there was sense to his question; I only could not find it.

"Her pose," continued the caterer, seeing that no instruction would come from me, "suggests lightness. I expect she would best complement a dessert, such as the bonbons or the jelly *compettes*."

"Wherever you decide," I told him, for I no longer cared about the Goddess of Liberty, though I had made Mr. Maillard send all the way to Boston for her. I cared only that Willie had taken no solid food for two days. Another of the gentlemen in white coats bore down upon me with a spun-sugar battleship. "You decide all of it," I said to the man holding the goddess, then ran back upstairs to my son's bedside.

That afternoon Doctor Stone recommended jalap for Willie, instructing me to mix the powder with jam to disguise the bitterness.

"You cannot recommend I attend the reception now," I said to him.

"Instruct one of your servants stay with your son," he told me. "And tell them to send for you if there is any change."

But I did not trust anyone beside Mr. Lincoln and myself to watch over Willie, save for the dressmaker Lizzie Keckly.

In the months since she had begun working for me, the mulatto mantua-maker I had first called "Mrs. Keckly" had moved in affection to the more informal "Lizzie"; although I could not persuade her – even when we were entirely alone – to call me anything but Mrs. Lincoln. During the weeks Lizzie worked upon my dress for the reception – a white satin gown with black lace trimming and a deep neckline – we spent many hours in my bedroom, Lizzie pinning swaths of satin over me. I believe it was that intimacy – the bedroom, her brown hands upon my half-clad body – which prompted Lizzie to tell me how the son she had lost in the fighting at Wilson's Creek had been fathered by the white man who waited for her every Sunday after church. I confided in Lizzie as well, telling her about the hoodoo hand and my stepmother. I think I would have told her, too, about how I had come to have my eldest son, but for the sense I had that she would have considered it improper, for the half-Negro dressmaker possessed a decorum as well-formed as that of any Southern dowager.

The white satin gown Lizzie made required careful lacing, both to fit me into it, and to ensure that with its neckline, none of me spilled out of it, and I asked my new friend to come before the reception and help me dress. She came early, and once she had laced me into my corset, obliged me to bend forward more than once to check her tying. The dress she had stitched was laid out upon the bed, the skirt spread the length of the mattress, as if the lady wearing it had collapsed there and been magicked out of it. As Lizzie made to retrieve the gown, I stayed her with a hand upon her wrist.

"I am anxious for Willie," I said to her. "And the housemaid is so fearful of Mr. Nicolay, I do not trust her to send for me if he turns worse."

Lizzie regarded me with eyes colored like her skin, and I thought again how handsome her face appeared, although it was too capable-looking for prettiness.

"I will be happy to stay with your son," she told me.

I think that it was lack of sleeping which caused me to embrace Lizzie – that and an overpowering gratitude. Like a number of Negroes I knew who had bought their own freedom, Lizzie Keckly possessed a formality among white people which was polite and unwavering, and though I pressed her strongly to my well-corseted bosom, she did not place her hands upon me.

I relaxed my hold and took a step back. "You are a good friend to me," I said.

Lizzie lifted the dress from the bed and assisted me into it, allowing her hands, now engaged in the practice of her profession, to rest lightly upon me. "You merit such friendship."

I smiled at her. "I have done little but hire you to sew too many dresses."

Lizzie moved behind me to do up the pearl buttons at the back of my gown. "You do not recall the letter you wrote me when my son was killed?" Her voice quavered, so lightly I almost believed I imagined it.

"That is only what women do for each other," I told her.

"That is what white women do for each other," she replied. "And what colored women – when they have writing – do for each other. But it is not often what a white woman does for a colored woman."

"I only imagined that your grief for your son was the equal of mine for Eddie," I said, "and wrote from that."

Lizzie finished the buttons and came to stand before me. "It is for that imagining," she told me, "that I am your friend."

When I was dressed and my hair done up with white winter roses, I brought Lizzie to the Prince of Wales room where Willie lay uneasy with cramping and fever. I was surprised to discover Mr. Lincoln, already dressed in his formal clothes, sitting upon the enormous mattress beside his sick son.

"Has he improved?" I asked my husband.

"Very much," he replied.

I could see by Willie's hard shivering that Mr. Lincoln was not being truthful; still, I appreciated the deception, for by it my husband showed me more kindness than he had since the arrival of the letter about Mr. Wood.

Willie began to thrash about, and Mr. Lincoln lifted his son's shoulders from the mattress. Before my husband could reach for the basin, Willie retched jalap and jam upon his father's trousers. Mr. Lincoln held his son upright, and when there was no more to retch up, he used his pocket handkerchief to wipe Willie's mouth. Cradling his son's head in one large hand, he eased it back upon the pillows.

I sent Mr. Lincoln to have his trousers seen to, for I do not believe he would have thought of it upon his own, and Lizzie and I remained with Willie until Mr. Nicolay came to tell me that all of my guests had arrived and that I must go down.

It seemed to me that the East Room had been made too bright – by the chandeliers I had insisted be scrubbed and fixed with clearer glass, and the light from them which reflected upon the satin of the ladies' skirts. I had bought much for this room which was polished and brass, and everything glittered with such hard light, I could scarcely squint against it.

At my appearance, the Marine Band, stationed now in another corner of the room, for there were no stains to hide, began to play an unfamiliar tune. It was, Mr. Nicolay informed me, newly composed and entitled "The Mary Lincoln Polka." The melody was gay and sprightly, and each measure of it made me wish to flee its cheeriness. But I could not leave. Eight hundred people had come to see the decorations upon which I had overspent – and I was First Lady.

Mr. Nicolay, who was in charge of protocol, positioned me in the receiving line and as each of my guests approached, consulted an oversized ledger so that he could whisper their name to me. I recall nothing I spoke to the distinguished gentlemen and ladies who reached across my skirts to take my outstretched hand, for my attention was too fixed upon my sick child's bile and his unending dysentery.

After an hour, I made an excuse to Mr. Nicolay and hurried to the second floor to check upon Willie. Lizzie had pulled one of the velvet chairs nearer the bed and now sat upon it, for once not sewing at something, but keeping her eyes instead upon my son.

"Has he stirred?" I asked.

"Only to tell me a dream about soldiers," she said softly. "Although I'm not certain he didn't believe me a dream."

"Did he take any beef tea?"

"A little. But it made him cramp, and I did not want to force it on him."

I stayed until Mr. Nicolay sent a servant to retrieve me, but came back twice more when the secretary was distracted by a party of European royalty.

At midnight the doors to the dining room were opened and the guests feasted on scalloped oysters and canvasback ducks. The smell of these luxuries made me feel that I would retch, and leaving my guests to gorge upon the delicacies, I fled upstairs to Willie's room, which smelled of bitter jalap and sickness, and did not distress my stomach so much.

I did not return to the reception until Mr. Nicolay sent word that it was time to make a formal farewell. I circled the East Room upon the arm of a gentleman I did not know, but whom Mr. Nicolay had chosen by the complicated hierarchy of protocol, while the Marine Band again played that too-bright polka. The moment I finished my circuit of the room, which felt as enormous as the entire soldier-crowded city, I rushed away, eager to free myself of the dress which made it difficult to stand near enough Willie's bed to catch his retching.

I stayed with Willie all that night, and while he got no worse, he also got no better. The following morning, Taddie woke complaining of cramps and dysentery. And by nightfall, Doctor Stone had diagnosed typhoid fever in both my sons.

"What can we do?" I asked him.

"Only what we have been doing," he told me.

I do not know how many days passed, for I slept only in the times between my sons' spasming. Upon Doctor Stone's instructions, I dosed them both with calomel and jalap, coaxing it down their throats and catching it in basins when it came up.

When he could, Mr. Lincoln came to ask if Willie or Tad had

eaten anything, if I could say they were at all better. These conversations, filled with information about jalap and chamber pots, were the first real discourse we had engaged in since I had confessed to him of Mr. Wood, and I cherished them as much as if they had been composed of poetry.

Lizzie Keckly came every day. I offered to pay her for her time, for I knew the hours she devoted to my sons cost her in dressmaking fees. Lizzie, however, would take no money, saying only that as any lady would do, she came out of friendship. She helped me wash Willie and Tad and went out for more Peruvian bark or jalap powder when we ran out. And when there was no nursing to be done, she sat beside me upon the velvet chairs, now stained with bile and jam, and distracted me with news of the world, which had become as foreign to me as the moon.

It was Lizzie who told me what the newspapers wrote about my reception; that the *Washington Star* had called it "the most superb affair of its kind ever seen here," that the *Tribune* had proclaimed the newly decorated President's House "an American Versailles."

"And no one had anything disparaging to say?" I asked her.

Lizzie compressed her mouth in a smile of some irony. "It would not be Washington City if no one had anything disparaging to say."

"Tell it to me, then," I said. "It will distract me better than the compliments."

"Some of it is unkind," she warned.

I glanced at Willie, his fingers plucking at the bedcovers in the anxious motion of the very elderly. "What can they say that will injure me?" I asked her.

Lizzie nodded and moved her chair nearer. "The *Washington Chronicle* has devoted much space to an editorial decrying your disgraceful frivolity and gluttony when the country is in mourning," she told me. "And a lady writer has published a poem in which a dying soldier with no blanket watches your reception through the window and expounds for many stanzas upon the heartlessness of the 'Lady-President.'"

"Did it possess any literary merit?" I asked.

"I would say the effect was more malicious than literate," Lizzie replied.

I counted upon Lizzie to bring me the news, to read to me the stories about Washington City politics, to tell me what was happening with the war. Only one story did I read for myself. One which I knew she would not have allowed me to see.

It was late afternoon, and I was hurrying down the corridor between Willie's sickbed and Tad's. Of late, I had begun to keep my eyes lowered when I made this journey, hoping the petitioners would take me for a servant in my sick-stained dress and unwound hair. On this day, my downcast gaze fell upon a newspaper which must have been dropped by one of the office-seekers, and the headline of it froze me where I stood. "President's Sons Hopelessly Ill" was what it said.

"Have you told the newspapers that my sons will die?" I asked Doctor Stone when he came, showing him the paper, forcing him to read that headline.

"I never call a case hopeless," he told me. "And I never speak to newspapermen. I do not like their manners."

"And my sons?" I asked.

"I wish you to increase their jalap."

I burned the paper, for if the headline could not be denied, at least it could be reduced to ashes. Still, the new quietness of the gentlemen who passed outside the sickrooms was evidence that the story had existed, and their hushed voices proof that they, too, had read of the hopelessness of my sons.

After a week, Taddie began to improve. His chamber pot did not need to be emptied as often as Willie's, and his did not contain the bits of pinkish material found in his brother's, which made it seem that having run out of digested matter, my middle son's body was now expelling its organs. But while Taddie retched less and kept down more of the beef tea, Willie fell into a kind of slumber from which he could not be wakened.

"He is badly dehydrated," said Doctor Stone, showing me Willie's cracked and peeling lips, pointing out the papery feel of his skin. But I already knew the diagnosis, for that morning Willie had begun to cry without tears.

Every half hour, upon the doctor's instructions, I dipped a cloth in water and swabbed the inside of my son's mouth, holding it open with a finger pressed to his teeth, teeth which had not so long ago broken through his flesh and had not yet had time to lose their scalloped edges. Willie's slumber, too much like death, frightened me, and I tried to call back my son by the sound of my voice. I talked without ceasing, describing for him everything we had done together and everything we might yet do. Even explaining to him how a train might travel from Chicago to New York in the space of a single day, to prove I had been listening well enough to have learned it by heart.

Two days passed without Willie waking.

"Is it hopeless now?" I asked the doctor.

Behind his beard, Doctor Stone appeared sorrowful, and no longer so certain of his opinions. "It is dark," he told me, "but never hopeless. If it is God's wish, anyone may recover."

I sent for Mr. Lincoln.

"What did the doctor say?" he asked.

"He has advised prayer."

My husband did not speak, but upon his face I saw the only sorrow on earth equal to my own.

Neither of us would leave Willie. We sat upon the mattress, upon either side of our son, each holding a small, still hand. As I waited beneath the headboard, which loomed like something about to fall upon me, I began to hate the enormous rosewood bed, for its imposing grandeur spoke of irretrievable events. *When this is done,* I thought, *perhaps I will burn it. And then throw myself upon the fire.*

As the day wore on, I remembered how we recalled Eddie's life for him before we let him go, and I thought we should do as much for Willie. *I shall mention how he watched Donati's Comet with opened mouth, as if to catch its brightness,* I thought. *I shall say how he stayed beside Taddie on the train to Washington City, translating his brother's imperfect speech for strangers.* But each of these recollections tore too mercilessly at my heart. *Do not think upon how he has always been a warm presence at your side,* I warned myself. *How if he dies, you shall never be able to look too directly into your own eyes, for their resemblance to his. Only set your entire mind to praying for his recovery.*

I believe that my husband prayed also for Willie. Mr. Lincoln was unused to prayer, he admired reason too much, but for all the time that we sat beside our son, I could see his mouth move, forming words so quiet they could only be intended for God.

As the sun began to set – early, for it was still February – Willie's ragged pulling at the air softened; then grew more shallow; then, with nothing to mark the change, ceased altogether. His going was so quiet, the stillness of his slumber already so much like death, it was some moments before I understood that the small hand I held could not – and would not again – know the pressure of my fingers. I gazed upon my son's face, thinned into a shape which made him seem older than his eleven years. But upon his face was the rapturous expression he wore when he prayed, the one I saw when I, less devout than he, sat in the church and studied him, my thoughts more upon my child than upon God.

Mr. Lincoln continued to hold fast to Willie's hand, and I wondered if he understood that his child was gone.

I must tell him, I thought. *Tell him that his rare and nearly silent prayer has not been answered.* But what issued from my mouth instead was incoherent, a sound which came from my grief instead of my thinking. And when it was over, I fell upon the bed and crushed my child against the aching in my chest, held his wasted body over my heart like binding meant to staunch blood from a wound. Willie's arms hung limp, the fingers trailing upon the bedcovers, and I think that I pleaded with him to lift them and put them about my shoulders. But I cannot be certain, because a kind of madness overtook me then. A madness which is generous and temporary, and protects the reason.

In the days which followed Willie's dying I alternated between the clouded derangement of mourning and a clarity made too bright by grief. I recall that the sight of my son's unclothed body – his ribs and the bones of his hips pushed so hard against the container of his skin they threatened to tear through it – made the room reel and sent me into convulsions during which I was certain I would choke upon my own terrible sadness. I possess a memory of Mr. Lincoln gazing at his son's dead face and telling himself, "It is hard, hard to have him die," as if disbelieving the hardness of it. And I remember enough to believe that it was Lizzie Keckly who removed my clothes, pulling over my head a dress which smelled of jalap and Peruvian bark. And that it was she who tended to Taddie, and who kept from him the news about his brother until he was stronger.

I know that it was Mr. Nicolay who left the mourning manual outside my door. *Sepulchers of Our Departed* was its title, and it recommended quiet grief for funerals, for "only Jews and the heathen howl in impious anguish." I knew also that the sight of the coffin lid being shut upon Willie's small, beloved face would turn me into the most unrestrained of howling heathens, and so I kept myself from the service.

It was Lizzie who described for me this first state funeral conducted for a child. She sat in a chair beside my bed and told me of the dignitaries and important gentlemen who had filled the East Room, so many that rows of wooden seats had to be constructed along the walls. She told me, too, how Willie's father had wept quietly into his hands.

"And Robert?" I asked, for my eldest son had come from Harvard for his younger brother's funeral.

Lizzie did not meet my gaze. "Robert wore a very fine suit."

"Did he grieve?" I persisted.

"He behaved very properly," replied Lizzie, "as Robert always does."

One week exactly from the evening upon which Willie died, I was pulled from my bed by an unearthly noise – a high-pitched wailing which came from the room where my son had succumbed to typhoid. I did not know the time, only that it was dark, and I suspected that my reason was addled – unbalanced by lack of food, lack of rest, and too much sorrow. Yet I was certain that the sound was my son, and that he was crying for me.

I leapt from my bed with such haste, I was struck to the floor with dizziness. Crawling across the carpet, I found my dressing table and pulled myself to my feet, then waited only until I was certain I would not fall again before crossing the corridor and trying the door to the Prince of Wales Room. But it was locked.

"I will come to you!" I told my son. And I leaned into the door as if I might will my flesh through it. From this position, I could hear the wailing better, hear it well enough to notice that there was something familiar in the tone, something which did not sound like a child. And it was then I understood that the keening belonged neither to Willie nor to his ghost, but to my husband.

Mr. Lincoln wept for his son with an unrestraint he did not allow himself elsewhere. The howling of his grief came as if he did not care if his sobbing shook him apart, untethered him from his reason.

"Let me come to you," I called through the shut door. "We can grieve him together."

I could not keep from recalling how it had been after Eddie, how we had come together in grief to make the child who had now been taken from us. I did not count upon anything similar now. It was too late, in too many respects. But I thought I might count upon the consolation of touch, of comforting a grief I knew myself.

"This burden would be lighter if we bore it together," I told him.

However, Mr. Lincoln would not cease his wailing, and he would not open the door to me.

I pleaded with my husband until my throat was raw and my back ached with standing. And only when I had run out of hope that I might be allowed past that unyielding door did I return to my room, sinking into my bed with a sorrow which felt heavier than when I had risen, weighted by the knowledge that even our shared grief would not repair the damage I had inflicted upon us.

(July 29) General Farnsworth has just been to see Mrs. Lincoln – Says she wrote him a note yesterday asking him to come – (This note she must have put in the office yesterday when she claimed to have written only to her sister.)
—Patient Progress Reports for Bellevue Place Sanitarium

The letters I posted in Batavia while the carriage driver Mr. Paddleford waited outside were more pleading than was proper. "I am being held very much against my will," I wrote in them. "Come! Come and see that I am sane."

Of the five important gentlemen to whom I had written, three sent back replies the following morning. These letters were penned in a style so simple, I suspected their authors had convinced themselves that my mind was not only deranged, but had also returned to childhood. "Those in charge of you at Bellevue Place know what it best," they all advised. "You must listen to the doctor and do all that he says." In none was there any mention of coming to see me.

I read these letters in my room, then tore them into pieces because I wished no one at Bellevue Place to know that I had written to any person who did not appear upon Robert's list, and because it was so very gratifying to tear them.

Two letters remained unaccounted for: one which had been written to General John Franklin Farnsworth, a hero of the War Between the States and a former congressman, and one sent to Judge James Bradwell. I had met the judge through his wife, Myra, with whom I had sat in the séance parlors of Chicago.

Surely one of these gentlemen will come to me, I told myself. Today, I think. For I have made the situation so urgent they will not want to take the time for writing. I paced my room, imagining the carriage of my rescuer coming up the asylum drive. But the thought made me too restless to stay in that room, even to stay within the limestone walls of the building. And suddenly it seemed the best thing would be to wait outside and meet the gentleman's carriage when it came.

I dressed in black linen of some lightness, for though it was still July, the day had already acquired an August mercilessness, then went to walk the dusty path which crossed the front of the asylum and gave a view onto the road. Mrs. Munger's husband came at noon. Mrs.

Johnston's arrived at one. The day grew sweltering, and my blood became too heated for my veins. Beneath the dark-colored linen, my flesh was sopping. A heat headache throbbed at my temples, and I knew that if I did not go in, my rescuer would arrive and find me collapsed upon the drive like a woman too deranged to know to come in from the hotness. But I could not make myself give up the path for the cool of the asylum. *If you go inside,* I said to myself, *that will be like giving up. And then no one will come and you shall only leave here when Mrs. Ruggles feeds you too much chloral and they do with your body whatever they did with Mrs. Matthiessen's.*

The carriage came to take Mr. Munger to the station, then returned for Reverend Johnston. My mouth went dry and my tongue stuck to my palate, and I worried that when someone did come I would be unable to speak to him. But still I did not go inside for water.

An hour after the carriage left with Reverend Johnston, it returned again, and I tried to recall which other mad lady had received a visit from her husband. But when the carriage stopped beneath the shade of the portico, it was not the husband of a lunatic who descended. It was instead the stiff-legged and portly figure of General Farnsworth.

Despite the heat, I ran up the drive, although to move so quickly in this temperature made my vision burn black at the edges.

"General!" I called out.

The general squinted through the shimmering air. "Mrs. Lincoln?"

As I came closer, I saw that General Farnsworth was frowning, and I slowed myself, for fear I would appear a madwoman to be racing about in such weather.

"You are a true friend to me!" I told him. I made to take his hand, but he had it employed in wiping the sweat from his forehead.

"It is very hot, is it not?" he replied. Indeed, the general appeared undone by the heat. His sparse hair was slicked flat across his scalp, and his shirtfront damp where his beard had dripped upon it.

"It is," I agreed. "But let us remain outside a while." I took General Farnsworth's arm and began to propel him away from the asylum.

"You do not believe it would be cooler inside?"

"We may find a breeze from the river," I promised him.

It was no easy thing to turn General Farnsworth from the asylum. Still, I kept a firm hold upon his arm and did not let him halt until we were some little way from the building.

"I am sorry to discomfort you," I said to him. "But outside is the only place we are assured of not being overheard."

The general regarded me curiously. "You believe yourself to be spied upon?"

"I live in a madhouse." He winced at the word. "I possess no privacy."

The general gazed about the grounds, at the rolling lawns, the gardens in summer bloom, the ladies playing at croquet – who from a distance appeared entirely sane. As was the case with my son, General Farnsworth appeared to find it all agreeable.

"You wrote that you wished to leave this place," he said.

"There are genuine madwomen here," I told him. "And I fear that if I stay too long I shall become like them."

General Farnsworth cast his eyes over me. "You appear well," he replied. "Better than I have seen in some time."

"I think when you saw me last I had just lost my youngest child," I reminded him. I took the general's arm and pulled him a few more steps along the path. "This is not a healthful place."

General Farnsworth looked again at the mad ladies playing at croquet. "It appears entirely beneficial."

I considered telling him about Mrs. Matthiessen, but recalled only how the story had made Robert believe more strongly in my madness.

"Ladies here can be sedated by force," I said instead. "Beyond what is harmless."

"You do not feel safe at Bellevue Place?"

The question seemed to hold something more than ordinary concern. "I do not feel I belong here," I told him.

He wiped a streaming cheek upon the shoulder of his jacket, then he moved a step nearer to the asylum. "You have been committed to this place by the court," he recalled for me. "I cannot see what it is you wish me to do."

"Appeal to Doctor Patterson," I pleaded. "Tell him you have seen me and that I am sane. Tell him it is an injustice to keep me here. Then go and say the same thing to my son."

"Is it an injustice?"

"I promise you that I am sane," I told him. "Entirely as sane as I have ever been."

While the general gazed at me with an unreadable expression, I watched a droplet of sweat course down his face, thinking that if he answered before the sweat reached his beard, it would be yes.

"Very well," said General Farnsworth. "I will speak with Doctor Patterson. But let me do the thing now, for the day is too hot for walking and I must return to St. Charles."

I clasped the general's wet hand and put it to my lips. "You are saving me," I told him.

I wanted to sit in the comfort of Doctor Patterson's office and hear how General Farnsworth would say that I was underanged and deserved my freedom. But I knew that the doctor would not tolerate it. Moreover, I knew that nothing could happen about my release until the gentlemen had spoken with Robert; so I brought General Farnsworth to Doctor Patterson's office, then returned to my room to rest in a dark place.

My room was not much cooler than the path outside; it was stuffy and felt as if it had been hung with wet laundry. But it was shadowed, and that – and the headache the heat had given me – made me long for my bed. I removed my black linen dress and put on a thin wrapper – only loosened my stays, for I did not possess the energy to undo my corset. Lying on top of the bedclothes, I fell to sleep in very little time.

I think that I dreamt of my freedom, for I slept with no sense of choking and woke with an expansiveness in my limbs I had not felt since coming to Bellevue Place. Stretching myself the full width of the mattress, I took in breaths which held no catch of entrapment, and did not notice until he spoke that a man stood over my bed.

"General Farnsworth informs me you have written to him," said Doctor Patterson.

Everything – breath and muscle – drew tight, and I started up, clutching at the wrapper which fell open.

"He tells me that you appealed to him to help you gain your liberty."

Blood rushed to my flesh at being so revealed, both in intent and by the thin wrapper. "This is my room," I gasped.

"And it shall remain so for a long while," Doctor Patterson replied. The damp heat had inflated the doctor's coarse, curly hair.

"I want my freedom," I told him.

The doctor shook his head. "You have practiced deviousness by writing to the general. And it is well-known that deceit is a symptom of insanity."

"I am not mad," I insisted.

Doctor Patterson scratched at his beard, which had turned black with his sweating. "General Farnsworth believes you to be."

The shock of this lifted me more from the bed, forgetful that I was near to unclothed. "What did he say?"

"That you did not talk like a sane woman."

"I cannot believe that."

The doctor sighed. "He said that you imagine you are spied upon. And that you have convinced yourself you will come to physical harm."

I thought back over my conversation with General Farnsworth, attempting to see how the reasoning I had used to persuade him of my leaving had worked to convince him of its opposite.

"Moreover," continued Doctor Patterson, "he tells me that your friends have believed you to be on the border of insanity for many years. And that it is his opinion were you to be released, you would do many unconventional things."

The general's betrayal was so complete that despite my loosened corset, I could not draw breath enough for speech.

Doctor Patterson glanced about my room, taking in the plates and lace Robert had brought me for decoration, Mamie's paper ladies. "It would be best for your overtaxed nerves if you reconcile yourself to remaining at Bellevue Place for an indeterminate period."

Then, as if my room were his and he was not required to bid me good-bye before quitting it, Doctor Patterson walked out, leaving open my door.

I flew from the bed and pushed it shut, wishing it could be locked from this side. I did not know what to feel first; pain at General Farnsworth's betrayal, shame at how Doctor Patterson was granted the right to see me unclothed, or the suffocating dread of being confined with Mrs. Ruggles and her bottle of chloral. But it was my body which decided, filling with a rage which threatened to shake my very bones through my flesh. Searching for something to spend it on, my eye fell upon the little mantle clock, which ticked loudly, despite the fact that I never wound it.

"You think that I shall be here forever," I said to it. "You think I shall be forced to stay here and listen to your ticking until I am dead."

I pushed myself away from the door and went to stand before the clock, hating it as much as if it were responsible for putting me here.

"Perhaps you, too, believe I have been on the border of insanity for many years," I said to it. "Perhaps you believe I am now in my rightful place."

For reply I got only its terrible ticking. The noise grew more loud, amplified until it became the sound of Mrs. Matthiessen's frantic beating. The sound of something attempting escape.

"I will not let myself die here!" I was shouting at the thing, but still it would not cease.

In a fury, I pulled open the face of the clock and thrust my hand into its workings. The pendulum swung past my fingers, knocking across the knuckles. I closed my hand over the brass disk which weighted it – hot in my sweltering room like something living, like a heart – and ripped it from its mechanism, bending and twisting the wire which held it so it could never be put back again.

I fell into the unbalanced rocker, the brass weight, like a heart hardened, clutched in my hand. My fury was suffocated by the heat of the room, as was my hope. I knew now that I would receive no help from the important gentlemen to whom I had written, who had come to see me at the President's House, who were friend to my husband. I squeezed the weight I had torn from the clock, felt the unyieldingness of it, and knew, too, that Robert would never set me free of his own accord.

If you do not want to die among lunatics, I told myself, *you shall have to devise your own way out of here.* And the only plan I could devise which would release me before the deceit of my other letters was discovered and Mrs. Ruggles dispatched to dose me with the chloral, was to run away, leave Bellevue Place after dark, after the rest of the madhouse was asleep.

I rose from the rocker and paced the room. But the day spent upon the asylum path had wearied my legs, and to escape Bellevue Place I would need to walk no small distance – at least as far as Batavia, though the next town, Geneva, would be better – before I would find a coach to take me to Elizabeth's house, the only place I could go without money. *No, I shall have to wait until tomorrow,* I determined, *after I have had opportunity to rest, and to persuade Mrs. Bunker to leave me unlocked again.*

For the first time since coming to Bellevue Place, I allowed the attendant to give me laudanum for sleep, swallowing enough to force myself to remain in bed until noon. In the early afternoon, I told Mrs. Patterson that my spine pained me too much for walking, and I passed most of the day sitting upon the back porch with Blanche, gathering my strength. I made only one journey, up to the third floor of the East Wing to Minnie's room to say farewell, and to tell her that if she wished to be in my company again she would need to eat so she might leave this place. But Minnie was in the unreachable sleep of shock – the bruising about her mouth showing that Mrs. Ruggles had fed her with the pump again – and I could do no more than say the words to her still face, and place my lips upon her fleshless cheek.

Shortly before supper I made ready to go, searching the drawers of my bureau for the few pieces of jewelry I had kept to wear in the madhouse – mourning rings and brooches of jet I had bought in memory of each my sons, trinkets I now hoped would convince a driver to take me. Spread over my blanket, these seemed too few to take me very far – although they were more than a mother should possess – and I wondered if a driver would recognize the value of such simple black stones.

Even if he does, I worried, *he might also recognize me and determine that a surer fortune lay with returning me to the asylum. Then again, what if he does agree to carry me to Springfield and Elizabeth refuses to keep me once she learns I have run away? You shall just have to persuade her,* I said to myself. *Her and the driver both. For you possess no way out of Bellevue Place save your own cleverness and your mourning jewelry.*

I packed the jewelry in a large reticule, adding an extra pair of slippers, in case I should wear through the first while walking. I set aside a shawl, in case the night grew chill, as well as a bonnet with a veil long enough to hide my face, taking care that both were very fine, so I might appear as respectable as possible while I pleaded with the driver.

I lost sense of time – and I did not have the mantle clock to remind me of it – so that when the sun fell low enough to slant into my window and there came a knock upon the door, I believed it was Sarah Bunker come to lock me in. I did not call out "Come in!" but sat upon the mattress and waited for the door to open, for at Bellevue Place a knock was only a pretence at politeness, as no member of the staff would wait for a mad lady to give or deny permission to enter. And indeed the door did open, although with more energy than I had ever seen displayed by Mrs. Bunker. And when it had swung fully on its hinges, it was not the night attendant who stood in the doorway, but Myra Bradwell, the lady lawyer.

I was too stunned for speech and could only take in Myra's elaborate traveling costume, which was fashioned out of linen and silk, and some other material which shone like actual gold in the slanting sunlight. Her bonnet was adorned with marabout feathers and an aigrette of spun glass, and in the coils of her hair she had pinned a scattering of gilded stars. Myra Bradwell had been trained as a lawyer – although the Illinois Supreme Court had not allowed her to practice because of her sex – and believed in the rights of women. But, she entirely put to rest the notion that suffragists were ladies of plain dress.

"I have spent too much of my dressmaker's time upon this ensemble for me to judge your speechlessness as anything but appreciation." Myra stepped into the room, brushing the lime-stone dust which coats everything in Batavia from the flounces of her skirts.

"It is only that I so want it to be true that you are here," I said, finding my voice, "I am afraid you are no more than a phantasm."

"I sincerely hope," Myra replied, "that if you have taken to conjuring up phantasms, they are considerably more romantic than a dusty lady overcome by heat."

She finished shaking out her skirts and came to sit beside me upon the bed. Without a word, she lifted my hand from my lap and held it within her own. I think it was her intent to recall for me the nights, five years past, we had spent together at the séance table, our hands clasped as we attempted to call up phantasms. Myra Bradwell had lost two of her own children, and it was their spirits she had sought at magnetic circles presided over by mediums. For though Myra is a lady of the law and possessed of a practical mind, she is also a mother who misses her dead children too badly. It was at these circles that I met her, when we both lived in Chicago, after Willie died, after my husband was killed. It was there that we sat holding hands as we did now.

"It has been no easy job to see you," she said. "Did anyone tell you that I came the day Judge Bradwell received your letter?"

I shook my head.

"Doctor Patterson would not let me go to you."

"But why?"

"Because I did not have a line from Robert."

I stared at her in amazement.

Myra raised her chin so she could see me more fully beneath the brim of her hat. "You do not know that no one is allowed to see you without permission from your son?"

"Robert approves my visitors?"

"In truth, he approves none of them. Have you not wondered why no one has been to see you?"

But General Farnsworth came, I was about to protest. Then I recalled that I had stopped the general before he reached the door; I had spoken to him outside, before Doctor Patterson knew that he was here. The realization came upon a hot tide and again I felt that fury which had shaken my bones, made me reach inside the clock and rip out its piece of weighted brass. But the clock was broken now, and I had no place to send my rage save at the son who had been keeping the world from me. I gripped Myra's hand more tightly, held it as fast as I had when I believed its contact would help bring Willie to me.

Myra held fast to me as well, as if she sensed the emotion which tainted even the taste in my mouth, as if we had formed a magnetic circle between ourselves which made such unspoken communication possible. She did not ask me to talk. Nor did she speak. But only waited until I had put down the hatred which had now risen toward my last living son.

"If you had no line," I said, when I was more calmed, "how, then, are you here?" Myra smiled and let go my fingers so she might take up a stylish bag made of the same shimmering gold as her dress. "I have discovered," she told me, "that gentlemen who are in charge of expensive lunatic asylums will agree to many things in order to avoid unpleasant press." From the golden bag came a newspaper. "And I am acquainted with a gentleman who writes for the *Bloomington Courier*."

I needed to read no more than the headline to see how Myra Bradwell had been permitted to see me without Robert's approval.

"Is the Widow of President Lincoln a Prisoner?

No One Allowed to See Her Except by Order of Her Son

An Account of a Remarkable Interview with Her Jailer and Physician"

I could not help but smile at the extravagantly dressed lady sitting upon my mattress. "You referred to Doctor Patterson as my jailer?"

"I only told the writer what occurred," Myra shrugged. "He is responsible for the prose."

I made to return the paper to her.

"I think you should keep it," she told me.

"I am not allowed it," I said.

Myra shook her head and took the paper back. "You must be very anxious to leave here."

"What makes you say so?"

She nodded at the things upon the bed. "You have put a spare pair of slippers in your reticule."

I said nothing, embarrassed before this sensible woman by my half-formed plan.

"If it is your intention to walk to freedom," Myra continued, "I should perhaps inform you that there is no underground railroad for former First Ladies who have convinced the courts they are insane."

I crumpled the shawl I had so carefully laid out. "I know it is a bad scheme. But I do not know any other way for me to be set free."

Myra rested a hand upon the *Bloomington Courier*. "I do," she told me.

I gazed into her face, at the features drawn there with such a clear hand. Myra possessed an exact turn of mind and I had never known her to utter a single statement she did not know to be fact.

"And you are willing to see me leave here?" I said. "You are not afraid what I might do?"

She smiled. "Are you planning something of which I should be fearful?"

"General Farnsworth believes so. He believes that if I am released I will engage in unconventional acts."

"I very much hope you shall," Myra replied.

Again I took a firmer hold of Myra's hand and looked hard into her eyes. "I need for you to tell me truly," I said. "Do you believe I am insane?"

Myra looked back, her gaze open and unwavering and impossible to disbelieve. "You are no more insane than I am."

Myra Bradwell's visit on this day has made me recall almost too powerfully my grief at the death of Willie, a grief which drove out everything before it, even, at times, thoughts of my recovering younger son. In the weeks which followed Willie's passing – and my husband's refusal to allow us to comfort one another – I was subject to fits of sobbing so violent my fingers became tinged with blue like one suffocating, and the salt flooding my eyes turned them blind.

I was unprepared for mourning and had to have a good number of dresses made in bombazine, a fabric chosen for its ability to take black dye. I was grateful for this task, for it kept me in Lizzie Keckly's company and permitted me to pay her for the time she spent with me. The mourning manuals dictated six months full mourning dress for the death of a child, and once my grief allowed me to rise from my bed, Lizzie came every day but the Sabbath to drape me in swaths of dull black bombazine.

But too often it seemed the black cloth worked to pull the grief through my skin. I would recall too strongly Willie's scent of almonds, the timbre of his boy's voice, and the remembrance would collapse me to the floor in a nest of unfinished mourning clothes. At such times, Lizzie set down her sewing and instructed the housemaid to bring a basin of water sweetened with chamomile. When it was brought, my friend sat upon the floor with me, my head in her lap, and bathed my eyes, smoothing the hair at my part with the hard polished pads of her seamstress's fingertips.

To keep her with me, I begged Lizzie for some unimportant piece of work I might stitch, and every afternoon we sat together in my bed-room, sewing the black cloth for my mourning wardrobe and speaking of the shared grief of having lost a son. But as the winter of Willie's death passed into spring, my wardrobe filled with enough mourning for three times the term prescribed by the manuals, and I was obliged to give up my friend to the other ladies of Washington City who required dresses.

With Lizzie gone, the President's House became gloomy. Taddie had made a good recovery from the typhoid, but the loss of his brother had turned him quiet, as if without Willie to watch, it was no longer amusing to ride the goat through the East Room, or conduct the hanging of his treasonous Zouave doll from the staircase. Taddie seemed also to require more of his father, and at least once a day burst into his office to throw himself upon Mr. Lincoln, chattering in the softened speech only we understood. Most days, he refused to leave the room unless his father gave him his glasses or a penknife to hold until he could come to him himself.

However, Mr. Lincoln could not come often to Taddie, for the war, which had so long seemed stalled, had turned murderous. That April, more than twenty-three thousand from both sides had been wounded or killed at Shiloh. My own half-brother Samuel, the oldest of Betsey's sons, had died there, fighting for the Confederates. My husband spent long hours at the War Office, waiting for better news to come in on the telegraph. In consequence, Taddie and I were left alone with our sorrow, and for hours at a time we sat together in cheerless silence, like people who have waited too long for a train.

My husband was so consumed with the war, I might have believed him to be done with his grieving for Willie, if not that every Thursday – the day of the week upon which our middle son had died – he locked himself into the Prince of Wales Room. I had ceased pleading with him to let me inside. And I no longer went into the corridor when I knew he was locked in that room, for I could not bear the sound of his hoarse sobbing.

As summer came and the city grew hot and pestilential, I began to fear that if we did not leave the President's House for a time, the three of us would succumb to either our sorrow or the Washington City malaria. I persuaded Mr. Lincoln to let us move into the Old Soldiers' Home, which was situated at the top of a shaded rise not more than two miles from the capital, and often used as a summer residence for the president's family. We moved in mid-June, taking nine trunks, a cook, a housekeeper, and Mr. Lincoln's valet.

Our new home was a porched and peak-roofed cottage in the Gothic style tucked beside the brick turrets of the Old Soldiers' Home, which was part hospital, part residence, built for invalided soldiers who had not the money to live anyplace else. Our cottage was shaded and cool, and filled with so many wicker chaises and settees, no matter where I felt like dropping down, there was one to receive me. An ancient wisteria tree grew twined about the porch columns, and upon the days which were warm enough to unlatch the windows, it blew its perfume through the house. But even in this setting, we could not forget the war. The windows of the north side of our cottage faced out upon a cemetery for soldiers which was dug up with too many fresh graves; and every morning, men with missing and mangled limbs took the air upon the bricked path which passed by our porch, creeping along on crutches and in wheeled chairs.

Still, Taddie regained some of the brightness of his disposition at the Soldiers' Home. He became friends with the injured soldiers, for each one owned a saber he was not reluctant to allow a nine-year-old boy to handle. Mr. Lincoln, too, seemed to draw comfort from our new surroundings. My husband returned from Washington City every evening no later than six – even on Thursdays – and made a small ritual of removing his boots on the porch, as if shedding the duties of his office along with his shoes. For the remainder of the night, he strolled about the cottage in carpet slippers, fanning himself with a broad palmetto leaf as if he were no more than a tropical eccentric.

Seeing both my husband and my son returned to better spirits eased my own, and because I possessed no memories of Willie at the Old Soldiers' Home, for he had never lived here, my sorrow, too, was lessened. As the summer advanced, I devoted my days to novels of no large literary aspiration, although I did not completely abandon the world, for each afternoon, that day's edition of the Washington City newspapers were brought to me by the legless Colonel Murton.

Colonel Murton, who was a resident of the Soldiers' Home, took all the Washington City papers, as he wished to be "cognizant of everything those scoundrels in the government were up to." I did not know if the colonel included my husband in that characterization, and I did not inquire; for I was fond of Colonel Murton, and he was generous with his newspapers, delivering them to me every afternoon in his wheeled chair. I looked forward to the noise of his wooden wheels upon the bricked path, and the sight of his large face, red with indignation at the scoundrels, and with the effort of pushing his wheels in the heat.

"A day like this will be boiling those rogues in Washington City!" declared Colonel Murton, upon a very hot afternoon in mid-August. A pile of creased and unevenly folded newspapers rested in his shortened lap, soaking up the sweat from his pant legs. "It'll surely prepare them for what they can expect from the hereafter!" he predicted with no little glee.

I stepped off the porch onto the path, so he would not have to wheel himself so far in the hot weather. "You are quite harsh in your opinions, Colonel," I scolded him, though it was this I liked best about Colonel Murton.

"The nation got my legs." He waved a calloused hand at his pinned-up trouser legs. "That sacrifice relieves me of the pretence of civility to politicians."

Colonel Murton handed me the newspapers, and then plunged into a lengthy tirade upon the misdeeds of the commander of the Army of the Potomac, General George McClellan, but I heard little of what he said, for at the top of one of the papers I saw the headline, "Mrs. Lincoln's Brother Killed." And below it, "Alexander Todd dead at Battle of Baton Rouge."

The sun was too hot, too bright for my eyes and my thinking, so that Colonel Murton's words came at me with no more meaning than the blasts of heat from the pavement. Not Aleck. Not my affectionate little half-brother – the child who had thrown himself against my skirts so frequently, I imagined I would find an imprint of his small self fixed there at the end of the day.

"I must go inside," I said to the colonel. "The heat has made me ill." And though I could see that he was speaking, that he was far from finished, I turned and ran back into the cottage.

When my three half-brothers had joined the rebel army, I swore that if they were killed, I would not mourn them. And when Samuel fell at Shiloh, I told myself he had made his choice and set aside any memory I possessed of him. But I had loved the little half-brother so near in age to my eldest son, and to learn that he was dead was too much like losing my own child.

Although it was stifling inside the cottage, I could not stay still, but walked the house, crossing the plank floors from parlor to sitting room, thinking to outpace the memories of Aleck which would not be set aside. But my roaming took me past the north windows which looked out upon the soldiers' cemetery, and the half-dug holes which waited for the newly dead made me imagine too much Aleck's slaughtered body. To wipe out that image, I worked to see my half-brother in his gray uniform, made myself a picture of him firing a musket at the heart of every Union soldier I had met. But this terrible likeness would not stay fixed in my mind. For I could not describe Aleck's heart-shaped face without seeing it filled with affection.

The crying I did for Aleck, like water spilled upon a parched plant, revived my sorrow for Willie, and soon I did not know for which dead boy I cried, only that I could not cease. My room was smothering, but I would not open a window, for I wished it hot, hoping that the heat would force my tears through my flesh, as there were too many of them for my eyes.

I asked the cook to give Taddie his supper; and when Mr. Lincoln arrived, sent down word that I was suffering from headache and could not eat. The sun dropped low, but it grew no cooler; and I remained upon the bed, crying into soaked sheets. After a time, I fell into uneasy sleep and dreamt that rather than the Washington City newspapers, the legless colonel had brought Willie back to me, riding him in his missing lap.

When I woke in the heated darkness my face was wet with tears. I rose from my bed and pushed open the window, but though the moon was up and the night was heavy with the sound of crickets, the air felt as hot as it had at noon. Not knowing if it was early or late, I wiped at my sopping face with the front of my muslin shift and felt my way to the door.

The only light came from Mr. Lincoln's bedroom, where I saw the flickering of lamplight and heard the cool rustling of pages being turned. I crossed the hall and stood watching him from the doorway. He was seated upon a wicker rocker set before the opened window, reading. Upon his bed, beneath the gauze of mosquito netting, Taddie lay sleeping, his limbs thrown about the mattress as if he'd been struck down in midst of leaping. Taddie slept most nights in his father's bed, for since Willie's death, he had been plagued by nightmares which woke him in such terror, even *we* could not understand his frantic jabbering.

After a while, Mr. Lincoln raised his eyes from the book. "Are you better?" he asked me.

"I have been dreaming of Willie," I told him.

"That he hadn't died?"

I nodded.

My husband looked out the window to the place where the moon shone white upon a patch of porch. "I believe those dreams to be a cruel and unjust trick of the mind."

From outside came the cry of a bird, one which sings at night, or perhaps one just bewildered by the heat.

"Aleck has been killed," I said.

My husband brought his gaze back to me, and I detected more sadness than usual in it.

"I have heard," he told me. "And I'm sorry for you. I know you had much affection for him."

His eyes rested upon me, and I did not know what picture I made. My hair, which had come undone from its plaits, hung hot and heavy upon my shoulders. My muslin shift clung to all the places where my skin was damp. My face, I knew, must be sleep-swollen, and my eyes inflamed by weeping. It was not an appearance for seduction, still, I crossed the threshold of my husband's room and knelt upon the uncovered floor at his feet.

"I need your company," I said to him.

"Sit with me here while I read."

"I need more than to watch you turn the pages of a book."

He pushed back in his rocker, lifting his knees away from me. "I will read a bit of this to you."

I rose to my own knees, put my hands upon his legs and pressed them down to me. "It has been more than a year since you have touched my flesh."

"I know how long it's been."

I gripped the hard bones beneath my fingers. "Come to my bed. Please."

He shut his book. "I am not ready."

"You do not have to come to me out of love," I pleaded. "You can come out of pity for my grief. Or remembrance of our affection. Come even out of disgust, if that will move you."

Not ungently, he removed my hands from his legs. "You should show more pride."

"I have no pride," I told him. "All I have is grief for Willie. And love for you. And the great wish that the second will help me overcome the first."

I grabbed hold of his shirtfront, which he had partially unbuttoned because of the heat, pushed my face into the dark hair on his chest, filling my mouth with the coarse strands of it. "I shall do whatever you wish," I murmured.

"I haven't the will for this," he said. But upon either side of my waist, his legs were trembling.

I raised my head and strained for his mouth, certain that if I put my lips to his my desire would be strong enough to carry us both. But he pushed me away with such violence, he knocked the book to the floor.

"I will allow you to strike me if you wish."

My husband looked upon me with horror.

"That is how hungry I am for your touch. I will take your hand in anger, hoping that once the anger is spent, it might rediscover tenderness."

He held me away from him with a hard grip upon my shoulders. "You mustn't talk like that," he said. "Such debasement will only make me want you less."

It was impossible to fight his strength, and his resolve. I sat back upon my heels, and after a time, he released me. When I could, I rose to my feet, using for support the wicker arms of the rocker rather than his legs.

"Let us say that it is grief which has driven me to such unwomanly behavior," I said to him.

Mr. Lincoln retrieved his book and set it upon his lap. "I have no doubt of it."

Turning toward the bed, I reached through the netting and brushed my fingertips across Taddie's hot forehead.

"I shall not distress you with begging again," I told my husband. I made my way to the door. "However, I wish you to remember that my invitation remains an open one, in the event I cannot summon the courage to repeat it."

He nodded, very slightly; and I returned to the hot darkness of my room.

To be so refused by my husband left an ache in my chest deeper and more empty than the grief-prompted desire which had driven me to force myself upon him, and for the remainder of the summer, I prayed for him to come to me. I left open my door, even if it meant being seen in my bed by the soldiers who sometimes came to deliver messages to Mr. Lincoln, and slept only in silk chemises, which I washed and dried in the sun, so they would smell sweet. Some nights, my wanting was so great I determined to go to my husband's bed and startle him into taking me before he had chance to wake and recall that he was repelled by the touch of my skin. But then I'd remember that my youngest son was likely sleeping in that bed, like a small, unaware sentry.

* * *

At the close of that summer, the Confederate general Robert E. Lee attempted to invade Maryland. Lee's rebel troops were met at Antietam Creek by General McClellan's Army of the Potomac, and by the end of that day, five thousand soldiers were killed. Twenty thousand more were reported wounded or missing. Despite the bloodshed, the Battle of Antietam was called a victory for the Union, for it had succeeded in forcing General Lee to turn south. Mr. Lincoln took advantage of the generous mood brought on by the victory to make public a proclamation which he knew would be received with mixed reaction, even in the North. A proclamation which granted emancipation to all Negroes still held in bondage in the South.

I was proud of my husband for penning the proclamation, for my friendship with Lizzie Keckly had only worked to increase my already long-held dislike of human slavery, and I prayed that Mr. Lincoln would not be talked away from signing it into law upon the first day of the New Year, as he had promised. The afternoon the proclamation was read, I was told that the President's House rang with hymns sung by great crowds of abolitionists who had gathered outside. However, at the Old Soldiers' Home, I heard only the digging of hundreds of new graves for the fallen at Antietam.

Through the end of September and into October, the soldiers killed at Antietam – and elsewhere – arrived outside my cottage in long lines of pine coffins; so many they seemed to constitute their own army. An army of the dead. At the same time, as if brought on by their coldness, came the chilling weather of winter. Weather for which the cottage at the Old Soldiers' Home had not been constructed, causing the servants to complain of freezing bedrooms, and Mr. Lincoln to talk of moving us back to Washington City.

While Taddie was eager to return to the President's House, having already handled every piece of weaponry belonging to the invalided soldiers, I did not yet feel ready to live in the rooms where Willie had talked to me of trains and journeys. I was rescued from that prospect by a note from Lizzie Keckly. "I am seeking a way to travel to New York where I can raise money for the Contraband Relief Association," she wrote. "Do you know of any lady who is going?"

"Come with me," I replied. "I will shop, and you will do good."

Since the war, "contraband" was the term used to describe runaway slaves who had fled to the North, for these Negroes were still considered the property of their Confederate masters, confiscated by the Union government in order to prevent them from being returned. These former slaves, most of whom could neither read nor write, possessed no skills, save those employed in fieldwork, which was of little value in Northern cities. With no work and no money, they were compelled to live in camps of barrackslike buildings, beneath conditions likely poorer than those they had known in slavery. Washington City possessed a number of such contraband camps, and the poverty and sickness she had witnessed in them had persuaded Lizzie to help form the Contraband Relief Association. "I understand that New York is filled with abolitionist ladies with private incomes," she said in her reply to my letter. "Now we shall see how willing they are to devote a portion of that income to assisting the colored people they are so eager to see set free."

Lizzie and I journeyed to New York in early November, where we stayed together at the Metropolitan Hotel. On our first morning, Lizzie went out early to meet with her abolitionist ladies. Left alone, I decided to go to the Ladies' Mile, where I might buy some mourning jewelry for Willie, which I had not yet had the heart to do.

A year of war had done little to dim the brilliance of the New York shops. Perfume and lace still arrived by boat from France, while bone china made the journey from England unharmed. At the beginning of the War Between the States there had been talk of organizing a boycott of goods from those foreign countries which continued to do business with the cotton merchants of the South. However, knowing that such action might cause France or England to ally themselves with the Confederacy, Mr. Lincoln had refused to put restrictions upon trade, and fine wines and British woolens continued to sail across the Atlantic as if there was no such thing as a civil war.

I traveled to lower Broadway by hackney, and I expect that no newspapermen followed me because I was so swathed in mourning – including an ankle-length veil – I was unrecognizable. Indeed, the New York streets were filled with women dressed in black bombazine; and when I entered the jeweler's – which carried a greater selection of mourning pieces than before – it was crowded with women who gave the appearance of crows picking through the collar brooches and rings.

The clerk was a pallid-fleshed man who spoke with the gravity of an undertaker. "Madam would like to see some jet?" he asked me.

I nodded, which to him must have seemed only the undulation of a black veil.

With a nod of his own, he led me to a marble and glass counter and set upon it a velvet-lined tray filled with mourning jewelry. "These are the most excellent examples in the shop."

The jet of the stones was darker than night, darker than the grave. I hesitated before touching them.

"Pieces like this, you will possess forever," the clerk informed me.

I lifted a bracelet. Despite its filigree, it felt solid and substantial.

"Can you not sense the permanence of it?" The clerk took the bracelet from my hand, and with nimble fingers fastened it about my wrist. It rested there, heavy upon the bones of my arm.

"Such a piece will last beyond your own lifetime," he promised. "Perhaps one day, a granddaughter will wear it to mourn you."

I removed one glove and put my bare fingers to the black stones which were set around the bracelet. They felt cool and hard and indestructible. *These will not succumb to fever, or fits of coughing, or the spasms of dysentery,* I thought. *Certainly to own something so imperishable would be consoling.*

"I shall take the bracelet."

The clerk nodded with solemnity, then reached for my wrist to undo the clasp.

"I should prefer not to remove it," I told him, drawing away the piece of jewelry and covering it with my ungloved hand.

I wore the jet bracelet all of that day, and that night slept with it upon my wrist. But the weight of it made me dream that it was Willie's hand which pressed me there, for my son had had the habit of holding my wrist when he was telling me something, as if to better fix my attention; and when I woke, it was into the sorrowful knowledge that I was held only by filigree and jet.

Nevertheless, I returned to the shop on lower Broadway and asked the clerk to show me his finest jet collar brooches. When the velvet-lined tray was placed before me, I again removed a glove so I might feel the unbreakable hardness of the stones.

"These will last beyond my life?" I asked him.

"Beyond the life of your children," he assured me.

I bought several of the brooches, and the next day appeared at the shop to purchase two jet rings of, according to the clerk, great durability. But all this mourning jewelry, these things I owned which would not sicken and die, could not long keep me safe from my grief. Once I became used to the new heaviness upon my finger or at my throat, I recalled how impermanent were the things which were most precious to me, and how impossible it was to believe that I would grow used to the weight of that knowledge.

For her part, Lizzie had endured an equally unsuccessful week.

"I have spoken before five societies of devoutly abolitionist ladies," she declared one evening. "And I have raised almost nothing."

We were seated together in the little parlor of our adjoining rooms, side by side upon a tufted settee, our feet very close to the fire, for the November weather had turned cold and sleet-filled, and we had both come back with wet shoes.

"What do they say when you ask them for money?" I asked.

"They wish to know who else has contributed."

"Tomorrow, tell them that President and Mrs. Lincoln have donated two hundred dollars. And tonight I will write to my husband for the check."

Lizzie dropped her sewing in her lap and threw her arms about my shoulders. Then with equal suddenness, she let me go and took up her sewing, concentrating upon it with an embarrassment equal to that of having mistakenly come upon me naked.

I caught hold of her fingers to stop their furious sewing and compelled her to look up at me. "I am quite used to affectionate gestures from my friends," I assured her. "Even when I have not just given them money."

"It is only that having you and Mr. Lincoln on the list of contributors will make the difference," she told me. "Some of these abolitionist ladies have never seen a Negro up close before. Much less a colored *lady*. I think they are too preoccupied with staring at me like I'm something from a traveling menagerie to hear anything I'm saying."

"Next time, take me with you," I offered.

"To speak about the contrabands?"

"I have seen their camps out near the Soldiers' Home," I reminded her. "And my powers of description are capable of achieving a high degree of drama as a consequence of my training beneath a French schoolmistress."

Lizzie looked down again upon her sewing. "I could not take you from you own pursuits."

"My own pursuits appear to be nothing more significant than the accumulation of too much mourning jewelry," I told her. "And that has only proved expensive."

With some further coaxing, Lizzie agreed to take me with her, an arrangement by which I was made more grateful than she. Every mourning manual I had opened maintained that ladies in bereavement would find solace in good works, and now I would be able to test the theory.

Over the next week, Lizzie and I were entertained by the ladies of abolitionist societies in the gilt and damask parlors of the mansions along Fifth Avenue, and even in the newly built private palaces as far northward as Twenty-third Street. After the tea and the sandwiches, I spoke to the ladies of the contrabands, how they lived together in barracks houses and had neither blankets nor clothes any better than those in which they'd escaped. I enjoyed speaking to these Northern ladies – if only to observe their astonished expressions that it was I who addressed them upon the plight of the contrabands. Like most abolitionists of the North, these ladies surely believed that my being born into a slave-holding family had rendered me in favor of human bondage, and I suspected they were secretly of the opinion that I kept chained-up darkies in the cellar of the President's House.

Unhappily, no amount of speaking about contrabands in gilt and damask parlors could soften my grief. Still, Lizzie and I did raise a large sum of money for the Relief Association, and to celebrate our success, we decided to have an extravagant supper sent over from Delmonico's, and eat it without wearing our corsets.

We ordered oysters – cooked and raw – and lobster Newburg drowned in sherry-ed cream, and ate it all upon a small linen-covered table before the fire.

"When I am like this," I told Lizzie, "I think I will remember how to be happy."

"You are unsure of the possibility?" she asked.

"I am if I think upon Willie." I leaned back in my chair and looked over the table covered with plates of cream and pearl-edged oyster shells. "It is death's finality which comes to me as cruel. Knowing I shall have to die myself before I can see my son."

"The ministers say we should be consoled by the anticipation of that heavenly reunion."

"It is too long a wait," I told her. I imagined that Lizzie would now quote me something from the Bible, some mention of Green Pastures. But my friend stayed silent. "Do you not feel the same about your son?"

"I did," she said. "Once. But I have since seen him."

"In dreams?" I asked.

"In séance parlors," she replied.

"*You* are a Spiritualist?"

Since the war the country had become full of Spiritualists, for more families now possessed a new member of the dead they wished to contact. A good many of the politicians of Washington City attended séances, and I had read in the newspapers that Queen Victoria of England employed mediums to call up her departed Prince Albert. However, Lizzie Keckly was a practical woman, and it was difficult to imagine that she could put her faith in table rappings and phantom appearances.

"I do not know if I am a Spiritualist," Lizzie replied. "But I do believe that I have spoken to my son."

"You talked with him directly?"

"He spoke through a colored medium in Washington City."

"How did you know it was he?"

"He mentioned things no one would know. He gave me the initials of his father."

I studied Lizzie's face; upon it was pure belief. "What did he tell you?"

"That in the afterlife he had ceased pretending to pass for white. And that the bullet which pierced his brain did its work quickly, and he felt no pain before he died."

"Did he say if he is happy now?"

"In the Summerland?"

"What is the Summerland?"

"That is what the Spiritualists call the place where the spirit goes once it has crossed over." Her eyes traveled something I could not see, but which appeared to please her. "He says that he is more content than when he was upon the Earth. He also tells me things which will happen."

"He knows the future?"

"All spirits do. It is why they come back to us. To help those they loved in life choose the right course."

I leaned across the table, watching the play of Lizzie's expression. "And your grief is less since you have seen the Spiritualists?"

"When he comes I smell the wax he favored to smooth his hair. Sometimes from the medium's mouth I hear *his* voice." Lizzie's features softened. "It is as if my son is not gone from me entirely."

I sat back and imagined how it would be to smell the almond scent of Willie's skin, hear again his boy's voice, which I had already started to misremember. "Do you know any Spiritualists in New York?"

"All the Spiritualists I know are colored," Lizzie replied. "But doesn't your writer friend, Mr. Willis, go to séances?"

Indeed, the magazine editor Nathaniel Willis, whom I had first met in Washington City, had once boasted that upon any given night in New York, one might take one's place at more than three hundred magnetic circles. Straight away, I rose from the table.

"You are going to write now to Mr. Willis?" she asked.

"I cannot make myself wait until I am dead," I told her.

Nathaniel Willis arranged for me to attend a séance the following night.

"You are in great luck," his note read, "for we are being visited by the celebrated sensitive, Emma Hardinge, who has sat for the Society for the Diffusion of Spiritual Knowledge, and is expert on the topic of communion with the spirit world."

We were to sit in magnetic circle with the celebrated Miss Hardinge at the home of a Mrs. Kellogg, a noted medium in her own right. I instructed Mr. Willis to introduce me to the gathering as Mrs. Picard, a widow, for I did not wish my identity to be known. Despite being widely practiced, Spiritualism was condemned from the pulpits as the work of Satan, and regarded by doctors of the mind as a symptom of insanity. I did not imagine that it would benefit my husband to have the newspapers report that Mrs. Lincoln had turned Spiritualist. Moreover, Lizzie had warned me that there was a certain amount of trickery practiced at séances, and it seemed I might better test the authenticity of the medium if she did not know who I was.

To disguise myself, I dressed in deepest mourning, covering myself in a voluminous dress topped by a tentlike sacque, which rendered me unrecognizable. Upon my head, I wore a mourning bonnet so elaborately veiled, I required Mr. Willis's assistance finding my way out of the carriage.

Mrs. Kellogg's rooms were in a building situated on upper Broadway. I imagined that this noted medium inhabited fantastic apartments. However, the parlor Mr. Willis led me into could have been the sitting room of a Presbyterian minister, it was so very ordinary. The chairs were covered in thin velveteen and the table at which we were to establish our spiritual telegraph was unpolished oak. The sole ornamentation was a collection of china dogs, some of them chipped, arranged in a curio cabinet. There was no carpeting upon the floor of Mrs. Kellogg's parlor, and the planks showed an uncommon amount of scarring beneath the table legs.

"Those are very odd markings upon the floor," I whispered to Mr. Willis.

"They are made when the table is rocked by spirit emanations," he told me.

Two ladies stood in a corner, the slighter of which Mr. Willis pointed out to be the celebrated medium. Miss Hardinge was somewhat plain of feature, save for eyes which were perfectly round and more gleaming than those of most people, as if they manufactured their own light. She wore a brown dress with a lace collar, a good many years out of date, and though I would have put her age at just beneath forty, she seemed settled in herself in a manner only those who become aged without becoming bitter achieve. The other lady, whom I took to be Mrs. Kellogg for the way she fluttered about the celebrated medium, making introductions and inquiring whether Miss Hardinge required tea or a chair, was as ordinary as her rooms; a little plump, with colorless hair.

My friend, Mr. Willis, was an author of some vanity, and at gatherings generally waited to be approached first. So I was much astonished when, forgetting that I stood beside him in my black tent, he flew across the room to take hold of Miss Hardinge's hand.

"I have heard you speak while seized by the spirits," Mr. Willis told the medium, "and continually come away inspired and edified."

"That is reassuring information," replied Miss Hardinge, "as I never know beforehand what words the spirits intend to send out of my mouth." The medium possessed a clear and ringing voice, rendered precise by a British accent.

"Allow me to introduce Mrs. Picard," said Mr. Willis.

Miss Hardinge released the gentleman's hand to take mine. Even through the netting of my veil, I could see the shininess of her eyes. "You are the lady who wishes to contact her son," she told me.

I made a surprised cry and very nearly pulled my hand away.

"Do not be astonished," said the celebrated medium. "The information comes to me by unclairvoyant channels. My source is Mrs. Kellogg."

"And mine is the esteemed Mr. Willis," added the ordinary lady at her side.

I loosened my fingers, thinking to step away so that another member of the group might be introduced, but Miss Hardinge kept a firm grip upon my black-gloved hand.

"I have the sensation that I must try especially hard for you," she said, her voice less ringing now.

"I have had difficulty with grief," I admitted.

"I see that," she replied. And it did indeed seem that her glittery eyes saw through all my veilings.

Once the celebrated medium had been introduced to all present, Mrs. Kellogg called us to seat ourselves around the oak table. Our circle was eight in number, four gentlemen and four ladies. One of the ladies beside myself was in mourning; two of the gentlemen wore black armbands fastened about their sleeves.

"Mrs. Kellogg," commanded Miss Hardinge, "would you turn down the gas in the lamps? Strong light produces motion in the atmosphere which disturbs the manifestations."

In the dim light, the clothing of those of us who made up this magnetic circle disappeared into the shadows, so it appeared we were no more than white faces floating above the séance table. Miss Hardinge allowed us to sit in silence for some minutes before she spoke.

"I like to begin by singing in chorus," she said, "to focus our intention upon a common purpose. I generally find a hymn is best."

With no further preamble, or even what seemed time to draw breath, Miss Hardinge began to sing. The medium's voice rang so pure, so much like the calling of a seraph, it seemed blasphemy to cover it with lesser tones. But after a stanza, Mr. Willis took up the song in a booming baritone, and within another phrase or two, the rest of us joined in. I had been expecting a Spiritualist anthem, something peculiar to the world of séance and table rapping, but Miss Hardinge had chosen a hymn I had sung many times in the Presbyterian church in Springfield, one which promised life after death.

When the hymn was finished, Miss Hardinge instructed the ladies to remove their gloves, and then had us take hold of each other's hands. My hand was held on the one side by the smooth one of Mr. Willis, and on the other by the slightly tremulous fingers of one of the gentlemen in mourning.

"You may engage in subdued conversation while we wait for the spirits," Miss Hardinge told us. "But do attempt to direct the talk toward the purpose of our gathering."

Everyone spoke about their dead. Both of the gentlemen in mourning had lost family in the war – a son at Shiloh, a brother at Antietam. The other lady in black had a daughter who had been taken by smallpox. I longed to tell about Willie, about the pitiless way the typhoid had taken him. But I kept silent. Lizzie had told me that deceitful mediums often coaxed information from those at their tables and then repeated it back as if such knowledge had come from the spirit world. If Willie did come, I needed to believe it was not deception.

"Your son is still a child!" declared Miss Hardinge.

The suddenness of this remark caused everyone to turn toward the medium. Miss Hardinge sat very straight in her seat; her eyes fixed upon me.

"I had assumed he was a soldier," she continued.

"You see Willie?" I asked, forgetting that I meant to withhold my son's name.

"He says that you should not miss him so much. That he is at your side as often as he was before."

But the entire country knew that my son had died.

"How can I know that you really see Willie?" I asked the medium.

"You are seeking proof that I am in communication with his spirit?"

"I am sorry if such a request is discourteous."

"When one is looking to lessen grief, courtesy has a small place," she said, "as does pride."

Behind my netting appeared the image of myself the night I begged my husband to take me at the Soldiers' Home. I saw the flame of Mr. Lincoln's reading lamp flicker, felt my nightdress flattening against my soaked skin. I heard even the crickets in the still-hot grass outside, and smelled the scent of my own sweat. It was a picture of such detail and clarity of the senses, I could not believe other than that Miss Hardinge had put it there.

"I will see if Willie can bring you some proof," said the medium.

Miss Hardinge cast her brilliant eyes across the room. I followed her gaze, but could make out nothing save Mrs. Kellogg's china dogs glowing softly in the darkness. Mr. Willis cleared his throat. One of the gentlemen in mourning let out a sigh. Then, moving with the otherworldly attention of trance, the medium reached for the pen and paper which had been placed before her and began to write. I felt Mr. Willis tighten his grip upon my hand, heard the other lady in mourning gasp. And taking my eyes from the paper, I saw for myself what was so extraordinary about Miss Hardinge's performance. The celebrated medium wrote without taking her gaze from the china dogs, as if it was not she who directed her hand.

The characters took shape swiftly upon the page, and as they did, I saw that Miss Hardinge was transcribing them upside down, so that the letters and numbers faced me and not herself. Still, between the dimness of the room and my veil, I could make no sense of the meaning of these characters, not until the medium set down the pen and pushed the paper toward me. Then, releasing my hand from Mr. Willis's grasp, I held the paper before my veil, trembling as violently as if Willie's own hand had moved through the spirit world to touch me. For there upon the page, in my middle son's slanting penmanship, was the timetable of a train traveling from Chicago to New York in a single day.

I took my other hand from that of the gentleman in mourning and put it also upon this paper which in some supernatural way had been touched by my son. It was not the same as weaving my fingers into his fine hair or placing them upon the soft curve of his cheek, yet the feel of the ink lifted the most hopeless portion of my grief, making space enough in my body to permit joy. For this paper tracking the journey of a long-distance train was proof that the dead could be conjured into rejoining the living.

I wanted to repeat what had happened at Miss Hardinge's magnetic circle as soon as I might, and upon leaving New York had Mr. Willis provide me with the names of Spiritualists in Washington City. This information brought me to the Georgetown home of Cranston Laurie and his wife, Margaret, who hosted regular séances. The large-bosomed Mrs. Laurie was considered an extraordinarily talented sensitive, while her red-haired daughter, Mrs. Belle Miller, was one of the finest physical mediums ever seen. Upon my first visit to their house, I witnessed Mrs. Miller transport a gold wedding band across the room with only the power of her mind.

Throughout that autumn and into winter, I traveled to the Lauries' house two and three times a week, hoping that one of the lady sensitives might bring me some token of Willie. Although neither Mrs. Laurie nor Mrs. Miller possessed the mediumistic ability of Miss Hardinge, they had some success. Mrs. Miller one time produced a rapping upon the table which she maintained was Willie – and it is true that whoever did the rapping knew precisely where Taddie had hidden a broken pocketknife belonging to his father. And once Mrs. Laurie called up my half-brother Aleck, who came to me as a warm wind which blew my skirts against my legs. This was little, but it was enough to lessen my sadness and send me back to the Lauries' bricked town house.

It was enough, too, for me to wish to bring Mr. Lincoln to these circles. It had not been a good season for my husband. He had at last replaced General McClellan as commander of the Army of the Potomac. However, the new commander, General Ambrose Burnside, had quickly led his troops to a defeat at Fredericksburg which had left twelve thousand casualties. Mr. Lincoln, too, was being discouraged from signing his proclamation emancipating those still held in bondage. Most Democrats – and even some Republicans – believed the declaration too radical, too likely to cause a flood of Negroes coming to the North, and should be delayed or given up altogether. Moreover, since our return from the Old Soldiers' Home, my husband had once again commenced every Thursday to lock himself into the room in which Willie had died.

It was Taddie who first noticed this, and after he told me, I waited behind my door until I heard Mr. Lincoln's footfall headed toward the room, then stepped out into the corridor.

"I am going to the Lauries," I said to him. "Come with me."

My husband stood before the door to the Prince of Wales Room, the key he used to lock himself in already in his hand.

"At worst it will be a diversion," I continued. "And at best, you might receive some sign of Willie."

Mr. Lincoln shook his head. "I don't know as I want to hear Willie's voice as raps on a table or through the mouth of a medium. I hear it well enough in memory."

I took a step, trying to place myself between him and the door. "Do you disbelieve that the Spiritualists have brought Willie to me?"

My husband turned the key over in his hand. "It's hard to say what I believe."

"The Scriptures say that the spirit does not die."

"But they do not claim that we can communicate with it."

"They do claim we can communicate with God. Which to me seems certainly a more fantastic feat."

He looked upon me with more concern than I had received from him in many months, and I thought for a moment that he was going to touch my hair. "I worry it is your great desire to believe that causes you to hear raps and feel breezes."

"I worry that as well," I admitted. "But even the possibility that the rapping is Willie comforts me. And how can you explain the paper in his writing?"

Mr. Lincoln's eyes went to the door of the room in which we had watched Willie die. "I cannot explain that except by what you've told me."

"Then come with me," I almost reached for his arm.

He turned over the key once more, then put it in the door. "I would prefer to have you deliver Willie's messages," he told me. "I think I can only bear to hear them from your mouth."

At the end of December, a young medium named Nettie Colburn arrived in Washington City. Miss Colburn was a trance medium – a sensitive who, during séance, was controlled by a spirit which made use of her magnetic energy to communicate directly with those in the circle. The young medium was much in demand, and upon hearing that she would be giving a demonstration at the Lauries', I hurried there.

I had been told that Miss Colburn was twenty-four years of age; however, the trance medium was much younger in appearance. She possessed a face as unmarked as blank paper, and her dark hair was arranged about her ears in the ringlets of a schoolgirl. When Mrs.

Laurie introduced me – rather grandly as Mrs. President Lincoln – I noticed that the young sensitive's fingers shook slightly.

"Have you ever seen trance mediumship before, Mrs. Lincoln?" asked Miss Colburn in a soft voice.

"I have not," I told her.

"I hope you won't find it unsettling."

We were a large group that evening, a group which included two congressmen, a senator, and a Unitarian minister who had given up the church in order to preach Spiritualism. At a sign from Mrs. Laurie, we seated ourselves around a table covered in black baize and took hold of each other's hands. The minister, Reverend Pierpont, initiated the circle with a prayer which still bore traces of Unitarianism.

The young medium took a breath, a nervous, fluttering inhalation. Then she fixed her eyes upon a clock which hung opposite, following with her gaze the swinging of the pendulum as if performing some feat of self-hypnosis. As I watched, I noticed that Miss Colburn's breathing became deeper and more robust, and that her fingers – which were held in mine – acquired a new firmness, as if they had been made stronger. Earlier, when the young sensitive had asked if I had ever witnessed trance mediumship, she had spoken in the light tones of a girl. Now when Miss Colburn opened her mouth to address the circle, her voice came weighted with the deepened timbre of a man.

"A distinguished assemblage!" declared the voice.

The entire circle started at the voice, and at the change which now came over the young medium's face. Slowly enough to be watched, Miss Colburn's delicate features were overlaid by a jaw grown heavier, a more prominent nose and brow. This new face seemed less mobile than the sensitive's own, the eyes did not blink, making it appear that Miss Colburn wore a mask of death.

"Who is with us?" asked Mrs. Laurie in a declarative tone.

"I am called Old Doctor Bamford," replied the voice, which carried the roughness of age, "because I was near to ninety when I passed into spirit."

"Why have you come?" said Mrs. Laurie.

"There is a young one on this side who has asked me for assistance." The phlegmy laugh of an elderly man emanated from Miss Colburn's altered face; and it *was* unsettling – enough to make me wish I had not been seated so near the medium.

"Even here," the voice continued, "the young have difficulty believing it requires time to concentrate one's powers."

With no warning, Miss Colburn turned that death mask to me, bringing it within inches of my unveiled face. I wanted to pull away, but the young medium held my hand so firmly to the table I could not put any space between us. I saw then a working about Miss Colburn's jaw and mouth, and I was terrified that Willie's face would appear superimposed over that of the old doctor. For as much as I wished to look upon my son's face, it would be a horror to see it melded with the features of another. I tried to shut my eyes against the sight, but could not. Very gradually, the lips of that death mask parted, the mouth opened, and the young medium exhaled a tremendous blast of air into my face.

I expected the air to be sour – the post-dinner breath of Miss Colburn, or the exhalation of the long-dead doctor. But the wind which blew upon me smelled instead of almonds. This weighted air did not so much move past me, but through me, heating my flesh, infusing it with the sticky warmth of a sleeping child. I felt as if I were holding my son, although my hands had not lost their grip upon those of Miss Colburn and the Reverend Pierpont.

The sensation did not last longer than the time it takes a breeze to blow by. And when it had passed, when I no longer felt my son's warmed weight upon me, I was left with a sorrowful love for what I could not have. If I could have found voice, I would have pleaded with the spirit who had remade Miss Colburn's face to blow upon me again. But that same inexplicable spell which had keep me from looking away now robbed me of speech, and it was the old doctor who spoke to the group about the table.

"I have been controlling this young lady since the time of her development," he declared, "and through her have worked upon a good many lives. Now, I have a notion to work upon history."

"We have a number of political men with us tonight," Mrs. Laurie assured the spirit.

"There is on this side of the veil, a congress of spirits," continued the old doctor, "composed of public men who have passed from the Earth. It is their desire to help guide the affairs of the nation."

"What is it they wish?" asked Mrs. Laurie.

"They wish that my medium be brought before President Lincoln."

To hear my husband's name said at séance was cause for suspicion, for I had encountered mediums whose emanations had been more political than spiritual; mediums whose spirit guides possessed the names of a remarkable number of living souls they believed should be granted government appointments. But here, with the scent of almonds still upon my clothes, I could not believe Miss Colburn no more than an actress.

"I would try anything for the spirit who can bring my son so much into this world," I said to the old doctor. "But Mr. Lincoln is not a believer."

"You will know how to convince him," he replied.

And then, because I saw Miss Colburn's delicate features pushing through the doctor's death mask, I pleaded with the spirit. "Tell me," I begged him. "Is Willie still with you?"

But the young sensitive's face had been returned to her, and with a small convulsion, she fell back into her chair.

I spoke to my husband that night, waiting up for him until I heard him come into his room. Covering myself with a woolen wrapper, I stood at his door. He did not see me right away. He was looking down upon Taddie, sprawled in a hard boy's sleep upon the bed. When he did glance up, he showed a face made elderly with fatigue.

"I have had a rare night at the Lauries," I said.

"Did the spirits make the table dance?"

"No. But they brought a message for you."

Mr. Lincoln rubbed at his eyes. "I don't think I have the energy for messages from beyond the veil."

"This was from the spirits of public men. Men who want to help you to guide the country."

He let out a cheerless laugh. "I already have plenty of those here on the earthly plane."

"But these men possess a wisdom no one living can claim. It is said that the spirits can see into the future."

"You want me to run the country on the advice of spirits?"

"I want you to hear them. In the end, you shall make your own decisions. As you always do."

He regarded me coolly, sure of his own reason over mine. "At the moment, I'm receiving more counsel than I can manage from those who continue to draw breath."

Before he had even finished speaking, he had turned away, pulling upon his collar in a manner which made me know that he wished to undress for bed, that he wished me to leave. But I could not leave with him unconvinced. I knew that what I proposed sounded like lunacy, that it was beyond what could be believed. But I did believe it. Because I had felt Willie's spirit move through me.

"Willie came," I told him. "Not as raps upon the table or spirit writing, but his actual presence."

My husband turned back to me. I saw no more of that cool sureness. "How can you know?"

"My flesh knew. It recognized the weight of him. And there was his scent."

"Almonds."

"It was still upon my dress an hour later."

"I would have liked that." His voice broke.

I wanted to go to him, but I no longer entered my husband's room uninvited. "Perhaps he will come again," I said. "If you agree to let me bring Miss Colburn to you."

Mr. Lincoln bent to pull the bedcovers more surely over Taddie, then stood for a while with his hand upon his face, as if he hoped to find the scent of almonds upon his own skin. "Do you think it's possible?"

"It is always possible," I told him. "But you must think of him."

He let the hand fall from his face. "I always think of him."

I sent my own carriage for the Lauries and Miss Colburn in order to keep theirs from being seen outside the President's House, for too many of the country's citizens already considered my husband unfit for his office. The party arrived at eight and I had them shown into the Crimson Room, which, with its scarlet carpeting and red-flocked wallpaper, had always seemed to me the parlor of a gypsy, possessing the proper atmosphere for divination.

"So this is the little Nettie I've heard so much about," said Mr. Lincoln, upon being introduced to Miss Colburn.

The young sensitive stood before my husband, her dark ringlets quivering as if they had been taken over by spirit. Seeing that Miss Colburn could not manage the barest greeting, Mr. Lincoln took her hand and led her to a cushioned ottoman, seating himself in the chair beside it.

"Tell me how it feels to come under trance," he said to her. "Does it tire you to be controlled?"

Despite my husband's soft voice and gentle manner, Miss Colburn blushed and stammered, and could do little more in reply than nod or shake her downcast head. Noting how the young medium wrung her hands in her skirt and did not meet his gaze, Mr. Lincoln spoke instead to Mr. Laurie.

"Well sir, and how do we do this thing?"

Mr. Laurie, who greatly enjoyed explaining all things Spiritualist, filled his rotund frame with air in preparation for discourse. "The spiritual telegraph is best accomplished by combining our individual magnetisms," he explained, "which we do by coming together in a spirit circle." The gentleman began to describe in comprehensive detail the various methods by which spirits can be summoned from the Summerland, but he had used perhaps only a portion of the air he had stored when Miss Colburn leapt from the ottoman.

For the first time since Mr. Lincoln had entered the Crimson Room, Miss Colburn raised her face to him. However, it was not the young sensitive's delicate features which presented themselves without shyness, but the heavy-featured death mask of the old doctor. Indeed, Miss Colburn's transformation into Old Doc Bamford was so complete her hair ribbons and silk dress seemed objects of our own hallucination. The change in Miss Colburn turned Mr. Lincoln bloodless, and my husband stared at the young medium as if at a corpse come to life.

"This is the message from the men who reside in the world of spirit," announced the old doctor. "You must not weaken. You must stand firm in your conviction."

My husband was still white-fleshed, but he had not removed his eyes from the old doctor's death mask.

"This proclamation shall be the crowning event of your administration," the spirit continued. "It is the mission for which you have been raised up by Providence."

The voice ceased. We stood about the young sensitive, uncertain what to do, for I do not think any of us had seen a trance medium taken over by spirit without the assistance of a magnetic circle. Then, just as suddenly as she had fallen beneath spirit control, Miss Colburn was released from it. The density of the doctor's face vanished and in an instant the young medium's eyes again belonged to the living. Without the spirit of the dead doctor to animate her, Miss Colburn's figure went limp. Mr. Lincoln had to catch her and help her back upon the ottoman.

"It is always some three to four minutes before the spirit returns the entirety of the medium's magnetism," explained Mr. Laurie.

And indeed, in precisely that time, Miss Colburn resumed her own personality and once again became shy before my husband.

"You possess a very singular gift, Miss Colburn," Mr. Lincoln told the young sensitive.

"It was useful to you?" she murmured.

With a fatherly gesture, he rested a hand upon the parting of her hair. "Enough that I might think your coming here was inspired by the same Providence of which you spoke."

Miss Colburn, who never knew what she said while under spirit control, looked up at my husband in bewilderment.

"If you will permit," said Mr. Lincoln, rising to his feet, "my spirit advisors have left me with a fair amount to think over." And shaking the hand of Mr. Laurie, he bid the company good-night.

My visitors remained until Miss Colburn was fully revived. After they departed, slipping into my carriage with covered lanterns, I went searching for my husband. I found him in his office, seated in an armchair beside the fire. Since the day he had confronted me with the letter about Mr. Wood, I had not come to this room, and now could not enter it without imagining my hairpins scattered across the desk, wondering if one or two of them remained caught in the seam of its leather top.

"Do you think it is the proclamation emancipating the Negroes the spirits mean?" I said.

"I cannot believe it is anything else."

I went nearer, seated myself in the chair which was opposite him. No lamps had been left lit, there was only the fire, and it made the rest of the room – the green walls and carpet – even more like the dark woods I always believed it to be.

"And do you intend to follow their advice?"

"Three-quarters of the Republican Party believe that the proclamation will make the country vote Democrat."

"They may be right," I told him. "But you cannot always consider politics."

I think that he smiled, for the shadows about his mouth deepened. "Careful, or I will believe you under spirit control."

"It is right to emancipate the slaves."

"But then what will happen to them?" He leaned back against his chair with a great weariness. "I would have preferred to colonize the Negroes. Give them land and money, and let them form their own nation in Africa."

"And what would Mammy Sally do in Africa?" I asked him. "She has lived in Kentucky all her life." I reached across the space between our chairs and rested my fingertips upon the back of his hand. "You do not know Negroes," I reminded him. "You were not raised with them. You count none among your friends."

"But according to a group of dead gentlemen, I have achieved this office for the sole purpose of freeing them."

I let my whole hand fall upon his. "There is no greater good that you can do."

"I have been looking for a sign that that is true."

"I believe the spirits have given you one."

For some time, we sat quietly together, and Mr. Lincoln let me keep my hand upon his.

"It is a remarkable thing," he said, his voice made softer now, "the change which comes over Miss Colburn. Do you think she truly speaks with the dead?"

"Yes," I told him. "I am sorry Willie did not come to you."

"Perhaps it's better," he replied. "I'm afraid that even the smallest part of him will make my grief that much harder to bear."

I heard again that breaking in his voice which spoke of the mourning he could not control, the sorrow he let overtake him only when locked in the room where his child had died, and this time I did go to him. I sat at his feet upon the carpet, resting my face upon his trouser leg and keeping hold of the one hand he had allowed me.

I meant no more than simple consolation, a sharing of the sorrow of which only we knew the depth. But the warmth of his limb beneath my cheek, and the scent of woodsmoke I knew I would find upon his skin, made me forget my motive of simple consolation, and my head became filled with the complexities of all that I might do to comfort him. I slid my arms about my husband's waist, letting the starched cotton of his shirt chafe at the inside of my wrists, wakening the rest of my flesh to the rubbing and binding of my own clothing. I prayed that he would pull me onto his lap, that he would unfasten the neck of my mourning gown and put his mouth to my throat. I prayed that he would raise my skirts and take me there, in the chair before the fire in the dark green woods of his office.

But my husband did none of these things. He touched me only to rest a hand upon the parting of my hair as he had done with Miss Colburn.

I had become enough used to his rejection to know how to put down desire. After not very long my breath came steady and, sitting back upon my heels, I tucked away some hair which had become disarranged. "Are you so unmoved by me?"

"I could not be unmoved by you," he said. "Although I have worked at it."

"Can you imagine a time when you will wish to lie with me again?"

"For a while I could not."

"And now?"

The shadowing about his mouth made me think again that he smiled. "I find that love promotes a certain forgetfulness."

I touched again the back of his hand, to see if he would allow it. "You still hold some love for me?"

His hand remained beneath mine. "Despite my best intentions."

"Then I will pray for it to hurry its work upon your memory," I said. "But I am middle-aged and some would call you old, and I worry that we are forfeiting too much time." I released his hand and rose to my feet.

"In that case, I will see what I can do about hurrying it up on my end," he told me, "since you believe me so near to joining the spirit world."

He had meant it as wit, as a way to lessen any embarrassment my actions might have caused me, and for this intention I smiled at him before I quit the room. But out in the corridor I pulled the woolen wrapper tight across my chest, more chilled than even that unheated space warranted.

On New Year's Day of 1863, the doors of the President's House were opened to the public for the first time since Willie's death. At nine o'clock in the morning, Mr. Lincoln and I took our places in the East Room, where we would greet the great crush of people who waited in the wide main corridor and overflowed out in the cold. The diplomats came first, followed by the gentlemen of Mr. Lincoln's cabinet, then the officers of the army and the navy, and then any citizen willing to wait in the freezing weather long enough to be presented to Mr. Lincoln and myself.

Although it had been ten months since the death of my son, I still dressed in mourning. For this occasion, however, Lizzie Keckly had insisted upon stitching dove gray insets into my sleeves and at the band at my waist, using for excuse that she worked these days too much upon black and that it wearied her eyes. As this was my first public appearance since Willie's death, all presented to me – whether acquaintance or stranger – felt the obligation to express condolence. I knew that this was kindly meant, that some had waited in the sleeting rain only to share with me their sorrow over the loss of my son. But as these well-wishers filled my ears with their regret, they made me think too much of my own, and I had to work to prepare a smile for the next visitor who wished to tell me of his or her sadness over Willie.

For three hours I stood in the East Room and had my fingers squeezed by gentlemen and ladies whose conversation reminded me of my dead son. And still the line stretched out into the cold.

"I am feeling indisposed," I whispered to Mr. Nicolay, who always stood beside us at these receptions. "I am going to return to my room." And without waiting for that Germanic gentleman to grant me permission I hurried away up the stairs.

Lizzie Keckly was waiting in my room to help me undress. "The reception is already over?" she asked.

"My part in it is."

"But I was so pleased with this gown," she said, unbuttoning the back.

"For the time that I was down there I would guess that several hundred people set eyes upon it," I assured her. "And by the end of the week *Leslie's Illustrated Newspaper* will publish a sketch of me looking too plump in it. Which will not prevent them from describing your handiwork as 'another of Mrs. Keckly's enchanting creations.'"

Lizzie lifted the dress over my head, then untied the waist of my hoops and helped me step out of them. "Has Mr. Lincoln signed the proclamation?"

"I do not think he has left the East Room."

She made to crush down the underskirt, but fumbled it, clattering the metal hoops upon the floor. I put a hand upon her arm.

"He will sign it."

"You are certain?"

"Now that he has promised, it would be dishonorable not to. And the one thing we can generally count upon with Mr. Lincoln is his commitment to honorableness."

"It is only that so many are counting upon him," she replied.

Lizzie stayed to help me unpin my hair, and then I sent her away, promising to have a message delivered when Mr. Lincoln had signed the proclamation. Then, though it was only midday, I dropped upon my mattress and fell to sleep.

I dreamt that I still stood shaking the hands of the crowds which moved through the East Room. However, in my dream, each gentleman and lady who approached carried not some expression of regret, but a keepsake which had belonged to Willie – leaded soldiers, tin trains, his pony. After Willie died I had had all of his possessions taken from the house, for it only added to my sorrow to see them. Still, the visitors continued to bring me these things, laying them at my feet until the pile rose so high I could not look past it.

I woke from this dream to find my husband seated upon my bed. I studied him, still dressed in the black suit he had worn to greet the New Year's crowd; shut my eyes, then opened them to see if he would disappear, for it had been so long since I had seen him in this room, I feared I had just slipped from one dream into another.

"I have signed it," he told me. "Though my fingers are so paralyzed from hand-shaking, my signature does not look so sure as I feel."

I lifted myself to lean against the pillows. Late-afternoon sun slanted through the window, falling upon the dress Lizzie had left out to air. "And you do feel sure?"

"I have never in my life felt more certain that I was doing right than I did signing that paper."

He rubbed at his eyes, a gesture which had become habit, and I caught a glimpse of his swollen hand. The flesh of it was stretched and purplish, the fingers stiffened into claws. I took hold of it and gently pressed upon the cramped tendons.

"I felt him there," he told me.

"Willie?"

"When I made to sign the proclamation. I felt the warmth of him beside my shoulder."

"Did it comfort you?"

He took away his hand to once again wipe at his eyes. "It only made me miss him more," he choked. Then he bent his head and began to weep.

I pulled my husband to me so he could cry into my hair. When still his weeping did not stop, I held his face between my hands and kissed him, taking each tear into my mouth.

"I did not expect to grieve so long," he sobbed.

With an embrace near to violence, he took hold of me. I knew that it was only consolation he was seeking, but I was too susceptible to my husband's flesh. The taste of his tears, the pressure of his arms, the hard bones of his chest against my uncorseted breast made me shake as if with palsy. I put my mouth upon my husband's and pressed myself more upon him until I had climbed into his lap. And even there, I would not release his mouth, for fear of what he might say if I did, fear that I would lose my reason if he refused me. But he did not refuse me. Instead he pushed more fiercely against my mouth, putting his teeth to my lip until the skin broke and I tasted blood.

My husband's paralyzed hand fumbled at the front of my dressing gown, his stiffened fingers caught in the ties at the neck, and I felt the vibration of his frustrated moan against my mouth. I pushed his hands away and undid the gown myself, tore open my own chemise. Then I reached for his clothes; unfastened his vest and shirt, and felt the pounding of his heart beneath my fingers; put my hand upon his trouser buttons, making him shudder with violence.

He took me there, at the edge of the mattress. I could not keep hold of my desire, but writhed against my husband's body as if I wanted to break myself upon it, propelled by a passion which for eighteen months had done nothing but increase until I believed such wanting would overwhelm all other thought. Downstairs the citizens of what was left of the country paraded through the East Room; upstairs we sought every pleasure to be found in the body of the other, until weariness finally overcame my husband's desire and he fell into sleep, tangled in wrappings of bedcovers and discarded clothing.

I did not sleep, but watched over my husband. The weak sun of winter cast its imagined warmth upon the bedcoverings, and from outside I heard the rattling of carriages come to take away our guests.

In the dimming light I studied my husband's sunken cheeks, the flesh of his face, which had aged too much in the past year, then turned my eyes upon the comforting rise and fall of my husband's chest. When the sun dropped and the room turned cold, I covered that chest with my loosened hair, as if the strands might protect him and keep him bound to me.

As the country moved into 1863, the war which no one – North or South – believed would last longer than ninety days, entered its third year. And so many on both sides were dead. Four thousand at Chickamauga. Four thousand more at Shiloh and at Chancellorsville. Seven thousand at Gettysburg. And it seemed to me that each drop of blood spilled upon these battlegrounds claimed some percentage of Mr. Lincoln's own.

Although my husband's age was fifty-four, he could have been believed to possess twenty more years, for the skin about his eyes had discolored to something so near black he appeared to stand perpetually in shadow. Mr. Lincoln rarely ate. His shirt collars circled his neck without touching the shriveled flesh of his throat. And his cheeks had become so sunken, his face had assumed the shape of the skull beneath it. On the occasions he came to my bed, it was like embracing a bundle of sticks. When he traveled to Pennsylvania to deliver a speech at the dedication of the cemetery at Gettysburg, he returned with a case of varioloid – a strain of smallpox – and could not rise from his bed for three weeks. "This war is eating my life out," he repeated in the delusion of fever.

I worried, too, over the health of my youngest son. The typhoid had left Taddie prone to mysterious fevers, which turned him delirious and made him rant in his incomprehensible speech. These sicknesses of Taddie's caused in me my own brand of delirious fever. I felt in a frenzy to keep Taddie well, and dosed him with castor oil mixed with molasses to improve the taste until he hid from me, bribed him with a dollar if he would consent to swallow his morning tablespoon of Professor Low's Liniment and Worm syrup.

Only Robert seemed safe from death, away at Harvard College where he was studying law. But my eldest son did not appear to wish to remain safe. Each week came another letter from him begging his father to grant him an army commission. "It isn't right that Robert stays out of the fighting," said Mr. Lincoln, each time another of these letters arrived. "Not when he is so willing to go."

"He may be willing to go," I replied. "But I am not willing to lose any more sons."

It did not pass unnoticed that Robert was not in the army. The newspapers called him coward and accused him of sharing the traitorous sympathies of his mother. Mr. Lincoln, they declared, was only disposed to sacrifice other men's sons to his war to free the Negro.

I was not easy with my decision to keep Robert from the war; it was not just. Other mothers had given up more than one son to the fighting. And I possessed no defense when even those who were our friends asked why Robert was not in the army – save that I wished to keep my son alive. This guilt began to plague me, and to ease my own remorse, and make some small compensation for the fact that I would not give the war my son, I took up volunteering at the soldiers' hospital at Mount Pleasant.

Like so many soldiers' hospitals which had been hastily built about Washington City, Mount Pleasant was not much more than a cavernous barracks occupied by wounded soldiers and blowflies. The ward held close to five hundred beds – never empty for more than an hour – and even the building's high ceilings did little to dissipate the smell of dysentery, unwashed men, and the sweetish stench of rotting flesh. Like all army hospitals, Mount Pleasant was plagued with gangrene. Each time I returned, soldiers I had originally met with two arms or legs, now possessed only one, as if the hospital had taxed them a limb. I had wondered what happened to these confiscated limbs until one afternoon when I stepped outside for some fresher air and glanced into a bucket left by the door. Inside I saw a pair of feet, black with the disease.

Although there was not any shortage of sick or wounded soldiers to fill the beds at Mount Pleasant, there were never enough nurses to care for them. Consequently, the ladies of Washington City – at least those with a certain strength of stomach – were pressed into tending the less grievously wounded. When I first began to visit, I brought gifts which had been sent to the President's House – baskets of whiskey and homemade cakes. But after learning that a great many soldiers suffered from scurvy, I always brought oranges, saving them for the victims of the illness, whom I recognized by their gums turned swollen and purple as grapes.

One of these was Sergeant Tobias Warne, who was of the same age as Robert and nearly as handsome, save for the scurvy, which had caused his gums to bleed over his teeth, dyeing them pink. Sergeant Warne had been wounded in the hand. A bullet had passed through the center of his palm, severing the nerves so that his fingers curled in upon themselves like a flower made of flesh. It was his right hand which was wounded, and on the day that I met him, I saw that he struggled with his left to peel his orange.

"Let me do that for you," I offered. I took back the orange and pulled off the skin, placing the sections into his uninjured palm.

"I don't expect anybody will believe that the First Lady fed me oranges." Sergeant Warne was from Indiana and spoke in a slurred drawl which reminded me of my husband.

"Nobody except my youngest son," I confided, "who does not consider any status I might achieve excuse to neglect my mothering."

I brought Sergeant Warne oranges for a week, and at the end of it he asked if I would help write to his mother.

"I could make do with my left hand," he explained. "But my mama was a schoolteacher and was always very strict about penmanship."

I found paper and ink, and sat beside Sergeant Warne's bed as he dictated a letter to his mother. The correspondence was nearly three pages long. In it he used the word "love" four times.

As summer shifted into autumn, I continued to visit with Sergeant Warne. His scurvy lessened and his gums no longer bled, but I still brought him oranges, still peeled them and placed them in his uninjured hand. Once, before I could drop the sections into his palm, he reached up and wrapped the fingers of that hand around my own. Held it long enough to let me know the gesture was done from affection, not to say that he did not want oranges or to relay any practical message. Another time I arrived late and discovered him struggling to write with a pen he had forced between the paralyzed fingers of his wounded hand, the ink beneath it smudged by sweat. "I would be much let down if you did not let me do this," I said. After I released the pen, I wrapped my fingers around his stiffened ones, held them longer than practicality warranted.

Each time I came, I was surprised to discover that the sergeant was still in his bed, for he appeared to me to be only lightly wounded. "Sergeant Warne is plagued with fevers," muttered Mount Pleasant's chief doctor, a man of near seventy who had retired and now resented the war from taking him out of it. I was sorry to learn that the sergeant was not entirely well, but I was always happy to see him there.

At times I pretended that Sergeant Warne was Robert, my eldest son gone to war, now returned, lightly wounded, but altered – made more affectionate toward the living when faced so forcibly with death. *If this were Robert,* I thought, *I would bring him oranges – and anything else he desired. And I would hold his injured hand and take it to my breast and kiss it. And for once I would be entirely successful nursing back to health a son who needed it.*

Upon an afternoon near the close of October, an autumn day of hard brightness, I came to Mount Pleasant and discovered another soldier in Sergeant Warne's bed. *At last he is recovered,* I told myself. And I went looking for the doctor to learn whether the handsome sergeant had been sent back to the war, or home to his mother – as I wished.

I found the irritable old gentleman stitching together a rough-edged wound in a soldier's chest which had pulled open.

"Warne?" he asked, in response to my question.

I pointed to the bed in which Sergeant Warne had passed most of the summer.

The doctor squinted through blowflies, then turned back to his stitching. "Dead," he told me.

"That cannot be right," I said to him. "Sergeant Warne had a small wound. And it was very nearly healed."

The doctor put the end of a new piece of stitching thread in his mouth, wetting it for the needle. "Poisoning of the blood," he muttered. "Happens with some frequency."

The stench of gangrene which the autumn afternoon could not blow away slid into my nose and throat, filled up my mouth until I tasted the sweetish scent of the body turning upon itself, poisoning its own blood, blackening its own limbs. *This is the smell of death,* I thought, *and it will find Robert upon a battlefield or in a hospital like this one full of blowflies. It will seep from here and it will find Taddie, too, feeding upon his fevers and turning his blood against him. Then it will come seeking my husband, lodging itself in his wasted frame which*

— 361 —

has no strength to fight it. It will come, this stench which carries death, to everyone I love, the way that it has already come to Willie and to Eddie. For I am cursed in a way which draws it to those who mean the most to me.

My oranges fell to the floor, rolling beneath the soldiers' cots, and I turned and ran between the long row of beds, hurrying past the men who had already paid the hospital's tax of an arm or leg, and those who stilled hoped not to. I needed to stand in the wind and let it blow the stink of death from my clothes so I would not carry it home.

I rushed from the building, my shoes sinking into the mud which always seemed to surround it, even on the driest days. A long line of men bearing stretchers was outside, stretchers upon which lay soldiers who carried the scent upon their flesh, released it in their exhalations. I ran to the first carriage I saw and threw myself inside it.

"Drive!" I cried to the man seated upon the bench.

"Where?" he asked me.

"Anyplace that is not here!"

As the carriage began to move, I pushed down the window, pulling in air until my corset bit at my ribs. But there were too many carts filled with wounded soldiers in these streets so near to Mount Pleasant, and I knew that I was only breathing in more of the gangrenous scent.

"Take me out of this quarter!" I called up to the driver.

"I need a destination."

I thought only for a moment. "Pennsylvania Avenue," I told him.

After Mount Pleasant, Pennsylvania Avenue's brilliant shops glowed with life. The windows showed silks instead of wrapping bandages, boots which were only sold in pairs, gloves fashioned for unfurled fingers.

"Let me down here," I said to the driver. For I needed to walk in this air which was sweetened only by the scent of perfume and new leather.

The pavement of Pennsylvania Avenue felt safe and solid beneath my feet. I walked until I had ceased to smell death, then slowed and gazed into windows filled with objects which were new and unbroken. In one a silver tea service sat shining upon a velvet-covered pedestal. The service was so bright with reflected light from the store's gas lamps, it seemed that it generated the radiance upon its own.

"I must see that service close," I told the clerk inside.

"It is made of a high grade of silver," he said, placing the shining pieces before me. "Very lasting."

I removed my gloves and ran my hands along the smooth, undamaged surfaces. All was unmarked, untainted, and if any of it should blacken, I could polish it back to brightness.

"Have this sent to the President's House," I said to the clerk, although I already owned a tea service and had no need of another.

When the service arrived, I had the boxes brought to my room where I sat upon the bed and unpacked every piece of it. I held the sugar bowl and the creamer in my hands and their gleaming weight seemed a promise that the infection which sickened limbs would not find Robert, that whatever it was which poisoned blood would keep from Taddie. The serving pot offered me assurance that my husband would survive the burdens of his office, that the war would not eat out his life. I kept the silver service in my closet where I might look upon it whenever I felt need of its unmarred durability. Two days later, when Robert wrote again begging to go to war and a hint of the gangrene filled my nose and mouth, I returned to the shop and purchased a set of silver cake plates to keep it company.

During the winter of 1863 and 1864, I practiced the protection of my family in the shops of Pennsylvania Avenue, buying anything which seemed destined to endure, as if I could build a fortress about my sons and husband made of silver serving spoons and forged-metal fire screens. When I ran out of room in my closet, I had the boxes brought to a room in the attic. Once each day, more if my husband appeared especially unwell, or if Taddie looked feverish, or if Robert had sent another letter, I raced there and opened the boxes, stroked the smooth surfaces of the undamaged objects which sat safe within them. Only to put my hands upon these pieces of marble and brass and precious metal, to stand in awe at the wall the boxes made, was as calming as a dose of laudanum. And as when one is beneath the influence of that drug, it was simple to disregard the consequence of its employment. So when my unpaid accounts became too high to be overlooked by the shopkeepers of Pennsylvania Avenue, I went to New York and purchased the safety of my family with new accounts in the shops of lower Broadway.

By spring, I had made several shopping expeditions to New York, visiting most often the marble palace of A. T. Stewart & Company. It was there, while purchasing a set of malachite bookends, that I experienced the first consequence of such unrestrained armoring, for the clerk, who had gone to wrap up the pieces, returned without the bookends, and with the message that Mr. Stewart himself would like to speak with me.

In the brilliant glare of Mr. Stewart's store, I mentally calculated what I owed the Gentleman Merchant. By my reckoning – not including the malachite bookends – I had purchased more than eighteen thousand dollars of safe-keeping. "I always experience the greatest pleasure in conversing with your employer," I said to the clerk. "However, I was meant to be at a review of the Empire City Regiment some time ago and cannot linger. Indeed, it is probably my hurry which has made me say I will take the bookends when I am not entirely certain about them. Please do me the favor of removing them from my account until I feel more sure."

The clerk nodded, and I rushed out of the store, my heart racing less from the possibility of confronting Mr. Stewart, than that I had left the bookends.

I went to no more stores that day, for Mr. Stewart was acquainted with all the merchants of New York, and I did not know if he had mentioned the sum of my account to any of them. I passed the rest of the afternoon in my hotel and only left it in the evening, to attend a séance in Mrs. Kellogg's simple rooms on upper Broadway.

I visited Mrs. Kellogg's every time I came to New York, hoping always for some sign of Willie. Thus far, the plump medium had been unable to call up my son from the Summerland, but I had seen her oak table dance upon its legs, and on one occasion witnessed one of her china dogs fly from the shelf and shatter itself against the opposite wall. Moreover, I enjoyed the corporeal company of Mrs. Kellogg's séance parlor, as that lady counted among her followers many gentlemen of politics. One of these was Abram Wakeman, an ambitious lawyer who held the position of postmaster of the city of New York. Although Mr. Wakeman was forty, and I forty-six, he paid me the type of attention gentlemen pay to younger ladies – without the perilous undercurrent of desire, for Mr. Wakeman was a great supporter of my husband. I often found myself holding hands with him at Mrs. Kellogg's magnetic circles, and I found him very agreeable – although his chin was just a bit too receding for beauty.

"Tell me, how have you been passing your time while in New York?" Mr. Wakeman asked me upon this evening. Our circle had concluded and we were seated side by side on Mrs. Kellogg's horsehair sofa, sipping at cups of the black tea she brewed so strongly only one cup made me feel as if a spirit had taken control of my own nerves.

"I am afraid I have been doing nothing more edifying than shopping," I told him.

"Then surely you have visited my friend Alexander Stewart's store?"

I gazed at Mr. Wakeman with surprise. "Mr. Stewart is a friend to you?"

"The Gentleman Merchant and I have a long acquaintance," he replied. "If you are returning there, I should be happy to escort you."

I took a sip of Mrs. Kellogg's tea, which had turned tannic upon my tongue. "I believe I have concluded my business with Mr. Stewart's store."

Mr. Wakeman smiled and shook his head. "I have never known a lady to be entirely concluded with Mr. Stewart's store." He brought his small-mouthed face nearer and spoke in a false whisper. "Let me take you there tomorrow, and I will make old Alex show you the merchandise he saves for Mrs. Vanderbilt."

I shifted my eyes away from him. "I am scheduled to visit the Brooklyn Navy Yard tomorrow, and be shown a new warship."

"Unless you are planning to sail that ship down to Charleston and recapture the harbor, I cannot imagine that the activity will consume the entire day." Mr. Wakeman refilled my cup with the bitter tea. "We may go in the afternoon, and I will oblige Mr. Stewart to keep the store open late for you."

"I could not impose upon Mr. Stewart's kindness," I protested.

"Alex cannot help but be pleased to be imposed upon by the First Lady of the country."

Unable to conjure another excuse, I stared into the black well of my teacup, feeling Mr. Wakeman's eyes upon me. When that gentleman spoke again, it was in a quieter, more confidential tone. "My friend Alexander Stewart is an amiable gentleman," he told me. "However, I have known him to display a certain unreasonableness regarding the payment of ladies' accounts."

I glanced up from my cup into Mr. Wakeman's almost handsome face.

"If there were any way that I might serve you with Mr. Stewart," he continued, "I would be happy to do it."

I studied the ambitious postmaster's expression with the same carefulness I brought to searching Mrs. Kellogg's parlor for spirits. "Mr. Lincoln's attention to the war has left me unusually situated," I began.

Mr. Wakeman held up an elegant hand. "Do not make yourself discomfited by speaking of it further," he insisted. "I will call upon my friend tomorrow."

I did not imagine that Mr. Wakeman would have any success with Mr. Stewart, for the Gentleman Merchant did indeed have a reputation for wishing always to be paid. But the following afternoon, the postmaster turned up in my rooms at the Metropolitan Hotel in a cheerful mood.

"We may take our excursion to Mr. Stewart's emporium at whatever time you like," he declared, seating himself upon one of the scroll-legged chairs in my sitting room. "That overanxious gentleman has been reminded that in times of national crisis, we must all learn to practice patience."

"He is willing to forego payment upon my account?"

"For as long as the First Lady requires."

"You are a sympathetic friend, Mr. Wakeman," I said. "I trust that I did no injury to your friendship with Mr. Stewart by sending you to speak with him on my behalf?"

Mr. Wakeman crossed his legs and straightened the crease in his trousers. The postmaster was always very finely dressed, and I wondered if he purchased his clothes at A. T. Stewart & Company.

"Alex can be peevish when it comes to money," he replied, "but that is just the Scots in him. Once our business was concluded, we had a very agreeable visit." Again, he adjusted the fine wool of his trousers. "Indeed, he spoke to me quite movingly about one of his employees, a Mr. George Butler. Mr. Butler's son, a lieutenant in the Union army, has lost an arm in the fighting in Pennsylvania, yet he has been unable to secure an order releasing him from duty."

"Let me assist Mr. Butler," I declared. "Write out the lieutenant's name and company, and I shall telegram the Secretary of War myself."

"Mr. Stewart will be very grateful," the postmaster assured me.

Mr. Wakeman, it turned out, knew most of the merchants in New York to whom I owed money. Indeed, he knew them well enough to recommend forbearance regarding ladies' debts during times of national crisis. Once I returned to Washington City, I discovered that the postmaster had influence with a good many of the merchants there. Often these businessmen who were so accommodating about my debts were familiar with a patriotic soldier who required a furlough, or a deserving relation who wished a government job such as lamplighter, and it felt ungenerous to refuse to help such patriotic citizens. *Patronage is practiced at every level of government,* I reminded myself. *And if these small bargains make it possible for me to purchase more safety for my family, what does it matter who is made lamplighter?*

But after a time, it seemed that no delay of payment or acceptance of a partial sum came without a request.

"Is there not one merchant who does not have some errand he would like me to undertake?" I said to Mr. Wakeman, when next I attended séance at Mrs. Kellogg's.

"Merchants are a penurious breed," shrugged the postmaster. "Even in time of national emergency, they are disinclined to forgive a ladies' debts without receiving something in return."

"What would happen if I were not the president's wife, and possessed no influence?"

Mr. Wakeman regarded me with more seriousness than I generally received from him. "We must hope very much that Mr. Lincoln is reelected."

In the summer of 1864, the summer before the presidential election, we moved once again to the Old Soldiers' Home. While I did hope, along with Mr. Wakeman, that Mr. Lincoln would be reelected, the prospect did not seem likely. No president since Andrew Jackson had served a second term, and my husband did not share that man's popularity, even within his own party. The abolitionist Republicans feared that Mr. Lincoln would negotiate a peace with the South that did not completely rid the country of slavery. The moderate Republicans worried that he would negotiate no peace at all. And no one, Republican or Democrat, was happy with a president who after more than three years of bloodshed, had been unable to propel the Union army to victory over a rebellious Confederacy a fraction of its size.

And the war had grown even more murderous since the spring, since my husband appointed Ulysses Grant commander of the army.

I considered General Grant a butcher, and I was not alone in this opinion, as it was evident that the general did not care how many soldiers were sacrificed to his push through Virginia. In May, he led his troops into the Wilderness, where he lost twenty-six thousand men to death or casualty in one week. In June at Cold Harbor, twelve thousand soldiers beneath his command were killed or wounded within a space of eight minutes. The country was appalled. So many husbands and sons and brothers lost, and still the rebels held Virginia.

And in July, they almost took Washington City.

Taddie and I heard the cannons from the porch of the cottage at the Soldiers' Home. The sound was like thunder, making me believe a storm was coming, though the sky was blue and cloudless. Then, like birds scattered from a tree by gunshot, the refugees came clattering past the Old Soldiers' Home, their wagons overflowing with roped trunks and chamber pots, feather mattresses and stick chairs, wide-eyed children and chickens.

"You best evacuate!" shouted a man, who did not rein his horse to speak to us. "A troop of Confederates have crossed the Monocacy River and are marching on the capital!"

The refugees came all morning, rattling down the road as fast as they could drive their carts. Taddie ran after them, jumping around the littering of ladies' petticoats and smashed crockery that had tumbled off the carts, shouting in his unintelligible speech for them to stay and help him "lick those rebels."

I watched from the porch, and each time a cart filled with refugees rumbled past, I thought frantically of the possessions I had stored in the attic of the President's House. I wanted to stand among the soothing boxes, lift out the marble mantle clocks and brass urns, rub my fingers over the solid glass of a paperweight, the silver serving platters, for I could not be certain of their magic unless I could touch them. But I did not know if Confederates stood between me and these objects of safety, and I could not risk making the two-mile journey alone.

At midday, General Stanton, the Secretary of War, arrived at the Soldiers' Home in his own clattering carriage, sending up a great cloud of dust. Edwin Stanton had become Mr. Lincoln's Secretary of War after old age and dropsy forced the retirement of General Scott, whose letter had put me upon the presidential train.

"We will be able to better defend you in Washington City," he told me. The general did not come into the house, but stood with one foot upon the bottom step of the porch, as if demonstrating for me the urgency of leaving.

"Do you have enough soldiers to defend us?" I asked, for all of the men who once filled the parks and green spaces of the capital had been sent into slaughter with General Grant.

General Stanton shrugged beneath his tunic. "I have given rifles to all the able-bodied government clerks and released from the hospitals any soldier well enough to stand and shoot."

The streets of Washington City were deserted. Only at the entrance to the President's House did I see soldiers, six men, each bearing both a rifle and a bandaged wound. These men, weak and feverish-looking, made my fingers twitch with the desire to touch the bowls and bookends and tea services meant to safeguard us. Once I entered the house, I did not wait to remove my hat, but raced to the attic and shut myself inside, plunging my hands into boxes filled with straw and precious metals, breathing easy for the first time since the morning's cannon fire.

It was lucky that these injured soldiers and the government clerks with rifles were not called upon to defend us. For two days, a small Union regiment kept the rebels out of the capital. Then a troop of infantry sent by General Grant arrived in Washington City and the Confederates retreated. Beyond the burning of some houses, there was little damage, save what was inflicted upon Mr. Lincoln's hopes for reelection. For it seemed that the entire country placed the blame for the rebels coming so near to capturing the capital entirely upon my husband.

By the end of the week General Stanton declared that it was safe for Taddie and me to move back to the Old Soldiers' Home. But once there, I could not stop recalling how undefended I had felt with the objects of our security so far from my hands. Before a day had passed, I returned to Washington City, going directly to Pennsylvania Avenue, where I purchased another attic's worth of safeguarding, adding to accounts which were already ruinous.

At the beginning of August, a note arrived at the Old Soldiers' Home from the Commissioner of Public Buildings, Major French.

"There are rumors that the Democrats are getting up something which will embarrass you and damage Mr. Lincoln's political chances," he wrote to me. "Can you imagine what that might be?"

"I cannot imagine what affairs of mine could be considered embarrassing," I responded, leaving splotches of ink upon the page where I had not been able to hold my pen steady. For I was full aware that the unpaid debts of a wife always reflected badly upon a husband.

After I replied to Major French's note, I sent off a frantic letter to Mr. Wakeman, pleading with him to contact every storekeeper in New York and Washington City, and convince them to say nothing of my bills. "Tell the merchants that once Mr. Lincoln is reelected," I pledged, "I will settle everything."

"The merchants have very little faith in that possibility," Mr. Wakeman replied the following day. "I expect that is the reason they are pressing for payment now."

I begged Mr. French for money for expenses I invented, borrowed what I could from the household accounts, sending everything I scrounged to those merchants whose letters sounded most impatient. Still, it was very little against the mountain of my debt. Knowing that if the Democrats were to gather enough information about my accounts to embarrass Mr. Lincoln it would appear first in the newspapers, I began to fear the sound of Colonel Murton's wheeled chair upon the bricked path outside the cottage. Each afternoon when he came to rave about the scoundrels and rogues of Washington City, I stood cold beneath the hot sun, my eyes fixed upon the newspapers resting in the place where his legs would have been, waiting to learn if I had been exposed as one of their number.

That August was a hellish month. The heat dried the ink at the tip of my pen before I could set it to the pages of my desperate letters to Mr. Wakeman. The air was too hot to carry breeze or birdsong, and all hung uncommonly still as if in suspense of some great disturbance. Even the nights were hot, and neither Mr. Lincoln, nor I, nor Taddie could sleep. We rose from damp beds and roamed the cottage like sweat-soaked wraiths, seeking coolness until the sun rose and so heated the air, it seared the skin to pass through it.

Now, too, we were obliged to listen to the ceaseless sound of digging as the soldiers General Grant hurled against the rebels came back to be buried. The strangling heat, the slow creaking of Colonel Murton's chair, the unending rasp of shovel biting into earth, and overall, the near certainty that Mr. Lincoln would not be reelected and my debts would come due robbed my breath, left me both agitated and faint. Some days, seeing the fresh graves outside the window and their promise of the earth's coolness, I had to hold back from throwing myself into one.

The heat continued into September and I began to believe that like the war, this terrible summer would never end. And then, after a day of heated stillness so oppressive I wanted to shriek against it, the house shook with a furious thunderstorm, the first of all that summer. Thunder rattled my bedstead and filled the room with rending noise until the booming felt to be inside my own chest. Lightning came so near, my skin sparked. Taddie and I were both driven to Mr. Lincoln's bed, where we each clung to one of his arms and quaked at each assault of sound and light. This storm, so violently purposeful, seemed what the world had been waiting for all that season.

In the morning the heat had broken, breeze returned, and the air thinned to something more breathable. When I went out upon the porch, I saw that the storm had torn every blossom from the wisteria bush. I saw, too, that the boots Mr. Lincoln had left there upon his return from Washington City had disappeared. I searched the lawn surrounding the porch in a circle wider than it seemed reasonable boots could travel in any wind. Then I sent Taddie out to look for them, but even after an hour combing the grounds, he returned without the boots.

"Don't fret about it anymore." Mr. Lincoln stood upon the damp porch in his stockings. "They were pretty worn anyway."

But I could not cease thinking about the boots, for though they had been taken by the storm, one of Colonel Murton's newspapers, which I had forgotten near them, had been left behind. This made the vanishing of Mr. Lincoln's boots feel to be some sign of prophecy. But I did not want to think too much upon a prophecy of missing boots.

And indeed, before the day was done, I determined I was wrong to fret about the boots, for news came that General William T. Sherman had taken Atlanta.

This was the victory for which the North had been praying, and the South had been dreading; for Atlanta was the Confederacy's most important city, and to lose it to the Union meant a turning in the war. With the swiftness of the storm which had broken the heat, both the fighting and Mr. Lincoln's chances for reelection changed to our favor. The radical Republicans who had been talking of running another candidate in my husband's place fell silent. And the Democrats, who had proclaimed the war a lost cause, rushed to revise their opinion so as to make it look as if there had been no revision at all.

As for my own situation, I no longer feared the approach of the legless general; for shortly after the newspapers reported Atlanta's fall, Mr. Wakeman wrote to me from New York. "It appears that the merchants who were so anxious to see a soon-to-be former First Lady's accounts settled have suddenly developed a new patience," he informed me. "However, as no president has served three terms, I suggest you make good on your promise to pay your debts." I wrote back to Mr. Wakeman, assuring him that now that the war was not so distressing to my husband, I should have no difficulty settling my accounts. In truth, I had no notion how I might settle debts which, at last reckoning, exceeded Mr. Lincoln's presidential salary. *Still*, I assured myself, *at least my family is safe.*

For the rest of that autumn, the war continued to go well for the Union. General Philip Sheridan took Winchester and Cedar Creek in Virginia. Admiral Farragut captured Mobile in Alabama. Meantime, General Sherman marched his troops toward the Atlantic, cutting like a saber through the very heart of the Confederacy. With no one disbelieving that the Union would win the war, and win it soon, few were surprised when, that November, Mr. Lincoln was elected to a second term.

The morning after the election was ugly and gray, the type of weather which makes any happiness appear misguided. I had gone into the oval-shaped library in search of a book of poetry, something hopeful, and had only sat down with a volume when Mr. Lincoln entered the room. My husband looked tired. I knew that he had been up late the night before, eating celebratory oysters with the gentlemen of his cabinet, but in truth, Mr. Lincoln appeared tired all the time. He sank into his rocker as heavily as if it had only just kept him from falling upon the floor.

"I am going to give Robert his commission," he told me.

The news did not startle me. I had always known that my husband's honor would send Robert into the army. I suspected that, for my sake, he had been waiting until the war was nearly over.

"Can you put him someplace where there is no fighting?"

"I don't think he'll be satisfied with that."

"Then put him with someone you trust."

"I intend to send him into Virginia with Grant."

My nose filled with the sweetish stench of the hospital at Mount Pleasant. "Grant is a murderer," I said.

My husband leaned back in his chair and shut his eyes. "If I ask him, he will watch out for Robert."

I heard that Mr. Lincoln believed this, and I tried to believe it as well. And when that proved difficult, I thought of the boxes in the attic, telling myself, *These will keep Robert safe better than the general will. Let Mr. Lincoln depend upon Grant to safeguard Robert. I will count upon the things in the attic. And when I begin to doubt their power, I will buy more.*

My husband and I sat in the library with only the small explosions of the fire for noise, sat long enough that I hoped Mr. Lincoln had fallen to sleep in his rocker, for he had lately grown so insomniac I did not think he ever slept. I was about to get up and fetch him a shawl, when he surprised me by speaking.

"I do not think I ever told you the dream I had the night after the election that put me here," he said. "I had forgotten it myself until this election made me recall it."

"Tell me then," I told him. "Especially if it is cheerful."

He smiled. "You should know better than anyone that I am not given to cheerful imaginings."

"Tell it to me anyway," I said. "It is bound to be better than this poetry."

He stared into the fire, as if watching the dream unfold there. "I was in the bedroom of our old house in Springfield, and was just about to lie on the mattress, when I caught my own image in the swinging mirror we used to keep on the bureau. There was something odd about it, and looking closer, I saw that the glass held two separate and distinct reflections of my face, one superimposed over the other. These reflections were identical in every aspect, except that one of the faces was paler than the other. I tried tilting the mirror, angling it one way and the other, but the two faces wouldn't become one." He looked away from the fire. "Do you imagine there is some meaning to it?"

The meaning of my husband's dream was so clear that no matter how I attempted to cloud it, I could not make it mean anything else. The two faces foretold that Mr. Lincoln would be elected to two terms as president. The paleness of the second face was sign that he would not live to complete that second term.

"I think," I said to him, "that it is just an oddity of sleep."

At this, he relaxed back into the rocker. "Maybe," he told me, "it's a warning not to look into any mirrors."

We said no more about the dream, and I worked not to think upon it. But the following day, I went to Pennsylvania Avenue and purchased lamps made of heavy brass with thick glass globes. Then, recalling that both times I had required mourning I had not possessed enough of it, I bought for myself one thousand dollars' worth of black shawls and bonnets, lengths of veiling and yards of bombazine, thinking that if I owned an abundance of mourning, I would never need it.

By the start of 1865, the South had run out of old men and children to send to war, and that April, Richmond, Virginia, the capital of the Confederacy, was captured by the Union army. Mr. Lincoln was invited to see the city where Jefferson Davis had kept his own President's House, and as the occasion would coincide with Taddie's twelfth birthday, we decided to make the journey together.

"Come with us, Lizzie," I coaxed, the next time my friend came with a basted dress for me to try.

"Your party includes a senator and a marquis," she reminded me. "I'm not certain I should be included."

"Senator Sumner is an abolitionist," I told her, "and therefore required to be kind to you. And the marquis de Chambrun is French. As such, he will determine you to be an exotic female, and will sit at your side and flatter you all the way to Virginia."

"That is a generous interpretation," replied Lizzie, tugging upon my bodice to test the fit.

"Please come," I said. "You more than any of them are entitled to see the end of the Confederacy."

"All right," she told me. "To see Richmond ruined would be proof that it is over."

We journeyed first to City Point in Virginia, where General Grant had his headquarters, and there met Robert, who appeared dashing – as well as consolingly unscathed – in his captain's uniform. We were joined also at City Point by Secretary of the Interior James Harlan and his wife, as well as their grown daughter, Mary. Miss Harlan possessed the type of hair which Italian artists give to angels – excess amounts of fair curls – and a habit of touching your arm when she spoke to you. And having seen her once or twice in my eldest son's company, I was very pleased to suspect that Robert was in love with her.

At City Point, we boarded a small steamboat which would take us to Richmond by way of the James River. Although the James had been cleared of Confederate torpedoes, it still ran with signs of war. Our boat was bumped by the twisted hulls of wrecked ships, the bloated bodies of dead horses, and Taddie, trailing his hand in the water, brought up the split barrel of a rusted rifle and a boot with the toepiece torn away.

During the journey downriver, I attempted to speak French with the marquis. The young nobleman, who possessed the flabby features of a good many of the European aristocracy, appeared to consider his visit to the New World as a type of anthropological expedition, for every example of American behavior he observed caused him to write furiously in a small notebook. Still, I was far more interested in observing Robert's courtship of Mary Harlan. That, however, proved no more edifying than the marquis' conversation – at least what I might understand of his conversation – for although Miss Harlan employed her charming habit of touching the sleeve of Robert's uniform with nearly scandalous frequency, my son responded by committing nothing more shocking than once taking the young lady's elbow so she would not fall overboard.

As I gazed out at the Richmond shoreline, I believed that I was looking upon a great black wall the rebels had constructed in order to guard the city. But as we drew nearer, I saw that this was not a dark wall, but an enormous crowd of Negroes. I do not know how they had learned of Mr. Lincoln's coming. We had been secretive about the visit, sending word only to Colonel Ripley, commander of the forces in Richmond, for to bring the Union president into the defeated capital of the Confederacy was to invite the risk of assassination. But they had heard. And they had come.

We had not moved very much nearer the shore, when a tremendous cry went up from the black mass gathered upon the riverbank. "Glory Hallelujah!" they cried. And, "It is the great Messiah!" As our boat reached the pier, the wall broke apart and surged toward us, accompanied by a deaf-making slapping of bare feet upon mud, like the sound of a thousand wings taking flight. And as we stepped upon the dock, the Negroes crowded around Mr.

Lincoln, calling him "Father Abraham" and "Marse Lincoln" and "The Savior of the Land." Some of the men had been digging reeds at the riverbank and still clutched bunches of the plants in their hands. One by one these men dropped to their knees, placing their reeds at my husband's feet, the way the faithful had laid palms before Jesus on his final journey into Jerusalem. Then from behind the low buildings of the dockside, came another streaming of colored men, women, and children. In one great mass they approached the dock – some weeping, others leaping as they ran – and all knelt before the savior who had set them free.

I gazed over the bent backs of these former slaves, still clad in homespun or the tattered ball clothes passed down from former masters and mistresses, saw my husband standing tall above them, a look of wonderment upon his face. Over the years we had known each other, the sight of my husband had called up from my flesh no little response. But none was as profound as that which came upon me as I watched the Negroes bow their heads before him. Here, upon the Richmond dock, I felt a tugging upon my chest as corporeal as that of Lizzie pulling upon my bodice to test the fit, and as indefinable as the tug of affection. If I had been forced to put a name to it, I would have called it admiration. But no ordinary admiration would have made me feel that my very heart wished to leave my chest, only so it might present itself to this man before me.

The marquis was writing with great energy in his little notebook. Senator Sumner stood beside Lizzie, he more near to tears than she. Taddie's face was such a study of amazement, I recalled Willie watching Donati's Comet. I looked about for Robert, found him a little way off, standing beside Miss Harlan, who was crying prettily, her hand upon his sleeve. At first, I believed that my eldest son's expression had been misrepresented by the deep shadows cast upon his handsome face by the spring sunshine. But then I knew the representation to be actual, and I felt a sharpness in my lungs like inhaling ice, for Robert was watching the scene with a look of bemusement, as if making Negroes kneel at your feet was no more than a parlor trick.

He is a young man in love, I told myself. *Nothing will impress him unless it has to do with Miss Harlan.*

Mr. Lincoln placed a hand upon the shoulder of the colored man nearest to him – a man who bore the puckered scar caused by branding upon his cheek. "You must kneel to God only," he said to him. "He's the one to thank for your liberty."

"I been so long in the desert without water," replied the man, his eyes still fixed upon the planking of the dock. "I can barely look 'pon the spring of life."

"People have all manner of excuses for not wanting to look upon my face," said Mr. Lincoln. "But this is the first one that sounded like a compliment."

My husband helped raise the man to his feet, clasped his black hand and shook it. Then all the Negroes rose and pressed forward, wanting to shake Mr. Lincoln's hand.

We moved through the sea of dark faces which parted for my husband; made our way up the pier to the open carriage where Colonel Ripley and some of his soldiers waited for us. As we took our seats, a former slavewoman in a pair of man's brogans like those Mammy Sally used to wear began to sing "The Year of Jubilee," and from every corner of the crowd, other voices took up the song, until the entire gathering of Negroes was singing the hymn. The singing moved the air as strongly as the James moved all that went into it, and as our carriage pulled away from the shoreline, I could believe that it was the singing itself which carried us as much as the horses.

Colonel Ripley, a deep-chested man with muttonchops like black caterpillars fixed to his cheeks, rode alongside our carriage, leading us away from the crowd of Negroes and into the city which had once been capital of the Confederacy. It was a warm spring day, the breeze soft and thick with the scent of flowering jasmine, and the streets were lined with more people who had come to see Mr. Lincoln. But here there were no black faces, only the white ones of the Southerners who had sent their sons and husbands and the men they might have married to fight against Mr. Lincoln's army. Southern ladies stood at the curbside, their white skin shielded from the April sun by parasols grown tattered from lack of sewing silk. Southern gentlemen, either very old or very young, stood beside them, staring in silence more ominous than the fiercest rebel yell. I searched their number for an unhostile face and saw a boy near to Taddie's age raise a burnt and blacked broom handle, aiming it at us like a rifle.

There was no sound save the creaking of our carriage wheels and the hoof-beats of the dozen cavalry soldiers who rode with us as protection. We received only one gesture of welcome, this from a young woman who stood upon the balcony of a hotel with a Union flag draped round her shoulders like a shawl. As our carriage passed beneath her, the young woman raised a white hand in a small and solemn wave. Raising his head, Mr. Lincoln returned the lady an equally small and solemn nod, and our carriage passed on.

We were driven first to the building which had housed the Confederate Congress. I had once seen an illustration of this building in Frank Leslie's magazine, a drawing of it white-columned and graceful upon a wide expanse of lawn. Now that lawn was turned to mud beneath the trampings of the hundreds of Southern refugees who had set up residence there. Every inch of the ground which surrounded the marble steps of the rebels' capitol was covered with tents fashioned from woolen coverlets and velvet draperies, and lean-tos constructed from burnt timber and stiff board. Pigs poked their snouts into piles of garbage that no one came to cart away, fires of wet wood sputtered and smoked, and ladies in dresses of dimity and lace, faded and four years out of date, walked about with sacks of cornmeal and dazed expressions.

"The rebels set fire to anything they thought we could use, even their own houses," said Colonel Ripley. "And then we burned the rest."

We descended the carriage, and the colonel and his men led us into the building. "The gentlemen of the Confederate Congress and their president took off in something of a hurry when they heard Grant's army was coming," explained Colonel Ripley. And indeed, the interior of the graceful building looked to have been the scene of some great riot. Desks had been emptied and thrown against the walls, chairs lay splintered in the stairwells, great piles of paper swirled around our ankles, blown by spring wind let in by shattered windows. Taddie stuffed his pockets with thousand-dollar Confederate bonds, unable to believe in their worthlessness. Lizzie found beneath her shoe a copy of the resolution which banned free colored people from entering the state of Virginia.

"This was Jeff Davis's office," said Colonel Ripley.

The office of the president of the Confederacy seemed the only room which did not appear to have been the scene of some violence. Its desk, large and leather-covered, much like that of my husband, sat upright, as did the regal-looking mahogany chair behind it.

"Is that the chair that belonged to Mr. Davis?" Lizzie asked the colonel.

He nodded, and she went over and sat upon its leather seat.

"How does it feel?" I asked her.

"Like only a chair," she replied. But I noticed she was a long time rising from it.

Colonel Ripley next took us to see the building which had been the President's House of Jefferson Davis and his family, a classical structure of gray stucco with many windows. The Davises had fled the city, leaving behind all of their possessions, including a Negro butler who had decided not to accept emancipation. This servant, still wearing his red footman's uniform, answered Colonel Ripley's knock and bowed us in with a stiffness I think came from both his sense of formality and his remarkable elderliness.

Although some senior Union officers had been using the Davis house, nothing had been disturbed. The furniture was upright and highly polished, the windows unbroken and covered by lace, and every one of Varina Davis's china plates sat undisturbed in her glass-fronted cabinets.

"It's all so lovely," breathed Miss Harlan.

The Negro butler tugged upon the hem of his scarlet vest. "Mrs. Davis tole me to have the house nice for the Yankees when they come."

In the foyer, we came upon two Southern ladies, both dressed in black and seated at either side of a rosewood table as if guarding it.

"Good afternoon, ma'am," said Secretary Harlan to each.

Neither lady acknowledged his greeting.

"These ladies lost all their menfolk fightin' in the Confederate army," said the Negro butler in the loud whisper of those whose hearing has lessened.

Colonel Ripley led us past the ladies, who did not raise their eyes to any of our party. However, when I looked back, I saw that they were staring at my husband as if he were Satan himself.

We were taken through all the rooms which the Confederate president and his family had used, and which were lovely, for Varina Davis was a lady of taste. But each time I turned from examining an eyelet-edged coverlet in the bedroom or a leather-bound book in the library, I discovered one of the ladies from the foyer standing close behind me, as if she believed Mr. Lincoln or I might wish to steal Mr. Davis's riding boots or his wife's sewing basket. As we made our tour, these black-clad ladies followed us from room to room, and I began to feel as if we were being following by death.

It was a relief when we were taken out behind the house to view the slave quarters, for the Southern ladies did not follow us there.

"We ought to hang Davis when we catch him," declared Senator Sumner. He stood in the small wood-planked rooms which the slaves had shared, surveying them with tremendous indignation, although in truth, they were clean and in repair, and no worse than those my father had kept.

"I would like very much to avoid hanging anybody," said Mr. Lincoln.

"Mr. Davis was against you," I reminded him.

"If I was to hang everybody who was against me," he replied, "I'd run out of rope."

Once our tour of the Davis house was concluded, Colonel Ripley escorted us to the south portion of the city, where the shops and storehouses and businesses had stood, before the rebels had burned them to prevent the Union from profiting from what had been inside. Our open carriage took us past smoldering chimneys and the burnt shells of warehouses and stores and houses. Blackened iron, twisted into unnatural shapes by the heat of the fire, lay in the street like mangled corpses, and the empty cavities of heat-exploded windows stared down at us with dark malevolence. In these streets the perfume of jasmine was buried beneath the greasy stench of charred wood, and the breeze was spiked with cinders. We saw few people here, only the odd disconnected soul rifling among singed remains with charcoaled hands.

"It is like traveling through a district of Hell!" exclaimed Secretary Harlan.

"The rebels possessed a powerful belief in their cause," Colonel Ripley informed him. "It has made them revengeful."

Our carriages turned northward, where the burning had been less. Here, between the scorched frames of stores and stables stood the odd house untouched by fire, like a soldier left inexplicably standing after the men on either side of him are struck down. My eye went to these houses still upright, to see what the city had been, and in the unshattered window of one, I saw a man in Confederate gray shouldering a rifle to take aim at my husband.

My skin felt as if it had been set to boiling, although it also seemed freezing. I squinted to see if I had truly seen a Confederate soldier preparing to shoot my husband, but the carriage traveled out of the shade and into the harsh light of a blinding sun. "There!" I cried. But before the word was finished, we were plunged back into shade, and I saw that there was no soldier.

Mr. Lincoln glanced across the carriage at me, worried-looking. I shook my head, as if I had only meant to show him something but had changed my mind.

I hid my shaking hands beneath the linen folds of my spring cloak. I had bought this cloak only the week before, one of the purchases intended to keep my family safe, and now I wished that my husband had been seated nearer to me, near enough so that I might cover him with it, like a cloak in a magical story.

One week after our return from Richmond, on the ninth of April, 1865, General Robert E. Lee surrendered to General Grant at Appomatox. The War Between the States, which had lasted almost exactly four years, was finished.

The following dawn, all of Washington City was wakened by the firing of five hundred guns. Church bells and schoolhouse bells rang without stopping. Drums were beat upon, tin trumpets blown until breath expired and the instrument had to be handed off to some-body else. Cannons were dragged into the streets and fired until the ground shook. And everyone in Washington City who possessed a firearm – nearly every citizen over the age of fourteen – came outside to fire it.

The President's House was filled with the bright cacophony of band music, for every marching band in the city came to the lawn outside our windows in order to serenade the victorious president. "The Star-Spangled Banner" was followed by the "Battle Hymn of the Republic," which was followed by "Yankee Doodle," and then all was begun again. Soon, the marching bands were joined by ladies, their skirts trimmed with red-white-and-blue bunting, singing hymns and marches and every song that could be deemed patriotic.

By nightfall there were bonfires and fireworks at every corner, and every house in Washington City, save for those which had belonged to Southerners, was lit up with gaslight and lantern and candle. Hanging from the pediment of the Capitol building, visible from any place in the city, was an enormous gaslit transparency which projected the legend "This is the Lord's doing, and it is marvelous in our eyes." Just after nine, a crowd gathered outside the President's

House, and Mr. Lincoln addressed them from the window with Taddie balancing a lantern over his pages.

Although I rejoiced with the rest of the city over the war's ending, I could not rid myself of the uneasiness which had settled over me since Richmond. The celebrating crowd in the night's blackness appeared to me like the billowing of some black ocean. And when I looked to my husband, I saw only how he was lit up by the lantern for even the most malevolent in that dark mass.

At midnight, after all but the most inebriated celebrants had gone home, I came to my husband's bed and made him take me. For once it was not passion which drove me, but that uneasiness. I required some proof that my husband lived, and this was the most alive thing I could think to do with him. Afterward, we slept. But not long after dawn, I woke to discover him leaned up against the bedstead, reading the Bible.

"If you are searching through Scripture because you feel some shame over what we have done," I said to him, "I assure you we have not committed any act even remotely forbidden in those pages."

"Strange how much there is in the Bible about dreams," he replied. "Sixteen chapters in the Old Testament, five in the New."

I pushed myself to sitting. "Have you had a dream?"

He nodded.

"One which sent you to the Bible?"

"I did not wish to sleep anymore."

In the weak light of dawn, Mr. Lincoln appeared indistinct, his edges blurred as if he were in the act of vanishing. I moved nearer to him so that I could feel the solid weight of his leg along mine. "Tell it to me," I said.

"I'm afraid it will frighten you."

"You have already frightened me." I reached for my nightdress, tossed at the end of the bed, and pulled it over my head.

"I was sleeping," he told me, "and was waked by the sound of crying. Leaving my bed, I went downstairs, where I heard that same pitiful sobbing, but I could find no mourners. At last, coming to the East Room, I saw an elaborate catafalque upon which rested a corpse wrapped in funeral vestments, its face covered. Around the catafalque stood soldiers and a throng of people, all gazing mournfully upon the wrapped corpse.

"'Who lies there?' I asked one of the soldiers. 'Who is dead in the President's House?'"

"'It is the president,' he told me. 'Killed by assassin.'"

Dread squeezed upon my heart until my blood barely beat, and I gripped my husband's arm hard enough to feel the solid bone beneath my fingers. "Do you believe the dream is prophetic?" I said to him.

He studied my face, as if determining his answer from what he found upon it. "Even in prophecy," he reminded me, "dreams don't always mean what they seem. A dream of assassination may mean only that I am laying to rest a wartime president for one of peace. Recollect that in the dream, a version of myself still wanders the house."

"Perhaps that is only your spirit which wanders."

He smiled. "That would be your dream. Remember that I am not a believer in Spiritualism."

"You must be more cautious," I told him. "Do not return to Richmond. And read no more speeches from lighted windows."

He rested his fingers upon my face, then glanced back at the Bible he had kept upon his lap. "God knows what is best," he said. But he spoke the words so quietly, I knew they were not intended for myself.

Four days later, on the afternoon of Good Friday, Mr. Lincoln invited me to take a carriage ride. The day was dark-clouded and cold, but I did not think to cancel the ride – even after the closed carriage was discovered to have an unsteady wheel and we were obliged to ride out in the open air; for it had been too long since my husband had ridden with me.

We rode in weather more winter than spring, weather which caused the budding cherry trees and lilac bushes to appear irrationally hopeful against the slate sky. I kept a beaver blanket over my lap and my hand in my husband's pocket.

"When this second term is over," Mr. Lincoln told me, "we should go to Europe with Taddie. And with Robert, if he'll come. After that I'd like to go to California. See the Sierras and the common men made rich by gold."

"You are uncommonly cheerful today," I said to him.

He brushed away a strand of hair which the wind had blown across my mouth. "I think from now on we must both be more cheerful," he told me. "Between the war and the loss of Willie, we have been very miserable."

At the mention of Willie my eyes filled with tears. I blinked, and they blew away in the spring wind.

My husband looked hard into my face. I waited for him to say something, but instead of giving me words, he gathered my face in his hands and pulled me into a kiss. He pressed his lips upon mine so powerfully, I had not the space to draw breath, yet I breathed nonetheless, finding my oxygen in his mouth. Our tongues twined, and I felt faint with the air he had already breathed, the wet that I found there. This was not the kiss of a consoling husband. It was the immoral seduction of an unprincipled lover. Every cord of my desire was pulled toward him, and I knew that I would consent to perform any indecency beneath the beaver blanket, no matter that we were within full view of the driver and all of Pennsylvania Avenue. And still my husband kept his mouth upon mine, until I began to sink into the carriage seat, unable to remain upright. Then he released me, and the cold air rushed across my fevered face, leaving me open-mouthed and panting.

"Perhaps if I continue to kiss you in that manner," said my husband, "you will give up your unhappiness."

"If you continue to kiss me in that manner," I told him, "I will give up anything so that you do not stop."

He laughed. "I should like to test you upon that," he said. "Tonight, when we have returned from Ford's Theater. I'll come to you and we'll see how much we are each ready to give up."

"You are not afraid to make me such a promise?"

My husband traced the upcurving of my mouth with fingers made cold by Calvary's weather. "I am tired of being afraid," he told me.

(August 7) Mrs. Bradwell went down in town this morning about 10 oclock – At 1 oclock pm (the Doctor being in Chicago) Mrs. B. came back attended by "Mr. Wilkie of Chicago" – Mrs. Lincoln came down to meet them. After being introduced to Mr. Wilkie she invited him up to her rooms and the 3 staid there in conference for 2 hours.
—Patient Progress Reports for Bellevue Place Sanitarium

This morning, Myra Bradwell, who is now always granted permission to visit, informed me that she would be bringing a Mr. Wilkie to call. The two of us were in the lunatics' parlor. I sat upon a chair, while Myra stood fluffing the bustling at the back of her skirt with the satisfaction of an ornamental bird, an impression rendered more apparent as the lady lawyer was the only ornamental object in the room.

"And why would you dress yourself in a promenade suit of such complicated bustling and go to town to bring this Mr. Wilkie to me?" I said to her.

"The suit is from a French pattern," Myra replied. "And Mr. Wilkie is from the *Chicago Times*. And the reason I must go into town and bring him is that the gentleman reporter is of the opinion that ravening madwomen roam unencumbered through the streets of Batavia and I believe he is a little afraid of them."

"Doctor Patterson will never allow me to receive a newspaperman," I said.

"You are not receiving a newspaperman," she replied. "You are receiving only Mr. Wilkie of Chicago." Myra paced about the parlor. "Moreover, it is Saturday," she continued. "And as is the case every Saturday, Doctor Patterson is himself away in Chicago."

"Deceit is a symptom of insanity," I told Myra, mimicking the doctor's words.

"That is what men always tell women," she informed me. "Save when it is them practicing the deception."

"Still, I do not see why this Mr. Wilkie of Chicago would leave that city to visit me."

"Because I have invited him. And because once he has interviewed you, he will declare to the very many readers of the *Chicago Times* – and any other newspaper which wishes to take up the story – that you have been unjustly and cruelly confined." Myra came to rest near the maple sideboard upon which one of the mad ladies had carved the word "redemption" a hundred times.

"My son will not like it," I told her.

"No, I expect he will not," said Myra, stepping away from the sideboard. "However, if you will do only what Robert likes, you may as well resign yourself to living forever with ladies such as the wild-haired one I observed conversing with a garden bench."

It was impossible to dispute Myra Bradwell's logic – indeed, it was a great pity the court had not allowed the lady lawyer to practice her profession. Still, I could not rid myself of the image of Robert reading in his morning paper that he had been cruel and unjust, and simply picturing it called up the stinging of my son's anger, a sensation like lye spilled upon unprotected skin. *I should argue this*, I told myself. *Tell Myra that I will not see Mr. Wilkie. That we must devise a plan which will not embarrass Robert.* But Myra had already repinned her bonnet – a straw edifice supporting twenty chiffon rosebuds – in preparation for leaving. And so I said nothing, feeling, as I generally did with Myra, that I was being swept along by her well-ornamented train.

"Remember that Mr. Wilkie is fearful of female lunatics," she told me. "And remember we want the gentleman to write that you are undeservedly confined. So be certain to behave like a sane person when you are about him."

I remained in the lunatics' parlor after Myra had gone, pacing the same course she had taken, as if I might acquire some of her surety by it. I did not want to think upon my son's reaction to a story saying I was sane, so I worried instead how I might persuade a newspaperman who was fearful of female lunatics that I was not one. Afraid that I had been at Bellevue Place long enough to have grown fuzzy upon the conduct of the underanged, I thought hard upon how I might emulate Myra's behavior – with somewhat less preening, as I did not possess the wardrobe for it – and attempted to forget all the actions of ladies such as Mrs. Munger. Finally, for luck, I stood at the sideboard and ran my fingers over the word which was carved into its surface one hundred times.

Myra and Mr. Wilkie arrived from the train station shortly after noon. I showed them into the lunatics' parlor, being careful not to describe it as such. Mr. Wilkie was a large man, big in the chest and with thick arms which strained his sleeves. His features, too, were large, and possessed a hardness which did not look as if it ever eased. His mouth in particular appeared unchangeable, fixed as it was into the shape of a line. From behind Myra's elaborate skirts, the newspaperman gazed curiously about the room, noticing the empty picture railing and the curio cabinet from which everything breakable had been removed.

"I believe I know you," I said to Mr. Wilkie.

"You have uncommon powers of memory, Mrs. Lincoln," he replied. "We did indeed meet once in Washington City. When I was wartime correspondent for the *New York Times*."

"As I recall, you accompanied a regiment into the field during the fighting."

"The First Regiment of Iowa Volunteers."

"I expect it was very harrowing."

"One might say so. We encountered the rebels on numerous occasions." He uttered this remark with the false offhandedness gentlemen employ when discussing their own dangerous exploits.

I offered the newspaperman a seat upon the sofa whose arms had been picked at by Mrs. Bartholomew. Myra and I sat across from him upon a settee with a back cushion which had been slashed open – with a hat pin, perhaps? – then stitched shut. For upward of an hour, the newspaperman asked me questions and I answered them. Mr. Wilkie inquired about incidents which had happened in Washington during the war, requiring me to supply the names and particulars. He asked for details regarding certain streets in London which I had visited with Taddie five years earlier. He wanted to know whether I recalled various New York families with whom I had only the barest acquaintanceship. The questions came quick and without cease, and I understood that they were meant to test my memory, as if forgetfulness were the same as madness.

My interrogation was interrupted only by the sudden appearance of Mrs. Patterson. With no warning, the doctor's wife stood in the doorway of the lunatics' parlor, clutching a basket of thorned roses. "I was not told you had a visitor," she declared.

Myra and I both started at the sharp sound of Mrs. Patterson's voice, for we had believed her to be engaged in going over the madhouse accounts.

Myra recovered first. "This gentleman is Mr. Wilkie from Chicago," she said by way of introduction.

Gaining the impression that the ruddy-complexioned lady with the roses was not lunatic, Mr. Wilkie rose from the sofa and bowed in the direction of Mrs. Patterson.

"You are a friend of Mrs. Lincoln?" she asked him.

I spoke before the newspaperman might reply. "Mr. Wilkie is an old acquaintance from Washington City."

The corners of Mrs. Patterson's eyes pulled tight. "You have traveled all that way to visit Mrs. Lincoln?" she asked him.

"Mr. Wilkie is now living in Chicago," I explained in his place. But I knew that Mrs. Patterson's curiosity would not be satisfied with only this. She would ask Mr. Wilkie what he had done in Washington City, and what occupied him here. In a very short time, she would know Mr. Wilkie's profession and would have the newspaperman escorted from the asylum before he might decide upon my sanity.

Seeing that Mrs. Patterson was about to form another question, I leapt from my seat. "I was just about to invite Mr. Wilkie to my rooms," I exclaimed. "So he might see for himself how well-situated I am."

Upon an impulse, I took hold of Mr. Wilkie's thick arm, as if we were indeed very old friends. The newspaperman flinched at my touch. Nevertheless, I did not release him, but propelled him toward the door.

"Are you a friend of Robert Lincoln?" Mrs. Patterson asked him, blocking our way with her thorned roses.

"At the time Mr. Wilkie and I were acquainted," I explained, "my son was away at Harvard." I took another step, praying that propriety would compel Mrs. Patterson to step out of our path.

"So you have no line from Mrs. Lincoln's son?"

I felt Mr. Wilkie, who knew nothing about lines from my son, stir, making ready to give Mrs. Patterson some answer which would surely result in his being forced from the asylum. In a panic, I cast about for some polite utterance which would deflect the doctor's wife, but before I might uncover anything, I was rescued by the uncommon force of Myra Bradwell's personality.

With a majestic flouncing of her skirts, Myra rose to her feet. "Mr. Wilkie has only a little time before his train," she informed the doctor's wife. "So we must retire to Mrs. Lincoln's room at once, if he is to see it at all." Then delaying only long enough to again perform that regal fluffing of her bustle, she swept across the room toward the door.

Only the Illinois State Supreme Court and the spirits of the dead had been known to defy Myra Bradwell. And though Mrs. Patterson could demonstrate much boldness if there was gossip to be gained, the doctor's wife did not possess a brave character. Demonstrating the expression of a woman with a train barreling down upon her, Mrs. Patterson stepped out of the doorway to let Myra pass. Taking advantage of the opportunity, I hurried Mr. Wilkie out of the room. As we moved away down the corridor, Myra turned back. "I expect you will want to get those flowers into water," she said to Mrs. Patterson, in the event the doctor's wife was contemplating following us. "Although I would advise you to remove their thorns. You would not want to find yourself stuck."

Mr. Wilkie appeared to find my little room more disquieting than the lunatics' parlor. He entered it hunched and wary, in the posture of one who fears something will drop upon him from above, and could not remove his eyes from the bars over the window, gazing at them as if it was his own exit they blocked. I wished that I owned something for him to sit upon other than the off-kilter rocker, but it would have not been correct to offer him the mattress, and the reporter was too large for my desk chair.

"What else might I demonstrate for you, Mr. Wilkie?" I asked, seating myself upon the edge of the bed.

"I beg your pardon?"

"I have already shown you the fitness of my memory. Is there some other area of my mind upon which you would like to test me?"

Mr. Wilkie looked into the little notebook in which he had been writing during our interview. "I should like you to talk to me about your husband's assassination," he said.

To hear him speak of this with no warning filled me with more grief than my body could hold, and I rose from the bed and walked the room to rid myself of the excess of it. "I wish instead that you had asked me to name every political gentleman I had ever met in Washington City," I said to Mr. Wilkie. "I wish you had set me to describe every boulevard and alley I have walked upon in Europe."

"Allow me to be as candid as yourself," the newspaperman replied. "It is said that the assassination of your husband is the event which has left the most powerful impression upon your mind."

"Could anyone imagine it would not?" I said to him.

Mr. Wilkie ignored my remark. "It is also said that your insanity had its origin in the incident." Again he consulted his notebook. "If I am to judge you sane, I must observe how you speak of it."

The newspaperman's words recalled for me why he had come, what I had to gain – and lose – by his opinion. I forced myself to return to my seat upon the mattress. "There was a time," I told him, "not long after it happened, when I told the story of my husband's killing ceaselessly. As if I might change it into fiction, turn it into something which had never happened, made up for dramatic effect. But I have learned, Mr. Wilkie, that all such retelling does is to fix the details more securely in my mind. And to make me sad."

Mr. Wilkie looked up from his notebook. "I am very sorry to make you experience anything sorrowful," he said. "But I cannot write that you are sane unless I am sure of it."

"I recall that you were always a very scrupulous journalist," I told him.

"Why do you think I went to the war with the Iowa Regiment?" he replied. For a moment, it seemed that a smile attempted to reshape the straightness of Mr. Wilkie's mouth. The newspaperman returned his attention to the notebook. "Tell only as much of the story as you want, Mrs. Lincoln. Only as much as you believe will persuade me."

Myra rose from the little desk chair and came to me. "I shall sit beside you while you tell it," she said, "and hold your hand."

She took a place upon the mattress and the room grew quiet, save for the faint trilling sound of a lady singing hymns out on the lawn. I fixed my gaze upon Mr. Wilkie's face, as if its set features might prevent me from becoming lost in remembrance; for it was possible for me to tell this story in too much detail, to speak aloud too much of how that night appeared to me, how it felt to have my husband killed while he had hold of my hand. Once I believed I could keep myself in the room, I opened a portion of my memory I had shut tight and began to tell the newspaperman the story of my husband's murder.

I told the story without falter, describing the smell of Mr. Booth's breath and the shrieking in the theater, but when I tried to tell about the twitching of my husband's face, the muscles, which, free of his brain, moved of themselves, my own blood and bones and body began to spin out of control, and I felt as if I were falling too far into memory.

Mr. Wilkie, who had not removed his eyes from me, did not miss this. His mouth was more a line than ever, and I was certain he had just judged me lunatic. I gripped Myra's hand, told myself we were only at séance; for what was this but a form of calling the dead? Her fingers, covered in rings, made me know I was not in that strange boardinghouse waiting for my husband to die, that all that was causing my dress to stick to my flesh was the hot summer day and the effort of proving myself sane. Filling myself with air from this time, this place, I resumed my story, skipping past those details which would sound too much the impression of a madwoman, telling Mr. Wilkie only of the rain-soaked night, and how word had come that Mr. Lincoln breathed his last.

When I finished, Mr. Wilkie let the story sit upon the air, undisturbed by sound or motion. The newspaperman's features had eased in a way I had not thought possible, rendered changeable by the softening of pity. Though I did not know if the pity was for what had happened to me then, or now.

"Does this satisfy you, Mr. Wilkie?" I said, when I could talk of other things. "Can you write now that I am sane?"

The newspaperman rose from the rocker and came to sit at my other side. He took hold of my hand. "I can write it," he said.

Mr. Wilkie told us he was eager to return to Chicago to begin work upon his story, and Myra accompanied the newspaperman to the train station, riding with him back to the city. I remained in my overheated room, agitated by a grief with which I had believed myself finished, and worried over my son's response to a newspaper story which would call him wrong for placing me here. Twice I went to my desk to write to Myra, instruct her to go to Mr. Wilkie and beg him not to print the story. But I could not finish writing the second word of her name without hearing her ask if I wished to live forever with ladies who addressed themselves to objects, and each time the answer made me tear the letter in two.

I did not leave my room all that stifling afternoon, for I had been made so uneasy by the story I told Mr. Wilkie, I could not say what I might do if confronted by any mad lady's shrieking. Even the knock upon my door before the attendant entered with the late mail made my heart hammer, for it seemed too much like the report of a gun.

"One for you!" declared the attendant, a plump farm girl who behaved toward us lady lunatics as if we were a form of livestock. The young attendant tossed my letter upon the desk like scattering feed for chickens, and left without farewell.

The hand which had penned my name and the address of the

madhouse belonged to Elizabeth. I rose from the bed and stood before the desk, my fingers resting upon the wood no more than an inch from the heavy linen my sister favored, afraid to open her letter and learn what was inside. Before taking it up, I touched the face of each of the four angels carved at the joinings of the desk's legs, angels I had come to think of as my four sons, trusting that the three who had already taken that form might prevail over the one still with me.

Elizabeth possessed a ponderous writing style, full of commas and extra phrases meant to pad the meaning of her sentences, as if too much clarity might be ill-mannered. "As to the request, you make, in your own letter, on the experiment of coming to me in Springfield," she wrote, "I have contemplated what events, might arise from the occurrence, and being certain, I have not misapprehended their nature, make formal declaration, that I am willing to receive you."

Never had I been so happy to receive a correspondence from my sister! Keeping the letter clutched in my hand – thinking I might not release it until I was let out of this place – I fell upon my desk. I had to write to Myra right away, had to get her to stop Mr. Wilkie from publishing. Elizabeth's letter made it unnecessary for the news-paperman to tell all of Chicago – all of the country – that Robert had been an unkind son.

I carried the note to Myra to Mrs. Patterson's office myself, telling the young attendant to make certain it was sent in that day's post. Afterward, I thought that I would go to Minnie and tell her my news. If she had not just been fed by the pump, if she was awake, I would show her Elizabeth's letter, for I had it with me in my pocket. I hurried down the corridor to the staircase, thinking upon my friend, wondering how I might turn my good news into hers, when I nearly collided with the hurrying figure of my own son.

"Robert!" I exclaimed. "This is not your day for visiting."

My son was red-faced, more than I could credit the heat of the day, and his left eye did not sit straight.

"Mrs. Patterson sent for me." Robert's tone made clear how distasteful he found having been summoned by the doctor's wife.

"I cannot imagine the reason she would so inconvenience you," I said, pretending innocence.

"You cannot?" My son's voice echoed off the limestone walls

of the corridor, giving me the sense he would continue to ask the question until I gave him a true answer.

"Let us go into the lunatics' parlor," I said. I did not ever spare Robert the full name of this room, wanting him always to know where he had shut me up. "It is accustomed to shouting." Giving him no opportunity to refuse, I hurried away down the hall.

Mercifully, the lunatics' parlor was unoccupied, although I sometimes imagined that one might live out the most private scenes of one's life before the bewildered eyes of the mad ladies who came here, and they would only consider it some entertainment produced by their own minds. I sat upon the sofa with the shredded arms. Robert entered the room in a great rush and did not sit, but stood above me.

"Mrs. Patterson sent me a note with the information that you were visited this morning by a Mr. Wilkie of Chicago." My son spoke as if he had been told of my committing some unpardonable offense.

"I made no secret of it."

"Mr. Wilkie does not have my permission to see you."

"Mr. Wilkie is an old acquaintance."

"Why is it that I do not know him?"

Robert stared at the empty picture rail and appeared to be trying to recall a context in which he might have heard Mr. Wilkie's name. I could not remember if my son took the *Times*, or if he was likely to make note of its writers' bylines, but I did not wish him to think too long upon my visitor's identity. I rose from the sofa, forcing Robert to back away from me. "Why is it that you must approve my visitors?" I said. "Apparently the reason I have seen none of my friends is that you do not allow them."

Robert took his gaze from me, cast it about the room as if searching its bare surfaces for something upon which to fix his attention. "I do not wish you to have contact with those who will disquiet your mind."

"I spend my day with lunatics," I reminded him. "It is unlikely I would find even the most excitable of my friends disquieting."

"Still," said my son, "in your present state I believe it advisable you be protected."

I recalled the letter in my pocket, Elizabeth's invitation issued upon heavy linen and embellished with commas. All I need do was show it to him and he would keep his promise. He would let me go to my sister, where I could be visited by any friend willing to make the journey to Springfield, and where I would have no need to entertain newspapermen who made me tell them stories which left me heart-sore.

"I have heard from Elizabeth," I said. "She has sent me an invitation."

Robert pulled his eyes narrow. "Let me see it."

I nearly kept the folded paper in my pocket, imagining Elizabeth's invitation being removed from me, its existence called the hallucination of a madwoman. But holding the letter in my pocket would not see me released.

Robert snatched the invitation from my hand and carried it away to read. He stood before the empty curio cabinet with his back to me, taking a long time over the words.

"You will keep to your promise." I said this firmly, allowing no question to come into it. "You will release me to live with Elizabeth."

Robert stood smoothing his fingers over the cabinet's bare shelves. When he spoke, it seemed more that he was speaking to himself, or to the cabinet. "I very much hope that my aunt does not change her mind."

"What would cause her to do that?"

"Aunt Lizzie's health is uncertain."

"Elizabeth's health has never been uncertain," I told him. "Not for one day of her life."

"But she is past sixty now. And upon reflection she may decide that caring for you is beyond her strength."

"I am not an invalid," I told him.

He turned toward me. "Your mind is fragile."

I saw him slip Elizabeth's letter into the pocket of his waistcoat.

"I should have the invitation back."

"It is very safe where it is." Robert pressed his hand upon the pocket where he had hidden my letter.

"It is addressed to me."

My son sighed and crossed the room to the window. "You recall my stipulation that Doctor Patterson approve any guardian willing to take you?"

"I do."

"Then is it not logical that I keep the letter to show him the invitation exists?"

He made a motion toward the door and it seemed that he

intended to leave, to go out of here and take Elizabeth's invitation with him.

"Myra Bradwell knows I have received the invitation!" I blurted.

The name of the lady lawyer caused my son to bite upon his mustache.

"I have shown it to her." It was a lie, but telling it made me feel safer.

Robert regarded me as though judging the truth of my statement. Letting my gaze rest upon his pitiless eyes, I was overtaken by a hatred so pleasurable I had to remind myself that this was my son.

"Do you not wish to see me leave Bellevue Place?" I asked.

Robert moved back before the empty cabinet. "I only do not wish to see you disappointed."

"I will not be disappointed to leave here."

"I only mean that suppose Aunt Lizzie decides after you have gone to her that her constitution is not robust enough to be your guardian? We might not then be able to place you into any facility as agreeable as Bellevue Place."

I would not hear the threat in this. "You are worried over nothing," I said to him. "Elizabeth is my family. She will not wish to be rid of me."

"Unless she has underestimated the challenge."

"Do you believe me so very difficult?"

Robert rubbed his defective eye. "I believe I should write to Aunt Lizzie myself. Confirm the invitation."

I felt the fluttering start of panic. "But you have seen her letter."

"We must be certain my aunt knows *all* she is committing to."

The emphasis he had placed upon "all" reminded me that I was as trapped within my son's authority as I was within these walls. I had been judged insane by a jury, and unless I could be sent to a place where I would be beneath someone's guardianship, even Mr. Wilkie's story would not free me.

"You will not make me seem too difficult?" I worked to remove all the anger from my voice, everything which might make it seem I possessed a will beyond Robert's own. "You will not give Elizabeth the impression that I am too disorderly to live with any but lunatics?"

"I shall only tell her the truth," he replied. "As it appears to me."

I examined Robert's face, trying to learn the emotion which pulled at his eye, but I had never been able to see into my son's heart, and only had to guess at what he kept there.

The story which Mr. Wilkie made me tell earlier this day has stayed with me, putting before my eyes images from that terrible night and filling my ears with shrieking and the sound of gunshot. I think that only saying the words of what occurred has moved it from my memory, and to send it back, I need to turn it into history. Like all the other history I have set down in these pages.

That Good Friday night at Ford's Theater, I would not release my husband's hand. I held it tucked into the folds of my skirt – no longer the black of mourning, but a gray much like my husband's eyes – and through three acts of the play was not called to set it free, for Mr. Lincoln never clapped for any performance, so self-conscious was he of his overlarge hands. The production was a comedy, light enough to be ignored, although even had it been Shakespeare and tragedy I do not believe it would have commanded me, for I could think of little save that unhusbandlike kiss in the carriage and Mr. Lincoln's promise to come to me and demonstrate all that he was willing to relinquish. Despite the chill of the theater – we watched the play in our coats – I felt my blood running very near the surface of my skin.

We were seated in the presidential box, which was raised and set at the side of the stage, so the audience could see us as easily as the performance. My husband was sitting in the red velvet rocker which was kept there for him. I sat upon a small chair I had placed so near, his legs were tangled in my skirts. Our company that night was Clara Harris, the practical-minded daughter of a senator from New York, and her fiancé, Major Henry Rathbone, who had seen the killing at Petersburg and come back melancholic. Miss Harris was primly pretty and Major Rathbone dashing, and the contrast of their types made them a pleasure to be among, despite the major's darkened outlook. Mr. Lincoln had wished Robert to join us as well, for my son was just returned from City Point. Robert, however, had declined him, claiming tiredness.

It was the smell of whiskey upon the breath of the uncommonly handsome man who entered our box which I noticed first. Whiskey and something stale, like the sheets of a sickbed. The smell first, and then the sight of him. Black-haired, with a profile he held slightly raised, as if knowing too well its fineness demanded to be traced. When I glanced down, I saw that something glinted in each of the man's hands, and when he raised an arm, directing one of those shiny objects at the back of my husband's head, at the hair he had forgotten to comb, I thought, *perhaps it is some portent of fortune, a blessing. Or perhaps he is only going to smooth the hair.* And at the same time, I heard a hard banging noise and felt my husband's hand twitch.

Then I could not see, for the air was filled with a blue-colored smoke; and I did not smell the whiskey or the sickbed any longer, but instead breathed in something very much like gunpowder. The smell frightened me, and I held tighter to the hand which had almost twitched away from me; and when the air grew more clear, I saw that the shining object in the handsome man's raised hand was a pistol, and that it was held too near my husband's head to have missed.

I heard then a cry, and the explosive breaths men release when they struggle against each other. Major Rathbone had thrown himself upon the handsome man; and in the fighting, the pistol, small enough to belong to a lady, dropped onto my skirts, singeing the silk. But the second object in the man's hands, longer and more shining than the first, struck at the major's arm, and I heard the tearing of fabric and the rainlike sound of blood falling upon my dress.

Something terrible has happened to my husband. But Mr. Lincoln's hand was still warm, and he sat quiet in his rocker with his chin sunk to his chest as if he were sleeping.

Then a hand clutched the railing beside me, so close I could see how very clean the fingernails were kept. I smelled whiskey again, and that odor of sickbed, and a handsome – but pale, very pale – face hung for a moment before my eyes. It was the face of a madman, burning and beautiful, with flecks of blood trapped in the waxed ends of its mustache.

Who is this handsome man with the glinting, dangerous objects? I wondered. *Do I know him?* The mouth beneath that blood-flecked mustache opened and I thought he would answer me, but what the handsome man shouted was "Sic semper tyrannis!" *Thus always to tyrants.* And the words were not directed toward me. Nor to my husband. The exclamation was meant for the upturned faces of the audience. And after it had been uttered, the handsome man leapt upon the railing and, as if intending to jump into their embrace, flung himself into the air.

I thought I saw him fly, for he did not immediately fall. But then I understood that he was held by Major Rathbone's grip upon the hem of his frock coat. For a moment the handsome man hung above the audience, that second object – a long-bladed knife – sparking in the gaslight. Then there was more sound of tearing, and the man's coat ripped at the seam and he tumbled over the railing, knocking crooked a portrait of the first president which hung outside our box. When he fell upon the stage, there came the loud snapping of bone.

The theater was filled with the hissing of the gas lamps and the rasped breathing of the assassin, who lay upon the stage, his left foot angled oddly beneath him, and the two sounded very much the same. The handsome man still clutched the knife in his hand, and he stabbed it into the floorboards of the stage, then used the handle to raise himself to his one working foot. "The South is avenged!" he cried out, as if this were no more than a performance, and he were no more than an actor. He waved the long-handled blade over his head, spattering the front rows with Major Rathbone's blood. Waiting for no applause, he hobbled from the stage.

"The president is shot!" screamed a lady. And I think it must have been Miss Harris, for she stood in a dress covered in blood and her mouth was moving. I stood then, too, and the rising made me let go my husband's hand, shattering the spell I had fallen beneath when I first smelled the handsome man's breath of whiskey and sickbed. I was like one wakened by chill water, overcome by urgency; for at last I understood that the handsome man had fired his gun into Mr. Lincoln's head, and that if we could not get help, my husband would die.

I flung myself against the door to our box, but it would not open. Major Rathbone, his arm bleeding, came too and pulled upon the handle. But the man who wished to be Mr. Lincoln's assassin must have found some way to barricade it once he had come in.

The major whirled and shouted into the crowd. "We are trapped in the box," he cried out. "And we must have a doctor!"

Everything fell to pandemonium. I believe I heard more bones breaking, but it might have been chairs splintering, for the people in the theater, trapped themselves in the aisles by each other, pulled up seats and hurled them against the walls. The building shook with a pounding which was the vibration caused by running feet. And there was screaming, panicked and sometimes muffled horribly, the effect of the screamer being pressed to the floor beneath the weight of fleeing bodies.

I think that I was screaming too. Screaming and throwing myself against the barricaded door. A door which was no longer still, but beat back, like the uproar's terrible heart. Hands took hold of me – Major Rathbone's, I think, for they were covered in blood. I struggled against them, but they would not relent, pulling me away from the door just as an ax broke through the wood.

"I am Doctor Leale!" shouted the first man to enter. He was young, not much older than Robert.

"You have to save Mr. Lincoln," I said to him, imagining he might not be old enough to understand his task.

The doctor nodded, then turned toward the major. "The president will be better lying down."

He clasped his hands across my husband's chest, and with the help of Major Rathbone, lifted him from the rocker and stretched him upon the red carpeting of the box. "His breathing is very shallow." Doctor Leale opened my husband's mouth and felt inside for his tongue. "Perhaps his lungs can be coaxed." The young doctor pressed his parted lips to those of my husband and breathed into him. When his breath ran out, he placed his fingers over Mr. Lincoln's heart and tried to rub it into stronger life.

I watched these intimacies; and the little effect they had upon my husband made me wish that it was I who lay over Mr. Lincoln, who touched his tongue and his heart. *I am the one who will save him,* I thought. *The way I have already saved him from the hypochondriasis, and the madness of his own passion, and the sickness which smells sweet and poisons the blood.* Seeing for himself the small effect of his efforts, Doctor Leale sat back onto his heels. The instant he was away, I fell to the floor beside my husband and put my mouth upon his, finding his lips still warm from those of the doctor.

I remained there, attempting to breathe for my husband, until Miss Harris pulled me away from my husband's mouth.

"We are going to move the president to a boardinghouse nearby," she told me.

"Should we not take him to a hospital?" I asked.

Miss Harris exchanged a glance with her fiancé.

"Doctor Leale believes he can treat him there just as well," said Major Rathbone.

It required four men to carry Mr. Lincoln from the theater, plus Doctor Leale, who walked behind, supporting my husband's head so it would not loll. It had been five days since Lee surrendered to Grant at Appomattox, and Washington City was still celebrating. Bonfires burned at every corner, and fireworks exploded from the rooftops. The street outside Ford's was thick with smoke, and with people, the crowd from the theater being added to those already in the street. Ladies in silks were forced against staggering drunks wearing Union flags draped about their necks. I held fast to Miss Harris's arm as we passed through them, and in the darkness, their faces – some weeping, others frantic with the ending of the war – appeared from the vapor with the suddenness of demons.

"Is that Lincoln they're carrying?" asked a stumbling man, who wore the ill-fitting jacket of a Union uniform. He held his torch above my husband's face, so near I feared he would burn him.

"Look! The widow's covered in his blood!" said another man, pointing his torch at Miss Harris, whose dress was nearly black from her fiancé's bleeding.

"Why do they stand in our way?" I said to Miss Harris. "Do they not see we are trying to save Mr. Lincoln?"

She did not answer, only held tighter to my arm.

They carried my husband up the stone steps of a narrow boardinghouse which stood across from Ford's Theater. Inside, a man in nightshirt and half-buttoned trousers pointed down a tight hallway to a little bedroom at the back. "Take him there," he said. "The tenant is away."

The bed was too small for my husband, and to prevent his feet from dangling off the end, the men who had carried him laid him across it at an angle. It was a poor room, turned crowded by a little spool bed and a pine dresser, and the unconscious body of my husband. I could not be made to leave him, could not be persuaded to let go his hand. During his fits of melancholy, my touch had kept my husband's mind tethered to his body. Now I believed it would do the same for his soul.

Doctor Leale stood at the head of the bed and ran his fingers through Mr. Lincoln's hair. "I must examine the wound better," said the doctor. "It might be best if you look away."

But I would not look away. *A soul might require more magic to stay than the holding of a hand. A soul might need to be watched.*

"The wound is clotted," said Doctor Leale. He pushed his smallest finger into the hole the bullet had made in the back of my husband's head and dug deep in that dark space. When he removed his finger, a black mass of what looked to be blood and bone fell upon the pillow. The sight of it was horrifying, and yet hopeful, for it seemed a kind of treating.

"Is that the bullet?" I asked. "Will he wake now?"

"The pressure on his brain will be less," Doctor Leale replied.

So he will wake, I said to myself, finishing the young doctor's statement as I wanted it finished. *Of course he will wake. He has survived the shooting. Look, he still breathes. Even if that breathing has the uneven and congested quality of a dove's cooing.*

The little bedroom became filled with gentlemen. Gentlemen who said they were doctors, who said they wished to examine Mr. Lincoln and that I should leave.

"I must stay with him," I told them. "Or his soul might fly away." And I would not release my husband's hand.

"They cannot save Mr. Lincoln unless you allow them to examine him," Miss Harris told me. The young lady had not been in the room earlier, and I wondered if the gentlemen had summoned her to persuade me.

"Do you think they will save him?" I said.

"If anyone can," she replied. "Short of God."

"You must call me back," I said to the gentlemen who were doctors, "the instant you are through."

I let Miss Harris take me to the boardinghouse sitting room and lead me to a tattered sofa. I noticed again the blood upon Miss Harris's dress, the blood upon mine.

"Where is Major Rathbone?" I asked her.

"He has gone to have his wound attended to."

I was consumed by a terrific urgency to offer Miss Harris some advice about marriage. I asked her whether she believed Major Rathbone was kind, and without waiting for her response, said that it was best to have a husband who was kind. It's possible that I offered this advice more than once, for Miss Harris's answer acquired the rhythmic quality of something much repeated.

When I was allowed back into the little bedroom, I noticed that it smelled sharply of mustard plaster, and for a moment was certain I would find Eddie lying upon the spool bed. Then I saw the broadcloth suit I had chosen for my husband to wear to the theater folded upon a chair. Someone had covered Mr. Lincoln with a woolen counterpane woven with harlequin diamonds. Beneath it, at my husband's hands and feet, I saw the rounded shapes of hot water bottles.

"The president's extremities have gone cold," explained Doctor Leale, following my gaze.

His words made me pull one of Mr. Lincoln's hands from beneath the bedcovers and hold fast to it. For the young doctor had made it sound too much as if death had already begun to take my husband, beginning at his hands and feet.

Robert entered the room. If one did not know him, one would have thought him bewildered by something, for such was the impression when his left eye was so strongly canted. But I knew the canting for distress.

"Come to me," I said to him. I held out my other hand for him to take, and when after a moment he did, I pressed his fingers to my cheek. Robert's flesh smelled of cigars, and it made me think that he was now more a man than my son.

"We must work to improve the president's circulation," advised a gentleman I recognized as Doctor Stone, the doctor who had attended Willie's and Tad's typhoid. "Let us see if he will swallow some brandy."

A decanter of brandy was brought and Doctor Stone poured a small portion into Mr. Lincoln's mouth, holding it shut afterward with a firm hand upon his jaw. A thin stream of brandy leaked into my husband's beard.

"Mr. Lincoln does not like brandy," I said.

When I turned back to my husband, I saw that the left side of his face had commenced to spasm. I took this working of Mr. Lincoln's muscles as the effort to speak and brought my ear so near his mouth I could smell the brandy which had spilled out of it. "Say something to me," I begged him. "I think if you will talk, you will live." *Perhaps if I kiss him,* I thought. And I pressed my mouth to his cheek, feeling the spasming muscles beneath my lips.

My husband made no sound. "Send for Taddie," I told the doctors. "He will speak to Taddie."

"He did not speak to me," said Robert. There was an anger near to tears in my eldest son's voice, and I could only believe it was for what the handsome man had done.

"Taddie will call his father back," I repeated to the gentlemen around the bed.

"I will not have a twelve-year-old boy brought here," declared General Stanton, whom I had not noticed in the crowded room. "This is not a place for a child."

"Please," I begged him. "If Mr. Lincoln remembers it is Taddie he is leaving, I do not think he will go."

"This is no place for a child," repeated the general.

I glanced at my husband, imagining, I think, that he would intercede for me. But Mr. Lincoln's face had ceased convulsing, as if the general's refusal had caused him to halt his effort at speech. Worse still, the spasming of the muscles had wrenched the left side of my husband's mouth into a permanent and uneven grimace.

Over the next hours, I sat beside Mr. Lincoln and pleaded with him to wake, uttering any endearment or indecency I believed might rouse him, careless that I spoke these things before the doctors and the gentlemen of his cabinet who had begun to arrive during the night. Once, while I recalled for him the day each of our children had been born, I sensed some movement under the coverlet, and Mr. Lincoln's naked arms sprang out from beneath the bedclothes. No change came upon his face, his mouth still held its grimace, yet my husband's arms thrashed in the air above his chest, struggling with some unseen opponent.

"Save your strength for breathing," I said. Then I caught hold of his hands and pressed them to my face, wept into their cool palms, for the moving of my husband's arms had been so like when we were courting and his nerves had made him dangerous to china.

When they wished to make examinations, the doctors sent for Miss Harris to coax me away, and she would lead me back to the boardinghouse sitting room, where I believe I continued to give her the same advice about marriage. Just before dawn, a steady rain began to fall outside the sitting room windows; and the light, when it did come, was so gray that no one thought to extinguish the lamps. Shortly after six by the clock upon the slate mantle, Doctor Stone came to say that I might return to the back bedroom.

It had been near to an hour since I had seen my husband, and in that time the flesh around Mr. Lincoln's eyes, particularly the right, had swollen and discolored, the skin turning the purple of plums, so that it looked as if the doctors had been beating my husband upon the face while I was absent. The mustard plasters must have been removed from his flesh, for I no longer breathed their sharp smell. Indeed, the room now held a new smell which was familiar, yet so distant in memory, it was some minutes before I could place it as the coppery scent of blood, the scent of pennies meant for the eyes of the dead, the scent of my mother's room before she had been taken by childbed fever.

I took a step nearer the bed and understood that this scent rose from the linen napkin tucked beneath my husband's ear. Each time I had been allowed back into the room, this napkin was an untainted white, although by the time I was sent out again, it had become stained with blood. At first I imagined this was some type of healing magic, that my husband's wound was recalling its lost blood. Then I apprehended that the linen was replaced before I was called back, to spare me the sight of the blood-soaked pillow beneath it. Now, however, the whiteness of the napkin had not lasted longer than it had taken to retrieve me, for already across its center it bore a seeping line of rusted red.

This scent of funeral pennies, this bloody piece of linen beneath my husband's ear, made me know the thing which all who were in this room had known not long after the handsome man had fired his lady's pistol into Mr. Lincoln's brain. My husband was going to die. And the knowledge of this, which I had denied by believing I might hold a soul by touch, or bring to consciousness a head-shot man by the summoning of a twelve-year-old boy, came upon me full, robbing my lungs of air and knocking me to the floor.

When I regained myself, I felt cold rain upon my face and the burning of salts in my nose. Doctor Stone and Miss Harris, each with a grip upon my arms, held me before an opened window. And I must have hung there between them for some time, for the front of my dress was soaked through.

"Is Mr. Lincoln dead?" I asked, brushing away the doctor's spirits of ammonia.

Doctor Stone glanced back toward the bed, as if he could not answer without checking.

"He still lives," replied Miss Harris.

Pushing free of them, I returned to my husband. Someone had placed Mr. Lincoln's hands above the counterpane, unconcerned now with keeping them warm. I lifted one of those hands and was grieved by its slackness. "One final time," I murmured to his bruised face. Unfolding his fingers, I rested the middle one upon my mouth, and, lightly as breath, traced the upcurving of my lip. I saw myself in the future, unable to keep my fingers from my own mouth, obsessively tracing the curve of my lip until the skin chafed, until it grew ragged and raw.

"Take me with you," I pleaded with my husband, as if his proximity to death granted him the power to bestow it upon me. "Do not make me live with you gone." I threw myself upon him, pressed my mouth to the side of his which was straight, where it still seemed the same, and tried to force a kiss. But his lips were cold and his mouth had no taste. "Please," I begged, not taking my mouth from his. And I shut my eyes and waited for him to do this one last thing for me. But when I opened them again and knew that I still drew breath, that he would go and I would have to stay, I sent up a wail which over-filled the little room, pushed out everything that was not my grief.

"Take that woman out of here!" came a voice so loud it rose above my wailing. *It is God,* I imagined, *furious that I would ask to die.* "Take her out now!" the voice commanded. And I knew it this time for General Stanton's.

Hands yanked me from the mattress. "Please let me stay!" I cried out. But unlike the general, I could command no one's attention. I clung to my husband, and the tugging of the men upon me knocked a hot water bottle to the floor. Only when the noise it made caused me to look up did I remember that Robert was in the room. My eldest son stood at the head of the bed, and I think from the wet upon his face that he had been weeping. Although now that he was watching me, whatever tears he had been shedding had stopped in the turning of his expression to horror.

I must say something, I thought. *Let him know this is grief and not insanity.* But the gentlemen who had hold of me pushed me toward the door and I was given over to Miss Harris.

"You must let Doctor Stone give you some laudanum," she said, leading me back to the sitting room.

"No!" I told her. For these were the final hours during which my husband and I would both be alive in the world, and I did not want them dulled in any way.

I knew in my body the moment that my husband died. For as I sat beside Miss Harris, both of us corseted into blood-stiff dresses, I was overcome by a hard desire which nearly shook me from the tattered sofa.

"Are you unwell?" asked Miss Harris in alarm.

I could only nod, as the sensation was too like the pleasure I experienced at the hands of my husband to describe to any lady; and even had I dared, my words would have contained no sense, so near to indecent was the craving's effect upon me. I clasped my hand over my mouth to stifle a small cry, and upon my own skin, I caught the scent of woodsmoke, and knew for certain that it was my husband. I felt the weight of him press upon me, the hard angularity of his bones push against my flesh; and though I was buttoned and laced into layers of fabric and whalebone, I felt his overlarge hands move across every inch of my skin, until my desire was as large as my grief. And it was by all this that I knew Mr. Lincoln no longer breathed in the back bedroom. For the quality of his presence was so like that of Willie's when he had come to me at Mrs. Laurie's séance table, I recognized it for spirit.

No one came to tell me that my husband was dead. Not Doctor Stone, nor Doctor Leale. Not one of the other gentlemen in the room. Not Robert. And while I sat and waited for someone to remember me, I understood that there was one aspect of having my husband gone which I had not considered. That with him would go any regard I had been able to claim for myself, even that which obliged the general to act kindly toward me.

The day after Mr. Lincoln was assassinated, I woke from a laudanum-induced sleep to the hard crack of the assassin's pistol being fired over and again. The shots came quick, one after the other, making it seem that my husband was being killed a hundred times in the space of a minute. My heart, still slowed from the opium, tried to race, tried to send enough blood to propel me from my bed before Mr. Booth – I had by now learned his name – came to kill Taddie or myself. But Doctor Stone must have dosed me heavily, for my limbs felt weighted and would not obey me. Panicked by the sound of the shots, I worked to free my muscles from their drug-induced paralysis, but by the time I forced myself upright upon the mattress, the noise had ceased. *It must have been some remnant of my dreaming,* I thought. *Left over like the laudanum in my blood.* However, after a minute the firing came again, and I began to be afraid that the sound was something produced by my own unhinged mind.

"Mr. Booth has murdered my reason," I said to Lizzie Keckly when she came with a basin of chamomile water to bathe my eyes. I had sent for her just before Robert brought me back to the President's

House, begged her to meet me there and stay with me. "The sound of his pistol has become locked in my brain, and I fear I shall hear it for the remainder of my life."

Lizzie sat beside my bed, placed the basin upon the marble-topped night table. "What you hear is the sound of hammers in the East Room," she told me. "They are building Mr. Lincoln's catafalque. When they are finished, it will stop."

"Where have they brought him?" I asked her.

She inclined her head toward the door which connected his room to mine.

"So near," I said. And what I meant by this was that, in truth, he was not near at all.

Still, when Lizzie left to fetch the sherry we used to cover the bitterness of the laudanum, I went to that door and tried the handle, but it was locked from the other side. Standing before it, my eyes began to tear of their own accord, as if the door itself could provoke sorrow.

"Come away from there," said Lizzie. She put an arm about my waist to lead me back to bed.

"The door has made me cry," I told her.

"That is the hydrochloric acid," she replied. "The embalmers are using it to replace Mr. Lincoln's blood."

"Tell them to stop," I said to her. For it seemed to me that the embalmers were forcing my husband to endure a second death.

"General Stanton has ordered it. The president must be preserved for the train journey."

"From Washington City to Springfield?" I asked, for that is where my husband would be buried.

Lizzie pulled the bedcovers over me and unstoppered the bottle of laudanum. "The gentlemen of the cabinet have decided to send Mr. Lincoln's body back to Springfield by the same circular route he took to come here," she said. "But in reverse. It will be some two weeks before he can be buried."

I recalled that original journey, undertaken so the country might set eyes upon Mr. Lincoln's face. Now, not much more than four years later, the country would again be given opportunity to set eyes upon that face, although this time the face would be dead, preserved by hydrochloric acid. And I would not stand beside him. I reached for the opium-laced sherry in Lizzie's hand, drank it in one swallow as if to render its oblivion more potent.

It required two days for the workmen to build Mr. Lincoln's catafalque. I did not go down to see it myself, but heard from Lizzie that it had been made to a height of eleven feet, and had been termed the Temple of Death. To allow it to fit into the East Room, one of the chandeliers had to be removed. The others were shrouded in black bags, as if they, too, were obliged to wear mourning. Six hundred guests had been invited, and the enormous hall was lined with tiered seating.

On the day before the funeral, I roused myself and sent word to General Stanton, asking him to come to me in the oval-shaped library which had been my family's sitting room. It was the first time I had left my bedroom since entering it the morning after the assassination, the first time I laced myself into a corset after removing the one made even more stiff by Major Rathbone's blood. And as I stepped into one of the black gowns I had so recently discarded, I could not stop myself from thinking that from now on, I would always dress as a widow.

General Stanton sat at the very edge of a brocade chair near the fire, as if to illustrate that he did not intend to remain long in my company. Noting this, I made my request directly.

"I wish to have a lock of Mr. Lincoln's hair cut for me," I told him.

The general stroked the beard which fell to his sternum. This beard, which in his youth must have been entirely black, had partly turned with age, so it appeared something white had dripped from the corners of his mouth. "I cannot give permission for any of the president's hair to be taken," he said. "The Beloved Remains must look well for the viewings."

I did not like this name by which the nation now referred to Mr. Lincoln, for it sounded as if they had already discarded him. "This is my husband," I reminded the general.

"He was also the president of the country." General Stanton uncrossed his legs, readying himself to rise. "I'm sure you possess other keepsakes."

I felt the energy of my anger push against the stupor of the laudanum Doctor Stone made me drink three times a day. But although I wished to fight the general on this, to feel anything save grief and the slowness of the opium, I would not let the anger up, for I had another request to make of General Stanton.

"On the train to Springfield," I said to him, "I would like Willie's casket to be placed near his father's."

The general recrossed his legs impatiently. "I was not contemplating putting any other caskets on the train."

"But you will have a funeral car," I reminded him. "And Willie has been all this time in a borrowed grave in Washington City."

"Five hundred dignitaries and political gentlemen believe they deserve a place on that train, and I have room for only three hundred." The general rose from his seat. "Then there is the honor guard, the soldiers to carry the casket, and the embalming surgeons. I have no room for a dead child."

"It is only a small casket."

General Stanton shook his head.

This gesture, which he performed instead of answering in words, turned my blood less sluggish. I stood and placed myself between the general and the door. "I wish Willie to be with his father," I told him.

"How can it matter now?"

"They are the same family," I said. "They should not rest apart."

General Stanton regarded me, determining, I think, how much he would be required to agree to move me from the door. "I promise nothing," he told me. "But I will look into whether it is possible."

In the end, I sent Lizzie Keckly to the East Room with the same sewing scissors she had used upon my dress for Mr. Lincoln's inauguration and my mourning clothes for Willie. The lock of hair she brought me was only as big as my smallest finger, for she did not want the general to notice it. I braided the strands together and tied them with a black ribbon. This I kept in my pocket, and each time I touched it, the coarseness of my husband's hair put me in mind of my mother's bavolet.

As for Willie's casket, General Stanton did agree to put it on the train. But only after I had Robert make the request.

I did not attend Mr. Lincoln's funeral. Few ladies did – of the six hundred guests, only seven were female. I knew I would be incapable of limiting my mourning to any standard prescribed by *Sepulchers of Our Departed*, and I feared that if I was made to see my embalmed husband eleven feet high in a Temple of Death, I would lose my reason. I stayed alone in my room – sending Lizzie, who had possessed a strong affection for Mr. Lincoln, to watch the ceremony from the corridor. Still, I knew when my husband's body was taken from the President's House by the sound of drum and fife, and by the rumbling of carriages carrying away those who had attended. This rumbling shook my windows and made me believe that my husband's spirit was trying to come to me. I left my bed and threw open the sash, standing in the way of the wind, letting it blow upon me. But the air smelled only of wet earth and horses, and I could not feel my husband in it.

"Bring me a medium," I said to Lizzie the following day. "The most adept that you know."

A great line of Spiritualists came to my bedroom, drew the curtains against the light, and formed magnetic circles with Lizzie and me. They fell into trance, or were taken by spirit control; and while we held fast to their hands, they searched beyond the veil for Mr. Lincoln's spirit. But though some claimed to reach him, I did not feel it. And after they left, I lay weeping upon the bed with the lock of my husband's hair so tight against my lips, some of the strands worked their way into my mouth.

Taddie had been stunned into silence by the killing of his father. The child who had once burst into cabinet meetings to tell the president a story in imperfect speech, now spent most of his time sitting upon his father's bed, handling the objects left upon the table beside it – Mr. Lincoln's gold-rimmed spectacles, a jay's feather which had once blown into his office. I did not like to go into this room, but the first time I discovered Taddie there, after the train had left with my husband's body, and with Willie's, I made myself go to him.

"You are uncommonly quiet." I sat beside my youngest son upon the bed, although to do so made my body yearn after something which was filled with hydrochloric acid and hundreds of miles away.

"I'm thinking," he told me.

I watched the spectacles in his hand, their lenses glinting in the spring light like gaslight upon Mr. Booth's pistol.

"What are you thinking?" I asked him.

"I'm thinking that Pa is dead. And that I am not a president's son anymore." The words, uttered with an acceptance which made him seem to possess more than his years, sounded at odds with his soft, defective speech. "I am only Tad Lincoln now."

I lifted his chin and looked into the face of my only dark-eyed child. "Tad Lincoln is enough to be," I told him.

Robert's grief possessed a different character. After my eldest son returned from his father's interment in Springfield, I noticed that his face had acquired the dry, haunted look of the sleepless, and that when he believed no one watched him, he chewed furiously upon his mustache. Lizzie, whose dressmaking work put her in the way of all gossip, told me it was said that Robert went to Ford's Theater three or more times a week, always during the day when no play was on.

"What does he do there?"

"He stands in the box where Mr. Lincoln was shot, not speaking and never moving, except for the times he is seen to sit upon the sofa and then spring up toward the door. I am told he does this over and over, as if he is testing the quickness of his reflexes."

The following morning, waiting only until Taddie had been taken from the family dining room by the tutor to whom he paid no real attention, I raised with my eldest son the subject of this rescue which had never happened. "You could have stopped nothing," I told him. "It was very quick."

Across the gray-stained wood of the walnut table, Robert raised bloodshot eyes to me. "I might have seen the assassin come in," he replied. "I might have had time to shout some warning."

It occurred to me then that as the youngest member of our party that night, Robert would have been expected to seat himself near the door to the box, the door through which Mr. Booth had entered. But I could not let myself think upon how Mr. Lincoln's killing could have been prevented, and to keep myself from it, I felt in my pocket for the coarse twisting of hair.

"He wished me to be there," Robert continued. "He asked me that afternoon. I told him no."

"You were made tired by the journey back from City Point," I reminded him.

My son rubbed at the black mourning band sewn to the sleeve of his jacket, as though it was his arm which pained him. "I did not love him enough."

I rose from my seat and walked round the table, intending to tell him, *you did love him enough. You loved him almost as much as he deserved.* But by the time I came to stand beside Robert's chair, the words felt too far from true to be spoken aloud, and I could do no more than place my hand upon his to stop him rubbing at the mourning band.

"It was just beyond me," he said.

"Beyond you to love?" I did not believe it was beyond anyone to love.

"So much so, I have always been persuaded that my share of the talent was inherited by Willie, and by Tad."

I sat beside him. "An aptitude for affection is not divided up among the members of a family."

"Then, let us say it is my own deficiency."

I had not imagined that Robert ever considered his capacity for affection, that he might think its meagerness a deficiency, and the realization made me place fingers upon my son's face near the corner of his imperfect eye. "It is not impossible to acquire the ability," I told him.

Robert jerked his head away, leaving my fingers in the air. "Even if I possessed faith in such a claim, it is somewhat too late."

"You are young still," I said to him. "Your character is not fixed."

"I meant that it is too late to practice upon my father."

"It is not," I told him, "too late to practice it upon me."

Over the next weeks, I looked for some change in Robert, but my son grew only more ashen, and his mustache more sparse. I heard from Lizzie that he went even more frequently to Ford's Theater, and that while there, he was sometimes heard to be moaning.

By the beginning of May, I began to wish us out of Washington City. And I was not alone in this sentiment; for President Johnson wished us out as well. Since the day upon which Mr. Lincoln's body was taken out of the house, Andrew Johnson, the man who had been made president only by virtue of Mr. Booth's bullet, had been anxious for us to follow it. Weekly, he sent messages through Robert, inquiring when his own family might take up residence in our rooms, and offering his servants to assist with our packing.

I knew that it was right to give the new president the house; I only did not know where I should go when I left it. Nor what I would have to live upon when I arrived. For Mr. Lincoln had left no will, and the settling of his estate could not be accomplished immediately. I put off Mr. Johnson, but by mid-May, the new president had so prevailed upon my son that Robert was compelled to ask Judge Davis to come and speak with me.

I had not seen Judge Davis in some time, despite the fact that Mr. Lincoln had appointed the judge to the Supreme Court, and the gentleman who possessed no belief in the political value of wives now lived in Washington City. While my husband continued his friendship with Judge Davis, I was successful in avoiding him, an undertaking made easier as I now had a cook to feed the always-ravenous gentleman. However, upon the morning that Mr. Lincoln died, Robert had telegraphed Judge Davis with the request that he handle our affairs. And while I would have preferred to be beneath the protection of a gentleman who thought more of me, I expected Mr. Lincoln's estate would be settled in a short time, and I did not wish to go against my son's decision.

We conducted this meeting meant to persuade me out of the house in the library; Robert and I seated upon chairs near the fire and the judge spread across the settee, for the man's bulk had swollen to such a size, he could no longer sit upon a normal chair.

"There is talk that it will require General Grant's troops to force you from the President's House," my son declared.

"It is unkind of you to repeat such gossip," I told him.

"Robert is concerned only for your interests," said the judge. He shifted his weight upon the settee, and beneath him, the legs creaked dangerously.

"It is just that it is hard for me to think where we should go."

"You should take Taddie and return to Springfield," said Robert.

"But where will you be?"

"I intend to go to Chicago. Father has friends there. One of them will give me an apprenticeship in his law office." Robert smoothed the trousers of a new suit. "But as you will have no male protection but Taddie, it is best to go where you have a house and relations."

"I cannot return to the Springfield house," I told them. "I have too many memories of the dead there."

"Until Mr. Lincoln's estate is settled," warned Judge Davis, "you shall have only the interest earned by it to live upon. Springfield is the only practical choice."

"I will not go there," I repeated.

Robert glanced at the judge, and I was certain I saw some communication pass between them. A telepathy which made me want to take my son's arm and pull him from the room, leaving the judge's malevolent bulk upon the settee where it could do no harm.

"Where do you propose to go?" Judge Davis asked me.

His tone implied that he did not believe me to possess an answer. But it was that complicity which had passed between the judge and my son which had caused me to acquire one. "Taddie and I will go to Chicago with Robert," I said.

My son sprang from his seat. "There is nothing practical in that idea!" He was near to shouting. "You know almost no one in Chicago!"

"I shall know you."

"I will be entirely engaged in the learning of law. I will have no time to spare for…"

But before I might learn for which aspect of myself my son would spare no time, Judge Davis held up a thick-fingered hand. Robert instantly ceased speaking.

"Your portion of the interest," said the judge, "will not be enough to keep you in even the meanest boardinghouse."

"But each of us – Robert, Taddie, and myself – receives our own interest. Is that not correct?"

"That is the law."

"Thus, if we live together as a family, we will be able to combine the amounts and afford something better."

"Even combined," said the judge, "you will have to board in a second-class establishment."

"Only until you have settled the estate," I reminded him.

"Which will require much labor," he replied.

"Then, we shall trust you to work swiftly."

At the close of May, forty-three days after my husband was killed, I arrived with my sons in Chicago. The sky that day was covered in rain clouds so eternal-seeming, all the bright spring days which had gone before felt to have been an illusion. I myself was covered in layers of veils, meant as much to hide my identity as my grief, for I did not wish it to be made public that the former First Lady and her sons would now live in a boardinghouse in an unfashionable part of town. Only the landlady had been told my name, and as she was only recently come from a country in the east of Europe, I do not think it meant much to her.

Our new home, the Clifton House, was a narrow-fronted tenement on Wabash Avenue, a peeling clapboard building which was not improved by the dismal rain. "I fear," declared Robert, even before he had cast eyes upon its chipped chamber pots and spotted mirrors, "that I would almost as soon be dead as remain three months in this dreary house."

"I do not believe Judge Davis will require that much time

to settle the estate," I assured him. And I hoped that I was right in this.

As Judge Davis had predicted, the Clifton House was a second-class establishment. The globes on the gas jets were cracked and the sheets so mended, it was impossible to stretch my feet without catching a toe upon a thick welter of stitching. Our carpeting was rough and stained in places by something which looked very much like gravy, and the two wing chairs which sat before the soot-blackened fireplace of our sitting room smelled of mold. Our fellow boarders were men looking to make their fortunes and become gentlemen, and ladies of uncertain income who claimed to be widows. Within a week, the fact that I took my meals in my room and never stepped into the uncarpeted corridor without swathing myself in black bombazine and veilings made me an object of curiosity to the other tenants. The ladies gazed at me from beneath the brims of their showy hats, and the men felt entitled to stare openly.

In Chicago, Robert quickly found a law apprenticeship and passed most of the day at his office. Taddie, I enrolled in a not-expensive academy which he attended until mid-afternoon. Myself, I did nothing. The mourning manuals were unyielding that the recently widowed should attend no social gatherings and pay no calls. They were equally adamant that those widowed beneath three months should receive no visits unless they were of condolence – which, as I had told none of the few people I knew in Chicago where I was living, never came. My only diversion from this carefully prescribed period of bereavement, which gave me too much time to think upon my grief, were the walks Taddie and I took together when his classes were over and the day was fine.

Upon one such afternoon, as my youngest son and I stepped out of our rooms, we found our way blocked by a member of the Clifton House's gentlemen-in-the-making. The man wore a slouch hat, which he did not yet seem to know to remove in the company of ladies, and in the close confines of the hallway, he smelled strongly of onions. The man looked hard at Taddie, and then at me, squinting, as if that might help him see better through my veils.

"I know you. You're the president's widow."

I nodded, hoping that this would be considered as much greeting as a first-year widow was required to extend a stranger in a boarding-house corridor.

The man pointed a grimed finger at my son. "And this must be Taddie."

Taddie, who had once spoken readily to anyone, gazed at the floor.

I took a step toward the man, to show him that I wished to pass by. But the narrowness of the corridor and the width of my skirts made it impossible unless he was willing to step aside for me.

"Is it true?" asked the man, who remained in his place. "Is it true what I read? That during the war, you spied for the Confederacy?"

Taddie made a noise which reminded me of all the times he had offered to fight the rebels, and moved toward the man. The man made his hands into fists.

"I think that the weather has turned," I said, taking hold of my son's arm. "It has become much too unpleasant for us to go out." Backing away from the man in the slouch hat, I pulled Taddie into our room and shut the door.

"How could he say such a thing to you?" my son asked me. "Right to your face."

"I expect it is because I am only Mary Lincoln now," I replied. "And not a president's wife anymore."

Despite this incident, my youngest son was mostly happy in Chicago. Taddie had not lived in the same house with Robert since before we moved to Washington City, and now that the three of us shared the Clifton House's unrepaired roof, his ten-years-older brother, with his cigars and his shaving blades, took on the aspect of a divine being. Each time Robert made ready to catch the streetcar, Taddie begged to be taken along, tugging upon his elder brother's sleeve and calling him "Bob." Taddie was the only one who used this name for Robert, only in part, I believe, because the letter R was difficult for him. On occasion, Robert did take Taddie with him. But he always made his younger brother change into clothes "more suitable," and instructed him to "say as little as possible to the gentlemen in my office."

At the end of October, after we had been living at the Clifton House some five months – Judge Davis having not yet settled Mr. Lincoln's estate – Robert took his brother on an outing and returned him with a cruel-looking steel brace fitted onto his teeth.

"What is this?" I made Taddie open his mouth for me. The inside of his cheek had been cut by the apparatus and was bleeding a little.

"It is a brace to improve Taddie's speech," said Robert.

"It does not look as if he will be able to talk at all."

Robert shook out his overcoat, then hung it before the window. "He is nearly grown and can barely be understood by anyone outside his family."

"It is the fault of the way his teeth are angled," I told him, for it had sounded as if Robert put the blame for Taddie's defective speech upon some obstinacy.

"That is the reason for the brace," said Robert.

I closed Taddie's mouth, and then touched his cheek, which was reddened, perhaps from the weather, which was windy, or from being pulled upon so the brace could be inserted. "How long must he keep it?"

Robert threw himself into one of the wing chairs, regarded with loathing the smell his weight had raised from its cushions. "Until I no longer have to translate his words for strangers."

I kept the steel brace fastened to Taddie's teeth – though I was sometimes obliged to rub cocaine upon the inside of his cheek to numb it, for it pleased Robert to know that his younger brother's speech was being corrected, and so little pleased my eldest son these days.

That year, I wished to give my sons overgenerous Christmas presents – those which would make Taddie forget that he was fatherless and ease Robert's reproachful melancholy. However, the interest checks I received from Judge Davis did not allow for the buying of presents which were even a little extravagant. I went to State Street every day and searched the shops, as if finding the correct present might undo what had happened to us. For Taddie, I at last bought a set of carved ponies which had been made affordable by their slightly misshapen legs. For Robert I was forced to settle upon a sateen cravat even the clerk who sold it to me knew reflected too much light for taste.

The week before Christmas, I spent too much upon branches of evergreen to decorate our rented rooms, and when the weather turned unseasonably warm a few days before the holiday, the branches dried out and dropped their needles into the fireplace. A sleeting rain fell on Christmas Day, keeping us in our rooms, where we ate the onion-flavored goose sent up from the kitchen and only Taddie seemed cheerful – having convinced himself that the ponies' misshapen legs turned them into a rare and marvelous breed of horse.

"You look well in that cravat," I told Robert, after I had coaxed him into tying the thing around his neck.

"Thank you," he replied, though his voice held more of bitterness than should be heard upon Christmas.

For the rest of that dull afternoon, Robert and I sat silent beside the fire, which threatened to scorch the dried branches over the mantle, and did not stir until Taddie bent a portion of the steel frame in his mouth upon a nougat from his Christmas stocking. Later, after Taddie had fallen asleep amidst a pile of ponies, Robert informed me that as he had begun to draw a small salary, and as the three of us were quite crowded into these rooms, he had taken an apartment for himself near the city's opera house.

My son's announcement felt an inevitability of this unhappy holiday, and I had no heart to argue it. But though Robert had been poor company these past months, I could not bear to have my family made smaller. And I knew how sad Taddie would be without his brother.

"Perhaps we can see about larger rooms," I said. "If we economize . . ."

Robert tugged at the cravat. "And what luxuries shall we do away with?"

"We could sell the carriage," I told him. "There are only a few months remaining of strong cold. And I have become too sedentary."

"You cannot do without the carriage."

"The coal for the fire, then."

Robert gripped the arm of his chair, meeting me with an expression I hoped was for the mold smell of its cushions and not myself. "I would rather die than stay another month in this house."

My vexation at Robert's complaining propelled me to my feet. "And do you imagine that I find it agreeable?"

"You appear to tolerate it well enough."

I stood before him, my voice made loud enough to cause Taddie to stir. "All that allows me to abide this house's smell of unwashed linen and the nighttime noises of other people's sleep, is that while we live here, what remains of our family is together."

"While I am made miserable," Robert said. He dropped his face into his hands, as if unwilling to gaze further upon the room. My eldest son displayed little in mannerism which was similar to his father, but this gesture was so like my husband's when the hypochondriasis was upon him that the energy which had driven me to my feet drained away. Defeated, I sank back into my chair.

For a time, we sat listening to the dropped pine needles crackling in the fire.

"We shall both miss you very much," I told him.

"I will come to see you," he promised. "Often." And, perhaps without knowing that he did so, he pulled off the bright cravat.

On the first afternoon after Robert moved away, near the time he would have come walking up Wabash Avenue, Taddie pulled one of the wing chairs to the window and sat watching the street, as silent as those first weeks after his father had been shot.

"Why do you not play with your Christmas ponies?" I said to him.

"They don't stand right," he told me. "There is something wrong with their legs."

After a week of watching my youngest son wait for his brother, I took Taddie to have the steel brace removed from his teeth. The way that it bit at the inside of his mouth every time he attempted speech had made him quiet, and I missed his glad, imperfect chatter. But even after I had replaced the brace with an elocution teacher, Taddie stayed mostly silent. With Robert gone, Taddie and I seemed reduced – not only in number, but also in ourselves. The two of us moved about our rented rooms with the sadly passive disposition of the infirm.

"We have been evenly divided," Taddie said to me one evening. It was well after dark and he was only just moving the wing chair away from the window.

"What do you mean?" I asked.

"Three of us are in Heaven," he told me, "and three of us are on Earth."

I felt a little sorry then that I had had the steel brace removed from Taddie's mouth, only so I might hear him say this more clearly.

"Though it doesn't feel so very even," he continued, "since only two of us live here."

I rose and helped him move the chair closer to the fire for the excuse to touch his face and his fine, dry hair. "It is only temporary," I said to him. "Only until Judge Davis settles the estate."

"I don't believe he will settle it," said Taddie. "Ever."

That night after Taddie had fallen into sleep, I wrote to Judge Davis. "I wish to make a loan against the money in my husband's estate," I told him. "I wish to buy a house for myself and my sons."

"I advised you against settling in Chicago," the judge wrote back. "I can send nothing until the estate is settled."

"Can you tell me when you will be finished with your work?" said my next letter. "It has been almost a year since Mr. Lincoln was killed."

"I have been lately incapacitated," Judge Davis replied, "by a painful carbuncle."

If he will not make me the loan, I determined, *I shall save the money myself.* And as the winter progressed, I worked to see how little I could spend. I had no new mourning clothes stitched, wearing the ones Lizzie had made when Willie died, and loaned out the horse so I would not have to feed him. I watered my writing ink to make it last, and saw no more Spiritualists. As time passed, it became a competition with myself to see how much I might do without. I told the landlady to give me less wood and during the hours Taddie was at school, I did not warm my rooms, wrapping myself in the coverlet, which possessed an oily feel from the cold. Most nights, I did not take supper, sending down word that only my son possessed an appetite. I did not mind this strict economy. Indeed, I found a pleasurable satisfaction in the deprivation; for every cent not spent felt one more credit upon the side of the ledger which would buy for me Robert's affection.

Each time an interest check arrived from Judge Davis, I added the amount to the sum already saved, scratching my figures upon the edges of old newspapers to conserve stationery, calculating how near I was to affording a house. But despite the mania which drove me to rinse out my chemises in my washing-up water to save the laundry fee, by April I still could not have bought even the meanest shack out near the slaughterhouses.

I had begun to lose hope that I would ever see my family together in a house when I received an unexpected letter from Simon Cameron, a gentleman who had been in Mr. Lincoln's cabinet. I had not even had a letter of condolence from him – an unsurprising fact, as that gentleman's resignation from the cabinet had been encouraged by Mr. Lincoln, after my husband learned that Mr. Cameron was selling the army blankets made of cotton for the price of woolen ones.

In exchange for this resignation, Mr. Lincoln had made Mr. Cameron ambassador to Russia and sent him halfway around the world. I had read in the newspapers that Mr. Cameron was lately returned to the United States, and had decided the country would be best served if he were made senator.

"I wish you to know that I have begun a Mary Lincoln subscription fund for the amount of twenty thousand dollars," the gentleman wrote to me. "It is to be used to provide a suitable home for the Orphaned Sons and Widowed Lady of our Martyred President."

That Mr. Cameron might start such a fund for me was not entirely remarkable. Such subscriptions for houses – meant to aid the families of men who had served in the war – were common. General Grant himself had benefited from a fund which had paid off the thirty-thousand-dollar mortgage on his home in Washington City. Still, I suspected that patriotism was not the sole motive behind Mr. Cameron's generosity; for what more efficient method of brightening a dulled reputation might be devised than assisting the Orphaned Sons and Widowed Lady of the Martyred President?

Whatever Mr. Cameron's motive, twenty thousand dollars would easily remove my family from the curiosity of the not-quite-gentlemen of the Clifton House. Straightaway, I sacrificed a piece of my stationery to write back to my benefactor. "When do you imagine we might realize this amount?" I asked him.

"It is my belief that the Deceased President's family has strong claims upon every Patriotic Man in the Land," he replied. "I expect the twenty thousand shall be raised with little delay."

The afternoon I received this response, I experienced a sensation very much like hunger, and thought how nice it would be to eat supper that night. The following day I wrote to the few ladies I had met in Chicago, mostly at séance, and asked if they knew of any modest houses situated in genteel neighborhoods which might be for sale. It was Myra Bradwell who wrote back and told me of a block of stone row houses near her own on West Washington Street. The houses were being sold by the builder, a man named Cole, and immediately I sent a note to Mr. Cole, asking him to show me a house.

Mr. Cole was a talkative man with a nearly hairless head – a feature which was difficult to overlook, as the builder did not wear a hat.

"I voted for Mr. Lincoln twice," he told me. "Although, if truth be told, I have no feelings one way or the other about Negroes."

Mr. Cole's houses were cream-colored stone and set too near each other. But their windows were high and their roofs pitched, and they looked very well beneath the spring sunshine.

"From here you can walk to Union Park," said the builder, waving his hand in a westerly direction. "The Bois de Boulogne of west-side Chicago." I took it as favorable sign that the builder did not mispronounce the French.

Mr. Cole walked me through one of the houses, which, though modest, possessed smoothly plastered walls and evenly set moldings. On the second floor, I saw a room for Taddie and one for Robert, which faced out upon a garden where a plum tree was already covered in thinly petaled white blossoms.

"I would not be able to give you the entire price of the house for a short while," I said to Mr. Cole.

The builder rubbed a hand over his hairless head. "How much could you give me?"

I named the entire amount I had set aside by my saving.

Mr. Cole regarded me, assessing, I expect, my mourning clothes, which were some years out of date. "Let us say that I sell you the house for that sum," he said to me, "with the promise that the rest would be paid within three months."

"That is a very charitable offer, Mr. Cole," I replied. And before the day was out, I had given the builder all my money, certain that three months would be ample time for Mr. Cameron's Patriotic Men of the Land to offer up their donations.

In June of 1866, my sons and I moved into the cream-colored house on West Washington Street. Although the summer was hot, I set to work in the garden, pulling weeds and planting iris and heliotrope and any other flower which was graceful, and which I believed would please my eldest son when he gazed out his window, for from the first day I showed it to him, Robert had been unenthusiastic about the little stone house.

"Have you lost your reason?" he asked me.

"No," I told him. "I have only bought a house." Then wishing to show him the rooms, show him the one which looked out upon the garden and would be his, I took the key from my pocket and moved up the walk. But Robert had remained on the street, staring at my house as if it contained ghosts.

"You will come and live with us?" I said, turning back.

"I expect I shall have to," he replied. "How would it look if I didn't?"

"It would look as if *you* had lost your reason," I told him. "For who would not wish to live with those who love him?"

I filled the rooms of my house with rosewood furniture I bought on credit, demonstrating my faith in Mr. Cameron's Patriotic Men of the Land. The mantles and shelves of the glass-fronted cabinets I covered with the objects I had bought before my husband was killed, the malachite clocks and silver tea services I had believed would safeguard my family. Robert joined a gentlemen's club downtown and only returned to sleep and fill his room with the smell of cigars. Still, Taddie was happy to see his brother every morning, and came to his room and sat upon a wooden washing stool while Robert shaved around the shape of his mustache, talking to him continuously in his slurring speech.

When the three months which Mr. Cole had given me to pay what I owed on the house were nearly concluded, I wrote to Mr. Cameron about my subscription. "Have you received any donations on my behalf?" I asked him. "My gratitude shall be as great as my hopes to see you returned to the U.S. Senate."

"As you are so sympathetic to my political aspirations," the gentleman responded, "I do not hesitate to tell you that the pursuit of the position which you mention has necessarily commandeered all my attention." And I began to fear that the brightening of Mr. Cameron's reputation had only required that he begin my fund, not that he solicit any donations for it.

Mr. Cole, on the other hand, had a good deal of attention to devote to my financial affairs. Once the date for the payment had passed, the builder sent me notes once a week, and then twice, asking when he might come round to discuss the matter of the outstanding balance on my house. As the only money I had was Mr. Lincoln's pension, which I owed to the merchants of Washington City and New York, I put off Mr. Cole by claiming incapacity due to headache. But Mr. Cole was not a gentleman and could not be put off indefinitely by a lady's indisposition, and I was unsurprised when, upon a cruelly hot day at the end of September, I discovered Mr. Cole standing bare-headed upon my front step.

"I was thinking," he said by way of greeting, "how this beveled glass gives your door such a refined appearance." The builder ran a callused thumb over my window. "Certainly worth the extra expense."

"I am very fond of it," I assured him.

The sun shimmered hotly off the top of the builder's hairless head. He wiped at his crown with a sleeve, gazing into the dark coolness of my hallway. "Do you reckon weather this hot in September means something? An omen, maybe. Some message from the Almighty."

"I expect that if God wished to make a point with us, Mr. Cole, He would send something more pestilential than Indian summer."

"Do you think I could come in, Mrs. Lincoln?"

"I am not prepared for company."

"I only ask as I expect it would be better if we discussed our business inside." He glanced to my neighbor's house, where someone had left the doors and windows open against the heat.

"Very well, Mr. Cole." I said, and showed him into the parlor.

"Do you know," he said, smoothing his hand the length of my mantle, "that this marble comes from Italy?"

"You mentioned the fact to me when I purchased the house."

"That was some four months ago, wasn't it?"

"Just after the one-year anniversary of Mr. Lincoln's assassination."

The builder flattened his wide palm to the mantle top. "And still, you owe me more than half the price."

I crossed the room, coming to stand before the window as if I had only required more air. "I am expecting funds from Washington City," I told him.

The builder came up behind me and, reaching so near my shoulder I could not keep from flinching, pushed open the curtains to look out at the row of houses he had made. "I was more than a little pleased when you bought this place," he said. "Having President Lincoln's widow living in one of my houses adds refinement to the whole block."

"Somewhat like the beveled glass."

"Exactly," he replied. "But the thing is, another widow lady – the wife of a judge – is extremely taken with your house. And she's got the entire price sitting in a Chicago bank."

I whirled around, a motion which brought my face too near to that of the builder. "You would give away my house?"

"I would return you your initial payment," he assured me, "less something for the four months' rent. That should be enough to set up you and your sons in a snug little boardinghouse."

My nose filled with the mold smell of the Clifton House chair cushions as strongly as if my face had been forced into them and not let up. Holding my breath against it, I moved out of the range of Mr. Cole's grasp. "I shall pay you the full sum tomorrow," I said.

The builder remained by my window, lifting and lowering the sash to test the counterweights. "You'll forgive me for inquiring whether you plan to have a headache tomorrow?"

"I shall be very surprised if I do not," I told him. "But, I will not allow it to prevent me from giving you all that I owe."

The moment Mr. Cole was away, I put on a bonnet with a double set of veils and pushed aboard a downtown streetcar, crowded and hot, and reeking of the wet horse which pulled it. It required more than an hour to persuade the manager of the Bank of Chicago to write me a check for everything in my account, and to prevent him from sending a note to Robert asking him to intervene. The streetcar back was no less jammed, and I arrived home with sopping hair and some of the dye from my veils staining my cheek.

I had been left light-headed by the heat, by the fear that the bank manager would not give me my money, and by the fact that once I had signed the check over to Mr. Cole, I would no longer possess anything with which to pay the merchants of Washington City and New York. I went to the little rolltop desk in my sitting room and pushed open its cover. There, filling all the pigeonholes, were the notices from the merchants of Pennsylvania Avenue and lower Broadway, notices I had folded into small squares and put away rather than paid or tallied even. Seized with a fatal panic, I began to pull out the bills, until the pile of them covered the polished surface of the desk. Once I had every one, I pushed them aside, took out ink, and began to add up the numbers of my debt.

Halfway through, I rose and loosened my dress, and then my corset, but still could not fill my lungs. Forcing myself back to the figures, I fought dizziness and a darkness which crowded my vision and altered the numbers on the page. Still, I would not let myself stop until the final bill had been tallied.

The total of my debts was nearly thirty thousand dollars.

I clawed open the collar of my dress, tearing off the buttons, then got to my feet and stumbled across to the mantle, laying my hot cheek against the marble for coolness, swallowing air with the avidity of the starved. *Taddie will be home soon*, I told myself. *And he should not find you gasping upon the mantle, the desk covered with evidence that you cannot keep him safe from the stares of strangers.* But when I lifted my head, my ears filled with the noise of my own blood, and I feared more that he might find me collapsed upon the hearth.

I stayed until I did not have to strain so to fill my lungs, until the roaring of blood in my ears was replaced by the delicate ticking of a small gilt mantle clock, for which I still owed M. W. Galt & Company of Washington City fifty dollars. The clock was an expensive-looking thing with gold numbers and filigreed hands, and I wished very much I had never bought it. And it was this wish which put the question in my mind. If Mr. Cole had been willing to give back my money for return of the house, perhaps Mr. Galt might do the same with the gilt clock?

I hurried back to my desk and shoved aside the billing notices and the pages of tallying. Taking up my pen, I wrote to Mr. Galt, who, until my bill with him had gone unpaid a year, had always proved accommodating, and asked whether he would consider the return of the gilt clock, as well as an onyx breast pin and ear knobs (value sixty dollars), a pair of diamond sleeve buttons (value thirty dollars), and one and one-half dozen silver nut picks and spoons (value fifty-six dollars).

A week later, Mr. Galt wrote back to say he would be most pleased to accept the return of my things. Immediately, I sat down to write to Mr. Kerr of Kerr China Importers to see about the return of two dozen teacups (never used) and three gilt-edged slop bowls (likewise). The following day, I penned a letter to Mr. Stuckey of May & Company regarding a lady's watch (unworn). Before another week had passed, I had written to every merchant from whom I had purchased something which had not been put to use. A number of these gentlemen were willing to take back what I had bought, but not at the price I had paid, citing the changing fashions of the season.

Only Alexander Stewart, with whom I carried the largest debt, refused to accept anything. The Gentleman Merchant replied to all my letters begging the return of unmade dress fabric and filigree fire screens with reminders of the great sum I owed to him, until at last, came a note telling me that he would be arriving in Chicago in a few days' time and that he intended on giving himself the pleasure of calling upon me. I wanted to tell Mr. Stewart that I was too indisposed to see him, but the recent appearance of Mr. Cole upon my doorstep had proved that ladies with debts lost the right to such excuses.

I arranged to meet Mr. Stewart in the ornate tearoom of the Bradford House Hotel, and went to meet him with my face covered by the most opaque of my veils. I arrived early, but found the Gentleman Merchant already waiting at a table, seated upon an empire chair with a horn of plenty cut into the wood behind his head.

Mr. Stewart was the only lean man of affluence that I knew; even his beard was narrow and shaped to a point. In the time since I had first met him, his red-colored hair had silvered, which suited him, perhaps because it reminded one of his wealth. He acknowledged me by casually extending his fingers over the thick linen of the tea table.

"Our mutual friend Mr. Wakeman asks to be remembered," he said, employing that accent in which Irish warred with Scottish. "And tells me to say that he misses you at Mrs. Kellogg's séance table with only the dead to speak with."

I sat in a chair decorated with small apples. "I am happy to hear that I am more engaging than the departed," I replied.

We ordered tea, which I found difficult to drink, for I could not keep the hem of my veil out of the cup.

"I was sorry to learn that Congress granted you a pension of only one year's salary," said Mr. Stewart. He leaned back in his seat, letting his silvered head rest upon the horn of plenty.

"It is generous of you to concern yourself."

"When one considers the enormous debt the country owes to your Noble Husband, it is most unjust."

"It is very little," I agreed.

"Still," continued Mr. Stewart, "it is sufficient to settle the debts which I am certain you find so cumbersome. The money to my own emporium, for example, which would take no more than two-thirds."

"That money is gone to pay another debt," I told him, happy for the opacity of my veil.

"Still," said the Gentleman Merchant, "Mr. Lincoln was a practical man. Certainly, he left an estate of some size."

"Judge Davis has yet to settle Mr. Lincoln's estate."

"It seems Judge Davis moves as ponderously in business as he does upon land. I do not trust a man of great corpulence; it points to an untidy greed." Mr. Stewart flicked at his teacup and listened to its chime. "Still, I expect to be paid."

I leaned across the table, dipping the edging of my veil into my tea. "Could you not grant me more time?"

The Gentleman Merchant shook his head. "If it is seen that some ladies do not pay their bills, other ladies will form the same notion."

"But who would learn of my bills if you did not tell them?"

"The debts of well-known ladies have a way of coming before the public." Mr. Stewart lifted his teacup, studied the marking upon the bottom. "I would not be surprised to find yours mentioned in the newspapers."

"You would publish my debts in the papers?" The thick veils over my face felt to be blocking out the air.

"Imagine what people might say were they to learn you spent five hundred dollars upon a shawl," he replied.

"Please!" I begged. "You cannot tell the papers what I have spent."

"I did not say that I would be the one to give them the information." He shrugged. "In truth, I seek only payment of what is owed me. And the courts are a more efficient venue for that task."

I sat back hard against the little apples. "You intend to sue me over my bills?"

"Only to recover my funds. It is a customary business practice." Mr. Stewart toyed with a silvered spoon. "If you wish to keep the particulars of the case confidential, you could always engage the legal services of your son."

"Robert knows nothing about my debts."

Mr. Stewart blew upon the bowl of the spoon to see how his breath steamed it. "That is remarkably closemouthed of you. Of course, I expect that Harvard gentlemen would consider their mothers' overdue accounts as subjects of some discomfiture."

Frantically, I thought of the last payment of interest Judge Davis had sent me and what expenses I might put off. "If I give you a check for some portion today," I said, "could you grant me a few months more?"

Mr. Stewart pointed his narrow beard at me. "How substantial would that check be?"

I thought of the money I had set aside for coal and kerosene. "Not above two hundred."

"I can grant one month," he told me. "And then, I must receive another, more sizable payment. If only to demonstrate your good faith."

I sent Mr. Stewart my coal and kerosene money that afternoon. That night, I woke with a longing for my husband so pointed, my breath stopped altogether. Since his killing, I worked not to think about my husband at night, for at night my flesh – which I was shamed to know yearned for him even more than my mind – was particularly susceptible to the memory of desire. However, on this night, my body was racked by desire so profound, it seemed that if I was not allowed to press myself against his hard bones, to rub the scent of his skin upon mine, my reason would leave me.

I cannot say how long I tossed upon the bed, twisting the linens from the mattress, setting them against my teeth in the anguish of my one-sided passion. Exhaustion arrived before madness, and when my breath had slowed, I spoke to my husband, sending my words into the blackness, into what I hoped was a gateway to the Summerland. "We are poor," I told him, "and I am running out of ways to keep us together."

My coal and kerosene money had bought me only one month's grace, and I did not know how I would raise the sizable sum Mr. Stewart would require when that time ended. But the merchant's mention of Mr. Wakeman recalled for me the gentlemen for whom I had performed small political favors in exchange for the delaying of those bills which now filled the pigeonholes of my desk. *Many of these gentlemen are well-off,* I reminded myself. *Many due to my assistance. How dishonorable could it be to write to them and ask for some small loans against Mr. Lincoln's estate? Certainly no more dishonorable than having done the favors for them in the first instance.*

I wrote the first of my begging letters a week after my tea with Mr. Stewart, and only after Taddie and Robert had gone to bed. The heated autumn had by then given way to a frigid early winter, and as I was conserving coal, my house was chill enough at night to turn my breath to vapor. Before going to my writing desk, I was obliged to dress myself in two woolen wrappers, one worn over the other. I chose black-bordered stationery for my letters to remind the recipients of my widowed status, and before first light, I had written to six well-off gentlemen, for the month was short and the amount Mr. Stewart required substantial.

At the close of three weeks, I had collected enough in loans to keep myself out of the courts. However, my payment only prompted Mr. Stewart to demand one of similar size in another month's time.

For all of that winter I made myself shameless, writing to wealthy gentlemen of the shabbiness of my mourning clothes, referring to Robert and Taddie as "Mr. Lincoln's Fatherless Sons." I mentioned amounts which would cover the cost of our coal, the feed for our horse, and after a time, did not insist so strenuously that I would look upon such generosity as a loan. The checks which arrived, I signed over to the punctual Mr. Stewart. And if there were any funds remaining, I spread it among the most insistent of my other creditors.

Assessing the tone of each of my dunning letters and devising new means to make myself sound pitiable became my main occupation at the house on West Washington Street. A portion of my other time, I spent engaged in the housekeeping tasks I had once so assiduously studied in Miss Beecher's *Treatise on Domestic Economy*; although I expect I did not perform these with any more talent or enthusiasm. In the afternoons, I helped Taddie with his letters, for my twelve-year-old son could not read more than a handful of words. All the time we had been in Washington City, Taddie had shown more aptitude for hiding from tutors than learning from them, and when appealed to, Mr. Lincoln had only maintained that his son might learn his reading later, "when such activity doesn't have to compete with something so interesting as a war." For diversion, I sometimes went to séance with Myra Bradwell, who seemed to sense that I did not have the medium's fee and would always offer to make me a present of it. During these magnetic circles I was oft tempted to call up my husband and ask his financial advice. However, Mr. Lincoln had never shown skill in the management of money. Despite the strangeness of this life, I was not unhappy. In the company of his elder brother, Taddie had regained some of his brightness of spirit, and as he had done with his father, he saved his treasures to show to his elder brother, bringing him a pointed rock he harbored no doubt was an arrowhead, or an old half-eagle coin with the left-facing head. After he had displayed his own treasures, Taddie would beg to be allowed to handle Robert's – a device like a guillotine used for trimming cigars, cuff links embossed with sailing ships. And on occasion Robert obliged him. For his part, Robert was less tormented than he had been in Washington City, and not as quarrelsome as he was at the Clifton House. And he did not chew so much upon his mustache.

With my sons made more glad and some portion of my debts cancelled, I began to believe I might keep my living family together in a house which was mine. But I had forgotten the spring taxes which were due on the house, and when notice of their payment date arrived with the early March mail, I had no money with which to settle them. I could only stand in the foyer with my head resting upon the beveled glass which Mr. Cole believed so refined. *I have run out of gentlemen from whom to beg loans, and will have to give up the house for the rent money, or lose it entirely,* I told myself, and it was some time before I could lift my head from the glass. When I did, I went to tell my sons.

It was one of those melting days which come in early spring, days upon which it feels that things long frozen are turning to water, and my sons were outside, seated upon a slatted wooden bench beneath the plum tree covered in white blossoms. They did not see me come out to stand upon the small back porch, but from that spot I saw that Taddie held a yellow-legged beetle in his palm, and that he was showing it to his elder brother as if he had invented it himself. Robert was listening to Taddie describe the beetle's most remarkable features, his head bent over the small insect. But what I saw most clearly from my place upon the porch, what impressed itself upon me most, was that my eldest son sat with his hand pressed to his younger brother's back.

That night, I wrote a begging letter of a different sort. The recipient was a gentleman by name of Harris C. Fahnestock. Mr. Fahnestock had been Mr. Lincoln's banker in Washington City and had recently taken a position with the firm of Jay Cooke & Company in New York. With no embellishment or pretense to favors owed, I explained to Mr. Fahnestock that I was impoverished and informed him that, like a lady who possessed no discreet personal acquaintance from whom she might make such a request, a lady who, in consequence, barely merited the term, I required a loan from Mr. Cooke's institution.

Within the week, Mr. Fahnestock sent me a businesslike reply stating that Mr. Cooke would be glad to make me a loan at a "rate of interest which has, as is customary, been calculated upon how likely it is that the borrower will pay back the full sum." By the rate quoted in Mr. Fahnestock's letter, I understood that word of my New York debts must have reach Mr. Cooke's ears.

I had no choice but to accept Mr. Cooke's terms, and when

the check arrived, I set it aside for the taxes. However, I had underestimated the cost of my gas; and in spring the horse developed sweet itch; and Mr. Cooke's interest was so high, I sometimes had to use a portion of the loan just to pay it. And by the date the taxes were due, I had only one-third of the amount.

I wrote one last desperate letter to Judge Davis, penning it with my watered ink which rendered my plea faint and indefinite. I begged the judge to settle Mr. Lincoln's estate, or to at least make me a loan against it so I would not be forced to give up my house. But the judge sent back word that my inquiries only served to delay him further.

I found tenants to live in my house beginning in May, and in April, I hired an auctioneer named Cornelius Butters to sell off my furniture – for enough, I hoped, to pay a good portion of Mr. Cooke's loan. I would have no more use for furniture. Robert was moving to a hotel, and Taddie and I were returning to the Clifton House. Mr. Butters was an impatient man who spoke in the rushed cadence of his profession, even when in conversation. He instructed me to remain at the house during the sale, and to wear black. "Buyers are less miserly when they see the money is going to a widow," he informed me.

The day of the auction, I had Robert take Taddie to Union Park, as I did not wish my youngest son to see his bed and bureau and bookshelves sold to strangers. Taddie had been made sad by the news he would no longer live with his brother. Robert had reminded me that it had always been his opinion that buying the house had been a type of insanity. Though the day was warm, I dressed in heavy mourning, placing several layers of dark veils between myself and those who had come to buy my possessions. I did not want to be inside the house, where I might overhear the buyers comment upon my taste, so I went to sit beneath the plum tree upon a wicker chair too unsteady to be sold.

Through the windows I watched gentlemen and ladies wander through my rooms, put their hands to dressers and tables, which, for the moment, belonged to me. Near noon, the time when Mr. Butters would sell my furniture by means of his rushing voice, a lady came to the window and looked into the garden. The lady wore a bonnet topped with the feathered replica of a bird, and she did not pretend to be examining anything in the garden, but stared at me openly and with an appraising frankness, as if I had been set upon display alongside my furniture.

I was startled by the lady's rudeness, yet found myself sitting very still, feeling somehow that I was obliged to behave as if I were another inanimate object upon which she might bid. The lady moved nearer the window, and as she did, she stepped into a slant of sunlight which caught the glass eye of the bird upon her hat, making it appear that both stared at me. This doubled stare seemed to see right through my veiling, and I felt how poor a protection were my yards of black-dyed crape. Indeed, all the silver tea services and woolen shawls upon which I had made my debts had all proved poor protection. For I had not understood that it was only money which offered refuge, which shielded one from the stares of ill-bred strangers and the disrespect of well-off gentlemen. And now, I had none. I had only trunks filled with the things I could not return – satin turned into dresses, velvet-tipped capes worn once to a ball – and I was obliged to sit beneath the gaze of impolite ladies as if I myself were for sale.

I wished then that I might burn everything in my trunks, all the embroidered slippers and fur cloaks and pale gowns I would never wear, for I did not ever intend to dress in anything but the black of widowhood. More strongly still, I wished that I could turn these extravagances back into the money I had spent upon them.

And in that instant, it occurred to me that I might. That instead of setting fire to my dresses and shawls, I could sell them – discreetly, of course, as ladies did not sell their clothing – but sell them nevertheless. For even a portion of what I had paid for these things would get my house back and keep me from having to beg a favor from another gentleman.

This plan seemed so hopeful, I could not keep myself from making a small wave to the lady with the odd bonnet. Startled, she stepped back, and the light left the glass eye of the bird upon her head, causing it to wink out like death upon the eye of the living.

(August 13) Mr. Robt Lincoln visited his mother to-day – He said that in regard to Mrs. Bradwell that she was a pest and a nuisance. Mrs. L seemed glad to see her son.
—Patient Progress Reports for Bellevue Place Sanitarium

Myra Bradwell came early today, dressed in French muslin and a skirt edged with chenille tassels. "Come with me outside," she said in an unquiet whisper. "Someplace where our conversation cannot be overheard by that gossip-mongering doctor's wife."

The day was brutally hot, with a too-bright sun which even the maddest ladies knew to avoid. Nevertheless, Myra dragged me from the shade of the portico and onto the empty lawn, the chenille tassels flying about her ankles.

"Where can we be where we are sure to have no company?" she said.

"There is a bench near the greenhouse. Nobody goes there." I pointed the way and we hurried over the rise which hid the bench from the asylum. I had not been to this place since the day upon which Minnie and I discovered Mrs. Gill in the Reverend Judd's carriage and my friend began to starve herself with more devotion. The slats of the bench's seat were covered with a thick dusting of pollen and limestone, and its untouched condition made me sad.

Myra wiped at the bench with a linen handkerchief before pulling me to sit beside her.

"What is it you require so much privacy to tell me?" I asked.

"I want you to grant Mr. Wilkie permission to publish his story," she said. "Immediately. Before he loses interest in it."

"But I do not need Mr. Wilkie's story to be set free," I reminded her. "I have the invitation from Elizabeth."

"I fear very much that Elizabeth will alter her mind about taking you in."

"But she has already invited me," I protested. "Robert has her letter."

Myra shook out her handkerchief, scattering pale green dust in the dirt about her feet. "Invitations can always be rescinded."

I recalled what Robert had said about writing to my sister, his great desire to confirm that she had not underestimated the challenge of taking me in. "You have reason to believe Elizabeth's will be?"

She glanced across the lawn, into the dark woods of which the lady lunatics were so afraid. "I have been to see Robert," she told me.

"He received you?"

"It is difficult to send away a large, noisy lady who appears upon your doorstep without warning." Myra appeared pleased at this description of herself.

"And he was cordial to you?"

"Actually, he called me the 'high priestess of a gang of Spiritualists.'"

"I am sorry he was rude," I said.

"I was not in the least offended," Myra assured me. "Indeed, I have always wished to be thought the high priestess of something."

"Robert is already troubled by the dead too much to go seeking them," I told her.

"I do not believe it is my communication with the dead which troubles Robert," she replied. "He made it evident that it is his belief I wish you freed only so I might get hold of your money."

"You have no need of my money!" I exclaimed, embarrassed by my son's discourtesy.

"I suspect that Robert knows that," she told me. "But I suspect also that he is sensitive to any depletion of your income."

"I do not understand. My son has a good deal of his own money."

"Perhaps," said Myra. "However it is no secret among Chicago bankers that Robert has invested in several ventures which have failed spectacularly. Keeping you here, and keeping conservatorship of your money, prevents more than one type of embarrassment."

The sun burned my eyes. "You believe that Robert is working against my release?"

"I know that he is."

I looked away from Myra, putting my gaze upon the unfinished greenhouse. *I could leave this bench and go inside there,* I thought. *Hide among Mrs. Patterson's overblown roses and not have to hear what Myra Bradwell wishes to tell me about my son.*

But I knew that it would be of no use if I did, for Myra would only come and find me.

"Do not tell me how you know this unless you are certain," I said to her.

I felt her fingers upon my jaw, turning my face toward her own. "Robert has in his possession a letter from Doctor Patterson which declares you fully recovered."

Without knowing I would do so, I slid to the edge of the bench, as if my body intended to take me to the greenhouse of its own accord.

"My son showed you this letter?"

"I saw it upon his desk"

"You looked at it unbidden?"

Myra shrugged. "He was called away to attend to some business."

I looked again at the greenhouse, shining irrationally beneath the sun. "Do you think that Doctor Patterson truly believes me sane?"

"I think that Doctor Patterson possesses too many debts," she replied. "And he can ill afford to have the wealthy Chicago gentlemen who send their wives here reading in newspapers that he is keeping the widow of the Martyred President a prisoner." Myra placed a hand upon my own and spoke more gently. "I do not believe Doctor Patterson is a very good judge of sanity."

"Does he say if I should be set free?"

"He has recommended to Robert that you be placed beneath your sister's care."

I let myself be a little hopeful. "Robert will not like to go against Doctor Patterson's advice."

But Myra did not answer right away, and I was troubled by how long she gazed across at the dark woods. "I saw another letter," she told me. "He was working on it when I came in, and when he was called away, he made a point of pushing it beneath some papers." She put her eyes back upon my face, and I felt her fingers tighten upon mine, the way they had in séance. "It was a letter to Elizabeth."

Now it was myself who looked into the ill-omened woods. "Even if I do not ask," I told Myra, "even if I say that I do not wish to know, you are still going to tell me what was in the letter."

"In the long run," she replied, "understanding a hard truth is better than believing a lie."

As always, it was impossible to make argument against Myra Bradwell's declarations.

"Robert wrote Elizabeth that you are entirely deranged," she continued. "He claimed to her that in the interest of protecting your dignity, he had prevented his lawyer, Mr. Swett, from using all the evidence against you. He said, too, that your insane behavior had nearly destroyed his marriage, and caused you to be a danger to his child."

I hated that Myra had forced me to hear this truth about Robert, and was full of bile which grew hot beneath the merciless sun.

"Why do you come carrying this tale?" I demanded, whirling upon her.

She spoke to me again in that gentled voice. "To make you give Mr. Wilkie permission to print his story."

"Why? So you might make me into one of your causes?"

Myra cupped my face in her hand. "So I can free you from the madhouse."

I put my hand upon hers to remove it from my face and felt beneath my fingers the jet ring which Myra wore for her dead daughter. It was this child whom Myra had tried most often to reach during the magnetic circles we had attended together, this child whom she most wished to call back. Yet despite her longing, Myra had never lied to herself about the unidentified knockings beneath the séance table, or the anonymous disturbances of air in the room. She had never turned these ambiguous communications into messages from her dead daughter. And she would not lie to me.

My anger fell away, replaced by shame that I would throw accusations at this forceful lady who had made me her cause. "I am unjust," I told Myra.

"And I think too highly of hard truths," she replied.

We sat together upon the bench and watched a harsh-calling jay fly through the greenhouse, noting how the bird knew which places were empty and which were not.

"When do you wish to write to Mr. Wilkie?" I asked after a time.

"Today," said Myra. "Newspapermen are easily distractable."

"Robert comes today," I replied. "Let us wait until I hear what he says. There is the chance that he has had a change of heart and did not send the letter."

Myra regarded me with an expression I had once seen her cast upon a medium who insisted that the flickering of a lantern was caused by the breath of her daughter's spirit.

"I am not as clear-eyed as you," I reminded her.

Myra nodded, then made me a smile which had much of sorrow in it. "Clear seeing is not always a lucky thing."

For the remainder of that morning, I wandered the asylum, drifting from stifling lunatics' parlor to sweltering porch, wishing for it to be the hour at which Robert was to arrive, wishing equally for that hour to never come. For my seeing was not as unclear as I had made out to Myra.

My son arrived in early afternoon, and I sent word that he should meet me in my room. He arrived, looking handsome in a finely tailored gabardine suit.

"I noticed that the porch was subject to a breeze." Robert wiped at his forehead with a linen handkerchief which matched the fawn color of his suit. "Do you not think we would be more comfortable there?"

But I did not wish Robert to be comfortable. I wished him to remain in my hot little room so he would feel for himself the unbearableness of being made to stay here. "I do not feel well enough to appear in public," I told him.

"That is because you are shut up in this overheated room."

"Indeed," I replied. "I am."

He studied me long enough to determine if there had been some meaning behind my words, and how easily it might be ignored. Then he moved to the window and, fitting his hands between the bars, attempted to force the frame higher than it would go.

"Have you heard from Elizabeth?" I asked him. "Has she confirmed my invitation for you?"

Robert turned from the window, his handsome features arranged in an expression of too-large regret. "I am afraid Aunt Lizzie has written saying she is not well enough to have you visit."

The heated air seemed to force itself down my throat. "Please do not tell me this," I said to him. And I meant, *Please do not lie; please do not make me know you would do anything to keep me here.*

"I warned you of the capriciousness of her health," Robert told me.

"Did you write to Elizabeth that I was too deranged?" I asked him, speaking the question like a dare for the truth.

Robert fixed the regretful expression more firmly upon his features. He moved from the window and sat upon my unsteady rocker, all the time keeping that sympathetic face turned toward me as if it would prove his sincerity. "You must trust me," he said. "There is nothing I wish so much as to have you with Aunt Lizzie."

It was the untruth, uttered with such manufactured honesty and unkind intent, which drove me from my seat, sent me to stand before the bureau and look down upon the objects which Robert had brought to keep me content inside the madhouse. *It would be so pleasurable to smash that delft plate into a hundred pieces,* I thought, *so soothing to rend the lace made by nuns.* And my fingers itched toward them. *But ruining one's possessions is the action of a madwoman,* I reminded myself, *and will only bring Mrs. Ruggles and the bottle of chloral hydrate.*

"Do not let yourself be disappointed," I heard Robert say, as if it were disappointment I felt. "I shall do all in my power to persuade Aunt Lizzie to take you in."

You are a liar, I silently accused him. I put my hands upon the strip of lace which had been made by nuns and pulled until I had torn the hem of it. Robert did not notice, and I believe it was this – this small, pleasurable act of rebellion – which allowed me to turn and face my son with a mother's countenance. "Do you think you can convince Elizabeth to alter her mind?" I asked him. My voice was calm and did not shake.

Robert's face acquired the sheen of earnestness. "I will work very hard at it," he assured me.

This shiny, false expression drew my next question, the one to determine how deeply my son would betray me. "What about Doctor Patterson?" I said. "Could you not persuade him to write a letter declaring that I am recovered?"

Robert shook his handsome head. "I wish that I might. But Doctor Patterson is not yet convinced of the restoration of your reason."

Once I had thought that Robert's gray eyes resembled those of his father, and I believe it was that resemblance which had made me imagine that my son shared also some aspect of his father's character. But now as I stood before the bureau covered with bribes, I could see that they showed no similarity. Could see, too, that Robert would never let me out of the madhouse.

This knowledge filled my mouth with the metallic taste of headache, brought on the hard-edged pain which was like an evil spirit pulling wires from my eye. I had borne four sons and lost three of them, been left only Robert, my changeling child, conceived in constrained circumstances and made counter to my own character, but still my son. And he wished only to keep me shut away.

"You have become pale," he said.

"It is what you have told me."

Robert rose from the rocker, put his hand in the pocket where I imagined his train ticket must be. "Think only upon the wholesome qualities of Bellevue Place," he advised. "And leave the persuading of Aunt Lizzie in my hands."

He crossed to me, and the taste of metal was strong as if I held a bit in my mouth. I wanted to retch, save that I knew retching would bring on the headache with the crashing of a sledge. Robert took my hand in the businesslike grip which was his custom upon leaving me, then stood examining the top of my bureau. "A small, locking box would look well here," he declared. "I shall bring you one next visit."

"You have already done more than you should have done," I told him. But he had already gone, and I do not think he heard me.

I went directly to my desk and wrote a hurried note to Myra. "Tell Mr. Wilkie he has my permission to publish," I told her. "Robert's heart remains unchanged."

I carried the note to Mrs. Patterson's office myself, for I wished it to be sent immediately. Then I returned to my room to think upon all that had occurred with my son. I did not know how Robert could want so much to keep me in the madhouse, did not know how he might believe that delft plates and lace runners would keep me content locked up with lunatics.

But above all this, I did not know how he could love me so little.

Perhaps it is because he is too different from me, I thought, *because he has never understood the reasoning behind my actions. Perhaps Robert loves me too little because he does not know me. For I have always believed that if most of us were truly known, even the worst of us would prove deserving of affection.*

What, then, if Robert were made to read the pages I write at night when I do not sleep? I asked myself. *Pages covered in the ink of my reasonings. Certainly such an exercise would lead him to acquire the understanding which eventually leads to love.*

These thoughts which came upon me this afternoon are why tonight I feel a terrific rush to finish this history, to write it to the end so I might deliver it to Robert. For I believe I am right in this theory of affection and must trust that thinking so is not my preference for unclear seeing.

* * *

On the evening of September seventeenth, 1867, I arrived at the St. Denis Hotel in New York, having come to that city for the purpose of selling my clothes and jewelry. The St. Denis was likely the most awful hotel in which I had ever stayed. The paint of its façade had been applied over the peeling layers beneath, and the narrow, five-storey building possessed the appearance of an elderly lady wearing too much of the white face paint used for daguerreotype sitting. The hotel was no more elegant inside. The gas lamps emitted light in hissing spits, and the lobby carpet smelled of dog.

Nevertheless, the St. Denis suited my purposes exactly. I required a hotel which was not expensive, and one which would preserve my anonymity, for which the St. Denis was remarkably fit, as Mrs. Lincoln, the wife of a president, would never have stayed in such a place. I, however, was traveling as Mrs. Clarke of Chicago, a lady who was presumably not as discriminating.

Once I had decided to sell my clothes, I understood that I would need someone to assist me. A gentleman would have been best, but gentlemen will always show first loyalty to their own sex and I did not wish to run the risk of Robert hearing my plan. A white lady would have been second choice, but all the white ladies I knew were too genteel for such an endeavor. The only person who would do was Lizzie Keckly. Lizzie would be loyal first to me, and was only as genteel as a lady who was half-colored could afford to be. Moreover, she was familiar with the dresses we would be selling, having stitched most of them herself. I wrote to Lizzie on the same day that my furniture was auctioned and suggested a business arrangement; if she would assist me, I would pay her New York expenses, and give her a percentage of all that we sold.

Lizzie had arrived at the St. Denis before me, and I met her in the servants' dining room, which was where those who were colored were made to wait. My friend was outfitted in the brown gabardine dress which she wore for traveling – a dress which smelled a little of engine steam and was always covered with the dust of someplace else. Together, we returned to the lobby and presented ourselves before the desk clerk – a thin young man named Furth, who was dressed as colorfully as an equatorial bird and scented as intensely as Asian lilies.

"I am Mrs. Clarke, and I have reserved two rooms together upon the second floor," I informed the perfumed young man.

Mr. Furth glanced at Lizzie's complexion. "We have no rooms on the second floor," he replied in a precise voice.

"But I have reserved them," I insisted.

He glanced at my ungloved hands. "There is only a room for you," he said to me.

"But this lady is my traveling companion."

"Colored guests must stay on the fifth floor," he informed me.

I glared through my veilings at the clerk, but before I could argue the point, Lizzie touched my fingers.

"I shall be quite comfortable upon the fifth floor, Mrs. Clarke," she said, placing emphasis upon my counterfeit name.

"If Mrs. Keckly must stay upon the fifth floor," I declared, "then put me there as well."

"Very well, madam," nodded Mr. Furth.

I had brought with me six trunks of clothing to sell in New York and arranged with the clerk to have them stored in a small ground-floor room. Then, leaving Mr. Furth scenting the lobby, Lizzie and I proceeded up an uncarpeted staircase to the fifth floor. As we climbed, the staircase grew narrower and more steep. By the third floor, my lungs were straining against the stays of my corset.

The fifth-floor rooms were shabby even by the standards of the St. Denis. The ceilings, which were just beneath the roof, sloped so severely, we were in danger of knocking our heads if we only stepped too near a corner, and the atmosphere of them was airless. The bedsteads were iron instead of wood, the washing-up basins sat upon the planked floor, as there was no stand for them, and over everything hung the syrupy scent of bedbug nests.

"Once I have caught my breath," I said to Lizzie, "I shall go downstairs and inform Mr. Furth that I am Mrs. Lincoln, and demand the two best rooms this unhappy hotel possesses."

Lizzie sat upon the bed, revealing that the mattress was filled with nothing more comfortable than straw. "If that young man learns tonight that you are Mrs. Lincoln," she told me, "tomorrow, every newspaper in New York will know it."

"I suppose you are right," I sighed. "I expect that at this moment, he is lurking among my trunks, trying to determine whether I am as white as I appear."

Lizzie and I were the only residents of the fifth floor – even colored guests knew better than to stay at the St. Denis – and our rooms stood across from each other.

"Will you leave your door open all night?" I asked her, as we made ready for bed. "I will sleep better if I can hear your breathing."

But I did not sleep, although I did listen to my friend's breathing, which came as even and measured as her stitching. I imagined that bedbugs worked their way under the wool of the stockings I had worn into bed, and that the sudden clattering of horse hooves upon the street outside was a carriage of thieves making away with my dresses. When I left off imagining this, I reminded myself the true thieves were likely the New York clothing brokers, who would cheat me and leave me with almost nothing.

The morning was bright, with the rare blue sky which comes to New York in the autumn interval between the gray heat of summer and the coal fires of winter. Lizzie and I walked up Broadway, stopping near a fountain decorated with stone goddesses for whom the sculptor had carved gowns as light and transparent-seeming as can be made in marble. This fountain marked the start of the Ladies' Mile, and all about – dipping lace handkerchiefs into the clear water, or holding the leashes of little dogs – were the ladies for which it was named; ladies dressed in walking suits of gold gabardine or plaid poplin, their heads covered not by veiled widow's bonnets, but cunning little hats of tulle and straw.

The New York ladies took less notice of Lizzie and myself than they did the marble maidens pouring water from their urns. I, however, paid much attention to them. It was the existence of these fashionable ladies which had decided me to sell my wardrobe in New York, as it was well-known that those who shopped upon lower Broadway appreciated fine clothing, and generally possessed the means with which to buy it.

Upon that first morning in New York, Lizzie and I journeyed to the less-fashionable end of Broadway and the showroom of W. H. Brady & Company, whose ad in yesterday's *Herald* had promised the "highest prices paid for jewelry of any sort." The interior of W. H. Brady & Company gave off a slightly faded glory. Standing in its high-ceilinged showroom, Lizzie and I were surrounded by marble columns, lightly crackled like eggshells, and very many statuettes of unclothed nymphs.

"Might I show you some jet, madam?" asked a frock-coated clerk, taking in my black bombazine.

"I have come with something to sell." My voice did not sound as firm as it did when I came to buy.

The clerk made a tutting noise, which I invested with more discontent than perhaps could be contained in such a small sound. "You shall have to consult with the proprietors," he told us. Then he turned and led Lizzie and me past the nymphs into a small room at the back.

This room possessed no more than an uncovered table and several wooden chairs. It was so overly lit by gas that none of the flaws of the occupants, and what they had brought to sell, could be concealed. After some minutes, we were joined by two gentlemen.

"I am William Brady," announced the stouter of the two. "And this is my partner, Samuel Keyes." Mr. Brady was portly, and Mr. Keyes so very thin, it appeared the one partner had stolen flesh from the other. In their lapels both gentlemen wore diamond stickpins of a dimension I would have deemed ostentatious, if the gentlemen had not been in the business.

"I am Mrs. Clarke," I told them. "And this is Mrs. Keckly."

The two men studied the shading of Lizzie's complexion, and I began to believe it would have been better to have introduced her as "Lizzie," or even "my servant girl."

"These are the items I wish to have brokered." I took from my reticule a velvet box containing my jewelry, and pushed it across the table.

The diamond brokers examined my pieces, raising a gemstone bracelet or pair of ruby ear knobs to the artificial light to determine how well the stones reflected. I watched the fleshy lips of Mr. Brady, the sparse eyebrows of Mr. Keyes, hoping the baubles which had driven me into debt would make them quiver with eagerness; but these gentlemen looked to have trained themselves into expressions of noncommittal scrutiny, even had they been presented with the Hope diamond itself.

Only when Mr. Keyes examined a small ring set with sapphires did his face register emotion, although it was not a happy one. "What do you make of this?" He handed the ring to his partner.

"What is it?" I asked. "Was I cheated about the sapphires?" I thought back to where I had purchased the ring – a small shop a block off Pennsylvania Avenue run by an affable man named Barksdale, who had taken it upon himself to please me by having my name engraved inside the band.

Before Mr. Brady might decipher the letters, I reached across the table to snatch the ring from his hand. "It was not my intention to sell that piece," I told him.

Mr. Brady closed his plump fingers over my ring and held it to his chest. "It says 'Mary Lincoln' inside there," he informed me.

"Indeed," I replied, "the ring was given to me by that lady."

The brokers exchanged unkind glances.

"I have heard very little regarding Mrs. Lincoln's penchant for giving away her jewelry," declared Mr. Keyes.

"I believe we are not enough in sympathy to do business."

I reached this time for the velvet box, but Mr. Keyes, who was closer, covered it with skeletal fingers. "Gentlemen in our profession are obliged to make known to the authorities any items we believe may not have been procured legitimately."

"You think that I am a thief?" I invested my tone with so much indignation, I likely sounded a thief.

"I think that you have not offered us a satisfactory explanation of how you come to be in possession of Mrs. Lincoln's ring," replied Mr. Keyes.

"Or why you hide your face behind a veil," added Mr. Brady.

"I cover my face with a veil because I am a widow," I told them. "And because I wish that I were not here selling my jewelry."

"That does not explain Mrs. Lincoln's ring," said Mr. Keyes.

The two gentlemen sat between myself and the door, and I feared that they would not let me leave.

I sat straighter upon my chair. "I possess Mrs. Lincoln's ring," I said, "because I am Mrs. Lincoln."

"And we are to believe that?" asked Mr. Keyes.

I lifted the veil from my face, hooking it onto my bonnet. "Some daguerreotypes of my likeness were circulated," I said to them, "although I am certain I appear far happier in them than I do now."

The diamond brokers studied my face as closely as they had my gemstones.

"I am unspeakably sorry to have mistrusted you," said Mr. Brady after a bit. "We had read nothing of your being in New York."

"And you introduced yourself as Mrs. Clarke," added Mr. Keyes.

"We are both loyal Republicans," declared his partner.

Mr. Brady returned my ring to the velvet box and called for the frock-coated clerk, commanding him to bring us tea. While we drank it, I explained my business in New York and asked the gentlemen if they knew of an honest dealer in secondhand clothing with whom they might acquaint me. In response, Mr. Brady sat back in his chair and pressed together his fingertips.

"I could give you a name or two," he began. "However, might I suggest a better plan?"

"I am willing to hear any plan," I told him, "for I do not possess the best confidence in my own."

"Then allow me to say with no little confidence of *my* own," the gentleman continued, "that if you would place your affairs in the hands of W. H. Brady and Company, we shall raise you one hundred thousand dollars within the week."

I could not help but smile at the stout gentleman. "I am certain that my need has caused me to overestimate the value of my wardrobe," I told him, "but even I do not believe it will fetch that high a sum."

"I do not intend to amass the money by selling your clothes," said Mr. Brady.

"Certainly, my jewels are not worth that much."

"Sadly," declared Mr. Keyes, pushing the velvet box back to me, "they are not."

"However," Mr. Brady went on, "were you to write a letter to Brady & Company asking us to dispose of your worldly goods, and describing the lamentable nature of your financial difficulties; and were Mr. Keyes and myself to show this letter to certain political gentlemen who count themselves loyal Republicans, I believe those gentlemen would lose no time in making you a donation."

"And why would they do that, Mr. Brady?"

"Because I would tell them that if the widow of Abraham Lincoln were to continue in want, I would feel compelled by simple patriotism to make her plight known to the voting populace – say, by passing her lamentable letter on to the newspapers." His fingers tapped again. "And if that voting populace were to read of Mrs. Lincoln's poverty, they might develop the idea that the Republican Party had turned its back upon the family of its Martyred President."

"Is that scheme not a form of blackmail?" I asked him.

"Only if the donor were motivated by self-interest," he replied, "rather than by the stirrings of charity."

Mr. Brady had uttered this opinion convincingly, but I knew that the plan was no better than blackmail.

"Could you not raise the money without threatening the gentlemen with publication of the letters?" I said. "Could you not just appeal to their charitable natures?"

The broker sat back and twirled his diamond stickpin. "I shall go only as far as their own dishonorableness demands."

I glanced at Lizzie, who, as a colored woman among white gentlemen, had not made comment during this exchange. Still, in the way of slaves, Lizzie possessed a silent and subtle method of showing disapproval, a straight hardness of shoulders I could now detect beneath her brown traveling suit.

"One hundred thousand dollars," Mr. Brady repeated. "And you will not have to sell even the plainest shawl."

"One hundred thousand less a modest commission to W. H. Brady & Company," amended Mr. Keyes.

I looked upon the velvet box of my jewels, which had excited no appreciable interest in the gentlemen. "Perhaps it will be enough that these politicians learn that I am in genuine want." I unhooked my veils, drawing them over my face.

"I suppose that is always possible," replied Mr. Brady.

In anticipation of the sum he felt certain he would raise, Mr. Brady made me a loan of six hundred dollars for my expenses in New York. Then he called for a carriage and sent me back to the St. Denis to write the letter he would show to the Republican gentlemen.

I penned Mr. Brady's letter resting my paper on a suitcase, for there was no desk in my room at the St. Denis. In this correspondence, I described my impoverishment and begged Messrs. Brady and Keyes to dispose of my goods "so that my sons and myself will not be driven into shameful destitution." The moment the ink was dry, I ran down the five flights of steps and instructed Mr. Furth to have the letter taken round immediately. Then I put Mr. Brady's loan to use, and moved Lizzie and myself to a less-awful hotel.

The Union Park possessed a décor of soft encasement. The carpets were two layers thick and the draperies three. With no unpleasantness, Lizzie and I were given adjoining rooms, for the Union Park was accustomed to housing ladies who traveled with their servants, and we had decided to allow Lizzie to pose as such, so that neither of us would be compelled to sleep with bugs. Once situated, we unpacked our suitcases upon overstuffed ottomans, unpinned our hair at velvet-covered vanities, and there, in the cushioned atmosphere of the Union Park, we settled in to wait for the diamond brokers to produce the one hundred thousand dollars.

However after a week's time, the gentlemen had collected nothing.

"The stirrings of charity among politicians are unusually sluggish," came a note from Mr. Brady. "I fear I have been too mild in delivering my threats of publication. I shall try the endeavor with more vigor for another week."

"Perhaps, we should attempt to sell the wardrobe ourselves," I said to Lizzie. We were seated together in the small parlor between our rooms, so surrounded by cushioning, I felt as if I were living in the velvet box which held my jewels. "If we are fortunate, whatever we get will supplement Mr. Brady and Mr. Keyes's one hundred thousand. And if we are less lucky, we will raise at least enough to pay for what it has cost for us to come here."

"We know nothing about the selling of expensive clothes," she reminded me.

"I know a great deal about buying them," I told her. "I expect I can acquire the skill."

We sent down for a newspaper and scoured the advertisements placed by secondhand clothing dealers in that day's *Herald*. At last, we decided upon a Mr. Forsythe because his ad was large and elegant, filled with a good deal of curling script. We sent a note inviting Mr. Forsythe to the Union Park to view my wardrobe and then paid a portion of Mr. Brady's money to the desk clerk, who was a plumpish young man with the pouched cheeks of a squirrel storing chestnuts, to assure us exclusive use of the Ladies' Parlor.

Lizzie and I worked the entirety of a morning, draping the thickly cushioned furniture with the most sumptuous of my gowns, and dangling from the curtain rods the richest of my fur and feather boas. At precisely noon, the two of us stood inside the door and watched Mr. Forsythe handle my clothing.

Mr. Forsythe's appearance was as elegant as his script. He was tall and slender, and his head was narrowed by fine breeding in a manner which put me in mind of the Kentucky thoroughbreds of my girlhood. "You have a discriminating aesthetic, Mrs. Clarke," he pronounced, holding to the light the seams of a changeable silk dress. "And you, Mrs. Keckly, do superior work."

For upward of an hour, Mr. Forsythe placed his refined hands upon every inch of my garments. Then, rather than committing the gaucherie of saying his offer aloud, the gentleman wrote a number upon a calling card and presented it to me with a small bow. Unfortunately, the gracefully rendered number was half of what I had hoped.

"This is somewhat less than I had anticipated," I said, risking vulgarity.

Mr. Forsythe shook his thoroughbred's head. "There are a great many widows in New York selling their wardrobes," he replied. "And not enough ladies out of mourning to buy them."

I sent away the elegant gentleman with regrets and determined that I should seek out a clothing dealer who did not spend so much upon his ad. In the following days, Lizzie and I entertained – in consideration of additional portions of Mr. Brady's money gifted to the desk clerk – a Mr. Post, whose advertisement was small and written in lettering as upright and straightforward as his name, as well as a Mr. Sweeney, whose listing was even smaller and without a border. Both of these gentlemen offered me less than the finely bred Mr. Forsythe.

"Perhaps we are going about this wrongly," I said to Lizzie, after we had shown Mr. Sweeney to the door. "Perhaps we should take the clothing directly to the shop merchants."

Lizzie, who was – for the third time – helping me remove my garments from the chairs and settees of the Ladies' Parlor, dropped an alpaca traveling suit. "We are going to carry the goods to the shops ourselves?"

I shrugged. "At least it will prevent me having to give the desk clerk any more of Mr. Brady's money."

Disregarding the great caution with which she generally treated the clothing she had stitched, Lizzie sat upon the traveling suit. "We should give this up," she said.

"You wish to end it?"

"In truth, I wish we had not begun it."

I dropped into the chair opposite, crumpling an ermine-edged cape. "If you did not agree with my plan, why did you come then?"

"Out of affection."

"It is a kindness to say so," I said, "but I do not believe that my one letter of condolence at the death of your son would be enough to send you to New York to participate in a scheme of which you do not approve."

Lizzie lifted the sleeve of the alpaca suit and examined her own stitching.

"You are the wife of Abraham Lincoln," she said, "who has done so much for my race. I could not refuse to do anything for you."

"At least it is a noble reason," I said. "Noble enough that we should not waste it."

The following morning, I hired us a closed carriage, which Lizzie and I filled with as many of the gowns as we could carry. Then we set off for Seventh Avenue, where were located the shops known to deal in secondhand merchandise. We stopped first at Rose & Company, a gilt emporium, nearly as opulent as those upon lower Broadway.

"We deal only with brokers!" exclaimed the Rose & Company clerk, waving white-gloved hands over Lizzie and myself, as if casting a spell of disappearance.

"I wish to see Mr. Rose," I told him.

Mr. Rose did not bother to greet us, only pushed a pile of corset covers from his desk to the floor and indicated that we were to spread my things in their place.

"We do not generally purchase private collections," he said, lifting the hem of one of my gowns. "One knows so little about where they have been."

"These clothes have moved in the most exclusive of social circles," I assured him, for the dress he was looking beneath had been worn in the presence of Prince Napoleon.

Mr. Rose offered a sum which was the smallest I had yet been told.

"That is not very much," I said.

"The dresses have been worn," he replied. "And only by you, Mrs. Clarke, whom nobody has heard of."

"That is only one store and one merchant," I said to Lizzie in the carriage. "We shall do better at another place."

But we did not do better. Lizzie and I carried our armloads of dresses through one gilted entrance after another, only to have the merchants inform us that such extravagant fashion was not suited to these times of Reconstruction.

The squirrel-cheeked clerk was waiting for us in the Union Park's well-padded lobby when we returned. "A man from the newspapers was here this afternoon," he said, "and was exceedingly curious about your trunks."

"Why would a newspaperman be interested in my trunks?" I asked him.

"It was the writing upon the side."

"Writing?"

"Come and see," said the desk clerk. He led us into the storage room behind the lobby, a crowded space filled with the trunks of guests and cast-off draperies. "The words are faded. But in good light, they are still readable."

"Let me see." I pushed past him, my arms still full of dresses.

"You see, it is just there."

The clerk pointed to two lines of chalked writing on the side of my trunk which must have escaped my notice. "Mrs. A. Lincoln, Springfield," spelled the letters.

"When the newspaperman saw it," the clerk continued, "he ran right out of the hotel."

"Make up my bill," I told him. "And call back the carriage."

Our weariness replaced by frenetic energy, Lizzie and I ran about our rooms, pitching slippers and nightdresses and unboxed bonnets into our suitcases.

"If the newspapermen never see me," I told her, "they cannot say for certain that I was here."

"But where can we go where you will not be recognized as Mary Lincoln?"

"I will send a note to Mr. Brady," I said, "and ask him to tell us a hotel."

We left the Union Park in a rush, instructing the carriage driver to take us first in the wrong direction before circling back to the hotel which Mr. Brady had suggested. As a further precaution, once we had arrived at the Brandreth House, I sent in the driver to report to me upon every person who might be lurking behind the lobby's very many potted palms. But the only gentlemen waiting there for me were Mr. Brady and Mr. Keyes.

"Might we speak for a few minutes?" asked Mr. Brady.

"You have news for me?" I said.

The stout man nodded and then, with a word to the desk clerk, led Lizzie and me into the Ladies' Parlor.

The Ladies' Parlor of the Brandreth House was not so tremendously cushioned as that of the Union Park, although it did contain a great many curio cabinets which held trays upon trays of impaled moths, their soft bodies pierced by needles.

Mr. Brady and Mr. Keyes seated themselves side by side beneath a flaming gasolier.

"I have been strongly impressed by the hard-heartedness of my fellow Republicans," began Mr. Brady.

"You have collected nothing?" I squinted against the light the gasolier reflected from the gentlemen's diamond stickpins.

"I fear the gentlemen believe you have been profligate," said Mr. Keyes. "And it is well-recognized that gentlemen disapprove of profligate ladies."

"I see no solution but to sell my wardrobe for whatever I can get," I told the brokers, "and hope that it is enough to pay back what I have spent here."

"That is not the only solution," declared Mr. Brady.

"How can it not be?" I asked. "I have already used too much of my money – and yours, Mr. Brady – attempting to sell my clothes. And as I have seen tonight, if I remain in New York much longer, the newspapers will expose me and my scheme."

"That is precisely our plan!" announced Mr. Keyes.

I looked with incredulousness upon the two gentlemen. "You must realize that I cannot agree to such a plan," I told them. "Do you not think it would result in much scandal if it became known that the widow of the Martyred President was peddling her wardrobe to pay her bills?"

"What I think," said Mr. Brady, "is that it will result in a good deal of money."

"I am afraid, sir, that the time you have passed attempting to acquire funds from politicians has altered your reason."

The stout broker smiled. "You have had very little luck selling the wardrobe of Mrs. Clarke, have you not?" he asked me.

"I have had no luck."

"The wardrobe of the former First Lady, however," Mr. Keyes continued for his partner. "Now, that would possess a more fortuitous outcome."

"Indeed," concurred Mr. Brady. "What lady would not wish to own the gown that danced at a presidential inauguration? The dress which dined with generals?"

I blinked against the flashing of the brokers' stickpins. "And do you not believe that such a venture would disgrace me?"

"I assure you, Mr. Keyes and I would handle the business with the utmost delicacy and discretion," replied Mr. Brady.

"How could you accomplish such a thing?"

"We would begin by placing your entire wardrobe on public exhibition."

I let out a disbelieving laugh. "That would be your notion of discretion?"

Mr. Brady tapped together those ample fingertips. "The exhibition would be handled in the most genteel manner. Only to give the ladies of fashion the opportunity to see for themselves the exquisite taste and richness of the items. Once your wardrobe has been displayed for some weeks – long enough to create a good deal of interest – we will sell all of it at auction."

"Auction provokes purchasers to greater expenditures," Mr. Keyes informed me.

"Still," I protested, "it seems I will be made very public."

"You shall be removed," said Mr. Brady.

"Yes, you should return to Chicago," agreed Mr. Keyes, "leaving Mrs. Keckly here to oversee your interests."

I did not need to glance at the sofa to know the set of Lizzie's shoulders. However, a day spent attempting to peddle my used dresses on Seventh Avenue had proved that my friend's opinion was one more of the luxuries I could no longer afford.

"Once you have left New York," continued Mr. Brady, "we will forward the letter you wrote to us to the newspapers."

"Oh no, Mr. Brady!" I cried out. "It is enough that I let you show it to the political gentlemen. You cannot publish in newspapers the letter I wrote to you about my poverty."

"But it is good business to do so," he replied. "Such a letter will create sympathy for your cause, and touch upon the tenderness of the ladies who will be bidding for your gowns."

"To be sure," agreed Mr. Keyes. "The letter alone could increase the proceeds by twenty-five percent."

I glanced into the curio cabinets, at the soft creatures, trapped upon velvet-covered boards. *Robert will not want this,* I thought. *He will not want me to say in the newspapers that we are poor.*

Then again, what choice am I left?

"All right, Mr. Brady," I told the broker. "I shall trust to your discretion."

I left New York the following day. Lizzie remained behind, moving to a house which belonged to friends she had met while raising funds for the contrabands, for no colored person could remain at the Brandreth House without a white companion. My letter to Messrs. Brady and Keyes, and the notice of my clothing sale, would appear in the New York newspapers in three days' time, the same day upon which my wardrobe would go on display in the windows of W. H. Brady & Company. Wishing to know if Mr. Brady had handled this as discreetly as he had promised, the morning after all was to occur I went early to a newsstand near Chicago's Union Depot which received the New York papers directly from the train.

The area around the railroad station was one I did not frequent. It was near to the slaughterhouses and the air which surrounded it was filled with the hot stench of frightened animals, and on occasion, a screaming which I sometimes mistook for human. Though it was early, the people coming and going from the station already appeared as frenzied as the doomed creatures; German families shouted at each other in their harsh tongue, gentlemen from the train chased after empty carriages, and Irish immigrants and freed Negroes fought over the right to carry ladies' trunks. This was the first week in October, and though the wind in the rest of the city possessed a chaste crispness, here at the depot, it was hot and fetid and full of agitation.

I wove among swarming newsboys, who waited to buy the papers they would sell for a penny more in the better districts, searching the stacks for the *Herald*, or the *New York World*. But I had arrived so early, the New York papers were still sitting upon the platform at the side of the newsstand, still tied up with twine. I bent to read them, raising the edge of my mourning veil, and between the lashings upon the front page, I read the words "Mrs. Lincoln" and "Secondhand Clothing Sale," and then could read no more.

This cannot be! Mr. Brady promised me discretion, not the news that I had been obliged to sell my wardrobe upon the front page! In a panic, I tore at the twine which kept the papers bound, pulling at it until it sliced my palm.

"You must wait!" shouted the vendor, a German man with the

white eyelashes of an albino, who was engaged in selling a packet of snuff to a woman in a calico dress. "I come with a knife."

When the lashings were cut, I grabbed up all the New York papers, for all of them carried stories about me. *Read these at home,* I told myself, *not upon this busy street where someone might recognize you.* But I could not make myself wait the minutes it would take me to return to the Clifton House, and I pulled aside my veil and read every paper.

"Mrs. Lincoln's gowns are hard-worn and overpriced," declared one. "They are stained upon the lining and beneath the arms." "Their taste is vulgar and they are unwearable," said another, "being cut too low at the neck in consideration of that lady's appreciation of her own bust."

It was not only my gowns which the writers criticized, but myself as well. One paper branded me a "mercenary prostitute," another a "termagant of cupidity." Still another claimed that in order to pay for such a wardrobe, I had received bribes in exchange for political office, stolen the silver from the President's house, sold my husband's speeches and even – after his death – his linen undergarments.

All that I read was so much worse than anything which had been printed of me before, worse than anything I might have imagined. I stood gasping beside the news vendor's lean-to, pulling at air rank with the fear of animals. By tomorrow, this scandal would be carried by newspapers in Chicago – as well as in Boston and Philadelphia and Washington City, and everyplace else in the country where papers were printed. By end of day, all the anonymity I had been at such pains to preserve would be torn away, and I would be left as exposed as if I stood naked beside my secondhand gowns in Mr. Brady's window.

I felt eyes upon me, and glancing up, I saw that one of the Irish immigrants was staring hard at my uncovered face. I tugged upon my veil so violently, a section of it tore from my bonnet and made to take a step into the street, but was yanked back upon the platform by the Irishman.

"You must let me go!" I insisted.

"You'll be trampled," he said.

Looking out, I saw he spoke the truth; for while I had been reading, a railroad car carrying hogs had been unloaded, and the entire roadway was filled with the careening bodies of pigs headed for the slaughterhouse. Holding my veil closed against the dust raised by the hogs, I waited, wishing I might also shut out their horrible squealing, which sounded as if the creatures knew where they were headed, and what would happen to them there.

I remained upon the platform only until the herders came whipping the last straggling hogs with bamboo poles, then lifted my skirts and ran into the street, dropping the New York newspapers in the mud churned up by the creatures' hooves. I ran all the way back to the Clifton House, my veil pressed so tightly against my mouth, I could taste the dye in it. Letting myself in, I hurried up to my room, yanking the mourning bonnet from my head with such violence, I sent pins skittering down the hallway.

My room was not empty. Robert was there, pacing the circle of my small hearth rug, as if he wished to force it through the floor with his feet. My son was pale – paler than I imagined myself to be – and his hands shook as severely as his father's had done when he was on the Blue Mass. I did not need to ask whether Robert had seen the New York papers, for there was one clutched in his hand.

"This is what was delivered to my club this morning!" He slapped the newspaper against the back of a ragged hearth chair. "This is what I am given to read while I drink coffee with my colleagues!"

I was short of breath from running, and had no defense for this disgrace I should have seen would come. Robert slapped the paper again upon the chair back, then unfolded it and began to read to me.

"*Why does this dreadful woman persist upon forcing her repugnant individuality before the world?*" declared my son, his voice tainted with as much loathing as the words. "*Why is she so unable to make herself attractively suppliant? If Mrs. Lincoln had kept to her true mission as a mother and wife, she would not have so discredited her sex and injured the name of her country and her husband.*"

I busied myself at the small bricked hearth. "Please do not read me any more."

"But there is just this last bit," he said venomously. "*The most charitable construction Mary Lincoln's friends can put on her strange course is that she is insane. It is the opinion of many that Mrs. L is deranged – has been for years – and that she will end her life in a lunatic asylum.*"

"Doubtless," I replied, "they would like me to begin now." I rose from the hearth and went to him, standing so near I could see how the ends of his mustache were broken. "I cannot help what the newspapers write about me."

"Do you know what all Chicago is saying about me?" my son exclaimed. "They are saying that Robert Lincoln neglects his lunatic mother."

"I am not lunatic," I told him. "I am only desperate."

"Are you so very certain?"

I wished that Robert had hit me with the newspaper rather than speaking this, and was obliged to tell myself it was only that the humiliation was so very public which had caused him to say what he could not mean. "I am sorry," I told him. "I know how little you wish to bring attention to yourself."

"I am not certain you do know it," he replied, "as it is an attitude so very foreign to your own nature."

"That is a cruelty."

Robert threw himself into the hearth chair with such force I thought it would splinter. "Do you wish to know what a cruelty is?" he said to me. "When you are a child and you possess an imperfection?"

Robert had never mentioned his flawed eye, even when he was a child. "You told me nothing," I replied. "I only remember that the other children were sometimes harsh about your eye."

"They waited for me, those other children," he said, "the sons and daughters of shopkeepers and political men who inhabited our neighborhood. They waited at the corner and followed me to any empty lot or deserted side street – any place there was no adult to watch them. Then they pushed me into the middle of their pack, surrounded me so that I would not miss it when they contorted their own eyes, skewing them until they had made themselves cross-eyed and they had turned their faces into the faces of idiots. All in imitation of me." My son rubbed at the canted eye as if to force it straight. "I believed it was my own fault they did this. That I possessed a defect more profound than a crossed eye."

I recalled Robert as a child – a stiff little boy made to look through keyholes to straighten his eye – and wished that he had told all this to me sooner, when he could have benefited most from the fierce comforting mothers save for sons. I knelt beside his chair and pulled his hand from his eye. "I have never believed you defective," I told him.

Robert glanced away, as if this did not matter. "I would like to live the rest of my life without any more of such attention," said my son.

I took hold of the hand which had rubbed so hard at his eye. "I shall try to see that you do."

He dropped his glance to the beaten newspaper still in his lap. "I wish you to call off the auction of your clothing."

"I wish that I might call it off as well," I told him, "but I must have the money."

Robert sprang from his seat, stood over me, shouting. "What is this obsession with money?"

"I have debts. Far more of them than you know about."

"Debts? From what?"

"From the clothing in Mr. Brady's window. From the trunks filled with gloves and stockings and unworn shoes. From all the things that I bought to keep us safe."

"To keep us safe?"

"It was the war," I told him, "and there was the stench of gangrene in Washington City." I raised myself from the floor. "Taddie was sickly. Men wished to assassinate your father. You wanted to go to the army. All I might do to protect you was to build a fortress made of slippers and tea sets and candlesticks."

Robert shook his head. "Judge Davis has said that you were not rational about money."

I looked up at him in surprise. "Judge Davis said this?"

"He is an important man and much information comes to him."

"What has he said exactly?"

"That you did not know how to control your spending, and that without controls, you would squander everything you were given."

With this, a recognition fell upon me which burned away even the shame of the stories in the New York newspapers. "Is that the reason the judge has delayed settling the estate? So that I would not squander my inheritance?"

Robert took so long to speak, my question no longer seemed to require an answer. "I want your assurance that you will call off this sale."

"If the auction of my clothing is cancelled," I told him, "the attention we shall receive will be even more discomfiting. Before the month is out, the newspapers will be declaring that not only is your mother a lunatic, she also does not pay her debts."

Robert hurled his crumpled paper into the hearth and turned upon me. "If I knew a way to make you stop," he declared, "I would use it."

Every afternoon, I visited a different newsstand to see if someone else's scandal had pushed mine from notice. I ran this errand beneath yards of bombazine, for I did not wish to be recognized. Still, I could never compel myself to move more than a block from the newsstand before stopping to scour the pages for my name. And I could never look away from what had been written about me, in the way that one cannot turn from the collision of two carriages.

As was usual with disgraces which absorb the public, mine acquired a name – "Mrs. Lincoln's Old Clothes Scandal." And for all that October not one week passed without some editorial upon my dishonorableness. "Will not somebody, for very shame's sake, go and take away those dry goods the widow of the late Lamented persists in exposing for sale?" decried one. While others contented themselves by naming me "intensely vulgar," "unprincipled and avaricious," and "a woman of incredible impulses." As the November elections drew near, the Democrats turned my clothes into politics, claiming they represented the rewards of favors bought from my husband's administration. One newspaper learned how the gardener Mr. Watt had padded his accounts for me, and this money, it was claimed, I squandered upon the clothing in Mr. Brady's window. I became the symbol of Republican corruption and could not have been more condemned had I committed murder in every city in the Union. Indeed, upon some days, I was certain that the passengers on the streetcar, the blood-spattered men coming from the slaughterhouse, the ladies in fragile hats on their way to State Street, all knew it was myself devouring newspapers on the corner, and that they would set upon me out of loathing.

I brought none of these newspapers back to my rooms at the Clifton House, for fear that my youngest son would see them. And when I took Taddie out upon the Chicago streets, I was grateful that his reading was poor. From Robert I heard nothing more, save for an abruptly worded note informing me that he was going for a time to Boston, where he believed he might "remain more anonymous."

The newspapers' stories did little to benefit the selling of my wardrobe. "The ladies who can afford your things do not want them,"

Lizzie Keckly wrote me from New York, "for they have been made to believe that such luxuries were gotten out of bribery and theft. Mr. Brady has had to turn his attention upon those gentlemen who might buy the dresses out of charity and pity at your poverty." I wrote to Mr. Brady myself and asked that he set the date for the auction as soon as he believed he had any buyers, for I could see that Mrs. Lincoln's Old Clothes Scandal would not disappear from the newspapers until my dresses did from the broker's window. The broker wrote back and let me know that the sale would be held in the second week of November.

One afternoon, in the week before my auction was to take place, I visited the newsstand upon the corner of State and Madison Streets. It was a large stand, constructed of plank-boards painted with advertisements for plug tobacco and the rolled cigarettes known as Turkish Orientals. I bought my paper from the vendor and stood reading it in the shelter of a wall upon which was drawn the image of a camel.

On this afternoon there was no story about my clothing sale, nor one about how I had cheated the government to buy dresses. I felt the easing which came upon the days the newspapers did not write about me, and was about to fold away the paper, when my eye was caught by a small, bordered notice at the bottom of the front page. "Announcement of the Settling of the Estate of Abraham Lincoln," read the headline; and near to the bottom was the information, "whereby the sum of $110,000 shall be equally divided between the widow and the two sons."

I lifted my veiling to know if what I had read had been only a distortion caused by the netting before my eyes, for neither my son nor Judge Davis had written to me that my husband's estate was near to being settled. Once I had examined the notice again and knew that it was true, I leaned against the painted camel and calculated. My third of this inheritance would come to a little over thirty-six thousand – a good deal of money, certainly. However, not enough, with what remained of my debts, to both buy a house and retain enough income to live upon.

There is always the clothing sale, I reminded myself, before the breathlessness could start. *That amount, if Mr. Brady is even a little successful, will make the difference.* And I determined to fix all my hopes upon the auction.

But, the following days brought letters from both Lizzie and

Mr. Brady. "As it has been made public that Mr. Lincoln's estate has been settled," wrote my friend, "interest in buying your clothing out of charity has vanished. No gentleman, no matter how philanthropic, feels obligated to assist a widow who will receive one-third of one hundred and ten thousand dollars." Mr. Brady's note was even more direct. "In light of your inheritance," he informed me, "there is no point in holding an auction – particularly when there are no bidders. With your permission, I shall remove your items from our windows and prepare a bill for our expenses and our time."

Ten days after I learned of my inheritance, Judge Davis arrived in Chicago to discuss the distribution of my husband's estate. Robert arranged for us to meet with the judge at his own offices in the Marine Bank Building on LaSalle Street. Robert was now junior partner in the firm of Scammon & Lincoln, having recently started a law practice with Charles Scammon, the son of the man with whom he had apprenticed. The furnishings of Robert's offices were spare, although he had hung a collection of watercolor landscapes – vistas in which appeared no people to distract from the contemplation of purpled mountains and artistically clouded skies. It had lately become popular among lawyers to hang a daguerreotype or painted portrait of Mr. Lincoln upon their walls; Robert's office, however, did not possess one.

The firm of Scammon & Lincoln was located up four flights of steep steps. Robert and I, waiting in the lightly furnished office, heard Judge Davis arrive long before we saw him, for the enormous judge announced his presence with a labored puffing which sounded very like a locomotive being forced to climb stairs. It was some time before Judge Davis stood in the doorway, gasping and wiping at his dripping forehead with a handkerchief.

Upon spotting him, Robert leapt to his feet. "Sit here, Judge!" he exclaimed, putting a hand upon the back of his own desk chair. "It is the most accommodating."

My son held the chair steady until Judge Davis had completed the process of settling his mountainous self into it, then asked him many solicitous questions about his journey, which the judge answered with no more than a wave of his soaking handkerchief. I waited only until Robert had finished before putting my own question to the judge.

"The newspapers are remarkably knowledgeable about the

progress of Mr. Lincoln's estate," I said to him. "Do you not think I should have been as well-informed?"

The judge wiped at his face one last time, then tucked the handkerchief into his waistcoat pocket. "I have brought all the pertinent documents if you wish to become well-informed now, Mrs. Lincoln," he replied. Judge Davis glanced at a leather satchel he had dropped upon the floor beside his seat, and which his bulk prevented him from now reaching. Robert sprang up to retrieve the satchel for the judge. From inside the leather bag, the large man removed a substantial stack of papers, and set them upon Robert's desk.

"As you can see, it has been a complex business and there is much to look over."

I reached for the papers, but before I could take hold of them, the judge placed a swollen hand atop the pile.

"Or," he said, "in the interest of time, we might proceed directly to the disbursement."

I left my hand upon the edge of the desk. "I should like to review all that you have done on our behalf."

"Do you imagine Judge Davis has been dishonest?" asked Robert.

"I am a widow now," I replied, "and must become accustomed to keeping track of my own accounts." In truth, I would have been surprised to learn that Judge Davis had been deceitful, as his regard for Mr. Lincoln would have made that impossible. I only wished to prove before the judge – and my son – that I was not entirely irrational about money. "I shall read them over with some speed," I assured the gentlemen.

I moved my hand nearer to the stack of papers, but Judge Davis kept the weight of his own upon them. For some moments, he stared hard into my face, and only when I did not look away did he raise his hand.

While the men waited, I read the details of the two and a half years which the judge had required to settle the estate, how he had invested the money and what amounts had been paid to whom. As I made my way through the documents, I tried not to glance at my son's knee jerking with impatience, the judge's heavy hands splayed upon the desk, as if the fingers themselves were anxious for the return of the papers. Indeed, I read more quickly than I would have wished, and nearly missed a number which looked to me an error.

"You must fix this," I told the judge. "It shows here that Robert has received more than twice the amount given to Taddie and myself." I placed the page upon the desk so he might see the mistake.

Judge Davis cast his flesh-narrowed eyes at my son. Robert leaned forward and dropped a hand over the numbers.

"I have taken some loans against my portion," he told me. "For one or two small investments. And to refurbish my apartments."

The shock of this drew bands about my throat so tight I do not know how I forced the question, save that I had to hear the truth behind it. "Judge Davis has made you loans?"

"The requests were reasonable," the judge answered for my son.

I turned to the bloated figure sitting behind Robert's desk. "I asked you for a loan to buy a house," I recalled for him.

"That seemed an extravagance."

"A house for myself and my sons is an extravagance?"

My voice came shrill, causing to pass between the judge and my son a glance full of telepathy, a glance which made me recall how Robert had said that if he could think of a way to stop my clothing sale he would. *Is it too much of a leap*, I thought, *to imagine that if Robert and the judge could engage in the duplicity of the loans, they might also engage in the duplicity of settling the estate in time to halt my sale?*

But I could not let myself think this. For if I did, I might come to hate my son, and I had already lost too much family.

"What can the making of any loans matter now?" Robert was saying. "When you are about to get all of your money?"

"You are right," I told him. "Let us sign the papers, and send Judge Davis back to Washington City."

The estate was settled in November, and by January my "vulgar" and "hard-worn" dresses were returned to Chicago. My jewelry came back as well, less one diamond ring kept back by Mr. Brady to settle the loan he had made me and provide for the time he had dedicated to my cause. As I had not sold any of the clothing I had taken to New York, I could not give Lizzie Keckly anything from the proceeds. But now that I had some money, I thought I might make her comfortable in Chicago, for I missed her company.

"Come here and share my fortunes," I wrote to Lizzie. "I have not inherited much, but it is enough to employ you for the winter stitching new dresses. Come, for you are my best living friend."

Lizzie did not reply to this letter, nor to the many others I sent her, and I began to worry for my friend. I wrote directly to those acquaintances with whom she had been stopping in New York, but they sent back a note which read, "Mrs. Keckly has moved, and left no address." Then I wrote to all her friends in Washington City, who informed me she had not returned there.

I feared some harm had come to Lizzie in that jeopardous Eastern city. I felt also responsible, for I had brought her to New York with the promise of money, and then had had none to pay her. I wrote to all the ladies I knew there, hoping she might have taken work as a dressmaker and I might find her that way. But no one had heard of her, and by April, I had run out of those to ask.

Meantime, Taddie and I had left the Clifton House and taken rooms on West Washington Street, not far from the cream-colored house which still belonged to me, but in which I could not afford to live. Although we continued to board, our rooms were much improved from the Clifton House, for they were furnished with velvet lampshades, heavy draperies, and rosewood furniture very much like that which Mr. Butters had sold for me. Robert kept an apartment near his office. It was very small, he informed me. Far too small for social calls.

Taddie continued at his academy, studying "not so diligently as would be wished," according to his instructor, but at least not hiding from him. Robert worked at his law practice. And I wrote letters, attended magnetic circles, and for the first time since my bills had found their way to Chicago, did not grow breathless at opening the mail. When the weather improved with spring, I went for walks, generally to the shops on State Street. I went not so much to buy, as to pretend I might buy, to run my fingers over the finely turned legs of a cherrywood table or the smooth hemmings of linen bedcovers, as if I possessed a house of my own in which to use them.

Upon one such outing, near the close of April, I stopped before the window of Everode's Booksellers. It was a changeable day, the sky alternately a vivid blue, then the color of coal smoke and spitting rain, and I had ducked beneath the awning of the bookseller's to get out of the wet. Thinking to indulge myself with a spirit novel by Edward Bulwer-Lytton or the lady writer Elizabeth Stuart Phelps, I gazed into the window, and saw there a boldly lettered sign, the writing so large it appeared to be announcing news of tremendous significance. "Newly published by G.W. Carleton & Company, a Literary Thunderbolt!" it declared. *"Behind the Scenes; or Thirty Years a Slave, and Four Years in the White House* by Mrs. Elizabeth Keckly."

To see my friend's name in the window of the bookseller's was a shock. To see it attached to a book about myself an even larger astonishment. But I could not believe that it was real. *Lizzie would never betray me in this way,* I thought. *It is somebody else posing as my friend, intending to ruin her name and mine for the profit. But I will examine the book, which can only be filled with lies and invention, and prove it false to the newspapers, and to the publisher. And they shall be forced to retract all that is in it.*

I pulled open the door to the bookshop, jangling the bell harshly. Inside the air was close and smelled of molding paper and silverfish. The shop was tiny, with tall stacks of books piled upon the floor and shelves set so close together there was not room for the skirts of the ladies who squeezed between them. However, space had been found near the front for a large table devoted only to the book which was supposed to be Lizzie's. It was covered with a great many volumes bound in green leather and another boldly lettered sign, this one proclaiming, "Great Sensational Disclosure! Having much to say of a startling nature in regard to men and things in the White House and New York!"

I did not want to buy the book – which cost two dollars, as much as a novel by Monsieur Hugo, or the Misses Brontë – for I did not wish to contribute to the publisher's deceitfulness. I only wished to read one lie in it, one invention which I might use to prove it false. Lifting a leather-bound volume from the table, I opened to the inside cover, where, below Lizzie's name, I read the words "Formerly a slave, but more recently modiste and friend to Mrs. Abraham Lincoln." Upon the facing page was a pen and ink drawing of Lizzie in a beaded capelet, which had once belonged to me. This rendering looked so very accurate, I wondered if Lizzie had ever had a daguerreotype made in this little cape. But Lizzie Keckly was not a vain woman, and as far as I knew, had only sat once for her likeness – before I had given her the capelet.

"Might I assist you, madam?" inquired a voice as dry as the turning of pages. The speaker was a pear-formed man with squinted eyes whom I took to be Mr. Everode.

"No, no," I told him, replacing the book upon the table. "I desire no attention."

I waited until the bookseller had moved away to help a lady find a volume of poetry, then retrieved the volume and carried it to a corner where I might look through it unobserved. As the book was new, its leaves had not yet been cut, and for every two pages I could see, two were hidden from me. I opened it to the middle and partway down the page read the following: "I am sorry to say that Mrs. Lincoln's foresight in regard to the future was only confined to cast-off clothing, as she owed, at the time of the President's death, different store bills amounting to seventy thousand dollars. Mr. Lincoln knew nothing of these bills, and the only happy feature of his assassination was that he died in ignorance of them."

My face inflamed behind my veils to find the debts, which I had debased myself to keep secret, not only revealed, but made larger, in a book which anyone might buy. Keeping an eye for the bookseller, I turned the pages of the volume in my hands, stopping to read when I saw printed there the name of my youngest son. The start of the story about Taddie was hidden in the uncut pages, but it did not matter for I recalled it well. Shortly after Mr. Lincoln was killed, I had begun giving Taddie lessons in reading – more, I think, to distract us both, than to make any progress teaching him his letters. Upon the day of the story recounted, we were going through a small primer containing woodcut pictures of animals, and I had just asked Taddie to tell me what the letters upon the page – A . . . P . . . E . . . – spelled.

"Monkey!" exclaimed my son, glancing at the picture.

"No," I said him. "It does not spell monkey."

"It does so," he insisted. And then he had shown the page to Lizzie, who was with us, and asked "Yib" for that is as close as he could come to speaking her name. "Yib, isn't this a monkey? And don't A . . . P . . . E . . . spell monkey?"

I remember then that Lizzie corrected him very kindly. But the Lizzie Keckly who had written the book wrote less kindly, ". . . it occurs to me that had Tad been a Negro boy," she said, "not the son of a President, and so difficult to instruct, he would have been called thick-skulled, and would have been held up as an example of the inferiority of race."

My face burned more hotly now, not with shame, but with fury at how my friend had exposed my son. Taddie was fifteen, and while he could not speak clearly, and could not read much better than he had when he had mistaken A . . . P . . . E . . . for monkey, he felt nothing lightly. My youngest son's affections were intense and furious – as was his sensitivity to slight.

What else has she written, I wondered, *while I have been writing letters to everyone in New York and worrying over her?* I rifled through the uncut pages, searching for the listing of chapters. Only the second page of them could be read: "Chapter XV, The Secret History of Mrs. Lincoln's Wardrobe in New York, Chapter XI, The Assassination of President Lincoln," and the Appendix, in which Lizzie had published my letters to her. Looking across the crowded bookshop to see that Mr. Everode was occupied, I removed a hat pin from my reticule and used its sharpened end to cut open the leaves. "Chapter VI," I saw upon the newly opened page, "Willie Lincoln's Death-bed."

Only to see the words – "Willie Lincoln's Death-bed" – rendered in printer's ink made it feel that my son's death was happening again. The bookcases, too filled and too close together, felt precarious, like impending doom, like grief about to break. I found it difficult to see – I might have been shedding tears without knowing it – and as I tried to put away the hat pin before Mr. Everode noticed me, I stabbed myself upon its point. I had to know what Lizzie had written about Willie's death, how much of our grief she had put upon the page for the world to witness, but I could not read the chapter in this place where the bookshelves might come crashing down upon me. I paid Mr. Everode the two dollars for the book, praying that the money – those very same coins – would find their way into Lizzie's palm and burn it everlastingly, like hellfire.

Once home, I took a knife to Lizzie's book, and in the small, heavily draped parlor of my rooms read about my middle son's death. Lizzie had recalled how Willie had grown "weaker and more shadowlike" as the reception drew near, how upon the night of the event, the playing of the Marine Band "came to the sickroom in soft, subdued murmurs, like the wild, faint sobbing of far-off spirits." She recalled, too, Mr. Lincoln's grief, and placed it upon her pages for the world's entertainment. "He buried his head in his hands, and his tall frame was convulsed with emotion," she wrote. "His grief unnerved him, and made him a weak, passive child." Of my own sorrow, she said, "In one of her paroxysms of grief the President kindly bent over his wife, took her by the arm, and gently led her to the window. With a stately, solemn gesture, he pointed to the lunatic asylum.

"Do you see that large white building on the hill yonder? Try and control your grief, or it will drive you mad, and we may have to send you there."

But there was no lunatic asylum in sight of the President's House; and though in the days which followed Willie's dying, I would have prayed for lunacy if it might remove the clarity of my grief, my husband had never spoken those words to me. Lizzie Keckly, the woman who had helped me bathe my dead son and come to me after the handsome assassin put a bullet into my husband's brain had not only taken the things which belonged to my family and set them down for anyone who possessed two dollars, she had also told lies to make the world believe that I was near to lunacy.

I stared at the volume I had let fall to my lap, and it was as if the green cover of Lizzie's book had turned itself to bile – bitter and putrefying. With a cry, I pushed the book onto the floor, unable to tolerate it upon my skirts. Skirts which had been stitched by this woman who had exposed all the failings and vanities I had not thought necessary to hide from her. Lizzie Keckly's fingers had been upon every inch of my dress, and like the book in which she had written my secrets, I could not bear to have her handiwork so near to my flesh. I filled my fists with the stiff, overdyed fabric and pulled upon it until Lizzie's careful stitching gave way and the skirt tore from the bodice. The noise of the stitches ripping, the undoing of Lizzie's labor, made me feel as if I had become buoyant, filled with a lightness which was intoxicating. It was the same terrible satisfaction I had felt upon the day I had torn apart Elizabeth's favorite gown, after she had encouraged me to put hoops in my shift. I kept tearing at the dress until it was little more than unsewn lengths of fabric, the way it had been before she had ever touched it. Then I pulled out all the thread which had traveled through Lizzie's fingers, throwing it into the hearth, where I set fire to it. I burned the book right after, though the leather cover filled my rooms with an oily, foul-smelling smoke.

Unlike the newspapers which had reported upon the scandal of my clothing sale, Lizzie's book did not send Robert to my rooms to slap the green volume against my furniture. I received instead a curt note instructing me to write no letters to newspapers denouncing the author, and advising me to not mention Lizzie's name in any of my private correspondence. "I shall go to my solicitor and see if we can have no more copies printed," he wrote. "Meantime, if we shut the book away from our notice, I believe it will cease to draw attention."

However, Lizzie's book did not cease to draw attention. For weeks, the newspapers continued full of mention of it. "Has the American public no word of protest against the assumption that its literary taste is of so low grade as to tolerate the back-stairs gossip of negro servant girls?" declared one. "What family of eminence that employs a negro is safe from such desecration?" asked another. And while this outrage was in some measure sympathetic to myself – due less to any regard in which the editors held me, than to my whiteness – it mostly served to place the book more in the public eye. Indeed, the volume was so well-known, within a month of its release, an anonymous satire of it was published; a similarly green-covered volume entitled *Behind the Seams; by a Nigger Woman Who Took Work in from Mrs. Lincoln.*

It was not only Lizzie's book which drew attention, but also myself and my youngest son. I expect that Robert was also subject to more scrutiny, but did not know for certain, as I heard very little from him during this time. I was protected by the veils of mourning, which I wore doubled over my face when I went out, turning the world into a filmed and dismal place. Taddie, however, was stared upon by anyone who recognized him from the daguerreotypes printed during the time he had been a president's son. The attention made him forget to place his tongue where it would render his speech clearer, and at times he become incomprehensible even to me. One evening, when I took him to a brasserie which was bright and noisy, and generally so crowded I did not think we would be noticed, a large lady at the next table exclaimed to her companions, "That is Abraham Lincoln's son!"

We attempted to ignore the lady, but she pointed at Taddie, and spoke in a voice which carried over the noise of the restaurant.

"He cannot learn to read," she announced. And then she told for her companions the story of how Taddie had believed that A . . . P . . . E . . . spells monkey.

For the rest of the dinner my son stayed quiet. I could not engage him in any talk, even of when Robert might marry Mary Harlan, a favorite subject of his. Not until we had left the brasserie and were in the dark of a carriage did he speak more than two words.

"Am I very stupid?" he asked.

I put my hand upon his cheek. "Not stupid at all," I said to him. "Your father always believed that it was your mind which worked most like his."

"That was Willie," he told me.

After that night I began to think about taking Taddie away from America, from the country which could too easily recognize him as Abraham Lincoln's son. I wanted very much to take myself away as well. The Old Clothes Scandal had convinced the public that I was dishonest, Lizzie's book had persuaded it I was debt-ridden and deranged, and as consequence, even fewer ladies than before came to call upon me. Even in the séance parlors, I received my own telepathic impression that those with whom I held hands in magnetic circle wished less to talk *with* the dead than to talk *about* me.

Europe would be better, I thought. *In Europe, there is royalty adept at committing more lubricious scandal than even I can dream up.* Moreover, the schools in Germany were very exact. A German schoolmaster would not only teach Taddie how to spell monkey, but also ourang-outang and every other species of animal.

By early summer, I had decided that I would move Taddie and myself to Europe as soon as was possible. To let Robert know of my intentions, I made an appointment at his offices on LaSalle Street, for my eldest son came so little to see us, we might well be in Germany before he realized we had gone.

Since the settling of the estate, the offices of Scammon & Lincoln had acquired several more watercolors and a Turkey carpet. Robert had also acquired a larger desk, decorated upon its top with a swirling gold pattern. This desk, and the fact that my son sat so far upon the other side of it, pencil and a notebook of blank pages before him, made me feel that I had arrived here seeking legal advice, and I explained my plans with a hesitancy of language I did not intend.

"You cannot travel to Europe without a male protector," said Robert.

"I shall have Taddie with me," I reminded him.

"My brother is not yet a man."

"He is as tall as one," I replied. "In any event, it is Germany I am going to, not darkest Africa. I understand that the Europeans have been civilized for quite some time."

"But how will it look?" Robert tapped the point of his pencil upon the notebook, as if preparing to list the diverse improprieties of such unaccompanied travel.

"I am hoping it will look like nothing," I told him. "That once I take Taddie from here, America will forget we exist."

Robert set down his pencil, and I imagined that he found this prospect comforting.

"Still," he said, "it would appear better if you made the crossing under the protection of some gentleman."

"After two years beneath the protection of Judge Davis, I am unanxious to place myself under the guardianship of any gentleman."

"Judge Davis performed his duties with scrupulousness," said Robert, "acting always only in your best interest. When were you thinking of making the journey?"

"There is a ship we can sail on in July."

"You cannot go in July!" my son declared. "As I am getting married in September."

My impulse was to embrace him, for this seemed the very best news. But the large desk between us, and the sense that we possessed no more than a legal relationship to each other, made such a gesture feel improper.

"I am so glad for you," I said, sounding too much a client seeking legal advice. "Of course I will wait to see you married. What is the date? Shall I host you a brunch at the Palmer House? Do you believe Mary Harlan's mother will make the journey to Chicago?"

"The wedding is not to be in Chicago."

"Where is it to be?"

Robert glanced over my head at the wall where he had not hung a portrait of his father. "We are planning to marry in Washington City."

I twisted hands made clammy into my black skirts. "I do not think I can go back there."

Robert picked up his pencil and began tapping it again upon the page of the notebook. "What do you imagine will happen?" he asked me. "Booth has been shot and his friends hanged. Everything that is terrible has already occurred."

To hear him say the assassin's name felt as sudden and shocking as the firing of that man's gun. "I am afraid I will feel it is happening again."

"The wedding must be in Washington," said Robert. "Mrs. Harlan has been unwell. Her doctors have advised her against travel."

I leaned across his desk, although it was so very large, my son remained at some distance from me. "Then let me leave for Europe in July," I pleaded.

"You do not think people will consider it peculiar that my mother did not attend my wedding?"

"They will understand why I cannot be in Washington City."

"I am not marrying in Ford's Theater!" Robert threw the pencil upon the desktop, and I heard again the shot. "I shall put you in a hotel in Baltimore, and arrange a closed carriage to transport you to and from the Harlans' house."

"That will not fool my mind into believing I am somewhere else."

He rose from his seat and crossed the room, went to study the spines of the law books upon the shelf, as if what he might require to persuade me would be written there. "What about Taddie?" he said, after a time. "He is very fond of Mary Harlan. And myself. He will not want to miss our marriage."

This was, of course, the one thing which could persuade me, for my youngest son asked every day if I believed his brother and Mary Harlan would marry, and when it might be. *Perhaps,* I told myself, *it would also be good to give Taddie some better memory of Washington City.*

"You must promise that the carriage will be entirely closed," I said. "And that immediately afterward, I can sail to Europe with no more talk of a male protector."

Robert returned to his seat and again picked up the pencil. "If you will promise me this," he said, pressing the point against the paper so that the soft graphite left a smudge, "that the next day, all anyone can say is that Mrs. Lincoln sat quietly and watched her eldest son be married."

I nodded, and was certain I heard the pandemonium of chairs splintering, but it might only have been the rushing of an aged carriage outside.

Despite the fact that it would bring me back to Washington City, I was happy about Robert's marriage to Mary Harlan. I recalled the affectionate young woman's habit of placing a hand upon Robert's arm, even when there was no reason for it, and such a habit seemed a lucky thing for my son's affections. In the weeks before Robert's wedding, I concentrated upon this idea each time the notion that I would be returning to where my husband had been killed called up a dread which made me feel as if my own blood had been replaced by acid.

As promised, my eldest son arranged rooms for me at Barnum's Hotel in Baltimore. Taddie stayed with Robert at the Harlans' house in Washington City, for we were to leave for Europe a day after the wedding, and he wished to be in his brother's company as much as possible. Upon the afternoon of Robert's marriage, I traveled by closed carriage to the city where I had become a widow, keeping my mourning veils dropped over my face and the carriage curtains drawn over the windows, a double layer to protect me.

"We are obliged to you for undertaking the journey to a city of such sad memories," said Secretary Harlan. As he assisted me from the carriage, I closed my eyes and let him lead me like a blind woman. Only inside the graceful house, away from the tall streetside windows, did I hook back my black netting.

Mrs. Harlan was waiting in the parlor to greet me. The bride's mother had a lightly consumptive look about her – pale cheeks spotted with a flush which could be mistaken for health, if one ignored that it burned too brightly. "I am sorry for bringing you back here," she said to me.

I took the lady's hands, which were dry and cold. "Do not be sorry for anything upon such a glad occasion."

The Harlans' parlor had been decorated for the wedding with an entire conservatory's worth of newly cut flowers: purple gentian mixed with layers of blue belladonna, lavender asters tucked amongst utterly white lilies.

"I had these at my own wedding," I said, bending above the pale lilies. I breathed in, expecting the sweet, thick scent of the petals, but what I drew into my lungs was not the perfume of flowers, but the smell of sickbed and whiskey.

The room spun about my head, and I clutched at the table upon which the lilies stood to steady myself, but it was newly polished, and my gloved hands slid across its surface. Mr. Harlan caught me by my elbow and Mrs. Harlan pressed a bottle of salts into my hand. I held the bottle beneath my nose and breathed in the ammonia, burning and sharp, but better than that odor of sickness and drink.

"Is my mother not right?" Robert stood in the doorway, wearing a wedding suit of black and gray. His words contained all the sharpness of the salts.

"It is all these flowers," replied Mrs. Harlan. "I, too, have been finding the scent overwhelming."

"It is only that," I assured my son. "The flowers and the journey in the closed carriage." Robert kept his eyes upon me as I returned the salts to Mrs. Harlan. "Perhaps if I just sat quietly."

Taddie came and took my arm. "I shall help you to a seat," he said, shaping his imperfect speech into the formal language he used in the presence of his elder brother. My youngest son now stood nearly as tall as his brother, and today, his unruly hair – much like his father's – was pressed flat by an abundant amount of Macassar oil and pomade. At fifteen, Taddie had entered the awkward time between boy and man, where each day a different feature of his face looked to have expanded beyond the proportion of the others.

"You appear very handsome," I told him.

My youngest son led me to one of the cushioned dining chairs, which had been arranged in the parlor in rows to accommodate the guests. Within the hour, these guests began to arrive – prominent politicians, some of whom I knew, and relatives of the Harlans. As I was greeted, I studied the faces of those who bent over me, trying to tell by the set of their expressions if they had read Lizzie's book.

After a time, a small birdlike woman, a Harlan cousin, began to play upon the ornately carved parlor organ. The small cousin played hesitatingly, allowing the instrument to wheeze between the chords. Although as I listened longer, the soft gasping which came between the notes sounded gentler, more like the uneven cooing of doves. And it did not halt, even when the Harlan cousin lifted her fingers from the keys, and it was that which made me know the sound was not made by the parlor organ, but was instead the noise of my husband's last breathing.

That is impossible, I told myself. *Because Mr. Lincoln has ceased breathing more than three years ago.* But still, I could not drive the sound from my ears. *Perhaps if I leave the parlor, it will stop.* I rose from my seat, and in that moment, everyone in the parlor rose with me. I imagined with some relief that they had heard it too and intended also to escape its mournful noise. But then I saw Miss

Harlan descending the staircase in bridal white, and I knew that they had risen for her, and that if I were to flee the room, I would give them all something to say other than "Mrs. Lincoln sat quietly and watched her eldest son be married."

I gripped the seat back in front of me, pressed my fingers into its velvet cushion to keep me from running. *I shall go mad with grief if I am made to hear this,* I thought. *If I have not gone mad already.* But when at last it felt impossible to remain, even to please my eldest son, Taddie bent to whisper some remark into my ear, and though I did not understand what it was he said, his oddly made words drove away the dovelike gasping.

Breathing deeply this air which now did not contain the sound of my husband's dying, I stood beside Taddie and watched Miss Harlan walk the length of the parlor, her fair curls twined with small white tea roses; watched her come to stand beside my eldest son, handsome in a waistcoat which caught silver in the light; watched as the bishop from the Washington City Methodist Church made them husband and wife. And through it all, I sat quietly and did nothing to draw attention to myself.

Afterward, I stood among the pyramids of flowers and waited for Robert to bring Mary Harlan to me.

"I wish very much to kiss my new mother-in-law," she declared.

I caught her hands, so much warmer than her mother's, glad to kiss her back, glad she had wished for it. But when I brought my lips to my daughter-in-law's offered cheek, I was entirely certain that beneath them I would feel the spasming of my husband's convulsions. I started, pulling away, and received a sharp glance from Robert. *If you feel the twitching,* I told myself, *you must remember it is your imagination. Mary Harlan is not Mr. Lincoln. She is not head-shot and dying.* I placed my lips upon my new daughter-in-law's cheek, and the flesh there stayed mercifully still.

Taddie escorted me into the Harlans' second parlor, where a table had been laid with white linen and piled with platters of roasted squab and buttered crab, scalloped oysters and three kinds of aspic. I possessed no appetite, but I let Taddie fix me a small plate, for I wished no one to say that Mrs. Lincoln would not eat her eldest son's wedding supper.

"Is this enough?" Taddie held out a china plate filled with what he had chosen; but when I turned my eyes to it, instead of squab and buttered crab and aspic, I saw there the plug of bone and blood which had been removed from the brain of my husband.

You cannot scream, I commanded myself, *although the shriek is caught in your throat and promising to choke you. Swallow it down, and then swallow everything upon your plate, no matter what it looks to be, or what you believe it is. Eat the delusion which your grief-addled brain has made for you. And do not fear that it can make you more ill, for it is already inside you.*

I took the plate from Taddie and ate without looking at what I put into my mouth, refused to notice its texture or taste upon my tongue.

As early as might keep from causing comment, I asked for the carriage to return me to Baltimore. Again, I passed through the streets of Washington City behind double veiling. This time, however, the images I had hoped to shut out – a face pulled into one-sided grimace, bloodied linen beneath an opened wound – formed themselves upon the lids of my eyes, where I could not escape them. *You are in Baltimore now,* I said to myself, when the carriage halted. *You are out of Washington City.* And after a minute, the images faded to the grainy darkness of seeing the world behind a veil. However, the effect of them, coupled with the effort of putting down the apparitions which had haunted me during Robert's wedding, must have left me weakened. For though the lobby of Barnum's Hotel was not large, I was not halfway across it when I dropped to the floor in a swoon.

I was revived with salts, and then helped to my room – which I did not leave until Taddie and I set sail for Europe.

Twelve days after setting sail, in the autumn of 1868, Taddie and I arrived in the German town of Frankfurt. Like so many of the cities in which I had lived, Frankfurt was situated on a river, in this case, the Main, a meandering course of a burnished olive color which made the water appear as ancient as the stone and timber buildings that hugged its banks.

"We have settled into the Hotel d'Angleterre," I wrote to Robert and Mary Harlan. "And it is difficult to say which is more aristocratic – the Old World lobby, or the English gentlemen and ladies who sip their afternoon sherry in it."

The Angleterre was located in the center of the city, near a cobbled square which was home to several Kaffeehaus – dark-paneled rooms where waiters in long aprons served streusel and Sacher torte, and coffee thick as cream. I went every day to these Kaffeehaus to read the letters which flew between me and my new daughter-in-law.

"We have settled into a three-bedroom house on Wabash Avenue," Mary Harlan wrote back to me. "And while the only aristocratic furnishing in it is the oak commode which you presented to us, I would put my exceedingly refined new husband up against any Englishman."

Mary Harlan wrote me frequently, calling me "Dear Mother." I saved her letters to read with the Sacher torte I allowed myself once a week, so I might fill myself entirely with sweetness.

"Taddie is now enrolled at the Institute of Doctor Hohagen on Kettenhofstrasse," I told Mary Harlan, "where he is studying German, French, and English grammar, and reading aloud two hours a day to correct his speech."

My youngest son missed his brother and his new sister-in-law terribly. But he liked the quaint buildings and narrow streets of Frankfurt; and he liked that here no one stared at him. I, too, liked Frankfurt, and began to understand how it is that Europe spoils women; for women upon the Continent were granted an independence which was unimaginable in America. English ladies were permitted to be as eccentric as they liked, pursuing pastimes such as searching the woodlands for fairies without causing any comment. And French ladies, even married ones, went about town accompanied by gentlemen who appeared very much like lovers, without exciting a moment's scandal. Indeed in Europe, my American disgraces – my debts, and the selling of my clothes – were considered too little disreputable to merit writing about in the newspapers. While by contrast, a New York paper reported some months after I had left the country that "the Widow Lincoln is set to marry the Count Schneiderbutzen," an entirely fictional member of Bavarian royalty.

While I did not socialize with the fictional Count Schneiderbutzen, I did in Frankfurt receive callers from among the city's English-speaking colony, for in Europe it did not seem that widows were required to be so set apart. And at least once a week I was invited to take tea with the invalid American ladies on their way to take the waters at Baden-Baden and Marienbad.

"I am penning you this letter even before the ink has dried on the one to my own mother," wrote my daughter-in-law, after I had been in Frankfurt some six months, "to report that the illustrious Mr. Lincoln and I expect to become parents by the fall; and to confess to you my fear of the process which I dare not confess to her."

"Do not listen to the married ladies who are so fond of making new wives pale with sensationally rendered stories of childbirth," I wrote back. "I have no doubt that all will go well; and to prove my confidence, I have gone straight out to all the lovely little shops along the Zeil. Expect soon to receive too many boxes of lacework buntings and hand-knitted caps."

It was during that spring, my first in Germany, that I discovered these lovely shops. Unlike the large marble and gilt department stores on lower Broadway and Pennsylvania Avenue, the shops which lined the *Zeil* were small and rich with carved-wood molding, and sold one thing – lengths of heavy crape or china figures painted by hand. There was little I could buy for myself, as I continued to dress in mourning. Although I had acquired a new dressmaker, a mannerly gentleman by the name of Popp, who had stitched gowns for European royalty – and to whom I told none of my secrets. I could, however, buy for Mary Harlan and my anticipated grandchild. And this I did with enthusiasm, and without repeating the reckless overspending I had practiced during the war, perhaps because I did believe all would go well with my daughter-in-law's lying-in.

"After eight *suffering* hours, I have produced for you the most perfect granddaughter," wrote Mary Harlan that autumn, after I had been in Frankfurt a year. "She is called Mary. Your devoted son says for me, but in my mind, for my second mother halfway around the world."

I read this letter in my favorite Kaffeehaus, one which had walls paneled with cherrywood and especially good pastries.

"My granddaughter has been born, and she has been named after me," I told the waiter, although I was never entirely certain if he understood my Southernly accented English. He was an elderly man with an overlarge mustache, the fair edges of which rippled when he said his words. After delivering this news, I asked him for two pieces of Sacher torte, even though Taddie was not with me.

I felt light that day, emptied, as if some portion of my grief had been breathed out. My family had gained Mary Harlan, and this new Mary – named for me – and at last my living outweighed my dead, and we were not so evenly divided between Earth and Heaven.

"I wish more than anything that I could look upon the face of my little namesake – and upon yours," I wrote back to my daughter-in-law. "Make plans to come – all three of you – as soon as you are recovered and the weather improves."

"Do you believe they will come?" Taddie asked me. The Germanic tongue, filled with hard consonants, had firmed my youngest son's speech into more clarity.

I thought he appeared thin, and ordered him streusel from the waiter. Frau Hohagen, the wife of Taddie's schoolmaster, did not serve pastry, as she believed it adversely affected the morals. "We may have to wait until it is summer again," I told him.

"Robert informs me that Europe in summer is likely to be too full of pestilence and a danger to little Mary," wrote my daughter-in-law. "He also wishes me to inform you that an embroidered cloak is entirely unsuitable for a child of less than a year. (Although, it is exceptionally lovely.)"

"Please tell my commendably cautious son that Europe is filled with young children in summer," I answered Mary Harlan, "and I have observed none of them perishing from pestilence. I have, however, seen a good many of them dressed in embroidered cloaks."

Just before I left America, Ulysses Grant had been elected president. I had not liked General Grant for his barbarous conducting of the war – I was never entirely certain the end had justified his means – and had always declared that I would leave the country if he were elected president. Now that the general had been in office a year, I passed many rainy afternoons in the reading rooms of Frankfurt, pouring over the American newspapers to know how the man who had led so many Union soldiers to their death was running the country. These reading rooms were lit by small lamps which cast circles of light upon the polished tables, and were a pleasant place to read disapproval which was directed at somebody else.

"Your granddaughter has been given a nickname," Mary Harlan announced in her next letter. "She is now known as Little Mamie. My daughter is a happy, easygoing child. Still, I am feeling much confined to the house. Robert believes that employing more than one nurse would be an unnecessary expense – and appear unmotherly. But I am afraid I am missing the world too much."

"It is impossible to be motherly when one is unhappy," I told my daughter-in-law. "If you would make Robert understand this, he would not deprive you." Before I mailed this letter, I wrote another to my son. "I have instructed my agent to give to you the rent from my house on West Washington Street to be used to ease the way for your devoted wife and new daughter."

With the rent from the house in Chicago now going to my son and daughter-in-law, my yearly income was reduced to twenty-five hundred dollars – an amount I had once been capable of exhausting in an afternoon. At thirty dollars every week, the Angleterre proved too costly, and I was obliged to leave its aristocratic Old World lobby and the well-bred English gentlemen and ladies I met there. I relocated to the Hotel Holland, which reminded me more than I wished of the Clifton House, although rather than onions, the corridors and suppers – and inhabitants – of the Hotel Holland smelled of kraut.

"Please excuse the nature of my last letter," read Mary Harlan's next note, which was some time in coming. "I was suffering from a hysteria of the womb, which the doctor believes was a result of Mamie's difficult delivery. I am recovered now, and agree with Robert that the money you have so generously transferred to us should be used for some more useful purpose than my convenience."

I did not agree with the logic of this letter, for it seemed to me that if Mary Harlan was suffering from some hysteria of the womb, then more should be done for her convenience. "Have you thought any more about coming to us?" I wrote back. "I want very much to talk to you within view of your expression, and without the time it requires to cross an ocean between our responses. Tell Robert that if he agrees, I shall send the passage money."

My daughter-in-law's next letter was scrawling and splattered with blotches of dripped ink. "Mamie grows more like her father every day," she told me. "When he is at home, I cannot make her come to me. No offers of hair-braiding or the reading of books can pull her from her father's side – even if he is so preoccupied with his own thoughts, he would not notice if she had gone.

"Robert believes that an Atlantic crossing in the autumn is bad for the lungs."

I worried over the change in Mary Harlan's writing, the ink splatters which could have been caused by tears rather than an inferior pen. *Perhaps it is only motherhood*, I told myself, *which can sometimes turn one irrational*. "For some years Robert ran away from us," I wrote to my daughter-in-law. "I am certain Mamie loves you.

"I wish that I were there to see you."

I did not hear again from Mary Harlan for some weeks. And when her next letter came, the handwriting was so unsteady, I could barely read it, even with the spectacles I was obliged to borrow from the mustached waiter at the Kaffeehaus.

"Was Mr. Lincoln an affectionate man?" my daughter-in-law asked me. "Did you believe in his love? Forgive the impertinence of my inquiries. Ignore them if you wish."

"My husband loved me in the way that any wife would wish to be loved," I responded, "more than I deserved. I worry you are not well. Write to me right away."

However, the next letter which arrived from Chicago was written in Robert's upright hand. "I have sent my wife to her mother, who is poorly," my son informed me. "If her last correspondence sounded disordered, it should be attributed to her anxiety over Mrs. Harlan's health."

I wrote to Mary Harlan in care of her mother's house in Washington City, but received no reply.

In the summer of 1870, when Taddie and I had been in Germany for almost two years, war broke out between the French and the Prussians. Overnight, the quaint, old city of Frankfurt changed into a military camp. Soldiers took over the old stone hotels and timbered boardinghouses, and the graceful carriages of European nobility could not travel the cobblestoned streets for the lines of cannons and crates of munitions. William Murphy, the American consul, warned all citizens to evacuate, for it was believed that Frankfurt would be the scene of a terrific battle. I had lived in a city caught in the midst of war before, and now, at the age of fifty-one – a number I frequently reduced to forty-six – I did not wish to do so again; and in the autumn of that year, Taddie and I left Germany for England.

We settled in London, where I found an English tutor for Taddie. My seventeen-year-old son could now read perfectly, and his speech was clear, though sometimes pronounced with the too-precise articulation of a German speaker. We found a place which was not too costly on Woburn Street, near the British Museum, where I passed my days wandering among the antiquities.

It was a month before Mary Harlan's letters followed me to England. In them, my daughter-in-law told me nothing of her visit to her mother, nor said why she had answered none of my letters. In truth, she told me nothing of consequence at all. For weeks, all her correspondence was bright and impersonal – and entirely legible. Then at the end of winter, came a scribbled note of which I could read only part.

"Mamie is with Robert and I am locked in my room," declared the only clear section. "Does Taddie say that he loves you? Did Mr. Lincoln kiss you after your children were born?

"Why do you write to me? How can you sign yourself with affection?"

I had brought this letter to the tea shop of the British Museum, a cavernous room of chintz-covered tables and Greek statuary, for I had kept with my habit of accompanying my daughter-in-law's correspondence with something sweet. However, after reading it, my little plate of profiteroles and scones with Devonshire cream felt the wrong accompaniment for such a letter. It had been my hope that Mary Harlan would work a miracle of affection upon my son, but it seemed that Robert's character had proved the stronger. The letters which traveled across the world from my daughter-in-law had altered, and I feared very much that it was Robert who was working a change upon his wife – as well as upon his young daughter. Although there was no mention of illness in Mary Harlan's letter, I felt the same as if she had told me Mamie had contracted smallpox, or herself scarlet fever, and it was impossible to put down the belief that my family, only so recently tipped toward the side of the living, was about to tip the other direction.

I should go back, I said to myself. *Return to Chicago and show Mary Harlan how it is that I can sign myself with affection. Show my granddaughter some emotion other than her father's restraint.* I knew that Taddie wished to go back to America, but it was myself who was reluctant to return to the country which considered me no better than a mercenary prostitute.

But perhaps I have been away long enough, I thought. *Perhaps the newspapers have found a new president's wife about whom to write scandal – although it is true that Julia Grant conducts herself in nothing save the most respectable manner. Still, remaining here in Europe with Taddie does work to further divide my earthly family.*

Taddie and I stayed in London only until we could make a spring crossing. In May of 1871, two and one-half years since we had left it, we returned to the country my husband would not let be split apart.

Our boat docked in New York, where we took a train to Chicago.

We arrived at the Union Depot in the late afternoon. The station was full of noise and steam, and the shouting of Americans. It had been so long since I had heard so much of that familiar form of English, the conversations tugged me in every direction. Taddie, who was taller, spotted Robert and Mary Harlan, with Little Mamie in her arms, standing beneath a girdered arch. I sought first the face of my daughter-in-law, and found the flesh of it puffy for one so young.

"Say hello to your grandmamma," Mary Harlan coaxed a child who possessed all of Robert's baby chubbiness.

"She is much like her father," I told her.

"Better than like me!" declared Mary Harlan.

I could not say what my daughter-in-law had meant by the remark, only that it had been uttered in a voice which was too loud. Robert cast upon his wife a harsh glance. Mamie regarded her mother with a steady gaze.

"Her curls are like yours," I told Mary Harlan, then used the excuse of the comparison to look more closely into my daughter-in-law's face. I had time only to note the pinkishness in the white of her eyes, before she turned away toward Taddie.

"Look at my little brother-in-law!" Mary Harlan exclaimed in that hard, bright voice. "He has become nearly as tall as his father!"

Taddie, unused to the attentions of young ladies, smiled widely. Then forgetting he was now a gentleman of seventeen, he threw his arms about his elder brother's shoulders. "Why didn't you come to see us?" he exclaimed. "Mama would have sent you the tickets."

"Taddie's speech sounds as Bavarian as Nicolay's did," Robert said to me.

"At least you cannot argue he is clear," I replied.

"I think he sounds and appears quite wonderful!" declared Mary Harlan. "Look how rose-colored his complexion is!"

Indeed, Taddie's cheeks were splotched crimson, as were Mary Harlan's own – although I knew Taddie's for fever. For the weather upon the Atlantic had been foul and wet, and my youngest son had fallen ill with a sickness of the lungs.

As if to illustrate this, Taddie was now taken by a fit of coughing, which bent him at the waist and forced him to release his brother.

"We should find a carriage," I said. "The crossing has been tiring for both of us."

Taddie and I were to stay for a time at Robert's house on Wabash Avenue. The house was not large, but my eldest son had been insistent. "Now that I possess a home," he had written, "it is proper that my mother and brother live with me." I did not examine too carefully what motivated Robert's wish to place us all beneath his roof, was only made glad that he would.

Although small, Robert's house was exceedingly fine. It was built of a pale-colored stone with black shutters, straight and graceful, and in keeping upon a street of other such houses. Inside, it was decorated with great taste. The parlor and sitting room furniture was made of dark mahogany, and all of it stood upon sabered legs.

"This is all very elegant," I said to my daughter-in-law.

Mary Harlan reached for her husband's arm, but before her fingers could come to rest upon his sleeve, she checked herself. "It is your son who possesses the talent for decorating."

"It was necessary for me to uncover it," replied Robert. "For my wife possesses none of the skill."

My daughter-in-law dropped her gaze as if admitting to a larger failing. "I fear I am fond of pine."

Only the kitchen appeared to belong to Mary Harlan. The rising cupboard was a light-colored pine, as were the shelves, which held a collection of batter bowls, cracked and the exact shade of butter. The big farmhouse table was pine as well, and scarred by tiny cuts.

"I like this room," I said to my daughter-in-law. But Mary Harlan only shook her head.

Taddie's fever had risen during the journey from the train station, and seeing that he was as unsteady upon his feet as his year-old niece, I helped him to the spare bedroom. I was given the room Mary Harlan generally shared with Mamie. My daughter-in-law moved to the bedroom which belonged to her husband.

The following morning there were only three of us for breakfast, for Taddie was too weak to rise from his bed. We took our meal in the dining room, as if there were servants to wait upon us, although Robert employed none.

"Let us go today to some grand hotel and have tea," I said to Mary Harlan. "I should enjoy nothing more than a long afternoon spent eating little cakes and discussing the female condition."

My daughter-in-law glanced up from the shirred eggs she had

prepared, and of which she had scarcely eaten. Her face was still puffy about the eyes.

"You have no nurse today," Robert reminded his wife.

"We will bring Mamie with us," I declared. "As a member of the female sex, she is entitled to come."

"My daughter is too young for tearooms," my son informed me.

Had it been my own husband – who, in truth, possessed no opinions about tearooms – uttering this statement to me, I would have used up a goodly portion of our time at the breakfast table to convince him otherwise. Mary Harlan, however, only nodded across the table. "I am sure Robert is correct in this," she said.

I tried again the following morning. "Come walk with me in Union Park," I suggested. "The nurse will tend to Taddie and Mamie. The day is fine. And we can at last converse without resorting to pen and ink."

Mary Harlan, who had spent most of breakfast resting her head upon her hands, glanced briefly at Robert before answering. "I am afraid I am stricken with headache this morning."

"The fresh air will help you recover," I told her. But I wondered at my own prescription, for the skin beneath my daughter-in-law's eyes was dark, as if the headache was so violent, it had bruised her there.

"I fear the suffering is so acute," she replied, "it has affected my digestion." And indeed, she remained in her room for the remainder of the day.

Nothing I offered my daughter-in-law over the following mornings proved enticement enough to gain me her company. Mary Harlan was too fatigued for shopping, and too distracted for visiting; neuralgia prevented her walking, and a recurring ailment of the stomach kept her from riding with me in the carriage. And upon the rare occasions she was not sickly, my daughter-in-law preoccupied herself so entirely with Mamie – although the child did not seem to notice whether her mother was present – I could not coax her to come and sit with me someplace where I might ask if she were truly well.

Most mornings, Mary Harlan served our breakfast with half-lidded eyes and the careful step of one suffering migraine. And twice, my daughter-in-law came to the supper table with the long row of buttons upon the front of her dress unevenly fastened, as if she had dressed herself in the dark. Her mood, too, seemed to suffer some ailment, becoming by turns too sorrowful and too bright.

I would have pursued my daughter-in-law more diligently over these days, but I was made too anxious over Taddie. The illness of his lungs did not improve, and it brought with it a fever which kept Taddie turning upon his brother's spare bed, his brain filled with strange dreams. No amount of plasters or poultices eased Taddie's breathing. Before long, he was required to sleep propped upon several pillows, or he would wake choking, and I spent many hours watching over Taddie's sleep.

I left the house only to hurry to the druggist for more plasters and bottles of cinnamon oil meant to loosen Taddie's breathing, and did not go unless I knew my daughter-in-law was well enough to watch over him. It was upon returning from such an errand that I arrived back at a house which was still and unlighted. I was surprised by the empty feeling of the house, for I had come to believe that Mary Harlan never went out; surprised, too, to find none of the gas had been lit, for it was well onto dusk. I wandered the ground-floor rooms, calling my daughter-in-law's name. But all I found was the parlor full of shadows and the big cast-iron stove in the kitchen cold, although Robert would be home for his supper within the hour.

"Mary Harlan!" I shouted up the stairs, and received for reply only the ticking of a wall clock. Such human silence frightened me, made me fear that Taddie's condition had turned, and I raced up the steps. But Taddie was alone in the spare bedroom, and no worse than I had left him, save that he was near to falling off his pillows. Setting the parcel of cinnamon oil and plasters upon a night table, I resettled my youngest son's shoulders more firmly and pushed the sweat-soaked hair out of his eyes.

Thinking I might find my daughter-in-law in the nursery with Mamie, I hurried to the end of the hallway. But when I pushed open the door, I saw only my small granddaughter, seated upon the carpet before a small neat pile of wooden blocks.

"Where is Mama?" I asked.

The child regarded me with a solemn expression.

I knelt upon the floor beside her. "Mama?" I repeated.

Mamie's eyes shifted to the shut door of the bedroom. I lifted myself to my feet and went to knock upon the door.

"Mary Harlan?" I called. "Are you well?" I waited a moment, but no sound came. "Can you answer?" I said in a louder voice. Still there was no response.

Afraid that my daughter-in-law had succumbed to an illness more serious than those which kept her out of my company, I entered the room. I heard first the sound of hissing, as if serpents hid within the walls, and the noise nearly made me go and search for Mary Harlan elsewhere. I put out a hand to help me find my way in the dark, and a few feet along the wall my fingers brushed upon a wall sconce. Noticing how the hissing had grown louder here, I knew that the sound was not serpents, but gas escaping from the fixture, which Mary Harlan must have turned on but forgotten to light. I felt for the small filigreed cock of the sconce and shut off the gas. Then keeping my hand upon the wall, I found the window and pulled it open to let in the spring air.

The light from the unshuttered window fell upon the bed, showing the figure of my daughter-in-law sprawled across the mattress. She was still wearing her dress, although she had unfastened the buttons of the front and taken her arm from one sleeve. Her fair curls were matted and she lay with her mouth opened.

"Mary Harlan," I said quietly, for I did not wish to startle her awake. "Have you taken ill? Can I do anything for you?"

She stirred, and passed her tongue over her lips, as if her mouth were too dry to shut. I sat upon the edge of the mattress, putting a hand to her forehead, which was almost as heated as Taddie's. With a suddenness which felt of desperation, my daughter-in-law took hold of my fingers and pressed them upon her eyes.

"I am very drunk," she told me.

At first I imagined I had not heard her correctly. But then I recalled Mary Harlan's headaches, and her uneven buttoning, and the puffiness of her young face.

"Why?" I asked her.

"It is a habit," she said. "One I cannot check."

"Does Robert know?"

She pressed my fingers more tightly to her eyes. "Robert does not approve of ladies who drink."

"But you are his wife. And he must love you."

"Must he?" she replied. "I imagine I am difficult to love."

I fought a little against the pressure of her hand, so I would not push so hard upon her eyes. "I have not found it difficult at all," I told her.

"I expect that is because you are subject to an excessively emotional nature."

"Is that what my son says of me?"

Mary Harlan sighed. "He says the same of me."

She released my fingers and pressed her elbows into the mattress, lifting herself higher into the light. Beneath the unbuttoned dress and loosened petticoats, the ribbons which held together the waist of my daughter-in-law's underdrawers were undone.

Mary Harlan's gaze followed mine, and she saw what I had noted. "The drinking makes Robert cold toward me," she explained. "Yet it is when I drink that I most desire him warm." She spoke this without shame, and I did not know whether to ascribe it to the drink or to some understanding of my own nature.

"You are in love with my son," I said.

"More than is seemly." My daughter-in-law's eyes shined darkly in the dim room. With some effort, she sat up and began feeling for her buttons. "I have left Mamie untended. And Taddie."

"I will see to them," I told her.

"There is also Robert's supper to get."

"I shall see to that as well."

Mary Harlan fell back against the mahogany bedstead. "I do not understand why you love me so well."

I reached over and pushed the damp hair from her eyes, the same as I had done for Taddie. "I have always possessed a weakness for those who love hard," I said to her.

I left Mary Harlan in the bedroom, sleeping off the effects of drink, and the desire she had satisfied for herself. In the time that I had been with her mother, Mamie had fallen into sleep, and I placed the child in her cradle. Assuring that Taddie remained in his own uneasy sleep, I went downstairs to the kitchen. There, I found a hen, plucked and naked, which my daughter-in-law must have intended to roast for supper. Robert was too near arriving home for me to have time to cook the chicken whole, so after I lit the stove, I placed the fowl upon the scarred surface of the farmhouse table and set about hacking it into pieces.

"Why is my wife not preparing supper?" Robert stood in the doorway of this one room in which the wood was light, and soft.

"Mary Harlan is not well."

My son waited to hear if I would say more.

"She is ill from drink."

"Too drunk to prepare dinner?"

I pushed the cleaver through the hen's breastbone. "You are prosperous enough to employ a cook."

"I wish to keep my wife occupied. It gives her less time to pursue unwholesome habits."

"You sound as if you dislike your wife."

Robert sat heavily at the table. "Even my father despised drunkards."

"Your father did not like drink," I corrected him. "He was too kindhearted to despise anyone for weakness."

"Unlike myself."

I let the knife come to rest. "What are you saying?"

My son spread his hands upon the table, touching his fingers to the scars which were cut there. "I do not deceive myself that in anyone's eyes I could be considered as kind, or as noble, as Abraham Lincoln."

The words had been uttered with bitterness, but there was also grief in his voice. Wiping my hands upon a towel, I sat beside my son. "You have compared yourself with your father?"

"As has the rest of the world. With the result that it is accepted opinion I do not measure up to a man who possessed no manners, education, or even the knowledge of how to match trousers to jacket."

I pushed away from the table, unwilling to stay so near to my son, hating the contempt with which he had spoken of his father, and reminding myself that it was only the contempt which I hated. I rose from my seat and again took up the cleaver. "Perhaps the weakness does not lie with your wife," I said to him, my voice brittle as the bones beneath my knife. "Perhaps the only unwholesome habit is your want of affection." The terrible words tumbled out, as unstoppable as the falling of the cleaver. "Perhaps that is the defect of which your canted eye is sign."

"Perhaps," replied Robert, rising, "I learned my aversion for strong emotion from you, for whom it is a kind of madness."

"It is not madness to love to distraction," I told him. "Nor to grieve to it."

"It is only your derangement which makes you believe so."

We regarded each other across a table scattered with the severed pieces of the hen. Carefully, I set down the knife amidst the bits of blood and bone. "You must help your wife," I said to Robert.

"I am sending her to her mother."

"To rid yourself of her?"

"Her presence is disagreeable for Mamie."

"And for you, also, I expect." My fingers twitched upon the knife handle.

Robert drew himself up. "You forget that this is my house."

"I wish only to help Mary Harlan."

"I know best how to deal with my wife."

I made my voice more pleading. "If you would only be more tender toward her."

"I have not asked after your advice."

"The smallest piece more affectionate."

Robert began to turn from me. "I cannot."

"Only a little more loving."

Whirling about, my son pounded his fist upon Mary Harlan's table. "Enough!" he shouted.

His eye tugged so violently, it was painful to look upon it, and although I was the one touching the knife, I felt frightened of him.

"I wish you to go from here," he told me.

"You wish me to leave your house?"

"I shall send a note to a nearby hotel."

"But Taddie is ill."

"I have asked only you to go. I shall see after Taddie."

"I would not leave him in your care."

"He will be adequately looked after."

"Nevertheless, I shall take him with me. Taddie is as much in need of tenderness as plasters. And for all his love of you, he has received very little of it at your hands."

Robert made an ugly laugh. "It is fortunate, then, that he has received so much of it from our father."

"Whom he has lost. Along with his closest brother."

"The sainted Willie," he muttered.

The shock of his venom was such, I could draw no breath to answer.

Robert turned and moved toward the door. "I would make myself ready," he said. "It looks ill to arrive unannounced at hotels after dark." He scratched at a bit of poultry blood which had stuck to his cuff.

"I shall endeavor to ascribe your cruelty to concern over your wife," I told him.

He regarded me with a cold stare. "Perhaps it is just part of my character."

"You are still half your father's child."

"I expect even the noblest among us can produce a disappointment."

"Tell Mary Harlan I did not wish to leave her," I said to his back. "And try at least to give her my affection."

I washed the blood of the hen from my hands and hurried to make Taddie ready for the carriage. I dressed him in woolens, for the night was chill, though his fever caused him to sweat right through them. Then I settled him into a chair so that I might pack up his plasters and cinnamon oil, and all the bottles of patent medicine which had not yet opened his lungs.

"Why are we leaving Robert?" Taddie asked me.

"You have a sickness and it is dangerous for Mamie," I told him.

"I won't let it kill her," he promised.

"I know that you won't."

"I'll let it take me instead."

I dropped a bottle of Wistor's Wildcherry upon the floor, where it shattered, spilling its sticky contents over Robert's carpet.

(August 17) Judge Bradwell and wife think Mrs. L should be allowed to go to her sister's and that her health is suffering in consequence of her confinement. So much discussion with the patient about going away tends to unsettle her mind and make her more discontented and should be stopped. She should be let alone and this I have told Judge Bradwell. It is now apparent that the frequent visits of Mr. and Mrs. Bradwell and especially the letters of Mrs. B. have tended to stir up discontent and thus do harm.
—*Patient Progress Reports for Bellevue Place Sanitarium*

After I sent to Myra Bradwell the letter giving Mr. Wilkie permission to publish his story about me, I waited to learn if it had been printed, and what effect it had caused. However, days passed, and I received no notes scrawled in Myra's overlarge hand, and not once did I look up to find her standing in my doorway. After a week, I took to waiting every afternoon upon the back porch for Blanche to arrive with her shears and her newspapers.

"Let me find you a smooth page," I would offer, settling myself upon the step beside her. And as she waited for a sheet I deemed perfect enough to cut into one of her paper ladies, I searched every page of her family's discarded papers. Ten days passed, but still I did not find upon them either Mr. Wilkie's byline or mention of my own name.

Myra has found a better cause, declared my traitorous voice. *One more likely to further the campaign of female suffrage.*

But Myra is my friend, I told it.

Myra Bradwell is a crusader for the rights of women. What good will it do her sex to free one mad, unliked widow?

To quiet the voice, I wrote letters to Myra, begging to know if she had spoken with Mr. Wilkie and if she were still my friend. When that left me too much time to imagine I had been forgotten and that the story which would free me would never be published, I took walks about the madhouse grounds, and, despite the August heat, weeded in Mrs. Patterson's kitchen garden.

Since I had first begun to believe that Myra would release me, I had fallen out of the habit of sitting with Mrs. Patterson. Thus, when I received a summons to come immediately to her upon the side porch, I imagined that the doctor's wife wished to reproach me for my neglect of her.

Although it was just after breakfast, the day was already over-heated. Mrs. Patterson had dressed herself in a high-necked muslin gown, and although she would not be seen by any but mad ladies, she had opened none of the buttons. She was seated in her usual wicker rocker and had at her feet the drawstring bag in which she kept her sewing. However, Mrs. Patterson's hands were not employed with mending, and upon her face I saw a wrath which pinched her features sharp as blades.

I had not imagined that my inattention would have angered her so, and was about to offer apology, for it would not render my continued existence here easy if I earned the dislike of the doctor's wife. But before I might utter my placating speech, Mrs. Patterson thrust herself forward in the rocker, making me believe she would spring at me.

"You assured me that Mr. Wilkie was an old acquaintance!" she accused.

I could not say if I should be made glad or anxious by Mrs. Patterson's mention of Mr. Wilkie's name. "It is no lie that I knew the gentleman in Washington City," I replied, keeping my voice even.

"And so you knew that he was a newspaper reporter?"

"I believe that Mr. Wilkie covered the War Between the States."

"Then I expect you are also aware of the reason for his visit to Bellevue Place some weeks ago?"

"I assume that he came to see me."

With a furious gesture, Mrs. Patterson snatched up the drawstring bag. "He came," she declared, "at the instigation of Mrs. Bradwell. He came," she pounded a fist upon her bag, "so that you might persuade him to write libel!"

If Mrs. Patterson is saying libel, I thought, *then Mr. Wilkie must have printed his story.* I felt again that loosening of my limbs which came when I thought of my freedom.

"Mr. Wilkie is a man," I said as calmly as I might. "And I am only a woman. You cannot believe I might induce him into any action."

Mrs. Patterson pulled her mouth into a vicious smile. "And why should I not? When I possess proof otherwise!" With a savage motion, she ripped open the sewing bag and pulled out a much-creased copy of the *Chicago Times.*

I wished for nothing more than to tear the paper from Mrs. Patterson's hands and read it for myself. I put out a hand. "If you will allow me to see what Mr. Wilkie has written, perhaps I may prove to you that I did not direct him."

The doctor's wife pressed the newspaper tight to her bodice like a shield, and stared up at me, her eyes full of the same confusion I had oft seen in those of her weak-minded daughter. "I acted toward you as though you were sane," she said to me. "I made you my friend."

I felt a sympathy for the doctor's wife, for I was familiar with how it was to be betrayed by somebody one imagined a friend. But seeing Mr. Wilkie's story pressed to her bodice, where she would not let me read it, banished the sentiment.

"Please let me know what Mr. Wilkie has written about me."

"I shall tell you what he has written," replied Mrs. Patterson. She unfolded the newspaper and held it before her face, just beyond my reach. "*Mrs. Lincoln,*" she read, "*called my attention to the iron bars upon the window, and said that they menaced her with the idea that she was imprisoned. She told me also that she was apprehensive over the wild and piercing cries of the insane people of the house, fearing that in time, they might unseat her reason.*"

I recalled saying nothing to Mr. Wilkie about my bars, or about wild and piercing cries of the insane. These must be some embellishment of Myra's, I thought, impressed at the lady lawyer's ability to induce a man, particularly a newspaperman, into any action.

Mrs. Patterson rocked her chair so feverishly, the wicker seemed in danger of unwinding itself. "You have told all of Chicago that you believe if you are left too long in my house, it will drive you insane!"

"Did he say that he considered me sane?" I asked. "Did he write anything about my being released?"

At the mention of my release, Mrs. Patterson ceased her rocking.

"Mrs. Ruggles!" she called.

And as if the matron had been waiting only inside the doorway, Mrs. Ruggles now stood upon the narrow porch, her bulk large behind me.

I felt the large woman's breath upon my neck, and was certain I could detect the bitter scent of chloral hydrate upon her person. *They are going to dose me! Dose me as punishment for what Mr. Wilkie has written. Dose me like Mrs. Matthiessen, until I collapse upon the floor and they can say that I died of my mania.*

I must escape! Run down that long drive, and all the way to Batavia. But I could not run, for I was caught between the bulk of Mrs. Ruggles and the width of Mrs. Patterson's chair.

"What do you want of me?" I asked them.

Mrs. Patterson rose from the wicker rocker. "In the presence of Mrs. Ruggles," she said, "I wish you to state whether you have ever been unkindly or improperly treated during your stay here at Bellevue Place."

It took me some moments to understand the import of what Mrs. Patterson was asking. The doctor's wife wanted my pledge – before a witness – that I had never been mistreated at Bellevue Place. That could mean only one thing: Mrs. Patterson believed that I would be released.

I glanced back at Mrs. Ruggles. There was no bottle of chloral hydrate in her hand. I looked again at Mrs. Patterson. The doctor's wife appeared less wrathful, more uneasy.

"I attest that I have never been unkindly or improperly treated while at Bellevue Place," I declared.

Mrs. Patterson glanced over my head at the matron. "You have heard her?"

"I have," said Mrs. Ruggles.

"Does this mean I am leaving?"

"That is always a question for Doctor Patterson," she replied, then stuffed the newspaper into her drawstring bag. "You may return to your own pursuits."

I thought that now there would be some word from Myra, and waited every day for her to write, or even to come herself. But there was no word, and I began to suspect that Doctor Patterson – and doubtless, Robert too – had forbidden her. With Myra Bradwell kept from me, I did not know how I would learn any more of what Mr. Wilkie had written of my release until I chanced upon the stalklike figure of Mrs. Munger hurrying down the limestone corridor, and saw that, though it was not yet Saturday, her hair was once again arranged into a neat chignon.

"Mrs. Munger," I said, placing myself between the mad lady and the door to the back porch. "I was just intending to ask you for a game of croquet. However, the day is so sultry, I wonder if you might instead come to my room, where we might hope for a breeze and enjoy one another's company?"

Mrs. Munger stepped nearer the wall, seeking a way past. The banker's wife may have conversed with objects, but she was still capable of harboring a grudge toward me for having supplanted her as Mrs. Patterson's confidant.

"If you do not come," I continued, "I fear I shall have a lonely afternoon. Being as my life has always been so full of society."

This reminder of my life, and what it once was, made Mrs. Munger hesitate. She appeared to be reconsidering how much resentment she should feel toward me, and I suspected she would determine it less, for it has been my observation that there is an aspect of celebrity which makes others wish to be in one's company, even if only to say that they had.

"I should enjoy that very much, Mrs. Lincoln," Mrs. Munger replied.

I brought Mrs. Munger to my room, and let her have my rocker. Then I asked her questions about her life in Chicago, and about her husband, whom she described as "an important gentleman of finance," pronouncing the phrase in a sing-song cadence, which made it seem she was saying something which had been repeatedly told to her.

"I know you are much in Mrs. Patterson's confidence," I said, when I possessed no more patience. "Has she said anything to you of what Mr. Wilkie has written about me?"

Mrs. Munger reached up, intending, I believe, to pull upon her chignon, which was tightly coiled, and to which she likely was not accustomed. However, at the last moment, the lady appeared to recall that she possessed a horror of touching her own hair, and halted, leaving her hand suspended in the air.

"I have lost some standing with Mrs. Patterson," I continued, "I think, in part, due to this libelous story. You would do me a terrific service if you would tell me what you know of it."

With her arm upraised, as if waving to spirits, Mrs. Munger weighed her loyalty to Mrs. Patterson against doing a service for a president's wife. "Mr. Wilkie printed that you are unquestionably compos mentis," she said, determining my former status more compelling than Mrs. Patterson's present one.

"He wrote that I am sane?"

"That is the meaning of the term." Mrs. Munger appeared pleased by the idea she was explaining the phrase to me. "He wrote that you were compos mentis and ought not to be deprived of your liberty."

I leaned nearer the mad lady in my rocker. "Did Mr. Wilkie say if I would get that liberty? Did he know when it might be?"

But Mrs. Munger had now fixed her attention upon my mantle clock. "That clock is not working!" she announced.

"It has not worked for some time," I told her. "Pay it no mind."

However, the madness of the banker's wife made her receptive more toward objects than people. "That will not do!" she scolded my clock. "Mrs. Lincoln needs to know the time."

I could barely suppress the desire to reach over and shake the lunatic lady in order to wring more information from her. "Mr. Wilkie," I said, trying to recall Mrs. Munger's mind. "Did he speak about my release?"

With reluctance, Mrs. Munger took her eyes from my mantle clock. "He interviewed Mrs. Bradwell."

"What did Myra tell him?"

"That she had called upon your sister in Springfield, and obtained an invitation for you to stay with her."

"Did she say anything else?" I asked.

"I think that if I speak loudly to it," said Mrs. Munger, "I can oblige that clock to work for you."

"Did Myra tell Mr. Wilkie anything more?" I repeated.

"She said that they are only waiting for Robert to return from his vacation in the East to release you."

It was possible that might be true. But it was equally likely it had been Myra putting it in the newspapers in the hope it would become true. I attempted to learn more from Mrs. Munger, but she was too distracted by the mantle clock, and then the torn lace runner upon my bureau; and finally, I was forced to pretend headache to send her away.

"It would be best if you did not mention our new friendship to Mrs. Patterson," I said to her. "I have fallen so far beneath her favor, it could only jeopardize your own."

Mrs. Munger reached again for her chignon and again left her hand hanging in the air. She nodded, and then was gone.

For the rest of the afternoon, I paced my room and thought upon what Mrs. Munger had told me and how my son might have reacted to Mr. Wilkie's story. Robert was passing some weeks with his family at Rye, New York; however, I was certain that someone – Doctor Patterson, perhaps – had sent him a copy of the *Chicago Times* which contained the story about my sanity. *Certainly he has seen it by now,* I thought. *And certainly he must hate it. Although, he cannot hate it as much as I hate being confined with lunatics.* Still, I hoped that Mr. Wilkie's story, and the fact I had allowed it, had not turned my son too much against me; for I continued to believe that the pages I pen at night will inspire some affection from him. Moreover, I could not help but suspect that there were still measures Robert might undertake to keep me here.

And indeed, the following morning, an attendant came to tell me I was wanted in the lunatics' parlor. Entering the room, which was dim, as the curtains had been drawn against the heat, I discovered a bald-headed gentleman with a white beard seated upon the shredded sofa.

"Good afternoon, Mrs. Lincoln," said the gentleman, without rising. Since coming to Bellevue Place, I had observed that gentlemen did not extend polite courtesies to mad ladies.

"I am afraid, sir, that you have the advantage of me."

"My name is McFarland," he replied. "I am a doctor of insanity."

I did not require the explanation, for I recognized the name. Doctor Andrew McFarland was well-known due to his involvement in the legal case of Elizabeth Packard – a lady who had been committed to the doctor's asylum by her husband as a result of the great distaste the man possessed for his wife's Spiritualism. It had required three years for Mrs. Packard to persuade Doctor McFarland of her sanity; and once she was at liberty, she petitioned the Illinois State Legislature to make it unlawful for husbands to commit without a trial those she referred to as "slaves of the marriage union." Doctor McFarland had worked very hard to stop Mrs. Packard's petition, for he also disliked Spiritualism, as well as ladies who questioned their confinement. Assuredly, if I had requested a sign that Robert did not want me to leave the asylum, I could not have received anything more clear than the white-bearded gentleman seated upon the sofa.

"Is it Robert who has sent you?" I waited in the doorway.

"Your son is concerned for your well-being."

"In other words, he wishes you to say that I am too deranged to be released." Doctor McFarland let his hand fall upon the portion of sofa which had been plucked into tatters by Mrs. Bartholomew. With a quiver of disgust, he pulled back his fingers. "Mr. Lincoln is afraid that, in order to avoid unflattering publicity, Doctor Patterson will approve a release for which you are unready."

"Does it seem likely he will do such a thing?" I asked.

Doctor McFarland did not answer the question, but gestured to a chair he had positioned across from himself. "I suggest that you allow me to interview you, for I always consider uncooperativeness a sign of irrationality."

I contemplated which action might win me a verdict of sanity. I could not imagine that Doctor McFarland would decide me anything save mad; but I did not wish to make it certain. With no little caution, I advanced into the parlor and seated myself across from the doctor.

"Do you believe in Spiritualism?" he asked me.

"Are you asking whether I think it is possible we can talk with our dead?"

"That is, I understand, one of the principal tenets of the practice."

"I wish to believe it," I said to him. "Does that make me lunatic?"

"The dead are gone, Mrs. Lincoln. They cannot be contacted."

"Do you have proof that is true?"

Doctor McFarland folded his hands in his lap and regarded me as one might a willful child. "Sane people do not visit mediums," he informed me. "They do not convince themselves that a charlatan's boot knocking against a table leg is a message from their dead relation."

"It is your opinion that the desire to have communication with those we have loved is insane?" I asked.

"If they are dead, yes."

I touched the mourning rings I wore for my sons, for my husband. "You believe speaking with the dead is sign of derangement," I said to the doctor. "But I believe that those I love are not beyond my reach. No matter if they are dead, or living. If I allowed myself to believe otherwise, that would drive me lunatic."

Doctor McFarland sat silent upon the sofa.

"I expect it would be pointless to ask me further questions," I said, rising from my seat.

"I expect that it would," he replied.

"When you make your report to my son," I instructed the doctor, "please repeat to him all that I have said."

My conversation with Doctor McFarland has caused me to think much upon those I have loved who are dead, and also upon a time in my life when I would have employed any means – no matter how desperate – to put myself in their company.

After Taddie and I left Robert's, we moved back into the Clifton House. I settled Taddie into the larger of the two small rooms, a combination bed and sitting room furnished with a wrought-iron bedstead painted black and one armchair covered in a brocade so worn it showed no more of its pattern than faint shadows. I took for myself the back bedroom, which was windowless and close, and so little the bed had to be pushed up against the wall. The time we had spent traveling abroad had taken too much of my income. And I needed money for Taddie's doctors.

My younger son was now never free from fever. His dreams exhausted him, and his breath was wet. To tend him, I called three doctors to our rooms because I did not wish to trust to the opinion of only one.

Doctor Gilman Smith rapped upon Taddie's ribs, listening for the sound of water. "Use poultices to dry his lungs," he advised me, "as hot as can be tolerated."

Doctor Johnson pressed his stethoscope between the prominent bones of my son's shoulders, and noted how he winced with deep breathing. "Feed him many doses of Godfrey's cordial," he said, "for the opium in it."

"The boy's lungs are not seriously diseased," declared Doctor Davis, who was known in all of Chicago as an expert regarding lungs. "Over time, his body will consume the fluid in them."

But over time, Taddie's inhalations took more effort, and his exhalations made it sound as if he were breathing beneath water.

Still, my younger son assured me every day that he was much improved. "My breath comes easier now," he would say. "There are not so many delirious dreams." And every day, I would place a hand upon his laboring chest and tell him, "Yes, you do not look nearly so flushed with fever," in the hope that my lie might turn his true.

To keep Taddie's lungs clear enough for sleeping, I had him rest upon pillows I piled higher as the days passed – taking them from my bed, and then begging more from the rooms which were not occupied. I did not miss my own pillows, for I passed the nights in the armchair covered in faded florals which I kept pulled near to my son. I grew used to waking to the sound of Taddie's coughing, the noise his lungs made as they worked to clear themselves of the night's flooding. However, one morning, after Taddie had been sick some two weeks, I was wakened by an uncommon quiet. Seeing that the room was lit by the slanted light of morning, I leapt from my chair, my body buzzing with alarm.

Taddie's face upon the pillows was wide-eyed and panicked.

"Can you breathe?" I said to him. "Nod to me if you can breathe!"

My son's head remained still.

I grabbed at his wrists and placed his hands behind my neck. "Clasp your fingers together and hold fast to me."

His fingers twined beneath my hair, reminding me of when he had been small. Grabbing hold of his shoulders and pulling hard, I yanked him upright. Taddie sputtered and choked, and after an endless moment began to breathe in a damp wheezing.

"It felt that a weight," he gasped, "something heavy, had been laid upon my chest."

That night, I put Taddie to sleep in a straight-backed wooden chair, which I borrowed from the boardinghouse dining room. To prevent him from toppling to the floor, I pushed the chair up to a small oak table which usually sat in a corner of the room, the edge of it pressed against his chest. But sometime before dawn, Taddie pitched forward and his head struck the table, a blow which left a purpling bruise above one of his eyes.

The following afternoon, I paid one of the housemaids to stay with Taddie and went out to buy what the gentleman in the apothecary shop called a "pleurisy chair." The chair was straight-backed and cushioned for sleeping, and had across the front of it a latching iron bar meant to keep the sufferer contained.

"Are you comfortable in this?" I asked him that night.

"It's better than a bed," he told me, pushing himself against the latched bar to test it.

He did not wake the next day choking, nor did he strike his head in the night. But his neck was so stiffened from sleeping in the chair, he was unable to entirely right his head.

During his sickness, Taddie wished often for his brother's company. I sent letters to Robert every day, asking him to set aside his feeling about me and come for the sake of his brother. After a week of such pleas, Robert replied, stating only a date and time.

I waited for my elder son in a corridor which had lost none of its shabbiness since I had first lived in this place. At the appointed time, Robert came striding around the corner; and in the interval before he noticed me standing outside the door to my rooms, I saw him glance at the greasy wallpaper with remembered revulsion.

"It will make Taddie sad to know that we have quarreled," I said to him.

"I do not intend to tell him of it," Robert replied. He took a step toward the door.

I stayed him with a hand upon his sleeve. "You are my eldest child. The one who made me into a mother. I regret very much what I last spoke to you."

Robert regarded me from over his shoulder. "I am sorry also, that I could not control myself better." He placed his hand upon the door handle.

"And Mary Harlan?" I asked the back of him. "She is well?"

He kept his gaze upon the door. "I do not think my wife an agreeable subject of conversation between us," he told me.

Robert stayed for half an hour, and only when Taddie asked after his sister-in-law did I learn that Mary Harlan had been sent upon an extended visit to her mother.

I prevailed upon my elder son to come and see his brother three and four times a week, for his company seemed the younger boy's best pleasure.

"Help me into clothes," Taddie begged each time his brother was expected.

"I do not think Robert will mind if you are in your nightshirt." I did not like how the effort of dressing left Taddie sunk into his pillows.

But my younger son would only keep pulling upon his buttons, insisting, "I don't want to look sickly in front of him."

After a time, I became frightened of how the work of putting on clothes left Taddie too short of breath, and I refused to let him change out of his nightshirt for his brother.

"At least put pomade on my hair," he pleaded. "Bob hates when it is untidy."

And I combed wax through Taddie's fever-soaked hair and buttoned his nightshirt high to cover the poultice on his chest.

Taddie also did not ever want Robert to see him in the pleurisy chair, and made me help him into the faded armchair before the time of his brother's visit. This desire to keep Robert from having to see how ill he was became a mania for Taddie, infecting even his dreams. One night, I was waked from uneasy sleep by a soft thudding, and when I went to inspect what appeared to be a bundle of clothing tossed upon the carpet, I saw that it was my youngest son.

"Why did you leave your chair?" I asked him. His nightshirt was sweat-soaked, and his breath rank with a scent I refused to name as decay.

"Bob is coming," he said.

"It was a fever dream," I told him. "Your brother won't come until tomorrow."

The following day, he was too weak to be moved for Robert's visit. Indeed, after that night, Taddie did not ever leave the pleurisy chair.

I dosed my son with Godfrey's cordial and draughts of mustard, spread upon his wet lungs concoctions of flax seed and cayenne pepper. But still he got no better. The morning I noticed a bluing about Taddie's fingertips, I called again for the doctors.

"The water in Tad's lungs is pressing upon his heart," said Doctor Davis. The two of us stood in the shabby corridor, for this is where I consulted the doctors, as I did not want Taddie to hear so much about his condition.

"But was his body not supposed to consume the fluid?" I asked.

"I am afraid that it has failed to do so."

"Are you saying that my son will die?" As soon as I had uttered the words, I wished that I could take them back.

"Death is something one should be always prepared for," the doctor replied.

But how am I to prepare for Taddie's death? I wondered. *Does Doctor Davis expect my body to consume the recollections which would cause me to grieve? My youngest son's brightness. His glad conversation, at last rendered clear.*

Perhaps some other mother Doctor Davis knows could heal herself this way; but like Taddie, my body, too, will fail, leaving these recollections to press upon my heart.

As the days passed, Taddie's ankles swelled, and then his legs.

"It is the fluid," said Doctor Gilman Smith.

His lips, like his fingers, acquired a bluish cast.

"That is the weakness of the heart," declared Doctor Johnson.

He grew too weak to hold himself up in the pleurisy chair, and I had to stuff pillows between his chest and the bar to keep him from folding over it.

"Be prepared," repeated Doctor Davis.

"The doctors have instructed me to be prepared," I wrote to Robert. "Do not wait more than a day to come to your brother."

Robert came that evening. Although the sun was low, I had not yet lit the gas, hoping that Taddie would sleep a little; but the pulling required to force air into his flooded lungs could only be done awake, and each time he tried to sleep, he woke choking. The scarcity of breath made speech difficult for Taddie, and when Robert entered, my younger son could do no more than reach his oxygen-starved fingers toward his brother. Robert touched Taddie's hand lightly, then sat himself in the armchair.

"I have brought you a daguerreotype of Mamie."

Robert reached into his pocket and brought out a small likeness which he put into his brother's hand. Taddie moved the portrait closer to his face to see it better. I went to light the gas, as I had the sense that, along with his lungs and heart, my younger son's eyes were failing as well.

"Can you bring her to see me?" Taddie's breathing had grown so shallow, it required an inhalation for each word.

"When you are more well," Robert replied.

Taddie regarded his brother. "It would be better sooner."

My younger son studied the daguerreotype, touching the captured likeness of his niece with a blue-tipped finger.

"You love her," he said to Robert. The ragged inhalations which came between the words made it impossible to know if he had meant this as statement or question.

"She is my child."

"And a father always loves a child," Taddie said. "Like brothers." He reached for Robert's hand, and when it was given to him, he laid it upon his drowning chest. "Like brothers always love each other?" This time he had found breath to make the words a question.

Tell him, I pleaded silently. *Tell him he is right about the way brothers love each other, for he is dying and cannot hold you to it.*

Taddie, perhaps from the breath it had taken to ask his question, perhaps from the breath he had held waiting for it to be answered, slumped back in the pleurisy chair.

"Yes," said Robert, speaking at last. "Brothers love each other."

I could not say if Robert had meant the statement to describe his own true feeling or to instruct himself upon what it should be, but it seemed enough to satisfy Taddie, for he smiled at his brother.

When the pain in Taddie's lungs grew too severe, I gave him a dose of opium. When he coughed up the syrup onto his nightshirt, I gave him another. This second dose put my younger son into a state of dreaming wakefulness. He watched us with clouded eyes, and had so much difficulty staying upright, I was obliged to take the daguerreotype of Mamie from his fingers so he would not crush it against the bar.

Evening turned to night. Robert stayed in the faded armchair, and once I observed him reaching to smooth Taddie's hair, which I had neglected to pomade. I sat upon the bed and worked to take the advice of Doctor Davis. I willed my body to consume Taddie's scent and the feel of his flesh, the soft timbre of his voice and the love I possessed for this last-born of my sons. But I had been tending to Taddie's sickness for six weeks, and my body was too wearied to eat up so much affection.

After a time, the sky began to grow less dark, and I imagined that the light of that dawn possessed a bluish cast, until I understood it was only that all of Taddie's flesh had turned that color. I rose from the bed then, and went to him. His legs had swelled to twice their normal size, and his breathing sounded like the sea.

"A mother always loves her son," I whispered against his cheek.

I prayed that my lungs would fill with the fluid which was strangling him; and when that did not happen, I went to the window and looked out upon the street, as if what we waited for was no more than a visitor.

Not until it ceased did I realize how much sound had been made by Taddie's breathing; and its absence plunged the room into silence so profound, I imagined that all the breathing in the world had stopped.

One week after Taddie's funeral, Robert departed for a resort in the Rocky Mountains which catered to nervous gentlemen, leaving me alone in his house on Wabash Avenue. Although I did not always remember that I was alone, for I had lived so long in Taddie's company, I continued to save up things I wished to tell him – bits of news which came in my letters about his Springfield cousins, a description of a three-legged dog I had seen from Robert's front window. I wandered my son's elegant house, speaking my stored-up pieces of information to the polished cabinets and saber-legged tables, as if to hold them inside would only cause my sadness to accumulate.

But the objects of Robert's house could not be substitute for communication with my youngest son, and I feared that if I did not speak with Taddie, I would become deranged. Prompted by this, I wrote to a medium of terrific powers whom I had met while traveling in the East, a lady by name of Eliza Slataper. "Come and stay with me," I urged to her. "And let us see if you can raise my son."

Mrs. Slataper came and moved into Robert's extra bedroom, and together we worked to call Taddie from the spirit world.

"Bring me something which belonged to Tad," she instructed me before our first magnetic circle. "Those who are on the other side will oftentimes return to hold what was once theirs." Mrs. Slataper was a large-bosomed woman partial to dangling ear bobs, which tinkled when she gave commands.

I searched through a trunk of Taddie's possessions and came up with a box of toffee I had bought before my son took sick and a jar of his hair pomade. These I placed upon the round saber-legged table we had chosen for séance.

After drawing the curtains so that all of Robert's elegant furniture faded into the dimness, Mrs. Slataper took hold of my hands and called into the other world.

"Thomas Lincoln!" she cried in a voice she made deeper than her own. "Your sorrowful mother seeks the comfort of your spirit."

We sat together for nearly an hour, Mrs. Slataper concentrating with such intensity, her ear bobs vibrated with it. However, neither the sweets nor the pomade levitated from the table, and I could feel nothing of Taddie's presence.

For the length of two weeks, we repeated this practice, putting upon the séance table Taddie's neckties, his barely used shaving things, and even the steel frame which had once been fitted into his mouth. But my son's spirit did not come.

"I sense that the vibrations in this house are not conducive," declared the medium. "And I do not like this table."

In search of more productive vibrations, Mrs. Slataper took me to a gathering of Spiritualists who met in a mansion on Dearborn Street. There I sat with a medium – a gentleman – whose spirit guide was a Spanish nobleman, and whose powers, Mrs. Slataper assured me, exceeded her own. But though the gentleman medium conversed in Spanish – a language he professed not to know – and called up the long-dead cousin of another lady, he made no contact with my son.

After that night, I told Mrs. Slataper I would sit at no more séances; for each time I waited and Taddie did not come, it was too like having him die over again. The medium returned to the East; and upon the day that she left, I shut the curtains of Robert's house and saw no one save the doctor who brought me draughts of laudanum to help me sleep.

During this time, I spent as much of the day as I could in sleep, not bothering to corset myself when I woke, for not long after breakfast – and a morning dose of laudanum – I would return to bed, for asleep, I did not store up things to tell to Taddie.

"Do not take too much of this," warned the doctor, when he came to replenish my supply of the opium. "A large dose might be lethal."

But if I drank too little of the laudanum, I dreamed that Taddie and Willie and my husband had never died, that Eddie was alive. And the sorrow of having to wake from such dreams made me incautious about my draughts. Indeed, as the summer wore on, I began to think more often upon never waking from the dreamless sleep of the drug.

So much of my family has passed into the Summerland, I thought, *leaving me behind to sit in dim rooms, hoping for the imagined presence of someone I have loved. Would it not be better if I, too, became spirit and went to the Summerland myself?*

I thought that Robert might mourn me for a time, but he had his own family. And as for Mary Harlan, I imagined her life might be made simpler if she did not have me to be kept away from.

The summer after Taddie died would not end. The days grew as brief as autumn, but the intensity of the heat remained, so that I seemed to be caught in a twilight season of fever and darkness. I stayed shut up in Robert's stifling house, either deep in drugged sleep, or sweating in a chair, my head filled with imaginings of how it would be to hold my children in the Summerland.

"The laudanum is not working as well as it did," I told the doctor when he came. "I am still plagued with sleeplessness."

Repeating his caution about the dose, he left me a larger bottle.

I would have swallowed the entire thing as soon as he was gone, but it was still early, and I feared that a neighbor, or the boy who delivered my food, might come by and discover me in time to stop the opium from doing its work. *It is best to wait until it is dark,* I told myself, *and I am less likely to be disturbed.*

But darkness would not come. Each time I pulled back the

curtain to check the sky, I saw an orange light which glowed in the west and never grew any less – an endless sunset to accompany the endless summer. I opened the window to see it more clearly, and my face was stung by a fierce wind off the prairie, so heated it smelled of burning. This smell of burning made me think of Taddie, who as a child had stood spellbound before every bonfire in Washington City, and I decided that the day was advanced enough.

I wrapped the body I would leave behind in a dressing gown, then put into my pocket a child's book of poetry which had belonged to Willie, one of Taddie's milk teeth, and a small bundle of my husband's letters, as it seemed that these tokens might help me find my family quicker. Once readied, I rebraided my hair, sat upon the bed, and swallowed the bottle of laudanum, following it with a few drops of peppermint oil so I would not die with the drug's bitterness in my mouth.

The next I knew was an insistent pounding, as if my heart were hoping to escape my chest. *Perhaps this is how you die,* I thought, *when your body is unready.* But after a moment I understood that the pounding was outside myself, and that it was more the sound of fists upon the door to Robert's house. *Maybe it is Robert,* I thought, *come to rescue me!* I tried to sit up, but could not concentrate my mind upon the control of my limbs. Only after some time was I able to rise, and when I did, I saw that the room was too bright for nighttime, too bright even for day, and was filled with a thick orange light.

The pounding came faster, faster than the beating of my drugged heart. I noticed then that the air was filled with roaring – *The roaring of my death disturbed?* Above that sound, and the pounding, I heard a man's voice shouting "Fire!" and "Run, if you want to save yourself!"

The laudanum had left me with no will of my own; I was compelled to run, forgetting that I had no wish to save myself. I stumbled down the steps and out into the orange light which was so bright, I could see nothing by it except its glare. I spun about in a terrible heat, felt the pricking of pins upon my shoulders and arms, the flesh of my face, and gazing up, saw that all around me burning cinders were falling like snowflakes.

The sky above my head was full of fire. Flames thundered in every direction, devouring the air, breaking apart in the incendiary wind. A woman knelt in the road with a crucifix clutched to her breast and her skirts on fire. A pack of drunken boys, as young as Tad and Willie when we had lived in Washington City, wheeled past, pouring the contents of a whiskey cask into their mouths. A man dragging a trunk stuffed with paper money knocked me to the ground. "Run!" he shouted. I pulled myself to standing and took off running down the smoke-filled street.

It was an unnatural fire, burning even the buildings made of brick; and it seemed that the smoke and flames were sickening the houses, causing them to spew the objects inside from their windows. Hoops sailed out of the blazing buildings like immense flower petals, crockery fell from roofs and crashed to the ground. A birdcage was hurled from a window, and as it fell to the street, I saw the yellow bird inside flying frantically against the bars.

A woman with a bureau drawer clasped in her arms dashed past, scattering behind her a trail of smoldering chemises. She was followed by a running child, a girl with long golden hair half consumed by flames. At the corner, I nearly tripped over a dead boy, his skull crushed by a marble tabletop disgorged from one of the buildings, his pockets stuffed with jewels. As I stood over him, I was overtaken by a dozen running coffins, upended boxes with their lids thrown open, each one occupied by a ragged boy clutching a dollar coin.

Taddie might be in one of these! I ran down the road after them.

I followed the dead boys to a street of shops. Here, everyone carried something – bolts of dress silks, armloads of hats. "Fire is the friend of the poor man!" shouted a man from atop a splintered piano. The man took a long swallow from a bottle of champagne. "It is God's scourge upon the rich!" Then he flung the bottle into the street, where it shattered against the wheels of a cart filled with harlots. The women in the cart wore little but their shifts, and their naked breasts glowed orange in the firelight, while their faces ran with rouge and soot.

It was then that I knew I was dead. And that I had been delivered into Hell – the reward of harlots and thieves and drunkards; the destiny of suicides. *I have swallowed laudanum, I told myself, and have not gone to the Summerland where my husband and sons wait. Instead, I have been sent to this place of flame and smoke and sin, where I will dwell forever with the damned.*

I fell to my knees upon the hot cobbles and retched, sick with the most terrible despair I had ever known, for there was nothing of hope in it. I had tried to bend God to my will, compel Him to send me to my dead family sooner than was His plan; and as punishment, He had sentenced me to Hell, where I would never see again my husband or my children.

"Run!" shouted a man, too panicked to step around my retching.

Why run? I thought. *When you are already condemned?* But everyone about me was running, and it came to me then that perhaps it was possible to outrun this terrible fate, and that was the reason the damned, even those already burning with Satan's fire, raced along the street.

I got to my feet and ran with them, my eyes stinging from the smoke of Hell's fires, my lungs burning from breathing in the hot cinders. If I made sound, I did not know it, for my ears were too filled with the booming of the flames, and the screaming of my fellow damned. My skirts brushed the corpses of burnt animals – pigs and a horse – and the dead face of a man or a woman, someone who had not run fast enough, someone so charred as to be left little human.

I slowed only when those around me did, when we had arrived in a cemetery, one in which the graves had been opened up, the tombstones uprooted and tossed about the dirt. *This must be the place where I am buried. And if I find my own grave and throw myself into it, perhaps I will escape this fiery place.*

I stumbled through the graveyard, tripping over the cracked and scattered headstones – "Beloved Mother," "Blessed Father," "Innocent Child" – but could not find one with my own name. *Perhaps I have run to the wrong cemetery. Perhaps they have already sent my body to Springfield, too far for me to run.* I threw myself upon the overturned earth, burying my face in its wet decay, for if I had been placed in the tomb in Springfield with my husband and my sons, then only our dead bodies would be near each other, never our spirits.

The doping of my reason lasted until morning, until the flames had consumed most of the city, until the only orange in the sky was a rising sun, smothered by smoke and less bright than the fire. With a mouth so dry my tongue felt papery, I raised my head from the dirt which had covered the dead and understood that I was not in Hell, but in the Catholic cemetery at the north end of town, which was being excavated and moved to make room for a park to be named for my husband.

Other souls who had fled the fire slept among the tombstones, some of them surrounded by their salvaged possessions – an elderly lady with a summer's worth of preserves, a young woman asleep upon her wedding dress. As I made my way through the cemetery – stiffly, for all the joinings of my bones felt parched – I saw that thousands had sought refuge in this place where there was little to burn, far more than the number of dead which lay here. Everyone appeared stunned, as if they, too, had drunk too much opium the night before; and their faces and hands were stained black, darker than any Negro. Glancing at my own hands, I saw that they, also, were black, and that the sleeves of my dressing gown were covered with hundreds of tiny burn holes.

I reached into my pocket, searching for Willie's book of poetry, Taddie's milk tooth, my husband's letters. But they were gone.

I knew that I would not again attempt to join my family by drinking poison. The fire which had burned so much of Chicago – and saved me – was warning enough. If I could not give up the wish to be in the company of my dead family, then I would have to seek them in the only manner which existed for the living – to sit in séance and wait for a medium to bring them to me. I could, however, improve my chances by sitting with only the most skillful of sensitives. Mediums who could be found in the Spiritualist communities of which I had heard tell.

There is nothing to keep me here, I thought. *Even if Robert's house has remained unburned, when Mary Harlan returns, I will not even have a place to live. Better that I go in search of these mediums of uncommon power, these clairvoyants who will, without condemning me to Hell, reunite me with my family in the Summerland.*

I went looking first for my deceased family in the Spiritualist community of St. Charles, Illinois. This small town, a morning's journey from Chicago, was home to more mediums than blacksmiths, and hosted more magnetic circles than church socials. Here, I took rooms at the Howard House hotel and went to séance with Caroline Howard, the wife of the proprietor. Mrs. Howard was the most well-regarded clairvoyant in St. Charles, having made her reputation by divining some years back the whereabouts of a missing corpse. She was a middle-aged, florid woman, plump, and without the pallor so oft found in the complexions of those who spoke with the dead. The wife of the hotel's proprietor conducted her séances in a yellow-painted house decorated with much gingerbread trim.

Mrs. Howard's specialty was spirit painting, and after I had been in St. Charles a week, she invited me to witness a demonstration of it. I arrived early at the yellow building and was shown into the séance parlor, which had been constructed in the center of the house so that it possessed no windows. Generally, Mrs. Howard had us sit in magnetic circle at a table covered with a damask cloth edged with fringe. This evening, however, the cloth was gone and the table was topped by a slab of cut glass, and after the clairvoyant had called us to the table, she did not clasp the hands of those who were seated at the sides of her, but instead put into her fingers a sable-tipped brush, which she then poised above a small palette of oils.

"Reverend Tweedale, might you secure the bandages?" said Mrs. Howard to a very elderly gentleman dressed all in black.

The reverend wrapped the lady's eyes in a white bandage, which he tied tightly behind her head, making it appear as though the clairvoyant had been blinded.

"Miss Spinny," said Mrs. Howard, nodding at the young lady seated to her left, "if you would see to the papers?"

A lady dressed in the short skirts and Turkish trousers of the hygienic-reform style reached for a small sheaf of blank pages, placing one before the medium.

"Spirit painting requires a great deal of magnetism," Mrs. Howard told us. "Therefore, I shall ask you to please allow your concentration to remain within this room."

Some minutes passed, and then Mrs. Howard shrugged her shoulders, a gesture she always made before trance, as if shrugging off her consciousness of this world like an over-heavy coat. The room was silent – even the clocks did not tick, for Mrs. Howard instructed her parlor maid to stop them before every séance – and it seemed that everyone seated about the oval table did not breathe, so hard were we concentrating upon the sable brush poised above the oils.

Then, with a gasp which came sudden and loud in the still room, Mrs. Howard let the brush fall into one of the oils and began painting.

I had seen the results of spirit painting before, the fantastical landscapes and strange scenes drawn by those who had passed beyond the veil. The Lauries had possessed a gallery of spirit art at their home in Georgetown, and I recall particularly a painting of a statue half-human and half-beast, and another of a man no bigger than a bee attacking the flesh of a giant being. But I had never witnessed such artwork being created, and the sight of the blinded clairvoyant painting in trance held me so mesmerized, I do not believe I shut my eyes to blink.

Mrs. Howard's painting arm moved with such speed, and with such independence from her stilled body, the limb appeared possessed. Paint moved from palette to paper with supernatural rapidity, shaping itself into landscapes and finely rendered portraits. Each time that the hand deemed a painting complete, it set down the brush and rapped loudly upon the table, and the young lady in Turkish trousers replaced the paper with a fresh one.

Each person appeared to know which painting had been done for him, or for her, and lunged across the table to take hold of it. And each time that Mrs. Howard began a new picture, I searched its colors, finding Willie's eyes in the blue that became sky, Taddie's undisciplined hair in the brown of any shading.

"Paint *my* dead," I whispered into the room.

After nearly everyone at the table had received a painting, Mrs. Howard's hand stilled, the sable brush hovering above blank paper.

Do not stop now, I willed the medium.

Then, with no warning or visible cause, Mrs. Howard drew her mouth into a smile which was familiar to me, as it was the expression of irrepressible pleasure which my youngest son's brightness had brought to all he turned it upon. With the smile still playing upon her mouth, the clairvoyant began to paint.

The image came with very few brushstrokes, yet all was there – the rounded curve of Taddie's cheek, the weighted lids of my sleepy-eyed child. Seeing it take shape was like watching the face of my last-born son appear beneath the glass of the table.

Like the others, I lunged for my spirit portrait the moment Mrs. Howard's possessed hand rapped upon the table, taking it into my hands the way I would have taken my son, had a more merciful God returned him to me.

I continued to visit Mrs. Howard; however, she was unable to again call any of my family from the Summerland, and she painted me no more spirit portraits. After two months spent in St. Charles, I traveled to Moravia, a Spiritualist community in upstate New York, seeking a sensitive named Sarah Keeler. Miss Keeler, the seventeen-year-old daughter of a farmer, was said to possess so much magnetism, she could sometimes lend the spirits corporeal form.

Miss Keeler conducted her séances in a small wood-framed cottage, atop which had been constructed an enormous cupola, more than half the size of the house below.

"The design for the cupola was given to my daughter by the spirits," explained Miss Keeler's father, a gray-bearded man in overalls who collected fifty cents from each of us who entered the overshadowed house. "The arches are how they come and go. The souls my daughter calls up don't seem to care for doors."

At Miss Keeler's séance, we sat with joined hands at a table, but in chairs arranged in rows before a thin wood partition. As my eyes adjusted to the dim lighting, I noticed that a small window had been cut into the partition, behind which was only blackness.

When all the seats were filled, the farmer led his daughter into the room. Miss Keeler was slight and wore her hair in childish braids.

"My daughter will now sit herself behind the partition," announced the farmer, "in order to lend her magnetism to the spirits."

"How do we know she won't play the part of the spirits herself?" asked one of the gentlemen seated in the row of chairs.

"That is the reason the partition had been made so thin." The farmer rapped upon the wood with his knuckles, producing a hollow sound. "If my daughter leaves her seat, you will hear it."

He then extinguished the lamps and we sat in the darkness, staring at the place we imagined the opening in the partition to be. This dark was so sudden, and so complete, it was like being rendered blind. And indeed, I began to fear that something had gone wrong with my sight, for after a minute had passed, I saw sparks of light, as if small stars flew through the darkness. However, a gasp from the lady beside me told that she, too, saw the tiny flashes of light. And then the man who had questioned the farmer let out a low whistle.

The sparks moved about in the opening of the partition, slowly drawing themselves together until they began to define a shape – until they took the form of what could have been the plump, cheerful face of a man in his fifties.

"That is my doctor!" cried a lady in a hoarse whisper. "He passed into spirit only one month past."

The face in the window seemed to dissolve and reform. And then the lady squealed.

"He has just patted my knee!" she told us. "He did that every time I went to him."

My flesh nearly shuddered from my bones with yearning for such a touch from one of my lost sons, from my husband. I thought hard upon the weight of Eddie against my chest, the feel of Willie's hair, the affectionate insistence of Taddie's shoulder pushing into me. I thought, too, upon my husband's hands, and of all the places – decent and indecent – they had touched me, until my breath quickened and my mourning-dressed flesh warmed, and the only respectable action would be to beg the farmer to let me out of the room.

And that is the moment I felt the hands come to rest upon my shoulders.

They were too familiar to be the farmer's hands, too large, with fingers which reached to my collarbones, and too accompanied by the scent of woodsmoke. In their weight I felt a great and terrible sadness, a sorrow too profound to be borne by the living, although I lived every hour with one of equal heft. The feel of these sorrowful hands made me glad, and I pushed myself more firmly into their grasp, trembling at how they were so much more flesh than spirit. Unlike the lady who had been touched by her doctor, I said nothing about my own contact, afraid that to speak would make the hands vanish. But after less than a minute, they did vanish. And all I felt against my shoulders was the scrollwork carved into the backs of the Keelers' chairs.

I remained almost a month in Moravia, going every day to the cottage. In the shadowed opening of the little window I saw only the faces of the dead which belonged to other people. And I never again felt the sorrowful weight of my husband's hands.

I went next to Boston, a city which possessed more clairvoyants than any other. All through that cold New England winter, I took my place beside the scions of moneyed New England families, held the hands of lady suffragists from Cambridge. Twice I thought I saw Taddie's face hovering behind a certain gentleman medium, mimicking the very precise manner in which he called up the spirits. One time I imagined that my lap felt Willie's weight, and at the end of the evening, I noticed that my skirts were creased by something I could not otherwise explain. And three or four times, I smelled woodsmoke, but I could not be sure if the scent had traveled from the spirit world or merely through an opened window.

In Boston, too, I visited the second-floor studio of the spirit photographer William Mumler. Mr. Mumler's studio consisted of a long gallery hung with examples of his work: daguerreotypes of lady mediums with the ghostly outlines of bearded gentlemen floating above their heads; images of psychics in trance, the viscous white substance of spirit ectoplasm emanating from their noses and navels. Standing among them, I felt as if I had entered an overcrowded séance parlor in which various manifestations of mediumistic ability were happening all at once.

"I have had an experience in séance of which I would like a photograph," I said to Mr. Mumler. "The spirit of my husband came and rested his hands – hands which were turned flesh – upon my shoulders."

"Sit for me, Mrs. Lincoln." The spirit photographer inclined his well-groomed head in the direction of a velvet-covered armchair. "And I will call up your Noble Husband for my camera."

I sat for Mr. Mumler, and when I returned to his studio some days later, the spirit photographer presented me with a daguerreotype he called a "blending of science and the supernatural." In the photograph, I was settled stolidly in the velvet-covered armchair, the black ribbon of my bonnet tied beneath a double chin, for all this sitting at séance had made me fat. Behind me, hovered the spectral likeness of my husband, his hands resting upon my shoulders.

I slept that night with Mr. Mumler's daguerreotype and dreamt that my husband's hands did not stay upon my shoulders, but traveled everywhere upon me; and I woke with the buttons of my nightdress undone and the daguerreotype pressed against my flesh. My body ached as if I had physically committed the acts of my dreams, still, I did not want to rise from my bed, for I wished to force myself back into sleep and return to my indecent dreaming. I placed Mr. Mumler's photograph upon the pillow near my face, imagining that the dream would come more easily if my last waking image was this picture of my husband.

But I saw now what I had not noticed in the dim light of Mr. Mumler's studio: the hands were wrong! Those hands which rested upon my shoulders in the daguerreotype, the hands which I had dreamed upon the most private portions of my flesh, did not belong to my husband.

As if I had discovered a stranger upon the pillow, I leapt from bed, pulling shut my nightdress. *How could I have believed that those hands belonged to my husband?* They were too large-knuckled, too coarse; gazing upon them I felt shame for all I had permitted them to do to me in dreams.

How could I not have seen this? Had my desire for the photograph to be true blinded me to its obvious fakery? The question sent me to the bureau to retrieve the spirit painting of Taddie. I did not need to hold the portrait to the light to know the likeness could be any boy, and that this was likely the handiwork of a lady who had learned to paint blindfolded. Recalling how I had kissed this painted image every night, I hurled the counterfeit portrait to the floor, rubbed at my mouth with the back of my hand, as if bits of paint were stuck there like a badge of my gullibility.

How long, I asked myself, *until I observe the viscid white matter emerge from a medium's navel, and believing it is one of my sons, reach for it? How long until I try to kiss a floating head, thinking it belongs to my husband?*

I turned back to the bureau, which was covered with Spiritualist journals and pamphlets endorsing communication with the dead, and saw nestled among these things the daguerreotype of my living granddaughter which Robert had brought to Taddie just before he died. *This is a likeness which needs nothing of the supernatural to bring it into being,* I told myself. *An entire gallery of daguerreotypes of Mamie could be made with only silver iodide and mercury and light.* Although one would not need to make so many, not when the real child existed to be held and kissed into sleep.

I knew then that I had been loving ghosts.

I returned to Chicago at the end of winter. I had been away only six months, but already the city was recovering from the fire which had consumed so much of it. New buildings, grander and taller than those which had stood before, rose everywhere upon the singed ground. Workmen hurried through the streets, shouting to one another in German and Polish for help with the donkey carts overladen with charred blocks of concrete and cindered wood. The sound of hammering echoed from every block, making it seem that the city possessed a hundred hearts, and that they were all returning to life at the same instant.

I took up residence in an unfinished hotel which offered reduced rates, for its upper stories were uncompleted and stood open to the sky. My rooms, situated just beneath these floors, were stuffed with an abundance of velvet chairs – my skirts tangled in their legs several times a day – and I suspected that most of them had been bought for the rooms above, and that the hotel had run out of places to store them.

My fittings were fine – damask at the windows and silk in the carpeting. However, at unexpected intervals my walls experienced a violent shuddering. At first, I imagined that my shaking walls were possessed by supernormal energy, and that I was being visited by unbidden spirits. The desk clerk, however, informed me that the vibrations were caused only by the wheelbarrows of bricks being hauled above my head.

As soon as I was settled I wrote to Robert asking if he would come to me, appealing to him to bring Mamie and Mary Harlan.

"My business demands much of my time now," he responded. "As the expenses of my family require a larger income."

I repeated my invitation for the following day, and the one after that. But for each date I suggested, my son made the excuse of the money he must earn to maintain his family.

You must be persistent, I said to myself. *You must give your living family as much chance to come to you as you granted your spirit one.* And so I continued every day to extend invitations to my son. Once the note was sent, I passed the rest of the morning arranging my velvet chairs around the tea table, as if the exercise were an enchantment devised to bring Robert. I was even careful to set out four of the chairs, thinking the number would act as a talismen to call up Mary Harlan. When Robert's regrets arrived, as they inevitably did, I replaced all the chairs against the wall, where they sat like audience to the sight of my disappointment.

After I had been back in Chicago some two weeks, I received a letter from Judge Davis, who, at Robert's request, continued to handle our estates and wished to know my desires regarding Taddie's inheritance.

"As Thomas Lincoln's mother," Judge Davis wrote, "you are entitled to two-thirds of his capital. A not-inconsiderable sum of $35,750."

I sat among my chairs and thought how two-thirds of Taddie's inheritance would allow me to leave this unfinished hotel and move back into the West Washington Street house. But of course, the idea of the house had been to live there with my sons.

"I believe I would be carrying out the wishes of my beloved Taddie," I wrote back to the judge, "when I suggest that an equal division of his inheritance be made between his brother and myself."

After I posted the note to Judge Davis, I sent off one to Robert, informing him of what I had decided about Taddie's inheritance and inviting him for tea upon the following day. "Please bring Mamie with you," I wrote in my postscript. "The hotel makes a very sweet white cake, much loved by little girls."

That morning, I rearranged my chairs and ordered the white cake. To strengthen the charm of the fourth chair, I asked the kitchen to send up that many settings, as if a teacup painted with blue roses might possess the power to draw my daughter-in-law. At the appointed time, there came quick knocking upon the door. When I opened it, I saw that Robert had not brought Mary Harlan. He had, however, brought me my small granddaughter.

Mamie was just six months past her second birthday, fair and delicately made like her mother, and possessed of the same bright hair which curled forward around her ears, as if seeking to touch her face. My granddaughter was dressed more neatly than my sons ever had been, in a camel-colored coat which matched her father's.

I dropped to my knees in the doorway and put my arms about her, feeling the soft wool of her coat and the hard fragility of the bones across her chest. It had been so long since the man holding Mamie's hand was this age, so long since any of my own sons were small, I had forgotten how much young children smell of new-baked bread – and how only breathing them in made one glad.

"You have come!" I exclaimed. "And you could not look more pretty in that coat."

"Thank you, Grandmama," Mamie replied. She formed her words perfectly.

Robert brushed granite dust from the shoulders of his coat. "This is a lunatic place to stay."

"It is a very great bargain," I told him.

"Such a bargain that you are required to entertain us in the doorway?"

I stood, stepping to the side to allow them in. "It is only that I am so pleased you have brought me Mamie."

My granddaughter sat straight upon her velvet seat, her white-booted feet scarcely reaching the edge of the chair. She held her china cup more confidently than any of my sons had ever done, more than her grandfather could on most occasions; and I found it almost disquieting to watch this child, small for her age, sit upright upon a velvet chair and with so much poise, sip milked tea from a china cup.

"You must have the white cake," I said to Mamie. "Lots of it."

I passed the plate of cake to her, but my granddaughter looked first to her father, waiting for some signal which I could not detect. Only after she had received it, did she take the plate from my hands.

Robert ate no white cake. And I ate too much of it, chattering away with Mamie upon the topic of dresses – about which she was uncommonly expert.

"Pantalettes should always have frills," she told me, as she fluffed the very many crimped ones upon her own. "And I do not think fur should be worn before the age of twelve."

I listened to all my granddaughter's pronouncements about fashion, wondering if they had originated with Robert, for I did not recall that Mary Harlan possessed such strictness about clothes.

"I expect you would prefer to discuss something other than pantalettes," I said to my son. "And are probably wishing Mamie and I would move the conversation into more gentlemanly topics."

"I did come with business I wished to speak with you about," Robert said.

"Tell me, then," I told him. "Before your daughter takes up the subject of sashes."

Robert set down his tea. "I wish you to make me a loan," he said. "Chicago is being rebuilt on a grand scale, and there is much speculation in real estate."

"The extra portion of Taddie's inheritance is not enough?"

"The scheme I am interested in has been devised by gentlemen of substantial means. A similarly substantial investment is required."

I set down my own cup. "Is it a very big loan that you want?"

"No more than ten thousand dollars."

I did not wish to show him my astonishment, for I knew what it was like to ask for money, although my son did not appear as uneasy – or as humbled – by the experience as I ever had.

"That is a large portion of my capital," I told him.

Robert shoved his cup away. "And I know how little fond you are of loaning money."

"I am only afraid of being poor again."

"You cannot be poor again!" Robert's raised voice caused Mamie to glance at her father, then myself. "Not if you do not misspend your money in shopping."

I poured more milked tea for Mamie. Robert was likely right in this, but it is not possible to lose as much as I to poverty and not be altered by it. Every dollar which I spent made me feel again the breathlessness of debt; any bit of money which left my hands – no matter how insignificant – recalled for me the image of myself as a black figure in the garden of the house I could not keep.

Robert got to his feet. "I think, Mamie, it is time for us to go."

My granddaughter hopped from her velvet chair and went to him. The two went to the doorway, where I had hung their coats upon hooks.

"Would you need the money for very long?" I said.

"Some few years," my son replied. "Until the houses are built, and sold."

He gave his daughter her coat.

"May we come to see Grandmama again?" she asked him.

"Perhaps," he told her.

I left the table and went to help my granddaughter into her soft coat, fastening the buttons to the base of her throat, because it was still more winter than spring outside, and because I wished to touch the fine vein I could see beating there. Mamie ran her fingers over the bones of my knuckles, lingering upon the jet ring I wore for Willie.

When she had done feeling it, I rose and stood before my son. "I shall loan you the ten thousand," I told him.

"You will not change your mind?" he said.

"No."

"I will have my office draw up the papers tomorrow."

"As quick as that?"

"Business opportunities in Chicago do not wait."

My son buttoned himself into his coat.

"Robert?" I put a hand upon his sleeve. "I would like to come to your house."

"I am afraid Mary Harlan does not wish it."

"She does not wish to see me?"

"She believes that you have interfered too much with the running of her household."

"She has said this?"

He nodded. The gesture was so definitive, I wondered whether Mary Harlan had made the comment, or if Robert had just told it to her.

"Then let us travel together," I persisted. "North, for the summer. Canada, perhaps."

"I am taking my family to Europe for the summer," said my son.

"I can assist you there," I told him. "My French is still serviceable. And I know people in Frankfurt."

"I already have letters of introduction for the important European cities."

"I could help with Mamie, then," I said, "so you would not need a nurse."

Robert took his daughter's hand. "I wish to make this trip with my family."

I had the urge to tell my son that I had just paid ten thousand dollars for the affections of that family.

"You and Mamie and Mary Harlan are what is left of *my* family," I told him.

As if set off by my words, the walls shuddered with a deep rumbling.

"What is that?" asked Robert, frowning at the wallpaper.

That is the portion of our family which is dead, I thought, *and cannot comprehend that you would wish to keep separate those of us who draw breath.*

"Only the workmen upon the higher floors," I told my son.

Robert shook his head. "I hope it is a very great bargain."

He opened the door, and they were gone down the corridor, leaving me with my chairs.

Before he left for Europe, Robert asked me for another loan. After I gave him the money, he brought Mamie again to my rooms for tea and white cake. When my son returned from his trip, he requested an additional sum. This money bought me an outing to the shops of State Street, where my granddaughter and I discussed the relative beauty of all the china-faced dolls in the windows. Some five months later, my son expressed an interest in purchasing from me the little stone house on West Washington Street. The price Robert mentioned felt less than the house was worth, but I let him have it, a generosity which purchased for me Mamie's sole company at a tea, during which we discussed with great seriousness when my nearly four-year-old granddaughter might acquire her first little girl's corset.

The pattern of my intercourse with my living family did not vary for all of these many months. Robert came to me for loans, and when I gave him the money, he brought my granddaughter to me. It was much the way it had worked with the mediums, although Robert could more reliably – and genuinely – produce Mamie than the mediums could conjure Willie or Tad. Still, no matter how large the loans I made to Robert, his house – and my daughter-in-law – remained as forbidden to me as the Summerland.

In the second spring after my return to Chicago, the turning over of a large sum brought me an invitation to accompany Robert and Mamie to the puppet theater in Union Park. In the nine years since my husband was murdered, I had not been inside a theater, and I wished my son had suggested some other entertainment. But I had seen little of my granddaughter all winter, and so wrote back that I would meet them in the park; then worked to remind myself that a puppet theater would be nothing like Ford's.

The day upon which we fixed for meeting was Palm Sunday, and like most of that year's winter, it was cruelly cold. The sky hung low with clouds, and the wind blew in gusts which pierced the flannel of my coat and tore the palm fronds from the hands of the children coming from church. I waited for my son and granddaughter on the gravel path outside the puppet theater, a red-painted building which was made to look like a small peaked-roof house.

"Why are you waiting out here?" said Robert, hurrying up the path.

"I did not wish to go into the theater alone."

"Look, Grandmama!" Mamie clutched a long frond of dried palm. "It is just like those the disciples carried when Jesus went to Jerusalem."

"You are very smart," I told her.

"Jesus was killed on Good Friday," she declared.

"So was your grandfather."

Robert and Mamie stared at me with no small astonishment. Indeed, I was astonished myself, for I had not meant to tell her this.

"Let us go inside," I said to them. "The day has turned too raw."

Inside, the small red-painted house was no more than a box containing rows of wooden benches. The puppets performed behind a window cut into a partition, an arrangement which made me think of the dark opening where Miss Keeler had caused the faces of the dead to appear.

You see that you were right, I said to myself. *This is nothing like Ford's.*

Save for that shrieking, replied my other voice, which preferred truth to comfort. *That is exactly the shrieking of the audience after they heard Mr. Lincoln had been shot.*

It is only the screaming of children, I told it, *made excited by the prospect of puppets.* Although I wished that the performance would begin and distract them into silence.

The story was Little Red Cap and the Wolf, acted out by puppets with painted faces and stiff little arms. I watched with Mamie's hand held in mine, my granddaughter so transfixed she was chewing lightly upon her palm frond.

You see, I told myself, *there are not even actors here.*

But when the wolf appeared, he seemed to me bigger than the other characters, more like a man and handsome in his little frock coat. *He is just bigger because he is the villain. And he cannot be handsome in the manner of a man, because he is made of wood and cloth and papier maché.* Still, as the character passed beneath a gas lamp, I imagined I saw something glinting in each of his hands.

Mr. Booth has been dead for nine years, I reminded myself. *And this is a puppet.*

Perhaps this is his spirit, replied the unfeeling voice, *inhabiting another villain.*

Why would Mr. Booth's spirit come to rest inside a puppet?

To carry out another plot.

In the story he is meant to kill Little Red Cap's grandmother.

Little Red Cap's grandmother is a puppet, the voice said scornfully. *Booth would not return to murder a puppet.*

Who then?

But of course, I knew. The assassin would come to kill whoever sat beside me, whoever had their hand in mine.

I felt there to be some flaw in this logic, but in the darkened theater with the shrieking children, my mind told me that the spirit of John Wilkes Booth was possessing the wolf puppet as surely as I had seen spirits possess the bodies of sensitives in séance, and that the assassin always killed in theaters.

And he always kills quickly. I grabbed my granddaughter from the bench, taking her up so suddenly, the palm frond whipped my across my cheek.

"What are you doing?" whispered Robert. He took hold of Mamie's boot.

"It is Booth!" I told him. "The wolf is Booth!"

The name made Robert startle and let go his daughter's foot. Freed, I turned and pushed my way into the aisle.

"Papa!" cried Mamie, her voice muffled by being pressed so close to my collar.

I heard behind me a frantic scuffling. *That is Robert,* I thought, *rushing from his seat so he might knock the gun and the knife from the wolf's puppet hands, and this time stop the assassination.*

With Mamie still in my arms, I burst into the daylight and did not leave off running until I stood upon the gravel path with the wind blowing upon me. And it was then, as if that wind was made so cold by an excess of clarity, that I knew everything I had done.

I set down my granddaughter, smoothing her disordered hair. "It was the theater," I told her. "And the wolf." But my explanation only made her stand silent with the palm frond between us.

Robert came rushing from the theater, reached me, and lifted Mamie into his arms.

"I believed she was in danger," I said to him.

"Your reason had become unsound," he told me.

"It is only that I cannot go to theaters."

He looked at me hard. "I am not certain you should be allowed to go anywhere!"

"Robert, please." I reached for his arm, for Mamie, but he stepped away.

"I have begun to wish you would disappear," he told me.

"You cannot mean that," I said.

"I can," he replied. "Even though it is unkind and improper for me to say it." He set his daughter upon the ground, his own legs standing between us. "I think it best that you not see Mamie for a time."

"Robert, please, no."

"You are unstable," he said. "It is not advisable for her to be in your company."

Like Mary Harlan, I thought, *when she is taking drink.*

"I shall find a way to be more calm," I promised him. "I shall consult a doctor."

Robert regarded me appraisingly. "One whom I choose?"

"If you wish. But please do not keep Mamie from me."

My son shook his head. "I cannot subject my child to madness."

"You know I am not mad."

"Then do not act like it."

"It is the Female Tragedy," declared Doctor Danforth some days later. "The Woman's Hell."

Doctor Danforth specialized in diseases of the organs of reproduction. Upon the wall of his office, which was furnished much like a gentlemen's club, the doctor kept a rendering of a lady whose flesh had been cut away in order to display these organs.

"It is an affliction which is not uncommon in women of your age," Doctor Danforth continued. "The organs of reproduction, having ceased to fulfill their function, suffer from a tumultuous state of irritation and disorder."

"And this would cause me to behave as if I am unreasoned?" I asked.

Doctor Danforth nodded with no hesitation. "What you are experiencing is a backup of vile humors in the womb."

"Can you prescribe me a remedy?"

The doctor shook his head. "There is no remedy for the Woman's Hell." He glanced at the rendering of the cutaway lady. "However, the symptoms of it can be lessened by avoiding all indulgences which cause an unnatural state of excitement. Dancing. Gambling. Rich food. Coffee, tea, and tobacco. And the reading of novels."

Doctor Danforth also prescribed frequent doses of Lydia Pinkham's Vegetable Compound – a concoction of black cohosh and chaste-tree berries preserved in alcohol. "Many ladies say that Mrs. Pinkham is the savior of her sex," he told me.

I followed Doctor Danforth's instructions without deviation – drinking nothing stronger than an infusion made from chamomile, and reading only the Bible. The absence of coffee, the Scriptures, and the frequent dosing with Mrs. Pinkham's elixir, all worked to make me drowsy, and I spent much time in sleep. But so much sleeping caused me to be susceptible to nightmares, and as the weeks passed, I was plagued by terrible dreams which I could not recall, but which frightened me awake to find myself half off the mattress, as if I had attempted to escape my bed. This dreaming left me with a steel-fisted pain in my chest, and I began to imagine that the demons which resided in such nightmares were able to reach between my ribs and squeeze my heart.

After such dreams, I could not allow myself to sleep again, but turned the gas on bright and sat in a chair until dawn.

For all of these months, I saw Mamie only one time, and only for a short while. Robert brought her to my hotel, saying it would be better if we went nowhere in public; and for the length of the visit, my granddaughter was very polite to me. However, though it was an early fall day and my rooms were warm, I could not persuade her to remove her coat. Once she had gone, I wondered if Mamie had wished to be prepared in the event I scooped her up and ran outside again, or if she had only wanted to be ready to depart more swiftly.

Once winter came, I was so deprived of sleep, I began to count upon the chill wind to sting me into wakefulness. Doctor Danforth recommended Florida. "The mild climate will work upon the agitation of your womb," he advised.

I made plans to travel to Green Cove, where the springs, according to Doctor Danforth, would cure everything from constipation to consumption. As Robert believed it improper for me to travel alone, I hired a companion – a nurse by the name of Mary Fitzgerald. Mrs. Fitzgerald, who was a widow, was shorter and plumper than I, and I had the impression that when we went about, we appeared no more than two squat piles of bombazine and veils. Before year's end, the two of us traveled to Green Cove by train, and there took rooms in an establishment with a name no more embellished than "Mrs. Stockton's boardinghouse."

Green Cove was overrun with plants which bore leaves bigger than a man's hand and grew to mammoth proportions, blocking the light and hoarding it for themselves. These plants seemed to sprout overnight, unfurling new leaves and sending out seeking tendrils which grew back as quickly as they were cut. The atmosphere of the place was damp and sulfurous from the great many natural springs nearby, and the clapboard sides of Mrs. Stockton's boardinghouse grew a creeping mold which made the wood soft and smell of rot.

I could not sleep in Green Cove. The hot, damp air oppressed me; and I swore that I could hear the plants growing. When I complained of this to Mrs. Stockton, a lady who appeared always damp herself, she sent me to an apothecary in Jacksonville.

"The only cure for insomnia is chloral hydrate combined with laudanum," declared the druggist. Although the man was not a doctor, he possessed the positive air of one.

"I have not taken chloral before," I told him. "Will it produce any unwanted effects?"

"Only some drifting of the mind when awake," he assured me.

"Does it prevent dreaming?"

"No one for whom I have prescribed it recollects any. Only keep the amount of chloral to forty grains. And water the laudanum with wine."

I followed the druggist's prescription, and for the first time in many weeks slept without dreaming; although in the morning, it took me some hours to wake and my thinking was muddled till noon. Still, I was well enough to visit the pump room at the Clarendon Hotel, where I went to drink Green Cove's sulfurous waters.

The Clarendon was a grand, columned building made of white limestone. The walls of its pump room were lined with tall windows of divided light, which gave out over a broad green lawn, kept clear of invading vines by daily gardening. Inside the high-ceilinged room, white-coated attendants filled small glass bottles with mineral-rich water, while a string quartet played soothingly. The wainscoting was white-painted and the floor laid with marble the color of fresh milk.

The gentlemen and ladies who came to the Clarendon to cure their consumption and gout, their liver ailments and neurasthenia, were all well-bred and polite. After a time, I made the acquaintance of several who came to take their water the same time as myself, including a chivalrous gentleman from Virginia, who offered to stand in the line and fetch me my bottle of water. The gentleman from Virginia was below forty and appeared to suffer from anemia of the blood, as he was as white-skinned as the Southern ladies who protected themselves beneath umbrellas.

The gentleman and I developed the habit of drinking our water together, talking lightly of horses, upon which the gentleman from Virginia was expert, and of the cities we both knew in the South.

"As a younger man, I went very often to Richmond," the gentleman told me. He placed his fingertips upon his dark mustache, a gesture he made when preparing to say something of deeper import than usual pump room discourse. "I believe that war is made more tragic when it comes to lovely cities."

I meant to agree with this poetical remark, but the gentleman had made me remember my last visit to Richmond, just before the war ended. I recalled the boy who had raised a blackened broom handle at us, the Confederate soldier I was not certain I had seen in the window, and it seemed to me that I had never heard the Virginian gentleman's accent so strongly before. Indeed, his speaking about Richmond had sounded more Southern than anything I had heard from him, and I wondered if that had been the gentleman's intention.

But for what purpose? To show me that he still held solidarity with the rebel states? To remind me of my own drawl and my traitorousness to the Cause?

It is only the vile humors of my womb which are making me think this, I told myself. And I drank an extra portion of the sulfurous water.

The following day, when the Virginian gentleman came with my water, I noticed for the first time how handsome he was. *He is as handsome as John Wilkes Booth,* I thought, *who was also from Virginia. He is as pale as him as well. And I will wager that his breath stinks of sickbed.* Intent upon proving this, I waited until the gentleman bent to hand me my bottle, then raised my face to his mouth. But his breath smelled only of old eggs from the water.

Drink more, I told myself. *Drown these organs which are making you think mad thoughts.* But the day after, when the gentleman from Virginia stopped by my chair to greet me, I saw flecks of blood caught in the hairs of his mustache.

That is the light, coming in at an angle, which gives the appearance of blood, I said to myself. *Unless it is not, for I do not see blood upon the marble floor or the whitewashed walls.* It occurred to me then that the blood might be a vision, one which had been sent by the spirit world as a warning.

But what action could the gentleman from Virginia intend of which I need to be warned? I thought.

The rebels from Virginia once threatened to murder your family, replied that other voice.

The war has been over for nearly ten years, I told it. *And no one has murdered me yet.*

Perhaps he has been waiting to find you alone, with no son to protect you.

I tried then to tell myself that my suspicions could be more logically traced to the Woman's Hell than to the spirit world, but I could not keep from watching the gentleman from Virginia as he fetched my water. And it was good that I did, for as he was returning to me, I observed something which made me believe it had indeed been spirits and not organs which had turned me mistrustful. He had come only partway across the room with my water, when he turned away and made a small motion of his arm. The same motion he would use if he were filling my bottle with poison.

I made no sound, only sat and watched him turn back and approach me with the poisoned water.

"The serving girl tells me the waters are particularly potent today," he said. "I could only agree, as the smell is especially strong." He made a little bow and held out the bottle.

That is my death in that glass, I thought. *If I drink it, I shall be seized with choking and retching, and the poison will eat me from the inside out.* And I threw up my arm and knocked the bottle from the gentleman's hand, splashing the poisoned water upon his well-cut trousers and leather boots.

"I will not allow you to assassinate me!" I told him.

The gentleman stared at me in perplexity. "I shall fetch an attendant for you," he said. "Please, stay and collect yourself until I return."

He made me another bow and moved away. Once he had gone, I noticed that the quartet had stopped playing, and that all the well-bred gentlemen and ladies had ceased sipping at their curative waters to stare at me.

They must believe I am insane, I thought. *For there is no way for them to know about the poison.* How could they? For I did not know it for certain myself. All that I could say was that the gentleman was pale like Mr. Booth and from Virginia. And standing in the cool whiteness of the Clarendon pump room with a spreading puddle at my feet, this seemed very thin evidence.

I must leave here. Before the gentleman from Virginia brings the attendant to hear something I cannot explain. And I gathered my skirts and ran from the room, my feet clattering upon the marble.

After that day, I did not return to the Clarendon's pump room, but sent Mrs. Fitzgerald for my bottles, instructing her not to allow them out of her sight. After the incident with the gentleman from Virginia, my nightmares returned, and I was forced to increase my doses of chloral hydrate and laudanum. To drink this much of the opium made me lethargic, and I spent a good portion of my day stretched out upon a damp sofa in my room, the wooden shutters fastened against the heat and light of day. Mrs. Fitzgerald asked me to accompany her on walks, but I always claimed tiredness, for I had come to believe that the spawning plants outside would attempt to wrap themselves about my throat.

To pass the time, I wrote letters, mostly to my son, although Robert's replies were brief and infrequent; and after a while, did not come at all.

"Are you certain you are posting my letters to Robert?" I asked Mrs. Fitzgerald, when I had heard nothing from my son for five weeks.

The nurse drew herself to all the height which she could rally. "I would never neglect your letters."

I did not believe her, and paid Mrs. Stockton's ten-year-old boy a nickel to take them. But still no answer came from Robert. This made me fear that my son had fallen ill, for it was impossible to be at Green Cove and not think of illness.

"Do you imagine that my son is sick?" I asked Mrs. Fitzgerald, when it had been eight weeks since Robert's last scrawled note. "Too weak even to write?"

"If Mr. Lincoln were seriously ill, he would send you word," she replied. "I'm sure he is well."

But how could she know this? Had Robert been in touch with Mrs. Fitzgerald when he had written nothing to myself? Had she been writing to him of my behavior? Did the two of them keep secrets about me?

In the event my doubts about the nurse were only the ravings of my womb, I went more frequently to the mineral pool to bathe, in the hope the waters would calm my offending organ. In the event my suspicions were correct, I ceased asking her to accompany me.

The mineral pool, which stood near to the grounds of the

Clarendon, had been constructed of the same milk-colored marble as the floor of the pump room. Broad columns stood at one end, and all about its edges, it was surrounded by dripping willows. On this day, nearly ten weeks since I had last heard from my son, I arrived there early, for despite the drugs, the certainty that Robert was ill with something mortal would not let me sleep.

Stepping into the ladies' changing house, I dressed myself in my bathing costume – a black wool coat which fell below the knee, worn over Turkish pantaloons, and then entered the pool at the far end. My fellow bathers were few: a young lady whose flushed cheeks and coughing showed consumption; a plump matron who breathed with the wheeze of an asthmatic and whose skin was so whitened as to be nearly blue; and an elderly lady who was suffering from a nervous disorder, which caused her to shake into spasm, agitating the water about her.

I circled the pool, my bathing costume drawing water, weighting me. As I came near to the young consumptive lady, she began to cough with more ferocity. At first, she attempted to hold in the cough, only let it sputter from between her colorless lips. But the young lady's lungs were too diseased to be controlled, and before long she was holding onto the marble edge of the pool, bent double by her hacking. Out of politeness, I did not glance at her as I passed; though there was something in her coughing which was familiar.

That is Eddie's coughing, said that voice which missed no opportunity to torment me.

Eddie has been dead for more than twenty years.

Still, do you not recognize it? It is the same hacking which lifted him from the bed.

I moved away from the consumptive lady, hoping to shut out her coughing, but this brought me nearer the elderly woman with the nervous disorder.

Notice how that lady's affliction brings on convulsions, said the voice. *Is that not exactly how Willie writhed upon the bed when the spasms of his dysentery were bad and it seemed he expelled his very organs?*

"Stop," I said – I believe, aloud. For the voice which taunted me was as loud as speaking.

And see how blue is the flesh of that asthmatic lady? That is precisely the shade Taddie's skin turned before he died.

I felt I was drowning, being pulled beneath the sulfurous water by the wet wool of my bathing costume and the recollections called up by the sicknesses of these ladies. I dragged myself to the edge of the pool. *Only the sickly ladies are real*, I told myself. *Not their resemblance to the mortal illnesses which took my sons. Even the voice is not real; it is just some portion of my own thinking turned against myself by the Female Tragedy.*

In the changing house, I threw off my soaking bathing costume, dressed myself with unlaced corset, and ran all the way to Mrs. Stockton's boardinghouse. "I must be alone," I told Mrs. Fitzgerald. Then, though it was not yet midday, I swallowed a large dose of chloral hydrate and laudanum and fell upon the damp sofa.

I hoped for sleep, but received only visions. Robert coughing so violently upon a mattress, he threw himself from it. Robert retching jalap and writhing with the spasms of dysentery. Robert turning blue and swollen in a chair, a bar pressed against the heart which was being squeezed by the waters of pleurisy. I knew these for visions, as I could feel that my eyes were open.

As the images repeated, I came to believe that I was receiving these mental pictures in the same way that a medium receives the messages which come from the spirit world. *This must prove that what I am watching has been sent by the spirits*, I thought. *From Eddie, perhaps. From Willie and Tad. These visions of my eldest son trying on the deaths of his brothers can only be a message saying that I am right. That Robert is sick.*

The surety of this conviction made the visions vanish, showing I had read them correctly. I felt, too, the effects of the opium leave my body, as if the spirits of my dead sons were drawing it away, so I might act upon their communication. I was consumed by a fearful energy which drove me to the door between my room and that of the nurse, made me pound upon it until my hands went numb.

"Mrs. Fitzgerald!" I called out to her. "We must return to Chicago at once! Robert is dying!"

(August 19) Mrs. L in a perturbed state of mind generally –
—Patient Progress Reports for Bellevue Place Sanitarium

Minnie Judd is dying.

Now that it is too dangerous for her to be fed by the pump, my friend has grown frail and elderly from starvation, and does not ever rise from her bed. Each afternoon, I go to her room and sit beside her, telling her stories of Mr. Lincoln, and of my life when it was happier. Minnie says little during our visits, but when she does speak, all the sweetness of her character remains undiminished, distilled as it is into her few sentences. It is impossible to see Minnie shrunken upon her bed and not know that she is dying. But I have worked at it.

This afternoon, when I came to see Minnie, I found an attendant stationed outside her door – a well-fleshed young woman with a chafed look about her, who, though she is recently arrived, is already a favorite of Mrs. Ruggles. The new attendant was seated upon a three-legged stool but stood when she saw me approach.

"No one can see Mrs. Judd," she told me.

"Is the matron with her?" I asked. "Is Minnie taking something?"

"Mrs. Judd is alone," she replied.

"Then why can I not see her?"

The attendant shifted her bulk before the door.

"Mrs. Judd requires her rest."

"But I am Mrs. Lincoln," I said. "I visit with her every day."

She raised her arms, placing a squarish hand upon either side of the door frame, as if she expected me to force my way in. "The order comes from Doctor Patterson."

"Is it because Minnie is dying?" I hated the attendant for making me speak the question.

"I can only say that Mrs. Judd requires rest."

I reached around the young woman and pressed my palm to the wood of Minnie's door, as if by that I could keep her breathing on the other side.

"If you do not go," said the attendant, "I will send for Mrs. Ruggles."

Seeing that the large young woman would be persuaded by neither position nor force, I left the third floor and made my way to the portico door. Once outside, I hurried along the path to the bench near the dark woods, for this spot felt as close as I might place myself to my friend. For some time, I sat before the uneasy-making forest and recalled all the things which Minnie had confided to me here. Then I dusted the limestone and pollen from my skirts and went back inside to wait for Sarah Bunker to come and lock me in.

Mrs. Bunker came some half hour early, a further sign that all was not as usual.

"You must leave me unbolted," I told her, "so that I can see Mrs. Judd."

The night attendant shook her head. "I have been ordered not to let anyone into her room. And the matron has instructed me to sit outside the door all night."

"But she is my friend."

Mrs. Bunker came more into the room. "You know that Mrs. Judd is dying," she said to me.

I was forced to nod.

"The doctor does not believe she will live longer than tonight."

"Is the Reverend Judd with her?"

Mrs. Bunker pulled her mouth tight. "He has told Mrs. Patterson that seeing his wife in such condition troubles him too severely."

"Then she is by herself?"

The night attendant nodded, then moved back toward the door, choosing a key from the sash she wore at her waist.

"Please," I said, following her. "Do not lock me in."

"I cannot take the risk," replied Mrs. Bunker. "You are watched more carefully now."

I took hold of both her hands. "She is my friend. I do not want her to die alone."

From this near, I could see the pattern of smallpox scars upon the night attendant's cheeks, and what I took as a sorrowfulness for Minnie Judd upon her features.

"You must leave when I tell you," said Mrs. Bunker. "Even if Mrs. Judd has not yet died."

"I shall," I promised.

"And this must be the last time."

"I fear very much that it is," I told her.

I let go Mrs. Bunker's hands and stepped back so she might shut the door. From the other side, I heard the metal scraping of the key as she pretended to lock it.

I waited in my room until the asylum had gone quiet, save for the random night-shrieks of the ladies whose madness tormented them in dreams. Then, I slipped into the dark corridor and up to the third floor, where I found the night attendant seated outside Minnie's room. She rose and placed a finger upon her mouth.

"When I tell you," she whispered.

And only when I nodded, did she open Minnie's door and push me inside.

Minnie's room was dark, and as it seemed worse to die in the dark, I lit the small oil lamp which sat at the side of her bed. But when the light showed me the form of my friend, I nearly extinguished it again. Minnie's coverlet had slipped to the floor, and the starved young woman lay shivering upon the mattress, her nightdress clinging to the angles of her famished bones. The sight of her recalled for me a daguerreotype Mr. Lincoln had carried with him during the war of a Union soldier who had been left unfed in a Confederate prison camp. The soldier's flesh was entirely gone, all that was left was the thinnest stretching of skin over bone, and he looked no more than a living skeleton. It pained me to see my friend so resemble this man starved by his enemy, and I retrieved the coverlet from the floor and placed it over her emaciated form.

"I missed you today," she murmured. Her voice was like that of someone grown ancient, the chords turned stiff and unlubricated.

"You are awake." I sat upon the edge of the mattress, taking care not to jostle the bed, for there was so little of substance between Minnie's bones, they seemed in danger of coming apart.

"I never sleep now," she said. "Sleep, I have learned, is a habit of the flesh."

I smoothed Minnie's hair, feeling the itch of the dry strands against my palm. Over the last weeks, my friend had become nearly bald, as if the hard bone of her skull had pushed so near the scalp, it had forced out all her lovely black hair.

"If I brought you some broth," I asked her, "would you take some?"

Minnie made what was meant to be a smile. "You still wish to save me."

"I will miss you too much if you die."

She shifted her gaze across the dim room, focusing upon something I could not discern. "I am doing what I must."

"For Reverend Judd?"

At the mention of her husband's name, Minnie's face softened into something which made me recall that she had once possessed prettiness.

"You believe you might still make him love you?" I asked her. "Even after you die?"

Minnie sighed, an abbreviated sound, for she had not breath to stretch it longer. "I think that is the only thing which will."

"That is insanity," I told her.

She turned her eyes upon me, overlarge and burning in their sunken sockets. "When I am dead, he will know how much I was willing to do for him," she said. "Then, he will send away Mrs. Gill and come to love me."

"And that will be enough? To be loved after you are dead?"

Minnie shrugged, sawing at the thin skin which covered the bones at her shoulders. "It is what I have."

What if he cannot love you? I wanted to ask her. *What if such affection is beyond him?* But I did not ask it. For I could see that my friend was as beyond the help of clear seeing as she was of clear broth. And I would not let her die disbelieving she had compelled her husband's love.

"Would you like me to read to you from the Bible?" I asked. "Perhaps it might comfort you."

"I already know too much of what is in there by heart," she replied. "And have had only sadness from it."

We did not speak for a long while after that. The light in the lamp grew dim as the oil ran out, but the early dawn of summer was already beginning to lighten Minnie's dark room. In that gray light, my friend appeared already dead: and more than once, I sought for the vein which had lately become prominent at the side of her fleshless throat, touching it with my fingers when I did not see it pulse. Minnie still lived, but the throbbing beneath my fingers was so unsubstantial, I believed it no longer originated from her heart, but from her will; and I thought that it must be only her passion which kept her alive.

"Please, Minnie," I begged, though I suspected she was past

hearing. "Take something. Tea. Or broth. Or watered milk. But do not let yourself die." I knew that this was senseless, that nothing would save her but the sight of her beautiful husband come to swear his love for her.

Minnie opened her eyes and glanced at me. She opened her mouth, but her tongue had turned white and swollen in her mouth, rendering her incapable of speech.

"You are right about what you think," I said to her. "He will come to love you."

Minnie gazed at me with what I took to be gratitude. But I did not imagine her gratefulness was for the reassurance I had given; rather, I think, it came from my believing her.

It took only another quarter of an hour for her to die; for her black eyes to become stones and her emaciated frame to take on the weight of surrender. When I saw that this had happened, I brought my mouth near her face.

"*I* love you," I told her. "I hope that will count for something."

I kissed her thinned cheek.

It felt only the length of a breath before Sarah Bunker opened the door.

"Is Mrs. Judd still alive?" she whispered.

I shook my head.

The night attendant slipped inside the room, came to stand beside the bed. "It is her heart that has killed her," she said.

"Yes," I agreed.

"It was weakened by too much fasting. A heart cannot live upon nothing."

"Hers could."

Mrs. Bunker looked down upon the scarcely perceptible form beneath the bedcovers. "It was madness which made her starve herself."

"No," I told the attendant. "It was not madness."

"Mrs. Judd was a food-refuser," she reminded me. "She was mad."

"It is only that she could not believe the one she loved was beyond her reach," I said, feeling a kind of horror in the familiar shaping of the words.

This is what I told Doctor McFarland about myself, I thought, *intending the observation as example of my rightness.* Only now, at the bedside of the young woman who had starved herself out of a wish to be loved, there did not seem to be anything which could be thought right about such conviction.

Mrs. Bunker was speaking some opinion about Reverend Judd, but I could not stay and listen to her. Pushing myself up from Minnie's mattress, I raced to the door.

"Don't let anyone see you!" warned Mrs. Bunker.

But I did not stop to check if Mrs. Ruggles or the chafed-looking attendant were in the corridor, only ran for the stairs back to my room. Almost since I had met Minnie, I had believed that we were twined; that our sanity and our passion made us alike. But now I saw that there was something darker which joined us. Something which sprang from need, and what we would do to satisfy it.

Once inside, I rushed to my bed and threw the bedcovers onto the floor. Shoving the mattress off the bedstead until I could reach the bundle of pages I had hidden there, I pulled out this memoir I have been writing almost since coming to Bellevue Place, falling upon the floor with the stack of it in my lap. Weeks ago, when the pages had become too many, I had tied the bundle with a ribbon I had ripped from an old nightdress. Now I tore at this ribbon, in too much hurry to read what I had written to unwork its knot; too anxious to know if Minnie Judd and I shared the same insanity.

Without taking time to right the bed or move to a chair, I sat upon the floor and read all the pages of my history, squinting at the letters until the daylight grew stronger, pulling off my wrapper when midday came and the room turned hot. In those hours, I read every incident of my life which I had set to ink, but it was what I read of Robert which most shamed me. For despite all that he had done to prove the opposite, still I had not believed him beyond my reach.

With shaking hands, I grabbed up the pages of my life, swearing I would burn them, for I could not bear to see myself so pitiable. But as I worked to fit the nightdress ribbon about the bundle, my eye fell upon a strand of Minnie's hair which had become caught in my mourning ring.

Never had I considered Minnie Judd pitiable. Not the day I first came upon her in the greenhouse, pressing rose petals to her mouth; nor the time when it had seemed she might win the love of her beautiful husband by reciting Psalms for him. I did not even feel pity for her when she had begun to starve herself, for it was impossible to pity anyone who could love so passionately.

Gently, I unwound Minnie's hair from my mourning ring, taking care not to break the strand before I had tied its black length around the ribbon holding together the pages of my history. It was true that I had recorded scandalous things which must have seemed insanity, but I would not let myself believe it was shameful to wish to be loved. It was, perhaps, only a type of madness to expect it from someplace it might never come.

I had possessed the hope that reading these pages would make my son stop loving me so little. Now that I was near to the end of writing them, it did not seem much risk to hold the hope a short time longer.

I hurried to the desk with the four angels carved at the legs, knowing I would not be able to wait for it to be night to take up my pen. But as I was gathering paper and ink, my door was flung open.

"They are going to release you!" shrieked Mrs. Munger.

I studied the banker's wife, seeing if her hair was combed, if she spoke the words to me and not to my clock.

"You are to go to Springfield!"

I sank against the back of my chair, made tired by the relief which comes after being given something you have wished for so long, you cannot recall never wanting it.

"Is this the doing of my son?" I asked.

"Oh no!" Mrs. Munger shook her head. "Mr. Lincoln is against it. He has sent Doctor Patterson a report stating that you are quite insane, and that it would be dangerous to release you to any place."

"Then why am I to be let go?"

Mrs. Munger lowered her voice to an unquiet whisper. "Doctor Patterson wants no more publicity. He has lost another lady."

"I know," I said.

The banker's wife nodded, unsurprised that I might have this information. She settled herself into my rocker as if we were beginning a social call, and I was not in my nightdress with my mattress and bedcovers cast upon the floor.

"I should very much like to visit," I told Mrs. Munger. "But if I am to be released, there is something I must finish."

Robert was not dying.

He was instead waiting upon the platform at the Union Depot in

Chicago when Mrs. Fitzgerald and I arrived, standing in the steam from our train like the resurrected rising from the mist.

"You are not perishing!" I exclaimed. And I threw myself against the front of his coat, pressing my face to the pearl buttons as if to fix their imprint upon my cheek.

"I am very much alive," he told me. I felt his chest move as he sighed.

"But I saw you sick like your brothers."

Robert removed me from his front. "You know very well that I have not experienced any illness for more than ten years."

I glanced into his unhappy face. "I am sorry," I said. "But I found Florida unsettling. A man tried to poison me there."

"In Green Cove?" He cast his gaze over my head, looking at Mrs. Fitzgerald.

"In the Clarendon pump room. A gentleman from Virginia put something into my water. Arsenic, I think. Maybe strychnine."

"You have proof of this?"

I shook my head, aware of how much more irrational this sounded in the March wind of Chicago than it had in the humidity of Green Cove. "I knocked the glass from his hand."

"Mrs. Lincoln accused the gentleman of being an assassin," Mrs. Fitzgerald told my son.

"You accused a gentleman of trying to assassinate you at the Clarendon?" Robert's voice rose. "I know people who winter there!"

"I am certain no one whom you know witnessed the incident," I assured him, though I did not know if this was true.

My son chewed upon his mustache for some minutes. "I think," he said, "it might be better if while you are in Chicago, I took a room near yours."

The wind upon the platform seemed more chill. "Do you believe I am in danger?"

"I only wish to watch over you," he replied. "In case you should find Chicago equally unsettling."

After sending word to Mary Harlan, who had returned to her house on Wabash Avenue, that I was unwell and required his company, Robert booked us into the Grand Pacific Hotel. Built since the Great Fire, the Grand Pacific had more than five hundred rooms, a courtyard overhung by a dome of etched glass, and three mechanical elevators covered in gilt. My son and I took adjacent rooms upon the third floor. Inside mine was a row of arched windows which faced out onto Clark Street and an immense mahogany bed with life-sized pineapples carved into the top of each of its posts. This bed was outfitted with a feather mattress, but I did not sleep much upon it.

I had left my chloral hydrate and my laudanum in Green Cove, imagining that once I was away from the town's damp atmosphere and spawning foliage, I would not require them. I had lately begun to believe that since taking the drugs, my thoughts had become more difficult to catch hold of, as if they, like the sidings of Mrs. Stockton's boardinghouse, had grown slippery with mold. But Chicago proved no more restful.

"Perhaps if I went out each day and walked the length and breadth of the city, I might make myself too tired for sleeplessness," I told my son. By this time, I had been at the Grand Pacific for three insomniac days, and had waited only until I heard his breakfast being delivered to come to his room.

"You do not intend to wander about the city alone?" he said, seating himself at the linen-covered table.

"Are you certain you do not believe me in some type of danger?"

Robert sighed. "I just don't want you imagining any."

I dropped into the chair opposite him. "I think to go out walking will wear down my restlessness."

"You have no laudanum to make you sleep? No chloral hydrate for your restlessness?"

"I did not like their effect upon my thinking."

"Perhaps you had the wrong dosage. I shall send a doctor to you."

Within the hour, Doctor Ralph Isham, a relation of Robert's law partner, came to my room. Doctor Isham was near in age to my son, and carried a leather satchel which was new-looking. I showed the young doctor to a seat and began to describe for him my symptoms. But Doctor Isham did not wait to hear them.

"Mr. Lincoln informs me you are much agitated and require opiates," he said.

"I only have trouble with sleeping."

"Insomnia is a symptom of too much disturbance upon the brain," he replied.

From his satchel, the young doctor removed two large bottles, one of laudanum and one of chloral hydrate, which he placed upon my night table.

"You may drink doses of both whenever you wish," he told me. "Particularly if your restlessness threatens to send you from your room in an unfit state."

That night, at the doctor's direction, I swallowed large measures of the chloral and the laudanum, and dropped immediately into stunned sleep. I could not tell how long I was unconscious, but when I woke, I heard the voices of men.

"You cannot dispute that a bullet to the brain is the most effectual," declared one, a man whose accent sounded refined, but falsely so, like the studied speech of stage actors.

"I'd rather strangling," put in a second man, whose accent was much coarser. "Hands placed directly upon the victim."

"Poisoning," replied a softer voice, "is the most tidy."

These men are plotting murder! I attempted to rise, to better hear where the voices originated. But Doctor Isham's prescription had been generous, and my limbs lay heavy upon the bed in an opium paralysis.

"As I shall be the one to execute the plan," continued the actor's voice, "I should choose the method."

"We are all in this thing together," insisted the coarse one.

"Either way, it must be done," murmured the soft tones.

Their voices are so clear! I thought. *They must be in the room next to mine!*

"Yes, it has to be done," agreed the coarse voice. "She has acted the traitor and the spy."

"And been unfaithful to the Late Lamented," cooed the softer one.

"She is the limb of Satan!" declared the actor.

Fear flushed the opiates from my veins and my heart compressed painfully. Trembling, I hurled myself beneath the bedcovers. *But this is lunacy!* I thought. *Bed linens are no protection from bullets. No, I must let them know they are discovered. Uncover their plot and thereby stop them.*

Throwing off the quilts, I stood upon the mattress. I was still unsteady from the drugs and had to take hold of one of the carved pineapples to keep my balance. "I hear you!" I shouted at the wall behind which I imagined they plotted. "I hear what it is you intend to do! And you will not assassinate me!"

It was then that I heard a small cry of startlement, and turning toward the doorway, saw Mrs. Gavin, the housemaid, with a breakfast tray in her hands.

"There are men on the other side of that wall," I informed her. "Assassins plotting to kill me."

The housemaid, a widow with a meek appearance, began to tremble and the teacup upon the tray chimed against its saucer.

"I shall fetch Mr. Lincoln," she said, and was immediately gone from the room.

Robert arrived in very few minutes, still tying the sash of his dressing gown.

"Why are you standing upon the bed?" he said to me.

"Men who are plotting to kill me are in that room." I pointed at the wall. "I heard them debating bullets versus poison."

"I am told that room is unoccupied," said my son.

"Do you believe that assassins would make their presence known to the hotel?" I asked him.

"You are very agitated," he told me. "Perhaps you should take a dose of chloral hydrate and rest." He put out a hand to assist me off the mattress.

I held more tightly to the bedpost. "If I rest, the actor will come and murder me."

"The actor?"

Robert sounded so disbelieving, I thought it best to say only what I knew for certain. "His accent is like an actor's," I amended.

Rubbing at his face in a manner which made me suspect Mrs. Gavin had woken him to come to me, he glanced doubtfully at the wall. "If you will drink another dose of Doctor Isham's medicine," he said, "I shall have someone stay with you."

"What about the assassins?"

"I will ask the hotel manager to search that room."

A porter came and sat outside my door; and once I saw that he was there, I swallowed more of the chloral and slept fitfully for the rest of the day. That evening, Robert came to tell me the hotel manager had discovered no men in the room beside mine.

"They must have fled when they heard you would have the room searched," I speculated; for if I could hear what was said in their room, it was reasonable to believe they could hear what was said in mine.

"The manager insists that the room is untouched."

"They are being clever and covering their tracks," I said, surprised that my son would prove so credulous. "Likely they recall how quickly Mr. Booth and his conspirators were captured."

"Your nerves are overwrought," Robert replied. "Do not neglect to take your medicine." And to be sure I would not forget, he fed me my doses himself.

But I heard the assassins again that night. And the night after. And every night for a week, although the hotel manager instructed a porter to sleep in the room next to mine. To counteract the agitation of my nerves, Doctor Isham prescribed more of the chloral and the laudanum. However, the more of the opiates I drank, the louder and more frequent came the voices of the assassins. And night upon night, I was forced to listen to them debate knife over pistol, my limbs fixed to the mattress by the drugs.

"There are no men in the room beside yours," Robert repeated, when the week was finished.

"Perhaps they are in the walls," I told him. "And that is why the hotel manager can find no trace of them."

Robert refused to inform the hotel manager that assassins lived within the Grand Pacific's walls. Instead, he promised that he himself would remain awake to listen for the killers' plotting. In return for this, he wished me to take my laudanum more frequently, so that I might pass the next few days soothing my nerves.

Such soothing, and the many draughts of opium required to accomplish it, kept me so tranquilized upon my enormous bed, I had little sense of time passing and kept count of the days only by how often I lifted myself to drink again from the bottles. When my count had reached five, it occurred to me that I had not risen once, even to bathe, and determined I would hold off swallowing another dose until I had washed myself and changed into a fresh nightdress.

Shaking my head as if that might clear it of the opium, I pushed myself to the edge of the mattress and got to standing. The room spun about me, and I wondered how long it had been since I had eaten. Breathing deeply, I swallowed air instead of laudanum, hoping to cure the blurriness of my vision enough to navigate the walk down the corridor to the bathing room.

I should cover myself in a dressing gown, I thought, *in the event I meet someone in the hallway.* But my dressing gown was across the room, and I was already so near to the door. *The light looks like midday. It is unlikely anyone else will be going to bathe.* But I had no sooner stepped outside, when I found myself standing before a man who had just come from Robert's room.

The man was a gentleman, at least by appearance; for he was dressed in finely woven wool and a well-shaped hat. His manner, however, was not at all gentlemanly. We could not have been more than a foot apart, yet he did not greet me, nor did he remove his shapely hat. Instead the gentleman examined me with sharp eyes, taking in, I imagined, my unwashed hair and crumpled nightdress.

"I have been unwell," I explained.

The man said nothing, only continued his scrutiny for a few moments more before striding away down the corridor.

I drank no laudanum that afternoon, and when I heard Robert return from his office, I went to his room and asked about the gentleman who had taken such a peculiar interest in me.

"He is a doctor," said my son.

Robert was reading a newspaper, and it seemed that he did not wish to interrupt himself from it too much, as if the gentleman's identity was of little importance.

"Then, you *are* ill!" I came near to his chair, scanning his face for excessive pallor or fever flush.

"I am fine," he told me. "He came for you."

I drew back in surprise. "Then why did he not examine me?"

My son returned his attention to the newspaper. "At present, it is sufficient for me to describe your symptoms."

"But I am already being seen to by Doctor Isham."

"Your case may require more than one doctor."

"But all that plagues me is the inability to sleep."

Robert looked up from his paper. "What about the men who are plotting to murder you?"

"They are not a symptom," I told him. "They are real."

My son studied me with an inscrutable expression. "I only wish to place you beneath the best possible supervision," he said.

And indeed, my son appeared to invest much time and trouble arranging my care, for from that day onward, I encountered many gentlemen I took to be doctors coming and going from his room. I attempted to be sociable to these gentlemen, nodding and giving them the opportunity to greet me – for certainly they knew me for who I was. However, few of them ever did. They preferred to stand silent in the hallway and stare at me. After a time, their scrutiny made me wonder exactly how my son had described my symptoms to them, and I took to hiding inside my room whenever I heard their footsteps outside the door.

It was after I had been living at the Grand Pacific for one month that the ten-year anniversary of my husband's killing arrived. Upon that day, I woke from my doped sleep with the headache which came to me every year upon that date. It pounded mercilessly behind my left eye as I scrabbled about the night table for my bottle of Pemberton's French Wine Coca – a nerve tonic made from kola nut and coca leaves I had learned of while traveling through Atlanta on my way to Green Cove – for the brown syrup could sometimes blunt the sharpest edges of my headache.

I poured an inch into a glass, filling the rest with water, then drank it down. When, after a few minutes, the headache seemed worse, I drank a second. Afterward, I placed my pulsing head upon the pillow and tried to sleep. But the Pemberton's Coca caused my skin to feel as if it were attempting to crawl off my bones, and I could not lie still. The linens tangled themselves about my legs, the pillow shifted beneath my head, and my body felt as if it might fly apart. To stop it, I swallowed a draught of chloral and laudanum. Once again, I forced myself back into bed, where I lay upon the mattress, my body shuddering with the rapid beating of my heart. Pressing my hand to my eyelids to keep them shut, I prayed for the oblivion of sleep.

Sleep came. But I could not stupefy my dreaming.

I dreamt my husband's head flopping limply as he was carried across countless streets; dreamt the bloated bruising of his face and his large, unconscious hands flapping themselves above the counterpane. My nose became packed with the scent of blood seeping from my husband's brain, and my ears were stuffed with the unnatural cooing of his breath. I woke weeping, with my hand pressed against my mouth. But rather than my own fingers, I felt instead the cooling flesh of my husband's lips.

"You should have let me come with you," I said into the empty room. Then I pressed my face into the pillow to weep, but the pillow slip carried the sickbed smell of Mr. Booth's breath.

I threw myself from the bed, but the force of the headache

knocked me to the floor. Unable to halt myself, I retched up my last dose of Pemberton's Coca onto the carpet.

A carpet which smelled of gunpowder!

I scrambled to my feet and stood with my back to the wall. But from the other side of that wall, I heard a scratching noise.

It is the assassins! They are burrowing through the wall to get at me! The coarse man first, for he is molelike with long, dirty claws. The soft-spoken man will be second, bringing his reason and his poison. The actor – the true assassin – will come last. He will make an entrance. Step through the ruined plaster of my walls in a frock coat and with breath which smells like soiled sheets, and of whiskey. He will be handsome. And pale. And he will fire a bullet into my bursting brain.

The clawing sound came again, and I pushed myself from the wall, searching for the door. I knocked against something unforgiving, and the pain of it against my cheekbone dropped me to the carpet.

Keep moving! For the coarse man is surely only moments from breaking through the wall!

And then I was outside. In the corridor.

I must get to the elevator! I shall be too slow upon the stairs. The actor is quick and he will catch me and shoot me in the stairwell. Leave me dying upon the floor. A blood-soaked pillow beneath my pounding head.

I began to run, which made the bile and what remained of the Pemberton's Coca rise to the back of my throat. *Do not stop to retch! If you do, he will catch you.* And as if I possessed clairvoyance, I heard footsteps chasing after me.

I reached the elevator, pounded upon its gilded doors. But it was caught on some other floor.

I am going to die! Die from being shot in the head. That is the reason for the headache. It is a premonition. A foretaste of how it will feel to have a bullet forced into my brain.

The footsteps came closer.

I beat harder upon the doors of the elevator, praying for the mechanical device to come and rescue me.

Hands fell upon my shoulders. Smooth hands with clean finger-nails. The hands of the actor!

"What are you doing out here in your chemise?" demanded a whispered voice.

Robert's voice.

I whirled around. The hands, too, belonged to Robert.

He is the assassin! And the others are his accomplices. Like the doctors who come and go from his room.

"Come away from there," my son whispered.

He tried to pull me from the elevator, but I struck at him.

"You are trying to murder me!" I shrieked.

Robert fastened a hand over my mouth. "Quiet! Someone will hear you."

I struggled against his hand, for it was stopping my breath.

"You cannot believe that I would cause you harm."

But I did believe it.

"I am your son. Like Willie and Tad. Like Eddie."

But Robert had never been like Willie or Tad. Or like Eddie.

"I am who is left," he whispered hard into my ear. "If you do not have me, you have no one."

I ceased struggling and let my son pull me from the gilded door.

"Come back to your room," he said, "and I will give you some laudanum."

Silently, we returned to my room, where the walls were still whole and the assassins quiet. I drank the concoction which Robert fixed, then asked him to sit with me until it had taken effect. We sat together until the opium made my heart slow.

"I am sorry," I said to him. "For imagining such ill of you."

"I do not believe you would have suspected Willie or Tad of being your murderer," he replied.

He was correct in this. But even doped, I could not say who owned the fault of that.

"I have no excuse," I told him. "Save this terrible anniversary. And perhaps the drugs."

"The chloral comes from Doctor Isham," he reminded me. "It cannot do you harm. Perhaps it is the world outside your room which agitates you."

"Perhaps," I said. "But I cannot shut myself up."

"It might be the best thing."

For the next week, I heeded my son's advice and remained inside my room. To pass the time, I read Scripture and stared out the windows which faced upon Clark Street, watching the people who were free to move about the city. When these pursuits left me too restive, I doped myself into sleep.

For all this time, the assassins stayed quiet, and I began to believe they had been frightened away by Robert's vigilance. *They see now that I have a son to protect me,* I thought. *Robert will ensure no harm comes to me.*

At the start of the second week, I woke to sunshine and the scent of hyacinths. It was one of the first soft days of April, and from my window I saw ladies in raffia bonnets moving with great determination into and out of the stores. Indeed, it seemed impossibly unreasonable to be obliged to spend such a day indoors, reading about the emancipation of the Israelites and drinking laudanum.

Robert will worry that I am agitating myself if I go out, I thought. *But I have not had to listen to anyone plotting my death for a week, and am much calmer now. Moreover, it is not as if he has locked me away here.*

I was a little unsteady upon my feet, and my hip ached from so much time spent upon the mattress, but I was able to dress myself without assistance. I did not possess a cunning raffia hat like the ladies on Clark Street, but I supposed it would only have been at odds with my mourning; for mourning clothes never could be reconciled with spring. I did, however, choose my prettiest black bonnet, one with a short veil and cream-colored lace at the neck, and after several attempts, at last had it situated upon my head.

Stepping into the corridor, I encountered no doctors coming from Robert's room. The gilded elevator was waiting for me, no one attempted to speak with me in the lobby, and before barely a minute had passed, I was outside in the bright spring sunshine.

It had been so long since I was out in the world, that at first all the commotion of the street – the horses made nervous by the sound of hammering, the workmen shouting to each other in the languages of Europe – disconcerted me, and I stood outside the doors of the Grand Pacific, unsure whether I should run back in. But as I listened to the newsboys calling out the headlines and the carriage drivers cursing one another, it all became soothing, for none of the dialogue was about murdering me.

I am safe out here, I told myself. *The assassins are locked inside the hotel.*

I walked along with the ladies in their fashionable hats, and their harmless purpose, and the spring air, sweetened with the scent of blossoming trees, made me feel almost tranquil. Once I reached State Street, I stopped to gaze into the windows filled with silks and glassware and gold; and at the great marble entrance to Mattock's Department Store, I stood rapt before curtains made of lace so fine they had to be Belgian.

I wish I might someday own a house for such curtains, I thought to myself. *I should like very much to live within the light cast by their fineness.*

If you should live at all, replied a voice in my head.

The voice did not belong to me, not even to my traitorous self. It possessed too much of the overarticulated refinement of the actor-assassin.

I put a hand to the glass protecting the Belgian lace to keep myself upright, and looked around. There was no one near enough to have uttered the words, no one glancing my way.

The assassin is in my head!

No, I told myself. *That is impossible. Assassins might live within the walls, but they could not live within one's skull.*

But what if I had been made more vulnerable to the killers? What if the terrible headache which had felt like my brain splitting open, and the round-number anniversary of my husband's death, and the large doses of chloral hydrate and laudanum, had opened a pathway into my mind? A pathway through which the assassins might enter me, in the way that spirits entered the bodies of true sensitives?

No, I insisted. *It is lunatic to believe that the assassins inhabit me. Lunatic to believe that they speak from inside my head.*

But I had sat with trance mediums too much to believe it too insane.

I intend to one day own a house for these curtains, I said to myself, pronouncing each word distinctly within my mind.

For answer, the murderers began to laugh – a noise which pressed upon my skull like the fiercest headache.

They are there! Living inside my head! Standing before Mattock's Department Store with the spring sunshine falling upon me, I pressed my hands to my ears. *I must make them stop this terrible laughter, or my skull will crack from it.*

I shall prove to you how much I believe in my living! I told the assassins.

With their laughter turning me deaf to other sounds, I rushed through the marble-arched doorway into the store.

"I must have that lace in the window," I demanded of the first clerk I could command. "Yards and yards of it. Enough to curtain every window in the biggest house."

The clerk, a frightened-looking young man, stared at me from behind his polished counter, and I realized that I was shouting at him, shouting over the laughter in my head.

"Please have all of it sent to me at this address," I told him, writing the street number of the Grand Pacific. "And please have it sent right away."

The assassins went still when the boxes arrived.

But the lace curtains only quieted the voices of the murderers for a short time, and the following afternoon, I was compelled to go out and buy two hundred dollars' worth of soaps to prove that I would continue to possess a living body upon which to use them. The day after that, I purchased three hundred dollars' worth of watches to demonstrate the vast amount of time which remained to me. And the day following, I ordered more perfume than I could wear in a year.

To shut up the assassins, I went shopping every day. My closet at the Grand Pacific filled with bolts of brocades to cover chairs I did not own, bracelets and brooches to be worn if I ever left off mourning, slippers I would never wear out even if I had a hundred feet. The sight of these boxes stacked in the closet made me remember the attic of the President's House, but where before I had shopped to keep my family safe, now I collected objects meant to safeguard myself.

Two weeks of this frantic purchasing passed, until one morning, Robert rushed into my room with the linen napkin from his breakfast still clutched in his hand.

"Mrs. Gavin has just told me she cannot open the door of your closet for fear of being crushed!"

I was seated at my own breakfast and did not rise from it, hoping to keep all seeming commonplace. "It is not necessary for the house-maid to clean in my closet," I replied.

My son waved his napkin at the closet door. "What is it you keep in there?"

"Only some things I shall use in the future."

"You mean you have been shopping," he accused.

"I have bought a few items."

Turning upon his heel, he headed toward the closet. I flew out of my seat after him.

"Do you not think I am too elderly to have my movements so closely regulated?" I protested. "And my privacy so disregarded?"

Robert got to the closet before I did and jerked open the door. I heard him gasp, saw the napkin drop to the floor.

"This is insanity!" he exclaimed.

"It is only shopping," I told him.

Still, peering around him into the closet, I saw how it could appear the work of a madwoman. The closet was filled from bottom to top with parcels, bolts of fabric, small Turkey carpets. Everything had been put here with no order, only crowded into the space as it had arrived, three layers deep in some places, large ones laid atop small, teetering all the way to the ceiling.

"These are talismans," I attempted to explain. "Charms. No more lunatic than carrying the foot of a rabbit."

Robert could not take his eyes from the closet. "There is more in here than you will use in your lifetime."

"That is what makes them lucky."

He regarded me with a hard eye. "How much money have you spent upon all of this?"

"Do not worry, I have not put myself into debt."

"What about your capital?"

"There is plenty of it remaining."

Robert glanced back at the boxes. "But for how long?"

I came around him and put my hand upon the door, thinking to shut it, but my son would not release his hold.

"Haven't you yourself assured me that I am not likely to run out of money for a good long while?" I said.

"I had not counted on you doing so much buying." He reached into the closet, shifted a few of the boxes. "Most of this is unopened. You can send it back."

"That would be dangerous!" I told him.

"Then swear you will not buy any more."

"But why?"

My son whirled upon me, his face flushed and almost ugly with his anger.

"Swear it, or I cannot say what will happen."

It was the resolve behind the threat which frightened me.

"I swear it," I said.

Pulling the door from my hand, he banged it shut. Something inside toppled.

"Remain inside if you find you cannot control yourself," he told me. "Drink the chloral if you have the urge to visit the stores."

I worked to keep my promise to Robert. Twenty times that afternoon, I opened the door just to look inside. Ten of those times, I was certain what was piled there was no more than fetishes against misfortune.

But ten of those times, I feared that I was mad.

To keep away the panic brought on by such thinking, I swallowed more chloral. And when I heard again the voices of the assassins, I pushed my palms against my ears. When my skull filled with their uncouth laughter, I bound a pillow about my head and sang hymns to drown them out. But the voices of the assassins were like knives, cutting through my singing as smoothly as Mr. Booth's dagger had cut through the flesh of Major Rathbone.

"Stop tormenting me!" I shouted into the empty room.

But the only thing which would make them stop was to buy something.

Robert cannot hold me to this promise! For he does not know how it is to have assassins in your head.

I dressed quickly, and before opening my door, listened first to make certain that none of Robert's doctors were in the hallway. Only when I was confident no gentlemen waited there to scrutinize me, did I slip from my room. I did not see until I had turned from locking the door that a man stood a little way down the corridor. His flesh was white and his hair was dark; and he was as handsome as an actor.

It is the actor! The assassin who lives inside my brain! And because I have bought nothing today, he has been able to assume corporeal form.

"I am going to the shops!" I shrieked at the man. "You cannot touch me!"

I fled down the corridor and ran for the staircase, taking the steps as fast as I could, praying my skirts would not trip me, leave me broken at the bottom for the assassin to find. I dashed through the lobby, not caring who stared, nor what they thought of my haste. Outside, I could not find an empty carriage, and certain I would be caught before one appeared, I lifted my dress and ran down Clark Street, moving much faster than a lady ever did.

It was cold for May, dark and damp and threatening rain. A cold wind tore petals from the trees and pushed my veil against my face, lashing the flesh of my cheeks with an icy stiffness. But the inside of Mattock's Department Store was gaslit and warm, and the oak shelves were filled with the things which would keep me safe.

I scanned the polished counters, upon which rested lengths of pale-colored velvet and summer bonnets with brims the size of carriage wheels.

I must have something small, I thought. *Something I can carry back myself. To protect me on the way.*

And then I spotted a clerk showing a pair of gloves to a lady.

Gloves! I can carry gloves. And as it is May, they will not be needed for some six months or more. Six months through which my survival will be guaranteed!

"Bring me all of these you have!" I commanded the clerk. "But only the warmest. The ones meant for winter."

The clerk returned with all the gloves he could carry and set them upon the counter before me. Tearing open the boxes, I put my hands upon the pieces of calfskin and suede which would prevent me being killed.

These, I took up a pair stitched of fawn-colored kid, *I shall wear next autumn. And these*, I caressed gloves lined with the fur of rabbits, *I shall give to Robert at Christmastime, proving I shall be here to give presents.*

I chose gloves of leather and of suede, all lined with the fur of animals, and none meant to be worn before the end of summer. In the warmth of the store, the feel of the soft gloves beneath my fingers lulled me, made me believe that each pair the delicate clerk added to my account removed another portion of the assassin's physicality, turning him back into spirit.

But when I looked up to give the clerk a final order, I saw the handsome assassin watching me from behind a display of unwashed woolens.

"I must have my packages!" I told the clerk.

He looked at me in alarm, and I wondered if he knew the assassin was there. "You do not wish them sent?" he said.

"They must be in my hands! Before it is too late!"

The clerk began to wrap up my boxes. But he was so slow I imagined he was the assassin's accomplice, tasked with keeping me here until the actor could place his lady's pistol against my head. I grabbed up the unwrapped boxes still upon the counter.

"Madam, wait!" cried the clerk.

But I did not wait. I ran through the store and up the marble steps into the street.

I must try to lose him in the crowd or he will be upon me!

Clutching the boxes to my chest, I pushed my way through the shopping ladies and foreign workmen, dashed across roadways, heedless of traveling carriages and trolleys. I worried more about motion than direction and soon became lost, finding myself in a strange neighborhood where dirty children stared at me – a running black figure with gloves held to her throat.

I lost a box on a street I could not name. Another beneath the hooves of a horse. I was certain that each box which fell from my hands brought the assassin closer, yet I knew it was death to stop and retrieve them. It began to rain and the wet weighted my veil and turned the boxes at my throat soft. I believed I would never find my way to the Grand Pacific. Then with no warning or reason, the hotel was before me! I threw myself at its glass-fronted doors, forcing my way inside, until I stood dripping upon the lobby carpet.

But the actor was there already, sitting in a chair beside a potted palm.

How could he be flesh? Why was he not spirit? I had the gloves!

I rushed across the lobby and struck at the assassin with the boxes. "You cannot shoot me!" I screamed at him. "I have bought something!"

The desk clerk hurried over, uncertain whether he should assist me or the man I was beating. The assassin covered his handsome face with his arms, and I struck harder at him, hitting him about the head, until I had lost all the boxes but one.

I must get to my room! If I have no more gloves, he will be able to murder me!

I turned and ran for the stairs, listening for the pounding of the assassin's footfall. When I reached the third floor, I raced down the corridor to my room, but halted just outside the door.

That is what he wants. For me to go inside where he is already waiting.

Reeling about, I threw myself upon Robert's door, pounding upon it until it was opened.

"The assassin followed me to Mattock's!" I told my son. "And now he is come here to kill me!" I pushed inside and shut the door behind me.

Robert regarded the mangled box in my hands. "You were out shopping."

"To preserve myself from the assassin!"

"Where is your chloral?"

"In my room." I gripped his sleeve. "But do not go yourself, I believe the actor is in there."

"I will send the housemaid for it."

"Yes," I told him. "He will not murder her, for she is not in our family."

When the bottle was brought, my son mixed it with water and made me drink a large dose. Once I had drunk it, I sat upon my son's bed and waited for the drug to work, fidgeting with the box of gloves in my lap. This was all that was left of the boxes I had snatched off the counter – a pair meant for Robert's Christmas, lined with the fur of rabbits. Lifting one from the box, I slipped my hand inside and felt the indefensible softness of the fur.

If I was mad, it was in this, that I had believed such a possession would protect me from the assassin. That was my lunacy. For no possession I owned had ever protected anyone I loved.

I laid the glove back into its box.

"I must go away from here," I said to my son.

Robert rose from his chair. "You would leave Chicago?"

"If those who wish to injure me are here, I must be someplace else."

"Such as?"

"Europe, I think. It is far, and I like it there."

"It would be better if you went to Springfield and let Aunt Elizabeth watch over you."

"I think I would prefer to settle in France." The idea felt the sanest thinking I had accomplished in weeks.

Robert hurried across the room to me. "In France, I will not know what you do. Or how you spend your money."

I handed him the box of gloves. "You will know. For I shall send back far too many packages for you and Mamie."

He held the box, battered from being struck against the assassin's shoulders, as if he did not wish it in his hand. "It is better that you send us nothing. And that you remain here."

"Why is it you are so anxious to keep me close?" I asked him. "Is it that you would miss me too much?"

Robert let the box fall upon the bed. "Yes," he said, "that is it."

But the time he had required to answer had been too much.

I lifted myself from the mattress – stumbling a little because of the chloral. "I shall travel soon," I said to him. "Ahead of the summer storms."

But I had not enough time to make my plans before the insanity lawyer knocked upon my door.

(September 6) Mrs. Lincoln's Pulse 90 to-day –
—Patient Progress Reports for Bellevue Place
Sanitarium

(Last entry in log for Mary Lincoln)

I write these pages from the train bound for Springfield. They are the last few, the end of my story. At any rate, they are my story as it has been up to now.

My son is uncurious about what I am writing. He sits on the opposite side of the compartment, watching the flat plains of the prairie pass by the window, land so featureless, it would be easy to convince oneself we were not moving. I expect this is what Robert wishes, that we were not moving away from Batavia and the madhouse. Or, at least, that I was not.

When the train sways upon the track, I can feel the shifting of the carpetbag at my feet, a bag covered in needle-worked roses which belongs to Minnie Judd. Although I suppose that now nothing belongs to her. Most of the roses have lost their thread, and their form is no more than dyed holes for the needle to pass through. Still, it is all I have of Minnie – this and the strand of her hair which I have tied around the ribbon holding these pages.

Early this morning, before I left Bellevue Place, I went to Minnie's room and saw that her lovely dresses had been packed away. According to Mrs. Munger, Reverend Judd is selling his wife's clothes – Mrs. Gill being too large of bone for them, I suppose. All that remained of the young woman's possessions was the carpetbag – it being more shabby than the auctioneer would likely accept. However, it is still serviceable, and large enough to hold these pages; and I took it for that. And because it feels to me some token of Minnie's hopefulness.

My friend's dresses made the first part of this journey with me – from Batavia to Chicago. Minnie also traveled that portion, her fleshless body stored in a cooled compartment. In Chicago, that compartment was switched to a train bound for Boston, where Minnie's parents will meet her. I had wished to say good-bye to my friend in Chicago. However, Mrs. Ruggles, who accompanied me that far, would not allow me to search for Minnie's car.

The station in Chicago had been busy, crowded with the curious who had come to get a glimpse of the mad widow and the son who committed her. Robert would meet the eye of none of them, and once we had been escorted into our compartment, he pulled the shades on all our windows.

"It will be a journey of some hours," he told me, as if I had never traveled it before, as if I had lived nowhere but the asylum. "It would be better if you rest."

"I am not tired," I replied, raising one of the shades. "And I wish to watch the other travelers. It has been too long since I have seen so many who are not lunatic."

That was all we said for some time; and I suspect that my son possessed no intention of speaking to me for the length of the journey, whether I was asleep or awake. He rested his head upon the square of muslin meant to catch men's hair oil, and shut his eyes, though I have never known him to sleep upon any train.

"Why is it you sent me to the madhouse?" I said.

Reluctantly, he raised his head. "You are out now. I don't see the point in asking me this."

"Is it because you love me?" I persisted. "Or because you do not?"

He pushed his fingers against the lids of his eyes. "Why is it that you want always to talk about love?"

"It is the most important thing."

"Not to everyone."

The train began to move away from the station. My son put his head back upon the muslin and again closed his eyes, as if this were a signal for his sleeping. Some minutes passed, and I determined he had decided against answering me.

"I sent you to the asylum," he said at last, "because it was best for me."

It felt the first true thing my son had said to me since sending me to live at Bellevue Place. Since long before, even.

"I know it is not something Tad would have done," he continued. "Or Willie. I suppose it is my own defect."

"Yes," I told him. "It is."

Robert had raised his head then, and regarded me from across the compartment, surprised, I think, that I would say such a true thing to him. And once I had said it, it felt pointless to say more, so I took out my pen and ink, and began to write these pages, leaning upon the asylum Bible, which I stole for what it had shown me of Minnie's character.

In an hour from now, our train will arrive in Springfield, where I will be taken to Elizabeth's house. Before that time, I shall add these pages to the others in Minnie's carpetbag. Then I will lock the bag and push it deep beneath my seat.

I expect it will be some days before the carpetbag is discovered. Some months before the railroad realizes no one is coming to claim it. After a year, perhaps two, if it is stored away from sight, an employee of the depot will stumble upon it and see that it is too worn to possess any value. If he forces open the lock, he will discover that it contains only someone's writing tied with a nightdress ribbon and a long, black hair. Irritated that he has expended so much effort upon something which has no worth, he will send all of it to be burned.

No one will read what I have written here. And I suppose in the end, that is as it should be. It is enough that I have read it myself.

Epilogue

Mary Todd Lincoln lived with her sister in Springfield for one year, after which the court declared her restored to reason and she moved to France. She remained in France for four years, returning to the United States only when her health began to fail. She died at her sister's house in 1882, at the age of sixty-three.

During this time, Mary Lincoln did not meet or correspond with her son. Not until the final year of her life did she agree to see Robert and her granddaughter, Mamie.

Robert Lincoln inherited his mother's money, a sum of $84,000, as well as sixty-four trunks of her possessions.

ACKNOWLEDGMENTS

To my agent, Amy Rennert, for believing in Mary from the very beginning, and to Anika Streitfeld for loving her first. Also to my editor Kate Nitze for coming to love her, David Poindexter for waiting for her, and everyone at MacAdam/Cage for being the kind of publisher writers dream about.

I am indebted to Jean Baker's excellent biography, *Mary Todd Lincoln*, which both informed and inspired me. Anyone interested in an entirely factual account of Mary's life should read this book.

Wendy Lichtman, Rosie Ruley Atkins, Anita Amirrezvani, Bonnie Wach, Karen Bjorneby, and Kat Meltzer read every word of my original 900-page manuscript, and helped me shape it into this story. All the good ideas are theirs.

And finally, to my son, Alex, whose obsession with John Wilkes Booth (the only person at Ford's Theater that night with both a gun and a knife) led me to Mary.

Once, Two Islands   Dawn Garisch

On the larger of two islands in the southern Atlantic seas, a baby girl is born one dark winter's day, while the spin-drift wind sings strange songs around the gullies and cliffs. But Gulai's mother dies soon after giving birth and her father, Dr Orion Prosper, the only medical doctor on the island, blames himself.

For days afterwards he stays locked in his room, refusing to talk to anyone. But Gulai never stops crying and her aunt is forced to seek advice from Sophia, the island's other healer, in secret. Thus begins Gulai's life on Ergo Island – betraying her father a mere ten days after her birth and becoming inextricably linked to the traditions he is working to eradicate.

Left to make her own sense of the world around her, Gulai is curious to learn more about the 'witch' the islanders publicly revile but privately visit, the 'madness' which drove a young woman to her death and the secrets which lie at the heart of all their lives. Secrets which will change everything once revealed. . .

'. . . earthy and refined; simple, yet beautiful. . . it took only a few pages before I was sucked into Garisch's magical island world. This is a wonderful story about the universal experience of growing up and growing away from your parents, but its elements add up to so much more than that.' Karin Schimke, *Cape Times*

'This graceful, pared-down tale of a young girl's coming of age on a far-flung South Atlantic island is deceptively simple, but full of wise magic. . . This book is a delight.' *Psychologies*

'Enchanting blend of ancient folklore and modern dilemmas. . . Garisch is good, very good. . . I eagerly await her next endeavour.' *The Weekender*

The Gift of Rain   Tan Twan Eng

LONGLISTED FOR THE MAN BOOKER PRIZE 2007

Penang, 1939. Sixteen-year-old Philip Hutton is a loner. Half English, half Chinese and feeling neither, he discovers a sense of belonging in an unexpected friendship with Hayato Endo, a Japanese diplomat. Philip shows his new friend around his adored island of Penang, and in return Endo trains him in the art and discipline of aikido.

But such knowledge comes at a terrible price. The enigmatic Endo is bound by disciplines of his own and when the Japanese invade Malaya, threatening to destroy Philip's family and everything he loves, he realises that his trusted sensei – to whom he owes absolute loyalty – has been harbouring a devastating secret. Philip must risk everything in an attempt to save those he has placed in mortal danger and discover who and what he really is.

'A powerful first novel about a tumultuous and almost forgotten period of history.' *TLS*

'A remarkable book. . . about war, friendship, memory and discipline.' Ian McMillan, BBC Radio 3

'. . . a stunning debut which heralds the author's arrival as a major literary talent.' *The Southern Reporter*

'An engrossing read, a hugely enjoyable emotional voyage.' John McRae, author of *The Routledge Guide to Modern Writing*.